The Aurora Marelup Saga

5 Year Anniversary Edition

Serenity Rayne

Content Warning

Content warnings are an important element to any novel. I don't ever want to harm a reader. So for this reason, I will list the warnings here.

- 6 mates total

- med-fast burn

- Two of the guys fall madly in love

- m/m - m/m/m/m/m

- PNR Why Choose

- Blood, death, decapitation, gut garland

- Wolves, Dragons, bears, eagle

- **pregnancy books 3&5**

- **SHIFTED WOLF ON MATE** book 1&5

- True/fated mates

- Strong Female main character

- Twin Sandwich

- Bonus content and deleted scenes added

This is a paranormal why choose romance with poly elements. It's a journey of self-discovery and personal growth.

There are many situations included that are intended for MATURE audiences (18+)

Throughout this book, there are references/ instances that may trigger some individuals such as: **decapitation, murder, beheading, skull collecting, blood everywhere, attempted murder, group scenes, near death experiences, birth, ancient burial rites. Other woman drama.**

FMC is slightly unhinged and has no issues ripping her enemies to shreds to accomplish her goals.

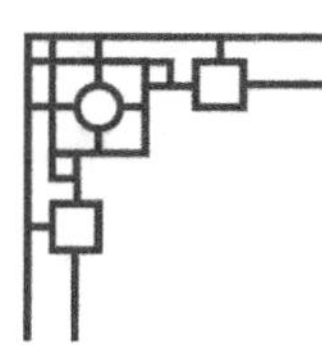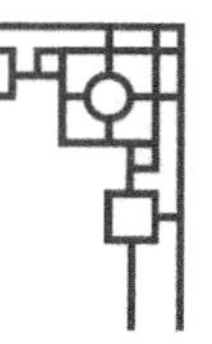

Inspiriational Playlist

1. Hail to the King - a7x
2. Welcome Home - Metallica
3. She-Wolf - Megadeth
4. Of Wolf and Man - Metallica
5. Crush'Em - Megadeth
6. Devil - Shinedown
7. Wish you were here- Pink Floyd
8. Nothing Else Matters- Metallica
9. Cemetery Gates - Pantera
10. Bulls on Parade- Rage Against the Machine
11. How Did You Love - Shinedown
12. Right Here Waiting - Richard Marx
13. Break Stuff- Limp Bizkit
14. Mission Impossible theme- Danny Elfman
15. Heathens- TwentyOne Pilots
16. The Blue Danube, Op.314 - Johann Strauss
17. Oh Tannenbaum- Sasha Cohn

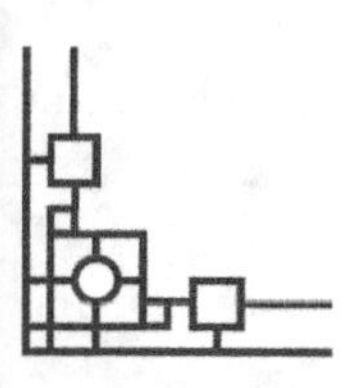

PT. 1

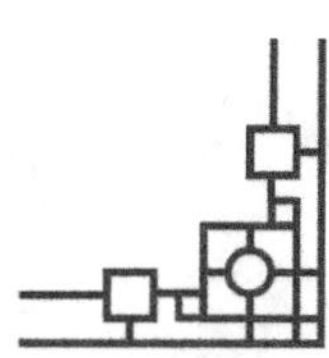

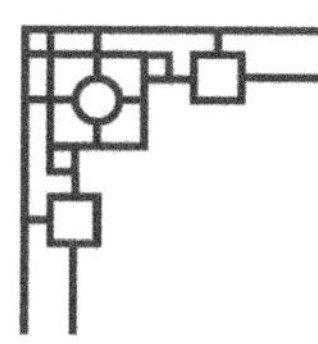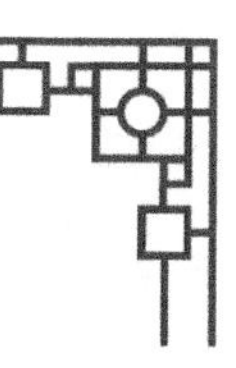

INSPIRIATIONAL PLAYLIST

18. Pony- Ginuwine
19. November Rain- G-N-R
20. Feel Invincible- Skillet
21, Sail- AWOLNATION
22. Silent Lucidity- Queensryche
23. Architecture of Aggression- Megadeth
24. You Could be Mine- G-N-R
25. Popular Monster- Falling in Reverse
26. Take What You Want- Post Malone, Ozzy Osbourne
27.Look What You Made Me Do- Taylor Swift
28. The Chain (Gears of War 5)- Evanescence
29, I Am the Highway- Audioslave
30. I Am the Fire- Halestorm
31. Killer Wolf- Danzig
32. Outlaws & Outsiders- Cory Marks
33. The In-Between- In This Moment

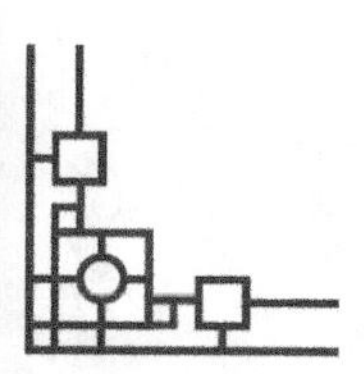

PT. 2

If Dominik chased you...

Would you submit?

Author Ramblings:

Dear Readers,

It's been a hell of a ride since I started back in 2019. As I continue on my author journey, it's been a path of growth and constant learning. I feel in the last year my craft has grown from the savage and aggressive in your face FMC's to the ones that have depth and problems like the rest of us. As silly as it sounds, I call them more realistic fantasy female main characters. I feel like my girls have become more relatable over time and their worlds are more immersive than before.

Aurora has always had a special place in my heart. She was my first FMC I ever wrote, and she helped me heal a part of myself. Each of her mates that she gathered along the way had a quality that made them stand out. It's hard to write a single male main character that has all the qualities we wish to find. Reverse harem lets us have our cake and eat it too. I expanded this edition, giving Aurora and her men the much needed additional time they deserve. For those of you that loved her the first time around. I hope you get to fall in love with them all over again, reading it as a continuous story.

Blessed be.

Serenity

CHAPTER 1
Dimitri

March-

We get to the other side and back on the main game trail. It's not long before the scent of other bears fills my nostrils; we are close to their camp. I can feel it. Out of nowhere, I get blasted in the side by something huge. Aurora goes flying, and I can hear her clothing rip as she shifts midair.

I hit the ground hard and scent the boar flying towards Aurora. She catches him and slams his bear to the ground. I can hear bones crack from the impact. Aurora is growling and drooling venom on the male's face. I go nose to nose with the male, and his eyes widen in recognition. Immediately he shifts back and looks up at me as Aurora releases him. "You're of the Kovac line, I know those markings," the man says in Romanian to me.

I raise my eyes to look at Aurora and explain what's going on through the bond to her. She runs and walks back to the bags and shifts back to her human form. Quickly, she dresses and returns to me with my clothes. I return to my human form and get dressed.

"Yes, I am of the Kovac line; my mother was Svetlana, and my father was Beck." I answer him in Romanian, and he nods slowly.

"They've been dead a long time, my friend. You cannot be their Dimitri. He should be long dead." He continues speaking in Romanian to me.

I show him the family brand on my forearm and the brand given to me the day I went to work as the queen's guard. Aurora silently steps up beside me and rests her bare forearm next to mine. She bares the Marelup seal as well as the seal of the Ice Dragon Royal House. The man visibly pales, looking at her markings. Quickly, he drops to one knee and apologizes for attacking.

Aurora walks over and gently touches the man's chin and raises his eyes to meet hers. Her steel-grey eyes examine him, then look back to me. "Tell him why we are here and that I forgive him. Make sure he realizes you're my mate and your life span was extended because of me. Tell him we seek your descendants," Aurora says, looking back down at the man. Slowly, she releases him, and she returns to my side where I hold her tightly to me.

Quickly, I relay what Aurora had said to the man before us. He's in shock that I'm almost a hundred and fifty years older than the oldest living Great Bear in our history. He gets up and grabs our bags, offering to lead us to the clan. Aurora is happy with this turn of events and smiles as we head towards camp.

Everything is almost how I remember it, except the clan is much smaller in numbers these days. My mother's hut is still standing where it was all those years ago. Planks have been changed out and the roof updated, but yet the same shape. A robust woman steps out of the hut, and she reminds me of my mother. I stare for several minutes while the man explains who we are to her and the others gathered.

Aurora looks up to me, and her eyes shift to that of her beast. I feel a tingle through the bonds as she attempts to pull some matrix shit with me. Aurora blinks twice, and the tingle stops; her attention turns back to the female. "She's of your blood, Dimitri, a grandchild. I can scent it on the wind." Aurora cants her head to the side, looking up to me.

I'm not sure what's more shocking right now, the fact Aurora just ravaged my mind and learned to speak Romanian in a matter of minutes, or the fact I left behind a child. "Who is your grandmother?" I ask the woman directly.

"My grandmother is dead, but her name was Irina. Her boyfriend left her pregnant to go work for the wolves." She spit on the ground after saying that. My chest hurt, all this time I had a child and never knew. Eventually, her mother emerges and I see my own eyes staring back at me. My chest tightens as I think about all of the years I missed with my daughter. I watch her run back inside and comes out holding a small canvas. I know that canvas; Irina painted my portrait just before I left to work at the castle.

Slowly the old woman turns the painting around, There's my face staring back at me. "Papa?" she asks hesitantly.

I nod my head slowly, looking at her. I'm all choked up from the power and emotion in this moment. She makes it past her daughter and comes over and hugs me without hesitation. I hold my daughter tightly to my chest. I explain a short version of what's happened in the last two hundred and almost thirty years. My daughter Katrina tells me her mom was going to tell me she was pregnant the day I left. I see tears rolling down Aurora's cheeks as she listens to my daughter's story. Katrina's daughter eventually comes around and starts talking to me about what I've missed. Aurora is silent, watching everyone like a sentinel. I also hear the whispers of her updating the others through the bond. I still have family; that in itself is a miracle.

Everyone gathers around the fire to talk, but Aurora remains at a distance. My people blame her people for my leaving and why so many never returned home after the coup. I believe that they sense she's more dragon than wolf, so they sort of relax in her presence. I make sure the entire camp knows who Aurora is and why we are here. I thought wolves were bad about shutting out other species, but apparently, the bears are worse. Slowly, I extract myself from the bears and walk over to the tree Aurora is leaning on. "Are you okay?" I just had to ask.

"It's just a lot to process." She kicks off the tree and starts to pace. Her hands shoot up and threads through her long, white hair roughly. "I'm the reason you didn't get to see your daughter born. *My* people are the reason so many of your people were slaughtered the night of the attack." Shaking her head slowly, she raises her eyes to look at me. The sadness there makes my chest hurt; by proxy she blames herself for what happened. "I'm not welcome here, it's okay. I understand why. If you want I'll have Marco come and get me, or I can call Alaric to me instead," Aurora says, her tone is broken and full of pain. Here, I thought this would be a joyous occasion, and now I'm having second thoughts.

Renee, one of the few sows in the camp that holds no ill will towards the wolves, brings Aurora some desserts and candies. They seem to get along well enough. Aurora isn't used to having a female friend, and Renee is trying to be that friend to her right now. Renee's three mates take turns bringing drinks and snacks over to them. Each male young and virile, muscles on muscles. Aurora doesn't even notice them at all. I can tell they are trying to be playful with her, and she seems to be lost in her own emotions again. I move back and forth between the family I never got to know and my mate. I'm torn. Both need me, and I can't be in two places at once.

A roar sounds overhead, and Aurora's eyes light up. They take on that ghostly glow when she talks to the dragons; it's frightening to those who don't know what's happening. Aurora tilts her head back and does that roar-howl of her beast, answering the dragon's call. I know it's Alaric, and he's concerned because of how Aurora feels through the bond. A bag falls from the sky, and Aurora catches it and runs off into the night. I get up to follow, and my granddaughter grabs my arm scared of what's to come. "Shh, little one, it's my bond mate, Alaric. He sensed Aurora was upset and came to her the fastest way he knew how."

"He's a dragon?" my daughter Katrina asks. She quickly pulls her daughter to her side, holding onto her tightly.

"Yes, he's a dragon, the Ice Dragon King to be exact, and Aurora is his queen. Everyone here shunned her because she's part Lycan. You should all be ashamed of yourselves." I make eye contact with each of my descendant's clan. I see the regret in their eyes, I can only hope it's enough to appease Alaric.

Alaric and Aurora walk into sight, hand in hand, and thankfully she appears to have calmed down. Well, all except both of their eyes are that of their beast. With the light coating of frost on them, I can tell Aurora is in deep conversation with Alaric. Dragons and their freaky shit, I think Ellis had it right. It's just weird how hard-wired they are to each other. "Greetings,

Dimitri!" Alaric says as he releases Aurora and embraces me. We pat each other's back then step back.

"I hope your flight was a good one, Alaric." I can tell he's mad. I know it's not at me but at my people. At this point, I can't blame him. I'm mad at them too.

"It was, Dimitri. It's just upsetting that my mate is distraught because of how speciesist your people are. Part of me, I want to burn them all to ash. Then again, Aurora tells me you have a daughter and granddaughter here, and both are anti-Lycan," Alaric says, trying to contain his temper. I can see the struggle he's having with his beast.

Aurora moves in front of Alaric and lays a hand upon his chest. Slowly, she brings her free hand up to lightly stroke his beard. "Love? My mother's Lycan mate did a lot of damage to a lot of species. In some ways, I understand why they have a dislike of the Lycans. But in other ways I don't, it happened two hundred and twenty-nine years ago, on my birthday of all days. My poor mother was drugged and unable to fight against Vladimir. I swear I will have my vengeance on him for what happened to my mother and all the other lives lost that day. I will make him suffer a thousand deaths." Aurora speaks with so much passion that it brings tears to the bear's eyes who can hear her clearly.

Alaric leans down and kisses Aurora passionately. You can hear the happy rumble of their beasts. Eventually, Alaric releases Aurora and she just smiles up at him, content again. "D? What do you say we head to the pit and let your people see who I really am? Maybe let them send four of their strongest boars into the ring with me? I could use the exercise." Aurora smiles at me sweetly then I see Dante, Edgar, and Marco flank Alaric. Oh boy, Aurora has a plan, and it involves siphoning energy from the other dragons if need be.

Several bulky males laugh and offer to take the "queen" up on her offer. Alaric and I both can't help but laugh. They have no idea whom they are fucking with. They assume that because she's female, she's going to be smaller and weaker. That is their first and last mistake.

I move to the training pit center and hold up my arms, getting everyone's attention. Aurora, apparently, wants to fight all four at the same time. I can almost bet she has a new move she's waiting to try out. "Attention bear clan, dragons, and hybrid, this is the challenge ring. We obey the old laws, fight to submission or knock out only. Does everyone understand?" I look between the four boar and Aurora. Aurora looks absolutely bored out of her mind right now.

Aurora walks up to Alaric and hands him the robe she was wearing. Slowly, she shifts to the form of her beast; her beast's bulk and mass are insane. More dragon features are now very pronounced as she turns to face me. Her entire muzzle is covered in white scales and up around her eyes to protect them. Her heavily scaled arms look like very aggressive medieval gauntlets with almost six inches of razor-sharp talons on the end. Aurora's legs even have scales on them from her paws to her knee. She starts tapping her talons together as her dragonic eyes regard everyone around her. I use the word regard very loosely; it's more like she's sizing everyone up, assessing them for strengths and weaknesses.

All four males make the mistake of shifting at once, and Aurora spins to face them. She roars at them, causing the dragons present to answer her call. All almost ten feet of Aurora's beast lowers its body into an attack stance. The bears don't know what to make of her at this point. Hmm, let's see here, an almost ten foot tall, approximately half-ton of heavily muscled and armored white Dragon-Lycan hybrid in the ring. I can only imagine what's going through their minds right now.

Two of the larger males charge simultaneously, and with a quick swipe of Aurora's talons, she cut both of their muzzles and sent them crashing to the ground. Her eyes lock on the last two, and she charges them. They move, trying to circle her. Aurora, on the other hand, is having the time of her life. The two boar decide to charge again at the same time, idiots. Aurora saw what they were going to do long before they did it. At the very last second, she leaps up and lands on the one boar's back, causing him to crash to the ground.

All four male bears are wounded, and Aurora's fur is still its ghost-white color. I can see how she's watching them, assessing if they will continue to fight or tap out. Her eyes land on me, and then I look to the boars still attempting to get back into the fight. "I'm going to count to five. If you cannot continue, lie on the ground. If you want to continue, then fucking do something. *One ... Two ... Three ... Four ...*" Suddenly, a boar leaps out of the crowd, heading directly at Aurora.

She spins just in the nick of time to grasp him by the throat and slam his body to the ground. She starts to growl and snap in his face; her venom is dripping from her canines, some of it landing in his mouth. He starts thrashing as his beast retreats deep within himself because of the toxin. Aurora backs up and narrows her eyes at him as her tail thrashes wildly behind her.

Apparently, the Alpha's son thought he had enough strength to take her. Obviously, he was wrong. Now he's going to be stuck as a human until the venom works its way out of his system. I finally yell five, and the match is over. Aurora looks back to Alaric and then me. We both bow our heads to her and raise our fists to our hearts. Slowly, Aurora looks at the gathered crowd, and one by one they mimic Alaric and me. I guess she earned the clan's respect in the ring, more by actions than by words. The old Alpha Vladimir would have disregarded the rules and killed all those who challenged him.

In one round of battle against five opponents, Aurora showed mercy and proved that not all Lycans are bad. Aurora steps up to Alaric and licks his face, then she turns and licks mine. Silly woman. Alaric throws her robe over her beast's shoulders as she shifts back to her human form. The clan Alpha comes to apologize for the way his son attacked out of turn, and Aurora accepts his apology.

Alaric raises an eyebrow, looking at me, shocked that Aurora is speaking yet another new language. I shrug my shoulders, looking at him. "She pulled some matrix shit with me earlier. Next thing I know, she's speaking my dialect." I shrug my shoulders at him again, then go back to watching Aurora greet the clan's people. Finally, they pull their collective heads out of their asses.

Alaric starts to laugh and shake his head. "I honestly can't figure out how she does that. Usually, only the ancients can pull that off. Maybe it's Aurora's hybrid status that helped. I honestly don't know. We'll have to remember to ask Nicodeamus about it when we return," Alaric says as if he's going to ask about the weather instead of an ability.

Aurora returns to us and looks back at the gathered bears before facing us once more. "Time to go home; there's not enough Great Bears to ask them to fight with us. Alaric love, summon Ellis and his Polar Bears; we'll need them. The winter storms are almost over; his people may be able to blend in." Aurora finishes speaking then turns her face to the sky. Soon, we hear Marco's, Dante's, and Edgar's call. Aurora extends her arms outward just as the snow starts to fall. I don't know if she sensed the snow or summoned it; either way, we have one last freak winter storm to deal with, and we need to leave. "I'll fly back on Alaric. Dimitri, you can fly back on Marco; we need to call a meeting of the clans' heads. Soon, I hunt Elena, then we head towards my mother's castle." Aurora's tone is cold and detached.

We watch Aurora walk to the field where the other dragons have landed; she seems to be in deep conversation with them. "What just happened, Alaric?" I had to question him, something isn't sitting right with me.

Alaric inhales deeply then slowly lets the air escape his lungs. "Apparently, she sent the trifecta to investigate a lead for her. They came back with the news that she needed to hear. She now knows exactly where Elena and the rogue pack are. They apparently have a small force of Wyverns with them. If I know my mate, she's going to ask those three to pick the best fighters to come and take them out." Alaric looks back to Aurora then back to me.

Before I have a chance to say anything, Aurora is yelling that we have to get moving. The two War Dragons take off, and the Black Dragon waits for me. I look at Aurora and Alaric as he jogs to join her. His shift is fast and fluid; apparently, that is one of his gifts from Aurora. I watch them take off, and I head over to Marco. He lowers his wing and stretches his front leg out so I can get on. This is going to prove to be a very interesting flight home.

CHAPTER 2
Alaric

APRIL-

Several nights have had heated discussions as to how we are going to handle the Elena problem. Ellis arrived this morning with over a hundred assorted bears that he trusts. There are not only Polar Bears but also Black and Brown Bears in the mix as well. Dimitri is in charge of getting the bears settled as I lead Ellis to the war room. A den of Siberian Tigers is due to arrive here by the afternoon.

I push open the double doors, and there's Aurora at the head of the table; her dress is ice blue and hugging her plentiful curves. She's not happy that she's a little thicker after the twins, but fuck, she is hotter now than she was before. Ellis stops in his tracks, and I practically have to pick his jaw up off the floor. At the table is a leader from each species of Dragon, Alex for the Dire Wolves, Klaus for the Lycans, and now Ellis for the Bears as a whole.

Aurora stops speaking the minute she sees Ellis and runs over and hugs him tightly. The look of fear in Ellis's eyes is totally worth it.

My twins come barreling through the door and start chirping at Aurora, and she releases Ellis. Ellis's eyes move from me to the twins, then back to Aurora again. "Aw, fuck no! Hell to the no... Bro, what the fuck!" Ellis throws his hands up in the air, and his dramatics catches Aurora's attention, and now she looks pissed.

"What do you mean fuck no?" Her arms instantly shift to her armored gauntlets as she stares Ellis down. He just made a huge mistake saying anything that can be perceived as negative about the babies.

Ellis begins to back up till his back hits the wall. "No disrespect, Aurora... I wasn't expecting there to be two baby dragons here. I mean, seriously?" He raises his hands up in defeat. I decide to take pity on him and get between him and Aurora.

"Love, what my buddy is trying to express is that his kind isn't strong enough to shift so young. So it's a shock that our babies possess the strength to be their animals so very young." I can tell I've got her by the way she's looking between the babies and Ellis.

"Fine, only cause my babies are awesome, and they can roast his balls off if I wish it." Aurora returns to the head of the table, going back to conducting the meeting.

"Alaric? Was she serious? Do your babies have fire already?" Poor Ellis is scared, and by the time he finishes his question, both babies breathe fire at the same time harmlessly into the air. I've never seen a man of color get so pale so quickly. Ellis looks about ready to pass out when the babies run over to sit near their mother.

Aurora mouths *sorry* then returns to what she's focused on. The strike teams have been made, orders are given, and new training regiments are given to prepare for the assault on the castle.

Everyone goes to leave, and Aurora stops Alex and Dante from leaving. Aurora's eyes find me, and she motions to the door. "Ellis, I hate to do this, but this part of the meeting I can't have you in on." Ellis gratefully nods and exits the room quickly.

We re-assume our seats, and Aurora pulls down a map she had hidden. "We strike tonight. Alex, I need six Dires with toxic bite." Alex nods, slowly jotting down names on a piece of paper then passing it over to Aurora. Her eyes glide over the paper quickly, and she smiles; Alex immediately takes his leave.

Next, Aurora looks to Dante and smiles. "She has Wyverns as we suspected. Thank you for that vital information. I want you, Edgar, and five others that would be able to take out Wyverns quickly." Dante nods slowly, raises his fist to his chest then leaves the room.

"My love, we need to move Father and the twins to the cavern I discovered under rubble not far from here. I'll send Jayce and Dominik with him to protect the babies. Dimitri and Klaus will run things here like nothing is happening." She glances down at her notes briefly. "The bear cub I saved from the slaughter will be sent home with one of Ellis's bears to raise." Aurora draws in a long-drawn-out breath before exhaling slowly. "Sundown, we leave. One thing I learned is that Elena can't see well at night due to her advanced age." Aurora smiles and kisses my lips lightly. "Let's kick this party off, love. Time to get revenge." My mate is entirely way too happy right now.

"As you wish, my love." I gently kiss her cheek before leaving the room. My twins follow behind me as I start to search for their grandfather. Lucky for me, I find Nicodeamus and the other twins together with a single bag apiece. "I'm guessing Aurora gathered everyone for me?"

Nicodeamus steps forward and lays his hand on my shoulder. "Yes, we've been given the task of guarding the family's greatest treasure. Which we will do proudly and with honor." Nicodeamus turns and gives the twins a look.

I know they want to go help hunt Elena. I reassure them through the bond that their job is just as vital. They collectively sigh and nod slowly, finally agreeing that they have just as important of a job as I did. "Marco will be carrying you three. The babies will be clinging to my back for the ride out. It's about time they are treated like the hatchlings they are." My statement makes Nicodeamus smile and beam with pride. A hatchling's first flight is important. They tend to test their wings, some learn to fly, others just enjoy the ride.

We head outside, and Jayce runs and climbs up onto Marco's neck and sits behind his head, ready to go. Nicodeamus makes his way to join Jayce up by Marco's head. Dominik is hesitant and climbs up to sit in front of Marco's wings. Without warning, Marco takes off, and Dominik screams like a little girl. I can't help but laugh. I look at my twins and smile down at them; they run in circles, getting impatient. Aurora makes it outside just as I pack my clothes into my bag. I love the appreciative look she gives me.

I run a ways away from everyone and shift into my dragon. The babies walk over, slowly chirping up at me. I lower my head and nuzzle the babies. Aurora joins us and climbs up onto my back, showing the babies the best place between my wings to cling to. I feel Aurora's talons as she strips away loose and dead scales so the babies don't fall off. It feels really nice to have my scales tended to by my lovely mate; my dragon croons his appreciation. My sensitive ears pick up on Aurora's rumbling in reply to mine. Once she's satisfied with my scales, she climbs down and moves to stand in front of me.

"You carry my greatest treasures on your back. Protect them fiercely, leave no enemy standing, burn them to ash." Aurora steps closer and kisses my dragon's maw, her beast's eyes looking deeply into mine. Slowly, I rise up and take off into the sky, en route to the hidden cavern.

I discover along my flight that Ladon is strong enough to fly with me. I had to slow down to gliding, but it's totally worth it to watch my son's first flight. I reach out through time and space through the bond to allow the others to witness Ladon's first flight. I feel Aurora get emotional; she's so proud of our son. Nicodeamus is beaming with pride, boasting how his grandson takes after him. I look over my shoulder, and Tiamat is hesitantly spreading her wings. It'll take time, but she will eventually fly.

Towards the end of our flight, Tiamat opens her wings and lets go of my scales. I turn to watch her falter, then slowly straighten back out. Ladon moves to fly beside his sister, and he's talking to her, instructing her what to do. I reach out to my family again and share the vision of both babies flying for their first time. Ahead of me, I hear Nicodeamus's dragon roar from the ground his joy and pride. I feel Aurora's pride and her emotional reaction to seeing her babies fly. I know deep down she wants to fly, but she can't. Little does she know I ordered her some wing suits that I'm giving her for this mission.

My theory is that she can jump off my back and glide into the camp and seek Elena while her forces concentrate on the rest of us. Is it a good plan? Quite possibly, I guess we'll have to wait and see. In the clearing ahead, I see Marco's dragon helping to excavate the cave entrance. Dom and Jayce are watching for the babies and me to arrive. Jayce has his mini camcorder, videoing the babies and me. I click and chirp at the babies so that they circle and watch me land first. My twins chirp in response to my instructions and start to circle, watching my every movement. This is absolutely the slowest and most important landing I have ever made in my existence.

Once I'm on the ground, I shift quickly and dress, waiting for the twins to make their first landing. Ladon takes the lead and begins his circling descent. I'm a bundle of nerves watching my son land for the first time. Usually, I hate landing in fresh powdery snow. Today,I'm very thankful for it for once. Just as Ladon is about to land, he gives his wings a few quick flaps, and his hind legs touch down first, then his front. I run over and hug my son to my chest, telling him how proud of him I am.

My eyes turn skyward to watch Tiamat. I thought the fear of Ladon crashing scared me; my daughter's landing scares me to death. Anxiously I watch her lazy circles. Ladon is right next to me, calling to his sister to give her instructions. Tiamat breathes fire, showing her aggravation at her brother's coddling. Tiamat's circles are getting closer to the ground, and my fucking heart is in my throat. One strong flap of her wings, and she stops about six inches off the ground and gracefully drops onto her feet. Tiamat prances over to me, her head held high. She remembered to protect her underbelly, unlike her brother. I scoop up my daughter and hug her tightly. I tell her how proud of her I am. Nicodeamus's and Marco's dragons click and purr at the babies, telling them how proud of them they are.

Dominik and Jayce make it over and kneel down close by. My twins break free of my arms and run over and knock Dominik and Jayce on their asses. Both babies happily chirping and purring to their other fathers. I listen to my bond mates tell my twins how proud they are of them. I then hear Dominik's phone ringing; it's Aurora's ringtone. "Little ones, your momma wants to talk to you." Dominik accepts the video call and turns the phone to face the babies.

I listen to Aurora telling them how very proud she is of both of them. She then focuses on Ladon and tells him he's a very good brother for talking his sister through everything that made her nervous. Aurora then looks to Tiamat and smiles, and tells her how proud she is of her for working up the courage to try. She then instructs Dom to turn the phone to me. Aurora tells me to hurry up and get my scaly ass back there because she has a plan to set in motion. The call suddenly disconnects, and I look to the others.

Nicodeamus herds the babies into the cavern then instructs Marco to move some of the stones back on either side of the opening. That way, if they are attacked, the enemies will be funneled right where he wants them. My father-in-law is a brilliant tactician. Dominik and Jayce strip and carry their clothes into the cavern with them. I see the glow of both sets of Dire Wolf eyes staring back at me through the darkness.

I'd hate to see what would be left of the fool that tried to attack my family. Nicodeamus sticks his head partially out of the cavern, inspecting what was done. I hear the click of his ignitor and then see the blue flames lick the ground. The entire area outside of the cavern is a huge skating rink. He then proceeds to make icicle bars to mostly seal off the cavern. There's enough room for a good airflow, but it's enough to slow any invaders down. Once I'm sure my babies, bond mates, and father-in-law are secure in the cavern, I take to the sky, my guards flanking me on the way back to the camp.

CHAPTER 3

Alaric

Tonight's a night of retribution; Aurora is out for blood. To be perfectly honest, so am I. The memories she's shared with me, and the pain that she buries down deep... I'm ready to burn the world to the ground and hear the screams of my enemies as they burn to death. The flight back is much quicker than the initial flight out.

Aurora is standing in the middle of the field, waiting with the other dragons as we breach the horizon. I notice at Aurora's feet is the box with the wing suits in it. Surprisingly, the box looks untouched. I circle the field twice before I land and shift back to human. "Hey, babe, let's get your present on you so we can take off." Aurora looks to me curiously, then back to the box, then back to me again before she tears into the box.

In the box, there are four wing suits, two black and two blue. Aurora squeals and starts trying to slip into the suit. I know for a fact she knows what it is since she's been begging me to order her a few so she can experience flight. I help her with the final straps and buckles and then have her open her arms to make sure the membranes are properly stretched out for her. After several minor adjustments, I send her up with one of the small Gold Dragons so that she can get the hang of the suit. Aurora glides around catching the thermals, and manages to stay in the air much longer than I had initially anticipated. When she finally lands, she runs up and kisses me passionately. Score one for me.

I break away from my beloved mate and smile softly at her before shifting to my dragon's form. Carefully, I lie down and she quickly climbs up and onto my back. Surprisingly, she sits just before my wings instead of up by my head like she usually does. *Is everything okay, love?* I question her through the bond, unsure of her decision of where to sit. Did I do something wrong?

I hear Aurora's laughter through the bond, and then I hear her. *Everything is perfect! I get to drop down out of the sky and kill my enemies when they least expect me. Best day ever!* She starts singing the song "Architecture of Aggression" by Megadeth. Yup, she's in her homicidal mindset for this mission.

I take off and join the other seven dragons flying towards the camp where Elena is hiding. I see Marco come towards us, and he lines himself up under me. Before I can question Aurora, she runs and jumps off my back and clings to Marco's Black Dragon. Through my mind's eye, she shows me her plan, and fuck me, it's solid. I didn't think about the fact that my dragon may be spotted because of its light color.

Marco expresses his concern and says he's sorry, but he can't disobey Aurora. Honestly, I can't blame him; after all, she took down an ancient Black Dragon almost twice his size alone. I watch them take a different path to the camp than the rest of us are.

Aurora enters my head again, telling me more of her plan, that the other dragons and I are the distraction. Marco will drop her within gliding distance, then he's going to lay down a circle of acid around the camp so no one can escape.

I'm almost stunned at the brilliance of the plan that Aurora has come up with. I know Aurora's false mate Sebastian had gifted her with a battle strategy, I just didn't realize she would still retain the gift after the bond was severed and he died. It's quite a curious state of events that I must investigate with Nicodeamus once this mission is over with.

I fly with the rest of the assault force and start laying waste to the camp that Elena thought that she had hidden so well. I get the pleasure of briefly watching my mate gliding through the air, then shifting last second to land upon what looks to be the Alpha House. Her giant, white Lycan visible only for the briefest of moments before she leaps off the roof.

Screams and the sounds of fighting fill the air; white snow turns crimson as my mate goes on her rampage. She calls to me through the bond. Apparently, Elena has a bunker underground and Aurora can't lift the lid. I land just as Marco starts to lay his ring of acid down around the campsite. Bloodcurdling screams fill the air as unsuspecting rebels step into his black acid fog. I pause in my forward momentum to watch that acid of Marco's melt the flesh off of whomever it touches. *What a way to go!*

A tapping catches my attention now, and I look down to my pissed off impatient hybrid mate. Fuck! I reach my taloned hand over and grip the stone disk and lift it free of its resting place. Several series of tunnels are below, each leading in a different direction. I watch Aurora look skyward, and then Marco circles and lands next to me. Aurora locks eyes with Marco then motions to the hole.

I hear Marco's ignitor click several times before he lowers his head and starts releasing his acid fog into the tunnels. Smart thinking on Aurora's part, the fog will creep along the floor and swiftly move through the tunnels. Aurora comes over to Marco's side and pats his cheek; his ignitor clicks again, and more acid fog comes out, this time thicker. Once that round finishes, he moves away and takes flight again. Now, we wait and listen. Eventually, we hear Elena screaming. The acid has found her. Aurora drops down on all fours and lowers her head to the opening. I hear the click of her ignitor, and Aurora breathes her blue flames onto the acid fog. Aurora leaps back quickly as the highly flammable acid ignites and the flames race along the mist. Elena's screams and cries are muffled then silenced.

Aurora nods her great wolven head then starts heading towards the building that suspiciously just went up in flames. Once reaching the porch, Aurora kneels down, sinks her talons into the wood, and starts freezing the house, effectively putting out the fire. By the time the house is frozen, I raided a house nearby and stole pants for myself to wear.

Aurora looks back at me then proceeds into the house cautiously. I feel like we are walking into a trap with each step we take. Aurora pauses and looks around; something catching her attention. I can watch her wolven ears moving in several different directions before focusing on a door. Her talons come up, and she cuts through the burned door with ease. The scent of burned flesh permeates the air that drifts up to us. Most of the staircase is missing, and what's left doesn't look safe to climb. Aurora kneels down and motions for me to climb onto her back. Hesitantly I wrap my arms around my mate's thick neck and my legs around her beast's waistline.

Without warning, Aurora drops down into the house's basement. Her head scans the area then she backs up a bit. I feel the vibration of her ignitor when it clicks to life, and she starts breathing her blue flames around the room. I follow the path of her flames, and she is burning away the last of the acid fog pockets. Slowly she crouches down, and I slide off of her back and begin to look around.

Lost artifacts from her mother's castle are here in what I'm guessing is a safe house for Vladimir's secret forces. I hear Dante and Edgar calling for us, so I holler and let them know we're fine. They leap down and motion to Aurora, still in her beast's form. "Something still isn't right; she won't shift back until the area is clear."

I motion to the walls, and the look of recognition flitters across both War Dragons' faces. "We need to secure all the treasures housed here. Send for others to come back and carefully pack this stuff up." Both guys nod, and we watch Aurora stalk down the hallway in full stealth mode.

The three of us are no more than ten feet behind her when she raises her tail and crouches low. A muffled moan and whine reaches us. Aurora's ears flicker, catching the sound. Slowly, her wolven head tilts as she listens to the room carefully. My gut tells me that Elena is in the room.

Aurora shifts back to a mostly human form, leaving herself three-quarters of the way shifted. Her taloned hand slashes at the damaged door, sending splinters flying in every direction. Bodies litter the floor and yet somehow, Elena is untouched at the back of the room behind the pile of charcoaled corpses. A guttural growl escapes Aurora's lips, the reverberations shake the walls in the room. Elena visibly pales, staring at Aurora in her partially shifted form.

"You killed my son!" Elena yells at Aurora.

The clicking of Aurora's talons is the only sound besides our breathing that can be heard. It's almost as if time has stopped. Shaking her head slowly, Aurora begins to prowl the room as the guys and I block the only exit. "You've caused so much damage and told so many lies, yet you dare yell at me, witch!" Aurora says witch with so much venom in her inflection the old woman cringes at the tone.

A brief huff of a laugh escapes Aurora's lips as she stares at Elena. "You meddled in the Elder God's plans for us, damaged sacred bonds, and falsified a bond for your own benefit." Smirking, Aurora crosses her armored arms over her ample chest.

"There shall be no Elysium for you or your bloodline, Elena. I swear on my blood and the blood of my ancestors I will make your bloodline go extinct." Aurora's long, white tail thrashes violently behind her as she stalks forward. Elena doesn't bother begging for forgiveness or mercy. Death has come for her in the form of the last Marelup.

Time slows to a crawl as Aurora moves forward, extending her taloned hands towards Elena. The tips of those long, white, curved talons press into the soft pink flesh of Elena's skin. As a last-ditch effort to save herself, Elena attempts to shift into her Lycan to try to break free of Aurora's vice-like grip. Black fur erupts all over Elena's body as it bends and breaks, trying to transform before she meets her demise.

The most sadistic grin crosses Aurora's lips as she allows her body to fully shift to that of her hybrid beast. The guys and I quickly back up as the sound of ripping and whining fills the air. Weakly, Elena's Lycan tries to fend off the much larger hybrid that has her suspended in the air.

Without warning, Aurora's muzzle comes down and clamps onto Elena's shoulder as her talons sink deeply into the black Lycan's flesh. The familiar clicks of Aurora's ignitor fill the air before the roar of the flames can be heard. Within minutes, flames erupt from Elena's body as the scent of burned flesh fills the air. Her cries suddenly silenced as her lungs are burned to ash. To add insult to injury, Aurora rips Elena's body in half then proceeds to burn the remains till there's nothing left. Aurora's pain and heart-break pulse through the bond as her memories of all the things that Elena damaged come to mind.

Aurora falters shortly after torching the room. Her body betrays her, and she shifts back to her human form without warning. "Guys, we need to get Aurora to the surface. We can send the others to gather the treasures and skulls later." As soon as I finish speaking, Aurora falls to her knees in front of me.

Dante quickly takes off the shirt he was wearing, and we wrap it around Aurora's shoulders. We make it back to the room we entered from. Edgar has found a ladder that we lean against the wall leaning towards the door. The ladder is about three feet too short. Dante climbs up first, then I follow, holding onto Aurora as Edgar braces my back as we move up the ladder. At the top, I hand Aurora off to Dante. Once she is out of the way, I climb up then help Edgar.

"After I'm in the air, send Marco to go get my family from where we hid them." Both men nod agreeing, and I back away to shift back into my dragon. I stretch out my taloned hand, and my beloved mate is laid in it. I look down at Aurora; she's so limp and exhausted. Slowly, I close my hand around her. Dante gently moves her limbs around so that she remains safe and comfortable. Normally, my dragon would not be happy with another male touching our mate. Today is an exception. He knows we cannot adjust her the way Dante can; we both are grateful for his assistance.

Once Aurora is settled, we take flight and clutch her close to my scaled chest. I wrap my other hand around the hand, holding Aurora to protect her from the cold and wind. I reach out to Dimitri and Klaus, telling them what happened and how Aurora is at the moment.

I can feel the slight tug at my strength as I fly with her. *Baby girl, I know you're weak. Please wait till we get home. I don't want to crash and kill us both.* I feel the pull lessen then stop completely. I just hope she took what she needs for now. In the distance, I see the camp and the bonfire that the residents have every night. I roar, alerting the pack to my arrival in the field behind the houses. I spot Dimitri and Klaus with torches waiting for me. Elsa and two other females are there waiting as well.

I circle twice and do the one thing I told my children not to. I land with my hind feet first, then gently my front foot. Dimitri and Klaus rush over, and I slowly open my hand to expose a very bundled Aurora, sleeping soundly. Both of my bond mates are worried and concerned for her. Gently, Dimitri lifts Aurora up. Klaus moves behind him and throws a blanket over her and Dimitri, trying to keep his body heat in for her. Elsa stands there holding a robe out for me as I turn my back away from everyone and shift back to my human form. I am not shy in any way, but I find it rude for the world to see what's for Aurora's eyes only.

I slip on the offered robe, and everyone follows Dimitri and Klaus into the house. Klaus directs Dimitri to the master bedroom on the main level, and he lays her down gently. Elsa moves and starts to examine Aurora from head to toe. She shrugs her shoulders then looks back at us. "I don't think she ate enough before heading out on the mission with everyone. I believe her beast burned through her available fat reserves faster than she anticipated."

"What happened that was different with this mission than in the past?" Elsa looked to me for answers. Oh, I had answers but not ones I was willing to give her.

"Not too much out of the ordinary, Elsa. She froze an entire house that was on fire. She managed to kill Elena and several of her followers. Oh, and we found some of the missing treasures from her mother's treasury." I shrug my shoulders as if it was no big deal. I know I'm hiding vital information from her, but I'm not sure if we have traitors here as well.

Through the bond, I shared the events that actually occurred instead of the edited version I gave Klaus's grandmother. Dimitri gives me a subtle nod, and Klaus raises both eyebrows then spins to look out the window so Elsa wouldn't question him.

Dimitri moves and climbs up onto the bed and lies down next to Aurora. "I'll keep her warm. You two find food for her, probably fresh raw meat would be best." Dimitri makes absolute sense with his request. More often than not, Aurora has been eating her meat rare to raw ever since the babies.

Klaus and I leave to head to the kitchen. We are all on the same page after the last debacle. We are not leaving Aurora alone when she's in a weakened state. Klaus wasn't happy with what was in the kitchen and led me across the village over to a house with several roe deer and boar hanging out front. A stout man with a long beard comes out onto the front porch; he looks to Klaus then to me and bows. "M'lord, Alpha, what brings you to my humble home?"

I smile and slightly bow to him. "Our mate requires sustenance. I was wondering if I could purchase a whole deer from you for her?" Klaus pulls out his wallet and holds out more than enough euros to cover the deer and a bit extra for the hunter's trouble.

"Put your money away, Alpha, it's no good here when it comes to providing for my Queen. Only the best for her. You need meat, you come to me, don't feed her that store-bought chemical shit. My family hunted for Anca; I will be more than honored to hunt for Aurora." Hanz, I find out his name is, moves to his rack of deer and picks off a plump roe deer and a fat piglet. "This should please my Queen, if not, let me know, and I'll see what else I can get for her."

We thank Hanz profusely, then carry our game home. It's nice to see that there are old families still faithful to the crown. We make it back home, and the twins must have arrived with my twins and father-in-law while we were gone. Aurora is sitting up in bed with our toddlers sitting on the bed with her. Klaus leaves to go slice up some of the fresh pork and venison for Aurora. I notice in the corner that Marco is sound asleep. "Aurora, did you play vampire with Marco again?" I tilt my head looking at her, and she blushes.

"Yeah, he told me too. He didn't like me looking so pale and exhausted. Dominik helped him over to the chair to sit back down." Aurora adjusts how she's sitting then looks over at me. "I feel much better now. I'm just curious if I can drain someone to the point of death?" Aurora has that look on her face that lets you know she is seriously contemplating this theory.

Elsa turns around quickly and stares at Aurora, forgetting for a moment that not only is she queen, but that she is her Alpha too. "How can you think such a horrible thing?! It's a monstrous thing for such a beautiful woman to think about."

Aurora smirks and slowly shifts her body to most of her beast. She moves till she's nose to nose with Elsa. "Haven't you heard? I am a monster. A beast of legend, according to the Fae." Elsa promptly pisses herself and backs up slowly. The stench of fear and urine fills the room. "Don't let this beautiful visage fool you. Deep down, my beast lurks, ready to destroy anyone who threatens what's mine." Aurora slides back to where she was previously on the bed; she's completely human again by the time she sits down. Elsa leaves quickly, and the cleaning girls come in and clean up the mess. Aurora is calm, but you can sense under the surface something is bothering her.

Ladon and Tiamat tackle their mother and start leaving sopping wet toddler kisses. My children have grown so fast because of their mother's plan to allow them the anonymity of being in their dragon forms in public. Aurora's plan is solid though, you can't abduct or harm a child that you have never seen. I watch my children play, and it warms my heart to see them so healthy and happy. I've been blessed many times over this past year with a beautiful mate, wonderful bond mates, and two beautiful, healthy children.

I watch over my family that I've made. My legions of dragons wait for orders. We all believe in restoring the last Marelup back to the Lycan throne. The Strigoi have been a thorn in everyone's sides for far too long. Tonight, other packs of shifters arrive for the celebration that we planned for this new alliance's birth.

CHAPTER 4
Aurora

APRIL-

My to-do list is gradually getting smaller. Found Elena and slaughtered her ass, score one for me. Klaus and Alaric seem anxious because of all of the species that have rallied to my cause. I have Jayce in my closet searching for an outfit for tonight.

Honestly, I don't give a fuck. My mates are the only ones I worry about looking good for. Dimitri is at the table by my window, going through some of the treasures recovered from Elena's camp. The thought that she had some of my mother's things all this time and she never told me pisses me off to no end.

Things around me start to freeze, and Dimitri gets up and wraps his thick arms around me, holding me tightly to his chest. I sigh and relax in his grip. Without warning, the big guy scoops me up and carries me back over to the table he was sitting at. He pulls a single necklace out of a velvet pouch and dangles it in front of my eyes.

"You should wear this tonight; it was a gift from the Siberian Tiger Alpha to your mother. It's a promise of allegiance and an offer to become his mate. Vladimir took the necklace and wouldn't allow her to wear it." Dimitri nuzzles my cheek before continuing. "I already told Alaric that I was going to show it to you. Having the tigers on our side would be most helpful. Like you, they can climb walls. Siberian tigers are one of the biggest cats, and thankfully they have the numbers to help us," Dimitri says and smiles before he places the antique cat-eye pendant in my hand.

I stare at its craftsmanship; the metal's delicate twists and turns must have taken a very long time to do. By the age and weight of it, I know this was made by hand by someone who was very interested in my mother. I place the necklace back into its ornate pouch. My plan is to put it in the present Alpha's hands as a sign of goodwill. I don't want an old promise to weigh down the new alliance. "I will take your suggestions under advisement, love. But I honestly feel I would rather my own be given to me of their free will. The person that gave this to my mom is more than likely either very old or very dead. Either way, I don't think the new generation would hold to that old promise too willingly. I know I wouldn't." Slowly, I stand and then bend to kiss Dimitri's full lips. I can hear the pleased rumble of his beast as I slowly pull away to go search my closet for Jayce.

There's Jayce with the closet torn apart and clothing everywhere. Yup, this was not what I was expecting to be walking into, at least not from him. In the corner of the room, I find Dominik sitting there holding three outfits over his arm. Neither of the boys realizes I'm in there until I clear my throat to get their attention. "So, I see we had a category Jayce hurricane in my closet?" I smile and go to kiss Jayce and then Dominik.

All I can do is shake my head, looking at the mess they made in my absence. "Do we at least have a clue as to what I'm wearing tonight?" Dominik and Jayce each hold up a separate outfit, and I have no fucking clue which one I want to wear. Then I have a brilliant idea; I reach out through the bond and summon all my mates to the room. Since I have five mates, one outfit will win over the other easily. I kick Jayce and Dominik out of my closet then; I hang the two options up then wait for the others to arrive.

When I hear the commotion in the bedroom, I know it's time to step out. "Okay, guys, I need your help. The twins picked two beautiful outfits for me to wear, but they can't agree on which one. Here are five post-it pads with pens. I'm going to wear each outfit and model it for you. Write the number of your favorite down. Fold your post it up and hand it to me when I come back out. I'll see which one receives the most votes, and that's the one I'll wear tonight. Sound fair?" I look between all of my mates, and they nod and smile at me. Okay, the worst is over, now on to the show. I look between the two outfits. Both fit my style, and honestly, I may do an outfit change mid-party just to wear both.

Jayce's selection is slinky and silky feeling. Black skin-tight satin stretch pants with rhinestones around the waist and down the legs' outer seam. The shirt is a bodice hybrid with a peasant blouse. The bodice is blood red with black stitching; it makes my breasts look absolutely huge as they almost bubble over the top. The peasant blouse is black and off the shoulder with long flowing sleeves that are long enough to hide if I shift my arms. Oddly for Jayce, he picked out my black Docs to be worn with it. I mean, I love the idea, but it's not a typical choice for Jayce. I put my hair up into a quick French twist, with the rest of my hair flowing out in waves from the top. I place my great-grandmother's ruby crown upon my head then walk out.

Alaric drops his glass, spilling his drink all over his lap. My sweet Jayce is beaming with pride, looking at me wearing what he selected for me. This outfit reveals all five bite marks from my mates. Strategically, I understand why he did it. The evidence of all five bites would strike fear into the hearts of those that may stand before me. I look at Dimitri next, and he makes the twirling motion with his finger. Slowly I turn, then pause when my back is to the guys. I bend over, stretching my body out so that my ass is on full display. Something else falls, and I look back, and it's Klaus who dropped his glass this time.

Dominik stands and rushes over to me; I stand up and look up at him, smiling. "Okay, love, Jayce wins. You have to wear this tonight; I understand now why he chose it." Dominik runs his fingers over my bite marks, sending pulses straight to my core. "Look at this brilliance. Our marks are on full display. No one would dare to approach her unless they believe themselves to be a true mate." Dominik gently kisses his mark then walks away, leaving me wanting.

"Okay, now that you guys have me all riled up, let's go get this party started, shall we? We have guests arriving as we speak, Dante and Edgar are remaining as their dragons behind where I am sitting for this party. They will be switching out every few hours to keep watch over everything. After the raid on Elena's camp, I wouldn't be shocked if Vladimir sends forces to retaliate." I look back towards my mates, and not a single one attempts to argue my logic. "Alaric and Klaus will escort me to my seat with my children. Dimitri, you head up security and make sure everything is up to your standards. Jayce and Dominik help Dimitri in any way he needs. I have a feeling before sunrise we will be in the middle of a battle." Deep down, I am hoping I'm wrong. The little devil inside is screaming, wanting a complete blood bath.

We make it to the main walkway and it's covered in red petals and almost looks like blood droplets covering my path. My children in their dragon forms trot alongside us as we make our way to my makeshift throne. I raise my eyes to see that it's made of skulls similar to the one I had at the American Lycan camp. I look between my mates, trying to hold back my tears that threaten to break.

Dimitri decides to break the tension. "Baby girl, Klaus, and Alaric made you the throne. Some of the skulls are from this latest mission; the rest came from the original throne. We know that Sebastian's betrayal did some damage with you, but we hope to erase that pain in time. His skull and his mothers are the ones in the front of the arms. Feel free to dig your talons in and cut them if it helps heal your heart." Dimitri looks down at his feet; he, most of all, knows the pain of his betrayal.

I hug Dimitri around the neck and kiss him on his cheek. "Would you like to scratch them up a bit too?" I hit a playful tone in my voice as I look up into his hazel eyes.

"Nu! I've already pissed on them both. Then I rinsed them off. Honestly, I felt better after doing it." Dimitri has a sheepish look after he admits to pissing on their skulls. I can't help but laugh at his antics.

"Thank you for rinsing them off for me. I appreciate it. Nu? That translates to no, correct? I get confused. You bounce between Romanian and Russian so often my head spins." I giggle a bit, looking up at him, letting him know I'm not upset.

"Da, you're correct. I can't help it; it's just so much easier for me, at times, to just use the words that first come to mind. Sorry for the whiplash, my love." Dimitri bends down slowly and kisses my lips, sucking on my bottom lip. Fucker just made my damn greedy core clench. Fucking party…

I shake my head lightly, then move back to Alaric and Klaus as we come into sight of our guests. As soon as we are visible, Dante raises his head and roars, announcing our arrival to the clans. I wink at Klaus and Alaric and step away from them. Each step I take from this point on, the ground freezes, leaving a trail of frost behind me. Jayce runs over, and queue's up G-N-R's "You could be mine" for my walk to the throne. I look over my shoulder at him and wink, approving of the musical selection. The opening line always gets me, and I love it still.

I march my happy ass up to my skull throne, spin dramatically and sit up straight, looking out over everyone gathered. My children sit on pillows at my feet in their dragon forms, watching the people in front of us. I do a flourish with my right hand and Dante and my children breathe fire at the same time. I see fear in the eyes of some, but most watch and stare in wonder at the sight before them. It's now that I decide to test the strength of my Alpha powers.

"Welcome one and all." My sultry tone booms out across the gathering crowd with minimal effort on my part. "Thank you all for making the long journey to get here. My mates, packs, and allies, thank you for coming." I maintain the strength and power of the tone of my voice.

Most are looking at me in wonder. Most times, the Alpha is male and pureblood; I am neither male nor pure blood. I look briefly up to Dante, and he snakes his tail out in front of me. I rest my hand on it then leap up to stand on the flat blade. Slowly he elevates me up and out over the crowd. "I seek additional allies in the hope of taking back my mother's castle in the Carpathian Mountains. I seek to utterly destroy the Strigoi stronghold and return my people back to their ancestral home." Dante moves me over the crowd, then back to my throne, and gently sets me back down.

I walk to the edge of my platform and notice new arrivals. I make Alaric aware of the arrivals, and he goes to escort the Siberian Tigers leader to me. The leader is flanked by four men, all of them appearing to be of various mixed bloodlines. Two men distinctly have an Asian appearance, two seem to be more Russian, and the third male is a perfect blend of the two. As they get closer, I slowly move and meet them halfway.

My father rushes ahead and greets the men in Russian. Part of me is pissed he interfered, but they relax in his presence, and well, I'm kind of a wild card. My father makes introductions so that I am aware that the Alpha's name is Kazimir. He greets me and attempts to move in to kiss me; my skin quickly coats with frost as I back up and into Alaric. Within seconds my mates surround me, placing a hand on me, offering comfort. Dimitri is the first to speak to me as my father apologizes to Kazimir.

"My love, he was just trying to greet you," Dimitri says to me softly. He knows deep down my beast doesn't like strange males near me.

"You know how I am. I don't like other males touching me. It makes my skin crawl. I can't help it. I'm sorry." I look over at the tigers and apologize in their native tongue, explaining my issue with touch outside of my mates. It then dawns on my father the grievous error he had made, assuming it would be fine. Nicodeamus leads the tigers off and into the crowd heading towards the food. I pull Dominik with me and plop him on my throne, and I decide to use him as a chair for a while.

Sometime around eleven in the evening, I hear Dante sound the alarm overhead. Edgar, who is behind me, looks down, and I motion for him to lower his head. Quickly, I scoop up one baby and Dominik grabs the other. We run to Edgar's side and place the babies between his wings and send him into the sky with my children.

My other mates are already shifting and battling Strigoi. Most of the clans are shifted and entrenched in battle with the Strigoi as well. I motion for Dominik to shift, and he does so quickly. I run back up, behind my throne and strip out of my nice outfit and proceed to shift. My beast was ready for this, waiting for the attack to come. We climb quickly to the tallest building we can find and look out over the masses, seeking out who appears to be the leader of this rabble.

Off to the side and far in the back is a man with a large staff and a beard that would make Santa jealous. He appears to be the one in control of the Strigoi. I leap from building to building, searching for Ellis. I find him surrounded by Strigoi and backed into a corner. Silently, I land behind the group surrounding him. With one swipe of my talons, I remove the heads of four. Quickly, I attack the others, ripping their heads from their bodies, leaving a trail of black blood in my wake. I shift back to human speedily, and so does Ellis.

I make the *shh* motion to him. "There's a man on the hill with a Santa beard and a glowing staff. I think he's controlling the Strigoi. Thankfully, there's still patches of snow in the shadows on the way up to him. Take some of your men and hit him from the back. I'll go hit him head-on." I look at Ellis as his eyes swirl to that of his bear.

"We're good." is all Ellis says before taking off to meet up with his crew. I watch the bear fade of into the blackness.

Through the bond, I reach out to Dominik and Jayce, their black fur would blend in perfectly with how dark it is right now. When the guys catch up to me, I shift and show them my plan. I'm heading straight for the man, and I want them to come in from the sides while Ellis and his bears attack from the rear. The man will be so focused on me that he won't have time to brace for the other attacks.

We reach the point of no return and charge towards the man. I swear he has a sixth sense because he looks right at Dominik before sending a wall of ice towards him. It's times like this I pray our bond has gifted my mates with immunity to ice. I don't stop or slow down as the man attempts to attack Jayce and me both with ice. He doesn't realize that Ellis is up on his hind paws behind him till it is too late. With one quick swipe of Ellis's Polar Bears paw, the man's head goes rolling downhill.

I nod my head towards Ellis, then move to check my two Dire mates. Neither are injured, more so in shock that the ice didn't harm them or stop them. Gently with my talons, I remove what ice is stuck to their fur. Honestly, they made out a lot better than I had anticipated. I have something I really want to try, but I had to wait till we got back in the privacy of our bunker. I walk around with the twins to find the rest of our family stacking Strigoi heads in a pile in the center of the camp.

Slowly, I draw in a deep breath, close my eyes and reach out, sensing all of the dragons. I feel my group's heartbeats, then I sense the faster beating of my babies' hearts. Gently, I give them a slight tug and reach out to Edgar to tell him the babies will fly to me. Soon I sense the excitement of my children's flight as they make their way back to me. I reach up carefully with my taloned hands to pluck both babies out of the air. I snuggle my hatchlings to my beast's body.

Out of nowhere, a white Siberian Tiger comes out from the tree line. He's not aggressive; he looks at me curiously and starts to circle, making my mates assume aggressive stances. Alaric has already shifted back to his dragon form and has summoned the babies to him. The tiger lowers his head to me then shifts back to his human form. I have to admit he's beautiful, but I'm not interested.

The Alpha Kazimir comes running from out of the tree line. "My Queen, please spare him. He's my only son." Kazimir skids to a stop and drops to his knees before me.

CHAPTER 5
Aurora

Ever the peacemaker, Jayce, comes up alongside me and offers me a robe so that I can shift back. Jayce opens the robe wide and I shift back quickly. Gently, I kiss Jayce's cheek and then reach my hand into the robe's pocket to find the necklace. I toss the pouch to Kazimir. "I wasn't going to kill your son. He should, however, know better than to approach a female with her young." I don't pay the young man any mind as another pack mate offers the man a towel to wrap around his waistline, so he's decent.

"My Queen," Kazimir continues. "Do you know what this talisman means?" He holds the talisman out, dangling it in my direction.

I lock eyes with my father, searching his memory for the history of the talisman. "Yes, I do. It was given to my mother as a gift, an offering of an alliance, as well as a marriage. I return it to you knowing that it once was made by hand by one of your ancestors.

I figured you would like it back." Dominik remains in his Dire Wolf form and comes to lean against my right side, waiting to see what happens. Out of habit, I thread my fingers through his thick fur, more to keep myself calm.

Slowly, Kazimir nods, then pulls out a box and offers it to his son to take. His son steps forward and kneels before me. He holds up the box to me and opens the top to see a similar talisman being offered to me. "My name is Jagger, firstborn son of Kazimir and Anastasia. I wish to offer you and your bond mates an alliance in blood." He sighs, forcing himself to continue. "I know a political marriage will never yield me cubs. Still, it's a smart decision for the safety and welfare of my people." Slowly, he raises his eyes to meet mine, and he attempts to smile.

"Who do you leave behind that has taken the light out of your eyes?" My eyes shift to that of my beast; my mercury dragon orbs search his features for any signs of deceit and find none. I do, however, feel his pain and anguish.

Jagger lowers his hands slowly and rests the box and his hands in his lap. "My light?" He glances down, and I see a single tear roll down his cheek. "I had two, once. One my father put to death for being male. The other, my Arabella, died in childbirth. I raise my daughter with the help of my mother." I watch his shoulders sag, and the fight drain out of him. I look at his father and then at my mates.

"Come in and talk to me." I look at my mates each, then at Jayce. "My beloved, please make Jagger comfortable while I go get dressed." I walk over and kiss Jayce's cheek, then I turn and jump on Dom's wolf's back. "Let's beat everyone inside." I hold on to his thick black fur tightly when he takes off towards the house.

We beat everyone in, and I hear Elsa yelling about wild animals running through the house. I can't help but laugh at her as we make the sharp turn into the bedroom.

I leap off Dominik's back and run into the closet. Quickly, I find the outfit Dominik had picked out for me earlier. Dominik has chosen a light, flowing silk shirt with a dragon pattern on it. The top is black and white, which covers most of my mate's colors. The pants are a dark-brown faux suede with stitched-in paw prints down the outer seam. One of the cleaning girls has returned with my ruby crown and my clothing from earlier. I look at the other three crowns I have on the shelves.

I reach up and grab the Elven crown Oberon had crafted for me. Quickly, I use the curling iron and give my hair a little bit of body. It's times like this I wish I had different colored hair other than snow-white. I take some of the hair ribbons the girls have given me and mix them into my hair, giving it a splash of color. Once I'm pleased with my appearance, I head out into the meeting hall. Everyone is sitting around the table, and I'm over here like, *oh, hell no*, "To the living room, we're not going to war again. This isn't an interrogation or a negotiation; we're talking like adults."

I make it into the living room first and take control of the coveted colossal bean bag chair. I plop myself right in the middle, soon to be attacked by my spawn. My twins run laps around me on the bean bag till they decide where they want to lie down. I softly laugh to myself, knowing full well that I am the only one to know which baby is which.

Alaric pauses and looks between the twins, then back to me. I watch his one eyebrow raise up as he points to the baby on my right and mouths *Ladon*. I shake my head no and laugh at him.

Alaric looks so mad that he can't tell. I twitch my finger at him, and he comes to kneel before the babies and me. "Tia's eyes are grey-blue like my dad's, Ladon's eyes are more grey-green like yours. Also, Ladon's eye ridges are more raised than Tia's." I lift each baby's head, pointing the features out to their father. My other mates watch intently as I explain everything.

"Jayce, love, will you take the children to go get changed. I want our new ally to know who he is protecting." Jayce nods, and the babies leave me to follow Jayce out of the room.

Klaus climbs up onto the beanbag with me as I turn to address Jaggar. "I will not trap you in a political marriage. It is against my belief to take away someone's right to a true mate." Gently, I rest my hand on Klaus's knee.

I'm still grateful the gods blessed me with him. I refocus on Jaggar. "If you wish to remain at my side as a friend and ally, I will gladly accept it. Your people have the protection of my house and my packs and legions." I shift my weight slightly and lean forward.

"In return, your people will come when called; when I plan to attack and take back my ancestral home. I request that if you know of any specialized fighting skills, my people may find useful that you teach it to us." I try my best not to have my resting bitch face in full effect, like I normally maintain through meetings. Alaric has slid up behind me and is gently rubbing between my shoulder blades to help me maintain a sense of calm.

Jaggar and his father look at each other; Kazimir speaks in their mixed dialect. I look between my father and Dimitri, being able to discern what is being said. "It is monumentally rude to speak in a mixed dialect in an attempt to speak around your host, Kazimir.

Do you wish me to challenge you for Alpha of your streak? I can promise you I can win without shifting and without ever leaving this bean bag." My mates start getting restless. Jayce returns just in time with my babies. My precious toddlers wobble their way over to Alaric, Klaus, and me.

Sweat beads run down Kazimir's forehead. He's not sure exactly how much I understood. Too bad for him. I understood everything. "I meant no disrespect, my Queen. Some things just shouldn't be discussed outside of the family." He's clearly fumbling for words, trying not to escalate matters further.

I stand slowly and stretch my body; with each step I take, the ground freezes under me. I watch Kazimir's eyes widen in fear as he sees me approaching. "Who was the last great dragoness to walk the Earth, Kazimir?" My eyes are that of my beast. As if on cue, Dominik hands me my great-grandmother's ruby crown and takes the Elvish one away from me. I place my great-grandmother's crown upon my head and stop to wait for his answer.

Kazimir swallows hard and looks up at me. "The Blood Queen, she ruled with bloody talons and little room for forgiveness. She was probably one of the scariest dragons in existence. She could summon dragons from far and wide and kill with a touch." Hmm, that last part I was unaware of. I raise an eyebrow as soon as he mentions the death touch. I wiggle my fingers, itching to test the theory out on him.

Klaus must have sensed my intentions and runs to get between Kazimir and me. "My love, please don't kill this man in front of his son. Jaggar has lost so much already. Do you wish to cause him more pain?" I search Klaus's eyes for answers, and all I see is his love and adoration for me reflecting back. I lean forward and rest my forehead against Klaus's chest as he moves me away.

Kazimir mutters under his breath, "She's no descendant of the Blood Queen. She's weak and foolish."

I raise my head off of Klaus's chest and shift my arms to my gauntlets, my long, white talons gleam in the light. I flourish both hands in front of me without hesitation, creating an ice prison to form around Kazimir. "You dare call me weak, you foolish kitty cat." I run my talons over the ice, causing the nails on a chalkboard sound to be made.

"Summon his generals here now. Jayce, pull the security footage and amplify his voice. I want his officials to hear what he has to say." I look back to Alaric and then Nicodeamus. "You two have a lot of explaining to do later."

My son and daughter come up next to me as the officials file into the room. They aren't happy seeing their leader imprisoned like he is. After watching the footage, they agree with whatever punishment I see fit as long as the alliance will be forged. I look to each of my mates: Dimitri, Dominik, and Alaric give an immediate thumbs down. Jayce and Klaus chose to spare him. I look to Nicodeamus, who gives an immediate thumb down. Next, my eyes fall on Jaggar.

"I know he's your father, but as future Alpha of your streak, what would your vote be if your ruler was spoken ill of?" I watch his eyes, and they harden in a second and immediately turns his thumb down.

"Hmm, maybe you shouldn't have killed the man your son loved, Kazimir. I sentence you to death in the most painful way I can think of." I shift my hands back to human and lightly touch his flesh. I feel the current of his life essence flowing steadily through his body. I reach out and grasp at it and start pulling it into myself.

Minuscule wrinkles form around his eyes, and the quality of his skin changes. The iris of his eyes begins to dull and lose color, and a haze coats his cornea. We watch Kazimir age before our eyes as I pull at his essence slowly. Panic slowly crosses his face as he realizes his body is aching, and his skin is wrinkling quickly. His muscle tone degrades rapidly; a once powerful Alpha is almost half the mass he used to be.

Kazimir begs for his life. Halfway through begging, he curses at me. Hoping that Tomas eats my heart for breakfast. That he should have signed the alliance with the Strigoi instead. There you have it; he was tainted by the Strigoi, and it's exactly why he killed off his son's lover to break his will. Talk about some fucked up shit. I shift my hand quickly and reach in and rip out Kazimir's heart to end it quickly.

My body is humming from all the extra life force I have stolen. It's time for me to make amends with my mate's grandmother. We didn't start off on the right foot, and I feel horrible for how I had treated her in the past. Elsa comes in to check on everyone and spots the Kasimir mummy in the ice prison. "That's new." Elsa says.

I have a moment of brilliance. "How much do you trust me, Elsa?" I look at her through the eyes of my beast. Her aura is all over the place; mostly curiosity is surfacing.

"I trust you with my life. You are my Klaus's mate and love. I know in my heart you wouldn't harm me." Elsa smiles, looking up at me. Time has ravaged this poor sweet woman, and her time is almost over. She has maybe another ten years tops if my theory doesn't work.

"Come here. Let me see if I can help you." Elsa willingly walks into my open arms. I lower my head and press my lips to her forehead and concentrate on that new life force flowing through me. Tentatively, I grip it and start to slowly feed it into Elsa. I pray to the gods that my plan works for her.

Slowly, I concentrate the energy into my hands, and I place them on Elsa's face and slowly draw them down from her temple to her chin. Through my mind's eye, I see my hands wiping away the years of wrinkles and sun-damaged skin. I see the layers of skin and muscles underneath rejuvenating and healing from the inside out.

Gasps are heard around the room as I continue to focus on the energy moving between my hands. I slide my hands down her shoulders to her ribs and down to her hips where I stop. I focus on feeling the energy rejuvenate every inch of her body. Finally, when the last of the stolen life force is spent, I stand up straight and open my eyes to look at Elsa.

Elsa is absolutely radiant; her hair is back to a solid dark brown, and her skin is almost as smooth as mine. I smile as I look down at her. "How do you feel?" I can't help but be excited for her and happy at the same time. Klaus and I get more time with her. Definitely a bonus.

"I feel wonderful, Aurora. What did you do?" Elsa then looks down at her hands, then back up at me. Her eyes are wide open, and she's looking at her hands as if they aren't hers anymore. Quickly, she runs to the closest mirror and stares at the woman she used to be about two hundred years ago.

"How? I don't understand. Thank you, thank you so much." Elsa runs back over to me and hugs me tightly, kissing my cheek repeatedly. Soon as the hug-fest starts, it's over, and out the door, she runs.

All I can do is shake my head and look at the others. My freak level just hit epic levels, and I'm perfectly okay with that. I kind of feel like Robin Hood: steal life from the wicked to give to the good. I look at my father next. Oh yes, he will get rejuvenated next, if I have anything to say about it. Life has just gotten a lot more interesting.

CHAPTER 6
Klaus

I can't believe what my mate just did. She literally stole Kazimir's life and gave it to my grandmother. I wonder what else Oberon did to Aurora. She said he settled her beast and unlocked new powers within her. My bond mates and I have been discussing it in private for days now. We are thankful she's calmed down and doesn't seem to be waging war within herself.

I head outside to catch up with my pack mates, who are currently training the new arrivals. We are leaving nothing to chance when it comes to the assault on the castle. The training pit is loaded with people training with not only weapons but also their shifted forms. Dimitri and Dominik emerge from the house, dressed for training.

The pit stops and the occupants turn to face Dimitri and Dominik. They explain the training for today and the new pairings for the training. Wow, their combined knowledge is impressive. I know Dimitri has been in service of the crown for years. Dominik, he said he was the weapons master and enforcer of his father's pack. I kind of feel inadequate compared to them. Aurora says we are all equals, but it kind of hurts that I feel like I have nothing to offer.

Suddenly, I have slender fingers covering my eyes from behind. "Hmm, I wonder who has taken my sight from me?" I know by scent it's my mate, Aurora. Her soft giggles behind me give me butterflies in my stomach.

"It's the big bad Hybrid," Aurora says, trying to be serious. Aurora leans forward and nips my shoulder over her mate mark. Her bite sends a thrill straight to my groin.

I look up and see Dominik and Dimitri watching me closely. They know all too well what she's doing to me. Both men smirk at me, then turn their backs to me. Shit, I've never done anything alone with Aurora. To be perfectly honest, my mate kind of scares me. She's so powerful, skilled, and experienced. I'm actually kind of embarrassed to admit Aurora was my first. I spin in Aurora's grip and kiss her lips. "My beautiful angel, what can I do for you, my love?"

Aurora blushes as she looks up at me. "I'm…. I was kinda wondering if you would have lunch with me today?" Aurora starts to fidget with the hem of her shirt. I can't believe she looks so nervous.

"Of course, I would love to, my sweet angel." I lean down and kiss Aurora gently. I take her hand, and she leads me off towards the large Douglas fir tree. There's a modest picnic setup just for us. We sit together, and Aurora starts to serve us lunch. I'm quite puzzled by our queen serving me. "My angel, shouldn't I be serving you?" I tilt my head, looking at her curiously.

Aurora draws in a slow, deep breath then grips both of my hands.

"I know I can be scary at times." Aurora lowers her eyes and looks at our hands. "I know, I must scare you. I'm sorry that I do."

I pull a hand free from Aurora's and gently cup her cheek. "Don't be sorry, angel, I've never dated anyone else but you. I've been waiting for my mate for what feels like forever." I bite my bottom lip as I watch her reaction to the news.

Aurora smiles softly and blushes. Slowly, she leans forward and kisses me. "I waited too. It just sucks it was that fucking rat bastard, scumbag of a false mate that I lost my innocence to." Aurora laughs softly then strokes my beard. "At least you got to lose yours with your true mate." Her smile is brighter than a thousand suns. I feel blessed to have her in my life.

"I knew that day that I came to your camp you were mine. I was shocked to see you had a Lycan male claiming to be your mate when clearly he wasn't. The sun rises and sets according to our mate's desires. He didn't seem to care if the sun came out at all." I bite my bottom lip again, feeling as though I may have gone too far.

"Klaus, I know that now. You've shown me what it's like to have a true Lycan mate. You, Alaric, and the others make me feel like I can take on the world and win. That may or may not be in the best interest of the rest of the world." Aurora laughs softly and scoots closer to me. "What is one thing your heart desires? If it's within my power, I will give it to you freely." I can see how serious Aurora is with her question. She actually wants to know what I covet most in the world.

I reach out to pull Aurora into my lap and wrap my arms tightly around her. Gently I rest my head on top of hers and sigh softly. "You've already given me two of the things I most desire. The third will come in due time."

Aurora moves a bit in my lap so she can look up at me. "I have?" Her voice rises at the end of her two-word question, as if I hold the mysteries of the world in my hands. I kind of do. I hold my hybrid queen in my arms, and she is the entirety of my world.

"You have, my angel. You've given me your heart and your love freely and in its entirety. You have given me bond mates that I call my best friends, lovers, and brothers, depending on the situation. The last will come in due time. I'm in no hurry. I'm blessed to have forever with you." I kiss her lips gently, then rest my hand on her stomach so that the third want is clear. She smiles against my lips, then lightly bites my bottom one. I can't help but laugh at my mate's antics.

I'm so lost in my happy little bubble I don't notice Jayce's approach. "Guys, I hate to break up the love fest, but a convocation has been spotted on the horizon, and Nicodeamus wants us all present for when they land." Jayce basically spits out his information then takes off to search out the others.

All I can do is shake my head and stand up, cradling Aurora like she's a bride on her wedding night. I love listening to her laugh because I refuse to set her down on her feet. Nope, this is my time with her, and nothing is going to end it early. We reach the porch of the Alpha house, and I set Aurora down.

Alaric comes up behind her and sets her ruby crown on her head. He then hands me the one that Aurora had made for each of us. I still can't get used to wearing this blasted thing. Aurora goes prancing from mate to mate, adjusting our crowns and kissing our lips before she moves onto the next one. A few of the house girls stand waiting with robes for our guests who are about to arrive. As the convocation gets closer, we can make out that they are Golden Eagles, the same as what Aurora's guardian was. Dimitri looks beside himself. I can't tell if it's excitement or pain. I mean, seriously, the man has perfected the male version of the resting bitchface.

One by one, the Golden Eagles land and shift to their human form. They appear slightly skittish around all of the apex predators in the camp. I can't blame them, to be honest. If I didn't know Aurora and Alaric, I'd be scared of them too. The last eagle to arrive lands the closest to the porch, shifting to his human form at the last moment. His eyes remain that of his eagle as he stares at Aurora without blinking.

I hear Aurora's breath hitch, then stop. The ambient temperature around us drops significantly. The man before us looks like that guy Jax from that motorcycle show that was on TV. His hair is a dirty blond, and so is his beard. If I didn't know better, he looks like he could be related to Alaric, you know, that Viking type. My guess is he is the Alpha of the Eagle Clan. Two others try to approach and he raises a hand, stopping them in their tracks.

We turn and watch Aurora, scales ripple up and down her arms and over the bridge of her nose. Her eyes are those dragon orbs of hers, the liquid mercury seeming to swirl around the black slit. Alaric reaches for Aurora, and her beast explodes into existence and growls at him in warning.

Her beast's massive head swings to regard the naked man before her. It feels like that t-rex scene from that dinosaur movie. Each step of hers shakes the planks in the porch. The air is heavy with anticipation, no one is sure what Aurora will do now. Half of the males' clan have shifted and taken to the trees nearby to watch.

I watch in horror as Aurora reaches the last step; she steps onto the soil, freezing it with every step. I give the man credit; he's standing his ground as Aurora's massive ten foot tall, half-ton beast looms over him. Slowly, she lowers her head and sniffs at his scalp first, then his neck. His Golden Eagle eyes remain focused on Aurora, not one ounce of fear evident on his face. Aurora proceeds to sniff his neck then she begins to circle him.

"We need to do something. Alaric, Dimitri, can't one of the two of you step in?" I look between Alaric and Dimitri, figuring since they both are the largest of us, they should be able to save him.

"No need. She's testing him," Nicodeamus states so calmly it's frightening. "Besides, if you step in now and he's unworthy, it will only give him false hope that he was accepted only to be shunned later." Nicodeamus slowly turns to head back the way he came, "We don't need another Sebastian on our hands." With that, Nicodeamus leaves the five of us staring at each other. None of us want to deal with the fall out of another mate that shouldn't be.

Aurora's beast looks back to us as she stands behind the male. Her gauntleted hand raises, and her talons come out in front of him. Her hand is level with his throat, and her beast has that gleam in its eye. Quickly she pulls her hand back, her talons heading for the man's throat. The five of us yell "no!" at the top of our lungs.

Before Aurora's talons can touch the man's throat, she shifts back to her human form and grips his throat. Quickly, she pulls him back to her and sinks her canines into his shoulder, as her eyes remain locked on us. Rivulets of his blood run down his chest as his eyes roll back in his head. The extreme pleasure from her bite makes him cum; his seed sprays wildly in jets out before him, landing in the dirt.

Besides the mate orgy we had a while back, this has to be the single hottest moment I've gotten to witness. Aurora slowly releases the man and licks his wounds, healing them instantly. Cautiously, she steps before him and looks up into his eyes. You can see the love and adoration he has for her instantly once his eyes shift back to human. His eyes are a beautiful shade of grey-green. Aurora's eyes sometimes turn a similar color, depending on her mood. Slowly, we all move to greet the new mate.

The new male looks down at Aurora, kisses her forehead and extends his hand to Alaric, who approaches first. "I'm Arnulf, Alpha of the Golden Eagles. Our ancestor came to the elders during meditation. He spoke of a female that was a daughter to him, that faces great peril ahead of her. He said she needs our wings, our sight, and our talons to help take back her mother's home." Aurora and Dimitri immediately begin to tear up looking at each other, then at the male that now holds her.

Tears began to stream down Aurora's cheeks, her bottom lip quivers as she tries to restrain the emotions fighting to surface. "Andre?" Aurora says, her voice a whisper as she looks up to Arnulf, hoping he is talking about Andre.

Slowly, he nods and kisses away her tears and hugs her tightly to him. "He was only able to cross the veil because the ancient rites were performed for him by a loved one. I can only assume he meant you." His hand caresses her cheek gently. "He said your name is Aurora. It's very beautiful and fitting for you." He gently kisses Aurora's forehead, and she loses it, crying hysterically.

Dimitri steps forward and takes hold of Aurora. The two of them cling ever so tightly to each other, crying hysterically. Nicodeamus feels a disturbance in the force, comes back out, sees Aurora and Dimitri crying, and runs towards them. Between Aurora and Dimitri, they fill Nicodeamus in on what is happening, and he joins in on the crying.

I extend my hand next to Arnulf and motion back to them. "Aurora performed the rites after Andre was murdered. She stood in her father's flames and watched his body burn. Jayce has the video if you want to watch it. You can see Andre's spirit leave the funeral pyre." As soon as I finish my sentence, Jayce is at our side playing the video for Arnulf.

I watch the emotions move across Arnulf's face; first pride, then amazement, then back to pride again. He looks between Jayce and me, then back to the major hug fest that now includes Dominik. "A dragon's flame won't burn her? That's incredible. We are truly blessed to have such a powerful mate." Jayce and I nod, agreeing with his statement. He has no clue just how powerful she truly is.

CHAPTER 7
Klaus

Arnulf turns to his people and screeches several times and they fly off, leaving him behind here at the compound. "I will call them back when we are ready to go to war. For now, all the larger predators are making them uneasy." Arnulf looks at me, then at Jayce. "Do either of you have extra clothes I can wear until my bags arrive tomorrow? I don't mind walking around naked, but I don't believe other females should see me like this now that I have a mate." That one statement from him catches all of our attention. He's going to fit in just fine.

Jayce and I lead Arnulf into the alpha house and into the master suites. Aurora's twins come running over and tilt their little dragon heads. Arnulf looks from the twins, then to me, then back to the twins. "Genetically, they are Aurora's and Alaric's babies. We all claim paternity when it comes to their care." I smile proudly as I look at the hatchlings before me.

"When the babies are in their human forms, we're all called Dad. Alaric is called Daddy; it's the only difference. They accept all of us as their father figures. It's really cool if you think about it. It definitely makes it easier on Aurora having multiple mates to help with the babies, so she's not so exhausted." I toss Arnulf a pair of sweats, and Jayce grabs him a T-shirt. Arnulf quickly dresses then sits on the floor to let the babies check him out.

"Children have become rare with my people. The occurrences of true mates are few and far between. I have been telling the elders that we must start looking outside our borders, to other species if we wish to survive." He sighs softly, the mantle of Alpha weighing heavily upon his brow.

"They fear change, and it will be the death of us. At least with me as Alpha, we have a chance to change our way of thinking, especially when they see me with Aurora and you guys." Arnulf is smiling broadly as he gets tackled by the twins. The rest of my bond mates and Aurora walk in, just as the babies go to attack Arnulf again. He rolls back, catching them gently and falls with them, taking the brunt of the landing. I have to give it to him; he's laughing hysterically at the baby dragons' antics.

Aurora stands there smiling and makes a noise only her hybrid can produce. Quickly, the children run to her and shift to their toddler selves. "Jayce, my love, please dress the children," Aurora says softly. She then moves forward swiftly, catching Jayce off guard and kisses him passionately before he heads off with the children.

"Arnulf, sorry about the..." She motions to where she had bitten him, looking a little embarrassed by her actions. "My beast got away from me. I'm sorry if I was a bit too forward. She did the same to Klaus a few months back. I feel bad when she doesn't wait for consent." Aurora lowers her eyes, looking at her hands as they grip each other, turning her knuckles white.

Arnulf moves swiftly and grips her hands. He tilts his head, trying to get her to look at him. "I am honored your beast chose me. Usually, a male makes a nest and hopes a female deems him worthy. You deemed me worthy without seeing my nest or what I was able to provide for you. Why?" He is genuinely curious as to what made him worthy in her eyes.

Aurora smiles and looks at each of us. She walks up to Alaric and places her hand on his shoulder. "Alaric's dragon called to my dragon side, his promise of protection and his loyal heart sang to my beast."

She next moves to stand beside Dimitri and smiles, looking up at him. "My beloved Great Bear, he has survived me from infancy. We have endured many hardships together and the loss of loved ones that is difficult to recover from." Aurora reaches up and gently caresses Dimitri's cheek; he leans into her caress, smiling at her. "His bear kept me sane, alive and protected. If it weren't for him and our initial bond, I would have been one of the lost ones without a pack. Lost to my animal, never to be human again. Dimitri saved me from me."

Next, Aurora moves over to Dominik and grips his shoulder. "Dom risked his life coming to me when I was my most volatile. I thought I was going to lose his brother and our fragile bond to the man he loved." Aurora's smile is radiant as describes hers and Dom's bond. "Dominik made the decision to ask my father to place him in a confined space with me. It wasn't the smartest move he could have made, but it's what forged our bond. He put my needs before his personal safety."

Jayce chooses now to re-enter with the twins in tow. "My sweet, sweet Omega mate, he guards my heart the fiercest. He's my snuggler and my chocolate hoarder." Aurora gently kisses Jayce's temple, then moves to me.

She looks up into my eyes and smiles softly. "Klaus here sees me as the woman I want to be. He calls me his angel when all I ever feel like is a demon. He leaped across a balcony to catch me before I fell, in my early stages of pregnancy. He knew before I did what we were, damn blood magic stealing precious time from me." Aurora kisses my cheek before turning to face Arnulf.

"Dimitri and Klaus were robbed of precious time with me because of Vladimir's tainted bloodline." She motions to Nicodeamus next. "My father was robbed of his mate because of Vladimir's treachery that knows no bounds. I swear, I will have my revenge, and I will dance on the bones of my enemies." She smiles, and her eyes flash with the power of her beast for a second.

"You know what I see when I look in your eyes, Arnulf?" She tilts her head for a moment. "Hope. I see hope for a better future. I see a future where I'm not constantly looking over my shoulder, afraid for my children's lives." She shakes her head lightly. "I don't need to see material things to gauge the man you are. You stood up to my beast when I know your bird wanted to fly. You trusted me enough to know I would never harm what's meant to be mine." Aurora smiles and kisses Arnulf on the lips. She lingers there for a moment then pulls away.

"Ok guys, enough mushy shit, I'm hungry. What's for dinner?" There's the Aurora we all know and love. Her request for food has us all cracking up and heading to the kitchen. Jayce is in charge of dinner tonight; I'm kind of curious as to what he has made for all of us. The kitchen smells divine. Between my mother and Jayce cooking, we will be well fed.

We find my mother and grandmother in a heated discussion, yelling at each other in German. It's not like German doesn't sound angry enough, even when spoken calmly. Just as I'm about to say something, Aurora unleashes a blast of her Alpha power that silences the room. Both my mother and grandmother are subjugated before Aurora because of the force she uses.

Slowly, she moves to stand before both women, shaking her head at them. "Enough of the bullshit! Tonight is a night of celebration! If I hear one more jealous or petty word, I swear to the gods heads will roll!" Aurora growls out the sentence as she looks between the women. Jayce chooses now to move behind Aurora and rub her shoulder lightly. Slowly, the oppressive feeling leaves the room, and Aurora turns away from my mom and grandmother.

Arnulf chooses now to turn to me and raises an eyebrow in question. "I'd love to say you'll get used to it, but I'd be lying. She's only getting stronger as time goes on. Each new mate brings a new power and more strength." I shrug my shoulders as I finish my sentence. I mean, seriously, what can I possibly say at this point?

"I would like to offer a mating present to you, Aurora, and to my new bond mates." Arnulf looks to each of us in turn, then back to Aurora. "I can help you reach your friend in the spirit world and possibly your mother. If you would allow me to try?" Arnulf doesn't realize the boon he just offered her.

Aurora's eyes light up, and she runs to grab Dimitri and Nicodeamus. "Yes, please, can we try after dinner?"

Arnulf smiles and nods his head slowly. "Anything for you, my mate. If it's within my power, it's yours."

The winner of the best and safest answer to date is now Arnulf. We all gather around the table, passing the bowls and baskets around. For now, the looming danger of the outside world is forgotten. Right now, everything is right in the world. We know the war is on the horizon, but it's nice to forget that part of life for a little bit.

Aurora chooses now to come to me and sit on my lap at the dinner table. She absolutely cracks me up at times. I don't think there's a single dinner that she's sat in her own chair the entire meal. Dimitri says it's because her beast needs contact to feel secure enough to eat in new places. Let's face it, this isn't her home, and we don't plan on staying here once the castle is liberated from the Strigoi.

Apparently, tonight I'm not allowed to feed myself; neither is Dominik. Aurora takes a huge helping of her favorite foods and alternates between me, Dom, and herself. Jayce starts laughing at Aurora's antics, and she flings a scoop of mashed potatoes at his head. Son of a bitch. Jayce moves just in time to catch the scoop, mostly in his mouth.

Aurora is cracking up, laughing at Jayce, who in turn flings some mashed potatoes at her. You know it's my luck that she moves at the last moment, and I get a glob of mashed potatoes on my face. Aurora is still laughing, looking at me before she starts to lick the potatoes off of my face.

The table silences as they watch Aurora lick my face clean. She turns and looks at everyone, who promptly starts to pretend like they weren't watching. "Oh, come on, guys, that was not the weirdest thing you've caught me doing," Aurora says, not skipping a beat. Poor Dimitri almost chokes on his drink. Alaric needs the Heimlich maneuver to dislodge the chunk of meat from his throat.

Jayce looks like he is going to say something for a moment, then he thinks better of it. Arnulf looks at Aurora and me and shrugs his shoulders. "They think it's odd for a mate to preen the other? I thought wolves are pack animals?"

"We are," Aurora says, then turns to look at the others. "They don't complain when I run my tongue in other places. But apparently, licking Klaus's face isn't normal," Aurora says with a sarcastic tone. I look at my bond mates, and their faces are various shades of red. "Don't act innocent, you heathens. You know you love it!"

This time it's poor Nicodeamus that almost drowns at the table. He's having one hell of a coughing fit. Dimitri is quick to pat Nicodeamus on the back, trying to help him clear the fluid from his lungs.

I decide to take this time to finally be a wise-ass. Then again, I have Aurora on my lap. Who in their right mind would fuck with me right now? "Welcome to the insanity, Arnulf!" I raise my glass to toast to our new bond mate. Poor guy has no clue what he just got himself into!

NEVER IN THE HISTORY OF MY PEOPLE HAVE ANY EVER CHOSEN A MATE outside of our own kind. Many live their lives alone or paired up with another, with no hope of ever having a hatchling of their own. Aurora fiddles with her phone and puts on "Silent Lucidity" from Queensryche, saying it was one of Andre's favorite songs. It's midnight now, and we gather around the fire in the tent that we had erected in a hurry.

Aurora sits next to me with some of Andre's belongings clutched to her chest. She anxiously fiddles with each item looking them over carefully. Nicodeamus has a single black braid in his hand. His sorrow is evident with how haunted his eyes appear. The hollow depths seem to almost stare through the braid in his hands. I watch him as he runs his fingers over the hair. I can only assume it's from Aurora's mom.

I start to toss the herbs into the flames, and they begin to change colors. Extending my hand, I reach out to Aurora on my right ,and Jayce who is on my left. One by one, we take each other's hands and form a circle. "Please close your eyes till we make contact." Slowly, we close our eyes as I begin the ancient rites to summon an ancestor.

After several moments of chanting, there's a soft scent of cologne in the tent, and I hear Aurora gasp as she grips my hand tighter. I open my eyes, and the ancestor that had guided me here stands within the smoke before me. His eyes sweep over everyone gathered, then locks on my mate. A fatherly gaze sweeps over her this time as he smiles softly.

"Baby girl." Andre's voice is like a whisper on the wind. His smile broadens as he tilts his head to the side, watching her reaction. At the sound of his voice, everyone opens their eyes. Aurora almost instantly starts to cry, looking at Andre. Dimitri and Nicodeamus are crying as well at the sight of their old friend.

"Baby girl, please don't cry. I can't hug you and make it better," Andre says, smiling at Aurora.

Aurora sniffles then reigns in her tears. "I'm so sorry, papa bird. I miss you so much. Don't worry, I made Sebastian suffer for what he did to you. I ripped his heart out then cut off his head. Oh, and I have babies." Aurora's eyes glow for a moment before her two baby dragons came running into the tent.

"I named them Ladon Uther and Tiamat Andrea. I didn't know I was having a son, but my daughter's middle name is after you." Aurora's babies sit on either side of her then shift to their human forms to look at Andre. Both children are blonde with grey eyes and chubby toddler cheeks.

Andre sniffles now, looking at the babies, then back to Aurora. "You make me so proud. I watch over you, even from here. I sent Arnulf and his clan to aid you. I figured since I cannot be your eyes in the land of the living, he can." Andre stares at Arnulf then starts laughing. "Son of a bitch. You're her mate." He points right at the mate mark that Aurora blessed me with. "You have to finish the rituals. Otherwise, she won't get a gift from you."

"Yes, my ancestor, I will. I am blessed and honored that you sent me to her." I lean over and kiss Aurora's temple. "Andre's twin brother is my great grandfather. His great bloodline lives on through me and us when we are blessed with hatchlings." Andre then takes the time to speak to everyone else present, as well. Aurora smiles, getting the chance to spend time with him, at least for a little while.

"My baby girl, don't worry, I'll be back in your lifetime. After all, we Golden Eagles believe in reincarnation. I will see you again, don't be afraid when it happens. For once, you will be the teacher, and me the student. Remember, death is but a doorway." Andre smiles one last time, then is gone as suddenly as he had arrived.

Aurora double blinks then leaps into my lap and kisses me passionately. I embrace her tightly, kissing her back with just as much enthusiasm. We hear Nicodeamus clear his throat, and we start to laugh and break apart.

"I'm sorry, Father, we got a little carried away. I need a few strands of your mate's hair and some of Aurora's blood to summon Anca here. I'm not sure how long I can hold her here, but I will try." Hesitantly, Nicodeamus offers the braid to Aurora.

Slowly, she lifts the braid to her nose to see if she can scent her mother. By the look on Aurora's face, no scent remains. Carefully, Aurora pulls six hairs out of the braid then hands it back to her father. I watch Aurora cant her head to the side and look at Alaric. He lifts his long blonde hair to show a snow-white braid woven into a braid in his hair. Aurora then looks to her father, and now Dimitri is braiding Anca's braid back into Nicodeamus's hair. Slowly, she nods in understanding before looking back at me.

I start adding different herbs into the fire and chanting. I toss the hair in, and the flames change color. I nod my head at Aurora; she slits her palm and holds her bleeding hand in the fire. I'm ready to flip the out when I notice the fire doesn't burn her. Slowly, she draws her hand back and shows me she's no longer hurt. *What the hell did I just witness?*

The smoke begins to swirl and whip about the tent wildly. Slowly, a form begins to emerge from the flames. She's beautiful, and if I didn't know any better, I would have thought my mate was standing in the flames.

"Nico!" The apparition shrieks. She tries to rush forward and passes right through him.

"Anca!" Nicodeamus screams as she passes through him. They keep trying to touch but can't. It's heartbreaking to watch them struggle.

"Mom?" Aurora speaks; her normally powerful, sure voice is reduced to a quiver. Quickly, the female spins and looks at Aurora.

Specters can't cry, but you can see it on Anca's face that if she were living, she would be bawling her eyes out. "Seraphina? My baby girl?" Hesitantly, her hand extends out and passes through Aurora's cheek.

Aurora winces and hunches over for a moment. "Mom, I ended up being named Aurora." Aurora's eyes drop, knowing fully well that her mother may be disappointed.

"Who the hell gave my Seraphina, my angel, the name Aurora? I chose her name." Anca's eyes are that of her wolves in a second. It's quite apparent that the dead queen is not happy.

"Vladimir did, my Queen," Dimitri answers and bows his head to Anca.

"How dare he. If he ever crosses over, I will make his afterlife a living hell." Anca's hands become clawed at the mention of whom named her daughter.

Aurora starts to laugh and stands up. She shifts before her mother, showing her the massive hybrid beast she can become. Aurora's babies shift and blow fire onto their mother showing she cannot be harmed. Aurora shifts back to her human form and stares at her mother.

"I already have plans to take his head and shove it onto a pike in the front yard. I'm going to make him suffer like he made my father suffer without you. His death will be slow and as agonizing as possible. On my blood, this I swear." Aurora promptly cuts her palm and holds her dripping blood into the flames.

"I'll be waiting for him on the other side. The other mates and I will torture him until it's your time to join us, and you can join in on the fun. It'll be a great bonding moment." Anca smiles at Aurora. "I am proud of you. Oh my gods, are those my grand babies!?" Anca almost squeals, pointing at the baby dragons.

"Yes, they are mine and Alaric's babies. Someone forgot to tell us that a dragon will always be chosen first, over all the other mates." Aurora looks between her father and Alaric. Both men say *"what?"* at the same time then start laughing together.

Anca and Aurora roll their eyes at the same time and both mutter *"men"* at the exact same moment. They look at each other, then start laughing. "Aurora, please take care of your father for me. He needs a babysitter, he has a bit of a temper and likes to burn things."

"Of course, Mom, I will. Hopefully, Arnulf can summon you again so we can talk more." Aurora looks to me, hopeful. I nod slowly that it is possible.

"Aurora will be able to sense what was mine. You can use a physical object of mine that will not burn next time. For now, I must go. I love you all. Take care of each other." Anca screams the last part as she fades from view. Aurora smiles, watching her mother fade, then looks around the gathering.

"Okay, well, now I know where the rest of my temperament comes from. Time to seek and destroy. Well, after I lock mine and Arnulf's bond in place." Aurora turns and looks at me. "So? To satisfy your animal's bond, what do we need to do?"

I look over to Alaric and smile. "We're gonna need your help, brother. Aurora needs to fly." Aurora's eyes light up, and she goes running out of the tent buck naked, to streak to lord knows where. "What was that all about?" I ask, looking back and forth between the guys, and everyone is laughing. I don't know if it's at me or because of what Aurora did.

Aurora comes running back into the tent after a few moments wearing what looks like a skydiving suit. She opens her arms wide to reveal it's a wing suit. "Ta-Da! I can fly. Well, glide. I've gotten really good at riding thermals, so hopefully this helps. Does this help?" She looks quite nervous and adorable at the same time.

"Yes, sweetheart, it does. I literally just need to grip you with my talons in flight, bite, then land somewhere to finish the task." I try to simplify the whole process for her, so it makes sense.

"Okay. That settles it. Alaric strip, the sun is about to come up, and I have a mate to finish claiming." Aurora reaches back and grabs both of our hands, dragging us out of the tent. She proceeds to shift her finger and use her talon to cut Alaric out of his clothing. Alaric is laughing hysterically at Aurora's antics.

Once naked, Alaric moves away from the now-gathering crowd and shifts into his dragon form. Shit, I didn't know he was that big. I really feel puny in comparison to Aurora and her other mates. Alaric's dragon roars then breathes fire harmlessly into the sky. He turns his massive head to look at us. Aurora just laughs, grabs my hand, and starts to run towards Alaric.

I'm a bit hesitant to climb onto the great beast's back, but Aurora doesn't exactly give me a choice. She moves us to stand between Alaric's wings. When she feels we're ready, she pats his back with her hand, and he takes off, launching us into the sky. I watch Aurora carefully; she's shifting her eyes to that of her beast. I can only assume she's in deep conversation with Alaric as we fly because he keeps changing course according to the direction she's looking in.

I can tell by the way the winds feel there are good thermals here. Alaric glides effortlessly for long periods of time just by adjusting his wings. "Time to fly, Arnulf." Aurora lets go of the spines on Alaric's back before I'm halfway stripped. She goes running for his tail as I get free of my pants.

The next thing I know, my crazy mate runs and jumps off of Alaric's tail and starts riding the thermals. *Fuck.* I shift quickly and fly to catch up with her. Gracefully, I swoop and glide along with her completing the aerial dance portion of the mating ritual. I watch Aurora watching me as I maneuver around her.

I honestly think she's a bit jealous. When every step has been completed properly, I move into position. I strike quickly, sinking my talons into the muscles of her shoulders. We fly like this for several seconds before I lower my beak. I bite her on the back of her neck, just under her hairline. I hold her, tasting her blood. I feel the bond snap into place instantly. The urge now to land is strong; we must finish the bond to make it permanent. I release Aurora and follow where she's leading me. I'm anxious and can't wait to land. For being a terrestrial being, Aurora makes a great landing then quickly strips out of her wing suit.

I feel like she's hunting me after I shift back to my human form. Suddenly, she jumps and tackles me to the ground. Her mouth descends, and she bites into my shoulder again. Aurora is dominating our mating; I feel her trying to line me up with her soaking wet sex. I grip my already leaking cock and tease her wet folds several times. Aurora's frustrated growls rumble a vibration through my chest. A quick thrust and I drive my length home; her gasp is music to my ears. Aurora may be on top and built heavier than I am, but I'm not about to be entirely dominated by her.

I roll her onto her back with all of my strength and begin to thrust deeply into her. With every stroke, I can feel Aurora's muscles tightening within her warm, wet depths. Her rhythmic gripping and pulsing around my shaft brings me closer to release. I feel her love, joy, and elation flowing through the bond to me.

It's times like this that I wish I were more like her species; I want to bite and mark her like this. I lean forward just as she screams her release and bite her shoulder with my human teeth. I can't break the skin, but it has the effect I was hoping to get. Aurora's orgasm intensifies and she begins crushing down on my shaft, milking every single inch. I'm fighting to hold on long enough for her to finish, but it's no use. Aurora bites me again, growling and bucking under me, and I cum harder than I ever have before—filling her womb with my seed.

We pant, trying to slow our breathing. We rock against each other, holding on tightly, riding out the final throbs and pulses of our orgasms. Reluctantly we release the tight grip we have on each other. Aurora begins to lick at her bite marks on my shoulders. Carefully, she cleans both wounds, making sure they will heal properly. I will proudly display her marks for all to see in the future. I raise my head to look down at my beautiful mate.

Aurora looks up at me; a soft smile plays upon her full pouty lips. Her hand slowly raises and caresses my cheek. "Do you know you're a beautiful man, Arnulf?"

I raise my eyebrows in mock shock. "You don't say? Hmm, it takes a beauty to know a beauty." I watch Aurora blush, and I feel a warmth in my chest. And then I'm assaulted by feelings and presences I cannot explain. I whip my head around, looking at my surroundings, trying to figure out what exactly is going on.

Aurora shakes her head gently. "That's the bond fully snapping into place. You can feel the others; we are all able to feel each other. I'm sorry, I forgot to warn you about that ahead of time." Aurora looks genuinely upset with herself and lowers her head for a moment.

CHAPTER 9
Arnulf

A DRAGON'S ROAR SOUNDS IN MY HEAD AS IF HE'S OVERHEAD. I MOVE away from Aurora quickly and begin to search the surrounding skies for the enraged dragon. Aurora shifts the moment the dragon's roar sounds; her massive beast locks eyes with me, and in my head I hear her animal's call. I'm lost in her gaze. In my mind's eye, I can see Alaric's dragon calling and Aurora's beast roaring back up at it.

To be able to watch these two titans in our mate link is insane. Alaric calms down then turns his massive dragon head to face me. He dips his head once in my direction, then fades from view. That was more than just the mate link; I believe I was just pulled into an astral plane—the mental realm that dragons can create to communicate over great distances and see each other. I've heard stories of the mythic beasts being able to do this, but to witness it for myself is massively impressive.

Aurora's beast stalks towards me, and up to this point, I've never gotten to appreciate the beauty of her. Several blinks of my eyes and we are back on the mountainside, and her beast is standing before me like in the astral plane. Cautiously, I walk around Aurora's beast and note its dragon and wolven features. It's a miracle that the two species produced a child in the first place. The delicate scales that adorn her eyes almost act like eyeliner. Her muzzle is thick and strong with bony plates similar to Alaric's dragon. Her beast has the size of Dimitri's bear but the Lycan body like Klaus's. I'm not sure where the twins' Dire Wolves come into play, but I'm sure it's just as impressive.

Aurora locks eyes with me again, and I hear her voice clear as day. *Let's hunt.* It's another astonishing development to be able to speak to each other without words.

I nod my head and shift to my eagle quickly. I fly a small circle around Aurora until she raises an armored gauntlet to me. I watch her turn her arm, so the smooth inner scales face up for me to land on safely. Apparently, it's my turn to be inspected by her.

Once I'm settled on her arm, I watch those dragon slits roam over my feathered form. Hesitantly, she presses her nose to my feathers and inhales deeply, learning my bird's scent. Soft rumbles resembling a purr sets my animal at ease. We both know she would never harm her mate. Aurora and I look at each other for several moments before I take flight, scanning the hillside, looking for quarries big enough for Aurora's beast to hunt. All I spot are several roe deer and what looks like other Lycans on the mountainside, heading our way fast.

Panicked, I call to Aurora through the newly-formed bond. I hear Alaric and Dimitri telling me they are on their way with the others. On a good headwind, it will easily take them over an hour to get here. I can't help but feel so useless. I don't have the weapons or the size of her other mates.

I watch in horror as the first two large Lycans reach Aurora. Honestly, I think her beast is smirking, looking at the much smaller black Lycans. They come to a sudden stop when they realize how much bigger my mate is than they are. Aurora is biding her time as I update her on how many Lycans in total are on their way up. When half of the rogue pack breaks into the clearing, they go on the offensive and attempt to attack Aurora from all sides. I'm in a state of panic. I screech into the wind, attempting to summon my people. It doesn't work; we are too far away for my voice to carry far enough to receive aid. So I change tactics and start knocking branches and pieces of trees down onto the attackers.

An odd sensation comes over me as the other mates' concern floods my system with emotions that are not my own. Alaric demands that I land and focus my eyes on the fight so they can see. How in the ever-loving hell is that supposed to work? I do as I'm told and watch Aurora rip a Lycan in half right before my eyes.

Her great white beast roars as blood sprays, drenching her white fur, painting it crimson. She throws the halves of her previous attacker at its pack mates, covering them in a viscous fluid. The other mates are cheering in my head, and I feel like I'm in the middle of some paranormal gladiator pit. I'm not sure what's more disturbing: the tingle in the back of my head because I'm basically live broadcasting the fight or the fact I'm able to.

By the time I can focus on everything again, Aurora has two more Lycans decapitated, and the fifth one is giving her a hard time. The guys are easily still thirty minutes out, and there are three more still climbing up the hillside to join their pack mates. The Lycan that was giving Aurora trouble is now headless and on the ground. Aurora tilts her head back and howls her death song into the wind.

I watch her ears swivel, picking up the rest of the rogue Lycans' footsteps approaching from the south. Aurora's beast seems to live for moments like this. Leisurely, she lowers her massive frame to the point that her talons dig into the blood-covered soil below her. Aurora's tail swishes side-to-side, impatiently waiting for the last of the Lycans to arrive.

The final three make it to the battle scene only to find their pack mates in various states of decimation. Aurora's beast is borderline in a frenzy from all the blood in the air. Its coppery tang hangs heavily in the air to the point I can taste it way up here. Aurora is clearly gearing up for something huge. I can see the frost gathering in her fur; her voice rings out in a roar-howl-like tone.

Aurora rises from her lowered stance, and without warning she throws her taloned hands up into the air. Ice spikes shoot up from the ground under the Lycans—impaling them where they stand. The bodies twitch and are frozen in a state of shock. They kind of remind me of those puppets on the sticks I use to play with as a child. I don't know if I'm more terrified or impressed with my mate right now.

Aurora's rage is palatable in the air as her beast throws its head back and howls its death song yet again. My eagle wants to fly and hide even though she's our mate. The fight-or-flight instinct is almost overwhelming. Alaric's dragon's roar answers Aurora's beast. She throws her head back a second time and lets loose a location call to help Alaric find us easier. In the meantime, Aurora is ripping the heads off of her attackers and piling them up.

It's now I notice that she's wounded, but from what I can see it's nothing life-threatening and barely bleeding now. Alaric's dragon lands hard on the mountainside, and the ground shakes from the impact. Aurora moves to stand before his dragon, and he bathes her in his flames. My eagle makes us hesitate briefly, still shaken up from the battle that had occurred. Eventually, we settle down enough and fly down to meet up with our bond mates. I shift quickly and fill everyone in on the events that transpired before they arrived—besides what they were able to see through my eyes.

All of us turn to watch Aurora still under Alaric's flames. Dimitri is the first to say something. "You never get used to seeing that. Amazingly, she can withstand the heat of his fire." Dimitri lays a large hand on my shoulder and pulls me in for a side hug. "Welcome to the family, Arnulf. We're just a little different from your average family, but it works for us."

As Aurora walks out from under Alaric's flames, I nod slowly, listening to Dimitri. She's back in her human form and looking at the surrounding carnage. "Fuckers ruined the nice evening I had planned. I wanted to hunt, feed, and fuck our way back home. But nooo, these assholes had to go fuck things up." Frost gathers around Aurora, and ice spikes randomly impale the headless corpses around the mountainside.

Jayce is the first to move to Aurora's side, and he nuzzles the back of her neck. We watch the tension leave her shoulders, and her stance relaxes as she melts into Jayce's embrace.

"Alaric, why didn't you go to Aurora? Or any of you for that matter?" My eyes shift to that of my eagle as I study the scene before me. Whatever power Jayce has over Aurora, it's working; she's calm and relaxed now.

"That's easy to answer," Dominik says, then moves to stand before me.

"Jayce is a natural-born Omega and built emotionally to be able to comfort. He's not a threat in any way, shape, or form. You'll learn each of our roles in this dynamic in time. I'll give you a crash course while he's soothing her. So..." Dominik moves and rests a hand on Alaric's bicep. "Alaric, our resident dragon, is an Alpha just like Aurora. Their word is law, and they rule fairly together. In moments of intense emotion, he's not able to soothe her, but she's able to soothe him as his mate."

Dominik moves over to Dimitri next. "Dimitri and I are what you would call Betas. We're second in command, so to speak. We plot and maintain defenses for the family. We're strong enough to keep the packs together but not strong enough to rule alone." Dominik taps his finger on his chin as he looks at everyone.

"Okay, so let me put it this way. If Alaric and Aurora are considered tactical nukes, we're the ones pushing the buttons," Dominick states. His military analogy makes perfect sense, so I nod along.

Dominik moves over to Klaus next. "Poor Klaus here, is a kind of anomaly. By birthright, he's Alpha of the German Lycan pack. But he's not strong enough to physically or emotionally hold the title. But he's not exactly Omega material either. I guess you can classify him as a Gamma. Not exactly a Beta, not exactly an Omega. He is also ready to jump into battle like the rest of us." Klaus nods along with Dominik's explanation.

Aurora and Jayce come walking over together just as Dominik finishes his explanation. Aurora is wearing Jayce's flannel shirt, and each male takes turns sniffing and nuzzling her neck. Alaric decides not to wait any longer and takes charge; he grabs hold of Aurora and leans her back against his chest. Aurora smiles at his possessiveness and sighs softly, finally fully relaxing.

"Now my brother, my twin Jayce, is an Omega through and through. But don't let his sweet disposition fool you. He has a toxic bite that can either kill you or make it so you can't summon your animal. Jayce is basically the bomb squad sent in to diffuse the nukes. Since he's an Omega, he's not perceived as a threat by the Alphas and allowed to enter their space." Jayce starts to laugh.

"Basically, what my overly-brutish brother is trying to say is that when either Aurora or Alaric are homicidal, I'm the only one with enough balls to approach them." To prove his point, Jayce moves over and snuggles right up to Alaric and Aurora.

"Arnulf, my guess is that you're also an Omega or maybe a Gamma in our family dynamic," Dominik says and shrugs his shoulders lightly. "Only time will tell, my friend."

I turn around to find Klaus and Dimitri gathering up the wolves' heads into several bags. "What are you two doing?" I ask.

"It's a dragon thing," Alaric answers before Dimitri has a chance to. "We tend to like to horde the skulls of our enemies. It serves as a warning and a reminder to those in our presence that we are much stronger than we look." Alaric smirks then looks back to Aurora, who's snuggled up with Jayce. "She likes decorating with skulls. Who am I to argue with her?"

Alaric turns his back to me and walks down to where he landed earlier. I feel the pull through the newly formed bond as he waits to have our attention. When Alaric senses he has our full attention, he walks away from the group and shifts, ready to carry us all back home. Aurora and Jayce take off running to Alaric for lord only knows what reason. Dimitri and Klaus carry their bags over to Alaric's dragon's talons and offer them to him to carry.

Aurora and Jayce are already sitting behind the crown of horns on the top of Alaric's head. Klaus and Dimitri have found spaces along the spines on Alaric's back to sit. Dominik takes his time, and I run to catch up. "What's wrong?"

"I'm not a fan of heights. Don't get me wrong, I trust Alaric with my life. I just don't like heights. Unfortunately, flying was the fastest way to get to Aurora and you." He shrugs his shoulders then looks up at the space left for him between Dimitri and Klaus.

"They try to make me feel safe, and it helps, but I still don't like flying." I can tell that Dominik is putting on a brave face as he approaches Alaric, ready to take his place.

Wow. I never expected someone so strong to have a fear, or a dislike, as strong as he does. I watch Alaric stand with a fluid grace I didn't think a being his size could manage. Carefully, he turns his body in the tight space and takes off running until he's able to clear the trees and spread his wings. Several strong flaps and he's off the ground and heading back to camp. My shift is swift, and I flap furiously to catch up to him. Alaric slows to gliding on the thermals, noticing I am having a hard time keeping up.

Aurora's eyes glow white as she looks back at me. I watch her shift her left arm to her gauntlet and stick it out for me to land on. I finally catch up and take advantage of the offered perch. Aurora carefully draws her arm in and rests me against her chest for the ride home. I am so very blessed to have mates concerned for me; I really got lucky to have joined the family they have created.

CHAPTER 10

Jayce

THE FLIGHT IS MUCH FASTER WITH ALARIC FLYING THAN ANYONE ELSE could have made on their own. Aurora decimated her enemies without breaking a sweat, yet again proving herself to be a phenom in battle. Alaric's dragon roars, alerting the camp to his arrival. Over the clearing in the center of camp, he opens his talons, dropping the bag of rogue Lycan heads. Elsa moves forward and sets some younger pack members to work removing and cleaning the skulls.

Alaric circles and lands gently in the field behind the Alpha house. Several of the maidens that work in the Alpha house come out holding seven robes, not knowing how many we may need. They are fully prepared for anything that may have happened. Everyone carefully disembarks Alaric's back and heads towards the maidens. Aurora moves first and takes three robes, then waves the women off. She passes the robes to Alaric, and Arnulf then puts the last one on herself.

"I was having a great time till those fuckers came and ruined it," Aurora grumbles as she shoves her arms almost violently into the sleeves of her robe.

Arnulf finishes tying his robe around his waist and then looks between Aurora and Alaric. "You would have been much safer with one of your other mates. I was completely useless in battle." Arnulf sighs as he kicks the dirt under his bare feet. His shoulders are almost curled in on themselves. His stance screams that he's mentally beating himself up.

Alaric moves forward and stands in Arnulf's way. "Not everyone can be warriors. You are skilled in the mystic arts, which we need in the coming battles." Alaric pulls him in for a bro-hug and then turns to head toward the house after the others.

Once inside the Alpha house, Aurora's agitation hits a new level and Dimitri is trying to talk to her. Suddenly, Aurora is standing on top of a chair in the middle of the room. I'm waving a leg of lamb at her, and Dimitri is asking her to calm down.

"D! Seriously? When in my *entire* lifespan, have I ever calmed down because you or Andre told me to?" Aurora flails her arms around several times like she's on the flag squad in high school.

"Aurora, be reasonable. It's nighttime, and a lot of the leaders may be sleeping or being intimate with their mates. Have some consideration, my love." Dimitri moves closer to Aurora and rests his large hand on her thigh. His eyes pleading with her for understanding.

"Fine! I want the seven leaders assembled here over breakfast tomorrow morning." Aurora crosses her arms over her chest, looking down at Dimitri, attempting to still look mad and failing miserably.

"Angel?" Klaus says softly. "Five of the leaders are already at your beck and call. Well, and technically in your bed." Klaus opens Aurora's robe, places a kiss just above her mound, and then walks away.

Aurora does a double take, watching Klaus kiss her so very close to her sex. Her eyes follow his movements closely as he smirks through his departure. She looks back down at Dimitri, and he shrugs at her, smiling. That is probably the quickest and easiest way to derail Aurora's anger. She leaps off the chair and into Dimitri's arms. "After him!" she yells just before Dimitri takes off running with Aurora in his arms.

I can't help but laugh at Aurora's antics. Alaric comes over and wraps an arm around my shoulders. "She's definitely one of a kind. We are truly blessed, Jayce. She's strong, intelligent, practical, and has her family and people as her top priority. Aurora is the queen that our people need." Alaric smiles, looking down at me, then kisses my temple.

"We definitely did get lucky with her. I can't believe how thoughtful and understanding she is with everything. Well, when it comes to our family, that is. Everything else with Aurora is fifty-fifty. You never know if she's going to start yelling 'off with their head' or hug them." I shrug my shoulder as I lean against Alaric and watch Dominik and Arnulf setting up for tomorrow's meeting.

~THE NEXT morning~

The meeting table is set and the leaders have gathered. Aurora stands at the head of the table, wearing her ruby crown. Alaric is directly on Aurora's right, and Dimitri is to her left. We each line up, heading down the table, leaving the Tigers and Ellis rounding up the table's end.

"We need to move on the castle sooner rather than later. We discovered Elena's hidden camp, and we have evidence from the house that Vladimir still lives," Aurora says and then makes sure to make eye contact with each leader in turn.

I stand and move to stand behind my brother; in diplomacy matters, he leaves the discussions up to me. "Our pack is ready, willing, and able to attack at your command, Aurora. We've created several teams within our pack, divided up by specialty, as you requested." I bow my head to my mate and my bond mates each in turn before returning to my seat.

"What numbers do the Dires bring to the table?" Jaggar—the Siberian Tigers' leader—stands, placing both of his hands flat on the table, staring up at Dominik and me.

Aurora's beast can be felt and heard as a low growl rumbles in her chest. The room temperature drops several degrees before Alaric and Dimitri place a hand on Aurora, attempting to calm her. My eyes move deliberately from Aurora down to Jaggar.

"Five hundred strong," I state flatly, almost sounding bored. "Five teams of a hundred wolves each, all given a specific task and target. How many Tigers do you bring, Jaggar?" I cross my arms over my chest and notice that my muscles seem bulkier than before. I'll have to question that later. Out of the corner of my eye, I see Aurora's tell-tale smirk that I just said something that pleases her sadistic side.

Jaggar's eyes glow the orange of his Tiger as he stares at me. I pull an Aurora and tilt my head to the side, staring right back at him. There's no way in fucking hell I'm going to let a fucking cat try to get the better of me. Jaggar breaks eye contact first then looks at the papers before him. "Three hundred. The last of my troops arrive tomorrow by sundown."

I look to the top of the table where Aurora is, and she lightly dips her head to me and then to Jaggar. I quickly take my seat, waiting for her next round of questions.

"Arnulf, are your eagles ready for their part in this operation?" Aurora glances down to the list before her, then back up to Arnulf.

Hesitantly, Arnulf stands and clasps his hands behind his back. He cautiously raises his eyes and glances at everyone in turn. "We are not warriors like everyone else here." He motions with his left hand to everyone at the table. "What we lack in strength, we make up for in skill and speed. I have a hundred and fifty eagles and various other birds of prey ready to fly at your command. The team you asked for is already en route to the target you requested. The War Dragons are flying with them for added security and to cut down on their exertion. For that boon, Alaric, I am grateful." Arnulf raises a closed fist over his heart and bows to Alaric and holds his gaze long enough to be respectful before taking his seat. Alaric returns the gesture, raises his fist over his heart, and lightly dips his head to Arnulf.

Aurora nods and makes a few notes quickly. "Ellis? I know it seems odd to request Polar Bears to be in the middle of a forest, but I have a good reason for it," Aurora says, then stands up and leans on the table. "Did you bring the fifty I requested?"

Ellis rolls his eyes and stands up, only to start pacing around the back half of the room. His dark brown eyes flickering back and forth between his human brown and the black of his bear. "Yeah, I still say you dragons are fucked up. For real! What the fuck is a bunch of white mother fuckin' bears gonna do in the middle of the forest? We can't hide. It's like throwing marshmallows on asphalt and expecting them not to be seen." He huffs as he flops back down onto his chair.

Aurora made the mistake of taking a sip of her coffee during Ellis's tirade. She ends up spitting her coffee out and across the table. Aurora starts hacking, coughing to clear her throat before she doubles over, laughing hysterically. "He called his people marsh-mallows!" Aurora is laughing so hard she falls off her chair. Alaric is shaking his head, looking down at her, and I can't help but mouth *sorry* to Ellis, who now looks pissed off.

Dominik decides to stand up and address Ellis. "I'm sorry, Aurora is a bit beside herself at the moment."

Dominik looks down at Aurora, trying not to start laughing himself. "She intends to use your group as a distraction for the main assault force. Your people will be heavily guarded by drag-ons. We want the Polar Bears to lead whatever force that comes out of the castle after them and straight to the dragons to get roasted." Dominik has developed Aurora's fascination with charred flesh. It's almost frightening, but then again, I'm not really shocked with as close as our bond has made us.

Ellis looks between Dominik and where Aurora once was, then back to Dominik. Alaric has finally gotten Aurora to get her laughter under control. "Okay. Sorry about that." Aurora regains her composure and draws in a deep breath.

"The short version is this: I need you to draw attention away from the side of the castle where the flooded tunnels are. My team and I intend to swim in and attack from within. My mates still on the outside will alert everyone to what needs to happen next as we progress." Her eyes churn liquid mercury as she regards everyone at the table.

"This whole mission is on a need-to-know basis. Everyone will be told exactly what they need to know and no more just in case there are still spies among us." Aurora flops down onto Alaric's lap and looks at everyone in turn.

Dimitri chooses now to stand and walk casually around the table. "Twenty Great Bears are en route here. They wish to fight and assist in any way possible to make up for our people's rudeness. They fear retaliation by the 'great white beast.'" Dimitri starts to laugh softly after saying that. "My recommendation is to set them with tasks that require great strength. Breaking defenses and such. The heavy lifting we can't do, we will defer to the dragons to use their size, strength, and fire to move what we cannot." Dimitri bows slightly to Alaric, and in turn, Alaric lowers his head to Dimitri.

"Okay, are you two done flirting so we can finish this meeting?" Aurora asks as she slides off of Alaric's lap. Aurora reaches out and grabs both of their hands and joins them. "There! Enjoy!" Aurora moves quickly and climbs onto my lap next and starts playing with my hair. Dimitri and Alaric look at their hands briefly and quickly pull their hands back.

Klaus takes this opportunity to stand and move toward the dry erase board. He looks over the plans and writes the number four hundred next to his species. "Between my pack and the American Lycans, we march with four hundred."

He moves back over to the table to look down at his notes. "My people have been divided into five groups as you requested, Aurora. I will not discuss the exact numbers at the moment. But all is ready and at your command, my angel." Klaus smiles at Aurora and lightly dips his head in her direction before sitting down.

Ellis almost chokes on his water when Klaus calls Aurora angel. Aurora's eyes take on that ethereal glow. Before Ellis has the chance to put the glass down, Aurora freezes the water in his glass. "Be careful, marshmallow. You may float away," Aurora says, then smirks. Her eyes fall on Alaric next. It's his turn.

Alaric stands, and the room falls silent. He truly has the commanding presence of a king. Nicodeamus walks in and lays his hand on Alaric's shoulder and gives him a nod. "All is in order; six species of dragon shall aid us in our attack. I will not name species in an open room, but we will have plenty of fire-power when we need it." Alaric smiles and bows to Aurora. She smiles and shakes her head at him.

Carefully, Aurora slides off my lap only to lean on Dominik's shoulders. "Thank you, gentlemen, for attending the meeting. Your contribution is most valuable in our future endeavors." Aurora looks at everyone and claps her hands together once. "Okay, the meeting is over, and I need coffee." Aurora climbs up onto Dominik's back and smacks his ass. "To the kitchen!"

We all stare in silence, watching Aurora leave. "That's our leader?" Jagger says under his breath.

We all heard him. Ellis, being closest, slams Jaggar's head into the table on purpose, knocking him out cold. "Fucking cats. Why the fuck do we have them here? Shifty motherfuckers. We can't trust them," Ellis says, looking down at Jagger.

"Three hundred Tigers is three hundred potential problems.

Nicodeamus, what's your suggestion?" If anyone would have the answer, it will be the original Dragon King.

Nicodeamus looks at the dry erase board and starts calculating the numbers in his head. "We cannot allow those numbers to arrive here. If they were to turn on us at the wrong time, it could be deadly. I'll handle it, don't even mention that this conversation took place." Nicodeamus's features harden, and it's suddenly obvious how terrifying he must have been in his prime. The old king leaves the room. With him, there are now more questions than answers.

Those that remain in the room watch Nicodeamus's back disappear down the hallway. Not a single word is uttered between us as we look at each other. Alaric's eyes cloud over for a moment before he and Dimitri move simultaneously to grab ahold of Jaggar and remove him from the room to points unknown. For now, I think I'll head to the kitchen and catch up with my twin and mate.

CHAPTER 11
The Recon – Erik

Under the cloak of darkness, the night sky serves as our canvas as three mighty War Dragons soar through the air in perfect formation. Their massive wings beat rhythmically against the cool night breeze, propelling us forward with a sense of purpose and determination. It's a sight to behold, the sleek, majestic creatures cutting through the darkness like shadows in flight.

We count ourselves fortunate that our queen has entrusted the War Dragons with the arduous task of carrying us to our destination. Their formidable strength and unwavering loyalty make them invaluable allies in our mission, allowing us to conserve our own energy for the challenges that lie ahead.

As we make our way toward the hidden Marelup castle nestled deep within the rugged mountains of Moldavia, anticipation courses through our veins like a wildfire. Fifteen of us have been chosen for this perilous mission, tasked with scouring every inch of the castle and its surrounding lands for any valuable information we can glean.

But our mission extends beyond mere reconnaissance. Tonight, we also have the important task of rendezvousing with the spies we left behind two weeks ago, gathering crucial intelligence that will aid us in our efforts to uncover the castle's secrets.

As we draw nearer to our destination, the imposing silhouette of the castle looms ahead, shrouded in darkness and mystery. It's a formidable fortress, its ancient stones whispering tales of centuries past, secrets waiting to be unearthed by those brave enough to seek them out.

In the distance, the imposing silhouette of the castle emerges from the clouds, its towering spires reaching toward the heavens like ancient sentinels guarding the secrets hidden within its walls. The sight is both awe-inspiring and foreboding, a testament to the castle's storied history and the mysteries that lie waiting to be uncovered.

As Edgar and his team touch down in a secluded field below, we take to the sky, our wings beating against the air with a powerful grace. The night is alive with the sound of our flight, the wind rushing past us as we ascend into the darkness above.

High above the rugged landscape below, we spread out in search patterns, our keen eyes scanning the terrain for any sign of activity. The thermals are in our favor, carrying us effortlessly on invisible currents as we glide through the night sky, each of us searching at different heights simultaneously.

It's a coordinated dance of movement and precision, our senses attuned to every shift in the air as we scour the landscape below for any clue that might lead us closer to our goal.

And then, at the base of the mountain, we spot it—the remnants of the tunnels that Nicodeamus spoke of months ago. The marking stone still stands sentinel over the entrance, a silent witness to the passage of time and the secrets buried beneath the earth.

But as we descend closer, we see that the entrance is now submerged beneath the waters of a natural spring, its once-hidden depths swallowed by the relentless march of nature.

As we cautiously circle over the dense cover at the base of the mountain, our keen eyes scan the rugged terrain below, searching for any sign of danger. The thick foliage provides ample cover for our teams, ensuring that they remain hidden from prying eyes as they prepare for the impending assault.

But amidst the tangled undergrowth, something catches my eye —a series of traps cunningly concealed among the rocks and foliage, poised to trigger an avalanche of rocks and mud at the slightest disturbance. It's a clever strategy, designed to thwart any attempt at invasion and deter intruders from approaching the castle.

With a sense of urgency, I reach out to our Alpha, Arnulf, forging a mental connection that allows him to see through my eyes. I show him the traps, the intricate network of mechanisms hidden among the rocky terrain, and the peril they pose to anyone foolish enough to venture too close.

And then, amidst the silence of our mental link, I hear a feminine voice, smooth as silk, echoing faintly in connection with my Alpha. It's a surreal experience, the sensation of sharing my thoughts and observations with another, and I obey without question as I change course and fly back toward the tunnels.

Several passes later, I'm instructed to resume my search of the mountainside, and I comply without hesitation, my senses alert for any sign of danger. As I circle the castle itself, a grim sight greets me—the road that once wound its way to the fortress has been utterly destroyed, the compacted stone roadway reduced to rubble by what appears to be explosions.

Huge holes and chunks are missing from the terrain, evidence of the devastating force unleashed upon the landscape. With caution, I continue my reconnaissance, circling the castle and landing on one of the lower windowsills to peer inside.

What I see confirms my suspicions—the first floor is submerged beneath at least six inches of water, a testament to the destructive power of the natural spring that feeds the castle's moat. It's a sobering sight, a reminder of the challenges that lie ahead as we prepare to confront the mysteries hidden within the ancient walls of the fortress.

As I fly to yet another window on the first floor, the room within appears to be relatively dry, save for a few scattered puddles that reflect the faint moonlight filtering through the glass. The air is heavy with the scent of age and decay, a tangible reminder of the passage of time and the neglect that has befallen this once-grand structure.

Moving on to several more windows, I finally come upon what must have been the throne room in ages past. Here, the room is divided by the cruel hand of fate—one half submerged beneath the murky depths of the castle's moat, while the other remains elevated and relatively dry. It's a poignant juxtaposition, a stark reminder of the castle's former glory now swallowed by the encroaching waters.

Hovering near the stairwell, I land in one of its windows, peering down into the flooded lower portion. The water level is rising slowly, inching its way up the stone steps with a relentless determination. From my vantage point, I estimate there to be around eight to ten inches of stagnant water pooling at the foot of the stairwell, a testament to the castle's gradual descent into ruin.

Turning my attention to the exterior walls, I observe several sections that bear the scars of time and neglect. Breaks and missing stones mar the once-imposing facade, their absence a testament to the ravages of nature and the passage of time. The structural integrity of the wall is severely compromised, with large sections now crumbling away and others bearing gaping holes that smaller shifters could easily pass through.

It's a sobering sight, a stark reminder of the castle's precarious state and the challenges that lie ahead for those who would seek to reclaim it from the clutches of darkness. As I continue my reconnaissance, it becomes increasingly clear that the castle may not even be safe to inhabit in its current condition—a grim reality that the queen and her mates will undoubtedly have to contend with once the castle is liberated from Vladimir's grasp.

As the sun begins its descent, casting a warm golden glow over the landscape, we take to the cover of the trees, our senses attuned to any sign of movement below. The forest comes alive with the symphony of the evening, the chirping of crickets and the rustle of leaves serving as a backdrop to our silent vigil.

As darkness falls like a heavy blanket over the land, the first signs of activity emerge within the courtyard below. Like shadows in the night, the Strigoi begin to stir, their dark forms moving with a sinister grace as they navigate the confines of the castle's interior. They move in groups of three, their movements fluid and purposeful as they circle the courtyard before ascending what remains of the crumbling walls.

There's an eerie sense of detachment to their actions, a mechanical precision that hints at a deeper purpose lurking beneath the surface. It's as if they are merely going through the motions, their movements dictated by some unseen force driving them ever forward.

Meanwhile, two out of three spires still stand tall against the night sky, their windows aglow with the soft flicker of light. It's a stark contrast to the darkness that surrounds them, a beacon of life amidst the desolation of the castle's ruins.

Though we were not expressly ordered to investigate the spires, I make note of their continued activity, a piece of information that may prove useful in the days to come. But for now, our focus remains on observing the movements of the Lycans and Strigoi below.

In the woods closest to the mountain, the Lycans move with purpose, their steps steady and unwavering as they patrol the perimeter. There's a sense of determination in their movements, a silent resolve to protect their territory at any cost.

Yet despite their differences, both species seem to be united by a singular purpose, blindly following orders without regard for their own safety.

As I summon the others, we swiftly make our way back to our awaiting dragon transports. The night air is crisp and cool against my skin as we climb onto the sturdy backs of our winged companions. Despite the success of our mission, a sense of unease gnaws at the edges of my mind, a lingering doubt as to whether our queen will view our findings in the same light.

Settling into our positions on the dragon's back, we brace ourselves for the journey ahead, the rhythmic beat of the dragon's wings providing a comforting backdrop to our thoughts. I remain in constant contact with our Alpha, relaying every detail of our reconnaissance mission and the troubling discoveries we made within the castle's walls.

The destruction and state of disrepair we witnessed are deeply concerning, posing a significant threat to the safety of our troops should they attempt to infiltrate the fortress. It's a sobering reality that weighs heavily on my mind as we soar through the night sky, the urgency of our mission driving us ever onward.

The flight back is swift, Edgar's flying infused with a sense of purpose and determination that hints at the gravity of the situation awaiting us back at our main camp. With each passing moment, my apprehension grows, wondering what exactly awaits us upon our return.

As we approach the camp, Edgar lands with precision in the center of the bustling encampment, a departure from our usual landing spot in the nearby field. It's a subtle yet telling sign of the urgency of our situation, and I can't help but brace myself for whatever awaits us as we disembark from our dragon transports.

As we land in the center of the camp, our queen awaits us with an air of palpable impatience, her silver dragon orbs fixed upon Edgar as he touches down. Flanked by her six mates, she exudes an aura of dominance and power that sends a shiver down my spine, reminding me of the formidable force she commands.

With a swift motion, she pushes her way free of her mates, her gaze locking onto us with an intensity that leaves no room for doubt. Arnulf, my Alpha, moves to her side, his presence a silent reassurance amidst the tension that hangs in the air. He gestures toward us on Edgar's back, a silent warning to tread carefully in the presence of such formidable predators.

Aurora's expression softens as she realizes the effect her presence has on us, her mouth forming a perfect 'O' of apology as she mouths her regrets to us. With a silent command, the rest of my team takes flight and heads back to the building where we are staying, leaving me alone to face our queen's scrutiny.

Extending her arm, partially shifted to bear a light coating of protective scales, Aurora offers me a perch upon her arm. I descend gracefully, my wings folding against my body as I alight upon the offered limb, feeling the slight dip as her arm accommodates my weight.

"Look into my eyes, Erik; get lost in the silvery orbs and let me in. I need to see everything you did," Aurora's voice, soft and silky, washes over me like a gentle caress, coaxing me to surrender to her will. Her hand, warm and comforting, rests lightly on the feathers of my back as she guides me toward a nearby bench, her presence a reassuring anchor amidst the swirling chaos of my thoughts.

As we sit together, her silver dragon orbs lock with mine, and a white glow emanates from within, casting an ethereal halo around her eyes. It's a mesmerizing sight, and I find myself drawn into the depths of her gaze, losing myself in the swirling currents of her consciousness.

Suddenly, the memories flood back, a torrent of images flashing before my eyes in rapid succession. I can feel the chill in the air as the temperature drops slightly, a tangible manifestation of Aurora's growing anger at the state of her mother's castle. It's as if her emotions are projected onto the very fabric of reality, their intensity almost overwhelming.

The mental probe seems to stretch on endlessly, each moment etched into my mind with crystalline clarity. Yet, just as suddenly as it began, Aurora breaks eye contact, her touch gentle as she strokes my feathers, a silent gesture of gratitude for my cooperation.

As the tension in the air dissipates, I can't help but feel a sense of awe at the depth of Aurora's power and the unwavering strength of her will. In her eyes, I see the weight of her responsibilities, the burden of leadership resting heavy upon her shoulders. And yet, amidst the turmoil, there is also a glimmer of hope—a determination to overcome whatever challenges lie ahead and reclaim her rightful place.

"Thank you, Erik. You and your team brought me very valuable intel today. I greatly appreciate it. Take the rest of the evening to relax." Aurora's words wash over me like a soothing balm, her gratitude a welcome reassurance after the intensity of our earlier encounter. As she turns her attention to Arnulf, her demeanor shifts, her smile softening into one of warmth and affection as she addresses him.

"Love, make sure your men are fed and spoiled tonight; my gift to them," Aurora says, her voice filled with genuine affection as she gazes up at my alpha. It's a tender moment, a glimpse into the deep bond that exists between them, and I find myself internally smiling at the sight.

Arnulf returns her smile with a nod of acknowledgment before turning his gaze to me, his expression one of gratitude and appreciation. "Erik, please carry my thanks back to your team for me. I'll come to visit later today and bring extra goodies with me," he says, his words laced with sincerity. With a light dip of his head in my direction, Arnulf conveys his gratitude, his smile a silent reassurance that our efforts have not gone unnoticed.

With a careful leap, I gracefully dismount from Aurora's arm and take flight back toward the cabin where my team and I are staying. The cool night air rushes past me as I soar through the darkness, the weight of the day's events still heavy on my mind.

As I approach the cabin, a sense of anticipation builds within me. It's odd, I reflect, that I didn't deliver the report in my human form. But given the atmosphere of secrecy and suspicion that surrounds us, I understand the necessity for caution.

With a final flap of my wings, I land softly outside the cabin and quickly shift back into my human form before entering. The warm glow of the fire greets me as I step inside, casting flickering shadows across the cozy interior.

True to Aurora's word, a bountiful spread of meats and cheeses awaits my return, laid out in a tempting display that makes my mouth water. Dinner has never looked so enticing, and for the first time in a long while, I feel a sense of belonging and purpose.

As I join my team at the table, I can't help but reflect on the day's events. Despite the challenges we face, we have a leader who keeps her promises and genuinely cares for our well-being. Working for a hybrid like Aurora may not be what we expected, but it's certainly a welcome change from the bleak existence we were led to believe awaited us. In her, we've found not only a leader, but a friend and ally in the fight against darkness. We were told working for a Lycan would be hell; working for a hybrid is fucking awesome.

CHAPTER 12
Alaric

Aurora must have come to my bed last night sometime after the Eagles and the War Dragons returned. I was kind of shocked to roll over to find her facing me with her hand on my chest. It's been forever since I have had Aurora in my bed alone.

My eyes roam over the features of her face, and it makes me smile. She looks so angelic in her sleep, so innocent and pure at first glance. Faint silver scars are marring her flesh from past battles, visible on a closer look at her features.

I run a finger over Aurora's cheek reverently; I am truly blessed to have such a wonderful mate at my side. Languidly, her eyes open; they are the mercury dragon eyes of her beast. A low rumble is audible from Aurora's beast, and it's now stalking me. I watch her rise up onto all fours with unearthly grace. Her beast is in full control, her mouth opens gradually, and her canines are visible and fully descended.

Her scent hits me in the gut hard; she's in heat again. My cock is as hard as titanium, and my beast urges me to breed our mate again. Through the bond, I reach out to my bond mates as well as Nicodeamus. I'm panicked, we've come so far, and we're so close to attacking the castle now. We can't take a chance of Aurora getting pregnant no matter how badly she wants it.

My door blasts open, and it's my bond mates first; their animals are almost on the surface as badly as I am. We are all struggling for control as we watch Aurora look at each of us in turn with that unmistakable hunger in her eyes.

Nicodeamus walks in and shakes his head as he raises one hand. Suddenly the temperature starts dropping in the room. Aurora focuses her attention on her father, and he locks eyes with her. But Aurora is almost stronger than her father because of the added Lycan Alpha powers combined with her dragon nature. With the combination of the two species' strengths, she's almost able to force her father into submission.

Quickly, I jump up and cover her eyes with my hand and attempt to restrain her. Aurora starts screaming and thrashing; she's not happy her attempt to breed was stopped. I give Nicodeamus the opening he needs. He rushes in quickly and lays his hand on her chest, dropping her body temperature. Ever so slowly, the fight begins to drain out of Aurora. Her scent isn't as powerful as it was before.

Just as quickly as it all started, it is over, and Aurora is asleep in my arms. I look up at my father-in-law, and he nods. "Carry her to my quarters; I'll look after her for the next three days. You boys have plenty of information to review and compile to formulate a battle plan. I'll watch over my daughter until her heat is over," Nicodeamus says with all the finality of a battle-hardened general.

I start walking with Aurora in my arms; I'm fighting my beast for control. Her sweet scent is driving us absolutely insane. Quickly, I carry her down the hall to Nicodeamus's room and lay her on the futon that he has. I smirk at Nico and shake my head. "I'm guessing you were prepared for her heat this time?"

"After last time? Yes. Yes, I am. We don't need her pregnant again, not now that we are so close to the end of the journey." Nicodeamus moves across his room with a blanket he had picked up. Gently, he lays it over Aurora, tucking her in for her slumber. "I'll keep her in the ice sleep, so her body goes through her heat without the pheromones. When it's over, I'll wake her up, and it will be back to business as usual. Till then, I'll watch over her and keep her safe. You need to be the king she knows you are." Nicodeamus rises and places his hand on my shoulder and smiles at me.

"I'll handle everything in her absence; thank you for watching over our mate for us." I bow my head and raise my fist to my chest as I look at Nicodeamus. He returns the gesture, and I dip my head slightly and leave his room, locking the door behind me.

Through the bond, I reach out to the other mates and call for a meeting in the war room. I shoot a text out to Ellis and tell him about the meeting. He's a wise ass as usual, but it wouldn't be Ellis if he weren't. I make it to the war room and shut the door, locking it behind Ellis as he enters. "Okay, everyone, as you can notice, we are two people down for the meeting. Aurora is indisposed and Jaggar... he's no longer breathing, and Tigers are on the extinction list." I cross my muscular arms over my chest, daring anyone to question me.

"Damn, bro! Harsh much?" Ellis questions. Ellis looks at each mate in turn, and none disagrees with my decision.

"Okay, so where is our Blood Queen?" Ellis looks around the room until he gets to Jayce, knowing he is the weakest link.

Jayce looks at me, waiting for my permission. When I nod my head to Jayce, he speaks, "She's with her father for a few days; there are important matters they need to attend to together." Jayce looks back to me again, this time seeking approval. I smile and nod my head again to Jayce, prompting him to smile in return.

"Okay?" Ellis says, but it sounds more like a question. "So, since I'm an outsider to this kumbaya shit you've got going on, mind filling in the blanks?" Ellis moves and leans against the closest wall looking at each bond mate in turn.

"Short version," I say as I start to prowl the room. "We couldn't trust the Tigers. Jaggar was acting shifty as all hell, and he was disappearing from camp more often than not." I move to the whiteboard and erase the Tigers part in the plan. I then flip the board over, and an entirely different plan sits there.

"I tried to believe that they were good, but in the back of my mind, I felt they were untrustworthy. So this is the real plan." I motion to the whiteboard then return to my seat at the head of the table.

Klaus casually stands and moves to the corner of the room and answers his phone. I watch him closely; his facial expressions are quite animated as he talks to whoever is on the other end. Eventually, he motions to the smart TV and casts the video he was sent to it. I get it now; it was Klaus's operative sent to explore the castle's flooded tunnels.

We watch as the male swims through algae-covered tunnels with all sorts of plant life filling the open space. The tunnel splits at one point, and we see him point to the right tunnel and shake his finger no. He swims to the left and cautiously emerges from the water. The room he enters appears to be the old armory in the southern corner of the castle.

The male looks around more and points to a very old sword on the wall. It bears the Marelup crest and appears to be in decent shape after all this time. At least a dozen swords have escaped the ravages of time because of the thick wax coating on the blades. I nod along, taking notes as to what I've seen. Klaus's man swims to the far side of the room to the partially opened door and looks out. All the lower chambers seem to be holding at least three to four inches of water.

The feed cuts out, and we look at Klaus. "Gus did well; he's one of our best swimmers, and he is the most stealthy when it comes to missions like this."

"Please tell him excellent work from all of us. Aurora will be most pleased knowing that there's an unobstructed path to the interior of the castle." However, I am not pleased that my mate wants to be the one to attack from the inside, but her logic is solid. With all that standing water, she can freeze her targets solid and minimize the damage to her infiltration team.

I roughly run my hand through my hair and try to quell my beast. He knows Aurora is in heat, and he wishes to go to her and fill her again with his hatchlings. It's not fun to be a rutting Alpha. I look up, and the room has cleared out. All except Jayce left. My good little Omega. He must scent my need, and he's waiting to see if I will accept what he's offering.

Deliberately, I slide myself to sit on top of the table with my legs spread, looking over at my Omega. His scent has changed, and he smells delicious; his scent almost mimics Aurora's. Bloody hell, his scent gets my cock hard and leaking. Jayce stands before me with the unspoken question in his eyes. Fuck yes, I want this boner taken care of! I smirk at him and lean back slightly, making it easy for his nimble fingers to make short work of my belt and buttons.

Carefully, he frees my throbbing cock from its prison, and he eyes it greedily. Jayce takes the rolling stool and sits upon it before me as he kisses and licks my balls. He's truly an expert when it comes to sucking cock. He knows how to rile me up and make me want him more. I feel his lips giving my length butterfly kisses from root to tip. I'm gripping the table hard, trying to resist the urge to thrust up and into his mouth before he's ready for me.

Slowly, Jayce tortures me; inch by inch, he slides my length to the back of his throat. What he can't fit in his mouth, he strokes roughly—knowing I like a firm grip. I can't resist anymore; I start to thrust up each time he takes me down his throat. Soon we find a rhythm that satisfies both of our needs. I release the desk and shove my hands into his hair for complete control. I'm so fucking close. Several more thrusts, and my seed starts pulsing down Jayce's throat, and he swallows every single drop.

Gently, I caress his scalp, running my fingers through his hair, showing my appreciation. His smile is rewarding enough right now. Hmm, what should I do for him? I'm still hard as steel, and his balls have to be aching. I reach out through the bond to Klaus—he's definitely the type to get in on some Jayce lovin'. Several moments later, Klaus enters the war room to find Jayce still licking at my cock and me smiling at him. "Come here, Klaus. I want you to suck Jayce's cock while I fuck his ass. If you're a good boy, maybe I'll fuck you to and have Jayce suck your cock as well."

Klaus's pupils dilate at the thought of what I just offered him. I turn my head to find Jayce naked and waiting. Gods, I love an eager Omega. I grab Jayce's hand and lead him over to the doorway that leads into the file room. I place each hand of his on either side of the doorframe. "Get to work, Klaus; make Jayce feel real good." Klaus takes the rolling stool that Jayce had used earlier and rolls it into position.

I reach around and feel how wet Jayce's cock is; feeling his pre-cum coat my hand, I pull away and rub it along my length. I give him a few more strokes, milking him some, then take more of his pre-cum and start to massage his rosette, getting the muscles to loosen up. Klaus is taking his time licking Jayce, making him moan and writhe before me. Oh yes, I'm absolutely fucking brilliant at times. As soon as Jayce is relaxed enough, I thrust deep inside of him—sinking balls deep. Jayce likes it rough, so I run my hand up his abs to his chest then his throat. I grip his throat, applying just enough pressure to have complete control. He moans and leans his head back and to the side in complete submission.

My dragon roars in the back of my mind, pleased with his reaction. I place my free hand on his hip and start thrusting into him hard and fast. I need this more than anything; I need my Aurora. Jayce is no Aurora, but his Omega status helps ease my rutting. I fuck him harder, occasionally making Klaus gag from the sudden forward thrust. I feel Klaus's free hand come back and grip my balls, and that does it. I come so hard into Jayce's ass that I end up biting him again, marking him as mine. My bite causes Jayce to come almost immediately. I watch over Jayce's shoulder as Klaus swallows every drop.

Between Jayce's and Klaus's involvement, they have managed to take the edge off my rutting for now. I look up at Jayce and the way Klaus is running his fingers through his hair. I have a feeling these two are involved in their own relationship within the bond.

Carefully I withdraw my now-flaccid cock from Jayce's ass, and I kiss his cheek. "Have fun, you two," I say as I turn and wave. "Be sure to clean up when you're done."

Both guys thank me as I depart, and I can hear them giggling to themselves as I close the door behind me. Yup, those two are definitely an item. The old-school thought is that each member had to be bonded to the other for the strongest connection. But the truth of the matter is, it takes time to forge a strong bond. The stronger the female, the stronger the bond is between the mates through her will alone.

We're lucky to have Aurora; she's probably the strongest, most understanding female I've ever met. The next three days will be hell for us without Aurora's presence. For now, I must talk with the others and plan our next possible moves.

CHAPTER 13
Aurora

Three days have passed, and yet to me it feels like only a few hours. My father had a brilliant idea putting me into a state of torpor to endure the heat until it passed. I pull out my amp and tune my guitar. It's been a while since I've played, and I decide to start playing "Popular Monster" by Falling in Reverse. It seems fitting for me.

It doesn't take long for the guys to locate me as my voice carries through the pack link. My voice fills the main hall in the Alpha House. I let my power explode from me and coat the room in ice. While I slept, my father dream-walked with me, filling me in on almost seven hundred years of our family's history. He taught me several new skills that I have yet to put into practical application. Today will be the day that those new skills will be tested.

My guys and our pack mates gradually begin to fill the hall as I go through the song. I feel my eyes shift, and my frost begins to coat the floor near me. It's slowly snaking out along the floorboards, plunging the room into winter. My mates look concerned as they watch as my skin flexes. My facial bones slide and shift, changing the structure of my cheeks as I sing. My beast wants out, and she absolutely loves this song and remembers what happens during the video. My pack mates stare in awe as I partially morph then shift back to human with very little effort on my part. I finish the song and set my guitar down next to my favorite chair.

"Today, we change up our training!" I announce as I leap up onto the closest chair to look out over my people. "Break out the swords, machetes, anything sharp that you can wield in your human form. They're expecting our animals; they will not expect some of us to fight as humans."

My eyes turn toward my father and Dimitri. "We're going to take the war to them—old-school. Their Lycans and most of their Strigoi won't know what hit them. Tactically, this will put us at an advantage, and we will reign supreme in the close-quarters battles. We must control the flow of the war; we must dictate how it begins and ends." By the time I finish speaking, my pack and my horde feed off my energy and power. Cheers erupt around the Alpha House and outside, where the rest of my people stand listening to my speech. I slightly incline my head toward my people, and they begin to exit the house.

Once everyone has left, I jump down and greet my mates, hugging and kissing each one in turn. "We need to prepare for all possible eventualities. Vladimir is old; he may or may not have taught his pack the old ways. We must make sure each pack member, as well as our allies, know how to use a sword effectively."

Dimitri nods gently then crosses his thick arms over his barrel chest. "Brilliant plan, my love. I've wanted to teach you how to use a sword for years. It's just, with as unstable as you used to be, it wasn't the smartest thing to do." Dimitri smiles his lopsided grin and tilts his head to the left, watching me.

My other mates back up slightly, expecting me to lose my temper over what Dimitri just said. I can't help but laugh a little; Dimitri isn't wrong in his assumption. "Good thinking, big guy; someone other than me would have gotten hurt," I purposely say it calmly and smile afterward. I walk over to Dimitri, wrap my arms around his neck, and kiss him gently on the lips before backing away. I give him a playful wink, then look at the others.

The twins and Alaric look at me, puzzled and in a semi-state of shock. Klaus and Arnulf have no clue how much of a hellion I was before Oberon helped me. "Are you feeling alright, baby girl?" Dominik comes over and kisses my forehead, and I grab his crotch.

"Yup, perfectly fine. Let's go train; I'm in the mood for a *twin sammich* and then a round of pass the Aurora." I start to walk toward the door in complete silence. I turn around in time to hear Arnulf ask the others what a *twin sammich* is in a whisper. Jayce is kind enough to lean in and tell Arnulf. I watch Arnulf's cheeks turn a brilliant crimson. Yup, that poor bird is going to lose his mind later.

Without skipping a beat, I head toward the training ring. Apparently, the town's blacksmith has a collection of swords from way back in the day. Boris, the Blacksmith, brings me over to the racks and allows me to choose first. I search through the swords and grab one that appears to be a heavily-built rapier. Its weight is just about three pounds, including the ornate hilt. Boris goes on to tell me that it is what's called a Munich sword. It's the perfect blend of speed and strength. He gives me a short history lesson on the sword's previous owner and its use. Apparently, this sword is a stone-cold killer, which just so happens to make it perfect for me.

By the time the guys come out and join me, I've decided this is the sword I will use. Alaric goes to the racks next and grabs a rapier and tests its weight in his hands. I smile, watching him as Boris stitches leather gauntlets over my forearms to keep my sleeves out of the way. Once everyone is ready, we pay for our equipment and then exit Boris's shop and head to the nearby field training area.

I crack my neck and close my eyes, remembering the lessons my father taught me while I slumbered. I find my center and gradually open my eyes. Confidently, I assume the stance I saw my father take a million times as I flitted through his and Dimitri's memories of my father's battles. Slowly, I raise my left hand and motion for Alaric to come at me. My breathing is controlled, and my focus is razor-sharp. I'm watching for any hint of his body telegraphing his move before he makes it. Alaric comes at me hard and fast, and I parry his strikes effortlessly. The blades caress several times, making that eerie scraping sound as they slide over each other.

I push off after the next clash of the blades, throwing Alaric off balance. My mate definitely telegraphs his moves before he strikes, and I'm anticipating them —which is starting to piss him off royally. His next move, I decide to end the match quickly and disarm him with a wide sweeping circle after the last clash. I stand now before him, holding both swords pointed at him. I smirk and toss him back his sword, then blow him a kiss. "Thanks for the warm-up, love."

"You move like your father," Dimitri says, looking between Nicodeamus and me.

"I should hope so, my love. Daddy taught me while I slept." I wink at Dimitri as Alaric passes his sword off to Nicodeamus. Father stretches and tests the weight of the sword in his hand. He eyes up the length of the blade then raises it briefly before assuming his fighting stance.

Father versus daughter, this should be most interesting. I stand en garde with my sword in a neutral position but my body in a combat position. Nicodeamus moves quickly, striking fast and efficiently. Luckily, I'm a quick study. We clash and lock several times, having to push off of each other multiple times. The battle is almost a draw, except my dumb ass gets a bit too cocky, and my father disarms me quickly. I smile at my father; we battled far longer than Alaric, and I did. I'm feeling quite accomplished at the moment. My mates begin to applaud my battle with my father, and I move in quickly to hug my dad and listen to him as he tells me where I went wrong so that I won't make the same mistake twice.

The rest of the afternoon, I sit beside Nicodeamus, enjoying some quality father/daughter time as he explains to me what each fighter is doing wrong. Out of my mates, Dimitri, Alaric, and—surprisingly—Arnulf are all skilled sword fighters. I watch as they and several pack elders take it upon themselves to teach the others to sword fight. Not everyone will get extensive training—mostly my assault force and the Lycans will.

By mid-afternoon, my father and Dimitri had switched out, and my other mates were replaced by elders. We watch the sparring matches, assessing everyone's weaknesses and strengths. Arnulf comes to stand before me and bows. "Would you do me the honor of sparring with me?" Arnulf has a bit of a mischievous look in his eye; the eagle is getting bold.

I rock back then flip up onto my feet before him. Casually, I reach back and grab my sword from where I laid it to rest earlier. "Let's go." I motion to the ring, and I can see the anxiety rolling off of him in waves.

Jayce comes over and caresses my arm and kisses my cheek. "Be gentle, love; he's new to our family."

I lower my eyes then look up to Jayce; I'm hoping my sadness is conveyed well. "I would be a bad mate if I took it easy on him. The Strigoi and the other Lycans won't take it easy on him. I won't hurt him, but I also won't go easy on him. I can't." I kiss Jayce's cheek then step into the ring with Arnulf.

I've barely entered the ring when Arnulf charges at me. It's then that I notice his eyes are vacant and not his own. Fuck! I know I killed Elena, but Arnulf is being controlled. I reach out to my mates, and they clear the area of all the others. I have to subdue my mate without killing him and figure out how the fuck someone got to him. Arnulf keeps charging, and I keep blocking and parrying his attacks. I watch, hoping for an opening where I can get in close and dominate him to drive the witch out of his head.

My other mates are concerned for Arnulf, knowing full well this may be a one-way ticket for him, but that thought to me is unacceptable. I will not kill my mate; I will fucking save him. Arnulf is starting to fatigue; his movements are becoming sluggish. I slap his ribs with the flat side of my sword to make the point he could have died right there. Nothing, no reaction from him. Mother fucking witch, I swear to the Elder gods I will slaughter her in the most bloody and painful way possible.

I reach out to Dominik and Jayce and let them in on my next move. I fake going to the right, and when Arnulf follows, the guys spring into action. They each grab an arm as Dimitri comes up behind Arnulf and wraps his arms around his ribcage. Arnulf is struggling, trying to get free, and I see it in his eyes that he's contemplating shifting.

I shift my eyes to that of my beast and force him to look at me. "I forbid you to shift!" I growl out the command, focusing all of my Alpha power just on him. The immense power he gets hit with makes his legs buckle under him; his bird goes and hides deep in his subconscious.

Slowly, I draw in a deep breath and grip Arnulf's head, and close my eyes. I force my way past the witch's defenses, delving into the mental prison that Arnulf is in. A kindly-looking older woman with a cane is walking in a circle around Arnulf's cage. This must be the Elder Dame I've been told about. She's definitely a blood mage, so I must take extreme caution. Arnulf looks up. Bringing my finger to my lips, I shake my head, motioning for him to remain silent.

"I know you're there, princess." The Elder Dame begins to laugh. "You're just like that fool of a mother you killed. You do know you killed her, right? You shredded her insides like cheese." The Elder Dame turns to finally look at me. She is short and withered, and I can see Elena's and Bash's features in her face.

"Oh, I know I killed my mother. Blood memories won't let me forget." I feel like I should be singing that Post Malone song, "Take What You Want."

I carefully stalk towards her, watching her movements closely. Raising my hand casually, I lightly touch my sternum where Oberon implanted an Elvish charm he said would protect me from blood magic. I stare the Elder Dame down and wait for her next move.

Her hand comes up to caress her chin as she studies me. "I should have broken your neck when I had your little body in my hands." She smirks, looking at me. "My idiot brother believes you will take him and accept him as a mate like your mother did."

I start to laugh. Honestly, I can't help it. "So you think by killing my mates or threatening to, I'll accept him." I shake my head as I feel my eyes shift.

"You honestly don't know who or what you're fucking with, crone." The eyes of my beast lock with hers, and the look of fear on her face is priceless.

"One huge *problem with your plan; I am my father's daughter." I shift my arms to my armored gauntlets and flex my talons. Arnulf winces, and I see blood on his head where my hands lay in the real world. Hmm, interesting development. If I hurt her here, she will be hurt in the real world as well. I tilt my head several times, studying her, seeing if she caught onto what I just figured out.*

"Abomination!" the Elder Dame yells, pointing at me.

"Yeah, I get that a lot; it's so unoriginal." I look at the ground under her feet and start to freeze it, trapping her in place.

"You're not the only one that's special, Elder Dame." With that being said, I create a mini ice storm and unleash it upon her.

I watch her wrinkled flesh be torn to ribbons before she fades from view. Arnulf's prison fades as well, and now he's free again. I close my eyes and lean my head back, focusing on returning to my body.

Sharply, I draw in a breath and open my eyes back in the real world and look around. My mates are in awe of what I have just done, and my father stands there proud as a peacock. "Just like your great-grandmother, I'm very proud of you, daughter." I smile and bow my head lightly to my dad, then look at Arnulf.

"Are you okay? I didn't mean to hurt you." I look down briefly as I remove my hands from Arnulf's hair. "I realized whatever I did there would happen here. I knew I couldn't physically attack her without killing you."

"Her who?" Dimitri asks as he pulls me into his arms and hugs me tightly.

"I met the Elder Dame," I say very matter-of-factly. "I sent her back, bleeding to her master." I sigh softly, looking over at Arnulf again. "Do you know how it happened? How did she get in?"

Arnulf moves close to me and touches my cheek. Through the bond, I feel how upset he is that he could have hurt me. "I saw her in my dream last night. I was trying to reach out to the ancestors for guidance, and she appeared. That's the last thing I remember." Arnulf shrugs his shoulders as he looks at me. I can tell he is hurting over all of this.

I look at Dimitri and he releases me. I immediately hug Arnulf and kiss him gently. "It's not your fault, love. You're new to the bond, therefore, your connection to me isn't as strong as the others yet. It will grow in time. Trust me when I say no one faults you for what happened here today."

My other mates all voice their agreement. I can see him attempting to smile through it again. I kiss him passionately as he grips me tightly, not wanting to let me go. I smile when I break off the kiss.

"Go shower, you stinky boys; we need some quality bonding time after dinner." My other five mates take off like someone lit their asses on fire.

Arnulf tilts his head to the side, looking at me puzzled. "Sex after dinner, Arnulf." When the real meaning hits him, his eyes light up, and I smack him on the ass sending him running off to shower. Silly males, what am I going to do with all of them?

CHAPTER 14

Dominik

The last twelve hours have been intense, to say the least. Aurora woke up with the fire of vengeance burning brightly in her heart. I don't know how the others feel, but I felt her rage as if it was my own. The underlining urge to hunt and kill all those who stand against us is spurring my beast on. He wants to kill and please our mate.

I head into the house, shower quickly, and race to the kitchen. Jayce is already in there, chopping and preparing dinner with Klaus as his sous chef. I watch them work in silence side-by-side, making dinner for everyone.

Lithe fingers ghost over my broad shoulders, then come to rest on my hips. Teeth nip at the muscle over my shoulder blade. I moan softly, shifting my weight slightly as I feel Aurora's fingertips move and trace each defined muscle across my back. Her hands rest on my shoulders as she moves to stand on her tippy toes. Her breath washes over the back of my neck, and I roll my head forward, granting her access. Aurora's lips gently caress my skin.

My wolf makes himself known, and he rumbles in my chest. I feel the smile move across Aurora's lips. My baby has a bit of a kink; she loves letting my wolf hunt her and have his way with her.

My cock is rock hard in my pants as I think about the last time we took her as a wolf. No, tonight, the man will have his way with his mate. Aurora gradually makes her way to stand in front of me. My beloved mate's scent calls to me; she's aroused and desires my attention. Bit by bit, I lower my head and nip at her throat, and listen to her moans fill the air. I look up, and Klaus's and Jayce's movements have stilled; they're watching us. I reach down and grab Aurora by the ass, slamming her back against the wall, and kiss her roughly.

I rub my hard cock against her crotch in slow teasing thrusts, knowing I'll have her begging for it sooner than later. Aurora arches her body, bringing her breasts close to my face; my canines elongate, and I use them to rip the fabric of her shirt, freeing her breasts. Her gasps are music to my ears as her hands grip my hair roughly, and she pulls my face to her chest. Who am I to deny my mate what she wants?

Aurora removes one hand from my hair and uses one of her talons to cut the remaining fabric free from her body. She obliterates her little booty shorts as well as the pretty lace bra she had on. My mate wants me as much as I want her right now. Then again, Aurora is always riled up after getting into a fight. Sex seems to soothe her beast better than anything else we can do for her. Aurora tilts her head, looking down between us at the offending jeans currently blocking what she wants.

I lean forward and bite her bottom lip as I take my free hand to undo my pants and let them fall to the floor. Aurora squeals with delight as she wiggles her ass until I'm lined up with her wet depths. I release her lip only to move and bite onto my mating mark on her shoulder while I thrust up into her and drive her body down.

Her muscles are already quivering and pulsing around my cock as I bury myself balls deep in her. Aurora squirts almost instantly when her orgasm comes crashing down on her. I thrust against the strong rhythmic pulses of her muscles, trying like hell to outlast her orgasm. The sneaky little minx bites the mate mark she gave me, and I fucking blow my load long before I wanted to. We cling to each other as we come down from our high. I can't help but smile at my beautiful mate. She's still pressed against the wall with me buried deep within her welcoming depths.

A sudden slap to my ass has me instantly growling, my black fur rippling up and down my arms. I'm in protection mode since my mate is cradled between me and the wall. I look around for my next victim and see Dimitri laughing.

"Couldn't wait until after dinner, huh?" Dimitri says, motioning to everyone, helping to set the table. Thankfully, it's just our bond mates allowed in the Alpha House after dark. Otherwise, it could have been quite the spectacle.

My brother Jayce comes over and offers us both wet towels, and Klaus has robes for both of us. I don't know if I should be embarrassed or strutting around like a peacock right now. Aurora rolls her eyes at me after she finishes cleaning herself up. Quickly, she bounces up and kisses my cheek before running to her seat to start eating.

I thought I would be used to Aurora's antics by now, but I'm not. I love that woman to death, but the invasion we're planning quite honestly has me terrified. I'm not scared for myself, per se; I'm scared of losing the only woman I've ever truly given myself fully to. Yeah, there have been many women over my lifespan—I'm a man, and I've got needs. But Aurora, even when I'm physically not touching her, I feel her deep within my soul. I'm never alone because of the bond she's forged between all of us.

Aurora always seems to be evolving, changing, becoming the woman we all need and our enemies fear. I guess my pensiveness has caught Alaric's attention. He stands before me, looking worried, and he motions with his head for us to leave the room. We walk in silence until we make it to the hidden bunker and shut it tightly.

"What's eating at you, Dom? Usually, you're very jovial after being with Aurora." Alaric tilts his head to the left then the right, studying me.

I exhale the breath I didn't realize I was holding. "I'm worried about Aurora. All these changes; new gifts, powers, and abilities. As she evolves, I fear she will lose herself in it all. I fear we'll lose her in battle. I fear if she dies, we all will either follow her into the abyss or be left to mourn her loss." I look down as a single tear rolls down my cheek and hits the floor.

"Ah, I see." Alaric moves and sits in his favorite chair. "Being a dragon has its benefits and its drawbacks. We live an incredibly long time, but it's also very lonely at times watching our friends of other species age faster than us and die."

Alaric strokes his beard before starting again. "What I'm trying to say, Dom, is that we don't know what's going to happen with Aurora. She's the second born of her kind, the first to make it to this stage of her evolution. The fact that the Fae King himself is watching over her brings me comfort."

"But... what if she dies? What if we're left behind?" I look away, trying to recompose myself. My heart feels as if it will break at any moment. "I don't want to live without her."

"Dom, let's hope it doesn't come to that." Alaric stands and moves to hug me tightly to his chest. "Do you know why Nicodeamus lived after his mate died? Which, I must add, is uncommon for dragons to do?"

"No." My answer is shorter than I had intended, but what else is there left to be said.

"He had his hatchling to live for, Dominik. We have Tiamat and Ladon to live for. They are our children, or as you wolves would say, they are our pack. Don't all members of the wolf pack tend to the young?" Alaric questions, making sure his understanding of pack law is correct.

"Pack takes care of the pack. Your hatchlings have the protection of the pack as well as the horde and swarm. They have mine and Jayce's protection for as long as we both shall live." I look into Alaric's eyes, making sure he understands what I said.

"But you don't consider them your children?" Alaric looks hurt as he speaks. It makes my stomach turn, and sadly, he's partially correct. I push off his chest and start pacing.

"Your babies don't freely accept the others in the bond completely. We're not dragons. They seek out the dragons or dragon hybrids in our family; the rest of us barely exist." I growl, thinking about how badly the babies' rejection hurts me.

"It sucks, Alaric! It fucking sucks! First, I think they are mine or Jayce's, and then now that they're here, they reject every fucking attempt we make at being close to them." Roughly, I drag my hands through my hair and huff out an exasperated sigh.

"I didn't know, Dom. I'm sorry." Alaric looks remorseful. "It's because as their animals, the others can't hear them. But now that they are older, they should be going to everyone equally. I'll have a talk with them posthaste." Alaric moves so quickly I'm almost shocked by it.

I run to catch up with him, and he's back in the kitchen with everyone else rather quickly. Aurora stares at Alaric curiously, as does Nicodeamus. By the color of their eyes, I know they are communicating amongst themselves. Both children come running into the room dressed in their clothing for the day. Aurora's been allowing them to spend more time as humans lately, which is quite a nice change.

"Children?" Alaric says.

"Yes, Father?" Tiamat and Ladon say in unison.

"Why do you not go to your other fathers within our bond?" Alaric asks them gently, trying to see where the disconnect is. The look of shock on Aurora's face tells me she was unaware of the problem. Tears form and freeze on Aurora's cheeks, her own pain over the situation evident.

"You are Father; they are Mom's other mates," Ladon says boldly, being defiant like always. Tiamat is shaking her head no and looking remorseful.

"Ladon, they are our dads. Father is our father, but they are all dads to us. Mom said so," Tiamat says with a slight growl to her voice. Tiny frost crystals move over Tiamat's skin, showing her agitation with her brother. Her little dragon is close to the surface as she stares down Ladon.

"Ladon, Tia is correct. They are your dads, and I am Father. They are to be afforded the same love and respect you do your mom and me." Alaric's eyes are that of his dragon, driving the point home.

Ladon looks away, which was a huge mistake on his part because Aurora is on him in a second. She picks him up off the ground and brings him up to eye level with her. "Do you love me less because I am not a full dragon like your father and grandfather?" Aurora is pissed off, thinking her son may be speciest.

"No, Mommy, I love you." Ladon tentatively reaches out to stroke Aurora's shifting facial bone plates.

Aurora snorts frost on her son and looks away. "If you cannot love my other mates like you say you love me, how do I know you love me? I am not and will never be like you or your sister. I will never know what it is to spread my wings because I have none. I will never know the freedom of flight without a wing suit or your father. Does that make me less than you or your father?" Aurora turns to look Ladon in the eyes, tears threatening to break again and roll down her cheeks. Deep down, we feel the conflicting pain versus the anger boiling under the surface.

We all start to rub the dull ache in our chests, feeling Aurora's pain as if it's our own. "Daddy Dom? Why are you rubbing your chest?" Tia asks as she looks up at me with her arms stretched, wanting me to pick her up.

"Because we all feel when your mommy hurts." I snuggle Tia to my chest, and Jayce soon joins us and snuggles up behind her.

"Only true mates can sense each other, little one," Jayce says softly before kissing the crown of Tia's head. She turns in my arms and wraps her arms around Jayce's neck, and hugs him.

"I'm sorry, Mommy. I'll be a better son from now on." Ladon

lowers his head in submission. Aurora gently sets him on the ground and watches his actions.

Ladon climbs up on a stool and looks at all of us. "I'm sorry I was mean. I didn't mean to hurt anyone. Mommy is very important to me, so I'm sorry because I was a weenie."

We all accept his apology and continue to play "pass the Tiamat" since she was the first to seek affection from us.

"You weren't mean, Ladon; you were an ass!" Tiamat screams at her brother, her dragon's growl making her voice sound that much angrier.

Her little dragon close to the surface, tiny scales ripple up and down Tiamat's arms. "I wanted to play with all my daddies, but you said no! You were an ass!" Tiamat is growling in Dimitri's arms, causing a light coating of frost to cover his shirt. Her little talons extend and retract, punctuating her anger. She looks exactly like a miniature Aurora.

"Two things, little one," Dimitri says softly as he kisses Tia's temple. "Don't say ass; it's not a nice word. Second, please don't freeze me; I'm not as frost-resistant as your mom and dad," Dimitri says as he smiles at Tia.

Tia looks quite sheepish as she studies the frost on Dimitri. Carefully, she passes her little hand over the frost, and it vanishes as fast as it had appeared. "Sorry, Daddy." Tia wraps her arms around Dimitri's neck and hugs him tightly. Her little dragon purrs its affections at Dimitri. Ladon, on the other hand, jumps down and starts passing out the hugs, telling everyone he is sorry for being a weenie.

CHAPTER 15
Dominik

Aurora still looks distraught over what her son has done. Alaric attempts to console her until Klaus comes over and takes Aurora from him. He raises his eyebrow at her and motions towards the door. Aurora smiles and shifts on the spot, heading towards the door.

"How are you turning the doorknob, you silly woman!?" Klaus yells as he chases after Aurora.

All I can do is shake my head while watching Aurora and Klaus leave. "Can we go play with them too?" Ladon asks as he pulls on my pant leg.

"I don't see why not." We all follow Ladon outside as he goes to look for his mother and Klaus. Looking at the distance between paw prints, they took off at a run and could be anywhere. I look to my brother, and we tilt our heads back and use a locating howl to gauge how far away Klaus and Aurora are.

Tiamat and Ladon both attempt to howl and can't it comes out more like a garbled roar. I cant my head to the side, listening for the return howls. Several seconds later, we hear their combined call. The children expectantly look at me; part of me wants to be an asshole and teach Ladon a lesson. The face he's making tells me he can't understand the howls at the moment, and that is enough of a lesson. "They're hunting by the lake. They are inviting the entire family to join them. They want the babies to see what Lycans can do."

Alaric looks in the direction of the lake. "It's about a mile away. We can fly there or shift and run as a pack."

It's my turn to raise an eyebrow at Alaric, knowing full well his dragon isn't able to run through the forest because of its size. We watch the children closely, and both shift to their dragon forms and start running in the direction of their mother. Dimitri shifts next, leaving his clothing in a pile. Arnulf follows Dimitri's example, as does my brother. It's then I notice that Alaric has a bag he's placing all the clothing in.

"How are you getting up there?" I ask him as I start to strip.

"Dimitri was kind enough to offer to carry me as long as I carry everyone's clothing. It's a fair trade to me; I never get to see the forest from this perspective." I hand Alaric my clothing and shift into my wolf. We take off running to catch up to Aurora and Klaus.

Jayce and I keep pace with the babies, making sure they don't get into anything they can't get themselves out of. Dimitri brings up the rear with Alaric on his back, going at a lumbering pace up the incline heading towards the lake.

We see Aurora's white beast as well as Klaus's black Lycan darting in and out of the thick trees at the lake's edge. The babies catch up quickly to where they last saw their mother and go on the search to see if they can find her themselves. From experience, I know better than to blindly go in the most apparent direction. I know what the babies are trying to do; they are attempting to track their mother. On the other hand, I decide to go the opposite direction, breaking off from my brother and babies to get ahead of the much faster Lycans.

By scent and instinct, I know that my quarry isn't far from where I'm standing. Now, the average hunter looking for a terrestrial being never thinks to look up. I, on the other hand, know better. I look up and see Klaus and Aurora hanging by their talons in a rather large oak tree. I watch them for several seconds before I trot off slowly, not giving away their position to the babies.

I watch the little ones weave in and out of the trees, following their mother's footprints in the freshly churned-up dirt. I see the rest of my bond mates make it up into the general area where our other mates are up in the tree. I sit down, wagging my tail, waiting to see who else gets smart enough to look up.

Alaric slides off of Dimitri's back and comes to sit next to me. I know that he knows exactly where our silly mate is. The babies are still running around in circles, checking every single tree, trying to find any sign of their mother. Alaric smirks as he keeps a watchful eye on his progeny as they search the forest floor. He glances up in the exact direction our silly mate is, and I follow his gaze and wink at her. Aurora raises her chin in my direction and gets a mischievous look in her eyes.

Aurora decides to be a bit of a wise-ass and starts jumping from tree to tree, using her talons to grip the thick bark. The sudden movement of her great white beast and the blur of white catches everyone's eyes. Tiamat is the first to look up, having heard her mother's talons grip the next tree when she lands. Ladon watches his sister and then looks in the direction that she's currently staring at. Both babies take off running, trying to catch up with their mother jumping from tree to tree.

It finally dawns on Tiamat that she can fly, and at a full run, she spreads her wings and takes off. Quickly, she flaps her wings and gains altitude, catching up to her mother. Tia tackles her mother, knocking herself and Aurora out of the tree.

Thankfully, Aurora's quick reflexes and maternal instinct get her to wrap her arms around her baby and twist just in time so that she lands on her hind paws. Tiamat is clearly very proud of herself at the moment for finding and capturing her mother long before her brother did.

It was a great training exercise for the babies. Now they have a better understanding of what the Lycan side of the family is capable of doing. Next up are Jayce and me to show the babies what the Dire Wolves can do. Jayce walks over to a sapling, tilts his head sideways and bites into its soft bark, then backs up. Within a matter of moments, the sapling dies and withers before our eyes. Alaric takes this moment to explain about the toxin that Jayce has. The babies look up to him curiously, and he opens his mouth, letting some of the yellow-green toxin drip freely from his canines.

Aurora does a short bark, and then when the babies are looking at her, she opens her mouth and lets the same toxin drip from her canines as well. Arnulf and the babies look between Jayce and Aurora with shocked expressions. Aurora decides now to shift back to her human form.

"I know it's confusing, but I am the last of my bloodline." She looks down sadly as she flexes her hands, looking them over.

"There will never be another like me born. I gain gifts from each of my mates; each mate has given me a weapon, so to speak." She looks up and motions to each of us in turn.

Aurora moves over to Jayce and threads her fingers through his fur. "Jayce gave me his toxin; his twin Dominik gave me his night vision with heat."

Aurora moves away from Jayce and heads to Dimitri. She runs her hand over his broad chest then smiles with pride. "My Dimitri here is one of the last originals of the Great Bear bloodline. He gave me his size and strength. I now possess the power of the Great Bear." Aurora bounces up and kisses Dimitri on the lips before moving to Klaus.

Aurora's fingertips move over Klaus's chest before she stops at his side. "Klaus is the last of the pure Lycan bloodline. I received from Klaus his speed and agility and my increased jumping ability."

Gently, Aurora kisses Klaus's muzzle, then bounds away from him and over to Alaric. She tilts her head left, then right, then back again. "Your father bestowed upon me the power of the dragon—access to the recesses of my bloodlines." Aurora gently runs her fingers down the bridge of Alaric's nose. "My final ascension, I'll be given a choice: evolve the rest of the way or remain as I am in between."

Aurora gently kisses Alaric then looks back at me. "What do you mean in between?" I ask curiously.

I watch Aurora draw in a deep breath, and her eyes go frost-white. The ground around her starts to freeze. "I have the choice to remain as I am or to become more than I am now."

The frost leaves Aurora's eyes and she draws in a deep breath then looks around as if she doesn't know what just happened. "Don't tell me of the prophecy I spoke of. To tell me will only stop it from happening. It's time to go home."

Aurora shifts and runs back down the hill toward the Alpha House. It's frightening to know that one decision can turn the tides, and it all depends on Aurora. We look at each other, then shift and start to head home. The final battle is on the horizon, and each day brings us a step closer.

Once the children are in bed over in Nico's cottage, Aurora starts to stalk the house. I get the feeling she's about to make good on her promise of sex. One by one, she finds her mates and whispers in their ears. I watch my bond mate's eyes flare to life before they turn and run toward our master bedroom.

Aurora stalks me last. She has that gleam in her eyes that tells me she's up to no good. "Dom, baby... I wanna play." Aurora drags a single finger down my chest to my abs. I watch her open her hand wide as she caresses my abs. I can see the hunger in her eyes; she needs her other mates and me. "Time to go, love." She winks at me, then turns and walks away.

My mate is going to be the death of me and the others. I head down into the hidden master bedroom and close the hatch behind me. I follow the delicious honey-tinged scent of Aurora's arousal. The master bath is lined with candles, and my bond mates are all in Aurora's tub. "Join the others, Dom," Aurora says softly.

Apparently, my mate has plans for us tonight. Her eyes lock on my fingers as I casually unbutton my shirt. I'm not going to give in as quickly as my bond mates did; I'm going to draw this out as long as I can. I roll my thickly-muscled shoulders, making my shirt slide down my arms to the floor.

Aurora is a sucker for a nice, thick trapezius muscle—after all, it's the same muscle that most of our mating marks are on. The ethereal glow of Aurora's eyes tells me I have her full, undivided attention. I make a big deal of sliding my hands down my abs to my belt. Since I'm teasing my mate, I maintain eye contact with her, daring her to approach me. A deep lust-filled growl escapes Aurora's lips; she's barely able to contain herself as I drag my zipper down. I do a small shimmy and my jeans fall to the ground, pooling at my feet.

Quickly, I toe off my shoes and saunter my happy ass over to the pool with my bond mates. Aurora is practically foaming at the mouth as she stares at me as I walk away from her. High fives ensue the moment I get into the water. We turn as one as Aurora shifts one finger and begins to cut the fabric of her shirt off of herself. We watch her with rapt attention as each shred of fabric hits the floor. My eyes rake over every square inch of her ivory flesh; I've memorized every scar and freckle from ankle to earlobe.

A slow roll of her hips is given before she loops her thumbs into the top of her leggings and pushes them down. Her ass and sex are on full display as she looks seductively over her shoulder at us. Sensually, she rolls back up to standing; her long, white hair falls in waves down her back and stops just above her hips.

Her pink tongue darts out between her ruby lips, and she draws her tongue teasingly over her front teeth and to the points of her descended canines. Aurora's beast lurks just under the surface as she begins to stalk forward, hunting us as if we are a herd of sheep. I watch Alaric's hands twitch at his sides—he wants what the rest of us want. We want to get our hands on our mate. Aurora languidly slinks into the water and dips under briefly. She rises up out of the water like a siren calling the sailors to their deaths. I watch every rivulet of water stream down her body, especially the one that runs between her ample breasts.

Aurora bypasses her usual choice for the first mate to attack and heads towards Arnulf. The poor bird is beside himself, watching this apex predator stalk him. "Shhh, baby, I won't hurt you... I just want your attention and affection." She speaks softly as she presses her cheek against his. Arnulf visibly relaxes as her hands slowly slide across the defined planes of his chest. Dimitri moves up behind her and presses his chest against her back. It might not be the *twin sammich* she was looking for, but she's definitely going to get what she's craving.

Without hesitation, Aurora climbs Arnulf like a tree and starts grinding herself on his length. Arnulf is struggling to hold onto Aurora and attempts to line himself up with her warm depths. Dimitri does Arnulf a solid and lifts Aurora up effortlessly and holds her suspended in the water for him. I can see the look of thanks on Arnulf's face as he is finally able to line up and sink balls deep into our mate. Arnulf starts to set the pace as he holds onto Aurora with Dimitri's help.

Dimitri, being the slick fuck that he is, slowly presses his length into Aurora from behind. Her back bows off of Dimitri's chest the minute the big guy hits home. Her gasps and moans from how deliciously full she is makes my cock pulse in time with her moans.

I'm so focused on Aurora that I don't notice till now that Jayce, Klaus, and Alaric are having their own fun on the other side of the pool. Alaric is sitting on the edge of the pool. Jayce has his mouth wrapped around Alaric's length, sucking his cock as deep into his throat as he can handle. Klaus has a firm grip on Jayce's hips as he teases him, sliding his rigid cock gradually in and out of my brother's ass. Jayce is in heaven; the happy moans he's making are only setting Aurora off more. Aurora screams as her orgasm crashes over her; Arnulf can't resist and follows quickly behind her. Dimitri is like a machine—he's still pumping slowly in and out of her ass like he has all the time in the world.

Arnulf quickly taps out and motions for me to slide in where he was. Hell yeah, I want in. Dimitri notices that I'm replacing Arnulf, and a wicked grin crosses his lips. Aurora squeals and leans forward, knowing I can easily support her weight. Aurora's arms wrap around me, and I feel like I'm home. I feel her love through the bond, and I hear her demands echo in the back of my mind.

Quickly, I line myself up and drive my cock deep into her warm pulsing depths. She's so full, and I feel the sliding of Dimitri's cock as he withdraws. We set our rhythm rather quickly—this isn't the first time we've had Aurora together. She writhes uncontrollably between us while the water sloshes all over; most of it being driven out of the side of the tub from our combined efforts.

Dimitri and I are both getting close, and we can feel the fluttering of Aurora's muscles just before they begin to tense. We'll be damned if we cum before she does. Silently, Dimitri and I agree to pull out all the stops. A single nod of our heads, and we both lower our mouths and bite Aurora simultaneously. The surge of power her lithe body unleashes is unreal. Every single fiber of my being reverberates with every single pulse and throb of her muscles as they contract and milk my cock. I can't hold back anymore; it's no longer possible.

Aurora is still whining and whimpering from her release. I roar out as my cock throbs, spilling my seed deep within her womb. Dimitri crashes over shortly after I do, which triggers another orgasm from Aurora. Her nails dig deep into my flesh as she turns to sink her canines into Dimitri.

Gradually, our breathing returns to normal, and I can finally open my eyes to look around. Everyone else left at some point during our intensive lovemaking. Personally, I feel like I've been reduced to Jell-O. Aurora is practically asleep in Dimitri's arms, and to be honest, if I weren't afraid of drowning, I'd probably fall asleep too. We drag our exhausted selves off to bed. In a few hours, our journey begins, and the war will be on the horizon.

CHAPTER 16

Dimitri

Morning comes way too quickly today. I've been dreading this day since Aurora started collecting her mates. Everything we could need has been packed in wagons that my people supplied for us, so we don't look out of place. Aurora was smart when she set up trail buddies. One dragon, one either Lycan or Dire Wolf with each wagon. We will be broken into four teams, taking four different routes to the same campsites each day. We are aware we won't hide our numbers for long, but the longer we can, the better.

I walk through the house, looking for the rest of my bond mates. I come across Aurora speaking to Elsa and Klaus's mother—whose name for the life of me I can't remember. I already know what's happening, though; Aurora is telling them it's their job to protect her babies. Elsa is honored, but her daughter doesn't want the responsibility. Aurora is at her wits' end when Nicodeamus walks into the room.

"Aurora, I need to speak with you." Aurora nods and moves to her father's side.

"You too, Dimitri." Oh fuck, shit just got real. His tone tells me there will be very little room for argument. We follow Nicodeamus into the library.

"I've already spoken to your bond mates, and there will be no arguments. I am staying behind to guard the babies. Not that I don't trust Elsa, it's just that she can't reach out to you if something goes wrong here. She can't call you back if we're attacked, nor do they have my fire," Nicodeamus says, making a very logical and sound decision. Aurora is borderline in tears. I reach for her and pull her to my chest.

"It makes perfect sense, my King. You protect one treasure; we will protect the other." I bow my head graciously towards my king.

Aurora shoves against my chest and goes to stand before her father. "Daddy, no! How am I supposed to protect you if I'm not with you? How am I supposed to keep you safe?" Aurora is crying, her tears freezing on her cheeks. The rest of the bonded enters the room only to be halted by Nicodeamus raising his hand.

"Aurora!" Nicodeamus says her name with a force I haven't felt from him before.

His ancient power crackles over his flesh, and his eyes take on an ethereal glow like Aurora's do. "I will have none of this nonsense. I'm well over a thousand years old, and I don't need to be babied. Your children, my grandchildren, will be at their safest with me. You know in your heart that I'm correct. I can sense them, call them all without words. I promise to reach out to you daily, so you know they're safe." Nicodeamus extends his hand to Aurora.

Aurora draws in a slow, deep breath, then rushes forward and hugs her father tightly. Frost coats them both—something I've never seen them do before. On the other hand, Alaric moves forward and hugs them as well, adding to the frost. It's getting stranger and stranger when Ladon and Tiamat come running in and grab onto Aurora's and Alaric's legs. They both end up covered in frost as well.

I shake my head slowly, watching this frozen hug-fest; I have no fucking clue what they are doing. Eventually, they break apart, and I decide now is a good time to question them. "What just happened?"

Nicodeamus starts laughing. "I'm sorry, everyone, it's an Ice Dragon thing. When we are to separate for a long time, we share our frost; it soothes our beasts. It makes communication between the dragons easier, and it takes less effort. I wish it worked for the rest of the family the way it works for us."

I can see the gears turning in Aurora's mind when she starts looking at everyone. "It might, Dad. I mean, if Alaric and I start and the guys hug on in order of binding. It's worth a shot; the babies will have to grab on before Arnulf. Dad, you'll have to grab on after Jayce." Aurora turns and looks at Alaric and opens her arms to him, wanting to start. Of course, Alaric gives in immediately and holds onto Aurora, starting the frost. Dominik and Jayce are next, but the frost burns them.

"Wait, I have an idea." I move forward toward Alaric and Aurora and touch them, and the frost moves inch by inch over my skin.

As I suspected, her wolf bonded to me first way back when. I hug Aurora and Alaric tightly, feeling their life-force move through me. Next, Dominik and Jayce join, and then Nicodeamus, then Klaus and the babies—Tiamat before Ladon. Finally, Arnulf joins in the hug, and we feel every single persons life-force as if it's our own. I close my eyes and see all of our animals on the astral plane.

Nicodeamus's dragon has all of its appendages, and he can fly again.

Aurora is standing beside a spectral form of her beast. "Here is our center; if anyone is captured, meditate, and come here. We can find you this way, even in death."

She breathes in deeply, trying to quell her emotions. "In death, this realm will give us time to say goodbye. Our loved one will only remain here as long as a fragment of their energy pulses through one of us."

Aurora looks to Nicodeamus. "Father has agreed to be the gate-keeper, my children the vessels. They will hold the lost ones here for as long as they can."

Now I understand why they were doing what they were. It's an ancient rite I haven't witnessed for over two hundred years. I nod, looking down at the babies. It's a lot of responsibility for them to hold and shoulder. Honestly, I don't think they understand the gravity of the situation.

Tiamat tugs on my pants leg, drawing my attention to her. "Daddy Bear?"

I look down at Tia and smile at her. "Yes, my Princess?" I kneel down to be closer to her level.

Tia scrambles and climbs up on my bent knee to look me in the eyes. Her little hands grip my face, her tiny fingers digging into my thick beard. "Don't worry, Daddy Bear, Pop-Pop told us what our jobs are. It's not difficult for us; we're big dragons."

Tia pulls my face closer to hers, and she leans into my ear. "We have Mommy's wolf strength and funny paws on our dragons. We're awesome; Mommy says so. No one can beat my Mommy."

Tia nods firmly, believing her words as gospel. "Mind your Pop-Pop; if he says to hide, you hide. We would be utterly broken if something were to happen to you and Ladon," I say gently and kiss Tia on the crown of her head.

"We understand, Daddy Bear," Tia and Ladon say in unison.

A knock is heard at the door, and we turn to face it as it opens. An Elven woman with bright pink hair comes walking in. Gracefully, she bows then stands up again. "King Oberon sends his greetings and well wishes. I was sent to assist with protecting the future Heirs." She bows again then looks at each of us in turn.

"I remember you..." Aurora says as she moves forward.

The Elven woman smiles and nods at Aurora and holds her hands out to her. "Yes, I'm glad you remember me. It's been a bit over two hundred years since I last saw you."

Aurora takes the woman's hands without hesitation. "Laurel, isn't it? You had butterfly wings the last time I saw you, if I remember correctly."

"You are correct on both counts, Aurora." Laurel looks toward the ceiling for a moment, and her wings shimmer into view. "I'm sorry my blessing went wrong all those years ago." Laurel looks down sadly.

"What do you mean your blessing went wrong?" Alaric and I manage to ask within seconds of each other. Dominik and Jayce move closer, as do Klaus and Arnulf.

Laurel shuffles her feet briefly and flutters her wings. "I was sent to bless Aurora; I was to help her manage her dual nature. Instead, I accidentally postponed her ascension." Laurel almost immediately starts crying with her admission.

We watch several emotions flicker over Aurora's face. Anger, pain, and finally, sympathy and understanding. Aurora shocks us all and pulls Laurel into a big hug.

"Thank you for being honest," Aurora says softly to Laurel.

"But please don't try to bless my children," Aurora says with a toothy grin.

"I won't, I promise! I'm here to help protect them and cast a glamor over the village to hide them in your absence. King Oberon sent the spell with me. Nicodeamus is the one who needs to cast it as the Elder Dragon. The concealment spell will last as long as he's breathing, or as long as he wills it to last." Laurel breaks away from Aurora and walks over to Nicodeamus, and hands him the amulet.

"It must remain close to your skin for it to remain active. As long as a dragon's heart beats under it, it will work." Laurel bows to Nicodeamus and watches him put it in his pocket for safekeeping.

"I'll put it on after everyone departs. How do you plan to protect us, little one?" Nicodeamus looks at Laurel, studying her now.

Laurel smiles and flourishes her one hand and produces a magnificent bow. She grips the string and draws back, and a magical arrow appears. Harmlessly, she shoots it into the air, and it turns to glitter. "I assure you, my Lord, I am more than capable of defending against attackers."

Aurora starts to laugh as she watches Laurel. "I like her. She's spunky!" Aurora turns and looks at the rest of us. "Okay, boys, let's get this show on the road. The sooner we leave, the sooner we can get back!"

Aurora kisses her father and both babies goodbye. She goes and hugs Elsa and gives Klaus's mother the evil eye. Just before we are ready to leave, a woman with black hair approaches Dominik and Jayce.

Aurora comes up and leans against my side, staring at the female, watching her interact with the twins. "D, I think that's my other mother-in-law. Hopefully, this one isn't a royal bitch." Aurora smiles as she bounces up and kisses my cheek before heading towards the twins.

I watch Aurora move towards the twins, and I hold my breath—this could be an epic disaster or the best moment ever. The twin's mother bows to Aurora and bares her neck to her in probably the wisest move I've ever seen done by anyone yet. Aurora watches the woman curiously, then scoops her up in a huge hug and spins around with her. I don't know what was said, but Aurora is happy and tightly held onto the twins' mother. Aurora catches my eye and drags the poor woman over with her. "D! This is Dominik and Jayce's mom, Helle!"

Helle bows lightly to me and then stares at Nicodeamus; her eyes are that of her wolf's. Nicodeamus feels her eyes upon him, and he turns and freezes. Aurora is bouncing up and down, excited as all hell. Dominik is the first to say something. "Um, Mom? Mother? Hello? Earth to Mom."

Jayce moves between his mom and Nicodeamus and looks between the two of them. "Holy crap! I think they are mates!" We look between them both when suddenly they embrace each other and kiss passionately like long-lost lovers. There is a thud, and we all turn to see Dominik passed out on the floor. Aurora shakes her head, looking at Dom then back to her father, happy he won't spend the rest of his days on this Earth alone.

I smile and turn to head outside and leave my best friend to meet his mate. I look out at our gathered troops and the caravans. So many are ready to head out into an uncertain future. Sadly, I know many may not make it back, but many more shall fight valiantly and help us rid the world of one of the greatest evils it has known in a while. My remaining blood descendants are here in the village, remaining behind to help keep things running in our absence.

So much more planning has to be done, but things appear to be in order for now. One of the stewards hands me the checklist for the trip for me to double check everything. He knows that when it comes to my family's safety, I don't leave that in anyone else's hands. I'll spend the next half an hour or so double checking as everyone gathers the last of their things.

CHAPTER 17

Aurora

AT LEAST I KNOW I LIKE ONE OF MY MOTHERS-IN-LAW, I SAY TO MYSELF as I throw the last of my supplies into the carriage that I'll be riding in. I'm not fond of the idea of hiding myself but let's face it, with my white hair, I stand out. Jayce has opted to ride with me for this section of the trip. I hate being contained, and it's a known fact that he's about the only one capable of getting me to relax.

I lie on the bench with my head in Jayce's lap with my eyes closed. I'm listening to our traveling companions talk amongst themselves. Ellis and Dante are in here with two others from Klaus's pack. Ellis and Dante are having a contest of what's the most fucked up Aurora moment you've witnessed to date. Dante has Ellis beat by a long shot, but he's sworn not to speak of me breathing fire.

"Man, when I tell you Alaric and Aurora are perfect for each other, I kid you not," Ellis says with his usual dramatic inflection for everything.

"Why would you say that, marshmallow man?" Dante asks and motions to me. Yeah, I let him in on that one. I can hear Ellis's bear rumble, and as soon as the rumbling stops, I crack an eye open to turn and look at him, waiting for him to say something to Dante.

"Um, well...They're fucked up! Sending presents of meat and skulls and then the trippy cutting a scale into their own flesh... *That* was the icing on the cake for me. They fucking scare me," Ellis says as he glances between Dante and me.

Dante starts laughing and looks at me, then points to Ellis. "Damn, marshmallow doesn't understand the significance of those presents and gestures. Do you wish to explain, my Queen, or shall I do it for you?"

I carefully sit myself up and look at Ellis. I can see he's nervous by the way he's fidgeting with the edge of his sweatshirt. "The skull, Ellis, was to show that Alaric is worthy of having a mate." Ellis's phone rings; it's Alaric, and he wants the phone to be put on speaker so he can be involved in the conversation.

I begin again once the phone is set up. "Alaric sent me his scale to show how serious he was about wanting the alliance with us. I followed tradition and implanted the scale over my heart." I show Ellis and Dante Alaric's scale alive and well on my chest.

"As you can see, scale lives. Which, if you didn't know, it would only live on a suitable mate. A true mate, to be exact. I had Dimitri retrieve my wendigo skull from my collection. Besides my cougar skull, it was my most valuable possession. I sent to Alaric, as you already know, the skull, one of my scales, and a braid of my hair."

I look down for a moment and smile. "Instinct told me to send the braid. To this day, I still don't know what prompted me to do it.

Do you, Alaric?" I tilt my head to the side, waiting for his response.

I hear Alaric laugh a little, then clear his throat. "Well, as Dante can tell you, it was your animal's way of scent marking me so that other females know I'm being courted. It's a little different with dragons than wolves and bears but similar to the eagles. The females, since there's so few of them, choose the males they deem worthy."

I raise my eyebrows and look to Dante; he nods, agreeing with what Alaric just told me. "Wow, that's an interesting take on things. I kinda like it. Especially since I will raise Tiamat to be like me and not take anyone's shit and torch a fucker if they deserve it." I nod to punctuate my seriousness, then smile.

Dante nods along with me. Ellis, on the other hand, looks like he's panicking. "Are you fucking serious? Alaric, please, no! The world can't handle two Auroras in it. One is terrifying enough!"

Poor Jayce almost chokes on his water from laughing. I gently pat his back and look at Ellis just as Alaric's voice booms through the phone. "What do you have against my mate, bear?"

I can feel through the bond Alaric is extremely aggravated. "Aurora, do something; I feel like his dragon is going to rip free any moment," Jayce says softly as he leans in close to me. Jayce's wolf is whining in response to Alaric's dragon.

I wink at Dante and close my eyes as I gently rub Alaric's scale. I concentrate on how much I love him, and I beg his dragon to forgive the silly marshmallow. His dragon is pissed that he dared to speak ill of his hatchling and his mate. I nod as I listen to man and beast at once.

I feel them settle, and then I turn to look at Ellis; my eyes are churning mercury with my black dragon slits pulsing as I stare at him. "My mate and his dragon are mad that you spoke ill of our angel, Tiamat, and me. I strongly suggest you apologize and mean it, furball."

Ellis audibly swallows and picks up his phone, taking it off of speaker, and walks to the back of the carriage to speak to Alaric. I look at Dante and wink again, making the coo-coo motion then pointing to Ellis. Dante laughs softly and nods in agreement. He then turns to look at Jayce, who now has his head in my lap, attempting to keep me calm. "How are you holding up, Your Highness?"

"Um, I'm okay, I think?" Jayce looks up to me, and I smile at him.

"You'll get used to the title, love. Dante is here for our protection. Marco switched out with one of the bears at the last minute and is riding up front. Alaric is bound and determined to make sure we are kept safe when we're separated from him." I run my fingers through Jayce's thick hair, trying to soothe his nerves.

Jayce sighs and closes his eyes as he attempts to relax. "I know, love; it's just when you and Alaric get angry, it's intense. I feel like my wolf wants to rip free of me and go on a rampage. Which, for me, isn't normal. I'd rather be in the background than the fore-front." Jayce opens his eyes and looks up at me, smiling.

Dante shakes his head as he looks between Jayce and me. "If only your mother could see the woman you've become, Aurora. You have her power, her will, and her presence. But you are one hundred percent a daddy's girl when it comes to vengeance and the need to crush your enemies." Dante raises his fist to his heart and bows to me.

"I am honored to be able to protect you. Thank you for letting me serve you." Dante is very sincere and smiling at me; he almost brings tears to my eyes.

"Thank you, Dante; I can't picture trusting another team outside of yours to keep my family safe. You must promise me one thing, above all else." Jayce scoots out of the way, and I lean forward towards Dante.

"Anything you wish for, Aurora, if it's within my power, it shall be done." Dante's visage changes, and he's back to being the serious warrior I know him to be.

Ellis returns with the phone back on speaker so I know Alaric will hear what I say next. "Dante, I need you to swear to me that no matter what happens to my mates or me, you will protect my children. They need to survive, no matter what happens." I swallow down the sob that threatens to escape as tears freely roll down my cheeks. "I know there are dark days ahead, and right now, my babies are my priority."

I hear Alaric agree in the background as Dante slides forward and takes my hands in his. We turn one palm up, slice into the flesh, and put the wounds together. "I swear on my blood that your children will be protected until my last breath. I will put their safety above all others and spirit them away in times of danger to ensure their survival," Dante says with such a finality that there is no room for misunderstanding his intentions.

We remain with our hands pressing together for several moments, just staring into each other's animal eyes. Our animals, apparently, are in their own meeting of sorts. I feel the wagon stop. The back flap opens and I sense Alaric enter. Carefully, we release our grip then turn to Alaric, and he nods slowly.

I stand swiftly and leap into his arms, burying my face against his neck. I'm not afraid for myself, but more so for my children. Alaric's dragon croons to me, trying to settle me down. But honestly, I'm in pain. I feel as though my heart is breaking. My children somehow scurry into the wagon and sit at our feet. *How did they get here?*

I release Alaric and kneel down in front of my babies. "Little ones, mommy's precious angels. Uncle Dante is in charge of your safety. If he or his dragon calls and says it's time to go, you go. There are too many evil people left in this world that want to harm us." I tilt my head as I swallow down the emotions that are attempting to well up.

"Uncle Dante is a strong and able warrior, which is why I have sworn a blood oath with him. You two are his priority now. If he ever comes for you, you need to go with him without question." I watch my children for understanding.

Tiamat and Ladon look between Dante and me, hesitantly they move and climb up onto Dante's lap. I nod, then look back to Alaric. In the back of my mind, I hear his whispers—he's proud of the decision I made for our children. "I will guard these angels with my life, my King and Queen." Dante gently hugs my children, looking at both of them. He points to the little dragon with the high eye-ridges and mouths *Ladon?* I can't help but laugh and nod, agreeing with him.

"What the actual fuck?" Alaric says, looking between the two babies then back to Dante. "How the fuck did you do that? Seriously! I have a hard time telling them apart."

Dante shrugs and starts laughing. Alaric moves forward and grips Dante's hand. "Thank you for this, brother. I know my children will be safe in your hands."

Both men shake hands, then Alaric comes back over to me and pulls me flush with his chest. "It was wise of you to enlist his help for the babies' protection. Remember, Aurora, I love you. Till death do we part." Alaric kisses me passionately then leaves the wagon as quickly as he had arrived. I can't help but sigh over his romantic gesture.

Nicodeamus arrives swiftly when I reach out to him that his charges had given him the slip. My father shakes his head at the twins and reaches out, taking one at a time out of the wagon to head back to camp where they belong. We didn't get too far from the Lycan camp, so my father's trip home would be a quick one. Edgar offers to fly them back, allowing us to travel quicker to make up for the lost time.

We travel for several hours before Ellis finally has enough courage to ask the question that's been plaguing him. Ellis clears his throat and looks between us. "Is there something I need to know that no one has bothered to tell me?"

Dante looks to me, and I give him permission to tell Ellis since he was absent from the previous explanation. "It's like this, Ellis; we are literally walking into the bowels of hell. Fire will rain down from the sky, and the dead will walk the earth. You see, the Strigoi will be strongest on their home turf. It's something about fighting on the soil where their bodies were buried. Now, if we can find the actual burial ground and turn it into consecrated ground, they would lose most of their power if not just turn to ash."

"Hold up! Back that motha-fuckin' train up. The Strigoi that are vampires, like old school horror movie vampires, would be affected by blessing their graves?" Ellis always did have a way with words.

"Yes, Father found something in an ancient tome that mentioned such. It's not exactly clear who would have to do it, but it's clear as to what's needed for it to be done," I say as I look between Dante and Ellis.

Dante starts to pace back and forth within the wagon. "I've seen the damage a horde of Strigoi can do. They can tear through their victims in seconds. When you are killed by a Strigoi, the legend says you may return as one if you lived a life of sin. Those who fall in battle must be burned to ash just in case." Dante crosses his arms over his chest, standing firm with his beliefs.

Aurora's eyes shift to her beast's for a moment, then back to human again. "Father says we can also drive a nail into the forehead of the fallen so a proper burial can be performed." Aurora pauses dramatically before continuing. "As for the graves, he thinks they are along the wall. So we need to bless water and pour it on the soil. We can bless oil and set it on fire before the attack, and whatever Strigoi comes in touch with the smoke will be burned by it. Maybe, if we're lucky, even be killed."

"We're almost at the first campsite for tonight. Once we arrive, let's make sure everyone is settled, and we can research more before bed," Dante says.

I move to the front of the wagon and peek out of the blinds to see the makeshift campsite we have for tonight. It's going to be interesting with everyone out in the open. I'm not very comfortable with the situation, but I know it's needed to be done. We're at the halfway point of our journey, and soon enough we'll be going to war. I can only pray that we make it out with as few losses as possible.

CHAPTER 18
The Betrayal Pt1

As the caravan trundles along the winding road, I sit amidst the jostling chaos, my thoughts swirling with frustration and impatience. Months spent in the American Lycan camp have revealed little beyond their weakness and disorganization. The Dire Wolves, with their vigilant watch, have kept us at bay, denying us access to the main compound and its secrets.

Now, here I am, trapped in this cluster of wagons, surrounded by strangers and uncertainty. Yet, amidst the frustration, there is a glimmer of hope. With each passing mile, I draw closer to home, to familiar faces and the comfort of my own pack. And best of all, amidst this sea of strangers, I remain hidden, my true identity concealed from prying eyes.

As we draw closer to tonight's campsite, a sense of unease settles over me like a heavy shroud. The landscape unfolds before us, a desolate expanse of barren plains and rugged terrain, offering little solace or respite from the harsh realities of our journey. Each step forward feels like a battle against the elements, against the unknown forces that lurk in the darkness.

The air is heavy with the scent of burning wood, the acrid smoke mingling with the tang of sweat and fear. Flickering flames cast eerie shadows that dance and twist across the landscape, distorting reality in their wake. It's as if the very environment itself is conspiring against us, seeking to obscure our path and hinder our progress.

With each passing moment, the tension mounts, a palpable weight pressing down upon us, suffocating and relentless. I grip my cloth bag tightly, my fingers trembling with anticipation and apprehension. Every sound, every movement, sends a shiver down my spine, a reminder of the dangers that lurk just beyond the edge of our perception.

As I follow the rest of the group, I stick to the shadows like a ghost, silent and unseen. The darkness offers a cloak of anonymity, shielding me from prying eyes and unwanted attention. Yet, even in the safety of the shadows, I cannot shake the feeling of impending doom that hangs heavy in the air.

The campsite pulsates with activity, figures darting to and fro like shadows in the night. Their faces remain shrouded in darkness, adding an air of mystery to their movements. I slip away from the bustling throng, my steps cautious and deliberate as I navigate the labyrinth of tents and wagons.

A cacophony of sounds fills the air, the crackling of the campfire mingling with the murmur of voices and the clatter of pots and pans. Yet beneath the surface of this apparent harmony, a palpable tension simmers, like a coiled serpent waiting to strike.

The scent of burning wood hangs heavy in the air, mingling with the tantalizing aroma of cooking food. It's a seductive fragrance that beckons to me, tempting me to linger. But I know that to do so would be folly, for lurking beneath this facade of warmth and camaraderie lies a deadly threat.

With each step I take, I can feel the weight of the task ahead pressing down upon me. Poisoning the camp and abducting Aurora may be the orders I've been given, but executing them will be no easy feat. Every move I make must be calculated and precise, lest I risk exposing myself and endangering my mission.

As I disappear into the shadows, a sense of foreboding settles over me like a suffocating cloak. The stakes are high, and failure is not an option. In this deadly game of cat and mouse, only the most cunning and ruthless will emerge victorious.

As I lingered in the shadows, a sense of foreboding settled over me like a heavy cloak. Despite the outward appearance of camaraderie and warmth, there was an underlying tension that seemed to hum through the air, palpable and unsettling.

The flickering light of the campfire cast dancing shadows across the faces of those gathered, creating an eerie contrast between the illusion of safety and the lurking danger that lurked just beneath the surface. Every laugh and every jest seemed to ring hollow, drowned out by the weight of my own apprehension.

The comforting aroma of simmering stew hung thick in the air, a stark juxtaposition to the turmoil roiling within me. It was a scent that spoke of home and hearth, of warmth and sustenance, yet beneath its deceptively pleasant facade, lurked the potential for harm.

My mind races with conflicting thoughts and emotions, torn between the desire to protect my brother and the fear of the consequences should my actions be discovered. The choice before me was a daunting one, a delicate balance between duty and morality, and I knew that whatever path I chose would shape the fate of those around me.

With a heavy heart, I am resolved to carry out my assigned task, knowing full well the risks that lay ahead. For the sake of my brother and all those who depended on me, I would do whatever it took to ensure their survival, even if it meant descending into the depths of darkness.

With a heavy heart, I steel myself for what must be done. Ignoring the protests of my conscience, I approach the vat of stew, its contents bubbling and steaming invitingly. In a swift, covert motion, I empty the contents of a vial into the pot, my actions concealed from prying eyes by the cover of darkness.

As I slip away unnoticed, a sense of guilt gnaws at my conscience. But I know that in this brutal game of survival, there can be no room for sentimentality. For the sake of my brother's life, I must do whatever it takes to ensure our survival, even if it means embracing the darkness that lurks within.

As the camp settles into a seemingly serene rhythm, my senses are on high alert, attuned to every subtle shift in the atmosphere. Aurora's unwavering vigilance looms over the scene like a shadow, casting a veil of uncertainty over my plans. Each passing moment feels like an eternity as I wait for the opportune moment to make my move.

The water container, left unguarded by Jayce, beckons to me like a siren's call, offering a fleeting chance to advance my agenda. Yet, the stakes have never been higher, and every decision I make is fraught with tension and risk.

For what feels like an eternity, I remain poised on the edge of anticipation, my nerves wound tight with apprehension. The container taunts me with its untouched contents, a silent testament to the challenge that lies ahead.

With a surge of determination, I steel myself for the task at hand, each step forward laden with the weight of impending consequences. The air crackles with suspense as I approach the container, my heart thundering in my chest like a war drum heralding the onset of battle.

In a single, decisive motion, I pour the elixir into the water, the liquid swallowing the potent concoction like a voracious abyss. Time seems to stand still as I watch the ripples dissipate across the surface, the tension in the air palpable as the fate of my plan hangs in the balance.

As I melt into the encompassing darkness, a flicker of satisfaction dances within me, momentarily eclipsing the weight of my treacherous actions. The air is thick with tension, each breath laden with the weight of impending consequence. For I know all too well that within the veil of shadows, secrets are born, and alliances forged in deceit can unravel with the slightest misstep.

Resuming my duties, I tread carefully, the burden of guilt heavy upon my shoulders. Every movement is calculated, every step a delicate dance between necessity and moral reckoning. Yet, despite the turmoil raging within, the mission demands unwavering resolve, and I am but a pawn in its unforgiving game.

Approaching Aurora's group once more, I extend the water bucket with practiced precision, concealing the turmoil roiling beneath the surface. Jayce's gaze meets mine fleetingly, a mere flicker of recognition before he accepts the offering without question. In that fleeting exchange, the die is cast, and the stage is set for the clandestine machinations to unfold.

With bated breath, I watch as Jayce retreats into the shadows, the weight of anticipation hanging heavy in the air. Every heartbeat reverberates with the cadence of impending consequence, as the tendrils of uncertainty coil around us, ensnaring us in their suffocating embrace.

And so, with a silent prayer whispered into the abyss, I resign myself to the waiting game, knowing that in the shadows of deceit, the true test of loyalty and resolve is yet to come.

With each passing moment, the tension in the air grows thicker, suffocating me with its weight. I find myself consumed by a sense of foreboding, a gnawing unease that coils tightly around my chest.

In the shadows, I am a silent observer, waiting with bated breath for the effects of my actions to take hold. Every second feels like an eternity, each heartbeat echoing in the darkness like a drumbeat of impending doom.

The plan hangs in the balance, poised on a razor's edge between success and failure. All it takes is one wrong move, one unforeseen complication, and everything could unravel in an instant.

But still, I watch and wait, my senses on high alert for any sign of change. The anticipation is palpable, a tangible presence that hangs heavy in the air, as if the very fabric of reality is holding its breath in anticipation.

And then, finally, it happens. A subtle shift in Jayce's demeanor, a faint flicker of disorientation in his eyes. It's the signal I've been waiting for, the harbinger of impending chaos. With a surge of adrenaline, I spring into action, my movements swift and purposeful. The time for hesitation is over; now is the moment of reckoning.

CHAPTER 19
The Betrayal pt2

AURORA -

So far, so good. Everyone is settling in well within the camp. The American Lycans are passing out water, and tonight they are in charge of cooking. Dominik and Klaus are out hunting for my dinner while I remain here to maintain order. Slowly, I extend my hands out to warm them by the fire. The flames dance, moved by the slight eastern wind that blows gently. Wolves are a funny bunch, if you ask me. If they don't have an Alpha, they go all primal and start reverting mentally to their animal base urges.

Moving back away from the flames, I move to sit on Dimitri's lap so that our pack mates take turns receiving my touch. Touch is yet another important thing for wolves to feel grounded, safe, and that they belong. Dire and Lycan alike each come and bow before me, wishing for me to touch them. A gentle stroke here, a caress there, some just wish to be close to their Alpha just for a little while. For as long as I can remember, it was Dimitri, Andre, and me; now my family has expanded a hundredfold. For the first time in forever, I feel like I am almost complete. I have my mates, children, and my pack and swarm. I'm not alone anymore.

Dominik and Klaus return with a roe deer for me and it's still warm—just the way I like it. Sliding off of Dimitri's lap, I move forward to investigate the deer that my mates brought me. Dimitri warns the others to back away because I get very possessive of my food. I strip out of my nice clothes and shift. I eat quickly, savoring every morsel. It doesn't take long for me to finish off the roe deer.

I keep a close eye on everyone that's mingling at dinner time. It's too quiet, and I hate to be the negative Nancy here, but it's too peaceful. Something makes the hair on the back of my neck stand on end. The air feels too still and calm for some reason. Raising my nose to the wind, I draw in all of the scents around me. Nothing seems off in that regard. A sudden chill moves down my spine as I search the camp once more.

My guys hang out; drinking, eating, and socializing with our teams. I shift back to my human form and get dressed, then come back out. It's about eleven at night, and I start noticing people moving off to go to bed. It wasn't a difficult journey, but not everyone handles stress the same as others. I go to our cooler and pour myself some water. It's been a long day, and tomorrow isn't looking much better.

Pouring several more cups of water, I pass them out to my mates. That's how it always is—the minute you get yourself something, everyone else wants what you have. We sit, watching the fire burn before us. Dominik tosses a fresh log onto the fire, and it pops and crackles as it blazes to life. The smoke keeps changing direction causing poor Klaus to keep changing his seat. For some blasted reason, it seems that the fire is following him. Laughing softly, I return to my favorite pastime of people watching. With everyone going to sleep so early tonight, maybe I might get some "lovin'" before bedtime.

I lean back against Arnulf, using him as my personal pillow, watching everyone in camp. My mates, one by one, start to yawn and become sleepy. Fucking yawns are contagious, and I start yawning right along with them.

Suddenly, I watch Alaric's eyes flash to his dragons. "Something's not right, Aurora." His voice is a whisper as he fights sleep. His movements are uncoordinated and sluggish. Alaric's eyes close, and he falls over, asleep.

I yawn again, looking at everyone, studying them. I'm fighting to keep my eyes open, and it's becoming a losing battle. We've been drugged. I try with all my remaining strength to summon Dante to rain fire down upon our assailants. He doesn't answer. Either he's dead or a victim like the rest of us. I struggle to get to my mates, to shield them from whatever may come. Sadly, I fall short and land face first in the shallow mud. I fight to open my eyes one last time; I see a man staring at me. Is this the end for me?

— The next day~

My hands gradually slide up my face to hold my throbbing head. My mouth is dry like I had been up all night at the bar drinking the night before. What the hell happened last night? I rub my eyes, freeing them from sleep. It takes several minutes before they focus enough for me to see clearly. I look around the camp, and everyone is in different states of trying to wake up. I reach into my pocket and pull out my phone to check the time. I stare at the time far longer than I should. It's noon. We should have been on the road for six hours already.

"Aurora?" I call for my mate and receive no reply.

My heart is pounding furiously in my chest; I can't feel her like I normally do. Quickly, I stand up and shed my clothing and shift, which helps tons to clear my system and help me focus. I tilt my head back and howl, calling for Aurora's beast to respond to me. I'm cheating, using a distress howl to get her attention. Still no response. This time I howl, summoning all the Lycans in my pack and the American pack. I've never tried an Alpha move like this, but it's an emergency, and right now I need help.

My pack gradually awakens and comes to me; we are two wolves short from yesterday's headcount. Alaric and the others come running over, and I shift back to human quickly.

"Has anyone found Aurora?" My bond mates shake their heads no, and the sadness is overwhelming.

"I can't feel her..." Alaric says, rubbing the scale on his chest. "She's alive but I... I... gods, why!!" He drops to his knees, holding his head. Alaric's anguished tone pulls at our own pain and fears. Jayce is crying; his face is buried in Dominik's chest. Dimitri is trying to be strong for everyone.

"Fuck this!' I growl with the tone of my beast. "Pack, we search!" I turn to face my pack and snap them all to attention and start barking out orders. Whipping around, I look at Dom, Jayce, and Arnulf. "Arnulf, take to the skies with your people to see if you can spot tracks leading away from camp." Arnulf shifts immediately and takes off to start his search.

"Jayce, gather your packs' best trackers and give them Aurora's scent and have them circle the camp." Without regard for his clothing, Jayce shifts and takes off towards where his pack mates are to start on his mission to track Aurora. "Dominik, you and Dimitri are the muscle here; start interrogating anyone who may have had anything to do with what happened last night." I've never felt this dominant in my life. My mate needs me, and I swear to the gods I will rip the world apart to find her.

CHAPTER 20
The Betrayal pt 3

Jacob~

Deep within the dark and dank cavern, I've hidden my quarry. This plan's major downfall is the amount of guano from the bats. I hate bats. The smell of musty-ammonia alone makes my sensitive nose burn. But of course, Vladimir thinks this is the best place to hide Aurora. I force her mouth open and drop more of the elixir into her mouth to keep her sedated and me safe.

The male I tricked into helping me, I killed and dragged his body in the opposite direction of where the cave is. Hopefully, it throws them off my trail at least for a little while. I send two texts to Vladimir and to Tomas, letting them know I have Aurora. I also send a picture of her as proof that she's my prisoner.

Two messages come in, and both are from Vladimir, warning me of how dangerous Aurora is. She's drugged and harmless right now; I'm not the least bit concerned that anything is going to happen. Several hours pass and my brother shows up. I rush over and hug him, thankful he's safe.

"Back off, Jacob, where's the hybrid bitch?" Josef says with a snarl. He was always the mean one out of the two of us.

I motion toward the back of the cavern. "Vladimir told me to keep her towards the back so her scent can't be picked up easily." I smile at my brother, proud that I pulled off the abduction mostly by myself.

"Wipe that smile off your face; you look like an idiot. We need to poison this bitch and be on our way." Josef holds up the poison, and I can tell it's a lethal dose of wolfsbane and something silver.

"What's in the syringe?" I move closer and take it from my brother. I slide the contents back and forth, looking it over, trying to figure it out for myself.

"Wolfsbane and Dimethylmercury, the combination should kill her in a matter of hours. After all, she's just a white Lycan, and the fucking abomination needs to die." Josef spits on the ground, then looks at the back of the cavern and heads down to investigate how I have Aurora situated.

I look at the syringe in my hand and then towards the back of the cavern. Honestly, I didn't think we would be killing her; I don't believe in hurting females. I think back to how I had positioned her in sleep in the back of the cavern. Aurora looks like an angel, innocent and sweet. My mom used to say that still waters run deep, and we never know what's happening in the depths.

Josef returns and looks down at his phone, then back up to me. "Don't fuck this up, or Vladimir will kill us both over it." Josef looks at me with his eyes so full of hatred. I don't know what happened to him, but this isn't the brother I once knew.

Once Josef is gone, I walk to the back of the cavern. I stare at Aurora, and honestly, I can't kill her. I can tell the drugs are starting to wear off; she should wake up in the next few hours. I need to slow it down and slow her down at the same time. My eyes fall on the syringe in my hand. I have a total of five milliliters of poison, and it seems the majority of it is mercury.

Tears flow freely down my cheek as I come to the decision I've dreaded. I'm a dead man if I don't do Vladimir's bidding. I grip Aurora's arm and turn it so I can inject from below, keeping as much mercury out of the needle as I can. I push the mostly wolfsbane solution into her vein, trying to avoid the mercury. It'll slow her down and make her sick but shouldn't harm her too badly. I accidentally push a little of the mercury in and silently curse myself for my stupidity.

I withdraw the needle from her arm and sit on the floor with the remaining poison that I have decided to use on myself. I shake it up real good and inject the contents into my own vein. It's pretty fast-acting as I feel it getting harder to breathe. My veins are starting to blacken as a result of the mercury. Falling to my side as I look at Aurora, her veins are faintly blackened. I can only hope she's stronger than me. I use my finger to write I'm sorry before I close my eyes. My body slowly starts to shut down, and all I can think of is how sorry I am for what I have done.

CHAPTER 21
Dominik

THE SEARCH–

WE RUN circles for what feels like forever, trying to pick up on any scent that may be left. The light rain this morning is hindering our ability to find any trace of our mate. Between the scent of rain, the rotting leaves, and the moist earth, my poor nose is working over-time trying to find any trace of my mate's scent. My paws hurt, and I feel like I may have a pine needle stuck up my nose, but I refuse to give up. In the distance, I hear Klaus's howl and run in that direction as fast as my paws can carry me. We all catch up to Klaus, and he's found some of Aurora's long white hair on a low-hanging branch.

We shift back to our human forms and start examining the area. There are two sets of footprints leading towards the mountain-side. Several yards away, there's a place where they must have laid Aurora down for a brief moment. Aurora's scent is strong here, so it wasn't too long ago since they were last here. I'd safely estimate within the last eight to ten hours at most. They had to be moving slowly to carry her this far. Dimitri notices an area where there appears to have been a scuffle, and blood paints the surrounding trees and leaves. Drag marks lead us to a shallow grave where the accomplice lays beheaded.

We double back to where we caught Aurora's scent the strongest; I shift back to my Dire Wolf and start searching for any scent leading away. My brother, Jayce, also shifts and starts working in tandem with me, searching the area. Alaric, Arnulf, and Dimitri remain in their human forms on the lookout for anything our animals may miss. Klaus starts circling with his Lycan, looking for any clues that may be higher up.

Jayce suddenly stops, and his form goes rigid. *Dom, double check this. I think I found the guy's scent. I think I smell blood from when he murdered the other guy.*

Carefully, I move through the leaves over to where my brother is and lower my nose to the ground. *You're right, Jayce! You found it! Everyone, follow Jayce!*

Our bond mates move quickly to join us as we follow Jayce, letting him take point. We find several more places that the abductor had set Aurora down before we come to a cavern. The acrid scent of bat guano burns my sensitive nose.

"This is the perfect place to hide her; there is no way we could catch her scent over the bat shit," Alaric says as he stands at the edge of the cavern.

Alaric shifts to his dragon and breathes his flames inside, coating everything in a layer of ice. Frozen bats fall from the ceiling and shatter on the ground. Jayce and I shift back to our human forms and start heading into the cavern. Arnulf turns on his flashlight and passes one to Dimitri. Jayce, Klaus, and I don't bother; the light from the two flashlights is more than enough.

Our descent into the cavern is slow and methodical as we search for clues and our missing mate. The overpowering ammonia smell of the bat guano burns our sensitive noses the deeper into the cavern we go. We notice the corpse of a man lying on his side near the wall off to the side. Klaus kneels down to examine him. His veins are blackened from whatever poison he took. The needle he used to kill himself isn't far away, and the silvery contents remain behind.

In the soil near his hand, a barely legible sorry is drawn. Not far from his corpse is Aurora, her veins are a light grey, and she's covered in sweat. Dimitri practically knocks me over as he rushes forward to pick Aurora up. I've never seen the big guy move so fast in the entire time I've known him. Dimitri runs outside with Aurora, and we follow hot on his heels.

"She's barely breathing, Alaric. You have to do something!" Dimitri's voice cracks as he fights the sobs that want to break free.

"I don't know what to do," Alaric says as he looks at a very limp and pale Aurora in Dimitri's arms. Reverently, his hand ghosts over her pale cheek, staring down at our pale mate.

I move forward and get Dimitri to sit with Aurora, and I look her over. "I remember when assmunch was poisoned, Aurora bit her wrist and bled into his mouth. Do you think that could work?" I look between my bond mates then to Klaus as he emerges from the cavern.

Klaus's normally calm demeanor has changed; rage bubbles just under the surface. Quickly, he schools his features as he moves to touch Aurora's cold, pale cheek gently. "The male was poisoned by wolfsbane and mercury-based poison. I'm not sure if there's anything we can do." The look of defeat on Klaus's face is soul-crushing. His eyes close slowly as he lowers his head.

Arnulf is shaking his head, digging through the bag Alaric was carrying. "I refuse to give up. We will not sit here and wait for her to die." Arnulf pulls out a mug and some herbs he brought with him. Quickly, Arnulf slices his palm and bleeds into the mug; he adds some vodka, then looks at Alaric. Arnulf doesn't even wait for permission; he slices Alaric's palm over the mug. Jayce and I move in unison, waiting for our turn to contribute. Klaus runs back into the cavern, retrieves the syringe, and starts flushing it clean with water and vodka. Arnulf saves Dimitri and Klaus for last, adding the largest amount of blood from them. Arnulf adds more herbs and starts chanting over the blood. Arnulf is schooled in the mystical arts, and he is pulling out all the stops trying to save our mate. Without hesitation, he draws up an ample amount of blood. He begins to inject it into Aurora's veins watching for any changes. He repeats the process till half the mug is empty.

Through the bond, the slow tingling of Aurora's essence can be felt once again. We can sense as her heart becomes stronger, and her beast begins to stir under the surface. The gray tint to her veins starts to fade away with each passing moment. Arnulf moves and injects more blood into Aurora's veins, trying to speed the process along. Aurora's mouth suddenly opens, and her canines descend. They're not entirely wolven anymore; they are longer and sharper, almost like a dragon's. We all turn to look at Alaric, and he seems to be just as shocked by what he sees as we are.

Aurora starts to thrash violently in Dimitri's arms; Alaric and I move to help him hold her so she doesn't hurt herself. Scales begin to ripple all over her body. Did her Wolf die? What has happened to her because of the poison?

"She's changed, evolved. She'll live." We jump, hearing the musical tone of Oberon's voice behind us.

Jayce moves and kneels before Oberon and lowers his head. "M'lord, what do you mean she's evolved?" Jayce doesn't raise his eyes, nor does he move a single muscle.

Oberon moves away from Jayce and kneels next to Aurora. His slender fingers brush her hair off her forehead. He bends down and places a kiss on Aurora's forehead, and the thrashing stops. Once she stops, he stands and dusts himself off, then turns to face us.

"She will live, but she's changed. Aurora was always more dragon than wolf, though she will never know flight. She will know her dragon ancestors' strength and longevity. She still retains the shape of the Lycan, but with more dragon upgrades, I believe the humans say; the wolf will sleep until it heals." Oberon taps his chin before disappearing in a wisp of glitter.

"What the fuck just happened?" Klaus growls, frustrated with the lack of real answers concerning our mate's health.

"I'm not sure. All I do know is between what Arnulf did and what Oberon did after, she feels stronger." I tilt my head to the side, watching Aurora closely.

Aurora suddenly gasps and shoots up, sitting up in Dimitri's lap. I think she scared years off of our lives with that unexpected movement. "I don't feel right," Aurora says, her voice raspy from lack of use.

Carefully, she rolls onto all fours and looks at all of us as her body starts to break and reshape. Her blood-curdling screams tell us she's not shifting of her own volition. She's watching her body reshape with a look of horror on her face. She seems afraid of what's happening to her, and that concerns me greatly.

This shift is different; she's in pain, and we all feel it and can't do anything to help her. It feels as if every square inch of her is on fire. Eventually, the burning and ripping feeling subsides, leaving her altered beast standing before us. Aurora faces away from us, and some changes are already apparent. She has sharp spines down the back of her neck all the way to her tail. There appear to be scales under her fur, especially around her neck for added protection. We watch her posture closely, and we can tell she's examining herself.

Aurora's fear and pain bleeds through the bond to the rest of us. She's afraid we won't like what we see. I nod to my brother, sending him over to look at her first. A soft whine escapes from Aurora's lips, though it still sounds wolven. Perhaps nothing else has changed with her.

We watch Jayce's facial expressions because he can't hide shit, and from what we can see, he's shocked. This can't be good; we know that Aurora isn't going to be happy. Carefully, Jayce grips Aurora's gauntleted hand and prompts her to turn to face everyone.

Aurora's beast's face has more raised bone ridges like a dragon does, and she has a nictitating membrane that moves to protect her eyes now. Hesitantly, she opens her mouth, and her teeth are definitely more dragon and not completely wolf anymore. Her tongue is still wolven, which is interesting.

Aurora's chest and stomach are now covered with a thick layer of scales to protect her vital organs. A light layer of fur covers the scales, so they can't be seen unless close up. Her feet are still paws but are now heavily armored, and the claws resemble talons.

Aurora's sadness is palatable; her eyes still roam over her changed form, trying to understand what has happened to her. Cautiously, she raises her eyes to us; her brows are knitted together in the middle. She looks as if she wants to cry but can't in this form. I'm the first to move and embrace her tightly. Her beast is running hotter than usual, and I can feel the heavy plated scales under her fur. Gently, I nuzzle her chest and let my wolf rumble softly to her.

Behind me, Alaric shifts and lowers his dragon's maw to her. I move out of the way and allow their two animals to comfort each other. It's now that I can really compare how Aurora looks versus how she was before. It's more pronounced now that Alaric's dragon was next to Aurora with the changes that have occurred.

I feel the loss as Aurora's presence leaves my mind. I sigh softly as I feel everyone reaching out to her through the bond to soothe and reassure her. Aurora finally calms down and shifts back to her human form. We rush towards her, all of us needing the contact. Alaric is the last to approach after he has shifted back to his human form; he lets the rest of us soothe our beasts first.

Aurora cautiously untangles herself from us and launches towards Alaric. He catches her mid-air and spins with her for a second. Aurora climbs him like a tree and kisses him fiercely; owning him, dominating him. The look of shock on Alaric's face is priceless. It's about time the big guy got owned. Carefully, Aurora slides down Alaric's body, mindful of the major hard-on she has caused.

"I'm tired; let's head back to camp," Aurora says, then promptly yawns.

I shift quickly, then run to her and lie down, offering her a ride. Aurora smiles and carefully climbs onto my back. As gently as possible, I rise to my paws and start the long slow journey back to camp.

CHAPTER 22

Aurora

Oberon's voice still haunts me. "Evolve and live, remain as you are and die." I look around at my mates as we walk back to camp. What kind of monster have I become this time? My wolven tendencies are not as strong as they used to be; she's sick and weak; I'm confused and scared at the same time.

My father reaches out to me through our familial bond, and I catch him up on what has happened. The delay in his response is answer enough for me; he's scared for me too. He also notes it was much easier to reach out to me, unlike before. I don't want to lose my wolven legacy, but I really didn't have much choice. The poison I was injected with targeted my wolven side. I guess Vladimir assumes that because my mom was a Lycan it would be my dominant nature.

My fingers thread through Dominik's thick fur as we walk back; he's refused to let me walk. Perhaps another mate can take over for him; carrying me can't be an easy task. My eyes connect with

Dimitri, and in my mind's eye I let him know I wish to lay upon his bear for a while and give Dom a break.

Jayce speaks to Dominik when he watches Dimitri shift and amble towards us. Dominik is still rather overprotective of me; he feels that he failed me as the pack enforcer. I lean forward and nuzzle Dominik's neck before sliding off his back. Dimitri sees me walking towards him and lies down immediately. Alaric and Arnulf each take a hand and help me climb onto his back.

To be perfectly honest, Dimitri's bear is the most comfortable to ride on. His fur is the thickest out of everyone's, and his movements the smoothest. I stretch out and lie on my stomach, trying to sleep a little. I'm still wiped out—almost dying tends to do that to a person, I guess. Dimitri's bear rumbles softly, pleased that I'm allowing him to tend to me right now. As we walk, each of my men, at some point, walk with a hand on my skin.

Arnulf, whose bond is the most fragile and new, spends most of the time touching me as we walk. Jayce brushes my hair away from my face, and Alaric keeps encouraging me to drink. I notice there's been a change with Klaus—it's as if a switch flipped in him. I study him and notice his strides are more self-assured, and his posture is more dominant than before. He's finally accepting the title of Alpha of the Lycans. After tonight, I'm not sure if I should still wear that mantle. After several minutes of study, he finally turns and looks at me. I smile softly and whisper "thank you" to him.

One by one, my mates tell me in their own way what one of the others had done to help find me. One thing that is consistent with each of them is that they all feel like they failed me. I close my eyes and focus on our individual bonds. Deep within myself, I can envision each bond having a unique color.

Alaric burns white like his scales in the sunlight, reflecting every fractal of light. Dimitri's is a warm burned umber; its tone reminds me of the woods where I was raised and felt safe. Dominik is a brilliant crimson, and it is bright and as bold as he is in times of trouble. Jayce is a baby blue—soft and safe. Klaus is an emerald green, as strong as the trees in the forest he hunts in. Arnulf is a golden color, like his eyes. His color reminds me of the early morning sun just breaking the horizon. I search further through my bonds and find my father; his color is a royal blue, just as deep as he is. Finally, my babies; their colors are intertwined. Tia's is a bright orange and is as fierce as she is. Ladon's color is dark red like dried blood; I sense he will be a warrior like his grandfather.

I draw in a slow, deep breath and run my silver aura over each thread in the bond. I send my love, appreciation, and hope to everyone. I feel their love flood back to me. Their collective affections feel like a warm, soft blanket wrapped around me. Finally, I can rest and close my eyes for a while. I know my mates will watch over me closely while I sleep.

I sleep most of the way back to camp, and Klaus and Dominik decide to be the ones to talk to the pack about what has occurred. Dimitri, Alaric, and Jayce took it upon themselves to see to my needs.

My dreams are plagued with the pain I felt through the bond as I fight to wake up. The intense burning, ripping feeling of my shift was the worst feeling I had ever felt in my life. Birthing shifted-dragon hatchlings was more pleasant than that shift. I rub my face in the fur that's under me, and I'm comforted by the scent that is my Dimitri. Anytime I was ill, Dimitri was the one to sit by me till I felt better. It's different now; he's my mate, and our love has finally been allowed to evolve. His bear is snoring under me, and it causes me to giggle. I wish I knew where my phone was. I would love to prove to him he snores in both forms.

How do you feel, baby girl? I hear Dimitri's voice through the bond.

I slide carefully off his back and move to sit in front of him. "I feel better, thank you, D." I lean forward and kiss his bear's muzzle.

It always impresses me when Dimitri shifts that this massive beast fits within a massive man. Casually, Dimitri leans back against the cot that's behind him. I crawl to Dimitri on all fours, slide onto his lap, and wrap my arms around his thick neck. His beast rumbles to me, making my greedy core clench. His thick cock rises up between us—hot, thick, and always ready. I can't help but smile into Dimitri's neck, feeling his need is as great as mine.

My hands grip Dimitri's neck as I move to position his cock below me. "Baby girl, are you sure? Are you okay?" He practically pants.

"I need this, D. Please..." I purr softly in his ear as I slide the tip of his weeping cock through my wet folds.

Dimitri's beast practically roars in my head as he roughly grabs my hips and slams his length deep inside me. I throw my head back, reveling in the fullness that only Dimitri can give me. I feel so complete and loved right now. Our movements are slow and sensual—we've never made love, and this is about as close as we are going to get. Each stroke brings us closer together; I feel our bond renewing and strengthening. My beast wants me to reclaim her mates, rebind all of them. Dimitri locks eyes with me, and he sees my intention. His beast rises to the surface just before he lunges forward and bites me over his original mating mark. The sweet burn of his canines sinking into my flesh feels like heaven. I scream my release, then lunge forward to sink my new teeth into my old mark on him. Instantly, our combined orgasm sends shock waves of frost out in all directions.

The metallic tang on my tongue brings me solace; I feel the power of my Great Bear mate. I feel Dimitri's love coursing through the bond stronger than before. My other mates stand at the opening of the tent, looking at us in wonder. I smile my bloody smile at them and beckon them to me.

"We need to renew our bonds." I look down between Dimitri and then back over to them. "One by one. So my beast is content and secure."

Carefully, I remove myself from Dimitri's lap and sit on the cot beside him. "The changes that have happened to me, I'm still trying to wrap my head around. I feel something is coming, something big."

I run my fingers through Dimitri's hair, not ready to separate from him yet. "Arnulf, Alaric, send three of the fastest eagles. We have to search the area and send Edgar with them for protection. We're about two days away from the castle, and I need at least that many days to regain my strength."

I watch both Arnulf and Alaric's eyes shift to their animals. Several moments pass before they both smile at me. "It's done, my love," they say in unison then high five like teenage boys.

I can't help but shake my head at the two of them and their antics. "I'm hungry. Can someone kill something for me, please?" Jayce and Dominik wink before they shift and run out of the tent to find me food.

Dimitri stands slowly, then bends to kiss me before he walks out. I smirk, looking at Alaric. "So? Are you ready?" I feel the power from my awakened dragon side; my eyes shift, and I call to Alaric's dragon.

White scales ripple up and down his arms and face like waves on an ocean. His eyes shift to his dragon's as he stares at me. Before I can react, Alaric has me flipped onto my belly with my chest on the cot and my legs spread. His thick, rigid length impales me, filling me completely. His hand finds my throat and holds it gently but firmly enough that I know he's in control. Alaric looks to Arnulf, and Arnulf climbs onto the cot in front of me.

"Kiss her," Alaric commands.

Arnulf attacks my lips, kissing me like he needs me to breathe. I kiss him back just as fiercely, our tongues battling for dominance. Arnulf grips my face, gently stroking my cheek. Alaric tightens his grip on my throat and starts fucking me harder, knowing I need to feel him and his dragon's power. My muscles start pulsing slowly, gripping his thick cock, and I feel the rumble of his beast against my back. His mouth lowers, and he drags his teeth over my shoulder, preparing to bite me. My breaths are coming in pants as I climb closer and closer to my release. Arnulf reaches forward and grips my nipples, applying just enough pressure to send that delicious feeling straight to my core.

Quickly, I pull away from Arnulf and scream as my orgasm crashes over me, my muscles throbbing around Alaric's cock. I feel myself squirt all over Alaric, and I can hear the drips of cum hitting the floor. Alaric growls, feeling my orgasm milking his cock for all its worth. Alaric's movements become erratic, and he sinks his teeth into his original mating mark. His bite intensifies the pleasure I'm feeling; my core tightens, and a second orgasm washes over me, dragging us both over the edge.

I feel my arms shift and my talons rip through the material of the cot. My canines drop, and I have the urge to bite him; I need to bite him now. Alaric withdraws his now-flaccid cock and spins me to face him. Before he can react, I lunge at him and bite his shoulder over my original mating mark. Alaric quickly re-bites my shoulder over where he had just bit me. My greedy core pulses, wanting to be filled again. I feel him come again on my stomach; the warm jets of seed hit my flesh and slowly slide down my abdomen. We remain in each other's embrace, tasting each other's blood, reveling in the feeling of our intense, primal love swirling between us like a hurricane. I feel our bond growing stronger as the new bond snaps in place.

Eventually, we release each other and lick each other, taking care of our new wounds. I look over my shoulder at Arnulf and flip onto all fours to stalk him. He scoots back till his spine hits the tent pole, preventing him from going any further. His eagle is visible and staring at me; I can tell he wants to shift and fly. I know I must look frightening, and slowly I lower my head and close my eyes. I don't need to see Arnulf to know exactly where he is. By scent, I know he's less than a foot in front of me. His scent reminds me of fresh-baked bread on a cold afternoon; he smells like comfort and home. I keep my eyes closed, move forward, and drop my head lower and nuzzle his crotch.

Arnulf's eagle makes that whistling noise I heard during our mating flight. Apparently, I have both of their attention now. I feel my canines descend again, and I bite at the offending fabric that's blocking me from my goal. I feel Arnulf's body move and shift, and his hands come between me and his pants. "I'd like to keep my member in one piece if you don't mind," he says in a soft but loving tone.

"Aye, my beloved, I'd like him in one piece as well." I make sure my eyes are human when I look up at him. My beast wants to dominate all of her mates, but I won't allow her to terrify my poor flight shifter. I'm curious to find out if he has gained any gifts from me that may make this mating easier. I slide between his legs and run my tongue up his exposed abs to his chest. His bird makes that excited whistling noise again, and I know I have him now.

Carefully, I climb into Arnulf's lap, leaving his hard cock between us. I lightly nip along his jaw, eliciting more whistles and clicks from his bird. It's a curious thing having a flight shifter as a mate. His noises, in one sense, trigger my prey drive, but in another excites me because I know he's aroused.

Scenting Arnulf's arousal, his thick musk causes my greedy core to start clenching again, begging to be filled. Slowly, I raise up onto my knees and reach down between us to move his cock into position. I slide down his length inch by inch, prolonging the pleasure of feeling him fill me. I notice Jayce enter and drop my meal by the door. I know he's there so Arnulf relaxes, but being the greedy bitch that I am, I want both of them. I look between Arnulf and Jayce, and to my surprise, Arnulf motions Jayce over to us.

Honestly, I'm starting to get tired, but I want them so badly. Jayce runs his hands reverently over my body, and I'm practically purring. I move slowly, sliding Arnulf's length through my greedy core. I'm absolutely soaking wet, and the delicious sounds our bodies make coming together even at this slow pace drives me nuts. Jayce gently reaches between Arnulf and me, gathering my sticky sweet essence. I feel his index finger massage my rosette to get the muscles to relax.

"Are you ready, baby?" Jayce practically growls in my ear as I feel him rubbing the tip of his leaking cock over my backdoor.

In a rather uncharacteristic move, I tilt my head off to the side, submitting to both of my mates. I need this; I need their animals to give me what I need. I want them relaxed to be able to form the strongest bond possible. Without hesitation, Jayce sinks himself balls deep within me then bites me over his original mating mark. The minute his teeth break my skin, I feel my orgasm rip through me like a tidal wave.

Arnulf isn't far behind me, crying out this orgasm from how powerfully my muscles milk his cock. Arnulf shocks me by pushing up and sinking his teeth into the flesh above my right breast. I feel the rivulets of my blood flowing down my chest from Jayce and now Arnulf. Their love for me pours through the new bond like a flood. I hold a hand to the back of Arnulf's head, encouraging his attempt at marking me. Honestly, I think he was successful.

Arnulf double blinks, then releases my flesh, he looks up to me with a blood-tinted smile, and I notice tiny canines. My hand comes up to gently grip his face to get a better look. His human canine teeth are about a quarter of an inch longer than normal. I kiss his lips and nip at his plump bottom lip before I move and bite him over the original mating mark. I feel my bond with Arnulf strengthen, and I sigh softly, then look over my shoulder at Jayce. He knows what's coming next, and he's ready for it.

Carefully, he slides free from my ass then comes to sit beside Arnulf. I slide free of Arnulf's now-flaccid length, then go to sit on Jayce's lap. I kiss him gently along his jaw until I come to my mark, where I rest my human teeth over it and I feel his cock twitch. Without warning, I let my canines descend and pierce

Jayce's flesh. His orgasm is instant and yet again, Jayce covers me with his seed; only this time I was expecting it and welcome it. I lick his wound clean then move to do the same to Arnulf. I'm tired, and I'm losing the battle with sleep quite quickly.

Arnulf moves off the cot and sets up a makeshift nest for the night. Tonight, I remain in the arms of my two most gentle mates. I sense, sometime later, the others come in and climb into the nest with us. I'm safe, and most of the new bonds are in place. Tomorrow, I'll hunt Dominik and Klaus down. For now, I dream, and I'm shown the past—oddly, not by my father, but by Oberon himself. Tomorrow will be different because I am.

CHAPTER 23
Klaus

I return to our tent after speaking to all the packs of wolves and Lycans with Dominik. We soothed their fear of Aurora having been recovered and still weak. But a new concern has arisen. They don't sense her as strongly as they use to. It's something we must address with Aurora when she wakes up.

Dom and I notice that Aurora must have woken up at some point and ate the deer that was left for her. She is curled up tightly against Arnulf with Dimitri right behind her. Jayce and Alaric each have a hand on her.

We watch Aurora awaken gradually, and her eyes are that of her beasts. She wiggles free of everyone, and a sadness moves across her angelic features. "We need to appoint Alphas for the packs." She swallows down the emotions that try to well up.

"I'm not wolf enough to control them at the moment. I fear she's sick and gone dormant for now." Her eyes drop, and I see tears roll down her cheeks. Her hand flexes over her heart before running up her neck and into her hair, pulling it almost violently.

"My connection to the packs has been damaged; I don't feel them like I use to." Her eyes narrow as tears threaten to break. Through the bond, we can feel how this pain is like a knife plunged through her heart. She feels so lost and frightened it causes all of us to break a little inside.

Quickly, I reach out and take her in my arms, holding her tightly to my chest. "Angel, Dominik, and I are strong enough to control the packs. We will initiate the ancient rites of battle to assume control for you." Softly, I kiss her plump lips then gently pass her off to Dominik.

"My love, my life, I will battle for you and be anything you need me to be." Dominik bends down and kisses her lips. "First, we need to renew our bond, love." Dominik scoops Aurora up in his arms and carries her over to the nest.

Our bond mates sense what's about to go down, and gradually they take their leave. Aurora is so wrapped up in the moment she barely processes that the others have left to give us time to form our new bond. I move quickly and lay behind Aurora and nip at her shoulders. Dominik lightly nips at Aurora's neck. We move in unison, mirror images of each other. Our wolves in sync with one another. Something within us encouraging our movements, driving us to mate and renew our bonds.

Aurora's aroused scent hangs heavily in the air. Our hands slide down her body and find her folds soaking wet. Our beasts rumble, pleased with our discovery. I draw up more of her sticky wet essence and start preparing her rosette—slow, methodical circles over that tight muscle. Dominik lifts Aurora's thigh and flings her leg over his hip as he plunges his length within her.

Dominik's strokes are slow and teasing as he waits for me to gain entrance. My cock is rock-hard and throbbing, begging for release.

I run my thumb through my precum to lubricate the tip before I start pressing against her rosette. Carefully, I slide in slowly, inch by inch, into her tight warm, welcoming depths. She's so full with Dominik and me within her. We find our rhythm and start making love to our mate.

Slow, steady strokes draw out the first of Aurora's orgasms. She goes to bite Dom, and I stop her by gripping her throat and growling in her ear. Her core clenches and ripples again so soon after her last orgasm. Her beast rumbles, pleased with the way we are taking care of her.

Dominik and I know we are both close through our bond, and we pick up our assault. I prop Aurora up slightly since Dominik's mark is on the side she's lying on. We feel her core tightening again, and that's when we strike. Our teeth sink deeply into the muscles of her shoulders. The power of her orgasm rips through all of us, causing a domino effect; Dominik and I follow her swiftly after. The aftershocks of our orgasms cause Aurora to go into a frenzy, and she breaks free of my grip, lunging herself at Dominik, and sinks her teeth into him.

I watch his beast's fur ripples over his skin, and I feel the power she's infusing into him. Eventually, they release each other and clean their wounds. Gently, I slide free of Aurora, and she turns to me. I still see a sadness behind her eyes. Slowly, she comes to rest over my length, leaning forward, and licks my lips.

"I need you to be my sword and shield; you must lead the Lycans, be the Alpha I know you are." Aurora nuzzles my jaw then kisses my mark from her. I feel her human teeth grip my mark, and then it happens. Her canines sink deeply into my flesh, and I feel like my body is on fire. The rest of the bond mates come running in, sensing what's going on. Aurora is growling deeply as she holds onto me. Suddenly, she releases me then licks my wounds. I look down, and I have come all over my own stomach, I didn't even notice my release because the pain was so intense.

"It is done." Aurora draws in a deep breath and stands up, walking over to Jayce, who holds out a robe to her. Aurora dresses quickly then moves to the center of the camp.

I feel her Alpha power reach out, calling out to everyone within our camp. "I am passing on the responsibility of being Alpha of the packs to my mates Dominik and Klaus. With all that is to come, it is better strategically to divide and conquer than to be one force." Whispers move through the group with questions about what was happening.

"I am invoking the right of challenge!" Aurora extends her hand to Dominik and me. "My champions, my mates, will accept all challengers for the right of Alpha of the respective species packs." Aurora takes two steps forward and shifts her arms. "This is my will, and it shall be done. Pick your strongest to battle. We start at noon!"

I watch Aurora walk away from everyone; she stops in an opening and raises her hands. A throne made of ice, shaped like a dragon, rises up out of the earth. Aurora walks over and sits upon her ice throne. Once she's settled, Dante shifts and lays down, wrapping himself around it. He rests his great horned head in front of her and she places a hand upon him, gently stroking his scales as she gazes out amongst her people, watching everyone.

I see Alaric lower his head and shake it slowly. Something major just occurred, and I don't understand it. Dominik and I move to his side then follow him into our tent. "What did we just witness, Alaric?" The rest of our bond mates enter before he speaks.

"There were stories I was told as a boy about a powerful drag-oness. She was stronger than the Blood Queen. She held the bloodlines of all the species of old." Alaric looks to each of us, waiting for us to connect the dots.

"It was said the ancient Fae would decide when the world would need this champion." Again, Alaric looks at each of us, but his phone ringing interrupts his explanation.

"Tell me it's not so!" Nicodeamus's voice bellows through the speaker.

"I believe it is, Father. Vladimir has no idea that he has opened the gates to his own personal hell," Alaric says, speaking directly to Nicodeamus.

I raise my hand and wave it a few times. "Mind spelling it out for the non-dragons in the room? Also, why did it feel like Aurora set my blood on fire?" As a Lycan, I wasn't raised knowing all the dragon histories.

"Wait, she did what?" Nicodeamus asks curiously.

"It happened to me, too. Aurora's bite burned. She looked really sad afterward," Dominik says, then looks back to Alaric.

"Damn Elves and their meddling. I hate to be the bearer of bad news, but one of two things just happened. She gave the last of her wolven powers to you two, or she only passed some of her Alpha power onto you because her wolf is dormant. Apparently, the poison did more damage than we had originally anticipated." There is a sad resignation to Nicodeamus's voice.

The weight of his words moves through us like a freight train. I move and look out the tent flap, watching our army move around, unaware of what has transpired today. There's so many questions burning in the back of my mind.

"Father? Is she able to shift?" I look to my bond mates then sigh softly before returning to the call. "If she can shift, what is she now?" My brows knit together. Apparently, I ask the question that is on everyone's minds.

The atmosphere crackles with tension, each moment stretching out like an eternity as we wait with bated breath. The silence weighs heavy upon us, oppressive and suffocating, like a noose tightening around our necks.

Aurora's sudden roar shatters the quietude, echoing through the night with a ferocity that sends shivers down our spines. It's a sound we've never heard from her before, primal and untamed, carrying with it an undercurrent of primal fury.

Beside her, Alaric struggles against unseen forces, his body contorting and convulsing as if battling against an invisible adversary. Scales ripple across his exposed flesh, a stark reminder of the dormant power that lies within him, yearning to break free.

As Aurora's gaze flickers toward us, a silent plea for under-standing and support, the tension reaches a fever pitch. With a sense of urgency, she clambers onto Dante's back, her movements swift and purposeful.

And then, with a mighty beat of his wings, Dante launches into the sky, carrying Aurora away into the darkness. The air crackles with anticipation, thick with uncertainty and foreboding, as we watch them disappear into the night, leaving us behind with our unanswered questions and mounting fears.

"What the fuck just happened!?" Dimitri screams in a panic as we watch the dragon swarm shifting and taking off after Aurora.

As Alaric relays the unsettling news to Nicodeamus, a palpable sense of dread settles over us like a suffocating blanket. The gravity of the situation weighs heavily on our shoulders, each word spoken by Nicodeamus adding to the mounting tension in the air.

"The last great Wyrm Force Dragon... an ancient. He defeated the last hybrid that went insane. If he's calling Aurora, it may be the end of his time or hers," Nicodeamus's voice crackles over the line, his words laden with ominous implications. The mention of Gallus sends shivers down our spines, his legendary status casting a shadow of fear over our already troubled minds.

Alaric's urgency is palpable as he speaks, his voice tinged with desperation as he warns of the imminent danger. But even as he races down the hill in a desperate bid to confront the looming threat, a sense of helplessness washes over those of us left behind.

With Nicodeamus's cryptic words echoing in our ears, uncertainty hangs heavy in the air like a thick fog. We exchange apprehensive glances, grappling with the magnitude of the situation and the unsettling realization that we may be facing forces beyond our comprehension.

As the wolves stare at us with unblinking eyes, their silent scrutiny only serves to heighten our unease. In the face of impending danger, we are left with more questions than answers, our nerves stretched taut like the strings of a bow ready to snap at any moment.

"We need the challengers from the Dire Wolves as well as the Lycans. Let the battles begin," Dimitri says, then starts walking to a nearby clearing to wait for the battles to start. Normalcy must be maintained, and dominance must be re-established within the packs before all hell breaks loose. I'll watch over it all, unbiased, while Aurora and Alaric take care of whatever needs to be done.

As I gaze up at the sky, a sense of foreboding washes over me like a dark tide. The once serene mid-day sky transforms before my eyes, morphing into an ominous, inky canvas that seems to swallow the sunlight whole.

From our camp, a swarm of dragons emerges, their majestic forms blotting out the once-pristine azure. Their scales shimmer with an otherworldly brilliance, casting a kaleidoscope of colors across the heavens. Each beat of their vast wings sends shockwaves reverberating through the air, a thunderous symphony of power and majesty.

As they sail through the heavens, their sinewy bodies twist and coil with a serpentine grace, catching the dying embers of the sun and casting them forth in a mesmerizing display of light and shadow. The collective roar of their voices echoes across the landscape, a primal chorus that rattles the very foundations of the earth.

Beneath their colossal presence, the earth itself seems to tremble, as if bowing in deference to their dominion over the skies. They fly with purpose, driven by an ancient calling known only to their kind, their destination shrouded in mystery.

I watch in awe and trepidation as their silhouettes disappear into the distance, leaving me with a sense of uncertainty and unease. What awaits my mate and bond brother on their journey northward, I can only imagine, and the weight of that uncertainty hangs heavy in the air like a suffocating shroud.

CHAPTER 24
Gallus

For thousands of years I have watched over the mountain ranges throughout what is now called Eastern Europe. Conquerors have come and gone, civilizations have risen and crumbled like dust in the wind. Oberon came to me earlier this year and told me of the ascension of a very special hybrid. This time a female was born, and she appears to be a welcomed balance between her species. If I was being called to put down another Elven creation, I don't know what I would do.

I lie in my cavern at the highest peak of the oldest mountain hidden from human view. I close my silver orbs and reach out, feeling the different life forces out there. The hybrid has changed and had almost died. Self-preservation kicked in, and her dragon side kept her alive. Lucky for her, she had a mystic in her group that knew what to do. Oberon had paid her a visit and now stands before me.

"Old friend, mentor, I need your help one last time." The sadness in Oberon's eyes tells me something is going terribly wrong.

It's been years, maybe centuries, since I last shifted to a human form. "What do you need, child?" Even being thousands of years old himself, Oberon is barely a quarter of my age.

"Aurora's wolf side is dying even after healing. Is there anything you can do to save her and her wolf? She must live and exterminate the blight called the Strigoi." Oberon's eyes are pleading with me, begging me for the one thing only I can give.

"She may not be able to survive what will happen to her if I do as you ask," I say as I slip my arms into the silk robe Oberon offers me.

"I admit, I may have made an error when I chose her bloodline." Oberon gets a very mischievous look in his lavender eyes. "Her grandmother is the Blood Queen. I believe she can survive, but what would she be after you change her?"

I shake my head at Oberon; his mistake inadvertently just made his request possible. "It depends on how strong her dragon side is, she would be more Force Dragon than Ice, but she would wield the powers of both." I run through my abilities in my head: invisibility, able to breathe water, strike terror like mania into my opponents, my breath weapon means utter destruction, pure force unbridled.

I pace my cavern more, then look back at Oberon. "I will call her to me. If she survives, there will be nothing left alive strong enough to kill her—besides Odin himself."

Oberon approaches me and wraps me up tightly in his embrace. "Thank you, old friend. I will see you in Elysium." Blasted Fae flitted away in his glittery freaking mess.

Carefully, I remove the robe that Oberon had given me, and I lay it across a rock in my cavern. I return to my dragon form for the last time and bellow out my call for the one called Aurora. My tone is rich, deep, and haunting as it carries over the miles that separate us. Only dragons and other dragon-kin will hear me; it's part of my gift and curse.

In what feels like minutes, a call is returned. It's her, and she does vocalize like a dragon. The wolf in her is dying or at the very least, dormant. Tiny black dots break free of the cloud cover and are heading my way. It appears the girl is riding on a War Dragon with her swarm behind her. But where is her dragon mate, I sensed?

The dragon swarm is halfway here when a white and gold dragon hybrid breaks through the clouds and speeds towards the War Dragon. I see him line up under the War Dragon and the female leaps from one dragon to the other. The War Dragon falls back, and the Hybrid takes point. It appears that the mate has arrived after all. Upon arrival, the female stands behind his crown of horns. She gives her orders to the swarm. They quickly obey and begin to glide circles around my mountain, protecting the female and the male dragon.

The dragon lands, and against his orders, she leaps down and strides over to me. She's beautiful in her human form, but I can feel the pain of loss in her soul. *Little one, do you know why I have summoned you?* I speak within the bond that all dragon-born share.

Her pale-grey human eyes shift to her dragon's, and she looks between the male dragon behind her and me. She drops to her knees before me and sits upon her heels, and places her folded hands in her lap. For one so young, she's showing me the utmost respect.

No, ancient one, I can only guess it's because of what has happened to me. She speaks softly with a sense of sadness through the bond. Which prompts her dragon mate to shift and kneel behind her, then rest his forehead on her shoulder to comfort her.

Aurora, is it? I whisper through the bond so as not to add to her stress. *I called you here for two reasons. One is selfish on my part, and the other is to aide you.* Cautiously, she looks up to me, and her eyes hold a curiosity and innocence I haven't seen in what seems like forever.

If it's within my power, ancient one, I would be honored to help you. Again, she speaks softly. A few tears roll down her cheeks, and her mate moves alongside her. I can tell she's tired; the loss of her wolf is taking its toll on her.

Fear not, little one. I shall make everything better. You need not fear losing your mates or your wolf. Come closer, and we shall begin. Your mate can assist you, but once you make contact with my scales, he must release you. I look to the young, virile male beside her, and he nods and bows his head gently, acknowledging what I said through the bond.

The male stands first and assists Aurora to her feet. She stops and stands before him and presses her nose under his jaw, then kisses his lips before walking to me under her own power. Her dragon's eyes look up to me curiously before she extends her hands out.

I look to her mate then move my head forward until my cheek comes in contact with her. I move my wings forward and encase her in them. Her much weaker dragon is frightened of mine, and that's completely understandable. I croon and soothe the young dragon, and she opens her astral plane to me. Within, I find my old friend Nicodeamus and two hatchlings. Ah, our girl is strong enough to bear live dragon young. I reassure her father I am doing what needs to be done to ensure her a long, healthy life. Nicodeamus bows lightly and fades into the background, taking the babies with him.

I assume my human form in the astral plane, and I look like a cross between Father Time and Saint Nicholas. Aurora smiles, studying me intently. I watch her just as intently as she tilts her head left, then right, then back to the middle. *My time is coming to an end, Aurora—prematurely— and so is yours because of Vladimir's poison. Without your wolf, the power your body contains will rip itself apart. I must heal your wolf and strengthen your dragon.*

I watch the gravity of the situation hit her, and she lowers her head. *I'm not ready to go yet; I have babies and my father and mates need me. I can't let Vladimir live after all he's taken from everyone.* Her eyes flare, and the ghostly essence surrounds her eyes, and even here, the temperature begins to drop.

To Aurora's surprise, I smile and clap my hands. *There's the fire I was waiting to see! You are strong enough to hold the gift I am about to give you. You must promise me two things before I bestow this great boon to you.*

I raise my hand, holding up one finger, and smile gently at Aurora. *The first, only your mates and immediate family can know the full extent of what I have done, that is until you go to war. Only let your most trusted allies have a clue about the power that you hold.*

Next, I raise another finger. *Second, I know your mother's castle has been a priority to you. You must search it and completely remove all the tombs to exterminate all the evil bore there.*

I watch her closely, making sure she understands what I am asking of her. *When I leave you today, you will have enough power to bring about Ragnarok if you desire it. I hope not, by the way.* That causes Aurora to giggle a little.

I understand your wishes, and it shall be done. Time and the Strigoi have destroyed my mother's castle to the point of ruin. It may not be safe to raise children in; I was planning on possibly destroying it and rebuilding on the site. She smiles and offers her hands to me, palms up. *I'm ready for whatever may come, Gallus.*

Gently, I take her hands and look deep into her eyes, searching for any fear or regret. I find none. I'm going to miss being alive to a point; I won't miss the isolation of being the last of my kind. I bend over slowly and press my lips to Aurora's forehead and begin to cycle our energies together. If I do this properly, it will be painless for both of us. I feel the tingle of my energy move over my flesh, and I crack an eye open to see the familiar purple current pulsing. I look at Aurora. Her flesh is covered in frost; her power's pathways are completely open, so I begin to guide my energy into her.

I concentrate on my living form and fold my wings back at my side so that Aurora can leave easily when I'm gone. Her mate would be watching his mate beginning to glow faintly with my power and slowly increasing with time in the real world. He would also notice my scales slowly starting to turn dull and stone-like. When I'm done, I will be a large, stone statue; a monument to my sacrifice today.

My energy moves over and through Aurora slowly in gentle pulses, making sure it seeps deeply into every fiber of her being. In my mind's eye, I see her dragon basking in the glow of my power —becoming stronger and evolving to be more like me.

I find her Lycan curled up under the wing of her dragon. It's in a deep slumber and weakening by the minute. I start focusing my life force on the Lycan, and bit by bit, it starts to move and awaken. Eventually, it stands erect and looks healthy again. My final move before I expire, I join the two on the mythical level, both able to access all of my gifts and powers. She'll never know flight, but she'll never know defeat either. I'm feeling tired, and I pull back so that Aurora can look me in the eyes before I expire. Her eyes glow now with the purple energy of my dragon's power, and I am so incredibly impressed with the woman before me.

I feel the last of my power draining from me. *Remember your promise, Aurora, remember your mission. I will always be with you. Remember me.* I slowly draw in my last breath and gently press a fatherly kiss to Aurora's temple. My final words echo in the astral plane just as my time on the earthly plane expires. The last of my life force enters Aurora. I feel my body becoming harder to move as my limbs turn to stone. It's harder to breathe as my muscles seize. My last conscious thought is that Aurora remains safe.

~Aurora~

I awaken from what feels like a dream, but I know it's not. The Great Wyrm Force Dragon has given up his life so that I could live. He bestowed thousands of years of knowledge upon me in mere moments. I look at the sleeping giant before me and place a kiss on his cheek. "I remember my promise, Gallus; I won't let your sacrifice be in vain."

Alaric runs to me and quickly scoops me up, hugging and kissing me. "I'm healed fully, love. Gallus sacrificed his life so that I may live and finish the fight." I kiss his full lips to punctuate my joy.

"Are you sure, Aurora? You feel better and different," Alaric says as we walk to the mouth of the cavern.

I shift my eyes to that of my dragon, call out to my swarm, and send them home—no noise, no call, just my will alone. "There's something I need to show you and the others. I made a promise to keep my new gifts a secret for a while longer."

Alaric tilts his head several times, looking me over as I watch the other dragons leave. "Why just us?" Alaric's panic is palatable in the air. "What happened?"

I draw in a slow, measured breath and reach deep within me, searching for my beast. There she is—healthy and stronger than ever. Slowly, I shift my form allowing every bone to break and reshape. My Lycan hybrid is still about ten feet tall, snow-white, and sits about an even half-ton. I hold my arms out before me, looking at my gauntlets and talons.

My scales look more like Gallus's, chromatic in nature, still serrated and heavily armored. My talons are still white but have a streak of silver running along the talons' top half, I guess, to hide them better. My thick fur now covers my scaled body armor. I'm back to looking more wolf than dragon. The greatest advantage is not being known as a weapon. Slowly, I walk over to the cliff edge and click my ignitor; my breath weapon is Gallus's force attack. I hear the gasp of shock from Alaric as I rein in my newfound ability. I turn and test my frost, and the ground freezes before me. Everything is back to the status quo for now.

"I think we should head back, love. The others are in a tizzy with us being gone so long," Alaric says calmly.

I shift back to my human form, nod, agree with him, and wait for him to shift and lie down. Quickly, I climb onto his back, and we drop off the ledge into a freefall. I squeal with delight at the speed he achieves before he opens his wings and levels out. It's time to see my mates again and my growing swarm that waits for me back at camp.

As we fly home, I ponder everything that has happened to me since the beginning. Initially, I believed I was just an oddball white Lycan. After my ascension, I gained access to some of my father's dragon's abilities. Now, having almost died, I've been given the power of the ancients. What the actual fuck! I mean, seriously, I have a horrible temper at times, and to give me the powers to bring about Ragnarok is kind of insane to do. I shield my mates from my present emotions. I have mixed feelings about all of this. One being shouldn't have this much power. But I do, and thankfully I was blessed with some level-headed mates to keep me from going off the deep end. Hopefully.

I run my fingers over the scales on Alaric's dragon's head, and I'm reminded how much I love them all. They are why I fight. My children's future is at stake, and if I'm the only one strong enough to protect it, then so be it. Tomorrow, I set my plans in motion.

CHAPTER 25

Alaric

As I fly back to camp, a sense of unease gnaws at the edges of my consciousness. Despite Aurora's apparent peace, I can't shake the feeling of tension lingering in the air. The hurried departure has left our group unsettled, each member grappling with their own doubts and uncertainties.

Descending to the hill's base in the clearing, I land with caution, mindful of the weight of responsibility resting on my shoulders. Aurora dismounts gracefully, her presence a beacon of calm amidst the storm of emotions swirling around us.

But as the rest of my bond mates come running downhill, their expressions betraying a mixture of apprehension and curiosity, I know that our journey is far from over. Three of Aurora's mates are wolven, their instincts and sensitivities markedly different from ours. It falls upon me to navigate this delicate balance, to ensure that harmony prevails amidst the chaos.

With a quick shift, I assume my human form once more, the transformation a physical manifestation of the tension coiling within me. Drawing upon my knowledge of Force Dragon powers, I guide Aurora through the process of mastering her newfound abilities, each word uttered with a sense of urgency and determination.

Slowly, the atmosphere begins to shift, the palpable tension giving way to a semblance of calm. As my bond mates approach, their movements cautious yet determined, I can't help but feel a glimmer of hope amidst the uncertainty that lies ahead. For in this moment, we stand united, ready to face whatever challenges may come our way.

Aurora moves and embraces each of her mates one by one, and tells them how much she loves them. Her eyes land on me then she looks back to the camp. "Is everything under control?" she questions before starting to walk back up the hill.

Dominik moves forward and takes her right hand, and Klaus takes her left. "We defeated all challengers and have assumed the title of Alpha over our respective packs. Everything we have done has been in your honor, my angel," Klaus says, then bends to place a kiss on Aurora's temple. I watch her smile and kiss both Klaus and Dominik as they lead her back to camp.

I move alongside Jayce and Arnulf and look between the two of them. "How are both of you handling what's happened to Aurora?" I move before them, blocking them from walking back up to the camp with everyone else. Dimitri joins me, looking at the two most gentle mates in the family.

Arnulf and Jayce look between each other, then between Dimitri and me. Arnulf is the one who chooses to speak. "We were scared that she was going to die on us after her wolf was poisoned. It got even scarier when she took off out of nowhere."

That made me raise my eyebrows, then I look between the three of them. "You didn't hear the dragon's call? The one that summoned Aurora and all the dragons to leave?" I look slowly between the three of them, and all three shake their heads no. *Interesting*, I say to myself as I look to Arnulf. "What do you know about the ancient dragon of the mountains?"

Jayce and Dimitri both shrug their shoulders, and Arnulf's eyes flicker to his eagle's then back to human. "There were stories of a dragon able to bring about the end of days—an entire species capable of mass destruction. The Elder Gods watched from their perch in the other worlds. One day, one of these Titans took their rampage too far, and the Elder Gods struck and wiped out most of the population. Only a yearling dragon was left behind; the Elder Gods explained why his people were taken from him. Gallus was raised on the mountain top isolated away from everyone else." I nod slowly, having listened to his story.

As Arnulf's words hang in the air, a palpable tension settles over the group. The mention of the ancient dragon of the mountains sends a shiver down my spine, and I exchange uneasy glances with Jayce and Dimitri.

The revelation of such a powerful and destructive force lurking in the shadows fills me with a sense of dread. It's as if the very air around us has grown heavy with the weight of impending danger.

I can feel the hairs on the back of my neck stand on end as Arnulf recounts the tale of Gallus, the last remaining survivor of his kind. The image of a lone dragon, raised in isolation atop a desolate mountain, paints a haunting picture of loneliness and despair.

As Arnulf finishes his story, a silence descends upon us, broken only by the faint rustle of leaves in the breeze. Each of us is lost in our own thoughts, grappling with the implications of what we've just learned.

In the midst of the growing uncertainty, I can't shake the feeling that we've stumbled upon something far more sinister than we could have ever imagined. And as the night wears on, the sense of unease only grows stronger, casting a shadow of doubt over our every move.

"I had heard the same story as a little boy, and I thought it was something to scare little dragons into behaving. I met Gallus today; he gave his life force to allow Aurora to live. She is now an Ice Dragon-Force Dragon-Lycan hybrid." The look on the guys' faces matches how I feel on the inside. Shock doesn't even cover it right now. I'm grateful we get to keep Aurora, but at what cost to her?

Jayce looks down and then back up to me. "What does that mean for the rest of us? You two were very close before, now it will be worse and we will be forgotten." Tears slowly begin to roll down his cheeks. His wolf's eyes surface and look at me—his heart breaking before me.

Quickly, I move forward and pull Jayce to my chest and kiss his forehead. My dragon rumbles to him, trying to calm him and his animal. I hear the soft little rumbles of his wolf answering my dragon. Arnulf moves close, and Jayce and I open our arms and pull him into our embrace. Arnulf's bird whistles and chirps, trying to communicate with our animals.

Eventually, Dimitri joins the embrace. The four of us stand together, hugging and rumbling, settling our animals with all the changes. Aurora comes up and bounces around all of us. "Whatcha doing?" Aurora practically sings as she bounces around, touching each of us in turn.

Jayce pops free then starts bouncing around with her. "Bonding time, my love!" he says, practically singing to her as they hold each other's hands as they dance in circles. He's doing a great job hiding the hurt that had surfaced just moments ago.

This is the oddest thing I have yet to witness the two of them doing to this date. "Are you two okay?" I have to ask them. Even for Aurora, this tops her weird scale.

"Why, Alaric? What could possibly be wrong? I'm healed, my mates are safe, and we're back together. The best part! We get to kill Strigoi really soon," Aurora says, and her smile reminds me of her father's. It's like Hannibal Lecter and Joker had a baby.

I step free of my bond brothers and walk towards my overly-jolly mate. Gently, I caress Aurora's arms and feel the power pulsing under her skin. Lightly, I kiss her full lips then smile at her. "I know what's happening; you're infused with the power of the ancients. It will take time for you to adjust to it, my love." Softly, I kiss her lips, then take her hand and start to lead her back to the camp.

We reach the wood line, and she looks out over all those that gather. Her presence alone, the dragons instantly kneel before Aurora. Klaus and Dominik come alongside her and take her hands, and the wolves kneel simultaneously. Aurora looks to her two wolven mates and kisses them in turn. "We have a war to wage and an army to lead. We march on my mother's castle in the morning. For now, wolves hunt and bring back tasty meat. Water Dragons fly to the closest water and bring back fish. We must eat well; the battle will be tough." Aurora stretches out her Alpha power, and the wolves can feel her beast back where it should be, their smiles evidence enough.

Our people depart as soon as the orders are issued. Aurora slowly turns to face us and smiles. "We will have a night to end all nights. We feast and enjoy our time together. Then tomorrow, we follow the plan we laid out." She smiles so sweetly between the six of us.

As Aurora and Jayce guide me back to our usual spot beneath the weeping willow tree, a sense of foreboding settles over me like a suffocating blanket. The air crackles with tension, every movement and sound amplified by the weight of anticipation.

Perched upon my lap, Aurora's presence feels both comforting and oppressive, her grip on my hands like a vise. Beside me, Jayce's lean form radiates an aura of quiet intensity, his eyes scanning the surroundings with unwavering focus.

As we watch the preparations unfold, each passing moment is fraught with suspense. The return of the wolves with their bounty of meat and the dragons with their haul of fish only serves to heighten the tension in the air.

The feast unfolds around us, a symphony of sights, sounds, and smells that threatens to overwhelm the senses. Yet, amidst the chaos, we remain huddled together, our proximity a shield against the looming uncertainty.

Offerings are brought before us, each morsel scrutinized with meticulous care by Dominik and Jayce. Every bite we take is laced with apprehension, each swallow a leap of faith in the safety of our surroundings.

The peace we feel is strange, all things considered. We almost lost Aurora twice, to only have her back in the flesh as she is now. I watch my mate closely; she's shifting her hands to her gauntlets. The scrutiny she's putting them under is quite intense. "My love?

Is everything okay?" I ask softly, only gaining the attention of my bond mates.

Aurora's eyes shift to her dragon for a moment, then back to human before she looks at each of us in turn. "I think so. I mean, it's a lot to process. One minute I'm in between worlds—dragon and Lycan. Then my wolf is targeted and almost murdered, leaving me no choice but to take into myself the ancient life force and have him rejuvenate my wolf. He changed my dragon side too; she's stronger than before."

Aurora draws in a deep breath and sighs softly before continuing. "I don't regret passing on some of my Lycan legacy to Dominik and Klaus. After all, they need it more than me now."

Aurora drops her gaze for a moment, then looks back up. "I feel every dragon I've ever come in contact with. I feel my children as if they are next to me. I feel you, Alaric, just as intensely. I feel every single wolf here, Lycan and Dire alike, and it's absolutely amazing."

Aurora smiles the sweetest and most affectionate smile I've ever seen from her. Slowly, she touches each of us, and I feel a warmth move over my body like a loving embrace. "I feel everything from each of you. I hear your whispers in my mind, and I see your animals when I close my eyes. It's a wondrous feeling to be this at peace finally."

Her facial expression changes abruptly. "When we go to war, and I tell you to retreat, go. My new advantage, we shall call it, will decimate anything in its path. Pull your troops back and run. Don't look back. I'll send the dragons to help evacuate everyone. I love you all too much to risk harming anyone."

Suddenly, Aurora stands and looks at us. "Klaus, the team that was supposed to go with me, will remain with the main army. I don't need them trapped in the rubble if I decide to rip my mother's castle apart."

"Aurora, no!" Dimitri says forcefully.

"The castle isn't safe, Dimitri, and practically in ruins already." Aurora gently cups Dimitri's cheek before kissing him softly. Dimitri's eyes slam shut, and fur ripples over his bare arms.

He nods slowly then kisses Aurora's forehead. He smiles. "I understand, my love." Then he goes to talk with the bears, including Ellis's team.

"What did you show him, my love?" Jayce asks as he slides up alongside her and snuggles Aurora against him.

As Aurora's hands extend towards us, a palpable tension hangs in the air, thickening with each passing moment. We exchange wary glances, uncertain of what awaits us in the depths of her vision. Yet, with a sense of trepidation, we reach out and touch her bare skin, bracing ourselves for whatever revelations may come.

In an instant, we are engulfed in the swirling currents of Aurora's vision, drawn into the depths of her consciousness. The scene unfolds before us like a nightmare, each moment dripping with suspense and foreboding.

We watch in awe and horror as Aurora navigates the labyrinthine corridors of the castle, her every movement fraught with danger and uncertainty. The tension mounts with each encounter, each confrontation with the Strigoi sending a shiver down our spines.

As Aurora unleashes her newfound power, a sense of dread washes over us, mingling with awe at the devastation she wreaks upon the castle. The air crackles with electricity, the suspense building to a crescendo as the vision reaches its climax.

Then, as suddenly as we were drawn in, we are violently expelled from the vision, torn away from the chaos and carnage that unfolded before our eyes. Gasping for breath, we are left reeling in the aftermath, the tension still hanging thick in the air like a heavy fog.

"I love you guys too much to chance anyone being harmed." She tries to convey with a look just how much we mean to her.

"No one will expect me to go in alone. I plan to signal everyone when I'm ready to bring down the castle. I'll wait until everyone is clear to destroy everything." Aurora smiles sweetly at us then walks off to talk to our people in the camp to ease their minds.

Honestly, I'm not sure if I'm more concerned about her safety or for ours. The visions she shared with us were some next-level shit. My sick side can't wait to see Ellis's reaction to Aurora's latest upgrade.

CHAPTER 26

Arnulf

THE LAST SEVENTY-TWO HOURS HAVE BEEN THE MOST INTENSE DAYS OF MY life. I almost lost the mate I just found. We get her back, and she's still not whole. Then the world's biggest mind fuck happens; an ancient dragon calls for her, and she leaves.

We stand here watching all the dragons shift and leave, following right behind Aurora. Even Alaric wasn't able to ignore the dragon's call. We waited for what seemed like forever for any word.

The mates left behind are a wreck; we felt the surge of power that went through Aurora and then the bond. Jayce and I remain together, hugging each other afraid of what may become of our beloved mate.

Aurora was reborn in a sense, from the gift that Gallus had given her. He not only gave her back her wolf, but he upgraded her dual nature. Alaric was kind enough to share with us the sight of our newly shifted mate. She's a Titan in a sense now, and there are several stories of what would bring about the end of days. Each religion and species has a different Titan.

The wolves believe it would be Fenrir. The dragons, Tiamat—the seven-headed dragon. The bears really don't believe their people would be involved at the end of days. My people believe we would be heralds of the end, warning others of what's to come.

Slowly, I move through all the shifters and make my way to Aurora's side. I run my right hand through Aurora's hair to get her to turn and look at me. Her angelic visage and soft grey eyes turn to face me. A gentle smile creeps across her full, ruby-red plump lips. I watch her move with a fluid grace I haven't seen her use before. Her lithe hands rise and caress my cheeks. Her thumbs move over my cheekbones as she looks deep into my eyes.

"Arnulf, you came for me. Is there something on your mind, sweet one?" Aurora rises up on her tiptoes and presses her full lips against mine.

I feel the raw crackle of power moving between us. The Titan within her is making itself known to me. My bird is pleased that our mate has the peace she so craved. The kiss breaks hesitantly, and I move to kiss her forehead. "My beautiful mate, I've missed you greatly. Will you join me? Will you have dinner with me?" I remove my hands from her face and offer her my upturned hand.

Aurora looks to my offered hand, takes it, and pulls it to her chest. The eyes of Aurora's dragon look at me, and its purple power crackles in the mercury of her eyes. "A meal would be divine, my love." Aurora's voice sounds like the sweetest love song ever sung.

I take her hand and lead her to the edge of the fire and have her take a seat. I move away briefly and return with fresh meat and a bottle of red wine. Aurora's eyes light up at the sight before her. I prepare the meat and wine for Aurora and offer it to her. A soft blush moves over her cheeks. "You don't have to serve me, Arnulf. We are equals in my eyes." I bend down and kiss her forehead.

"You know you scared me this last time. I know it wasn't your fault what happened. Hell, we were all drugged. We could have been slaughtered, and there was nothing any of us could do." I shrug my shoulders and see Jayce approach, so I motion for him to join us.

Jayce looks down and sighs. "I'm sorry for barging in. I just really need to be near Aurora for a little bit. I hope you don't mind, Arnulf?" The stress radiates off of Jayce, and his body is tense.

"Not at all, brother. If you wish to call the others over, we'll gather more food and eat together here by the fire." Jayce's face lights up, and he gets up quickly to tell the others. "Thanks, Arnulf."

Aurora is giggling as she sips at her wine, looking at me. "You're a good man, Arnulf. I've been blessed with six of the kindest, most thoughtful mates a female could ever ask for. Thank you for being you." Aurora punctuates her statement by leaning over and kissing my lips.

Aurora's look turns serious. "I'm sorry I scared you and everyone else." Aurora looks up and makes eye contact with all of us. "Everyone could have died because of me, and my heart hurts thinking about it." We watch scales ripple over her arms and down the bridge of her nose.

Aurora stands and begins pacing around the fire in deep thought. Oddly, her frost isn't coating everything right now. Apparently, I'm not the only one who notices—Dominik and Klaus are studying Aurora's every move. Alaric and Dimitri are also watching her very closely; Aurora is acting like her typical self but with no frost.

"Babe, are you okay?" Alaric asks and steps in Aurora's path.

Aurora looks up at Alaric. Waves of purple energy crackle through her hair, and then she smiles. "Yeah, I feel bad that everyone almost died because of me. I feel bad that my wolf almost died. I feel bad that Dom and Klaus had to step up because I was not wolf enough to control the packs for a while." A pang of sadness washes over her face then vanishes just as quickly. "I just hope I am enough to end all of this. End the reign of terror Vladimir and the Strigoi have brought to what used to be my mother's lands and people. She must be so disappointed in me that I'm not the pup she brought into this world." A single tear rolls down Aurora's cheek then evaporates. The evaporating tears is a new development. I'll have to ask Alaric about it later.

There you have it, the root of what's really troubling Aurora. Dimitri opens his arms to her when she looks at him. To my surprise, she comes to me and presses the bridge of her nose against my throat under my jaw. Cautiously, I wrap my arms around my mate and pull her flush to my chest. She chose me, the one least capable of protecting her, for comforting her.

I raise my eyes and look at my bond mates. Each of us trying to process what just happened. Lightly, I run my fingers through Aurora's hair, trying to soothe her. Her beast rumbles to me. I feel it through my very being and through the bond. My bond mates all turn sharply to look at Aurora. Apparently, they can feel her beast too. It's trying to soothe all of us, sensing how stressed we all are.

One by one, the guys step forward and wrap their arms around us. I can feel Aurora smiling against my skin. Eventually, Aurora lifts her head, and the hug-fest ends. The guys slowly let go and step back. Aurora takes her time going to each mate and kisses them, then presses the bridge of her nose to their throat. It's a trust thing she does with us. When she's done the first round, she stands before each of us, baring her throat to us. We each return the gesture and smile at her.

I look behind me, and all of our dragon warriors have gathered. "They're looking for their Queen, my love."

Aurora's eyes shift to her dragons as she looks at her swarm. Their eyes all shift and stare at her. A faint glow seems to envelop their eyes as they look at her. Alaric steps forward and rests a hand on Aurora's shoulder, looking at the other dragons. He then turns to us and extends a hand to us. We each make contact with his skin and now hear Aurora's voice boom through the bond with the dragons.

I close my eyes and suddenly, I'm on the astral plane with Aurora and all of the dragons. Aurora's upgraded Lycan beast stands before all of the powerful and ancient dragons, and she looks each in the eye, showing no fear at all. There're more dragons here than at the camp, and Aurora is imploring them to join her battle to rid the earth of the blight that is the Strigoi.

A great Wyrm Black Dragon steps forward and lowers his head to her, swearing to join the fight. Others in his swarm come forward and join him, offering support. Apparently, there are multiple nests of Strigoi throughout Europe and Asia. Aurora wishes to strike them all at once. The meeting ends soon after the directions for the strike to occur, and we are pulled out of the astral plane with her.

Aurora turns to look at us and smiles before walking off towards our tent to go rest. I turn and look to Alaric, who seems to be in deep thought. "What just happened?"

"Her connection to the dragons is impressive. I'm not sure why she didn't pull all of us in with her when she met with them. I'll have to ask her later what that was all about... I have full confidence that we will be victorious " Alaric says, contemplating the meeting.

"Alaric, I have a question. Aurora's tears used to freeze, and now they disappear. What changed?" My bird is on edge, nervous about the answer we may receive.

"Ah, you saw that. Well, it's part of her being changed. I'm guessing it's part of the destructive nature of the Force dragon," Alaric says, then gives me a quick hug before hugging our other bond mates. He turns and walks off with Dante and Edgar in deep discussion.

I look at each of the bond mates remaining. Dimitri is the most relaxed I've ever seen him; the twins are rather calm as well. "Relax, Arnulf, our mate will be fine. For once, I'll be able to sleep tonight, not afraid of what may come. With any luck, Vladimir believes she's dead and won't expect our arrival in a few days."

Klaus comes up alongside Dimitri and nods along with what he's saying. "We thought we had a tactical nuke before; we literally have a nuke now." Klaus, Dimitri, and the twins have known Aurora far longer than I have, and I already understand what they are getting at.

My thoughts wander then I look up to Dimitri. "What was Aurora like before her having mates?"

Dimitri almost chokes on the drink that Jayce has handed him. He motions to the logs near the fire for us to sit. He takes a seat, looking at the four of us. "She defined the word hellion. But from what we've recently learned from Oberon, it really wasn't her fault. Aurora has always been a loving and curious creature." He starts to laugh then shakes his head before starting again.

"I remember this one time this female decided to track me back to where we lived. Aurora was a little over a hundred and fifty years old at the time. The woman, another bear shifter, was trying to get me to accept her as her mate. Aurora happened to be the one to open the door. She yelled in the woman's face in a blend of her wolf and human voice that I was hers and to fuck off." Dimitri starts laughing then goes pale, seeing Aurora approaching.

"That was a fun night indeed, D. I thought my wolf was insane 'cause D showed *zero* interest in me. I launched that bitch and we proceeded to brawl across the whole front lawn and into the woods." Aurora smiles and laughs a little.

"Poor Andre was beside himself, and Dimitri didn't know what to do to stop two possessive females from fighting." Aurora starts to laugh softly. "D took the hose and started spraying our animals with water as we came rolling out of the woods. My beast hated to get wet unless she wanted to swim." Alaric comes and sits next to me, listening to the story.

"So there I was, hose in hand and two drenched females. I knew I was a dead man the way Aurora was looking at me. Soon as the other female got the hint and left, Aurora shifted and walked up to me." He tilts his head to the side and smirks. "You know how impossible it is to not look at her naked? She stood there, looking deep into my eyes, then broke down crying. I didn't know she felt I was hers, at least not till that point. My bear kept telling me she was ours, but I guess that tea that Elena had kept sending us kept me from connecting the dots."

Dimitri draws in a deep breath and shakes his head slowly. "I've got a chubby at this point, and she's in hysterics. I did the only thing I could think of. I scooped her up and carried her into the house and let Andre try to calm her down. Me? I went and took the coldest shower in the history of cold showers so that I could be there for her. You think a mad Aurora is scary, try one that's sad; that switch can flip in seconds flat." Dimitri smirks as he looks over to Aurora and snaps his fingers to help visualize the switch flip.

Aurora rolls her eyes, then stands up and walks over to hug Dimitri. "Do you have a clue how many times I woke up standing in the doorway of your bedroom in the middle of the night because my wolf wanted you? She wanted me to bite you and make you ours since I was about a hundred." A single tear rolls down Aurora's cheeks and evaporates before it hits her jaw. "So much time was stolen from us." She gently cups Dimitri's cheek looking up into his eyes. "Vladimir is going to suffer as no one has ever suffered before. I swear this to you, my love." Aurora raises up onto her tippy toes to kiss him before leading him off.

Dom and Jayce share a look then turn to the rest of us. "They have been royally fucked over by Vladimir's bloodline. Over two hundred years together. Almost a hundred and thirty, they could have been mates." Dom shakes his head, then looks at each of us. "If any of us find Vladimir or any of his relatives, we take them prisoner till Aurora and Dimitri can handle them. They deserve payback." Everyone nods in agreement with Dominik; he's right, after all, they've suffered enough.

"We should get some rest. We don't know what we're going to run into over the next few days," I suggest gently. After all, I am the new guy in the group.

"Arnulf is correct; we should rest. The next two days' journey could be the most dangerous just before reaching the castle," Klaus says, his eyes becoming that of his beast. I look over to see Dominik's and Alaric's eyes are also shifted. I can feel through the bond they are setting up sentries and telling everyone it's time to sleep. I follow suit and reach out to my clan, relaying the same message to them as well.

We decide to sleep outside the tent tonight, giving Aurora and Dimitri the time alone they so desperately craved earlier. The next few days will definitely be a challenge, but I know that we will be up to it as a team.

CHAPTER 27

Jayce

The camp is broken down quickly, and barely a trace is left behind in our wake. I'm back in the same wagon as Aurora, but there are no dragons in the wagon with us this time. Ellis, Klaus, a Dire Wolf, and one of Ellis's Polar Bears are with us. Aurora has decided to use Klaus and me as a pillow and a footrest. Oddly, she doesn't allow the others onto the bench we're on.

"How much longer?" The Dire Wolf asks.

"As long as it takes, pup," Aurora says, then cracks an eye to look at him. "I may not be your Alpha anymore, but I am still just as dangerous." As Aurora's arms transform into gauntlets, a surge of power pulses through the air, tingling against my skin. The faint crackle of purple energy dances over the tips of her talons, casting an eerie glow in the dim light of the campfire. The scent of ozone hangs heavy in the air, a potent reminder of the raw energy coursing through her weapons.

The wolf's eyes widen in astonishment as it beholds Aurora's formidable arsenal, the strange energy crackling ominously over her gauntlets. Ellis, ever the jester, decides to test her newfound power, dropping an apple into her outstretched hand. In an instant, the fruit disintegrates upon contact with the pulsating energy, leaving behind nothing but a fine mist.

Unfazed by the display, Aurora offers a playful wink in response, shifting her hand back to normal with ease. Her smile is radiant as she turns her gaze towards me, her fingertips tracing lightly along my jawline. As the crackling energy envelops us both, I feel a curious sensation wash over me, a strange mix of warmth and tingling. Somehow, against all odds, I remain immune to the potent effects of the newfound energy.

"What the actual fuck!" Ellis screams and flails his arms around like he's trying to take flight.

"What seems to be the problem, E?" Klaus asks as calmly as possible, studying Aurora and me.

"She just obliterated a mother fuckin' apple, and she's touching him with the same energy. You fuckers are scary as fuck." Ellis exclaims, then looks to the others in the wagon.

As Aurora sits up, the air seems to crackle with anticipation, her energy pulsating with an electric intensity. My senses are overwhelmed as her eyes lock onto mine, sparkling with mischief and a hint of danger. The air feels charged, almost tangible, as her fingers trace over my face, sending shivers down my spine.

I can practically feel the crackling energy coursing between us, a vivid display of her power that seems to dance through her hair like tendrils of lightning. The scent of ozone fills the air, sharp and invigorating, as her purple energy envelops us in its electrifying embrace.

"Awe, baby, the poor marshmallow can't handle me," Aurora teases, her voice a playful taunt that sends a thrill through me. With a wink, she rises gracefully from her seat, her movements fluid and confident, reminiscent of a powerful storm gathering on the horizon.

With a sudden burst of energy, Aurora strides over to Ellis, her presence commanding attention like a force of nature. In an instant, she seizes him by the neck, her grip firm and unyielding, and he cries out in surprise and fear he screams like a little girl and passes out. Ellis drops like a ton of bricks to the floor of the wagon and his clan mate thinks it's the most hysterical thing he's ever seen. This big, bad Alpha passed the fuck out.

"That was the shit. Dude, you gotta do it again." The bear that came with Ellis says. Without hesitation, he extends his hand to Aurora. "I'm Lamonte, Monte for short. It's an honor to fight with the one who brought down that giant ass Black Dragon in Alaska. That shit was dope."

Aurora examines his hand then shakes it gently. A wicked gleam in her eye tells me she's up to no good. I watch that purple energy race down her hand to Monte. He doesn't flinch in the slightest when it flirts with touching his skin. He just smirks and nods his head lightly. "Did I pass, ya Highness?" Monte says in a humorous tone.

"Yeah, you're cool for a marshmallow," Aurora says, letting a giggle slip before she resumes her position with her head in my lap.

"I've been called many things in my life, but a marshmallow is definitely new, as you can see," he motions to his body, "I'm far from being white." He's still smiling. He's more curious than anything at this point.

"Funny story, that is," I say as I run my fingers through Aurora's hair. "We were having a meeting about the attack plans. As you already know, you're supposed to draw troops away from the castle grounds towards the dragons." Monte nods, following the course of conversation. "Well, your genius of an Alpha made a comment to the effect of it being like throwing marshmallows on blacktop or asphalt."

Aurora again starts hysterically laughing, as does Monte. I shake my head, looking at our fearless leader. I motion to Aurora, who's in the middle of a massive giggle fit. "This happened last time too. So the nickname of marshmallow stuck."

"Got ya. I'll explain to my people what really happened," Monte stresses the word *really* and rolls his eyes.

"Thanks," I say, then run my fingers through Aurora's hair again.

"Hey, Klaus, how are you making out with getting your people organized?" I ask. Klaus looks up from his phone, then plugs in the solar charger and sticks the charging plate outside on the bench next to the driver.

"He's doing good. As Jax can tell you, there have been a million questions that we can't divulge answers to yet. Some are happy that Dom stepped up and took over; others still want Aurora to be in control for fear Dom is going to be like your dad was." Sadness washes over me, hearing that, which makes Aurora sit up.

"If Dom wants me to, I'll talk to your people; I'll reassure them he's nothing like your dad." Aurora smiles softly at me as we hear Ellis finally starts to wake up. "Hey, marshmallow, you missed half the battle, you lazy fuck!" Aurora says, staring down at him.

"No fucking way. You almost killed me. I didn't miss shit." Ellis says as he goes to stand up. Monte reaches out and places a hand on his shoulder, stopping him.

"Remember the apple, E. You don't want to piss that female off now, do you?" Monte winks at Aurora, and she slightly lifts her chin at him. It looks like she has a new ally in the bear camp.

Ellis looks between Monte and Aurora, then quickly sits up on the bench next to Monte. They bump fists, and Ellis mumbles something about "good looking out."

My phone goes off numerous times and catches everyone's attention. Aurora's phone goes off next, and her eyes go distant. "We need to go." Aurora sticks her head out the front near the driver giving him instructions. The wagon stops and Aurora bolts out the back. We are currently four days' journey away from home, and I'm not sure what has happened but whatever it is, we are leaving now.

The seven of us sprint in the opposite direction of the caravan and keep running till they are way out of sight. Alaric strips and shifts to his dragon; Aurora jumps onto his back, immediately taking off. As for the rest of us, when Dante, Edgar, and Marco catch up to us, we climb on their backs and take off. Dante and Edgar flank them quickly, and Marco brings up the rear. We are seriously packing some firepower going into this fight.

Alaric starts to bring us up to speed as to what has happened. Our original camp is being overrun with Strigoi. Apparently, one of the bears betrayed us. Nicodeamus, the twins' mom, and the babies are hidden down in the bunker I built. Nicodeamus didn't reach out to Aurora because he didn't want her charging into this alone. It's about ten in the evening, and we can see the Strigoi still fighting and attacking the camp in waves. I reach out to my clan that was left behind and tell them to hide in their houses.

When we get close enough to the ground, Aurora jumps off and shifts before landing on the alpha house. She goes on a rampage, her Lycan beast tearing through the Strigoi as if they are made of tissue paper. Body parts go flying, then the familiar click of her ignitor is heard, and she uses her breath weapon for the first time. A small pack of Strigoi is destroyed in a matter of moments and turned to ash. Her beast stalks through the camp as the rest of us spread out and search the houses for stranglers.

Nicodeamus and the babies come running out and stop short, staring at the mythic beast before them. Aurora almost looks like her old self, except she still has the visible spines running down her back that weren't there before.

"Is that my baby?" Nicodeamus asks, the level of disbelief evident in his voice.

"Yes, sir." It's all Alaric had to say.

Aurora finishes her attack and turns, having heard her father speak. Tia and Ladon go running to their mother in their dragon forms. Slowly, Aurora drops to all fours and greets her children. Her beast's muzzle definitely looks more dragon than it did before. It takes longer for her to return to her human form than for her to become her beast. I run up and help Aurora get dressed.

"Hi, Daddy." Aurora cringes slightly, her voice a bit rough from the use of her breath weapon.

Nicodeamus runs over and wraps his arm around his daughter, holding her tightly to him. Aurora flings her arms around Nicodeamus, holding him and starting to cry. She keeps apologizing for her wolf almost dying and disappointing him and Anca.

"Now, you listen here, little one," Nicodeamus says with a force he rarely uses with Aurora.

"If the Great Wyrm did this to save your life, then it's a blessing, do you hear me?" Sheepishly Aurora nods, so Nicodeamus continues.

"You didn't hurt your wolf; that was that bastard Vladimir's fault, not yours. Do you understand that?" Nicodeamus raises Aurora's head so that she's looking him right in the eye. Reluctantly she nods yes.

"Good! One of Dimitri's bears ratted us out that you were gone. I killed the betrayer before the Strigoi began to attack." Nicodeamus kisses Aurora's forehead.

"One of my people betrayed us?" Dimitri throws his head back and roars. His anger and pain are felt through the bond.

Aurora cautiously moves over and runs her fingers in circles across Dimitri's shoulder blades. I can hear the soft rumbling of her beast as it tries to soothe Dimitri's bear. "My love, it's okay. We're here and safe, and so are the babies."

Dimitri draws in a slow, calming breath then lowers his gaze to Aurora. A smile slowly creeps across his lips before he nods and presses his forehead against hers.

"We need to return to our troops. We are so close to reaching the castle's borders. Father, take your mate and babies underground again. I will send Marco for you once the battle is over." Aurora runs over and hugs her father, then looks to Alaric.

"Time to go, love." Both babies run to Aurora as their father shifts back to his dragon form. "Be good, my little fire starters. Don't accidentally burn your new grams. I'd like to keep her around for a bit."

Aurora and Helle move toward each other and hug tightly. Helle kisses Aurora's cheek. "Don't worry, daughter. I will take care of your father and children. After all, Jayce gets his venom from me." Helle smiles and shows her canines and the venom she allows to leak slowly from them.

Aurora passes off both babies to Helle and kisses her cheek in return. Dom and I hug and kiss our mother and head towards Marco and Alaric, ready to fly. Dimitri and Klaus stand waiting to assist Aurora up onto Alaric.

Alaric launches up into the air and turns towards the last camp that we will have before the battle begins. I sit snuggled next to Aurora, watching the trees and mountains move swiftly around us as the dragons carry us to our destination.

Several hours pass, and we can see the campfire light ahead of us. *We'll land far off from the camp and walk in. I don't want to alert any spies as to where we are. The less Vladimir and his group know, the better for us,* Alaric says through the bond.

We land in a field not far from the camp and slide off of the dragon's back onto the ground. Alaric shifts back quickly, and I offer him his clothing. I watch him dress, and I'm thankful every day I get to witness this fine specimen of a male dress and undress. Alaric notices me watching him and winks at me; I know my alpha appreciates my attention. "Come on, Jayce, tomorrow is going to be a very long and tiring day." Alaric comes up alongside me and slaps my ass. I can't help but laugh as I playfully bump into him before running towards the camp. Tomorrow starts the assault on the castle. We better sleep good tonight. Tomorrow, we march into hell.

CHAPTER 28
Klaus

As I gradually awaken from the depths of sleep, I am enveloped in a comforting warmth, surrounded by the familiar scent of sweat and desire lingering in the air. Aurora's head rests gently on my chest, her soft breaths a soothing rhythm against my skin. The tangle of limbs serves as a testament to the passion we shared throughout the night, seeking solace and reassurance in each other's embrace.

With tender affection, I press a gentle kiss to Aurora's forehead, savoring the intimacy of the moment. Turning to Jayce, I find him blinking away the remnants of sleep, his eyes gradually focusing on me with a sleepy warmth. There is a deep love that binds us together, a sense of belonging that transcends mere words.

I offer him a reassuring smile, a silent acknowledgment of the bond we share. As he nods in understanding, I watch him extricate himself from our tangled nest, his movements graceful and deliberate.

The tent is filled with a sense of tranquility, punctuated by the soft rustle of fabric and the occasional murmur of voices. Dimitri stirs next, moving quietly in the dimly lit space. With a tender gesture, he leans in to kiss Aurora's lips, a gentle caress that rouses her from her slumber.

In a moment of confusion, Aurora reacts with instinctive protectiveness, her canines bared in a display of primal aggression. But as the haze of sleep clears, she recognizes the familiar faces surrounding her, her features softening into a smile of recognition.

With a playful nip at Dimitri's lower lip, she returns his affection. "Evil female," Dimitri mutters before he too gets up and leaves.

Aurora looks at Dom and Alaric next and starts laughing. Alaric is spooning Dominik, and Dominik has Alaric's hand held tightly to his chest. Hmm, I carefully reach over and snap several pictures. Quickly, I send the copies to Jayce and to Dimitri. Aurora carefully leans over and nips Alaric's lip. He tightens his grip on Dom and starts grinding his cock against his ass. Suddenly, Dom's eyes fly open, and he starts struggling to get away from Alaric.

Alaric mumbles for Aurora to stay still, unaware of anything wrong, and he tightens his grip again. "Babe, it's not me you're holding." Aurora sings, laughing the entire time.

"What the fuck!" Alaric says when he realizes he's holding Dom, he rolls away then stands up, adjusting himself.

"Almost time to roll out, love. You need to give the dragons their tasks. Dom, you and Klaus organize the wolves as we discussed." As Aurora moves to the suitcase, a sense of anticipation fills the air, mingling with the faint scent of aged leather and the subtle rustle of fabric. With each movement, the soft swish of clothing against the suitcase echoes in the room, adding to the tension that hangs palpably in the air.

As Aurora retrieves the outfit chosen by her father, the rich aroma of well-oiled leather fills the room, intermingling with the faint scent of lavender that clings to her skin. The fabric of the pants is smooth beneath her touch, molding to her form like a second skin, while the supple leather of the bodice whispers softly as she fastens it around her waist.

As she dons the outfit, the room seems to come alive with a sense of adventure and excitement. The soft clink of metal against metal fills the air as Aurora pulls out her sword and scabbard, the sound of the belt tightening around her waist reverberating with a sense of purpose and determination.

Caught in a moment of shared understanding, Aurora meets my gaze with a playful wink, her eyes sparkling with mischief and anticipation. In that brief exchange, I can sense the weight of our shared history and the unspoken bond that binds us together.

With each adjustment and movement, Aurora transforms before my eyes, her appearance reminiscent of a character from a dystopian steampunk tale. Yet, beneath the facade of bravado and adventure, there is a vulnerability that lingers in the air, a reminder of the challenges that lie ahead. One thing I notice is she's not wearing the shoes this time.

"Angel, did you forget to put on your boots?" I hold up her favorite knee-high boots and wave them in the air at her.

Aurora rolls her eyes, then comes over and kisses me on my lips. "No, silly, I can't swim with those heavy things on."

I nod slowly, then bend down to kiss her lips again, savoring the moment. "Stay safe, angel. I love you." My chest hurts thinking about her entering the bowels of the castle alone.

"I love you too. You better stay safe too." Aurora boops me on the nose then leaves the tent quickly.

As I prepare for the upcoming assault, the weight of my sword strapped to my side serves as a constant reminder of the impending danger. The metallic clang of the weapon against my belt resonates through the air, accompanied by the rustle of fabric as I adjust my attire.

Amidst the hustle and bustle of the camp, my pack mates and I exchange greetings and strategize for the impending attack. The tension in the air is palpable, each of us acutely aware of the gravity of the situation.

My gaze flickers skyward, instinctively seeking guidance from the position of the sun. Its warm rays cast dappled shadows across the forest floor, a stark contrast to the impending darkness of our mission.

As the signal sounds, my pack springs into action, dividing into four groups and dispersing to their assigned positions. With a sense of purpose, we move swiftly, our footsteps muffled by the forest undergrowth.

Arriving at our designated rendezvous point, I scan the area, searching for our leader. High above, Aurora perches in the branches of a tree, her silhouette outlined against the azure sky. From her elevated vantage point, she surveys the landscape with a keen eye, orchestrating the operation with precision.

Under her command, our teams spring into action, methodically disarming the traps that litter the perimeter of the castle. Jayce and I look at each other, pondering why we are here if Aurora is issuing the orders.

As the group of approaching Lycans draws near, a surge of adrenaline courses through my veins, heightening my senses to a razor-sharp edge. The thud of their footsteps against the earth reverberates in my ears, each pounding beat a warning of imminent danger.

Jayce's swift shift into his dire wolf form sends a ripple of tension through the air. The scent of fur and musk mingling with the earthy aroma of the forest. In contrast, I remain rooted in my human form, gripping my sword tightly as I prepare for the impending clash.

As the Lycans draw closer, confusion flickers across their faces at the sight of me brandishing a weapon. Their hesitation is palpable, a momentary pause that grants us the advantage we need to strike.

With Aurora at my side, our swords gleaming in the dappled light of the forest, we charge forward with a primal ferocity. The clash of steel against flesh fills the air, accompanied by the visceral sounds of grunts and cries of pain.

It becomes evident with each swing of my sword that some of our adversaries are ill-equipped for combat, their movements clumsy and uncoordinated. I relay this crucial information to my comrades with urgency, ensuring that they are aware of the enemy's weaknesses even amidst the chaos of battle.

As we continue to fend off the attackers, every sense is heightened to its fullest extent, each moment fraught with danger and uncertainty. But amidst the chaos, there is a sense of unity and determination, driving us forward in our fight against Vladimir's forces.

Aurora is having the time of her life parrying and twirling out of the way of the attacking Lycans. It's almost as if she's dancing while she battles, and then I hear it. She is singing Taylor Swift's "Look what you made me do" while she's fighting. Every battle, a song is tagged to it. This battle is no different than any other.

I swear that woman is going to put us all in an early grave. We clear the attackers quickly then return to the task before us. Aurora moves to survey the entrance to the flooded tunnel. My scout goes to stand beside her and goes over his discoveries on his previous mission...

Aurora looks to Jayce and me, then back to the scouts. "Guys? Can you come here?"

"Yes, angel?" I ask, looking between Aurora and my scout. Jayce shifts back and pulls on his pants.

Aurora's features give nothing away at the moment. "I've reconsidered my original plan. Jayce, pick two of your men. Klaus, you do the same. The eight of us will enter through the tunnels."

Aurora's eyes take on that ghostly glow as she reaches out through the bond. She tells the rest of her mates her amended plans, and I sense the relief from the others. We start getting updates that Lycan forces have been testing our groups for the last hour. Several hundred have fallen by our swords.

Through the trees, I spot Arnulf coming through carrying his medicine bag. "Thank the Gods for Ziploc bags." he says, patting his bag. He needs to bless the ground the Strigoi are buried in to weaken or kill them, hopefully.

Aurora turns and approaches Arnulf and kisses him gently. "Are you prepared for everything?" Aurora asks in a soft tone.

Arnulf tilts his head, then smiles. "Yes, my love, I am fully prepared."

"Good. Jax will be your personal guard. When we find the graves, Jayce will shift and remain at your side for added protection. After all, his venom is unrivaled." Aurora's tone holds nothing but love and pride for her mates.

Arnulf nods, then looks at the rest of us gathered. "So, what's the plan?"

I step forward and motion to my scout. "Gus here was the one that scouted the caverns originally. I figure he will be the one to lead us to the old weapons' chamber that he discovered. Arnulf, one of us will hold your clothing. We can have you shift and fly through some of the chambers, giving us a little bit of recon before we proceed."

"Sounds good," Arnulf says.

Aurora looks to the cavern then back to us again. "Be prepared for anything. Each Lycan must have a Dire with you. My mates will tell you when to shift and climb. If I have to freeze everything, you'll need to be out of the water." Aurora looks to the entrance then back to Gus. "Let's get this party started."

The dampness of the surroundings seeps into our bones, a constant reminder of the cold, dark depths that await us. The faint sound of dripping water echoes off the walls, creating an eerie symphony that reverberates through the cavern.

As Gus takes the lead and disappears into the abyss below, the anticipation grows palpable. The water is frigid against our skin, sending shivers down our spines as we follow suit, each step a test of our resolve. The darkness envelops us like a thick blanket, obscuring our surroundings and heightening our senses.

With each passing moment, the tension mounts, our senses on high alert for any sign of danger lurking in the depths below. The sound of our own breathing fills the silence, a rhythmic cadence that serves as a reminder of our vulnerability in this unfamiliar environment.

As we plunge deeper into the darkness, uncertainty gnaws at our insides, a nagging reminder of the perils that await us on the other side. But with Aurora's guidance and Gus leading the way, we press forward, our determination unwavering in the face of the unknown.

CHAPTER 29

Dimitri

In the heart of the Lycan lands, nestled within a desolate wilderness, I find myself in a dark and foreboding forest preparing for war. For centuries, this place has guarded its most enigmatic secret, the fall of the Marelup empire.

Towering trees with gnarled, twisted branches loom overhead, their leaves creating a perpetual shroud, hiding the secrets of the past.

The air is heavy with an eerie silence that resonates with the whispers of the years gone by. I can smell the damp earth, decaying foliage, and ancient stone intermingling. I gaze upon a once-majestic fortress that now lies in ruins.

Four spires reach defiantly towards the heavens, their stone walls chipped and scarred by time's relentless passage. The grandeur of the castle has faded, but its shadow still clings to the earth, casting a somber reflection upon the land.

The surrounding area was once a lively, prosperous town, where the joyful laughter of children echoed through vibrant streets and the enticing aroma of freshly baked bread filled the crisp air. Now, only remnants of a bygone era remain, faint whispers carried by the wind. Decrepit cottages with sunken roofs and weathered walls, adorned with scars of forgotten conflicts, crumble into the embrace of encroaching vines and thick undergrowth.

The once bustling town square, a center of mirth and trade. Now lies hidden beneath a tangle of thorny bushes and suffocating foliage, as nature relentlessly reclaims its territory.

Evidence of the war of yesteryear is still visible in the cracked cobblestones, bearing the marks of long-forgotten battles. Worn and weathered, the cobblestones display the scars of conflict. Rusty, shattered weapons lie scattered across the landscape like grim reminders of a bygone era, their jagged edges and faded colors speaking of past violence.

Tattered banners of the fallen Marelup Empire flutter weakly in the breeze, their faded colors barely visible against the gray sky. The tales of bloodshed and valor have been consigned to dusty, neglected tomes in the annals of history, but the land itself refuses to forget.

The forest surrounding the castle seems to hold its own secrets, its ancient trees whispering stories of lost souls and long-forgotten mysteries. The towering trees, their gnarled branches reaching towards the heavens, cast eerie shadows that dance beneath the dense canopy. The occasional hoot of an owl pierces the silence, the haunting sound echoing through the gloom.

The air is thick with a sense of foreboding, as if the land itself has become a keeper of the past, guarding the tales of tragedy and triumph that play out on this forgotten stage. The scent of damp earth mingles with the musty smell of decaying leaves, adding to the atmosphere of history and decay.

The cracked cobblestones, worn underfoot, tell a story of countless footsteps that have trodden upon them. The rough texture of the shattered weapons, once instruments of destruction, now serve as reminders of the violence that once ravaged this land.

As the fiery sun sinks beneath the jagged silhouette of the horizon, its dying light casts elongated, spectral shadows across the land. A shiver dances down my spine, as if the very air is electrified with the awakening of the ancient castle and the crumbling remnants of the once-vibrant town.

In this ethereal twilight, their eerie beauty is illuminated, drawing me in with a magnetic pull. The dim light paints a haunting tableau, where the past and present intertwine, leaving an indelible mark on my senses.

The air carries a faint scent of moss and decay, mingling with the distant echoes of forgotten voices. The dark, foreboding forest envelops the scene, its ancient trees standing tall as solemn witnesses to the passage of time.

The castle, now reduced to a haunting ruin, stands stoically, its walls weathered by the ages. Together, they bear the weight of forgotten memories, their whispers echoing through the annals of history, reminding me of the fragility of our existence.

The day of reckoning is finally upon us. I stand beside ten of my kin, ready to wage war in the name of my mate and my fallen queen, Anca. The Polar Bears are getting restless, waiting for their part in this master plan. Alaric and the dragons line the forest surrounding the castle. Nothing will get in or out without our knowledge.

Under my command, the Dire Wolves have searched the perimeter, stopping at the edge of where the next group takes over. It's twilight and so far, all we have seen is the occasional Lycan raiding party break free of the walls to test our strength and numbers.

The dragons are under strict orders not to shift until nightfall and not to engage with anything other than swords until told otherwise. Ellis looks uneasy as he leans against the tree, not far from me. Damn, marshmallow is scared because there's no snow to hide his beast.

"Dimitri." I turn to face Alaric and walk towards him.

"Da? What's on your mind?" I keep searching the woods and looking back towards the castle.

"Aurora took a team with her into the tunnels. Klaus, Jayce, and Arnulf are with her as well as two other Lycans and Dires," Alaric says, the relief evident in his voice.

I nod my head slowly and crack a smile briefly. "Good. I feel better she's not in there alone. Why is Arnulf with them?"

Alaric looks around then leans in close to me. "He's going to bless the graves if they can find them. That's their primary objective. Vladimir is in one of the remaining towers with the Elder Dame, from what we can tell. We are saving them for last. Besides, I'm sure Aurora would love to unleash the full fury of her pain and anger on him." Alaric has that wicked look in his eyes. It is the same kind of look that Aurora and Nicodeamus get just before something gets destroyed.

I look thoughtfully up at the two remaining towers. "Vladimir always favored the north tower; it has the best view of Widows Lake, where he loved to go hunting. I believe there's a cabin there, if I'm not mistaken."

I ponder what I just revealed and reach out through the bond to Dominik. *"Dom, to the north, there's a cabin near the lake. Vladimir used to like to hunt there. Send your most stealthy scouts to go check it out."* Dom agrees, then I go back to focusing on the forest around us.

Most of my clan is in their bear form, ready to take down the southern wall so the Polar Bears can lead the enemy straight to the dragons to get roasted. I keep looking at the sky, watching the sun move slowly. Soon it will dip down low enough for the Strigoi to emerge, and the real fun will begin.

It's just about dusk, and the alarm is raised by the eagle shifters flying overhead. It's about to get real interesting quick. On the other side of the wall, the location screeches of the Strigoi start. Their calls fill the night air and send a slight chill up my spine. The first of the Strigoi have risen. If my suspicions are correct, there's a mass grave in the courtyard and a second one some-where deep within the castle. Hopefully, Aurora and the guys are safe and ready for the evil they are about to face.

I shift and rally my clan and roar the order to bring down the wall. We charge, hitting the broken section with our shoulders, the full weight of our eleven bears hitting at once. Stones begin to fall around us and we back up quickly. We take turns in pairs, rearing up and pushing at the stones with our paws. Slowly, we make progress and the wall begins to tumble down. On the other side of the barrier, we hear howls and screeches from the stones hitting Lycans and Strigoi. I send my clan mates back and hit the wall one last time, making most stones fall in toward the courtyard. I haul ass back to where Alaric has shifted and is waiting for them to chase me.

The screeches and howls are getting louder; they're closing in on my position fast. Ahead of me, I see Alaric behind a small grove of white ash trees. Quickly, I slide between the trees and under Alaric's dragon. The Strigoi and Lycans break through the tree line and come to an abrupt halt. The click of Alaric's ignitor is deafening in the sudden silence. The roar of fire fills the air as he unleashes the full magnitude of his breath weapon.

In the distance, the clicks of other dragons' ignitors can be heard. The roar of flames and the screams of the Lycans and Strigoi fills the air. So many voices are being silenced. Hopefully, we have thinned the numbers enough to make it easier on Aurora and her team inside.

About a hundred yards behind us, the Black Dragons have set an acid perimeter. The plan is if there's a way in or out of the castle we haven't discovered, the acid will kill the reinforcements.

During the dragons' recharge time, I reassemble my team to head back to the wall. I look back at the wall in time to see more Strigoi pouring out of the breach. I tilt my head back, roaring, raising the alarm. The answering roars fill the woods before we charge the breach. I stand on my hind legs and swipe my talon-like claws at the Strigoi. I guess my claws got an upgrade from my mate. Game on, leeches!

At least a dozen or more Lycans climb out of the breach and begin attacking my troops in sync with the Strigoi. Natural enemies fighting on the same side? It must be the work of the Elder Dame.

I am so busy pondering what is happening at the breach point that I don't notice the Lycans sneaking up on me. Thank the Gods for Alaric. He shifts back to his human form and grabs his sword, decapitating a Lycan.

"I've got your back, D!" Alaric shouts as he fights another two Lycans.

We cut through the assailants like a hot knife through butter. With every swing of the sword, a body falls. Black blood and ash are everywhere—Lycan bodies and crimson cover the forest floor around us. Alaric takes a moment and gets dressed between attacks. After all, it would suck if his dick got clawed off in battle.

The next wave comes and hits hard. The Wyvern has joined the fray. Alaric gets that cocky smirk of his, and then his eyes glow. The roars of the War Dragons fill the air as at least a dozen takes to the air setting the sky on fire.

I don't know what's more frightening to me, the roar of the flames overhead or the bodies of the charred Wyverns falling from the sky. Alaric smiles, looking at the battle overhead, then turns his gaze on the Strigoi coming at us. I feel a shift in him, and he pulls an Aurora and pulls ice spikes up from the ground from under their feet. Un-fucking-believable. Just what our family needs, two of them able to impale at a thought.

"Hell yeah!" Alaric screams before shifting his arms to his gauntlets and sending ice spikes up and through the Strigoi. It doesn't kill them; it only slows them down. Alaric impales them, and I dash forward and cut their heads off with my talons. It seems to be a very good working relationship.

I hear Alaric yell my name, and I look up in time to see a Wyvern falling right at me. I roll and try to get out of its way. Unfortunately for me, its tail catches my hind leg, cutting my thick hide with its spike. I roar and slip off the rest of the way. Alaric runs over when things settle down, and he takes a look at the gash in my hide.

"That's gonna leave a mark," Alaric says with a slight chuckle. I watch him shake his head, then study the wound more carefully. "If you shift, it may heal it most of the way. Though, I'm afraid it will leave a scar no matter what we do to heal it."

Alaric backs away from me while there's still a lull in the battle, and I shift back to my human form. Damn, even shifted back my leg looks like shit. At least it's not bleeding anymore. Alaric crouches down at my side, getting eye level with the side of my leg to get a good look at the wounded area.

"It's not bad, D. It looked a lot worse when you were your bear. I'd say give it a few minutes, then shift back." Alaric's fingers gently palpated the angry red skin, checking it for further damage. Alaric double checks the length of the wound twice, and at the very end he finds a solid mass. One finger shifts to a talon, and he cuts my skin open without warning. I grit my teeth and growl through it as he pokes and prods the hole he made. Several moments later, he removes a splinter of the Wyvern's tail spike.

Alaric offers me the splinter once he removes it and all of its fragments. It doesn't matter how fast we heal as shifters, leaving anything in a wound can lead to a massive infection. The screeches fill the air again as another volley of Strigoi comes pouring out of the break in the wall. I drop the splinter and shift back to my bear's form and prepare for battle. The Strigoi spread out, going in all different directions this time. Something changes in their behaviors; the puppeteer is pulling strings a bit differently this time. I just hope everyone else is safe and ready for this next assault.

CHAPTER 30
Dominik

Wave after wave of Strigoi keep coming. It's like the waters rising at the change of the tide. Lycans occasionally attack from behind, but we are lucky that Arnulf's people are in the trees, keeping an eye out for us. We bite and claw our way through the attackers and still, they just seem to keep coming.

Desi, Arnulf's second in command, notices a tunnel near the castle's wall's southern border. Fluidly, he shifts back to his human form and gets dressed quickly. Sword drawn, he approaches the hole cautiously. I walk up beside him and lean against his leg slightly so he knows he has the security of my wolf.

Desi turns his head to look at me and rests his free hand on my back. I move forward and sniff at the tunnel entrance. It reeks of death and stagnant water. It's safe to assume the Lycans with their sensitive noses would not be traveling this way. If anything used this, it would be the Strigoi.

Dante isn't far from where we are, and Desi signals him to come over. Dante ambles over to us, and Desi explains that we want to seal the hole up. Dante's large dragon head lowers to look at the hole, and we watch him tilt his head several times. Dante turns toward an oak tree and bites into it, pulling it out of the ground. Desi and I back up quickly as Dante shoves the tree with its roots down the hole. One problem solved.

Dante raises his head suddenly and launches into the air. Several minutes later, we see why he left so abruptly. A group of Wyverns fly past the castle towers trying to burn our troops. Alaric joins the fight; he's not as big as the War Dragons, but he's more maneuverable than they are. Fire rains down from the sky; screams and howls of pain echo through the valley.

The Wyverns hit some of their targets, but not all of us. I reach out through the pack link, telling my people to take cover under anything they can find. Most of the dragons in our ranks on the ground are opening their wings to provide shelter. Thank the Gods that they are with us. The smell of smoke starts to fill my nostrils, causing me to start to sneeze to try to clear them. The woods are on fire, and currently, we are trapped. We have two choices: enter the castle walls and possibly die or remain in the woods and hope the Ice Dragons can extinguish the fires in time.

I reach out through the bond to Alaric and inform him of our situation. I hear his answering roar in the distance. The ominous beating of wings can be heard long before they are seen. Several Ice Dragons swoop in and start breathing their frost flames, stopping the fire in its tracks. I watch the dragons, and it amazes me how each species' weapons work.

Aurora wanted us to stay out of the castle, but it's getting to the point that it's the next logical decision for us to make. I notice that Dimitri and his bears are starting to knock down more of the wall in the distance, making more sections unstable. The Ice Dragon that is with us sees the instability, lowers his head, and pushes at the stones. The wall starts to crumble and give way, falling in all directions.

The noise and vibrations awaken more Strigoi. I watch them claw their way up and out of the earth in the castle courtyard. It's probably one of the most frightening things I have witnessed in a long time. How many beings have been killed and turned into Strigoi over the years? I hope to live long enough to see my love and brother again.

The Strigoi keep coming and coming like a never-ending flood of death. We can't keep fighting like this, so I give the order to fall back. We need to rest and regroup. I can see the fatigue starting to wear on my troops; this isn't good. My eyes fall on my pack mates, and I can't believe what I'm seeing. They are still determined even though the odds seem stacked against us.

Alaric's roar can be heard echoing through the valley shortly after the sound of paws hitting the dirt can be heard. Our second wave of troops has arrived. Yes! We swap places with the new arrivals and hang back, catching the stragglers. Aurora's plan for splitting up the teams seems to be most effective. Healers move through the ranks at the back, patching up those who need it most first.

Ellis ambles over and shifts back to his human form before me and leans against the nearest tree. "My man, this is the craziest shit I've ever seen! How many deadheads do they have in there?" Ellis flails his arms around then drops them at his side.

I shift back to my human form and look at my flesh slowly, making sure everything is okay. Carefully, I listen to Ellis, and his concerns are quite valid for once. "Well, to be perfectly honest,

I'm not sure. It seems like they have stockpiled an army of Strigoi." Honestly, I'm exhausted, and our outlook seems bleak. I keep looking back towards the wall, watching the others fighting with everything they've got. We really need to find the puppet master and kill them off to stop this flood of Strigoi.

I signal Desi, and he flies over and shifts before landing. "Yes, Dom?" He cants his head, studying Ellis closely.

"Can you send one of your smallest flight shifters to go investigate the towers? I have a feeling one of them holds the person controlling this entire mess. If we can cut off the head, the troops should lose their will to fight." I look from Desi back to Ellis then back to Desi again.

"We have four in our ranks. I can send one to each tower and the others to investigate the castle and courtyard. If they are here, we will find them." Desi looks to me then over to Ellis before shifting and flying off. His calls fill the air, and other calls answer him quickly. Four little Merlin Falcons come flying out of nowhere, blowing past Ellis and me so fast we can barely tell what they were.

"What the fuck is that?" Ellis looks at the little slate-blue streaks that fly past us.

I shake my head and start to laugh at him. "Those were our eyes in the sky—small, incredibly fast, and super agile Merlin Falcons. They're perfect for checking out the towers and castle. Now we just need to wait for Desi to report back if they find anything good." I turn to face the castle, watching the tiny blue blurs buzzing the towers. Occasionally, they stop and hover for a moment, then take off again.

"So, we are basing our future attacks on flying Smurfs?" Ellis asks, sounding exasperated.

"Well, since marshmallows can't fly, yeah, we are relying on flying Smurfs," I smirk, looking at him. I can tell I pissed him off. It's all good; he needs to be knocked down a peg every now and then.

Ellis rolls his eyes and stares at the battle before us. "Fucking marshmallows… When the fuck are we going to live down my fuckup? Fuck, man, it was a bloody example of how bad we stand out here." Ellis suddenly looks defeated; I guess the nickname hurts him more than we knew. I reach out through the bond and fill everyone in quickly.

"Dude, I'm sorry, I'll talk to the others about it." I give him the typical clap on the back and look around the forest, making sure no one is sneaking up on our forces. In the distance, I see movement. it looks like an old Crone moving through the trees.

I reach out through the bond to Alaric and Dimitri. They would be best to help identify the Crone once we're able to get close to her. It doesn't take the guys long to catch up to me, and I point in the direction I saw her go. We take off through the woods; Dimitri and Alaric in their human forms, and me back in my Dire Wolf form. The Crone has the distinct scent of patchouli oil and saffron. She's easy to track, which in hindsight is quite concerning.

Alaric stops short and begins to look around. "It's a trap!" We're quickly surrounded by ten Lycans and the Crone on the hill.

How the ever-loving hell did they get the drop on us? I whip my head from left to right, trying to determine my best course of action. Dimitri rolls his neck and draws his sword, Alaric mimics him, and they stand back to back. Me, I bare my canines at the Lycans. They don't know if I have venom or not. It becomes clear that this was a last-minute attack. Even though the beasts look vicious, their body language screams uncertain. I relay what I see to my bond mates, and we are in agreement. They do not present a united front, and we will use that to our advantage.

Several Lycans attack at once, and Alaric and Dimitri move with fluid grace, using their swords to cut through the attackers. I notice between the attacks that they keep dipping their swords back into the scabbards. Ah, I see it now; they have Dire wolf Venom in the scabbards.

I lunge at a Lycan coming in from the side, going for his Achilles tendon, and rip it out. There's no running once the tendon is severed. He howls out in pain and tries to chase me with no luck —too bad, so sad. I repeat the process with three more Lycans, downing them so that Dimitri and Alaric aren't overrun.

We finish off the Lycans that were sent to attack us. We carefully begin to track the Crone that happened to disappear again. We find an old shack on the edge of the woods, and it looks like it's been used quite a lot recently. Alaric and Dimitri hang back as I choose to circle the building, investigating it. After two laps around, I come to two conclusions: one, she's definitely in there; two, there's only one visible way in and out.

Dimitri charges the door, and Alaric is at his back to shield him if there's an attack from the side. The door shatters from the force Dimitri hits it with. The Crone screams, and we hear her body hit the ground. There's a six-inch long piece of the door through her shoulder on her right side. In her left hand, a shattered vial that she was preparing to throw at us.

Dimitri grabs the Crone and drags her up onto her feet. Quickly, he ties her hands behind her back and searches her robes. "Boys, I would like to introduce you to the Elder Dame. She's the bitch responsible for the hell our mate has gone through." Dimitri's bear is close to the surface, and his beast's growl can clearly be heard in his voice.

"Easy, big guy... Aurora will be ecstatic if we hold this one alive for her," Alaric says, trying to get through to Dimitri.

I watch as Dimitri battles with his bear, and it seems to be a losing battle for him. "Dimitri, is it? That Lycan whore's guard? I guess you failed that task, didn't you? I could have saved the bitch, but what for? She didn't deserve to be Vladimir's mate," the Elder Dame says, venom dripping with every word she speaks.

There's that moment in time where things just flash before your eyes. Except this time, the world slows down horribly; I can't move fast enough. Dimitri's eyes become that of his bear, and I watch the bones in his face shift. The Elder Dame's hands break free of the bonds, and her nails turn to twisted claws. Even in slow motion, Dimitri still moves faster. One hand grips the Elder Dame's jaw, the other her shoulder. I watch his fingers change and take on the elongated claws of his bear. The Elder Dame's skin flexes then breaks as his claws sink deeply into the muscles and sinew of her neck. The deep crimson rivulets of ichor stream down her neck, streaking her pale-white, withered flesh. We can hear the tearing of sinew and tendons, snapping like breaking rubber bands. Her eyes go wide as she realizes he is going to end her. Little by little, her last spell's strength wanes as her life force escapes her flesh. Alaric and I can almost move again, but still not fast enough to stop Dimitri. With an unearthly roar that rumbles the cabin, he rips the Elder Dame's head free from her shoulders. The spell breaks almost as soon as the Crone's body hits the floor. Dimitri stands there looking like Hercules holding Medusa's head.

"Aurora will forgive me," Dimitri states flatly as he stares into the dead eyes of the Elder Dame's eyes. He stares at her for entirely too long before he spits in her face. His lip curls up as he growls, staring at her. Shaking his head, he storms out the door ahead of us. Something deep down snapped in him; we can only hope that Aurora can heal whatever is broken within him.

CHAPTER 31

Vladimir

As I stand in the tallest tower of the castle, the air carries a chill that seeps through the stone walls, sending shivers down my spine. Despite the cold, my senses are heightened, attuned to every sound and movement in the surrounding area.

With each passing moment, the tension in the air grows palpable, a tangible presence that hangs heavy in the stillness of the tower. I can hear the faint rustle of papers as I slide my hands over the map on my desk, the soft scratch of quill against parchment as I jot down notes.

The map beneath my fingertips is worn and weathered, its surface marked with countless lines and symbols that tell the story of battles fought and victories won. I know every hill and stone for miles around, my mind mapping out potential strategies and defenses with meticulous precision.

But as I switch to a different map, my focus shifts to the courtyard below, where the tombs of the Strigoi lie in silent repose. The weight of their presence hangs heavy in the air, a reminder of the countless lives lost in centuries past.

Lost in thought, I barely register the sound of battling dragons buzzing the tower, their roars echoing off the stone walls. But even as chaos reigns outside, I remain steadfast, my gaze fixed on the maps before me, ready to face whatever challenges may come my way.

"Vladimir?" Tomas says as he leans in the doorframe looking at me.

"Spit it out, leech." I'm so over having these vermin in my castle— look at it, it's in ruins.

"The water is being disturbed in the lower chambers as we speak," Tomas says slowly, stepping into my space.

"Either handle it or ignore it. Don't you see I have a war to win?" I say, practically growling.

TOMAS-

I ROLL MY EYES, make my way out of the office, and start down the spiraling stone stairs. I stand at the opening to the stone wall of the castle. My black eyes scan the forest, looking at all the gathered species battling. Hundreds of my people will die this day, and Vladimir in his ivory tower doesn't care. Hell, several hundred or so Lycans will die today also. Again, the head honcho still doesn't care as long as the usurpers are killed off. I head back inside and down the stairs into the bowels of the tower. I gather some of my people's oldest and leave through a tunnel that we made for ourselves.

I stand at the window, looking out over the carnage around me. My visage gives nothing away, my deepest thoughts a mystery to those around me.

"M'Lord? The Elder Dame has fallen," the young Lycan male says as he lowers his head.

"Really now? Who was strong enough to kill my sister?" I narrow my eyes as I stare at the young man before me.

The young man breathes in deeply and lets his breath out slowly. "It smelled like a bear, a dragon, and a wolf, M'Lord."

"All the Great Bears are dead!! I saw to their extinction myself!" I roar as I flip the nearby table over.

The young male throws himself back against the closest wall, then points out the window. "There, M'Lord... I believe that's the type of bear I scented."

I move quickly to the window and look out. Suddenly the anger fades from me as I stand there in shock. "How? I slaughtered hundreds of them..." I look back to the young Lycan then back out the window. I feel as though I have seen a ghost.

Calmly, the young male Lycan addresses me. "M'lord, what are your orders?"

As I pace the confines of my office, the weight of my delusions bears down upon me like a suffocating cloak. My fingers rake through my hair with frantic desperation, strands tangling beneath my trembling touch. The air hangs heavy with the scent of sweat and fear, my own frenzied breaths echoing in the suffocating silence of the room.

Turning my gaze to the young man before me, I unleash a torrent of madness, each word dripping with venomous fervor. "Everything must die. Send more Wyvern, tell them to burn them to ash. I am king! No one will take that from me!" The sound of my own voice rings in my ears, distorted by the twisted depths of my fractured mind. The young Lycan's eyes widen in horrified realization, his body recoiling instinctively from the palpable aura of insanity that envelops me.

As he retreats from my presence, the weight of my madness follows in his wake, casting a shadow of dread over the castle courtyard. The young Lycan hurries to relay my deranged commands to the waiting Wyvern, his movements quick and furtive, driven by a sense of urgency and dread.

Above, the sky darkens as the Wyvern take flight, their mighty roars echoing through the air as they heed the call to arms. With each beat of their wings, the promise of destruction looms ever closer, a harbinger of chaos descending upon the unsuspecting invaders below.

Meanwhile, the young Lycan slips away into the depths of the castle, disappearing into the shadows as swiftly as he had emerged. Left in his wake is a palpable sense of unease, a lingering reminder of the madness that lurks within the heart of the castle walls.

As I sit at my desk, the scent of ink and parchment fills the air, mingling with the acrid tang of anger that coils within me like a serpent. My fingers trace the lines on the maps before me, their surfaces worn and faded from countless hours of scrutiny. Each contour, each landmark, is etched into my memory, a testament to the land that was once mine to command.

But now, that land lies ravaged and desolate, a mere shadow of its former glory. Rage simmers beneath my skin, a relentless fire fueled by betrayal and loss. I clench my jaw, grinding my teeth together in a futile attempt to contain the torrent of emotions raging within me.

In my hand, I hold a small braided piece of cloth, a relic of a time long past. Once, it held the sweet scent of Aurora, a reminder of the daughter I had longed for with every fiber of my being. But now, that scent is but a distant memory, a cruel reminder of the dreams that were shattered by deceit and treachery.

Grief washes over me like a tidal wave, threatening to drown me in its depths. The loss of my daughter, my blood, fills me with a profound sense of emptiness and despair. But beneath the grief lies a simmering fury, a primal instinct to seek vengeance against those who have wronged me.

With a growl of frustration, I push aside the maps and rise from my seat, my movements tense and coiled with barely contained rage. The weight of centuries of betrayal bears down upon me, a burden too heavy to bear alone. And in that moment, I can't help but wonder if my ally, Lucian, relished the opportunity to rid the world of Nicodeamus, just as he claimed.

But for now, vengeance will have to wait. There are battles yet to be fought, enemies yet to be vanquished. And as I stand on the precipice of war, I vow to reclaim what is rightfully mine, no matter the cost.

As I sit at my desk, the smooth surface cool beneath my fingertips, I retrieve the white scales sent to me as proof of my enemy's demise. They feel weighty and substantial in my hands, each one a testament to my victory. I run my fingers over their surface, tracing the intricate patterns etched into the scales, my senses heightened as I immerse myself in the moment.

The scales emit a faint scent, reminiscent of earth and blood, a lingering reminder of the battle that was waged. I bring them closer to my face, studying them closely, the faint aroma stirring memories of triumph and vindication.

With a sense of satisfaction, I flip the scales end over end, the movement fluid and rhythmic. They catch the light, glinting softly in the dim glow of my chamber, their pearlescent hue a stark contrast against the darkness that surrounds me.

As I reflect on my accomplishment, a wave of adrenaline courses through my veins, mingling with a heady sense of satisfaction. The taste of victory is bittersweet, tempered by the knowledge of the sacrifices made along the way.

Lost in thought, I can't help but wonder if perhaps I've crossed a line, if my thirst for vengeance has driven me to madness. But in this moment, as I hold the evidence of my enemy's downfall in my hands, all doubts fade away, replaced by a steely resolve to continue on my path no matter the cost.

As I raise my hand, the faint sound of nails shifting to claws fills the air, a subtle reminder of my innate strength and ferocity. The sensation of my nails transforming, becoming deadly and razor-sharp, sends a shiver of anticipation down my spine.

With a satisfied nod, I turn away from the window and return to my desk, the cool surface beneath my fingertips a grounding presence amidst the turmoil of thoughts swirling in my mind. The scent of parchment and ink lingers in the air, mingling with the faint aroma of dried blood, a testament to the battles waged and victories won.

Lost in contemplation, I ponder my next move in the ongoing war, the weight of responsibility pressing down on my shoulders like a heavy cloak. Despite the invaders' relentless attacks, I remain steadfast in my resolve, confident in the strength of my pack and our ability to prevail against all odds.

Tomorrow, I decide, will mark my return to the battlefield. The thought of joining my pack in combat stirs a primal excitement within me, igniting the flames of determination that burn deep within my soul.

With a sense of purpose renewed, I lean back in my chair, the creak of wood echoing softly in the silence of the room. Tomorrow, I vow, victory will be ours once again, and the invaders will know the full extent of our fury.

CHAPTER 32

Jayce

As I observe my comrades slip beneath the murky surface, a wave of revulsion washes over me at the thought of plunging into the stagnant depths. The air is heavy with the scent of decay, and I can practically taste the musty, earthy odor that emanates from the water.

With a sinking feeling in the pit of my stomach, I watch as Aurora stands at the mouth of the tunnel, her gaze fixed on Klaus as he disappears beneath the surface. A shiver runs down her spine, visible even from a distance, as she contemplates the dark, forbidding waters before her.

In the dim light filtering through the trees, the water takes on an ominous hue, its surface rippling with unseen currents. It's a stark reminder of the dangers that lurk beneath, hidden from view but ever-present in the depths below.

"Need me to go first, my love?" I speak softly as I approach Aurora. She pivots to face me and smiles.

"I'm good, Jayce. I've just got a lot on my mind. My gut tells me Vladimir is in a tower watching everything. But for the lack of a better reason, we need to clear the castle out. I can't stand to think that those leeches have infested my mother's home all these years." Aurora's beast makes itself known to punctuate her agitation.

"Then that's what we shall do." Gently, I caress her shoulder then pull her in close for a hug. My Queen, my love, my life, I would move heaven and hell for this woman in my arms. I may not be the warrior my brother is, but I'm deadly in my own rights.

Aurora looks up to me, and a smile slowly creeps its way across her crimson lips. Her eyes are that of her beast and slowly fade to their human steel-grey. "I love you, Jayce. Thank you for being my rock and my comfort." I watch her raise up onto her tippy toes and place a feather-light kiss on my lips. I sigh softly at the emotionally tender moment and smile at her. "Let's get going, love, time to fuck some shit up!" Aurora says as she starts to bounce her way over to the tunnel. There's the take-no-prisoners mate I know and love.

As I watch Aurora gracefully slip beneath the surface of the water, a surge of adrenaline courses through my veins. With a deep breath, I steel myself for what lies ahead and plunge into the cold embrace of the water below.

The sensation is jarring, the icy chill seeping into my bones as I begin to descend into the murky depths. My senses come alive as I immerse myself in this underwater world, my eyes adjusting to the dim light filtering through the water.

Around me, the underwater landscape unfolds in a mesmerizing display of color and movement. Algae-covered walls line the tunnel, swaying gently in the current like ethereal dancers. Delicate underwater plants reach out with tendrils, their forms twisting and undulating in the water.

Amidst the foliage, tiny fish dart and weave, their shimmering scales catching the faint light. Their movements are swift and graceful, a testament to the vibrant life that thrives beneath the surface.

As we navigate the twisting tunnel, each bend revealing a new vista, I can't help but marvel at the beauty that surrounds us. Despite the darkness and the chill of the water, there is a sense of serenity in this hidden world beneath the waves.

Eventually, we reach a small chamber, a sanctuary of sorts in the midst of our journey. With a sigh of relief, we surface, our lungs grateful for the precious air above.

As we hover in the cool night air, a sense of tranquility washes over us, a welcome respite from the tension that has gripped us for so long. Each breath we take is crisp and invigorating, the night air tinged with the scent of pine and earth. In the darkness, we can hear the faint rustle of leaves and the distant calls of nocturnal creatures.

Amidst the calm, we check in with our bond mates, the connection between us strong and reassuring. Arnulf's voice cuts through the stillness, his words carrying a weight of authority and urgency. He confirms Aurora's suspicions, informing us that Vladimir has indeed taken refuge in the eastern tower of the castle.

The news sends a shiver down my spine, a palpable sense of unease settling over me. But amidst the apprehension, there is also a glimmer of hope. Desi's small group of Merlin Falcons have provided invaluable intel, their keen eyes spotting the figure of an aged man in the solitary tower.

As we digest this information, a sense of determination settles over us, driving us forward in our mission. With each passing moment, we draw closer to the confrontation that will determine the fate of our loved ones and our pack.

Aurora's eyes flicker and glow; the crackle of purple energy races over her skin as well as a light sheen of frost. Aurora slowly turns and looks at all of us as she's embraced by the ethereal glow. "The Wyvern has been removed from the equation, as well as most of the Lycan force. Our only remaining hurdle is how many Strigoi are left roaming the grounds." Aurora steeples her fingers in front of her, closes her eyes for a moment, and then opens them quickly.

"Once the castle is empty, I will raze the majority of the courtyard and outer towers to the ground with the help of the dragons. When it's time, Jayce, love, I need you to summon all the venom-bearing wolves and Dom. We won't leave Vladimir any possible escape route." Aurora breathes in a slow, measured breath then smiles. Her beast's vicious teeth have descended. "Vladimir is mine." Our team nods slowly, agreeing with Aurora before we start to swim again.

As we navigate through the murky waters and navigate the labyrinthine caverns, the air grows thick with the scent of damp earth and mildew. The sound of our splashing footsteps echoes off of the stone walls, creating an eerie symphony that reverberates through the cavern.

Finally, we reach our destination: an old armory hidden deep within the depths of the cave. The air is heavy with the musty aroma of rust and decay, mingling with the metallic tang of old weapons. With each step, the water laps at our legs, sending ripples cascading through the dimly lit chamber.

Aurora's movements are deliberate and purposeful as she surveys the remnants of the armory. The dim light casts long shadows across the room, adding to the sense of foreboding that hangs in the air. Despite the destruction wrought by years of neglect and moisture, the remnants of the armory still hold a haunting beauty.

As Aurora reaches under a ragged cloth, a glimmer of excitement dances in her eyes. With a sense of reverence, she retrieves two large maces from their resting place. The weight of the weapons feels solid and reassuring in my hands as she passes one to Klaus and the other to me.

In this moment, surrounded by the relics of a bygone era, I can't help but feel a surge of determination. Armed with these ancient weapons, we stand ready to face whatever challenges lie ahead, united in our quest for justice and redemption.

"Arnulf, love, can you take a quick flight through the lower level and let us know what we're dealing with down here?" Arnulf simply nods and starts to strip. I can't get over the lithe planes of his body—he's defined and sleek like most flight shifters. His skin is sun-kissed and bears very few visible scars. I hear Aurora giggle and realize that I'm busted; she's caught me staring at Arnulf. Klaus also looks quite sheepish as he tries to act like he wasn't looking either.

Out of all of us, I believe that Arnulf has the most beautiful shift. His bird seems to just emerge into existence, unlike the rest of us where our beasts break our bodies. Aurora is left holding Arnulf's belongings while he goes and scouts ahead for us. We remain still standing in the knee-deep water. Every movement sends out ripples, traveling who knows how far through the water.

It seems like forever before Arnulf returns and shifts back to his human form. Aurora helps him dress before he starts speaking, "For the most part, we are alone down here. I did, however, find a mass grave in one of the chambers. It appears it's one of the burial sites for the Strigoi. Light covers the entire room so they cannot rise if they wanted to. Unfortunately, for our teams outside, the trees provide enough cover for the leeches to move about." Arnulf digs in his bag and pulls out herbs and bottles. "We need to fill these bottles with water and put the herbs in. The herbs are blessed and will kill the Strigoi in their slumber. We will sanctify the earth, thus killing them in the process." Arnulf nods, sure of his statements.

"You heard the man." I say, then look toward the door and make a sweeping motion. "Lead the way, Arnulf. You're in charge."

Arnulf looks at me, shocked, and then begins to move forward. Klaus quickly grabs him by the shoulder and stops him. Klaus makes the shh motion with his index finger to his lips. My eyes fall to the water, and I watch the ripples moving toward us. Someone, or something, is walking around down here, and it's not one of ours.

Aurora reaches out through the bond to me, Klaus, and Arnulf. *Draw your swords slowly and quietly, just in case. Stay clear of the door. If I have to, I will use my breath weapon on whatever is trying to get in here.* We nod and motion to the others to get ready.

We can hear the faint click of Aurora's ignitor fire, and her eyes blaze with the power of the ancient. She is one hundred percent in seek and destroy mode. Gradually, the door opens; whoever is pushing on it is quite hesitant. When the door is three-quarters of the way open, a teenage boy sticks his head into the room. Aurora immediately freezes him in his place and covers his mouth with ice so he can't scream.

The young male is frightened, and his scent screams Lycan. Aurora growls deep in her chest. Her oppressive Alpha power fills the small room, making those not in our bond start to whine. She moves with an unearthly grace and gets right in the face of the young Lycan. She uses the wolves pack link to speak directly into the mind of the pup. Klaus and I can hear her clear as day. *Who sent you?* She growls out as she stares at him.

The young male starts to cry and pisses himself from fear. *Vladimir. My entire family has died today. I don't want to die in his war. Please tell me you're the ghost-wolf sent to kill him."* His eyes convey all the pain and anguish he is feeling. Aurora smirks and frees the boy.

"Gus, take the boy back through the tunnels to safety. Give him to Dominik." Aurora reaches into her hair and cuts free a small white braid. She reaches out and fastens the braid to the boy's wrist. "Show this to my mate, Dominik, and to my dragon mate, Alaric. You are safe now, pup." In an uncharacteristic move, Aurora grips the boy behind his neck and presses her forehead to his. "Go" is the last word spoken to the boy and to Gus.

"That was odd," I say softly, thinking I wasn't heard.

Aurora smirks and looks at me. "He's of my grandfather's blood-line, diluted but related to me. One of his parents was probably a product of one of the old king's flings with the help." Aurora shrugs her shoulders then starts through the door into the lower chambers.

Room by room, we clear them, ensuring nothing that isn't part of our team lived. Twenty-some odd rooms later, we come to the chamber in question. We take every precaution in securing the room. So far, no hidden passages or other ways in and out have been found. Arnulf gathers his herbs, and we all take turns filling the flasks up with water for him to bless and sanctify the ground. As the last grave receives the blessed herbs, screams and howls start to rise from the soil below. Arnulf continues with the blessing ritual with Aurora at his side as his personal guard.

Several Strigoi attempt to rise, and we decapitate them immediately. Aurora stands like a sentinel over Arnulf. She's watching over him, making sure nothing interferes with the important work he's trying to accomplish. I can feel it in my very being when Aurora starts reaching out to every mate in our bond. I feel her tug on the threads that bind us, making sure each one of us is okay. Her breathing hitches when she senses what has occurred with Dimitri.

A twisted smile plays upon her angelic lips. *I want her head*, is all Aurora says through the bond before we hear the answering roar of Dimitri's bear.

It shall be done. The link fades quickly after that, and Aurora's determination to end this war is doubled.

"We are done here, my love," Arnulf speaks softly as he looks up to Aurora from where he is kneeling on the ground before her.

Aurora slowly turns and looks at Arnulf with so much love and adoration, it makes my heart swell. She extends her hands to him, offering assistance to stand. Hesitantly, Arnulf accepts her help and stands, and she promptly kisses him then sets him loose. "Okay, now that the leeches are under control and the lower level is secure, let's head upstairs and clear out the next level," Aurora states, leaving no room for argument or questions. The Aurora we all know and love is back with a vengeance, and she seems ready to rain hell on earth.

We watch her walk out of the room with Arnulf reluctantly in tow behind her. We stand there collectively watching her walk out; she's a woman on a mission with a beast out for blood. On to the next level, I suppose. Here we go again.

CHAPTER 33
Klaus

As we ascend the stairs, each step is a deliberate movement, executed with precision to minimize any sound that might betray our presence. The musty scent of aged wood fills the air, mingling with the faint aroma of dust that hangs in the stale atmosphere of the castle.

My heart pounds in my chest, the adrenaline coursing through my veins heightening my senses. Every creak of the stairs beneath our feet reverberates through the silence like a thunderclap, urging us to proceed with caution.

As we reach the first floor, I peer cautiously around the corner, my senses on high alert. The dim light filtering in through the windows casts eerie shadows along the corridor, obscuring any potential threats that may lurk in the darkness.

A faint sound reaches my ears, a soft shuffling that sends a chill down my spine. With a series of hand signals, I communicate to my companions the presence of someone nearby, prompting them to prepare for whatever may lie ahead.

In a seamless display of coordination, Arnulf begins to shed his clothing, his movements fluid and silent. With a sense of anticipation, I watch as he transforms into his avian form, his majestic wings stretching out before he takes flight, disappearing into the darkness beyond the doorway.

With Arnulf scouting ahead, we wait in tense anticipation, our senses on high alert as we prepare to navigate the unknown dangers that lie in wait within the depths of the castle.

We wait patiently, hiding in the darkness of the hallway in which we are standing. The top landing is a little crowded with all of us standing here. Still, we should be all together waiting then to hastily charge out into the hallway into the unknown. After what seems like forever, Arnulf comes back to us, landing and shifting back to his human form. Aurora assists him, and he gets dressed quickly before he begins to speak to us. "It appears that there is a much stronger Lycan presence on this floor. At least two dozen, if not more. Aurora, do you think you can make them submit? Klaus?" Arnulf's eyes dart between mine and Aurora's.

"If we combine our Alpha powers together, without a doubt we can drive them to their knees and make them submit to us and our will. The real question is, though, will they be loyal enough to be trusted to live, or is it more humane just to kill them now and end their suffering at Vladimir's hands?" I rest my hands on my hips, looking back and forth between my sweet mate and our even more delicious Omega. I know in my heart of hearts, Jayce does not like us killing without provocation. But I also know that Aurora will kill without question to keep what's hers safe and do it for the greater good. My eyes drift over to Arnulf, who is the newest of our group, to see exactly where his heart and intentions lie.

Aurora simply nods then looks between Jayce and Arnulf. "Out of all of my mates, the two of you are the most in touch with your emotions and feelings. I would love to be able to save everyone." Aurora sighs then begins again.

"Realistically, though, it may not be the best decision to make at this time. On the one hand, I see the possibility of expanding the bloodlines available to the Lycans in Klaus's clan." Aurora holds up her left hand.

"On the other hand, I see possible dissension in the ranks and potential uprisings in the future." She raises her right hand and makes a see-saw motion.

"The possibility of traitors in our midst just like it was with the American Lycan pack. Extinction should never be an answer, but in times of war, we must do what is best for the greater good," Aurora says with great finality. Her word is law, and her law dictates the masses' safety over the preservation of a few. For a moment, I see a sadness creep across her visage, and just as fast as it's seen, it flickers away into that stone-cold-killer gaze.

As I step forward and clasp Aurora's hand, a surge of adrenaline courses through me, heightening my senses to a razor-sharp edge. The cool touch of her skin against mine sends a shiver down my spine, a tantalizing reminder of the bond that binds us together.

Turning to face the others gathered on the landing, I meet their gazes head-on, my eyes locking with each individual in turn. There's a tension in the air, palpable and electric, as we stand on the precipice of something momentous.

With a silent exchange of glances, I convey my unspoken trust in Aurora, my mate. Beneath the surface of her skin, I sense the simmering energy of her beast, coiled and ready to spring into action at a moment's notice. It's a potent reminder of the power she wields, both formidable and awe-inspiring.

Yet, despite the urgency of our mission, we must proceed with caution. We cannot afford to reveal our trump card too soon, lest we tip our hand and alert our enemies to our presence. And so, we stand poised and composed, a picture of unity and determination.

Drawing in a deep breath, I straighten my posture, allowing a surge of confidence to fill me. With a subtle shift of my body, I puff out my chest and square my shoulders, projecting an air of strength and resolve.

"Jayce and I will shift everyone else will remain in your human form with swords at the ready. I will attempt to use my Alpha powers first to make them submit. If they do not subjugate themselves before me, recognizing me as Alpha, then we slaughter them. If they do submit, we will take them to the lower level, and Aurora will seal them into the room that the Strigoi had once been in." I leave no room for argument when I finish my statement.

As I catch Aurora's smile out of the corner of my eye, a surge of warmth spreads through me. Her silent encouragement gives me the resolve I need to face the daunting task ahead. With a playful smirk in her direction, I convey my determination to her before turning my attention back to the group.

Every movement is deliberate, every glance purposeful as I convey the seriousness of the situation. Gone are the days of carefree abandon; now is the time for action, for leadership. I can almost feel the weight of responsibility settling on my shoulders, a tangible reminder of the task at hand.

With a steady gaze, I lock eyes with each member of our group, silently seeking their support and assurance. And one by one, I receive it, their unwavering determination reflecting my own.

With the unspoken acknowledgment of my comrades, a sense of clarity washes over me. The time for hesitation is past; now is the time for action. Together, Jayce and I begin to shed our clothing, preparing to shift and face whatever challenges lie ahead.

As the fabric falls away, I can feel the adrenaline coursing through my veins, heightening my senses and sharpening my focus. The air is charged with anticipation, every nerve tingling with the knowledge that we are on the brink of battle.

As I observe Aurora's reaction, a wry smile tugs at the corners of my lips, mingling with the tension that hangs heavy in the air. Despite the grim reality of our surroundings, there's a brief moment of levity as I catch her gaze wandering over my physique.

The scent of blood and death lingers in the air, a stark reminder of the violence that surrounds us. Yet, amidst the chaos, Aurora's eyes betray a fleeting sense of fascination as they rove over the planes of my muscular-toned body. It's a strange juxtaposition, the juxtaposition of beauty and brutality that defines our existence in this unforgiving world.

I can't help but chuckle softly to myself as I watch her, her gaze flitting between mine and Jayce's frames with a childlike curiosity. In the midst of all the death and bloodshed, she still finds time to appreciate the male form, a testament to her resilience and strength of spirit.

But my amusement is short-lived as I clear my throat, breaking the spell and drawing her attention back to my face. A faint blush colors her cheeks for a fleeting moment before she rolls her eyes playfully, her focus shifting once more to Jayce.

Her lack of shame brings another soft chuckle to my lips, a brief respite from the darkness that threatens to consume us all. And as my body begins to contort and reshape into the form of my Lycan.

As I glance to my left, I catch sight of Jayce mid-transformation, his muscles rippling beneath his skin as he shifts into his Dire Wolf form. The air is charged with tension, anticipation hanging thickly around us like a heavy shroud.

Despite the gravity of the situation, I can't help but admire Jayce's form, his physique sculpted and powerful. His movements are fluid and graceful, a testament to the strength and agility inherent in his lupine nature.

My senses are heightened, the scent of earth and pine mingling with the musky aroma of the shifting bodies around us. Adrenaline courses through my veins, heightening my awareness and sharpening my focus on the task at hand.

But amidst the chaos and tension, there's an undeniable undercurrent of desire that pulses through me. Jayce's playful smirk and wink plays in my mind only serve to stoke the flames of my arousal, igniting a fire within me that burns hot and fierce.

For a fleeting moment, I allow myself to indulge in the primal allure of the moment, the raw energy of the impending battle fueling the flames of passion that rage within. But even as desire courses through me, I know that now is not the time for distractions. We stand on the brink of war, and our focus must remain unwavering if we are to emerge victorious.

In typical Aurora fashion, she rolls her eyes at the two of us. It's as if she can't believe that we were ogling each other. After all, she's the one who gave us permission to be intimate outside of her bedroom, and besides, she started the ogling first. Jayce motions with his head towards the doorway as if provoking me to go first. Well, you don't have to ask me twice to go on the attack. We charge out side-by-side, taking the unsuspecting Lycans out quickly. Alpha power be damned; they had silver weapons ready with the full intention of using them. Aurora casually strolls out into the hallway and surveys the scene before her. She just leans against the wall, watching us rip our enemies apart. It's not like her to hang back, but then again, the larger half of the battle still rests on her shoulders when we find Vladimir.

Arnulf and the two last Dire Wolves that are with us come walking out into the hallway, drawing their swords and dispatching those that are still moving. The first room is a quick cleanup, thankfully. Part of me almost feels bad for them. A lot of them were young, untrained, and had next to no fighting skills. The other half of me knows that in the long run, this was safest for our family to do. After the dissension in the ranks with the American Lycans and all the problems they had caused us, we definitely learned our lesson. The worst part of all the betrayal was discovering we had an assassin living amongst my people. We can't take that chance again; we can't take the chance that we won't be so lucky the next time and that everybody survives the attack.

I motion with my clawed hand towards the back of the room, where there's a single door that appears to be closed. Aurora gives me a slow nod and sends Jayce and his two pack mates to investigate the door. A low growl rumbles deep in Jayce's chest. His hackles stand on end as his muscles bunch, and he lowers his body to the ground—he's ready to launch. His pack mates split up and draw their swords, one on either side of the door. We start stalking closer, and then I notice Jayce is counting off when to open the door. His tail taps the ground—one, two, three—and the door is suddenly thrown open; he lunges inside quickly into the darkness. His pack mates follow closely on his heels, providing backup for him. I rush over, only to find the entire room has already been decimated. Jayce and his pack mates have killed off another ten hidden attackers.

Today has been a day of many firsts. The biggest one that I take note of is that Aurora is not leading the charge this time. She's hanging back, watching every single move that everyone is making in her presence. Not to say that Aurora hasn't raised her sword several times to deflect the blows of those who tried to sneak up behind us, but abnormally, Aurora's not in the thick of it. I can count the number of times today that her eyes flickered and glowed as she reached out through the bond to the rest of our bond mates, checking up on everyone. In the background, I know she's issuing orders and strategically planning every move that everyone is making outside of the castle walls. I know the exact moment that our dragons start to battle with the Wyvern that are flying overhead. I watch the scales flicker, rising and falling on the flesh of her forearms. The urge to shift and fight is strong; the pull must be incredibly difficult for her to ignore. The internal battle that she must be dealing with having to restrain her beast until the time is absolutely necessary just speaks of her strength. I look over, and I watch my two bond mates that are here with me, each moving independently, both fighting with all that they've got. Our resident eagle is the lightest built out of all of us; he also carries the biggest chip on his shoulder—feeling he's inadequate.

CHAPTER 34
Klaus

We move room to room, clearing out any and all that we find. The death toll on the first floor alone is in the twenties for the other side. I'm not saying that we're coming out of this unscathed but we are doing much better than they are. All the extra training that Nicodeamus and Alaric made us go through is paying off hugely. Vladimir's men were not expecting us to remain in our human forms and to be using swords. I know that they trained for hand-to-hand and beast-on-beast battles. We're kicking it old school and bringing the pain with the metal of our blades. Not to say that Jayce and I didn't have a fun time letting our animals loose to tear through the small rabble that was waiting for us in the foyer.

The first floor is cleared quickly, and there are two sets of stairs leading up to the second floor. We divide our team into two sets of three. Aurora and I take one of the Dire Wolves with us. Jayce, Arnulf, and the other Dire Wolf go up the other flight of stairs. I watch Aurora's eyes flicker, knowing that she is speaking with

Jayce directly, trying to figure out exactly where they are in relation to the landing for the second floor.

"It's time to go. They're ready. Let's move." Aurora is very concise in her statement giving the order to move without hesitation.

As we ascend to the second floor, the air feels heavy with anticipation, each step echoing softly in the dimly lit corridors. I strain my senses, trying to pinpoint the location of our comrades through the unspoken connection we share. Though they're not within immediate sight, I can sense their presence lingering tantalizingly close, a comforting reassurance in the midst of uncertainty.

Beside me, Aurora's restlessness is palpable, her hand flexing nervously at her side. I imagine the faint click of her gauntlet's talons tapping against each other in agitation, a silent testament to her impatience. It's as if she's a caged tiger, her primal instincts urging her to pounce upon her prey, even as it remains just out of reach.

The tension in the air is almost suffocating, each passing moment stretching on like an eternity. Though the endgame is within sight, it still feels frustratingly distant, teasingly out of reach. For Aurora, the desire for victory burns bright, a hunger that cannot be sated until she can taste the sweet fruits of triumph.

I can't imagine what it's been like for her for the last almost two-hundred and thirty years of training and preparing for this day to finally come. I know that Dimitri has trained her well. She wouldn't be as lethal as she is if it weren't for him and his training. That man has been so many things to her: friend, guardian, trainer, disciplinarian, and now mate. He has seen Aurora at her best and at her absolute worst. I can't imagine what's going through his mind right now, with her being so far out of reach. All of our protective instincts are heightened when it comes to her. Still, he's had over two-hundred years of protective instincts ingrained into the very fiber of his being. He doesn't know anything other than protecting her at all costs and loving her unconditionally. I watch my warrior queen, my beautiful angel, stand there as she plots which way for us to go.

As Aurora leads the way down the dimly lit hallway, a sense of urgency permeates the air, palpable in the tension that hangs between us. The faint echo of our footsteps reverberates off the cold stone walls, a constant reminder of the perilous journey that lies ahead.

With each step, the musty scent of age-old dust fills my nostrils, mingling with the faint aroma of decay that lingers in the air. The corridor seems to stretch on endlessly, shrouded in shadows that dance and flicker in the dim torchlight.

Aurora's determination is evident in the set of her jaw and the determined glint in her eyes. She moves with purpose, her every movement calculated and deliberate as she leads us forward.

As we reach the spot where Jayce and the other team should be, a sense of unease settles over me like a heavy shroud. The passageway ahead is sealed off, a stark reminder of the obstacles that lie in our path. It's clear that someone, at some point, has taken measures to impede our progress, adding another layer of complexity to our already perilous mission.

As Aurora motions for us to step back, a surge of anticipation courses through me, mingling with the palpable tension in the air. Her eyes briefly illuminate with an otherworldly glow, a silent command communicated through their gleaming depths. I can almost feel the energy crackling around us, charged with the promise of impending destruction.

With a knowing glance in my direction, Aurora's smirk speaks volumes, a silent acknowledgment of the power she is about to unleash. The rhythmic clicking of the igniter reverberates through the air, a precursor to the cataclysmic display about to unfold.

As Aurora steps back, a surge of energy builds within her, culminating in a dazzling spectacle of light and frost. Her breath weapon erupts from her throat in a torrent of purple lightning tinged with frost, an awe-inspiring display of raw power and elemental fury.

I watch in awe as the stones before us crumble and disintegrate under the force of Aurora's onslaught, reduced to nothing more than a pile of dust and ash. The air is thick with the smell of scorched earth and ozone, the remnants of Aurora's devastating assault lingering in the air.

For a fleeting moment, time seems to stand still as we take in the aftermath of Aurora's display. The magnitude of her power leaves me utterly speechless, a testament to the strength and determination of my mate. As the dust settles and silence descends upon the scene, I am left in awe of the indomitable force that stands before me. Everything that her breath weapon touched is still crumbling and falling to the ground in a heap of dust and ash. I stand there, utterly amazed at the new power that my mate wields.

Aurora calls down the stairwell, beckoning Jayce and his team to come up, telling them that it's safe now. The look of shock and awe on my bond mate's faces is more than enough to confirm that, like me, they had no clue she was able to do this. Aurora studies the structural stability of what's left of the wall in front of us and motions for us to move quickly away from it, not trusting how far the stone will disintegrate.

As we advance down the dimly lit hallway, tension hangs thick in the air, suffusing the atmosphere with an almost palpable sense of apprehension. Every step echoes loudly against the stone walls, reverberating through the corridor like a foreboding drumbeat.

Rounding the corner, we are met with the chilling sight of four formidable Lycans standing before us. Time seems to stand still as we lock eyes with our adversaries, each of us frozen in a tense standoff. The air crackles with an electric energy, charged with the anticipation of imminent conflict.

In the silence that follows, Aurora's smirk cuts through the tension like a knife, a harbinger of the impending storm. With a slow, deliberate movement, she raises her right hand, a gesture laden with ominous significance.

As her hand ascends, a sudden chill permeates the air, sending shivers down our spines. Ice crystals materialize with startling rapidity, forming a frosty shroud around Aurora's hair before cascading outward in a relentless wave. In a matter of seconds, the four Lycan males are ensnared in a prison of ice, their forms rendered motionless and helpless against the frigid embrace.

The scene unfolds with an eerie sense of inevitability, the icy grip of Aurora's power serving as a chilling reminder of the ruthless determination that drives us forward. In the face of such raw elemental force, resistance seems futile, and we are left to confront the grim reality of our mission with a heavy heart.

"I'm not completely heartless. These males are young and could quite possibly be saved. They'll hibernate for now; we'll deal with them later." This act of mercy that we have just witnessed is rare, especially with all things considered. Aurora moves swiftly down the hallway to the next room that's on her left. She pauses at the door and then motions for the Dire Wolves to come up to sniff at it. Silently, Aurora draws her sword and gives us a nod that she's ready to go in. Aurora suddenly kicks the door open and flails her sword as she charges into the room. We follow swiftly behind her, but by the time we enter, the room looks like a winter wonderland as most of it is encased in various degrees of ice. Several young Lycan males are frozen in ice up to their jaws, immobilizing them. I get to observe my mate put the young males into deep hibernation. She takes excellent care preserving their lives for now, until we can determine if they should be spared or not later. Four older males lie dead by Aurora's sword and the bites from the Dire Wolves at her side.

I survey the scene quickly; this appears to be one of the primary studies in the castle. Through the bond, I alert Alaric to the discovery that we have just made. Ancient tomes line the western wall from floor to ceiling. Their age is apparent by the thick leather casing in which the pages are bound. Undecipherable glyphs line the spines of the tomes. From what Alaric can relay to me quickly, these tomes are probably thousands of years old and can bear witness to the magic of ages. Answers to how and why the different blood magics work on the different species may be found within these walls.

Arnulf digs deeply into his bag and pulls out two flasks and a large chunk of meat. Aurora comes to his side, takes a container and the flesh. She begins to gorge herself on what she's been presented with. I happen to find out that the flasks are filled with blood and vodka to help prevent coagulation. She hasn't used the full magnitude of her power yet, but the biggest fight is yet to come. It is wise that she sits here and refuels while she can. She waves off the second flask and tells him to hold it till later. For now, she's content, and the room is secure.

She motions for us to leave the room, and once we're all out, she closes the door and encases it in ice, making sure that nobody else can gain entrance. Satisfied with her work, she puts her sword away and begins down the hallway again, heading towards the next room that we need to clear. We repeat the process several more times on this floor until we have the entire second floor under our control. We double back to the staircase that we used to get to this floor, and she seals both entrances with ice.

On the northern side of the second floor is the staircase, which leads to the third and final floor in this part of the castle. A silent conversation is held between Aurora and Jayce before he and his two pack mates head up the stairs before us. We hear a growling begin above us, signaling that Jayce and his pack mates have found more attackers.

Cautiously, we approach the landing, and to my surprise, Jayce and his pack mates have it all under control. Only two attackers met them at the landing, and they were dispatched quickly. Aurora approaches Jayce slowly and runs her fingers through his thick fur. Her right hand gently caresses his left ear as she moves past him and into the hallway.

We watch Aurora's eyes flicker as she moves down the hall. She's always looking over her shoulder, checking where all of her people are at all times. "The dragons have taken control of the courtyard. We just need to clear the castle then take over the towers. Arnulf, you take the lead on the third floor; we've got your back." Arnulf nods then heads into the hallway and draws his sword.

"Let's finish up here so we can go the hell home." Arnulf smirks then catches up with Aurora and moves slightly ahead of her.

Just like that, Arnulf takes the lead, and we follow behind them. It's coming to the end of our journey, and now we work on clearing the final floor.

CHAPTER 35

Arnulf

I'm ecstatic that my bond brothers see me as someone capable of running the mission on the third floor. I pass Aurora and give her a smile and a slight nod as I walk past her. She smiles at me, seemingly impressed that I decided to take point on this part of the mission.

I have to admit, I'm kind of having second thoughts here. I'm not a warrior like Aurora, Klaus, or Jayce. I'm not built as heavy as the three of them. I don't have the bulk or the strength of their beasts. What I do have on my side is speed and agility. I approach the first door that is on my left-hand side. I lay my hand gently upon the wood, feeling for any kind of vibrations or disturbances with it. With my heightened sense of hearing and eyesight, I notice that the door has been moved. More than likely, someone has entered the room probably within the last twenty-four hours. I motion to the Dire Wolves to approach the door and take a sniff at it.

Just as I suspected, the room is loaded with our enemies. From what Jayce can tell me through the bond, there has to be at least eight to ten wolves in there waiting for us. There are only six of us in our group currently since we sent Gus back with the young male earlier.

Aurora smirks, hearing the internal dialogue between Jayce and me. She bends down and presses her hand to the floor, sending a wave of ice into the room. Within seconds we hear the howls of pain echo from inside. Aurora looks up to me and smirks before freezing the locked door. Aurora stands up, then looks at Klaus and motions to the frozen door. With a decisive nod, Klaus comes forward quickly and rams the door with his shoulder, shattering it. Icy wood splinters fly across the frozen floor and stop when they hit the now-frozen Lycans. This isn't the ice of hibernation; this is a killing blow.

Aurora motions to the room and then looks between Klaus and me. "Off with their heads," she says like the Red Queen in the fairy tale.

I watch Aurora prowl the room, looking through all the desk's draws and cabinets. Klaus gets to work almost immediately, and I watch him in almost abject horror. How can he be at peace with this? My eyes drift down to my sword, and I stare at it for several minutes. I hear a faint click and something sliding open. Quickly, I lift my gaze in time to see the barrel of a gun being pointed at Aurora. Without hesitating, I take my sword and throw it at the person in the hidden passage. I nail the arm that was holding the gun to the wooden frame. The gun falls to the ground almost instantly, luckily not going off in the process. Aurora spins quickly, shocked to see that someone had gotten the drop on her.

"Do you know who I am, bitch?" he screams as he tries to free his arm.

Klaus moves in to flank Aurora as she hops up to sit on the desk. I watch her arms shift, and the ice races from the floor and door frame, trapping the male in place. "Should I?"

Aurora sits there looking her talons over, studying them intently. She's barely giving the male the time of day, aggravating him further. Her beast's eyes scrutinize every scale and curvature of her long talons. The way she's looking at them and her gauntlets, it's clear that she is doing it on purpose just to agitate the male before her.

The eyes of the male's wolf blaze to life as he stares at her. The veins in his temples throb angrily as his face starts to turn bright red from the anger that is building. "I am Josef, brother of Vladimir, heir to the Lycan throne," he says as he grits and grinds his teeth angrily. His canines are bared at her, looking as if he could launch and attack her at any moment.

Aurora doesn't even bother to lift her gaze to acknowledge the angry male before her. She lets out a huff of breath tinged with frost. Exasperated with the male's attitude, frost starts to cover the desk around her. She crosses and uncrosses her legs twice, wiggling her toes out in front of her as she examines her nail polish. I swear to the gods above that my woman has been sent to personally aggravate the fuck out of this poor bastard. She rolls her eyes slightly and then tilts her head to the side as she looks up at him finally.

"Okay, and what is that supposed to mean to me?" She tilts her head to the side as she stares at him.

"As far as I'm concerned, I'm staring at the brother of the usurper that assisted with the death of my mother. Also, as far as I'm concerned, your brother is a dead man, be that it may be at my talons or my father's." She smiles sweetly at him and tilts her head to the other side.

"You, my friend, are going to die a very slow and painful death," Aurora says slowly, enunciating every word in her final sentence to the male.

She rises slowly from the desk, her bare feet landing on the thin sheet of ice that she has created on the floor. She raises up onto the pads of her feet and walks over to Josef, staring at him at eye level. She doesn't even bother keeping her eyes shifted anymore. Her pale-grey, human eyes stare into the eyes of his beast, and she just smiles at him.

Then we feel the sudden influx of her Alpha power being forced onto this male. We watch him attempt to fight it, but it's a losing battle, his sad attempt to maintain eye contact. He apparently thought that just because she's a female means she's not strong enough to make him submit. That was his first and last mistake— assuming she is like any other female that ever walked this Earth. Yeah. He just doesn't know.

She is the first of her kind, but the last of her name. There is no equal to my mate. Aurora is making this male want to bow and genuflect before her. It doesn't help that I had nailed his arm to the wall with my sword. He would probably be in a tight ball on the ground instead of standing, whining and whimpering like the wuss that he is.

Aurora looks at the sword and how badly he's pulling on his arm. He's trying to drop down to his hands and knees to save himself from the power she's bathing him in. She places her hand on the sword and quickly pulls it free from the wall making sure to slice his arm a little further than it was previously. He's already in an extreme amount of pain from the power that she's pressing on him; the additional slice to his arm is barely even registered by him.

Aurora hands me my sword and smiles ever so sweetly at me. One would think that she's borderline insane. Aurora can flip back and forth between being a vicious monster and then back to the sweet angel that we know behind closed doors in seconds. Her eyes bore into Josef as she stares at him curled up on the ground. His blood is slowly painting the wood floors crimson, and it brings a smile to her ruby-red lips. He's one of Vladimir's bloodline; therefore, he must die. Boy, this is going to be an interesting one. She releases the grip of power that she has on him. Immediately after, he starts coughing and sputtering. He struggles to draw in a deep breath after being released from the oppressive force. He digs his now-shifted claws into the wood to try to help himself stand up.

Aurora just stands there smirking at him. We watch this massive male try to stand up as weak as a newborn calf. "You are no Alpha. You're not even strong enough to be considered an Omega in the pack." Aurora waves her hand dismissively in his direction. "How dare you even think that you are male enough to stand before me."

As soon as she finishes speaking, Aurora sends another wave of her Alpha power down upon him. Josef crashes to the floor much faster and harder than he did the first time. She stares at him with sadistic glee. I can only imagine what Aurora's going to do to Vladimir when she finds him. I didn't know my mate was capable of this level of cruelty that she's inflicting on him, but then again, he was sent to kill her if he found her.

"My love, we still have so much more to search for," I say to her gently, hoping to appeal to her on some base level to remind her of the mission that we have before us.

Klaus decides to speak up at this moment also. "My angel, my love, do you wish me to end him for you?' He gently places his hand on her lower back, offering support. "That way you don't bother getting your talons dirty with this scum's blood," he says to her ever so sweetly.

Aurora seems to contemplate his offer for several moments before she shakes her head no. Aurora's eyes take on a feral appearance. I feel the tension through the bond as our other mates reach out, sensing her rage. They use the bond to see through her eyes to see what or who stands before her. The click-click-click of her talons reverberates in the room as she contemplates precisely how she wishes to end Josef's life. Through the bond, I hear her speaking to herself. She's debating between ripping out his heart or taking his head and then the third option of both.

I understand the need and the pressure of her being judge, jury, and executioner when it comes to those who have betrayed her bloodline. Things would have been much different for all of us if Aurora's life hadn't been disrupted the way that it had. Aurora moves slowly around the male that's before her. The tension is thick, and I can feel the weight that's upon her shoulders. Suddenly, she reaches down and shifts her hand back to human as she grips the back of Josef's neck. She lifts him off the floor and dangles him in front of us. His feet aren't touching the ground, and I can see the tension in all of her muscles as she struggles to hold him up in her human form.

Then it happens. Her body starts to bend and break and shift into that of her enormous, white Lycan. Now holding the male off of the ground is absolutely no problem. Her talons slightly dig into the flesh of his throat as she wiggles him a little bit. He makes the stupidest move in the history of stupid moves—he decides to take this moment to shift. I know it's a last-ditch effort to save himself from the death that is surely upon him. He just doesn't seem to realize he just switched her into full-on predator mode. There are a few major issues with our current situation. One, she has three mates in the room with her. Two, he poses a threat to her family just by breathing. And finally, if I know her, she believes he had a hand in her abduction and everything that's happened since.

The much-smaller, black Lycan male turns slowly and looks up at the almost ten foot tall, half-ton hybrid standing before him. If a Lycan can smirk, then Aurora is definitely trying not to laugh at the pathetic male before her. I'm guessing Josef is on a suicide mission since he tries to lunge at her, thinking that he may over-power her. The minute his flesh touches hers, he leaps back, howling in pain. Aurora has coated herself in permafrost and burned his flesh instantly because of how cold it is. Through our bond, I can hear Nicodeamus telling Aurora exactly what role in Vladimir's family Josef played. That is more than enough to push Aurora over the edge; two swipes of her talons come at him quickly. The first one disemboweled him, spilling his intestines upon the floor. Aurora stands there, watching the state of panic he is in. Her second swipe comes the minute he looks like he may attack again. Crimson ichor sprays the room, painting her white fur vermillion. After the blood settles, we watch him dangle there with unseeing eyes just before his head rolls free of his shoulders.

I stand there in shock, watching how easily my mate dispatched the man before her. Even though he was purely evil and held nothing but hatred in his heart towards my mate, sometimes I question the necessity of killing our enemies. It's times like this that Dominik usually pulls me aside and explains the failed justice system in most countries. That they would rather sit there and lock people away for the rest of their lives than dish out punishment that matches their crime. The dark ages are long over, and the weights and measures are in their place for a purpose. If we were to attempt to hold a trial, too many species have been harmed or entirely driven to extinction, there would be no unbiased parties available. Nicodeamus says I'm the voice of reason within this bond. But unlike his daughter, my sense of justice is different than hers. While hers is strictly black and white, mine has all the different shades of grey in between. What can I say? Being a Mystic, I have a very soft heart, and I feel that all life that walks this Earth, no matter how sick and twisted it is, has value.

The rest of the third floor appears to be empty. We double check all the rooms, leaving no stone unturned and no door unopened. The final assault on the tower that we know Vladimir is in is upon us. The night is falling quickly, and the unique sounds of the forest are starting to come alive. All the nocturnal creatures are beginning to wake up and go about their evening. Aurora's beast turns and looks at me; her eyes take on that ethereal glow. I watch the crackle of the purple energy coursing through her snow-white fur. She's been waiting for this moment for over two hundred and twenty-nine years. She runs to the open window that's in the hallway. Her talons grip the ancient stones, and she tilts her head back, howling her death song into the night.

Her howl echoes through the valley and the courtyard of the castle, reverberating off of every structure for miles. I turn just in time as Klaus's and Jayce's wolves rip from their bodies at her call. Every wolven ally tilts their head back and answers her. The night is filled with these deep, haunting howls, all of them calling for blood and vengeance. Their death song is sung for the last man left standing that has destroyed a bloodline.

Aurora goes silent for a moment, as if listening to something. She tilts her head slowly left then right. Her grip tightens on the stones under her talons before she throws her head back a second time. This call is unlike anything I've ever heard escape her lips; it's pure dragon. It's a deep, guttural roaring sound that makes the hairs on my arm stand on edge.

Within seconds, the sky is blackened with the wings of the dragons that are on our side. They all begin to roar and unleash their breath weapons into the air. It's a singular show of force to strike fear in the hearts of those who stand against us. The faint click of Aurora's ignitor can be heard, and then she unleashes a stream of what looks like purple lightning and her frost breath. The courtyard practically glows from the color of her breath weapon.

Her eyes now focus across the yard at the last tower that hasn't been touched. Her suffering ends here. Her wait is over; revenge is a short trip across the courtyard. Aurora makes yet another dragon sound before launching herself out the window and into the air. Thankfully, for my poor heart, I see Alaric come swooping in under her and catches her as she starts to free fall. I can feel the pull through the bond that Aurora is summoning every single solitary ally she has brought with her. Without question, I shift and take to the sky. I will not be the last mate left behind simply because my animal can't fight. I will be her eyes. I'll keep watch over her target until she's in place.

CHAPTER 36
Aurora

The time has finally come, and I can exact my revenge on the man who helped steal my mother from me. I look out the third-story window at what used to be, at one time, a grand castle with a beautiful courtyard. I take several moments to appreciate the architecture that's before me. Every stone in this structure was cut, chiseled, and placed by possibly one of my ancestors. Every room had a different feel to it as we explored the castle. I can tell that there'd been additions made over time because of the difference in the technique used to place the stones.

Taking Josef's head, knowing full well that he was probably involved with my abduction, and more importantly, the assault on my mother's people was immense. His death was just an added bonus that has prepared me for my final battle with Vladimir. Part of me, deep down in my heart, I want to capture Vladimir alive. I want to bring him gift-wrapped to my father. I think that is probably the most selfless thing that I can do. I want Vladimir's head and heart; I want Vladimir's skull resting on a pike in my front yard for the birds to shit on for all eternity. My pain is nothing like the pain my poor father has had to endure for the last two hundred and thirty years.

Not only did Vladimir take my father's fertility, but he also took his arm, his wife, his child, and his freedom all in one fell swoop. He may not have been the one to chop my father's arm off physically, but he may as well have been for inviting the Strigoi into the castle.

I grip the stones of the windowsill, sinking my talons into the granite that is under me. I howl my death song into the night, unleashing my full Alpha power. I know full well that I am ripping the wolves free from my allies and my mates. I understand it's an asshole move on my part, but our animals are more in sync when we're all shifted. We move as one as a pack. It's much easier for us as a whole when they can anticipate my next move.

I tilt my head back a second time—this time calling to my dragons, summoning them all to me. I'm ready to rain Hellfire down on those who stand against us. I'm out for blood, and my thirst will not be sated until either Vladimir is dead or in my custody. I answer my dragons' calls when they unleash their breath weapons into the sky as a show of force. I feel the hum of the ancient power that rests within me now. My igniter clicks and I open my maw, unleashing that massive force of energy out of my mouth. I have finally figured out how to combine both of my breath weapons into one massively destructive force. The Force Dragon breath weapon utterly decimates anything that it touches, rendering it to nothing more than dust and ash. The Ice Dragon breath freezes everything it touches. It has varying degrees of cold depending on the intention that I weave with it.

I sense Alaric calling to me through the bond, telling me now is the time to attack. That we must get to the tower before he makes any attempt to escape. I can't agree with my mate more. I launch myself out of the window, knowing full well that he would never let me fall. I make sure that when Alaric is under me, I protect him by curling my hands so that my talons don't rip into his scales. He flies me close to the tower, and I leap off, landing about a quarter of the way up the tower stones. We have several smaller dragon species that would be able to fit climbing up the tower staircases. I send three of them up, accompanied by my mate, Dominik, and five other Dire Wolves.

Through the bond, I show my mates precisely what I intend to do. Klaus volunteers to be the one to go up the stairwell with the dragons behind him to be able to get Vladimir's attention away from the window in which I plan to go through. I agree, and Alaric goes back quickly, as Klaus makes the jump out of the window, probably scaring poor Arnulf and making him think that the rest of us are absolutely batshit crazy. Arnulf's eagle starts to circle the tower. Through the bond, he tells me he sees a man sitting at a desk. He's moving pewter figures around as if he's still playing out the battle in his head; this bodes well for us.

I wait long enough for Klaus to be in position with the dragons. I advise them to travel slowly so that they don't alert their quarry that they are on their way. Slow and steady, I sink my talons into the granite of the tower. Foot by foot, I climb, my muscles strain and flex, pulling my half-ton beast up the stone wall. I turn my massive head and focus my eyes on my troops down below. Some of the wolves have discovered an escape tunnel and have gone to explore.

My pack tells me of their findings, and I pause my climb to direct them on how they should proceed. Alaric is concerned that I am hanging off the tower's side, having a full-blown conversation instead of finishing my ascent to the window. I shake my head and send my love to the big guy. I know he means well, but my people needed me, so I answered.

Klaus reaches out to me through the bond and tells me that he's three-quarters of the way up the stairs and asks about my progress. I look up, then back down, and realize I'm holding the group up. I laugh softly to myself and begin to climb again. My heart is pounding in my chest—not from fear but excitement. The end of this journey is so close I can almost taste it.

The wind shifts slightly, and I can finally catch the male's scent. It's not much different from Sebastian's and Elena's scents. Vladimir's scent isn't the usual woodsy scent of most of the Lycans. It's a perversion of dragon and rot. He's sick from whatever experiment he's been doing to himself to live past his species' years.

Father? I call out through my bond with my father. I need answers, and I need them now.

Yes, daughter? Nicodeamus's voice echoes in my head. I feel his love and pride when he addresses me.

Vladimir's time has come. I am within striking distance of him. He smells sick. Like rotting dragon blood and death. Is it safe for me to bite him, or should I place my toxin on my talons and cut him? I don't wish to make myself sick in the process of capturing my enemy.

I feel that familiar hum of his dragon, its pensive noise, and the feeling that I know he's in deep conversation with his beast. Though we are one with our animals, sometimes they have secrets that we don't know about.

Don't risk biting him. Cover your talons with your toxin. We are not sure what he's done to himself. It's better to be safe than sorry, Nicodeamus says with a finality that only my father can pull off.

Slowly, my father leaves our connection. Before he goes, I feel his love and pride over who I have become, flooding the bond one last time. Quickly, I reach out to the packs and horde, telling them of what I just learned. I warn Klaus to be extra careful around Vladimir.

Several moments pass, and I am poised just below the window. Everyone is in position; my dragons are waiting for my signal. Carefully, I lift one hand at a time off of the stones and run my talons along the length of my canines, covering them with the toxin Jayce has gifted me with. Once I am sure each talon is sufficiently coated, I tell Klaus to knock on the door.

The moment of truth is upon us. I hear Klaus knock and then the shuffling of papers on the desk. A chair slides along the wooden planks of the floor. And the sound of a lock being disengaged prompts me to climb up to the windowsill and slide silently into the room. In my head, I can hear the guitar intro for "Hail to the King" from A7x. The lyrics fill my head as I sing it through the bond.

The world seems to move in slow motion from this point on—pivotal times seem to do that. I watch Vladimir's hand extend and grasp the doorknob and turn it to the left. My heartbeat thunders in my ears, almost drowning out the music. Vladimir opens the door; inch by inch, I begin to see Klaus. My beast looms over Vladimir, looking down on his sickly form. I can tell by his bone structure he was once an impressive male. Now he's a sick and twisted husk walking around due to unnatural magics used to extend his lifespan.

The door opens fully, and I see Klaus standing there with his sword drawn and dripping with venom. Vladimir backs up and walks into my beast. My taloned hands rest now on his shoulders as I sink the tips into his flesh. My growl is deep—almost demonic sounding because of the mix of dragon and wolf. I fling the once-mighty ruler across the room and into the bookcase on the opposite side. A sickening crunch is heard as his body breaks the wood and probably several bones.

While he lies on the floor, I shift back to my human form and steal Klaus's flannel shirt from him. I dress quickly, roll the sleeves up above my elbows and turn my forearms and hands back to my gauntlets. From past experience, I know I look like my mother. I know the only real difference between us is my hair color. Other than that, I am almost a carbon copy of her.

Klaus comes to stand beside me, and we both wait and watch Vladimir stand slowly. He dusts himself off and then turns to look at me. Sebastian had the very same color blue eyes. I can see the similarities; the eyes, nose, and lips are the same. It makes me ponder precisely how much inbreeding was encouraged to keep his bloodline "pure."

"Greetings, daughter," he says with a sneer.

"Vladimir..." I say, practically snarling at him. I maintain my human eyes for the moment. I let him see my mother's trademark steel-grey eyes stare at him.

"You look so much like her," Vladimir says with an almost sense of wonder in his voice. "My baby Aurora."

I narrow my eyes at him, and my beast rumbles. Its tone is a perfect blend of dragon and Lycan. "You mean Seraphina, don't you, Vladimir? After all, that's the name mother wished to give me." I smirk as I lean back against Klaus. I will not kill Vladimir, but I will enjoy pissing him off for a bit before sending him to the horde.

Vladimir growls, and his wolf's dull-gold eyes can be seen. "Where did you hear that name?" He leans forward and places both hands on his desk. His fingernails are barely able to become claws. I take note of the fact that he more than likely cannot shift at this point.

I tilt my head left, then right, then move forward and place both of my hands flat on his desk. My talons digging into the wood beneath it. Vladimir finally takes note of the heavy chromatic dragon scale gauntlets that cover my arms. "Mother told me. One of my mates is a mystic and brought her to me through the veil. I know all of your dirty little secrets, Vladimir. You will pay for every single one of them."I smirk, looking at him, knowing full well I struck a nerve. "With my blood, this I swear."

I speak the ancient oath, and he knows his time is almost up. He makes the mistake of lunging at me from over the desk. I grip him with one hand and push Klaus out of the way with the other. "Go, Klaus, leave. He's sick. I've got this." Klaus hesitates and moves to the doorway, out of my way.

Vladimir grapples with me for several moments, and I can tell the exertion is wearing him down quickly. I fling him halfway across the room. It's not as easy to toss a full-grown man as a human. But I have to admit it's much more enjoyable this way.

Through the bond, I send my mates to get onto Marco's back and get airborne. Klaus goes running down the stairs to join the others. I carefully remove Klaus's flannel and shift back to the form of my hybrid beast. I summon Dante to me and watch him circle the outside of the tower. I run my talons over my toxin-covered canines, making sure they are entirely coated again.

This time when Vladimir charges me, I sink my talons into his flesh deeply and hold him there, waiting for his eyes to revert back to human. Dante calls, letting me know he's just about in position. I move towards the window with Vladimir screaming and pulling at my gauntlets. His fear must be overriding his pain because he's shedding his fingertips on my scales. I throw Vladimir out of the window and let Dante catch him midair. I watch as Dante circles the castle, waiting for me, and I can't help but smile at what I've accomplished.

I shift back to my human form and slip Klaus's shirt back on. Standing on the windowsill, I reach out to my allies and ask them to see the castle's clean-up and its grounds. We won the battle and the war. I congratulate them on the victory and advise them to take care of the wounded, and we will bury the dead in three days. Cheers erupt in the courtyard as my allies chant my name. I wave to everyone just before I leap out of the window to land on Alaric's back. There's one more piece of business left to handle, and that's back at the German Lycan camp. I rest comfortably, sitting on Alaric's dragon's back. Eventually, the events of the day catch up to me, so I lie down between his wings with my arms wrapped around one of his spines as I fall asleep.

My love? Wake up. We're home. I told Dante to remain airborne until you summon him, Alaric says through the bond, rousing me from my nap. Damn, that felt like the shortest nap in the history of naps.

Alaric lands, and my father, children, and his mate come running towards me. "Daughter? Were we victorious?" Nicodeamus asks with such a hopeful look.

"We were, Father. We were victorious, thanks to all of your planning and knowledge." I motion to Dimitri, and he comes forward with two cloth bags. I furrow my brows for a moment, and then it dawns on me.

Nicodeamus makes the Joker look sane with the way he's smiling. "First, Father, I would like to present you with the Lycan head of Josef. He died at my talons, though honestly, he wasn't a worthy opponent at all," I say, then pull Josef's head out of the bag and offer it to my father.

Nicodeamus pulls me in tight for the best hug ever. It's excellent being Daddy's little hellion. My own toddlers pull at my legs, and I drop Josef's head on the ground. Dimitri clears his throat, drawing our attention back to him. He pulls out the Elder Dame's head, drops to his knees before me, and holds the head up. His thoughtful gift brings tears to my eyes, and I lean down to kiss him passionately. Ladon screams,"eww!" Tiamat says, "awe." Helle says, *"get a room"*, and my other mates just smile at the two of us.

I motion to Alaric, and he comes to stand behind my father. "Forgive us, Father, but I wish your gift to be a surprise." With that, Alaric covers Nicodeamus's eyes just before Dante lands with my prisoner in tow.

Dimitri rises and quickly moves to grab Vladimir. I take some knotted fabric and make a ball gag and shove it into Vladimir's mouth. Honestly, I can't wait to see my father's reaction.

CHAPTER 37
Nicodeamus

THE LAST TWO WEEKS HAVE BEEN HEAVEN AND HELL. HEAVEN BECAUSE the gods saw fit to grant me a second mate. I was sure I would die alone, with my only joy being my daughter and her children. Speaking of my daughter's children, they are indeed a breath of fresh air. The last hatchling I was able to see run around was actually her mate, Alaric.

I swear this war that she's waging has aged me faster than anything else I could ever have imagined. Then there's all this technology that Helle is helping me learn and master. It's kind of sad that my grand babies have a better grasp of things than I do.

Klaus has this thing called a Switch, and the little ones sit there for hours like tiny zombies making a mushroom-looking man bounce all over the screen. I have no idea how any of this stuff works. But if it keeps them happy while their momma is away, I'm all for it.

Helle has been an angel, accepting Aurora's babies and me so quickly. Then again, it helps that she's Jayce and Dominik's mom.

To my surprise, Aurora actually likes her—that's huge. If my daughter doesn't like someone, she's not afraid to let them know.

I feel the height of the battle waging in what used to be my mate's home. I can almost track where Aurora is on the battlefield. She's left her bond with me wide open. All I have to do is close my eyes and focus on her. I have been guiding Aurora through the entire castle. I have been giving her the history of the castle as well as where hidden passageways are.

Sadly, in a way, I am glad that Anca has passed on. If she could see the state of her father's castle, she would be heartbroken. Aurora is still on the fence whether she wants to destroy the castle and build a new one or just resurrect this one. I watch her kill Josef and then her leap to Alaric. I have never been so proud of my child in all of my days.

She lands on the tower then proceeds to climb. I have a perfect view of how her talons allow her to grip the stones as she moves. It's impressive, to say the least, that she moves with such ease up the rocks. I regret that she wasn't born a dragon; she would have been a very deadly dragoness. She pauses as she catches Vladimir's scent; he's got a blood sickness that's slowly poisoning him to death. Idiot used dragon blood to prolong his life span. I guess he didn't realize it doesn't work that way.

I advise my daughter how to approach the situation, and then suddenly, I can't see through her eyes anymore. It is frightening in the first few moments, and then it dawns on me that she really needed to concentrate so as not to be distracted, so she closed the link.

What seems like forever passes, and finally, Aurora reaches out to me. *We won, Daddy! On our way home, see you in a few hours.* With that, I feel her lie down and go to sleep. I reach out to Alaric, and he fills me in on the entire battle from his perspective. My daughter is courageous and made me very proud of her.

Anca can rest in peace now, knowing her castle is no longer under Vladimir's and the Strigoi's control. It took so long to liberate her ancestral home, but in the end, it was more than worth it.

I run and tell Helle and the babies that Aurora and her mates are on their way home. She squeals from excitement; not only is her daughter-in-law on her way back, but so are both of her sons. Helle runs to the kitchen and gets the staff to start cooking various meals for the family.

"Love." I rest a hand on Helle's forearm. "Aurora may not eat what you are having prepared. Please don't take offense over it." I look down at my feet, then back up at my mate. Tears threaten to break and run down her cheeks. "It's not you, my beloved. She's been hunted all of her life. She needs time to trust you the way she trusts her mates. The last woman that claimed to love me tried to kill her." I furrow my brows and look at her, hoping she understands.

Helle nods her head slowly and wipes her eyes before looking back up at me. "I understand, my love. I just hope she can trust me like she does my sons one day."

Smile at her and press a kiss to her forehead. "Without a doubt, it will happen. You're a good woman and my true mate. How could she not love you?" Helle's laughter is like music to my ears; I love seeing her smile. I freeze suddenly as I sense Alaric reaching out, letting me know that he can see the village from where he is. "Hurry! We need to go outside! They are almost ready to land." I grab Helle's hand and drag her through the house. All of the commotion I'm making awakens Aurora's children, and the toddlers chase after us.

Our eyes raise up, looking skyward; dawn's early light casts a multitude of colors across the clouds. It's then, I see them. Alaric is in the lead, flanked by Dante and Edgar, with Marco, the Black Dragon, bringing up the rear. Dante appears to have something in his hand, but he's staying higher in the sky than the others. Alaric lands gracefully, and my daughter leaps off of his back. She shows me Josef's head and tells me about the battle. Dimitri shows Aurora the Elder Dame's head, which is probably one of the most romantic moves I've witnessed my old friend do.

Aurora is up to something as I see Alaric move to stand behind me. His hands cover my eyes, and I hear movement around me and a thud. Helle gasps, and I feel her hand on my left side. "Release him, Alaric," Aurora says, her voice so commanding and powerful, and I am already beaming with pride until I see what she has brought for me.

"Vladimir..." Frost begins to coat the ground around me as I stare at the one man who destroyed my life. My dragon wants to break free and plunge this bastard into a block of ice. Meanwhile, my daughter has the most sadistic smile on her lips that I have ever seen on her. It concerns me to see her like this. Alaric looks concerned, as well as her other mates.

Aurora cuts the gag free from Vladimir and drives him to his knees. Her taloned gauntlet keeps applying pressure to his left arm. I see what she's contemplating already, an eye for an eye. I look at her other mates, and I'm pretty sure they have no clue what's going on in that pretty little head of hers.

"Father?" is all Aurora says, and I give her a nod. Without a second thought, she slices through Vladimir's shoulder like a hot knife through butter. Her talons are covered in permafrost, and she cauterizes the wound as she amputates his arm. His severed arm falls to the ground, making a sickening thud.

In an uncharacteristic move for Aurora, she bows her head to me in submission and backs away from a cursing Vladimir. Dimitri stands between Vladimir and me, holding a pillow with my sword and a second sword. I remove my sword and test its balance several times before standing en garde. Vladimir makes the connection and grabs the other sword. Aurora had evened out the playing field by removing one of his arms. Now she stands on the sidelines, watching over my mate and her children. I know I will not fall in battle today; Daddy's little Hellion would never allow it.

Vladimir is angry, and we all know you should never fight angry. You become sloppy and make mistakes that if you were level-headed, would never have happened. He isn't used to fighting and only using one arm to balance himself. Welcome to my hell for the first twenty years of my imprisonment. I'll be honest. I'm toying with him, enjoying watching him suffer. "You are the last of your bloodline, Vladimir. How does it feel?" I ask him as I cut his calf.

"You bastard, Nicodeamus! Coward! You have your abomination of a daughter wound me!" he screams, practically foaming at the mouth. His rage is palpable in the air, and no matter how hard he tries to shift, he can't, and it's just making him angrier.

"Actually, I did that for the fuck of it, you bastard. I should really have castrated you like you did my father. But alas, you won't live long enough for it to matter much," Aurora says, staring Vladimir down, her eyes taking on that ethereal glow. The ancient power of the Force Dragon starts crackling through her long, white hair.

Vladimir is frozen in place, staring at Aurora as she starts letting the power she contains possess her fully. Frost and the crackling of that purple energy begin to radiate from her. The influx of power is to the point her mates pull my mate and her children away from her. Through the bond, I can feel the rage and pain in her heart. She stares down at the man that took so much from her. She suddenly throws her arms out at her side, and a wave of frost hits Vladimir full-force and sends him flying into a tree.

"I hold you responsible for my mother's death. I hold you responsible for the deaths of Dimitri's people. I hold you responsible for my father's imprisonment. I hold you responsible for making me the monster I am today." Aurora starts to laugh, and I think she's become unhinged the way she's looking at him.

"I have a fate planned for you far worse than death, Vladimir." Aurora tilts her head several times, side to side, as she watches him cower.

"For now, it does my heart good to watch my father kick your worthless ass." Aurora flops down onto the ground and pulls her babies to her.

Everyone is in a state of shock over how quickly the switch flipped with her. Aurora begins to run her fingers through Tiamat's light-blonde curls as Ladon does the same to his mother's long, white hair. I'm not sure who is soothing whom, but Aurora seems calm at the moment. Arnulf hands her a flask of something.

Out of the corner of my eye, I see Vladimir begin to charge me. I parry every attack he makes. The blades caress several times, and I have to admit, I didn't think he still had it in him to fight like this with as sick as he seems.

Laurel appears out of nowhere and passes popcorn out to my family as she goes to take a seat next to Aurora. Vladimir is an accomplished sword fighter, and I'm genuinely enjoying myself fighting him. He's all anger, and I am as cool as a cucumber, taking my time making sure that I block his every attack. Helle is being held by both of her sons as she watches me fight. I feel like a knight back at court trying to impress all the young maidens. Who knows, I might get a little extra lovin' tonight after my decisive victory in the ring.

Apparently, I got a little too cocky too soon; Vladimir manages to disarm me. Just as his blade starts to head for me, Aurora stops the sword with the scales of her gauntlet.

"Remember, I said you were going to die an excruciating death?" Aurora asks with a very soft and seductive tone. A light, playful smile plays upon her full blood-red lips.

Vladimir is frozen in fear as I feel the Force Dragon gift of intimidation being pressed upon him. His wolf's eyes skip between this blade and her gauntlet. I watch as the fur starts to ripple over his body. I see the look of concern on Arnulf's face as he watches Vladimir begin to shift to his Lycan.

Aurora unleashes the full magnitude of her Alpha power on Vladimir. "You will not shift!" Her voice booms as she stares at him with her beast's eyes. He attempts to resist her command but ends up falling to his knees—still human. He's panting hard, holding his chest, her power physically hurting him.

"You've stolen so much from me, Vladimir." She reaches down, grabs him by his jaw, lifts him off the ground, and starts encasing his body in an ice prison.

"You've stolen my mother from me; my father could have healed her if he was by her side instead of fighting the Strigoi." Aurora's talons press into the soft flesh of his cheek a little more. His skin flexes, straining to hold up against the sharpness of her talons.

"You stole my father from me. I could have turned out so much different if you didn't betray your own people." Her eyes narrow as she tightens the ice prison a bit. The tinkling noise of the ice as it moves and constricts can be heard.

"Your sister damaged my bond with my mate, Dimitri, at your behest. I thought I was insane because of you." Aurora is scarily calm as she speaks to him. Her talons lightly cutting into his face now. Rivulets of blood slowly flow from around her talons and drip onto the ice below.

"Payback is a bitch, Vladimir... It just so happens I am that bitch." Aurora's eyes begin to take on the ethereal glow; scales ripple up and down Aurora's nose and cheeks. The bone plates in her face begin to shift and move. It is as if her beast is about to break free at any moment.

Suddenly, she grabs Vladimir and lifts him off the ground, breaking him free from his ice prison. Her talons sink swiftly into his flesh. He appears frozen in a state of horror. What is my daughter about to do?

CHAPTER 38

Aurora

THE BONE PLATES IN MY FACE START TO SHIFT AND MOVE. I FEEL AS IF MY beast is about to break free at any moment. Suddenly, I grab Vladimir's throat roughly and lift him off the ground, breaking him free from his ice prison. My talons sink swiftly into his flesh. He appears frozen in a state of horror. His eyes are open wide, and his mouth hangs open in a voiceless scream. I watch the color drain from his face as he realizes how deep of shit he is now in.

I feel the rage boiling under my skin as I hold him off the ground, looking into his pale blue eyes. This thief has stolen so much from my family and me. Without hesitation, I throw him away from me towards the center of town and stalk slowly after him. I hear the gasps and whispers of my family around me. Part of me knows this isn't something my children should bear witness to.

"Laurel, take the children to the pond to swim." I don't bother to look in her direction, and without hesitation, I hear her gather up my children and feel them leave.

Once I am sure my children are far enough away. I tilt my head to the left, listening to my beast call for the blood of Vladimir.

Rip him to shreds. Tear him limb from limb. Rip his heart out and keep it as a souvenir. Bathe in the blood of our enemy, my beast says with a growl in my head. A wicked smile plays upon my lips as I shift entirely to that of my hybrid beast.

Vladimir smirks as he attempts to dust himself off. "Oooh, I'm so scared of an abomination like you. You're nothing but a whore's spawn, a genetic misfire." He sneers and waves a hand at me dismissively.

My family's voices sound as if they are underwater as my singular focus is on Vladimir and his heartbeat. Movement out of the corner of my eye shows my mates holding my father back. Vladimir is using me to bait him back into battle. I'm mentally shaking my head. Oh no. This asshole's time has come. I feel my power course through my veins and rise to the surface as the ice begins to form on my fur. An arctic wind begins to blow from behind me, sending small ice shards at Vladimir. I increase the storm's power in increments; more and more of the shards start to slice and rip at his clothing. The wind howls as its intensity increases, adding to the destructive power of my storm.

Alaric moves to stand behind Vladimir, his hands clamped on his shoulders as my ice has no effect on my mate. He has the same wicked smile on his face as I did a moment ago. From my father's memories, I pull forth one method he taught me. I remember the torture called Ling-chi—the lingering death, otherwise known as death by a thousand cuts. I reach out to Jayce, and he brings me his flannel. My shift back to my human form is slow and painful since my last upgrade. My storm falters for a moment and almost gives Vladimir a chance to attack. Thankfully, Alaric is swift and recaptures him and holds him in place for me.

"Tsk, tsk, tsk." I shake my head. "Good try there, Vlad, *old* boy," I say, emphasizing the old part. His eyes narrow on me as I smile sweetly, trying to get on his last nerve before I start the ice storm back up again.

"You're a bitch just like your mother was, thinking so highly of yourself. You're nothing! Not a Lycan, not a dragon." He motions to his feet. "You're lower than the shit on the bottom of my shoe." Vladimir spits his venomous words at me, yet I remain unaffected.

Tilting my head to the side I say, "I don't need my beast to kill you; you're already dead and don't even know it yet." Straightening myself, I look him in the eyes. I raise my hands and ice shards begin to gather and swirl all around me violently. *Alaric move!* I say through our mental bond.

Suddenly, I throw my hands forward, and the ice storm flies at Vladimir, slicing his flesh like a thousand razor blades. I watch my ice shards rend the flesh from his muscles and down to the bones in places. A mass of vermillion fluid oozes down his body and starts to pool at his feet. I focus on his heartbeat, listening for the moment it begins to falter.

Lub-dub, lub-dub, lub.... Lub-dub. There's the falter I was waiting for. The ice storm stops almost as quickly as it had started. He's weak and beginning to sway on his feet. I immediately encase most of him in ice before moving over to him.

My human eyes scan over his remaining features; his blue eyes remind me painfully of my first love. Or what I thought was my first love, Sebastian. If that poor man wasn't tainted, maybe I wouldn't have had to kill him. It's not worth pondering at this point.

My mind wanders to Andre, the only mother figure I had. He was my best friend and someone I loved greatly, and he's dead because of this fucktard before me. My mother, gods rest her soul, died because of his greed and lust for power. My father suffered for over two hundred years because of Vladimir. Dimitri and I could have been together all this fucking time if not for this man's meddling.

Drain him… Make him die. Make him feel fear and suffering. My beast demands retribution, and I will not deny her any longer.

Vladimir stares at me. "You look so much like her… My Anca."

I feel the ancient power spike in me. How dare Vladimir say my mother was his. "By the powers vested in me, by birthright and Gallus," my head tilts to the side as I study him, "I sentence you, Vladimir, to death eternal." I grip his head and shift my hands to my armored gauntlets. My talons sink into his flesh till they scrape his skull. At first, I channel all the pain I've felt at every turn throughout my journey. I give him the pain from all of the losses I've suffered over the last few years. I pour into him all the pain from never being able to stay in one place, always moving to stay safe. I give him my loneliness that I suffered from being isolated from everyone and everything. Vladimir's mouth hangs open in a silent scream as he relives all of the horrors of my life.

Casually, I look over my shoulder to my father to see tears rolling down his cheeks. *Fuck, I left the bond wide open.* Everyone connected to me feels what I am feeling, right at this exact moment. "There will be no Elysium for you, Vladimir. I won't allow it." His face is now ghost white, eyes wide, showing pure fear as he feels me starting to pull on his life force. He starts muttering "no" over and over again. His pathetic no's mean nothing to me.

My Force powers begin to manifest and run like streaks of lightning through my long, white hair. Frost starts to coat the earth surrounding where I'm standing, plunging the camp into winter. I see Alaric shift into his dragon and move to sit behind me, helping me drop the temperature further. Vladimir's body starts to wither slowly before my eyes as I drain his life from him. I pull at each strand of every year, one by one, taking his power into myself.

Oddly enough, I gather as I pull on his mana; he has no special gift. He had absolutely nothing he could have offered my mother beside his seed. This pathetic excuse of a male was never meant to be a mate to my mother *ever*. There's not a single thing about him that would have been found worthy. Vladimir stopped making noise a while ago, and his heart has fallen silent. I steal the last fibers of essence from him before releasing my grip on his husk.

Burn him, turn him to ash. Leave nothing behind. He's not worth remembering, my beast says to me. *Heal father, give mate more years. Make him whole,* my beast tells me as I look at my father and Helle. I know what I have to do; I know what I want to do. The question is... *Is it possible?*

I reach back and touch Alaric's dragon, then motion to the rest of my family to move back. I click my ignitor and open my mouth, breathing my force weapon upon Vladimir's husk. I pour all my pain into the weapon at my disposal. He burns until not even ash is left, just a black mark upon the soil. I draw in a deep breath, silencing the weapon in my chest. Jayce comes running over to me and offers me water. I sip slowly from the offered cup, then hand it back. Gently, I kiss his cheek and move to my father next. Out of the corner of my eye, I see Elsa. She knows what I'm about to do because she was the recipient of my prior gift.

"King Nicodeamus Tepish of the Ice Dragons, I ask you, not as your daughter but as your equal to kneel before me." I'm not sure how my father will react to this, but I must try—the power of the ancient pulses through my hair and over the scales of my gauntlets.

My father tilts his head slightly then drops to his knees before me without hesitation. "I, Nicodeamus Tepish, kneel before our Sovereign Queen, Aurora Marelup-Kraus, true leader of the Ice Dragon and Lycan packs'."

I lean forward and press my lips to my father's forehead. Ever so slowly, I start feeding the stolen life force back into him. In my mind's eye, I reach out and grab hold of his dragon's form. I focus a majority of the power on my father's dragon. Being mythical creatures, things work differently for them. Gallus taught me the extent of his power as well as my own. As Gallus had done for me, I am doing for my father. I focus my love and my intention on his dragon. We remain locked for what must seem like forever to everyone else. For me, it was but a blink of an eye. A light coating of frost remains on my father's whole body when I pull away. I offer my hands to him to assist him in standing. He rises to his feet, looking at me curiously. I didn't reverse time for him as much as I would have liked. I gave him a better gift than years, I almost can't wait to tell him.

"Helle, would you come here, please?" I extend my hand to my father's mate. I don't have much left for her but I can at least give her something. Helle comes to me quickly and grips my hands tightly.

"Yes, Aurora?" She beams up at me; the joy and love in this woman's eyes almost erases the hell I relived today.

"I need you to relax and trust me." I smile as I look down at her. The minute she nods, I press my lips to her forehead. I shift my gauntlets back to my human hands. And ever so gently, I place them on her face and slowly drag them down to her jaw. Next, I run my fingers through her hair, rejuvenating it too. I wish I could do more, but unfortunately, I used most of the stolen mana on my father. I feel the last of the stolen energy leave me, and I stand up straight, looking at Helle. She could easily be confused for an older sibling to her sons than their mother. I release her hands and look back over at my father.

CHAPTER 39

Aurora

"Hey, dad?" I smirk knowingly. "Would you mind shifting? I want to see if what I tried worked." Nicodeamus looks at me curiously, then moves away and shifts, shredding his clothing. His dragon stands tall and proud; everything is status quo till he spreads his wings. I may not have been able to give him back his leg, but I was able to give him back the skies. His great dragon turns his head and looks at his wings, then roars happily. He takes off into the air, and Alaric joins him for his first flight since my mother's death. At least Vladimir was good for something.

I look back to my mates after watching my father fly for a little while. *Once they are done, we need to return to the castle and finish up there.* The guys nod at me, agreeing with my plans I shared with them through our bond.

Out of nowhere, Helle hug-tackles me, crying. "Thank you, daughter, for this wonderful gift!"

Helle kisses both of my cheeks, still hugging the life out of me. I smile down at her before I kiss her forehead. "No need to thank me. I love you both, and I would walk through the fires of hell itself to see my father happy again." I look back to the skies, watching my father riding the thermals.

"My family, I've prepared dinner for everyone, figuring that you would be hungry upon your return," Helle says, smiling, looking at each of us expectantly.

My father and mate both land not far from the Alpha House. I look from Helle, who announced dinner, then to the direction that Alaric and Nicodeamus will be coming from. I'm not used to eating someone's cooking. Still, I doubt that this meal is any threat. After all, this is the woman who gave birth to two of my mates. Now she's my father's mate. Part of me is scared of eating something that my mates have not caught. But the other part of me accepts the fact that I need to move on and accept that not everyone is trying to kill me all the time.

Watching Helle and her sons interact, I'll be honest... I'm jealous. I wish I knew what it was like to have a mom. It's one luxury that even being a princess, now queen, I was not granted. My eyes drift to my children, and I smile at them, knowing that they are the future. Every day I strive to be the mother that I wish I had growing up with. I went to war to ensure that my children would never have to live in the hell that I have for over two hundred years.

Carefully, I bend down and pick up my daughter, Tiamat, holding her to my chest. Her tiny dragoness purrs happily, being reunited with me. I missed my babies. From this day forward, we will never be separated again. My son's dragon sits at my feet, rubbing his scaled face against my leg. I understand his reasons for not wanting to shift to his human form. He wishes he could have been on the battlefield fighting next to me, cleansing my mother's castle. One day my boy will be a formidable warrior. I will make sure that he and my daughter can defend themselves against anything.

Once my father and mate have rejoined us, we enter the house and sit for dinner. I must lead by example when it comes to my children, even though it scares me. Alaric looks at me then looks towards the door, questioning if I need him to hunt. Gently, I shake my head no. I must learn to trust. It's beyond my comprehension that my father's mate would dare cause me any harm, so she is the first one whose food I shall eat. Hesitantly, I reach out with the serving fork and take portions from several of the bowls in front of me.

Silence falls at the breakfast table as my mates watch me fill my plate. Anxiety rolls off each of them to different degrees. I fill two more plates, offering one to my daughter and then put the second on the floor for my son, who still refuses to shift. I take my first fork full of the sausage that Helle made fresh today. Out of habit, I give it a quick sniff before biting into it. I swear I've developed a form of anxiety when it comes to eating. My nerves are on edge as I chew the sausage.

Everyone watches me expectantly to see how I react. Through the bond, they sense my anxiety. They sense that I'm on edge and fearful that something still may happen. I finish off the sausage and take a sip of my wine; so far, so good. I smile at my new stepmom and lightly incline my head to her.

"I can tell from the taste of this that the sausage was made fresh today. It's still full of flavor." Hesitantly, I look down. "I'll be frank with you; eating cooked food scares me." I lower my head slightly, having admitted to being afraid of something.

A few moments later, lithe hands rest upon my shoulders, and I hear Helle's wolf whine. Turning my head, I face her and nuzzle her cheek, trying to settle her wolf. Honestly, I'm not sure which of us needs comfort more. Helle needs my acceptance because I'm Nicodeamus's daughter. Me? I need to know I'm safe in her presence. Helle's fingers thread through my hair, and my beast rumbles in response. Is this what having a mother is like? I freeze in my movements, unsure of what's happening.

"Shh, baby girl, you're safe," Helle whispers to me.

Hearing her words, I start to cry, finally able to release all of the pain I've held within all these years. *I am no longer alone.* My father's mate is acting like the mom I never truly had towards me. Gently, I nuzzle her throat and press my forehead to shoulder. Quickly, I wrap my arms around her waist, holding her tightly to me. Taking a leap of faith, I roll my head all the way back, offering my throat to Helle. Her breath hitches when she sees what I have done. Gently, I feel her place her lips over my vein before she nuzzles my neck. At this moment in time, I am assured that I can trust her with my life.

Carefully, I bring my head back down and press my lips to Helle's cheek. Drawing in a deep breath, I inhale and memorize her scent. My eyes slowly drift around the room to each of my mates in turn. They have no idea what I'm contemplating doing. I need to forge a bond with this woman to be able to find her if need be. My eyes shift to that of my beast, and I pull back to look at her.

Carefully, I lock down my alpha powers so that eye contact with me doesn't drive her to her knees. My beast calls to her wolf and brings her close to the surface. In the back of our minds, there's an understanding that comes between the two of us. I observe Helle rolling her head to the opposite side of where my father's mating mark is. She exposes her bare shoulder in full submission to me.

Without hesitation, I take the bulk of her trapezius muscle in my mouth. Quickly, my canines descend, sinking into her flesh, sending the sharp tang of coppery blood into my mouth. I roll my neck to the side, hopefully exposing a bare spot to her. Tentatively Helle bites my neck in return but not as large of a bite as I did. We taste each other's blood, and I feel a familial bond snap into place with her. From this day forward, she will have my protection without question.

Gently, I release her muscle making sure not to rip her tender flesh. Slowly, I cleanse the wound, licking it, making sure that it seals properly. Tenderly and lovingly, I press a kiss to her temple before standing up and walking away from her. My wound still sits wide open and bleeding, and I'm okay with that. I move over to my father and place the bridge of my nose under his chin seeking his approval. My father bands his strong arm around me, holding me tightly to his chest. His joy floods the familial bond making my heart swell with happiness. I swear to myself in this moment I will find a way to give him his arm back in the material plane.

For the first time, I hear my father's voice tremble with emotion. "Thank you."

Honestly, I don't understand why he's thanking me. Drawing back slowly, I look up into my father's tear-filled eyes and raise a single brow. "Why, Daddy? I don't understand." His gratitude absolutely puzzles me. My actions shouldn't require thanks. I only did what I felt was the right thing to do in my heart. Inquisitively, I tilt my head left, then right, then straighten it back up again, trying to figure out what my father means.

Gently, he raises his hand and caresses my cheek before he presses his lips against my forehead. "I know trust is hard-earned with you." His eyes drift to his mate, then over to my mates, and back to me again. "Too many times your trust has been betrayed. If I am to be so bold as to speak frankly, you don't exactly have the best track record with other females." His eyes drift, yet again, to his mate and then back to me. "To forge a familial bond without prompting speaks volumes to me." Again, my father kisses my forehead and then backs away.

His actions puzzle me even further as I watch him move around to each of my mates. He lightly touches each of their foreheads with his hand. Upon contact, a light sheen of frost coats their skin. Their eyes shift to that of their individual animals as they look up to my father. I'm not exactly sure what's occurring right now, but it must be a big deal. Alaric smiles and bows his head deeply to my father. He's the only one that my father presses his forehead to initially. Maybe it's a dragon thing; perhaps it's an alpha thing. I'm not one hundred percent sure as to why Alaric is receiving special treatment.

"Father, why is Alaric different from my other mates?" My beast shifts underneath my flesh. She's uncomfortable with the thought that one of my mates is held to higher standards than the others.

A broad smile crosses over my father's lips as he coats Alaric in frost. "Daughter, it is quite simple. I accepted them through Alaric into the swarm." One by one, I watch my father go and touch each of my mates, forehead to forehead before he returns to face me. "I needed an anchor, something or someone that they all had in common. Besides you, that anchor is Alaric." Casually, father motions back to my mates. "Goddess forbid anything ever happens to you. Instead of perishing from grief, they are now bound together." He tilts his head slightly as he watches me, knowing that this is a touchy subject. "They will be able to survive after your passing with or without hatchlings."

Softly I sigh, having the gravity of the situation finally hit me. I know personally, I wouldn't want to survive if I lost my mates tomorrow. In reality, there are too many other lives that count on us and our survival to protect them. This has now become greater than just our little family. We have so many species that have aligned themselves with us that look to us for guidance and protection. As much as passing on when our loved ones leave us would ease our pain, it would cause far worse pain for those that we leave behind.

The wisdom I find and my father's logic warms my heart that he can think that far into the future. There are so many fractured souls that have been damaged and or enslaved under Vladimir's reign that it will take years for us to help heal them. That is if they can be treated and rehabilitated. "Thank you for your counsel, Father, your wisdom and forethought are much needed in the dark days ahead."

Slowly, I approach Arnulf and reach to his right side and draw his sword from his scabbard. Gently, I place a kiss on his temple before walking back over to my father. "Please kneel before me." I observe my father lower himself to the floor to kneel in front of me. Gently, I tap each of his shoulders with the sword's broadside, essentially knighting him.

"Nicodeamus Tepish, old King of the Ice Dragon Court, I Aurora, Queen of the Ice Dragons and the Lycans, grant you sovereignty over the foundlings." The sword rests on his left shoulder as I speak. "I grant you the position of high council as an advisor to the crown of both the dragon and the wolven clans." Carefully, I move and rest the sword on his right shoulder. "I give you dominion over my people. To rule in my place in times where I am unable to, for whatever reason that may be," I state clearly with my full Alpha power behind my words.

The bonds between my dragons and my wolves are wide open. That way, everyone hears my words and sees through my eyes my actions on this day. I have secured my father's place in power for the rest of his days for the generations to come. Goddess forbid anything should happen to myself or my mates, he will be able to take over and protect those who are weaker than ourselves. He will be the one to determine which of my children will be the rightful rulers of each of the clans and the swarm. My eyes lovingly gaze over each of my mates, knowing full well that they are with me on this decision.

"Nicodeamus, rise and stand before me." Once he stands, I kiss both of my father's cheeks, then I step back to admire him. "Rule well, Father, as I know you were meant to do."

My eyes gaze back to my mates, and I smile sweetly at them. For now, we must retire and sleep for tomorrow; we all return to the castle of my origin. We will finish cleansing the land and heal it from the damage that Vladimir had done. From tomorrow forward, it will no longer be known as the Marelup Castle. It will be known as the Castle of Wolves. I will give it to whomever of my wolven children is deemed to be best suited to rule over both the Dire Wolves and the Lycan packs.

I will not show favoritism when it comes to any of my children that are born. The rightful seat of power is stated as by blood. My Lycan daughter should be the one to preside over the Castle of Wolves according to the bloodline. Should I not birth a daughter, whichever of my Dire Wolf daughters, if I have any who are suited to rule, then they shall inherit the title. I pass this edict without hesitation. Everyone within the different pack links, and through my bond with my dragons hears my words clearly. There is an understanding that passes between all of us through me. My words are spoken without question, my authority is accepted without argument.

Tonight, we rest; tomorrow, we fly. Through the link with the rest of my people that are still at the castle, I give them a list of things that they need to accomplish tonight before bed. Nothing major, just enough to secure their safety throughout the night until I return tomorrow. I motion to my mates and then lightly bow my head to my father.

"Good night, Father. Good night, Mother. Tomorrow is the dawning of a new era. Sleep well and go in peace," I say as gently as possible just before departing to retire for the night.

CHAPTER 40

Alaric

As the first light of dawn breaks across the horizon, a symphony of colors unfolds before me, painting the sky in shades of gold and amber. The air is crisp and still, carrying with it the earthy scent of the forest and the faint aroma of lingering smoke from the dying embers of the hearth.

Standing alone amidst the quiet remnants of our camp, I feel a sense of solitude settle over me like a comforting cloak. The crackling embers cast dancing shadows across the ground, their flickering movements a poignant reminder of the trials we've faced and the resilience that resides within us.

With each stretch and flex of my weary muscles, I am keenly aware of the toll that yesterday's battles have taken on my body and spirit. The ache and exhaustion weigh heavily upon me, yet beneath it all, there lingers a profound sense of gratitude.

Gratitude for the simple yet profound gift of witnessing another daybreak, for the quiet promise of hope and renewal that it brings. In the soft embrace of the morning light, I find solace and strength, ready to face whatever challenges lie ahead with unwavering resolve.

As we gather our belongings and make ready to depart for the castle, a sense of solemnity settles over the camp like a heavy shroud. The air is thick with the weight of grief, each breath tasting of sorrow and loss.

The reports of our fallen comrades weigh heavily on my heart, a burden too heavy to bear alone. Their names linger in the air, whispered prayers for the departed, their memories etched into the very fabric of our being.

I can feel the knot of sorrow tightening in my chest, a physical manifestation of the pain that grips us all. It's as if the very air is heavy with the weight of our collective mourning, pressing down upon us with relentless force.

But amidst the sorrow, there is a sense of purpose, a solemn duty that we must fulfill. As we begin the solemn task of planning funeral rites, I am reminded of the sacred obligation we bear to honor the fallen. Each detail, each gesture, is a testament to their bravery and sacrifice, a final tribute to their unwavering dedication to our cause.

But amidst the grief and mourning, there's a flicker of determination burning bright within me. For every life lost, there are countless more who still stand, resilient and unbroken. Their spirits may be bruised, their resolve tested, but they remain steadfast in their commitment to our shared cause. And as we gather our strength and steel ourselves for the road ahead, I draw comfort from the knowledge that we do not walk alone. United in purpose and bound by our shared struggle, we will rise from the ashes of our losses, stronger and more resolute than ever before.

As I stand outside the hunter's store, the weight of responsibility sits heavy on my shoulders, a silent burden that threatens to overwhelm me. The anticipation of awakening my beloved Aurora and our bond mates gnaws at my conscience, knowing full well the urgency with which she'll want to depart. With each hesitant step, I feel the weight of their expectations pressing down on me, a silent reminder of the trust they place in my leadership.

As I approach the bounty of game hanging before me, a surge of conflicting emotions washes over me like a tidal wave. The sight of the roe deer and boar, once symbols of abundance and prosperity, now serves as a stark reminder of the fragility of life in a world ravaged by conflict. With trembling hands, I carefully calculate the provisions needed for our morning meal, each selection a testament to the delicate balance between sustenance and scarcity.

With a heavy heart, I exchange payment with the hunter's wife, the weight of the coins in my palm a tangible reminder of the sacrifices made in the name of survival. As I arrange for the delivery of the meat to the Alpha House, a sense of duty compels me forward, driving me to fulfill my responsibilities even in the face of uncertainty.

But beneath the veneer of stoicism lies a wellspring of raw emotion, a torrent of fear and longing that threatens to consume me whole. With each passing moment, the knowledge that this may be the last morning of peace we'll know for some time weighs heavily on my soul, a bitter reminder of the ever-present threat of the Strigoi lurking in the shadows.

Drawing in a deep breath, I steel myself for the challenges that lie ahead, knowing that the road ahead will be fraught with peril and uncertainty. But amidst the chaos and turmoil, there's a glimmer of hope, a flicker of determination that refuses to be extinguished. And as I turn to make my way back to the Alpha House, I carry with me the unwavering resolve to protect those I hold dear, no matter the cost.

As I step inside the warmth of our home, the familiar sights and sounds wrap around me like a comforting embrace, a sanctuary amidst the chaos of the outside world. The sight of my two toddlers waiting eagerly at the door fills me with a swell of parental pride, their innocence a stark contrast to the harsh realities we face.

Ladon's refusal to take his human form speaks volumes of his youthful impatience, a desire to prove himself in a world that demands strength and courage. And though his determination tugs at my heartstrings, I can't help but feel a pang of concern for his safety, a father's instinct to shield his child from harm.

My little girl, Tia, with her long, blonde curls snuggles up, hugging my leg tightly. "Daddy, can I come with you, please?" But its Tia's sweet voice and gentle touch that truly melt away the weariness of the day, her unwavering love a beacon of light in the darkness. As she clings to my leg, her innocent plea reverberates through me, a reminder of the precious bond that binds us together.

With a tender smile, I crouch down to meet her gaze, the weight of responsibility softened by the warmth of her embrace. "Of course, my darling," I reply, my voice laced with a mixture of affection and reassurance. "You and Ladon can come with us. It's safe now."

The joy that lights up her face is like a ray of sunshine breaking through the clouds, a radiant reminder of the simple pleasures that make life worth living. With a flurry of excitement, she dashes off to her room to gather her belongings, her laughter echoing through the halls like music to my ears.

As Ladon's dragon gives me a solemn nod before retreating to the safety of their shared sanctuary, I'm filled with a sense of gratitude for the bond that unites us as a family. In their laughter and innocence, I find solace and strength, a reminder that no matter what trials may lie ahead, we face them together, bound by love and unwavering devotion.

As the aroma of sizzling meat wafts through the air, a tangible sense of comfort settles over our home, wrapping us in a cocoon of warmth and familiarity. The rhythmic sounds of chopping and sizzling mingle with the soft murmurs of awakening, signaling the start of a new day in our makeshift haven.

With each passing minute, the tantalizing scent grows stronger, coaxing my mate and bond mates from the depths of slumber with its irresistible allure. Dimitri's weary form shuffles into the kitchen first, his movements sluggish yet determined as he makes a beeline for the coffee pot, a lifeline in the early hours of the morning.

One by one, the rest of our family emerges from their rooms, their faces bathed in the soft glow of dawn as they take their places around the table. The twins, with their mischievous grins and boundless energy, are followed by Klaus, Aurora, and Arnulf, each bearing the weight of their own worries and burdens.

As Dimitri distributes steaming mugs of coffee with practiced ease, a sense of camaraderie fills the room, a silent acknowledgment of the trials we've faced and the battles yet to come. And as my mate takes her first sip, a soft sigh escapes her lips, a fleeting moment of contentment amidst the chaos of our lives.

For in her happiness lies our collective strength, a beacon of light in the darkness that guides us through even the bleakest of times. As we sit together, sharing in the simple pleasure of a meal prepared with love and care, I'm reminded of the importance of these moments of respite, these small pockets of joy that remind us of what we fight for.

In the warmth of our home, surrounded by the ones we hold dear, I find solace and strength, a reminder that no matter what trials may lie ahead, we face them together, united in our determination to protect one another and preserve the fragile threads of hope that bind us as a family.

"My love, I know you're anxious to return to your mother's castle, but please consider resting at least till noon before we head back." A soft smile plays upon my lips as I wait to see how my words are received by my mate.

"My love, I understand your concerns, and I appreciate you looking out for all of us." She smiles softly. "You're always trying to make sure we are in the best condition possible." A slightly frustrated sigh escapes her lips. "I worry about everyone that we left behind." Aurora stands and moves around the kitchen island so she can face everyone. "There may or may not be stragglers still roaming the woods or hiding in the catacombs. It weighs heavily on my heart that I am not there to help protect them." I watch Aurora move across the room gracefully as she comes to stand before me.

Her fingertips lightly touch the buttons on my shirt and then glide over the muscles of my chest. "My love, would you feel comfortable leaving the children or me in that environment without you?"

I shake my head firmly. "No, I wouldn't."

"Then please understand." She places her hand upon my cheek.

"I feel as though I am their mother, they are my children." She sighs softly and then looks up into my eyes. "I don't want to chance anything happening to any more innocents." She moves away from me slowly and then leans against the island in the kitchen with her back to everyone else.

"There are a bunch of young Lycan males that I put into hibernation during the battle that I feel in my heart." She rests her hands on her chest, imploring me to listen with my heart and not my head. "I believe that I can save them. That I can heal them from the damage that Vladimir did." Her eyes drift over to Klaus and then back again.

"If there are young males, there are young females somewhere." She takes two steps forward towards me again. "We must find them. I don't know what conditions they're living in, and it scares me." She speaks with so much emotion that it pulls at my heartstrings that I am driven to help her.

"We must do whatever is necessary to ensure the safety of these young females," I state firmly. "We will leave as soon as everyone finishes eating." I walk forward and kiss her forehead. "I hope this pleases you and brings you some sense of comfort that we will hopefully find these new females." I smile confidently. "We will save them and heal them. We will bring them back into the fold with the rest of the Lycans here." My eyes move over to Klaus, who is smiling broadly.

"They will not be alone or endangered anymore." Gently, I kiss Aurora's lips and smile. "With my blood, this I swear." My eyes flash to that of my dragon and lock with hers, and we have an understanding. My word is my bond, and I will not break my vow to my mate.

CHAPTER 41
Nicodeamus

The wind embraces my scales as we take flight back to where it all began. My mate is giggling and enjoying flying with me. Never in a million years did I think I would be blessed with a second chance.

My mind roams, remembering all the things that have been accomplished since I was freed. My incredible hatchling has been through so much in her short life. She definitely has some impulse control problems because of it. I blame that on Vladimir. If Aurora had her mother and me, she would have turned out so different. The thought of my hatchling all alone, trying to figure things out makes my ancient heart ache.

With a slight tilt of my wings, I move myself closer to my daughter and her family. Tia is standing on her mom's lap waving her arms in the wind. Ladon's dragon is using his talons to hold onto his father's spine. His wings are spread, and he's enjoying the air moving over his scales. Slowly, his head tilts, and I know he wants to join me. Carefully, I maneuver myself over him and reach down with my taloned hand. Ladon reaches out and grips my scales. Slowly, he climbs up my body to sit with Helle.

Twins are so rare with dragons, yet my daughter birthed fully shifted hatchlings. In all my years, I have never seen that before. My grandson has figured out the accelerated growth table while staying shifted. He's a brilliant young man already, and to figure this out amazes me. I can feel that he's chosen to lay between my wings on my back to rest. Grandkids... I never thought this day would come. To make it even more special, they were born in the same cavern I was. This makes me wonder if when Tiamat is ready to give birth, will she migrate? Most times, a dragoness will return to where they were born to deliver their young. It's an ancient instinct. The question is: *does she possess it?*

Our flight takes us across Germany and its numerous towns and rivers. The predominant wind sends us down into Austria and over various mountains and their large national parks. Spring is around the corner, and we can see some of the trees starting to gain their leaves in the lower elevations. Higher up, some of the mountains are still covered in thick layers of snow. Mentally, I sigh. So much has changed since the last time I was able to fly. Kingdoms have fallen, and new civilizations have risen. One thing remains the same: the mountains are still here.

We take our first break at Lake Balaton in Hungary. I'm quite thankful we did because I was starting to get really thirsty. I don't bother shifting back. I lay down and let my grand babies use me as a jungle gym. The wolves in the family shift and take off into the woods. Aurora hesitates for several seconds before shifting and joining them. I don't understand her hesitation, but then again, I was never hunted like she was.

Helle doesn't leave with the rest of the wolves instead, she plays with Tia by the lake's edge. I tilt my head questioningly at her, and she just smiles at me. "Let the pups hunt, my love, I wish to enjoy the little ones," Helle says with conviction.

Carefully, I lower my horned head near her and rumble softly. *I wish I could give you more pups,* I huff, blowing frost out of my dragon's nostrils. *Unfortunately, that gift was stolen from me years ago.* I close my dragon's nictitating membranes, then my eyelids. My past causes my heart to ache. What if my mate wanted more babies? I hope I don't disappoint her.

Lithe hands rest on my dragon's maw, and I open the eye closest to her. "I have everything I need, my love." She kisses my scales, looking into my eye. "I have two strong sons; I have your daughter and all of her wonderful mates." She starts to laugh, and it's music to my ears. "I have grand babies now! Best day ever!" She claps her hands and bounces around a little bit. I feel the joy she's feeling, and I know in my heart she means every word she's said.

I can't stop counting my blessings. The level of gratitude I have to the Goddess above is immense. Quickly, I lift my head and use my wing to pull Helle and Tia closer to me. After everything that's happened, I find myself constantly on the defensive. Aurora, Klaus, and the twins come back to camp dragging and carrying their kills with them.

Aurora and Klaus drop their deer then run back into the forest. Jayce and Dom drag two deer over to their mom and me. Gently, I nuzzle Helle and the babies towards the larger deer. I devour the second one in a single bite and wait to see how much is left from the first deer. Helle cuts a hind leg free and holds it up for me. Carefully, I shake my head no and look to Alaric for assistance. He approaches and gets the hint. Helle holds the leg high above her, and he carefully blows his flames upon it.

Helle smiles broadly, looking at her cooked deer leg. She and Tia sit on my front leg, ripping chunks off and eating their fill. Ladon, on the other hand, is eating directly from the carcass and enjoying himself immensely. Aurora and Klaus return again and feed two of her guards before running off for a third time. They repeat the process till everyone has been given at least something to eat.

Aurora comes and stands before Alaric, and she bathes in his flames. When she emerges from the fire, she's shifted back to her human form. Quickly, she dresses and looks at everyone who's gathered. "Let's get this show on the road. We're burning daylight." Aurora doesn't hesitate to run to Alaric's side and climb up onto his back to get comfortable. Tia quickly runs over to her parents, and Aurora has to climb back down to help Tia up. Ladon rolls his eyes before climbing up onto my back again.

I can't help but laugh at my family's antics—they make life worth living. Dante and Edgar launch into the sky first, then myself, Alaric, and lastly Marco. We shift direction again, heading more southeast into Romania. Anxiety builds in my chest as we glide over the forests and mountain ranges. My scales rustle and shift with my unease. Part of me wants to turn around and go back. It doesn't take long before I feel a weight land on my back and walk up my spine.

The next thing I know, Aurora is on my head, hanging upside down, looking into my eye. *Daddy?* she says through the bond. *Are you okay? You don't feel okay.* Her eyes are that of her beasts, staring into my eye.

Slowly, I draw in a deep breath and try to release some of the tension I'm feeling. Leave it to Aurora to be so in tuned with me to pick it up before my mate. *Yes and no, little one. Yes, because I have to be.* My dragon huffs a breath of pure frost. *No, because there are very few happy memories waiting for me. Too many ghosts.*

Alaric roars at Aurora and she lifts herself up, sitting now on my forehead, and does her roar-howl call. *I'll protect you, Daddy. Always.* Gently, she runs her hand over my scales before leaping off my head. I whip my head around and watch her free fall and land on Alaric's back in a crouch. My baby definitely doesn't fear death in any way, shape, or form. I regret not being able to fight side by side with her in hopefully what was her final battle. Carefully, I shake my head to clear it. Every day is a gift, and it's time to stop being haunted by the past.

As we break over the horizon of the final mountain range, the castle's spires can be seen in the distance. Aurora and Alaric call out in unison, then quickly are followed by their guards and then myself. It's been forever since I had to roar and announce my arrival into royal airspace. My anxiety kicks up another notch, and I feel Helle trying to soothe me. Dante circles the castle first then lands in the clearing of the courtyard. Landing takes a while since room is so limited.

When it's finally my turn, I land in the center and can't help but look around at the devastation. Memories start to flood my mind as I remember what was compared to what is. I walk forward, towards the castle and reach my head up to what used to be Anca's room. I peer into what's left of the window, seeing what little is left of the room. My heart aches, remembering seeing Anca for the very last time, lying there on her bed. Unmoving and lifeless. From what I can see through the window, her bones lay scattered upon the floor from the attempts of someone who must have put the fire out. The fire *I* started to cremate her where she had laid.

Seeing the image laid before me, I suddenly back up and shift to my human form with swiftness. Clutching my chest, I feel haunted. Destroyed. My mate was never given a proper burial. I let out a guttural cry of anguish. Falling to my knees, Aurora cups my face with both hands, and within seconds she knows. I don't need to tell her what's transpired.

I dress quickly before we take off running, not listening to the others yelling for us to wait. Nothing and no one will be able to stop us from getting to our destination. We take the stairs two at a time to get to the second floor. Upon entering the corridor, Anca's room is blocked off by stones. I start crying and hitting the stones with my bare fist in a fit of rage. My heart is breaking all over again. Tears flow like rivers down my cheeks, and honestly, I don't care who sees.

Aurora places a hand on my good shoulder to stop me from hurting myself. "I've got this, Daddy. I'll get us in," she says all choked up. Her eyes are red-rimmed from her own tears that are falling freely. She quickly strips out of her clothes and shifts to her Lycan beast. She uses her taloned gauntlet to motion me to back up. Seconds after, I hear the click as it echoes all through the empty corridor as her ignitor fires up. She opens her mouth, and her force-breath weapon is unleashed upon the stones, disintegrating them all. If I didn't see this with my own eyes, I never would have believed it. I knew her weapon worked on flesh, but I was unaware of its effects on stone.

Minutes tick away like hours as I wait anxiously to get into Anca's room. Aurora finally reins in her weapon and then blocks my path. She shifts back to her human form and redresses quickly. Her mates have finally caught up with us, and Jayce hands her a bottle of water. I watch her eyes assess the stone, then she steps into the room, moving the debris as she goes.

The waves of emotion coming off my daughter drives me to my knees. I watch her move quickly and drop to her knees near Anca's bones. It's now that I notice the much smaller set of bones. Far too small to be Anca's. Aurora gently scoops them up and cradles them to her chest. She throws her head back, letting loose the most hauntingly, deathly howl I have heard from her to date. The tones she hits speak of loss and heartbreak. I feel like my heart is being ripped out all over again, listening to my daughter's pain.

I move hesitantly closer to her and see the tiny bones she's holding. The baby's skull is shaped like her beasts. Aurora had a twin. Taking my eyes from the tiny bones, I glance at Aurora. Her eyes look haunted. She brings her gaze to lock on mine, staring at me like she's asking for help.

"Daddy?" she says in the softest, weakest voice I've ever heard from her.

Jayce is the first to rush to her and wraps her up in his arms. It's now that she finally breaks and starts crying hysterically. Aurora snuggles in close to Jayce, holding onto him like he's her only lifeline. Had the baby lived, she wouldn't have been alone all those years.

Dimitri moves forward to see what Aurora is holding and starts crying immediately. "I didn't know... You have to believe me. There was no movement, I swear!" Dimitri keeps looking from Anca's remains then back to the tiny bones in Aurora's arms.

"There's no way you could have known, Dimitri. I saw Anca myself; there was no movement." I move forward and take my daughter from Jayce and kiss her temple. "I'm sorry, little one. We will build a pyre for them tonight and perform the rites that are long overdue." Aurora nods slowly, still cradling her sibling's bones to her chest.

Dominik enters the room with two silken cloths that he had found and offers one to me, and holds the other out to Aurora. Klaus and Alaric move alongside Aurora to support the cloth for her. Reverently, she arranges her sibling's bones, then carefully closes the cloth over them. "Klaus? Please go with Arnulf and gather enough herbs for mother and Seraphina." Aurora sniffles before continuing. "Mother wanted to name her daughter Seraphina, so I am naming this daughter Seraphina." Klaus and Arnulf leave swiftly after Aurora settles down enough to assist me.

"What was my mother like?" Aurora asks as she kneels beside her mother's bones. Her sister's bones lay bound, resting on her legs.

I can't help but smile at the thought of Anca. "She was wonderful; a strong and fierce leader. Not very different from you, to be honest. Sometimes I have to look twice to make sure it's not your mother talking." I chuckle softly as I help the best I can to get the cloth situated. "Unlike you, Anca refused to eat raw meat. Everything had to be cooked." I can't help but laugh at the disgusted face that Aurora makes at the thought of cooked meat.

"Father, I'll perform the rites in the pyre like I did for Andre. The fire won't hurt me," Aurora says softly. Somehow this is hurting her more than Andre's passing.

"Shall Alaric and I breathe fire upon them?" I tilt my head, trying to see where my daughter's head is with this. She nods, then begins to arrange her mother's bones on the silk. Aurora uncovers a necklace, earrings, as well as several rings. Carefully, she sets them aside so she can focus on her work. My daughter's emotions hit us like a freight train; her pain and sadness is almost overwhelming. Aurora's emotions feel like a storm upon the ocean; waves of grief hit like a sledgehammer, only to build up to hit again. My eyes focus on Aurora's stoic face. Beneath the surface, I observe the slight shifting of bone plates. It's terrifying to think how calm she appears doesn't betray the raging emotions' turbulent waves ripping her apart on the inside.

Carefully, Aurora closes up the silk and passes her mother to Dimitri. With a gentleness I didn't know my daughter possessed, she cradles her twin's remains. "I'll meet you in the courtyard at dusk," Aurora says, then exits the room quickly with Dimitri in tow.

"Will she be okay?" Dominik questions as he absently rubs his sternum. His action betrays how badly my daughter is hurting.

My eyes drift from where Anca's remains were to where Aurora had gone. "I'm not sure. Finding the pup was a shock to all of us." My chest aches all over again, just wondering if my second daughter would have survived if I had gotten there sooner. My gaze sweeps the room as I gather what worldly possessions Anca had.

"Alaric, would you and Dominik be so kind as to help organize the building of the pyre in the courtyard?" I don't bother facing them; I already know they will agree. By the time I look up and over to where they were, they are gone to work on their tasks. I have a feeling tonight's going to be a very long night.

Close to my chest, I carry the sibling I never got to meet. My heart breaks thinking of all the what ifs that come along with this discovery. Why didn't she survive? Did someone try to kill us in utero? I'm plagued by these questions that keep circling in my head. I wander aimlessly through the castle, searching for a room with a suitable table to tend to my mom and sister.

My precious sister, poor defenseless, tiny little thing. She probably didn't even get the chance to take her first breath of air. It makes me wonder if she passed on, and that's what caused me to be born early. Several turns later, I find the great library with a large oak table sitting in the center. *Perfect.* Through the bond, I reach out to my children and my mates. I wish for everyone to witness the final rites. Father taught me, and now I will teach my children. Dimitri enters silently and gently places my mother's remains on the table.

Eventually, everyone gathers around the table. Luckily, my father had somehow managed to acquire suitable types of cloth to do the wrappings. Arnulf offers to assist me with the herbs and wrappings. "Please explain to the children why I am doing these steps, so I don't break my concentration." I raise my eyes to him, and his sadness mirrors my own. A slow, steady nod is given as he positions himself near our children.

Quickly, I shift my hands to my gauntlets, and I begin to cut the strips I need. Klaus and Dominik start using their claws to cut fabric for me. Slowly, I draw in a deep breath, trying to be strong through all of this. "Arnulf? Is there a way to reach my sister in the great beyond?"

I look from her remains up into his eyes. They shift to his eagles then back to normal. "I'm sorry, my love, the elders say no. She was far too young to make that kind of connection." He feels like he's failed me.

I set the cloth down that I was holding and move over to hug him tightly. "Thank you for asking." I kiss his lips gently before returning to my task at hand.

Almost an hour later, I've applied the herbs to the cloth and then wove them like they are supposed to be. Dimitri offers my mother to me, and I draw in a deep breath before accepting her. The silk falls away in slow motion and reveals her bones to me. It's a surreal moment for me. I collect skulls, and this is one I don't wish to keep. My father is telling stories of my mother in the background as I start arranging her bones.

This is much more difficult to do than when Andre died. A physical body has a defined shape. Bones move because nothing is holding them together anymore. Every time I think I have them arranged perfectly, one piece moves, and I have to start all over again.

Alaric must have noticed my frustration and raises an eyebrow at me. "May I help, my love?" he asks tentatively.

"Please, I can't get it right, and I'm running out of time." My gaze moves to the sky, noting the change in color as the sun starts to set.

"I've got you," Alaric says, then kisses my temple. He moves his hand over my arrangement and uses a thin sheet of ice to hold everything where I wanted it. *Fuck me sideways, why didn't I think of that?*

Alaric pulls me into his side for a moment and hugs me tightly. "We are all here for you, my love. Your burden is our burden. Your pain is our pain."

Alaric kisses my lips so tenderly then passes me off to Klaus. He holds me and nuzzles my cheek before kissing me. "Whatever you need, angel, tell me, and it's yours."

Klaus passes me to Jayce, and my omega gives me the best hug ever. He lightly kisses my throat. "I love you." His words alone make me start crying all over again, and I squeeze him tightly. "I love you too." I nuzzle his cheek then get passed to Dominik.

Dom just looks down at me and gives me that bad boy smirk of his. "Hey, don't you have something you need to be doing?" He rubs his chin, causing me to give him a quizzical look with a raise of a brow. "Like kissing me?" Dom can be an ass at times, but he's my ass. I bounce up and nip his lip, drawing blood.

"Maybe," I say before he passes me to Dimitri.

My teddy bear, my rock, and may as well say my foundation. He has saved me more times and in more ways than I can begin to count. I look up into his hazel eyes, then throw my head back, exposing my throat. My emotions are all over the place. I need to feel grounded, even just for a little while. The soft rubbing of his beard over my throat almost tickles; the silkiness of his lips makes me feel something other than pain. "Not like this, beautiful," he whispers next to my ear. His large hand cups the back of my head and forces me to stand up straight. Gently, he kisses my temple again before passing me off to Arnulf.

Arnulf accepts me with open arms and hugs me tightly against his lithe frame. I hear his bird making soothing noises under his breath. I can't help but smile at how far he has come. No longer does he shy away from me or act skittish. His hands lightly grip my face as he looks me in the eyes. "Forever, from this life to the next." His words grip my heart tightly like a hug. I can't help but hug him and kiss him passionately. In a single moment, Arnulf managed to set my heart and mind at ease. I break the kiss and look back at the table. "Let's finish this."

Arnulf and I work quickly side by side, finishing the wrappings on my mother and finally my twin. To think I had a twin really fucks with my head. It takes several minutes before I finally can mostly process what could have been. When both wrappings are complete, we receive word that the pyres are ready as well.

We make our way out into the courtyard, and numerous pyres line the courtyard. One dragon shifted per pyre, ready to ignite it. I take my mother's and sister's remains and climb to the top of the pyre. The moon is full above us, and the veil is at its thinnest tonight. I set my mom and sister upon the sanctified cloth and raise my hands to get everyone's attention.

"We gather tonight to lay to rest our loved ones according to the old ways." I look to the other pyres, then down to mine. "Through fire, rebirth is possible. We free the souls of the departed to someday rejoin us." I rest my hands upon the bundles. "Tonight, I release the soul of my mother, Anca, as well as my twin, Seraphina, who passed before birth." I feel my frost starting to ghost out over the pyre as my emotions start to get away from me. "I seek safe passage for all those who fought to free our ancestral home from the blight of the Strigoi." A crack of thunder is heard in the distance with no storm visible.

"Dragons! Light 'em up! Time to send our loved ones to the great beyond." My eyes shift to that of my beast's, and my dragonic eyes lock on my mate and nod to him to release his flames. Alaric's ignitor clicks, and his fire rains down upon me. I look to my father, and he releases his frost flames. Fire and ice hit the pyre at the same time. My father's flames are so cold that they burn. I watch my clothes burn from my body and then look to the bundles before me. Eventually, their spirits' wisps burst free from their earthly bonds, and two smoke Lycans rise to the heavens. I look to the other pyres and start seeing the souls leave their earthly bonds. Our work is done here.

I launch out of the blaze and land near where my mates are gathered. Dimitri takes off his T-shirt and slips it over my head, and smirks at me. "Show off." His large hand lands firmly on my ass. The crisp smack sound gets everyone's attention. All I can do is laugh at the big guy.

"Aurora?" Arnulf says softly. "You did good tonight. It's the first time I've seen the ritual performed by so many species at once." He smiles then approaches me to snuggle into my side.

I know the amount of apex predators has him on edge. "Thank you, sweet one," I say, then kiss his temple.

"Bedtime everyone, we have a lot to figure out come morning," I say loud enough for it to carry across the courtyard. I grab

Arnulf's and Jayce's hands and start heading back into the castle.

After searching the west wing, we gather enough mattresses to make a bed for us all to sleep together. Like a little child, I run and jump into the middle, and my babies follow me, laughing hysterically. Ladon sleeps as his human but remains as his dragon during the day. He already appears to be at least three to four years older than his sister. I shake the thought from my head and pull both children to me. My mates surround us, keeping us in the middle for protection. Jayce and Dominik sleep as their wolves because of their heightened senses. Dimitri moves closest to where we are lying, and I use him as a pillow. Both my children use me as a pillow, so everyone is happy, I believe. My eyes follow Alaric around the room as he double checks everything.

Dimitri's fingers thread through my thick, white mane as his bear rumbles, trying to get me to relax. Klaus has pulled my legs over his as he leans back against Jayce. His nimble fingers massage my arches, washing away tension I didn't know I had. Silently I count my mates, and I keep coming up one short. I close my eyes and search for Arnulf through the bond. A soft smile plays across my lips when I feel his location. When I open my eyes and look up, his eagle is resting in the rafters looking over everyone and everything.

"Baby?" Dimitri says softly so as not to disturb my sleeping children.

"Hm?" I respond quietly as I lie back fully to be able to look him in the eyes.

"Andre used to do the same thing. He would stay in the highest point he could find to not miss a thing." Dimitri's eyes glow the gold of his bear as he looks up at Arnulf. "He worries about his place with us. That he's not strong enough to protect you or the children." Dimitri cups the back of my neck, massaging it gently.

"I'll make sure to speak with him in the morning. Thank you for your insight, D." I rub my face against his chest as I allow my eyes to close. I'm in the safest place on the planet. All of my mates are with me, and my children are safe. It just doesn't get any better than this. For the first time that I can remember, I have a dreamless sleep—no night terrors, no nightmares where I wake up ready to decimate anything.

CHAPTER 43

Aurora

Morning comes entirely way too soon, and I don't want to wake up. I slide my hands down my body, then pop an eye open. My children are gone, most of my mates are gone. Somehow Dimitri slid out from under my head and slipped Klaus in. Sneaky bastards, I swear one of them is a fucking magician. I look up into the rafters, and even Arnulf is gone. Hmm, I believe this is a setup. Sneaky mates. Brilliant, but sneaky.

With bated breath, I maneuver myself with the finesse of a cat burglar, every movement measured and deliberate, as if the slightest noise could shatter the fragile tranquility of the moment. My heart pounds in my chest like a drumbeat, a symphony of nerves and anticipation, as I inch closer to my target.

As I begin the painstaking task of unbuttoning Klaus's shirt, each button becomes a miniature conquest, a victory won through sheer determination and patience. With each one that comes undone, I'm rewarded with the tantalizing glimpse of his well-defined chest, a sight that sends a thrill of excitement coursing through my veins.

But despite my careful efforts, time seems to stretch on endlessly, each passing moment filled with the anticipation of what lies beneath. It's like unwrapping a precious gift on Christmas morning, the thrill of discovery mingling with a hint of nervousness, as if I'm venturing into uncharted territory.

Finally, after what feels like an eternity, his shirt lies open before me, a testament to my stealth and cunning. With a silent victory dance in my head, I turn my attention to his pants, knowing that the real challenge lies ahead. His pants are like Fort freaking Knox, and I'm trying to break in without being discovered.

There are three logical options. Cut the elastic; effective but destroys his favorite pants. Attempt to work the pants down without slapping his cock with the elastic; probability of failure fifty percent. Finally, wake him up; definitely not an option. With my heart pounding in my chest like a drumbeat, I steel myself for the daring task at hand. Option two seems like the best course of action, despite the inherent risks. As I position myself over Klaus, a surge of adrenaline courses through my veins, fueling my determination to see this through to the end.

With a silent prayer to the gods of stealth, I lower my head to the top of his pants, my canines descending in anticipation. With a steady hand, I lift the fabric and sink my teeth into the elastic, my breath catching in my throat as I prepare to execute my plan.

As I begin to inch his pants down, every movement is calculated and precise, my fingers dancing delicately over his hips in a dance of stealth and finesse. With each passing moment, I can feel the tension in the air mounting, the weight of the task at hand hanging heavy over me like a shroud.

But as I continue to work in full stealth mode, my focus remains unwavering, my eyes locked firmly on my prize. The probability of failure looms large in the back of my mind, but I refuse to let doubt cloud my judgment.

And then, just as I begin to see the light at the end of the tunnel, a sudden movement beneath me sends my heart racing. With a quick reflex born of desperation, I adjust my angle, narrowly avoiding disaster as I continue to lower his pants with painstaking precision.

But even as my breath hitches in my throat, I can't help but feel a sense of exhilaration coursing through my veins. For in this moment of daring and audacity, I've embraced the thrill of the unknown, risking it all in pursuit of a moment of mischief and playfulness. And as I finally succeed in my mission, my heart soars with the sweet taste of victory.

"Angel?" Fuck, I'm busted. Having heard Klaus, I look up, his pants' elastic still in my canines. I raise my eyebrows at him and provocatively wiggle them. If I let go now, it's going to be the mother of all cock slaps, and it's gonna leave a mark.

Fuck finesse. I firmly grip his pants and pull them swiftly down past his ass to mid-thigh. "Yes, love?" I finally say after releasing his pants from my mouth. My eyes drift down to his engorged member. Gently, I blow my hot breath upon it before I look back up at him.

As Klaus's Adam's apple bobs with a nervous swallow, I can sense the shift in his demeanor, the subtle change in his scent as arousal begins to permeate the air around us. My smile widens in anticipation, my senses heightened by the heady musk that fills my nose, igniting a fire of desire deep within me.

With a playful glint in my eyes, I lower my lips to brush against the sensitive skin of his cock, relishing in the softness of his flesh beneath my touch. The mere proximity to his arousal sends shivers of pleasure coursing through my body, my own desire mirroring his in a primal dance of passion and longing.

"Sleep well?" I murmur teasingly, my voice husky with desire, just before my tongue traces a tantalizing path along the ridge of his cock. The taste of him is intoxicating, a heady blend of salt and musk that ignites a firestorm of need within me.

As I continue to tease and torment him with my mouth, I can feel the tension building between us, the air crackling with electricity as desire threatens to consume us both. In this moment of raw intimacy, there are no words, only the shared ecstasy of two souls united in a symphony of pleasure and passion.

And as Klaus responds to my touch with a soft moan of pleasure, I know that we've entered a realm beyond reason, a place where the only truth that matters is the overwhelming need that binds us together. For in the heat of the moment, there is no past, no future, only the delicious agony of the present, as we surrender ourselves completely to the irresistible pull of desire.

His breaths are ragged. "Yes, angel." He sounds breathy; his tone makes my muscles clench with need. I'm starting to be able to scent myself. Game on, bitches.

"What does my mate desire?" I inquire as I slowly run my tongue from root to tip with my eyes locked with his. I'm at war with my beast; she wants him and wants him now.

"You, always you, my angel." I could easily bring Jayce up right now, but I know their relationship is different. Klaus reaches down and grabs my arms, and pulls me up his body.

As I shed my top, tossing it aside with a sense of abandon, the anticipation thrums through my veins like a symphony of desire. But before I can even catch my breath, Klaus's hands are upon me, tracing patterns of fire across the curves of my body.

With practiced ease, he slides my leggings down, his touch igniting a blaze of need that threatens to consume us both. The rush of sensation leaves me reeling, my senses overwhelmed by the heady mixture of pleasure and longing that courses through me like a tidal wave.

But as I move to regain my balance, Klaus is quick to assert his dominance, pinning me to the floor with a force that leaves me breathless. The sudden shift in our dynamic sends a thrill of excitement racing through me, my heart pounding in my chest as I surrender to the pleasure of his touch.

With each caress of his hands, I can feel the beast within me awakening, its primal instincts urging me to abandon myself completely to the ecstasy of the moment. And as Klaus's lips find mine in a searing kiss, I know that there is no turning back, no escape from the fierce hunger that burns between us.

In this moment of raw passion and unbridled desire, there are no rules, no inhibitions, only the overwhelming need that binds us together in a frenzy of lust and longing. And as we lose ourselves in each other's embrace, I can't help but revel in the intoxicating thrill of surrender.

As Klaus's hands assert their dominance, roughly lifting my ass into the air, I can't help but gasp in surprise, the thrill of his commanding touch sending shivers of anticipation coursing through me. With each movement, he exudes an aura of power and control, his actions speaking louder than words as he takes charge of our intimate encounter.

I feel the head of his cock teasing my slick folds, sending waves of pleasure crashing over me with each tantalizing glide. But before I can press myself up to meet him, Klaus swiftly takes control of my arms, his growl of dominance sending a shiver down my spine.

In that moment, I realize that Klaus has been reading from Alaric's playbook, embracing his primal instincts with a newfound sense of confidence and authority. And as my forearms are pressed together behind my back, restrained by his firm grip, I can't help but feel a surge of excitement at the thought of what's to come.

With a suddenness that leaves me breathless, Klaus thrusts forward, his cock sinking deep inside me in a single, powerful motion. The sensation is overwhelming, a symphony of pleasure and ecstasy that threatens to consume me whole as he claims me as his own.

As Klaus's intensity grows, I'm overwhelmed by the sudden shift in his demeanor. His once tender touch has transformed into something primal and fierce, igniting a surge of exhilaration within me. Despite the shock of his newfound assertiveness, I find myself drawn to the raw passion that radiates from him.

With each forceful thrust, a wave of pleasure crashes over me, sending shivers down my spine. Klaus's grip on my hip tightens, adding a delicious edge of urgency to his movements. The air is thick with the heady scent of arousal, mingling with the sound of our ragged breaths filling the room.

Suddenly, the door bursts open, and Dimitri strides in, his presence commanding and powerful. His bear instincts are close to the surface, evident in the primal gleam in his eyes. I can feel the tension crackling in the air as he takes in the scene before him.

"Klaus, she's going into heat... She shouldn't be," Dimitri's voice cuts through the haze of passion, his words tinged with concern. Through the bond, I sense the urgency in his tone, and my heart clenches with unease.

As the gravity of the situation sinks in, Alaric makes the swift decision to remove the children and our companions, Nicodeamus and Helle, from the escalating tension. The weight of his decision hangs heavy in the air, casting a shadow over the once-ignited passion between Klaus and me.

As Klaus withdraws abruptly, a warm sensation spreads across my back, evidence of his release. His semen trickles down my skin, leaving a sticky residue in its wake. I feel his grip on my arms loosen, and then his lips meet mine in a tender kiss. Confusion clouds my thoughts as I gaze at him, my brow furrowed in perplexity. "The guys and I decided that Dimitri should have his chance at being a dad first." Klaus smiles and grabs his clothing, and leaves.

"Let's get you cleaned up, my love." Dimitri moves to my side and assists me in standing up. "If I am to fill you with my cub," he swallows deeply, "we do it the right way, not like savages. I am more than just my animal." As Dimitri helps me to my feet, his touch is gentle yet firm, grounding me in the present moment. I feel the warmth of his hand against mine, a comforting sensation that soothes my nerves. The weight of his words hangs heavy in the air, each syllable carrying a depth of emotion that reverberates within me.

His voice, deep and resonant, fills the space around us, sending shivers down my spine. I can hear the sincerity in his tone, the raw vulnerability beneath his words. It's as if each breath he takes

is infused with passion and longing, a silent plea for understanding.

As he leans in to kiss my lips, I am enveloped in a whirlwind of
sensations. His touch ignites a spark within me, setting my skin
ablaze with desire. The taste of his lips is intoxicating, a heady
blend of sweetness and longing that leaves me breathless.

CHAPTER 44

Dimitri

Klaus was so close to having what I desired most, so bloody close. Why in the Goddess's name did I agree to leave? I know why my sense of duty is too strong, and I had to set the clean-up crew to work.

Klaus is right. I can sense the change in Aurora almost immediately as I come through the door. Being the gentleman that he is, Klaus bows out and takes his leave. As a group, we decided that I would be the next to father the children. I am beyond blessed to have such wonderful bond mates that are so understanding. I have had the longest time with Aurora and have been in love with her, though I thought it was inappropriate at the time, for what feels like forever.

As I watch Aurora, her eyes flicker with an intensity that sends a shiver down my spine. They oscillate between the pale-grey hues of her human form and the primal gleam of her beast. It's a mesmerizing sight, one that fills me with a mix of awe and apprehension.

With each passing moment, the air grows thick with anticipation, charged with the primal energy of the hunt. Aurora moves with a predatory grace, her movements fluid and deliberate. The low rumble of her growl reverberates through the air, sending a chill down my spine.

As she draws closer, I can see the hunger in her eyes, the primal urge driving her forward. Her mouth hangs open, revealing the sharp gleam of her descended canines. The scent of her arousal hangs heavy in the air, mingling with the earthy musk of the forest.

"Dimitri, my love… I need you," she breathes, her voice husky with desire. The sound of her words sends a jolt of electricity through my veins, igniting a fire within me that burns with a fierce intensity.

Before I can react, Aurora pounces, her body crashing into mine with an unstoppable force. I am overwhelmed by the sheer power of her presence, powerless to resist her advances.

As she presses closer, her scent envelops me, filling my senses with an intoxicating mix of desire and need. My bear stirs within me, responding to her primal call with a deep and primal rumble of its own.

In that moment, there is no escape, no hesitation. There is only the raw, untamed passion that binds us together, fueling the flames of desire that burn between us.

As Aurora's fierce assault on my clothing ensues, I'm engulfed by a whirlwind of sensations. The fabric tears and shreds beneath her relentless onslaught, leaving me exposed and vulnerable to her predatory gaze. The sound of ripping fabric echoes in the air, a stark contrast to the otherwise quiet surroundings of the bedroom.

With each shred of fabric torn away, the cool air brushes against my skin, sending shivers coursing down my spine. The sensation is jarring, a stark reminder of the perilous situation unfolding before me.

Aurora's eyes, ablaze with a half-crazed hunger, pierce through the darkness, sending a chill down my spine. There's an intensity to her gaze that sets my nerves on edge, a primal instinct that warns of the danger lurking within.

Before I can react, I'm forcefully pushed onto my back, the hard ground unforgiving beneath me. Aurora's presence looms over me, her gaze sweeping over my exposed form with a mixture of hunger and appreciation. It's a disconcerting sight, one that leaves me torn between fear and anticipation.

As her head lowers, a surge of adrenaline floods my senses, heightening my awareness to every touch and movement. Her lips graze against my skin, sending a jolt of electricity coursing through my veins. I can feel the dangerous proximity of her sharp teeth, a stark reminder of the primal instincts that drive her.

That long, pink muscle slips between her crimson lips to lap at my length from root to tip. I feel my own fingertips shift to my claws and dig into the rug beneath me. Maybe I've died and gone to heaven, if there is one. She keeps licking me like I'm a lollipop or her favorite ice cream cone, making sure not to miss a single inch. Sweat beads on my brow as the tension begins to coil in my lower stomach. She's getting me so fucking close I can feel my balls drawing up tight with every lick. And then she does it, she grabs my balls tightly but not painfully, and gives me one final lick from root to tip and I blow my load. I feel like a randy teenage boar just getting my first taste of a girl. It's almost embarrassing how easily I shot off.

I then look down and watch my beautiful, fierce mate licking up every single drop of my seed. She reminds me of a little kitten chasing after rivets of milk that's spilled on the floor. The throaty rumble coming from her tells me she's enjoying it immensely. Once she's finished, she crawls up my body and then puts her teeth to my throat. For some fucked up reason, she thinks I'm going to just lay here and submit. Never fucking happening. I grip her body tightly and flip us over so she's pinned on the floor. I take her hands and hold them high above her head, using my free hand to hold her hips down. Oh yes, this is going to happen, and it's going to happen my way. I line myself up with her dripping wet sex and thrust forward without any warning.

She does that roar-howl of hers that absolutely makes my fur stand on end. I can feel and see the scales rippling up and down her arms as she struggles, trying to gain some semblance of control. Never going to happen. I set my rhythm, hitting against her back wall hard, feeling every inch of her muscles quiver with each thrust. She's getting close, and that's all I can ask for. It's common knowledge amongst us shifters. If you can get the female to orgasm in heat, your ninety percent guaranteed that your seed will take.

Without delay, I drop my head quickly and suck one of her nipples into my mouth, lightly my teeth grip the engorged bud, and start flicking my tongue over it. Her body starts to writhe almost uncontrollably under me. I go in for the kill and pick up speed, pistoning in and out of her hard and fast. It's just when I'm getting ready to cum, I move to the other breast, and her muscles clamp down on me crushing my shaft. She starts to milk me for all I'm worth, her body begging for my seed to fill her womb. Who am I to deny her? Several pumps later, my orgasm overtakes me, and I feel my seed shooting out and into her womb: every pulse, every quiver from her dragging out my orgasm.

Slowly, we come down from our blissful high and I lick at her throat gently. For good measure, I bite her over my original mating mark, shooting her over the edge again. This is going to be a very long day for me. I will not leave her side until I'm sure my seed has taken root and my child grows within her. I know at some point later this afternoon I'm going to have to tap out, there's only so much a man can take. But I want to give myself the absolute best chance of being the one to father the children this time, so I will keep going. I will push myself to the edge of exhaustion and then some. As long as my mate is safe and sated, I'm a happy man.

We spend the better half of the morning falling in and out of bed, barely taking breaks to use the restroom. By lunchtime, Klaus bravely arrives with a tray of food in hand, hoping to not interrupt anything. Aurora is finally out cold, sleeping in the middle of the absolutely destroyed bed. I'm barely sitting up at this point. I'm so tired, but damn, do I feel good.

"Damn, bro, you okay?" Klaus questions with his head tilts to the side watching me.

"Define okay. I'm exhausted in the best way possible." My eyes drift to Aurora for a moment, then back over to Klaus. "Honestly, I think my balls are just shooting dust at this point." We share a good chuckle over my situation.

"Anytime you're ready to tap out big guy, I'm your man," Klaus says and then points both of his thumbs at himself with a big smile on his face.

"I may just take you up on that. As much as Great Bears are known for their stamina, a bitch in heat can definitely push you beyond your limits." A yawn escapes my lips. I just can't. I'm done. I'm beyond done. I think I've honestly invented a new level of being done.

Klaus tilts his head, looking at me and then over at Aurora. "This may just end up being a team effort. If she's wiped you out already, I'm worried for the rest of us."

I nod my head in agreement with Klaus's statement. "I just need a couple of hours to rest without being attacked." Carefully, I slide myself off the bed, hopefully without disturbing Aurora. "I'm going to go oversee the construction and destruction of the main courtyard." I shrug my shoulders as I look from Klaus to Aurora.

"Try and nap, man, it may take all of us to keep her sated." Klaus moves and sits on the bed, his back to Aurora. "Without Alaric here, we all have a shot at fatherhood." Klaus smiles broadly, looking at me. He's just as excited as I am.

A yawn escapes my lips, and I quickly raise a hand to cover my mouth. "Maybe a nap is in order before I check things out." I clap Klaus on the shoulder. "Good luck, brother."

As I start to leave, Aurora awakens, unbeknownst to Klaus. He's so focused on me that he's caught off guard when our mate pulls him back to her. I can't help but laugh at the look of shock on his face as I leave the room.

Several minutes later, I find myself in the courtyard, and I start assessing everyone's progress. Dominik is the first to approach me, and his pupils dilate almost immediately. "It's that time again?" he asks as his eyebrows shoot up.

"Yes," I say tersely, just before yawning yet again. Lord help us over the next three days.

"That explains Alaric's swift departure sometime last night. He took Nico, my mom, and the kids with him to the summer palace." I watch Dominik pace in front of me as he ponders the gravity of it all.

"He was truly serious when he said he would leave to give us all a fair shot at fathering a child." I smile then bro-hug Dominik. "Klaus is up there now, and she was already voracious this morning. You may want to check on him in about an hour," I say smiling at him, knowing full well Klaus may tap out in about two hours.

"Thanks for the heads up, D. Maybe I'll grab Jayce and bring him with me." Dominik shrugs, still smiling like a fool.

"Do what you feel is best. Aurora's going to be of a singular thought until her heat is over. We need to work in shifts." I start laughing like a madman. I'm completely serious about working in shifts, and Dominik knows it.

"I'll check on him in about two hours and bring Jayce with me. I'll let Arnulf know to check in about three to four hours after we head up." Dominik smirks, knowing full well that this isn't going to end well for any of us.

"Sounds good to me." I dip my head slightly to him before heading off to talk to the dragons in charge of knocking down the walls. We decide structurally it's safer to remove the walls and the towers and rebuild if Aurora wants the walls back. Knowing my mate, she won't want the walls. She's more of an open floor plan kind of gal. I find a place in the courtyard that's untouched, where a large, old apple tree stands alone. Slowly, I walk around the tree and find the spot I had carved my name into its bark. Carefully, I climb up into the branches and find a good place to rest. I'll close my eyes for a little while, then go grab something to eat. I hope the others fare well while I rest.

CHAPTER 45

Arnulf

It's been three days of switching out to take care of our mate's needs. I feel like such a wuss. I can only last a little over an hour before tapping out. Eagle females don't go through heats. Twice a year, if we are lucky, they are fertile and that's it. Not this every three months insanity that poor Aurora goes through. Poor Aurora, who am I kidding? Poor us! I mean, it's fun for the first day or two. After that, it's like is it over yet?

Slowly, I drag my exhausted ass out of Aurora's room and head towards the kitchen. Upon arrival, I find my other bond mates all hunched over their cups of coffee, trying to wake up. "Morning," I mumble as I flop into my usual seat.

Klaus shoves the bacon down towards me. "Eat up. Try to regain your strength," he says, sounding beyond exhausted.

"Look at poor Dimitri. He looks like he's lost weight." I say and flail my arms around. Stressed out doesn't even begin to sum up how I'm feeling.

"Good news is her heat has ended. I don't smell her anymore," Klaus says on an exhausted exhale.

Dominik's eyes shift to his wolf, then back to his hazel-green. "Alaric has been informed. They'll be back by lunchtime." He starts to laugh softly. "I elect Alaric to be on Aurora duty."

It's pretty much unanimous that we all need a vacation from the last three days. I pick at my breakfast; exhaustion is real. My bacon is delicious. I just barely have the energy to eat it. Several times I catch my head falling towards the plate.

Jayce comes over and snuggles up to me and holds me tightly. "You need sleep, brother. Take a quick nap." Jayce leads me over to the window bench that we built for Aurora. He sits down and places my head in his lap. "Close your eyes for a little bit. I'll watch over you," Jayce says as he runs his fingers through my hair.

His gentle strokes soothe me to the point I fall asleep quickly. My sleep for once is dreamless and fulfilling. In my dreams, I see the babies to be born. A bear and I believe a Lycan pup and a third I can't see clearly. Wow, Aurora is going to be upset carrying three babies at once. Then again, my visions haven't always been one hundred percent accurate.

Blinking several times, I finally open my eyes to find Jayce leaning back against the wall, also napping. Carefully, I remove myself from his lap and gently lay a throw blanket over him. Smiling softly, I lean forward and kiss his forehead. You honestly can't help but love Jayce. He worries about everyone and takes care of them without any prompting. He just knows when you need him, and he's there.

I glance around the kitchen and grab some pastries before heading to check in on Aurora. Silently, I creep down the hallway and reach Aurora's door. I open it a crack and peer inside. She's nowhere to be seen; perhaps she's left already. I close my eyes and reach out through the bond to locate everyone. Alaric is back with the children and is in the courtyard. Aurora and the guys, minus Jayce, have joined them. Gently through the bond, I reach out to Jayce and rouse him from his slumber.

As I wander the hallways, I notice the signs of reconstruction that's been taking place over the last week. We still haven't settled on where we are to live yet; I'm sure that we will make that decision in the upcoming days. Once I arrive in the courtyard, I get tackled by Tia and Ladon. I can't help but laugh as I fall back, cradling both children to me. "I missed you two so much!" I rub my face against theirs, letting my bird whistle its greeting to them.

"Daddy Arnulf, your animal sounds silly," Tia says, giggling as she pets my short beard.

I can't help but laugh with her. "That's because I'm not an animal, sweetheart. I'm an Eagle otherwise known as a raptor." Tia's eyes go wide as she looks at me.

"You can fly with me?" She gets off my lap and starts jumping up and down. "Momma! Daddy Arnulf can fly with me too." Tia says with enthusiasm. "I have Daddy and Father that can fly with me." Tia hits that high pitch squeal that makes all the wolves in the family cringe.

"Okay, little one, we can fly, but first we need to make sure everyone eats and is settled after your vacation." I raise my eyebrows at her. I can see how tired she is.

"If I must, Daddy Arnulf. Will you tuck me in for my nap, please?"

She tilts her head, looking up at me, and I can't help but smile at her.

"Of course." I stand up, scooping her up in the process. Ladon is fast asleep in his mother's arms and in his human form for once. He could easily pass for a six-year-old versus Tia, who appears to be about four.

I follow Aurora up to where the twins have their room. We set up their bed to be a nest where they would be comfortable as either their animal or as children. Aurora climbs to the middle of the nest and lays Ladon down. I follow suit and snuggle Tia in next to her brother. They instantly reach for each other and have to be touching in some way, shape, or form.

Silently, we leave the room and walk swiftly down the hallway. "Sorry about before, Arnulf," Aurora says. She softly sighs then looks over at me. "Honestly, I can't help it. I hope I didn't hurt you." Her eyes convey her concern as she looks me over.

I smile as I lean over to kiss her temple. "Definitely much different than the way Eagle females are." Lightly, I trail my hand down her abdomen to gently rest over her womb. "I, for one, cannot wait to see who joins our family next." Aurora's smile brightens immediately.

"Neither can I, to be honest." She starts to laugh softly. "It'll be tough to tell the difference between Jayce's and Dominik's pups." She shakes her head still giggling. "Eye color is a dead giveaway unless they have my color." She shrugs her shoulders.

A hearty laugh escapes my lips. "I guess we will worry about that when the time comes." Gently, I pull Aurora to me as we head back out to the courtyard.

Several shifted dragons work on knocking down the remaining walls and the towers after they were emptied. "My Queen?" Marco says, then bows deeply.

Lightly, Aurora places her hand on Marco's shoulder. "Yes, my dear Marco?"

"We are almost finished with removing the walls as well as the towers." He motions to all the work going on behind him. "Do you wish a new wall to be built?" He tilts his head to the side, awaiting an answer.

I watch Aurora's facial expressions as she surveys the courtyard. "Yes, we will rebuild them. This time stronger than before." Aurora pulls away from me and starts to turn slowly. "Construct the walls with my children's safety in mind." Marco nods slowly.

"As you wish, my Queen," he says as he brings his fist to his heart and bows deeply before taking off.

Aurora has a look on her face I can't quite decipher. "Something on your mind, my love?"

A soft sigh escapes her lips. "Yeah, Marco and my other guards are well over five hundred years old. None have met their mates yet." She looks longingly at me then my other bond mates. "Now that the war is over, I can only hope they find their mates."

I understand where she's coming from. In reality, I never thought I'd be blessed with a mate. "All we can do is hope. I'm curious, though."

Aurora spins to face me, and her eyes narrow. "What do you know that I don't know?"

Crap on a cracker, she's gotten good at reading me. "What if one of your daughters ends up being one of their mates?"

Aurora looks quickly between Dante, Edgar, and Marco. "I couldn't ask for more loyal and protective males for my children." She smiles and nods slowly. "It'd be cool."

"What if it's Tia?" I raise an eyebrow trying to gauge her reaction.

Aurora's eyes dart from the guys then towards where Tia is in the castle. "I'd be happy for her. Alaric may or may not be as accepting." She busts out laughing. "Who am I kidding? A king of a powerful nation could be her mate, and he'd still try to keep her from the world."

Another hearty laugh escapes my lips. "As long as he doesn't lock her away in a tower, it's okay." We share a good laugh as we walk around the courtyard.

"Angel?" Klaus says softly. "Don't forget we have all of those young males you spared to deal with."

Aurora rolls her eyes. "I know, did we retrieve the females from where they were being held?" She takes on a very serious demeanor.

"Yes, angel. Grandmother and Helle are seeing to their care." He smiles softly, knowing that has appeased her.

"Please have Elsa visit with me later. I wish to be checked over and start my vitamins," Aurora says as she lightly touches her stomach.

"Do you think it took?" Klaus asks as he and I look at her excitedly.

"My heat is over, and well, all of you took very good care of me," Aurora says, smiling. "We'll know for sure in a few weeks."

Klaus and I look at each other before he takes off running towards where Dante is. Dante strips and shifts almost immediately, and they take off. I start laughing hysterically. "I guess he's a bit excited." I lean in and kiss Aurora's cheek.

"I bet you all are as excited as I am." Aurora leans into my side before kissing my cheek and heading back inside.

Slowly, I make my way over to where Dimitri and Alaric are. They are looking over plans for the reconstruction. "Need any help, guys?"

Alaric lifts his head, and a knowing smirk crosses his lips. "So?" He starts to chuckle. "How was your first heat?" Alaric can barely contain his chuckle at my expense.

Exhaustion is evident on my and Dimitri's faces. There are dark circles under our eyes; we've both lost weight. Generally, we look worse than we did when we went to war. "How often does this happen?" I ask as I run my hands down my face.

"About every three to four months, give or take a few weeks," Dimitri says on a yawn. "That is unless she's given birth. Then we're safe until the babies are done being breastfed." Dimitri rolls his eyes then runs his hand down his face.

"My children didn't need to be breastfed long, so her heat came back three months later," Alaric says, then tilts his head. "There are herbs we gathered while we were away that will stop Aurora from going into heat. Well, that is until she wants to." Alaric starts to laugh again. "Depending on who managed to have a baby this time." He shrugs his shoulders. "I figure we have at least four more heats and vacations for me."

Honestly, I never thought about it that way. I look around the courtyard at the various other mates that are present. Any one of us can be the father this time. Granted, Dimitri and Klaus have the best chances since they were with her first and tended to last the longest.

Then again, you have the twins, so it's twice the chance that the child is a wolf. I don't mind either way; I know that eventually, my time will come and I will have a child as well. I'm just happy to belong to a family that is so loving and caring. Alaric doesn't have to leave to make sure that each of us has a chance at fatherhood, but he does.

"I'm going for a flight. I'll be back for dinner," I say to my bond mates before stripping out of my clothes. Carefully, I fold them and leave them on the nearby bench. Shifting to my Eagle is always so freeing for me. For now, I'll scout the area, making sure there's nothing left uncovered.

CHAPTER 46

Aurora

Life is technically back to status quo. My heat is finally over, and I'm able to regain some semblance of control of my life outside of it. As I descend the stairs going into the castle's main hall, my mind wanders to those I left in hibernation. There are about a dozen to a dozen and a half young males that I spared during the assault. I believe today is the day that I will go and determine if they live or die.

At the foot of the stairs, my beloved enforcer and mate, Dominik, waits for me. "What's your desire for today, my love?" He flashes me that debonair smile of his and leans upon the banister.

As I reach the foot of the stairs, I gently cup his jaw and draw him to me. Softly, I press my blood-red lips to his till I hear his wolf grumble at me. A smile plays gently upon my lips as I pull back to look him in the eyes. "I need you to come with me; we need to attend to those young males that I spared." I start walking down the hallway holding Dominik's hand as we head towards the dungeon. "It's not fair or conducive for them to spend their life behind bars." I shrug my shoulders, then sigh softly. "I truly detest being judge, jury, and executioner for such young ones."

Dominik stops me suddenly, and comes to stand in front of me, blocking my path. Gently, he grips both of my hands and holds them together in between us. "Do you wish for me to take that burden from you?" he asks softly, not wanting to overstep his bounds.

"I would do it in a heartbeat, without question, just to make your life is easier and spare you some pain." Dominik's eyes flash to that of his wolf, and I can see how sincerely he wishes to shoulder the pain that I'm sure to feel.

It's moments like this I realize that I am truly blessed. Someone somewhere has really been looking out for me. I go from being an orphan with no parents to finding my father, finding my mates, to having children of my own. Through Arnulf, I got to meet my mother. It's moments like this that I start thinking about all the little things others take for granted. Gently, I nuzzle Dominik's cheek then kiss his lips again. "My love, just you being with me is a blessing. Your desire to shield me from pain and unsavory situations means the world to me." I shrug my shoulders lightly. "I know I don't express this often, but I love you, and I'm grateful for everything that you do for me."

Dominik smiles and draws me close to him again, holding me tightly to his broad chest. "You've come a long way Aurora. You've gone from barely able to show any affection to being the best mate a male could ask for." He gently presses his lips against my temple and stays there for a few moments before pulling away.

"It's nice to hear the words every once in a while, but I feel it in my heart and my soul how much you love me." He gently places his hand over my heart and smiles at me.

"I know I have a place in here, and that's all that matters." Dominik grabs my hand again, and we begin the long descent into the dungeon.

Alaric has long since woken the young males up from their slumber. Most prowl the cage lost and confused. A couple look angry, almost too aggressive for their years. My gut tells me that at least four of these young males will not submit and will die by my talons.

After releasing Dominik's hand, I step forward and place my hands on the bars before me. My eyes shift to that of my beast as I observe each of these males within the cage. I hate the fact that we have to have them caged up, but I also don't know if we can trust them outside of it. One young male comes to the cage's edge and stares at me. He's a bold one; this should be interesting.

I start unleashing my Alpha power little by little, watching the rest of the young males cringe and submit. The one still standing at the bars is a potential Alpha, therefore a threat to my mates. I increase the amount of power that I'm using, slowly watching him buckle before me. It doesn't take all that long to drive him into submission, but he has not yet gained my trust.

By the time I drive this one male into submission, Marco and Edgar have arrived with Dante in tow. Dominik fills them in on what I'm doing, and one by one each of them takes out one of the young males to stand them before me. I step up to the first one and lock eyes with him. Almost immediately, his eyes drop and he whines. "Do you accept me as your Alpha?" I question. In silent submission, he rolls his head to the side and exposes his throat to me. I give Edgar a nod, and he walks off, removing the young man from the dungeon.

Next, I move to Marco and the young male that he's holding. This young male doesn't even attempt to look me in the eyes and rolls his head to the side. "I accept you as my Alpha," he says quickly and without hesitation. I study him for a moment longer and decide by scent he's an Omega like my Jayce. I give Marco a nod, and he walks off with the young man.

Dante just so happens to hold the male I had to drive into submission. He's still being a bastard. The defiant look in his eyes just tells me he's going to be nothing but trouble. "I don't even have to ask you if you accept me because you don't," I say with as much venom as I can muster.

"I would ask if you yield, but I know that you won't." The young man just smirks at me.

"I grant you the gift of death eternal." Without hesitation, I lunge forward and sink my canines into his throat. Instantly, I inject him with as much venom as I can pump into him. Stepping back, I look at him, my lips covered in his blood as it drips onto my chest. His body starts to convulse in Dante's grip. The venom is fast-acting, causing almost a seizure-like condition before all the blood vessels in his body explode. Dante drags the corpse off into an empty cell then goes for a new male to test.

By this time, Marco and Edgar have returned, and both are going to the cage to pull out two new males as well. The next three submit rather quickly and fully without hesitation. Part of me, I'm almost slightly disappointed that I didn't get to dismember anybody else. Still, I guess it could be a good thing. Dominik remains at my side as I test each of the males that were left. Only one more gives me a hard time, and we saved him for last.

Dominik goes in and has a scuffle with this young male. Part of me wants to send an ice spike up this male's ass and have it come out the top of his skull. The other part of me wants to look at the fear in his eyes as I rip his heart out and drip his blood across my scales. Maybe I can do both at the same time? Nah, I might accidentally harm Dominik, and I really don't want to do that to him. He finally gets the young male out of the cage and pins him to the wall. The young male just starts to shift, and I lock eyes with him.

"You will not shift!" I say with my beast's growl filling my voice.

The unearthly tone I hit makes my three dragon guards cringe. They know I'm on edge; they know I can instantly lose my sense of control and decimate this male. I'm trying not to be that ruler; I'm trying not to be the monster I've been made into. But fuck it, it's one of those days. In the back of my mind, Limp Bizkit's song "Break Stuff" is playing loud and clear.

Dominik releases the male, and he immediately charges me. Without hesitation, I use one of the tricks that Gallus taught me. I use his gift of intimidation, pressing that and my alpha power upon this male. I was almost starting to get concerned when he didn't immediately buckle. Then again, my sick side was kind of loving it, looking forward to a fight. I finally break his resistance, and he falls to his knees, cradling his head. Fur randomly ripples across his body as he tries to fight for control.

Eventually, I lessen the pressure upon him. Some might have called that a mistake; I call it an opportunity for a kill. He lunges straight up at me, his claws extend ready to sink into me. It all seems to happen in slow motion, at least to me. When he is halfway to me, I shift both of my arms quickly, bringing my talons out and sinking them into his chest and throat at the same time.

My right hand grips his trachea and the muscle surrounding it. My left hand wraps around his heart, feeling it beat against my palm. Every beat of his heart sends blood streaming down in between my scales. The crimson stands out so beautifully against my iridescent white and silver scales. The look of fear in his eyes is delicious. He's not able to hold his shift anymore; his claws have retracted, and he's just a mere man.

"I sentence you to death for attacking your ruler. I do give you credit, though," I say as I tilt my head to the side. "Most don't make it this close to me before I kill them." I shake my head back and forth.

"I wish you had chosen a different path. You are young and strong and could have lived a long time." Suddenly I pulled both my arms back, taking with them his heart and a section of his trachea.

He sputters and gasps for several seconds and then falls to the floor like a ton of bricks. I watch the blood slowly drain out of his body and coat the stone floor. Two lives were wasted today, all because Vladimir had poisoned their minds. On the bright side, I managed to save fifteen young males.

Through the bond I learned from Klaus, three young males know where additional females are being held. Klaus, Alaric, and Dimitri leave immediately with the three young males and four other dragons to retrieve them. I want to go with them; I want to help bring these females back. Dominik slides up behind me and rests his hand on my lower stomach, reminding me of my possible precious cargo. Mother fucker, at least the females will be safe, and having Klaus with the rescue party should help put their minds at ease.

"My love, we need to get you cleaned up. You wouldn't want to meet the new females looking like you stepped out of a horror movie." He smiles at me, then motions to the fact that my dress is now covered in blood. I'm still holding the man's heart in my hand and part of his throat. I shrug my shoulders because to me, it's no big deal. I offer the body parts to Edgar and watch him cringe. I start to laugh as I do something completely out of character for me. Quickly bouncing up, I kiss him on his cheek, leaving a bloody outline of my lips on his porcelain skin. I can't help but laugh as I walk swiftly down the hallway back towards the staircase.

These stairs leading to the dungeon absolutely freaking suck. What were they built by, smurfs? They're too damn short and too close together. I don't take long going upstairs and getting changed and cleaned up. I have way too much I want to accomplish today to get lost in a hot shower.

WHEN I FINALLY STEP OUTSIDE OF my bathroom, I find Jayce sitting on my bed waiting for me. My sweet, beloved Omega, he's absolutely my heart and the pride and joy of my family. Without a second thought, I run over to him and nuzzle his cheeks. I'm always excited to see him. Jayce brings out the best possible me that I can be. He makes me want to be a better person and to be more even-tempered and kinder. What I used to accomplish through fear, he's able to achieve faster through kindness. Perhaps I can learn a few things from him and start doing things more his way than mine. Without his knowledge, I've made him the diplomat in the family. I mean, why not? The guys already use him to propose ideas that they already know I'm not going to be happy with. Why can't I do the same? Have Jayce propose the ideas that the others may fight me on?

"How are you feeling, beautiful?" Jayce asks as he kisses both of my cheeks softly and then nuzzles my jaw.

"Doing okay so far today. No real complaints other than I wrecked another dress, and I had to kill two of the males." I shrug my shoulders lightly.

"All things considered, it's really not that bad when you put it into perspective," Jayce says, pondering the numbers that he had in his head from before. "Two out of seventeen, I'll take those odds." He starts tapping his chin looking at me. "Let me guess, the guy with the white-blonde hair and the one whose hair was almost black."

Immediately, I start laughing because Jayce hit the nail on the head. "Correct as always, my love. You know me way too well," I say as I laugh.

"It's not a question of knowing you too well, it's that I know how much bullshit you'll tolerate." He says as he lightly strokes my chin, then trails his fingers down my neck to my shoulders.

"Very true. I won't let anybody question mine or any of your authority in this pack." I rest my head on his shoulder and wrap my arms around his waist, just needing to be held for a moment. The last thing I need is for some young upstart to join the pack and poison it from the inside.

"We completely understand, my love," Jayce says as he rests his head on top of mine and wraps his thick arms around me. "You're only doing what's best for everyone involved, not just in the short term but for the long haul."

"Some days, I feel like an absolute monster, something that Mary Shelley would have written in one of her books." I shrug my shoulders lightly and nuzzle Jayce's chest as I close my eyes, listening to his heartbeat.

"We wouldn't let you become that kind of a monster, my love." His fingers run through my hair, removing any knots from my shower. "It's not like you don't give people a fair chance to prove that they're worthy of your leniency."

"Yeah, I guess you're right. It still sucks having to play judge, jury, and executioner." I sigh softly and squeeze him a little tighter. "It's not a weight or a burden that my conscience would allow me to place on someone else." I pull back to look up into his eyes to make sure he understands what I'm trying to tell him.

"We all have our demons that we hide, my love. You shouldn't be the only one haunted when there's six of us able to share the burden." Jayce keeps running his fingers through my hair, trying to soothe me.

"I know, baby, I'm trying. It's just so hard to let go." I try to smile even though I feel a little guilty for not opening up more. I raise a single brow looking at Jayce. "I wonder what demons Arnulf is hiding?" I wiggle my eyebrows at him.

"The man can talk to the dead. I'm pretty sure he has lunch with whatever demons he has," Jayce says matter of factly. I can't help myself, and I start laughing hard.

"Aurora, remember we all love you. I love you." Jayce presses his lips to my forehead and stays like that for a while. Eventually, he pulls away and starts to lead me out of my room. "Let's go see how everyone is making out."

Laughing softly, I follow behind him. He knows exactly what to say and do to make most of my concerns melt away. Jayce always manages to put my heart and mind at ease with simply his presence. He mentions heading outside to enjoy the beautiful day and the nice breeze that's blowing across the courtyard. We wind our way through the castle and out into the fresh air.

CHAPTER 47

Jayce

I lead Aurora outside and surprise her with an impromptu picnic under the apple tree. My mother, Klaus's grandmother Elsa, and the Fae Laurel, all sit under the tree waiting for us. Aurora's smile lights up immediately as she spins around to hug and kiss me. She moves quickly and sits between Helle and Elsa, then starts filling her plate. Well, I've officially lost my mate for the afternoon.

My excitement is at a fevered peak. I can't wait to find out whose babies are going to be born this time. The order really doesn't matter to me; I know eventually I'll get to meet my children. But for now, I can't wait to see the little ones that will be born into the family soon.

Looking across the courtyard, I see Dimitri, and he waves me over to join him. Happily, I walk over and sit close by. "I never thought I'd live to see the day that Aurora would willingly sit with other females," Dimitri says with wonder evident in his voice.

My eyes move back to observe Aurora more closely. She's all snuggled up to my mom, leaning on her and accepting her affections.

"She was telling me the other day that she was excited to finally have a mom." I shrug slightly and look back over at Dimitri.

"I can't fathom a female not being raised with a mom. Though it kind of explains why sometimes she's emotionally distant." I start to fidget with the edge of my shirt, looking down at it.

"You're right Jayce, it was tough raising her. We did the best we could. But... we're guys. What the hell did we know?" He lowers his head and sighs softly.

Gently, I embrace Dimitri and lean my head on his shoulder. "You both did fantastic with her. Look at how great she turned out." I motion towards Aurora.

"She is intelligent and can take care of herself, and it's all because of you!" Lightly, I touch his cheek to get him to look at me. "You did a fantastic job. You were a great authority figure." Smiling, I look into his eyes and make a goofy-looking face at him until he laughs.

"Okay, okay, I get it. I just feel bad when she has problems." He shrugs his broad shoulders and goes back to watching Aurora.

Gently, I pat him on the shoulder before walking off. Alaric is over by what's left of the wall, watching over the dragons as they remove what remains. "How's it going, Alaric?"

"Slow but steady Jayce. Where's Aurora?" He looks around the courtyard then he notices her sitting with the other women. Alaric raises his hand and checks his pulse in his neck. "When did that happen?" He motions back at Aurora and the other females.

"Scary, isn't it?" I say half-jokingly.

"Scary isn't the word for it. Remember when Aurora was ready to slaughter Klaus's grandmother?" He gestures in their direction.

"Now they're besties, it seems." Alaric tilts his head to the side as he studies the gathering. Out of nowhere, Ladon drops down out of the sky, startling us. "Holy shit, little man. Don't do that to Daddy." Alaric and I jump, both clutching our chests from the mini heart attacks I think we both had.

My hand is still firmly pressed to my chest as I try to calm my racing heart. "Is your sister with you, Ladon?" He shakes his head no and stretches his wings.

Tia's giggles carry through the courtyard as she runs from a shifted Klaus. His black Lycan giving chase. Honestly, he could easily catch her, but she keeps leaving ice patches that he keeps almost falling over. You would think he would learn by now to quit while he's ahead. Tia stops suddenly and shifts her arms to gauntlets like Aurora does. Klaus's Lycan stops and starts to back away from her. Thankfully for him, Aurora gets between him and Tia. They have a mini staring contest before Tia shifts her arms back to normal and joins the other women.

Aurora makes eye contact with myself and Alaric and shrugs her shoulders, rolling her eyes. I can't help but laugh at how similar the two of them are. "I think we're in trouble with those two, Alaric," I say it so matter of fact.

"No doubt, my friend, no doubt." Alaric half chuckles to himself, watching the two of them sit together with the rest of the women.

"How did bringing the rest of the Lycan females back go?" I look between Klaus and Alaric.

"It was rough. Most just need a good bath and a hot meal." Alaric looks down. "Some are carrying pups, most are not." His tone tells me that it was not a joyful discovery.

"Oh." There are no words to express what's going through my mind. Klaus comes walking back over after grabbing shorts.

"It wasn't a happy situation where those females were. Our healer is going to give them options." Sadness washes through the bond from Klaus. Lycans are being hit the hardest with infertility and to possibly lose these pups is a hit to the species. Aurora comes up behind Klaus and wraps her arms around his waistline. I can hear her beast rumbling to his, trying to soothe him. Gradually, she makes her way around to face him.

"Elsa and I will be going to sit with the females shortly." She lowers her eyes for a moment then presses her forehead against his chest.

"Any who do not wish to raise the pup they are carrying." Aurora swallows hard and draws in a deep breath. "I wish to adopt them and raise them. They shouldn't have to die because a sadistic asshole made a choice that wasn't his to make." Hesitantly, Aurora raises her eyes, looking up at Klaus. Doubt of her decision flickers over her before she schools her features to betray nothing.

"Do you mean it?" Klaus's smile brightens immediately. He grips her hands and looks into her eyes.

"I wouldn't have said it if I didn't mean it." Aurora's eyes move from Klaus, then to Alaric, and then me. Alaric and I look at each other then smile and nod, giving her our blessing.

"Angel, besides the birth of my own pup, this is a blessing. Thank you for this beautiful gift of life." Klaus kisses Aurora's forehead and sighs happily. "We have couples in my pack that can't have children. We can place some of the pups with them as well," Klaus says hopefully.

"Whatever you think is best, handsome. We can personally take the pups to meet with prospective parents," Aurora says, smiling up at Klaus.

"Let's take Gram's with us and go talk to the pregnant females. We can give them the option of letting a childless couple adopt instead," Klaus offers Aurora his open hand; without hesitation, she grabs it and pulls him with her.

I watch Aurora stop by the picnic and grab Elsa and my mom. It's probably one of the smartest moves she could make besides bringing me. The three women lead the way into the castle and head towards the wing where the rescued females are resting. "That went a lot better than I expected, to be honest," I say, then look at Alaric.

"Either way, those pups, if they are allowed to be born will find loving homes. Be it with another family or us," Alaric says with a confidence that gives me goosebumps.

Eventually, Arnulf returns from scouting the surrounding areas. He shifts back to his human form, and one of the staff members brings him a robe. He surveys the scene before him, making sure that everything is safe and that he could speak freely. He comes up alongside me and Alaric, waiting to make sure it is okay to talk about his discoveries.

Alaric's eyes shift to that of his dragon as he looks around the courtyard. He leads us off and out through one of the openings towards Mirror Lake. We pass over what he calls Apple Tree Hill and then down into the lower area. The lake is off into the distance, and the sun is just starting to set. Once he is sure that we are out of hearing range and no place for anyone to hide, he motions for Arnulf to start.

"As Dimitri had earlier stated, there is a hunting cabin to the north on the far side of the lake." Arnulf motions in the general direction in which he had spotted the cabin. He finds a stick nearby and uses it to draw in the dirt so that we have a rough map to go by.

"There's several different caverns with chambers that extend far underground that aren't too far from here." Carefully, he draws those additional chambers and tunnels and how far he suspects that they go.

"Generally speaking, if there are any Strigoi left, they would be in this tunnel system here." He circles the area in which he suspects is the deepest of the cavern systems.

"I suggest that Marco and at least one other Black Dragon go to both of the openings to the cavern system." He draws X's on the ground where he would position the two Black Dragons.

"Since their acid breath is dense and heavier than air, it should creep slowly along the cavern floor. With any luck, if they breathe enough of it into the caverns, it should reach our targets if any exist."

Alaric studies the drawing on the ground carefully. He reaches out through the bond to Dimitri and updates him as to where we currently are. He also calls forth for Dominik to join us to make sure that everybody is on the same page. The only mate he does not summon is Klaus because of his important work with Aurora at the moment.

It takes several moments before everybody finally arrives and starts studying the map that's on the ground. Marco and another Black Dragon arrive shortly after and shift back to their human form. Both men come over, exchanging handshakes and back claps with all of us.

Alaric goes over the suggested plan yet again, and seeks Dimitri's council and knowledge of the area. Dimitri confirms the suspicions that the caverns do run much deeper underground than we originally suspected. "There is a secondary entrance to the same cavern system from another smaller one," he says calmly as he draws the second system with its entrance on the map as well.

Dimitri issues suggested orders to Marco and his friend, Damien, as to where they should focus their acid breath. Tonight would not be the best time to do it. If the tunnels do hold any Strigoi, they would be able to escape out into the night.

Since the Strigoi are creatures of habit and tend not to roam far from where they were laid to rest, this is the most logical place to find them. We agree that this is the best plan to make sure that the last of them fall.

We head back to the courtyard to help with the final bits of construction and destruction. According to Aurora's wishes, she just wants to have a low-lining wall close to the castle but a more formidable one further out. Her thoughts are that the babies, as they grow, need a safe place to play. She doesn't want them growing up feeling like they are trapped or prisoners, like she did. She wants them to know freedom but also safety as well. I really do commend her for being able to see past everything that she had been through. Most people in those circumstances would have been broken, but not our Aurora. Thankfully, everything that she lived through only made her stronger.

Dominik decides to head in and double check on how the renovations inside are going. Dimitri heads back to make sure that the bears are doing well with the woodworking in the throne room and main foyer.

For now, I head over to where I last saw my mother and request for her to follow me. We walk over to the small gardens that manage to be preserved and have a seat. "What's on your mind, Jayce?"

Helle knows me all too well. After all, she is a mom. I fidget with the bottom of my shirt yet again, like I always do. "To be honest, Mom, I'm a little worried. I want to be a good dad. I want to be the best mate that I can be, but I didn't have the greatest example."

Mom smiles and wraps her arm around my shoulders, and holds me tightly to her. "Yes, it's true your father was a horrible man, but you are the exact opposite of him. I don't think there is a spiteful or hateful bone in your entire body." Mom smiles and kisses my temple.

"It's easy to say that, Mom, but I have killed. I killed Sinclair of all people because he went after Aurora." I hang my head in shame, having killed someone I had once loved.

"Oh please Jayce! That drama queen had it coming to him. He went after your true mate. If you didn't kill him, I'm sure that she would have." Mom releases me and stands before me, looking me dead in the eye. Her wolf surfaces for a mere second and then recedes just as quickly. "You have a good heart, Jayce, don't ever let me hear you speak ill of yourself again." She lightly pats my cheek and smiles.

"Okay, Mom, you're right." I sigh softly and lightly shrug my shoulders. "I just don't want to fail any of the children born because I'm not good enough at being a dad."

"See, this is exactly why you will be the best dad ever. You are so worried about failing that you are going to do everything within your power not to." She gently grabs hold of my hand and starts leading me back into the castle. "Let's go have a nice cup of tea and sit in the library and find something new to read. I hear there's a new Poe retelling in there." She wiggles her eyebrows at me and starts laughing softly.

Mom and her horror stories. I swear I have no clue how she doesn't have nightmares every night. The descriptive writing of her favorite author makes my fur stand on edge. If it were me, I would be waking up in the middle of the night whimpering like a puppy. It looks like this is how I will be spending my afternoon, having tea with mom and reading books. There are worse ways to spend my afternoon, but there are also better ways. Our parents are only with us for a little while, so I'm going to enjoy the time I have with her. Maybe later this afternoon I can catch up with everybody else and see how their days went.

CHAPTER 48

Klaus

Aurora's steps never falter on her way to the east wing of the castle. My hand remains on her lower back as we move through the corridors, with Elsa on her left holding her hand, showing support. It's a very emotional and touchy subject that we're about to discuss with these females. A painting down the hallway catches my attention. As we get closer, it looks exactly like Aurora but with black hair. "Angel, look. It's a beautiful painting of your mother." I motion to the painting, and Aurora pauses to look at it.

"Mom was younger than I am now when she died." Softly, she sighs and moves forward to touch the picture frame. "If memory serves me right, mother was a little over a hundred and fifty years old when she had Seraphina and me." Sniffling, Aurora turns away from the painting to get back on track.

"Little one? Do you wish to talk about it?" Elsa asks softly as she strokes Aurora's bicep.

"No, thank you, Grams, some things are better left to rest than to dredge up." Aurora's eyes flicker between her human grey and her beast's mercury.

"It's not good to repress things, angel," I say gently as I brush my fingertips on her shoulder.

"I know, but right now there are unwanted pups that can possibly be saved. I wish to focus on them rather than deal with what's rolling through my head." The depth of her pain is evident in the way she's looking at me. I nod slowly and give her a break. It's only a temporary solace for her. I will question her mental health later when all of her mates are present.

Softly, Aurora knocks on the door to the suite the females are being kept in. A blonde female named Sophie opens the door, and her jaw drops seeing Aurora standing there. Quickly, she lowers her head and bows as she opens the door wide. Time moves slowly for the next several moments. Shock and recognition cross the faces of each of the eleven females in the room. A female with darker brown hair comes over and grabs Sophie. "Do you know who that is?" she whisper yells at Sophie.

"Duh, Riley, that's the last Marelup." Sophie points at Aurora's family brand on her right forearm.

Aurora raises a brow, looking at the two bickering back and forth about who she is. She extends a hand out to the females. "I'm Aurora, Anca's daughter." Her eyes flicker between her human grey and her beast's mercury.

Both Sophie and Riley lunge for Aurora's hand and take turns shaking it. I can tell by Aurora's posture that she's uncomfortable with all the attention and contact. "Okay, ladies, let's let our queen into the chambers so she can visit with everyone," I say as gently as possible, as I place my hand on Aurora's lower back.

Aurora draws in a deep breath and nods her thanks to me, and allows me to lead her to the sitting area. Slowly, she lowers herself onto the pillows and gets comfortable. "I wanted to come see you all myself." Her eyes roam over each female, acknowledging them. "I am truly sorry for what Vladimir and his officers had put you through. Most died at my talons." Aurora shifts her right hand to her dragon-scaled gauntlet, her talons gleaming in the light of the room. Her eyes are fixed on her talons as she flexes her hand for the females' benefit before her. Quickly, she shifts her hand back and rests both hands on her lap.

"I understand some of you are with pups and were taken as mates against your will. Is this correct?" Aurora asks as gently as she can.

In unison, the females all murmur that what Aurora said was correct. "Do you sense the males that formed the bonds are dead? That the bonds have been severed?" Aurora looks anxiously between the females.

Only one still holds her head down. "Who is the male that took you as his mate, young one?" Aurora questions hesitantly.

The young female's head shoots up, and she looks panicked. "Please don't kill Sven. He's my true mate. He kept the other males away from me." Tears begin to stream down the female's face.

Aurora closes her eyes, and through the pack bond, she searches for the male in question. A smile crosses her lips as she locates him. "He's been summoned. He'll be here shortly to collect you."

Joy instantly crosses the female's features as she jumps up and runs over, throws her arms around Aurora and hugs her. My poor angel looks panicked. She's not used to affection outside of our bond. *"Think of her as Tia,"* I say to Aurora through our bond. Aurora instantly relaxes and snuggles the female, and starts making the soothing sound of her beast.

Moments after, three knocks sound at the door, and Aurora stiffens. Without hesitation she moves swiftly and puts herself between the door and the females. Frost begins to gather in her hands as she watches the door closely. I move to open it and Aurora cocks her head to the side as her eyes land on the male standing there. It's the same young male she spared and gave a braid of her hair to. He still wears it around his wrist. "Ioana!" he yells and bolts across the room towards her. They embrace tightly and cry tears of joy.

"My Queen, thank you for sparing me that day in the tunnels. I was trying to find a way to get to my mate during the war." He furrows his brow then looks down at the braid on his wrist. "Why did you spare me?" Ioana looks at the braid, then back to Aurora as well.

"You are a descendant of my grandfather, the King." Aurora tilts her head as she looks from the couple then to me.

"You are the last living relative I have from my mother's side," she says as she returns her gaze back to him.

"Your family is my family. Pack protects pack," she states matter of factly.

"You mean I'm a Marelup?" He furrows his brows.

Aurora slowly shakes her head. "Sadly no, Sven, that name is passed from female to female. You are a Constantine, my grandfather's family name." Aurora moves and extends her hand to Sven. "I'm guessing your mother is the offspring of my grandfather and one of the females that worked in the castle." Aurora rolls her eyes. "Apparently, he liked to take liberties with some of the young females."

There's a look of shock that moves across Sven's and Ioana's faces. "Vladimir was the same way, my Queen," Ioana states flatly. "It's why five of the other females are with pup."

The temperature in the room starts to drop immediately. Not long after, Alaric comes barreling into the room with Dimitri hot on his heels. "Do you know what Vladimir did?" Aurora shrieks, venom dripping from her descended canines. Her rage is palpable in the air.

Alaric goes to comfort Aurora, and she immediately rejects him. The look of shock on his face is priceless. Jayce, Dom, and Arnulf arrive just in time to witness the whole thing. Dimitri tries his hand at getting close to her, and she immediately melts into him. Out of curiosity, I start to approach and she grabs me and pulls me into the group hug. Hmm, this is an interesting turn of events.

The other mates watch with great curiosity at the new dynamics. The last time Aurora was pregnant, she only wanted Alaric. Now so far, it's Dimitri and me. Wait! Does that mean I get to be a dad next? My eyes dart over to my grandmother and she smiles at me. I think I may be onto something. Eventually, Aurora wiggles free from our embrace and moves before the five pregnant females.

"It doesn't matter to me who the father of your pups are. I would like to make a request." Aurora sits in front of the females, making eye contact with them. "Let them live. There are families in Klaus's pack that are childless." Aurora looks down and rests her hand on her lower stomach. "I would consider it a favor to me if we can give those childless couples a pup." Aurora keeps her eyes lowered as she listens to the females speak between themselves.

"My Queen?" A young female says softly. Her stomach is huge, and she appears to be close to giving birth.

Slowly, Aurora raises her head to look at the young female. "Yes, my dear?" she says tenderly, watching the female's stomach move.

"I would like my baby to go to a family." She steps side to side, appearing nervous.

"May I request to meet the members of your mates pack? Maybe my true mate is there?" she states the last part as a question, not sure where Aurora's thoughts may be.

"Fair enough. You can even meet the family that will be raising your pup, if you wish." Aurora's soft voice shocks the rest of us. She's so tender with these females. It's quite odd and almost unsettling the way Aurora is gently handling these females. Maybe it's because she, too, is pregnant, or perhaps motherhood has changed her some. Either way, it's strange to watch this inter-action amongst Aurora and all the females.

Nodding slowly, the female extends her hand to Aurora. When Aurora reaches out, she places her hands on her stomach. A broad smile creeps across Aurora's lips as she feels the baby moving. "Thank you for this gift. I hope we can find your mate, sweetheart. Everyone deserves their happy ending." Aurora leans forward and kisses the female's forehead, then looks to the others.

"Who else would like to accept my offer?" All but one female accepts. The last one wasn't far along and decides not to endure the pregnancy. I could see the war waging in Aurora's eyes. Being an Alpha, she could force the female to endure the pregnancy. But then again, it's not Aurora's style to force anyone to do anything if she doesn't have to.

Aurora motions to my grandmother, and she has the girl that didn't want the pup to follow her. Without hesitation, Aurora stands and leaves the room with her head held high. Through the bond, we can feel the pain she's in even though she's refusing to show it. We make it into the royal suite, and she starts to cry the moment the door closes behind us.

I move in quickly and scoop Aurora up into my arms and pull her flush to my chest. Her tears flow freely down her face as I run my fingers through her hair, trying to soothe her. "I don't understand… Why?" Aurora manages to get out between sobs.

Gently, I kiss the crown of her head and sigh softly. "Angel, you have to understand. That mating was forced, and the female is young and can't work through it." I nuzzle her hair, then rest my cheek on the crown of her head. "We managed to save four of the five pups. Lucky pup number six is going to be raised by its parents."

I pull away slightly and look into her pale-grey eyes. Lightly, I run the backs of my knuckles along her jawline and smile at her. "You did good today. Before you went in there, those pups had zero chance of survival." Tipping her chin up further, I gently kiss her plump lips. "I'm so proud of you, angel, so fucking proud."

Aurora's face lights up at my praise, and a smile graces her blood-red lips. "Thank you, Klaus, it's tough to see the big picture at times." She snuggles in close to me and rests her head on my chest again. With the way things are up to now, I never thought I'd be in the position I am in now. It was always Alaric and Aurora. I'm guessing it's because of the babies and who has paternity.

"I'd hate to break up this love fest, but Elsa sent me to gather Aurora for her check-up and vitamins," Dominik says and extends his hand out to Aurora.

"If I must!" she says with a mock sigh and rolls her eyes.

"Yes, you must, sweetheart. We need you and the baby healthy and strong." Dominik tilts his head, studying Aurora.

She smirks at him again, then runs and jumps on Jayce's back. "Let's go cutie! Time for momma to get tortured!" Aurora and Jayce take off laughing.

Shaking my head slowly, I approach Alaric, who looks beside himself. "You ok, buddy?"

"Yes and no. I mean, I knew the day would come when she would be carrying one of her other mates' babies, but I didn't think I'd be rejected." He shrugs his shoulders then looks between Dimitri and me. "If I had to venture a guess, I believe you two managed to father the next clutch of babies," Alaric says as he strokes his beard.

"I suspected the same thing," Dimitri says with wonder in his voice. "I can't believe I'm going to be a father." He raises his eyebrows, looking slightly shocked as reality sinks in.

Dimitri sways on his feet, and Alaric and I have to catch him and assist him to the floor to sit safely. "I'm going to have a cub. An actual cub, Klaus. Alaric, what do I do?" His bear flares to the surface, his eyes that golden hue of his bear.

"It's a miracle for sure, big guy," Alaric says as he grips Dimitri's shoulder.

"Since Aurora is a twin, you factor in wolves and bears have multiple births." He shrugs his shoulders slightly.

"She's carrying at least two babies with the way she's seeking you both out." He smiles and claps me on the back.

"Congratulations, gentlemen. Welcome to fatherhood!" Alaric says, laughing as he leaves the room. I have a gut feeling we are in for a wild ride.

CHAPTER 49
Dominik

Holding Aurora's hand, we walk through the halls of her mother's castle. She glances around, not really looking at anything. Just looking lost in thought as we make our way over to where Elsa has her makeshift medical office. "Are you okay, babe?" I lightly bump her shoulder, trying to get a reaction out of her.

Her hand moves over her lower stomach then motions to the castle. "Is it wrong that I'm not ready to be here yet?" She turns to fully face me and her eyes are that of her beast, betraying her stress level.

"Not at all, love. We can go anywhere you wish." Gently, I place my palm on her lower back and lightly rub it. "You've made some tough discoveries here. You tell us where you want to go, and we'll leave immediately," I say softly, kissing her temple.

Aurora breathes in deeply before letting the breath she was holding out slowly. "I'd like to go back to Klaus's pack lands." Her eyes lock on mine before she stands on her tippy toes to kiss me softly.

"Your wish is my command, my love." I hug her tightly before we approach Elsa's door. Three short knocks later and she opens the door, ushering us inside.

"So good to see you, sweetheart." Elsa embraces Aurora tightly, then hugs me as well. "So you think you're with pup again?" She smiles as she leads Aurora over to the lounge chair and helps her lay down.

"Elsa, it's only been a few days since my heat ended. I don't believe it's possible to tell already, is it?" Aurora asks curiously.

I shrug my shoulders when Aurora looks at me then we both turn our focus on Elsa. "There's always a way to tell, little one. Especially for a female that has given birth before." Elsa smiles then starts to palpate Aurora's stomach. Apparently, Aurora has a ticklish spot near her hip bone I wasn't aware of. Interesting.

"Hopefully, making me laugh will give us answers, Elsa," Aurora says, still giggling, trying to keep a straight face.

"Well, on the bright side, you are definitely carrying offspring." Elsa smiles, then looks at me, then back to Aurora. "The end of next month, I'll have a better idea of a due date." Elsa helps Aurora back up to her feet then kisses both of her cheeks. "Congratulations, momma." Elsa hesitates coming over to me but does so anyway.

The look on Aurora's face says it all. She's pretty sure whose baby she's carrying by her beast's reaction. She lowers her eyes and looks away from Elsa and me. Once Elsa releases me, I move to embrace Aurora and kiss her.

"Babe, mine and my brother's time will come." Gently, I kiss her lips and nuzzle her cheek. "I love you, and that's all that matters." I pull back slowly and lick my lips. "Besides, you get some sexy curves when you are pregnant." I wink playfully at her, and she lightly slaps my arm.

"You're so naughty, Dom!" Aurora smacks me several more times and each smack makes her laugh even harder.

"Ow ow ow, I'm being attacked by the great white beast." I shriek in mock horror and fake tremble in terror. Elsa rolls her eyes at me, and Aurora giggles louder. The rest of our bond mates join us just in time to watch Aurora slap my ass. The crisp sound of her hand impacting my muscular ass echoes around the room. The sting left behind makes my cock stir in anticipation. Apparently, I enjoy being spanked these days. More than likely, it's because my beloved mate smacked my ass.

"Dom! You hurt my hand with your firm ass." Aurora waves her injured hand in my face.

Quickly, I snatch her hand and examine her red palm. Softly, I kiss every single inch of her hand, making sure the booboo is all better. I smirk at her then scrunch my nose. "All better precious?"

Aurora takes her hand back and looks at it. "Yes, much. Thanks, Dom." She kisses my cheek then turns to our bond mates. "I'm definitely pregnant again, according to Elsa." Aurora looks over to Elsa and smiles at her.

She steps away from me and sighs. "I'm not ready to reside here yet. I'd like to return to Klaus's pack lands." She locks eyes with Klaus, and he smiles and dips his head, then leaves the room.

"Please make preparations for our departure. I'd like to leave as soon as possible," Aurora says softly, then reaches back for me.

Moving quickly, I grab her hand, and she drags me out of the room and down the hall.

Several twists and turns later, she has us outside and heading towards the woods. I have no clue what my mate is up to. She's up to no good, whatever it is. We walk for at least twenty minutes before she stops and looks around. I prepare to say something, and she raises a single finger to me as she focuses on the sounds around us. Aurora has that wicked gleam in her eye as she sizes me up.

"Dom, baby, it's been a long time since you've hunted me." Aurora hits a sultry tone that has my cock hard and throbbing in seconds.

She approaches me and starts unbuttoning my shirt painfully slow. Gunmetal-grey eyes lock with mine as she pulls my shirt free from my pants. Fingertips ghost over my shoulders and slide my shirt down my arms. I feel like her prey; I feel as if I am to be the one hunted. With sure fingers, my belt is removed and the buttons on my jeans undone. Aurora slips her hands inside my pants, her palms flush with my hips as she slides my jeans to the ground. On her knees before me, she looks up at me, her beast fighting for control. Her tongue darts out of her mouth and lightly touches the underside of my hard shaft from root to tip. Aurora stands before me and begins to unbutton her shirt. I feel her eyes roam over my body like a lover's caress. She drops her shirt on top of mine, then removes her leggings, adding them to the pile.

"Catch me if you can!" Aurora says before taking off, running deeper into the forest.

My Dire Wolf rips free of his human shell, and my paws hit the ground at a run. I dare not howl and call the others to me. This is what my mate desires, and I shall do exactly what she wishes. Aurora darts in and out of the trees, keeping just far enough ahead that she's barely out of reach. I nip playfully at her heels, enjoying the chase.

Up ahead, I see a nice mossy area, and my gut tells me this is where the chase will end. Aurora stops suddenly and drops to all fours facing me. Her head tilts to the side in submission, awaiting my approach. Lightly, I press my wet nose to her throat. Carefully, opening my mouth wide, I take her delicate throat in my teeth. A low growl escapes my lips as I apply a tiny bit of pressure. Her scent shifts immediately, her arousal intoxicating and makes me start to salivate.

As I release her throat, she begins to whine and wiggle her ass in the air. Her scent surrounds me and drives me insane. I circle her several times before I come up behind her and lick her wet folds. Aurora's beast rumbles in appreciation as I lap up her sweet sticky moisture. My cock is throbbing and starting to protrude from its sheath. My muzzle rubs along her hips, and she drops down onto her forearms, fully presenting herself to me. I want to howl so badly right now; my dominant alpha mate is in full submission. Quickly, I rear up and mount her, shoving my engorged shaft deep within her.

My thrusts are slow and methodical. It's something about taking her like this that I savor so much more. I'm mindful of my dewclaws, making sure they don't rip up or tear her delicate human flesh. My paws grip her tighter as I feel her channel starting to quiver around me. Turning my head sideways, I bite her back, sinking my teeth into her flesh. Her orgasm detonates around my shaft, pulsing and milking it for everything I'm worth. It doesn't take long for my balls to start to draw up tight. Several more thrusts, and I sink my shaft deeply into her, my mating knot locking me in place. My seed spurts out in pulses, coating her womb. Carefully I shift back to my human form and release her flesh from my mouth. I'm still locked deep within her as I wrap my arms around her and roll us onto our sides. The aftershocks from our orgasms still rack our bodies for a while longer. Lightly, I trace Aurora's ribs down to her abdomen. Lovingly, I place feather-light kisses along her shoulder.

"Hmm, I've missed that, Dom," Aurora says breathlessly. She reaches back and runs her hand over my arm.

"It's definitely something special between you and I, love," I say as I run the tip of my nose over her shoulder blade. Sighing softly, I press my lips to her skin. "It's nice to just relax and not be on edge all of the time." I wrap my arms tightly around her, holding her flush to my chest. My mating knot is finally loosening up, and I can start to move again. My hand slides down her body to her mound; I circle her clit, drawing out soft moans from her.

Suddenly, she pulls away and shoves me on my back. Her beast is in full control, and her canines have descended. "Such a bad boy, Dom." She smiles, looking down at me as she takes my length deep within her.

Slowly, she rocks her hips setting a rhythm that is maddening: not fast, yet not slow. It's a pace that keeps you on the edge of falling into absolute bliss. I go to grip her ass, and she slaps my hands away and pins them to my chest. A low growl escapes her lips as she presses down on my wrists. "I'm in control here, baby. You lie back and be a good mate and stay hard for me."

She winks at me as she changes her angle, and I feel the first quivers of her impending orgasm. I'm fighting like all hell trying to hold off from coming before her. Apparently, I love being dominated by her, just like she does with me. Suddenly, she pulls me to sit up, pushing me deep within her. Finally, I have control of my arms again. I use one to brace me to say upright and my free hand goes straight to her clit rubbing it furiously. Her orgasm hits her like a tidal wave, and her mouth descends, and her canines sink deep into my shoulder. My mouth grips her shoulder as I sink my teeth deep into her flesh. We buck and writhe together, riding the wave of our orgasm.

Aurora's giggles break me out of the bliss bubble I was in. I pull back gently to look into her eyes, and she points up to the tree. Arnulf apparently watched the whole thing. I wave at him. "Taking notes, brother?" I say half-jokingly.

Arnulf drops from the tree and shifts before his feet hit the ground. "Kinda? But seriously, everyone is ready to leave when you return." He looks back in the direction of the castle.

"Nicodeamus and Helle are opting to stay behind to oversee the construction. Um, I'll meet you back at the castle." Before we have the chance to say anything, he shifts and takes off, heading back home.

"I guess we should get going," I say as I shrug my shoulders at her.

"Sadly, yes. Damn adulting..." Aurora giggles and shifts into her hybrid beast, then takes off in the direction we came.

Shifting quickly, I close the distance between us. I swear I think I've gotten faster since becoming her mate. We tear through the forest and head back to where our clothing was left. By scent, I know my brother was here. Jayce thoughtfully left baby wipes as well as drinks for us. Aurora smiles as she lightly touches the presents Jayce had left for us before cleaning herself up and getting dressed.

She passes me the wipes and then a drink when I'm all cleaned up. We pick up our garbage and start walking back hand in hand. "You're a good mate, Dom, I'm lucky to have you," Aurora says softly as she wraps her free hand around my bicep. She hugs my arm tightly and leans her head on my shoulder.

Moving fluidly, I slide in front of her, dropping the bag and gently grip her chin to raise her gaze to meet mine. "I'm the lucky one, love."

A smile crosses my lips as I tilt my head. "You saved Jayce and my people from our father's reign of terror." Gently, I stroke her jawline. "You gave Jayce a choice to accept you or to stay with his boyfriend. I don't know of anyone who would have done that for him." Lightly, I kiss her lips. "I've seen monsters, first-hand, love, *you* are not a monster." Tears well up in her eyes as she looks at me. Her plump bottom lip quivers as she tries to hold back the emotions she's feeling.

"I love you, Aurora, now and forever." I pull an intricate band out of my pocket and show it to her. It's made in the shape of a wolf. Raising my hand, I run my fingers through her thick, white tresses till I find a braid. Carefully, I pull it out and undo some of her braid, and then weave the charm into it. The wolf sits in the middle of her hair braid where she can pull it forward and look at it.

Aurora grips her braid and touches the wolf sitting there. Her eyes flicker to her beast for a moment, then back to human as she regards my gift. "Jayce and I had it made so you would have a bit of us with you always," I say, watching her examine the present.

"It's perfect, Dom, you and Jayce did wonderfully." She smirks, then bounces up and kisses me. "We better get going before they come looking for us." She giggles then takes off at a sprint, following the path back.

It doesn't take long to make it back to the castle, and not shocking the dragons are all shifted, and everyone is waiting. Aurora shrugs her shoulders and mouths *oops* at me, then runs to Alaric and the babies. I hate flying... Unfortunately, it's the fastest way to get us where we need to be. Marco is apparently my ride today. My goofy twin is dancing on his back, singing to himself.

Hesitantly, I climb up onto Marco's back and take my seat between his wings. Jayce comes and sits beside me and leans against my shoulder. "So? Did she like it?"

Nodding slowly, I pat my brother's thigh. "Yeah, she loved it. I braided it right into her hair." Jayce visibly relaxes.

"Do you think we'll have pups next?"Jayce asks hopefully.

I can't help but laugh and shake my head. "How would we tell whose is whose? We're twins." Laughter escapes my lips as I try to contain it. Other than eye color, there would be no real way till they come of age.

"You're right. It'll be nice to have pups running around the den, though." Jayce starts laughing as Marco takes off.

"Alaric will be more at a loss with more wolves in the house." Jayce has a point, and I start laughing right along with him.

"Only time will tell, brother. For now, let's enjoy each litter as they come and wait for our chance," I say confidently, trying to reassure my brother. He nods slowly and moves to lie on his stomach. Damn, he's got a great idea. Moving carefully, I lie on my stomach with an arm wrapped around a spine on Marco's back. Jayce shakes his head at me before closing his eyes to sleep. I look around one last time before closing my eyes to enjoy a much-needed nap.

CHAPTER 50

Alaric

The flight back to the pack lands was uneventful, thankfully. It feels odd to me that I'm not the center of Aurora's universe. She's not ignoring me or anything, I'm just used to being the one she always came to for comfort. Now... now I don't know what my role is. The dynamics have changed and I'm guessing that's going to happen with every birth. I carry my mate and my children on my back. It's not that I don't trust the others... Okay, I'm a bit of a control freak and want to personally oversee their safety. After everything my mate has endured, I just want to give her a happy and safe life. Is it wrong of me to take every precaution? Nicodeamus is in full agreement with me. Then again, he's a father who only met his adult daughter a year ago.

The field we use to land on has been cleared, and most of Klaus's pack has returned to the town. I circle several times, making sure that our guards have landed first to ensure our safety. The winds are with me and help me gently glide to the ground. Three strong pumps of my wings and my touchdown is flawless. Slowly, I lower my massive form to the ground and extend my wing so that it's easier for Klaus to get onto my back.

I feel my babies awaken first, their little taloned feet moving along my scales and then a push before they launch into the air. I watch them having fun riding the wind that's moving through the field. It's only been a few short months since their first flight. And each time they take off, my heart swells with pride, knowing that my bloodline continues on.

I turn my head slowly to watch Aurora awaken and go into Klaus's arms. It tugs at my heart the way that she's holding on to him. A few months ago, I was where he's at right now. Am I jealous? Yeah, I'm man enough to admit that I am. I guess this is how the others have been feeling since Aurora became pregnant with my children.

It's now that I notice that Dimitri is waiting at my side for Klaus to help Aurora down. It's a modified game of pass the Aurora because Klaus scoops her up in his arms then drops her straight down to Dimitri. Aurora giggles upon impact and wraps her arms tightly around Dimitri's neck. Yeah, I'm jealous. I shouldn't be jealous because she never puts anybody above the other. But I'm still just a man, that for a time, was the center of her world.

As soon as Klaus is off my back, I shift to my human form and stretch my muscles. The flight always takes a lot out of me, especially carrying my precious cargo, but I wouldn't have it any other way. Aurora comes bounding over with a pair of pants for me and smiles. "Hey, no looking bummed out, you."

She pokes my chest several times. "I know it's going to take some adjustment for you. And that's my fault. I clung to you like a small child to her teddy bear." She sighs softly and shakes her head back and forth.

"I love you, Alaric. Time nor space will ever change my feelings for you." Aurora goes up on her tippy toes, and I wrap my arms tightly around her waist, holding her to me. She kisses me passionately and reminds me exactly how strong our bond is. Her beast rumbles to me, causing my dragon to answer her. This woman owns me on a primal level. Mind, body, soul, and beast all belong to her without question. It's my own insecurities that cause me to question my place with her. Carefully, I lower her back down to the ground and onto her own two feet.

Klaus's grandmother comes running over to us and offers her hands to us. "My King, my people have food prepared in the main house for you and your family," Elsa says happily as she tries to pull the two of us towards the house.

"Elsa, you don't have to address me as king. I'm just Alaric." I shrug my shoulders and smile at her, trying to be reassuring with my statement. Aurora pokes my side and starts laughing at me. Apparently, what I'm saying versus how I look are two different things.

"For a man, my beloved, you have the most epic resting bitch face," Aurora says with a giggle. She, who is the queen of the resting bitch face, just said that *I* had one.

I smirk, looking down at her and then school my features to be cold and emotionless. "I took lessons from you, my beloved ice queen," I say as gently as possible and then kiss her temple, hugging her tightly. The next thing I know, my thigh is ice cold, and it feels like my pants weigh a ton. Aurora skips away just before I look down and see that she froze my pants solid. Leave it to my mate to make her point.

Elsa attempts not to laugh but to be honest, I can't help laughing at it myself. I finally make it inside after I thaw my pants out.

Everybody's already sitting at the table digging into the wonderful meal the ladies that run the kitchen have prepared.

Interestingly enough, Aurora is sitting between our two children, trying to get them to use utensils. Ladon has almost perfected using a knife and fork. Tiamat, on the other hand, has her hands shifted to that of her gauntlets. She's using her talons almost like chopsticks to pick up her food after she cuts it. Aurora's laughing her ass off while attempting to be serious. Her attempts are an epic fail but valiant nonetheless.

Dimitri moves over to Tiamat next and whispers in her ear. "Okay, Papa Bear, I'll try, but just because you asked me to."

Tia does her typical pout with her little rose-colored lips before shifting her hands back. An ethereal glow surrounds her pale-grey eyes for a moment. I can feel a slight tickle at the back of my brain. Shit, my daughter is in my head. I turn quickly to face her, watching exactly what she's doing. I'm not sure exactly what she's searching for, but as fast as it occurs, it ends. Soon after, she picks up the knife and fork and starts cutting her food properly. Of all the things that she could have searched my memory for, she took the ability to use utensils. Thank the Goddess above for her innocence. The things that my poor child could have seen would have aged me at least a hundred years.

Aurora sits there staring at me with a brow cocked. Through our mate bond, I show her exactly what our daughter was searching for. A chuckle escapes Aurora's lips before she looks at her daughter. With a quick roll of her eyes, Aurora goes back to eating her breakfast at last.

I reach out through the familial bond to our patriarch, Nicodeamus. He fills me in on the fact that the ability to search others' memories is a throwback to his grandmother, the Blood Queen.

He also tells me that Tiamat retaining scales along her spine, shoulders, and across her hips is another Blood Queen trait. It makes me start to wonder if my son also has the scales down his spine that I haven't noticed. I look over to Aurora quickly and share with her the information her father just shared with me. Nonchalantly, she plays with the collar of Ladon's shirt. She pulls it back and looks down into his shirt. By the slow shake of her head, I know that he does not bear the scales along his spinal column. It makes me start to wonder if it's just a female trait in the family. Aurora has random scales down her spine but nothing like the pattern that Tiamat does.

Klaus and Jayce clear the table and set everything into the dishwasher to be cleaned. The rest of us head into the living room to just relax. Once there, Aurora goes over to her guitar and starts playing with the strings. It's now that I notice there's a full drum set and two other guitars sitting in the middle of our living room. I raise a brow at her, and she starts laughing.

"I fully intend to have everybody in this family playing something in the near future." She walks over and hands the drumsticks to Dimitri, who looks at her quite puzzled. She locks eyes with him and places her hands on his temples. The glow from her eyes can be seen from my place on the couch. I can feel the tension rolling off of Dimitri through the bond. What in the world is my mate up to?

Several moments pass before she releases his head, and he walks behind the drum set. He takes a seat and starts testing out the drums. Once he's comfortable, he starts playing a song I'm not familiar with. Aurora smiles, grabs a guitar, and starts playing. She looks over at Jayce and Dominik, and they give her a quick nod. They get up and go grab two of the microphones. They start singing a song that I've yet to hear. It's the song called "Outlaws and Outsiders" by some man named Cory Marks. The main vocals are handled by Dominik, but the more aggressive singing is handled by Dimitri from behind the drum set.

Aurora sits there, happy to be playing her guitar in the corner, letting the guys have fun singing the song that apparently they've been working on. Part of me is jealous I wasn't included in this, but then again, neither was Arnulf. Arnulf and I run around the room, opening up the windows letting the music drift out to the pack.

It doesn't take long to start noticing a gathering outside. Ever since Aurora gave birth, no one dares come into her personal space when the babies are present. Babies—my daughter appears to be four years old, yet she's less than a year. My son appears to be almost seven and yet five minutes younger than his sister. It was a blessing and a curse to keep them in their dragon forms to keep them safe. The blessing was that they were able to defend themselves. The curse is that they grew up much faster than we had anticipated. My son is bound and determined to reach adulthood quickly, to learn to fight and defend his family. I didn't realize that he felt so defenseless being so little. A hatchling should never have that feeling, and part of me feels that I failed as a father. Speaking of hatchlings, Klaus comes into the room with both of my children hanging on his legs as he's trying to walk.

I run my hands down my face, trying to clear the negative thoughts. Aurora tilts her head, looking at me, picking up on my emotions, and I force a smile to try and ease her mind. Her happiness is what's more important than the turmoil swirling in my mind. That poor woman has dealt with so much in her short life span; I don't know how she's kept it together. Females are revered in our culture because they are so rare. Yet, she's been hunted, poisoned twice and still remains standing. It's a testament to how powerful her bloodline is and her resolve to win. Most females would have buckled, bent to the will of others, and gave in under pressure. The six of us are truly blessed to have her as our mate.

Aurora decides to do one more song and switches it up a little bit. This is a song I definitely recognize from having heard her play it a few times already. It's her favorite song from In This Moment; the title is "The In-Between." The lyrics are very fitting, especially for her. The looks of an angel and the rage of the devil itself reside within her form. I guess you could say she is the embodiment of being in between. Not completely Lycan, not completely dragon; to me, the perfect mix of the two. She's always at war with herself, though, not as bad as it was before. Instinct versus logic seems to be her biggest fight these days. The beast within wants to destroy, the human side tries to find a decent middle ground.

The tones that Aurora hits as she sings this song make my scales stand on edge. The raw, unadulterated power that comes off of her brings me to my knees. I watch my daughter, Tia, start to mimic her mother's moves. Halfway through the song, Tia is standing in front of Aurora with her back to her mother and mirroring every movement. Lord help the man that ends up with my daughter. He's going to end up with a mini Aurora with a full-blown dragon form. Hell on Earth? It's possible, but I'm going to do everything I possibly can to prevent it.

The song ends, and the crowd outside erupts in applause. Aurora smiles and lightly bows to the crowd gathered outside through her window. It's now that Klaus suggests the wolves go for a run and stretch out their tight muscles. Aurora, Klaus, Dominik, and Jayce all head to the back door, shift, and disappear into the woods within a heartbeat. The three of us that remain look at each other then head off to handle our respective duties now that we've returned.

CHAPTER 51

Dimitri

My bear is driving me up the wall. He wants me to follow Aurora into the woods during her hunt. My other instinct is to provide a safe nest for her to return to.

After pacing around the house for about half an hour, I go into town. Several of the stores have reopened, and I go and investigate. The linen store is my favorite; I purchase several of the softest blankets and sheets I can find. With bags in hand, I run home and down into our private quarters. There's a room down here that's supposed to be for storage, but it's currently empty.

Several text messages go off, alerting me to my other purchases being delivered. Multiple trips are made to bring my items downstairs. "Do you need help?" Arnulf asks, startling me and half scaring me to death.

Grasping my chest, I turn to face him. "Sure, there's still boxes outside." I motion towards the front of the house.

"Okay, on it." Arnulf takes off, leaving me to ponder how the fuck he managed to sneak up on me.

Back in the room, I start ripping open the boxes and pulling out pillows. Dozens upon dozens of pillows line the one side of the room. Arnulf finds me in the middle of a sea of pillows and starts laughing. "If I didn't know better, I'd say you were building a nest." He sets the boxes down just inside the door. The look on my face must have spoken volumes to him. He immediately stops laughing and starts opening boxes to help.

We work in silence for hours, using the sheets to hold groups of pillows together. Carefully, we set it up in the corner then used the rest of the sheets to make a "den." The super-soft blankets go over the top of the pillow nest to make it extra soft. While I put the final touches on the nest, Arnulf installs the lock on the door.

Soft twinkle lights and a natural sounds radio are installed easily. Arnulf claps me on the back and smiles. "This is a nest any female would be proud to use." Nodding slowly, I usher him out of the room and lock it behind us.

"You really think so?" Sighing softly, I head over to the sitting area and flop into a chair. "I've never had the urge to build a den before. It's so important and scary at the same time." Roughly, I run my fingers through my hair before leaning against the back of the couch.

"At least with your species your worth isn't determined by the nest you build," Arnulf says and sighs, looking down and away.

"I've built grand nests, and none were ever chosen." Arnulf shrugs, then looks back to me, his eyes the gold hue of his eagle. "I guess fate had other plans for me," he says smiling, his joy so very obvious.

"With bears, only the strongest boars were ever chosen to be mates." I look down, rubbing the cut on my thumb that Irena and I made. "I was chosen, but it never felt right. I did my male duty."

I look away and exhale deeply. "When I was chosen to serve at the queen's side, I went without question. I didn't know Irena was with cub." Roughly, I slam my fist on the arm of the couch. "Duty will not pull me from my cub again."

"Settle down, big guy, this time is different." Arnulf smiles and shakes his head.

"You are mated to the queen. On top of that, the biggest threat to us has been destroyed." Arnulf gets up, walks over to the bar, and pours us both a bourbon on the rocks. He comes back over and offers me the glass.

As I take the glass from him Tia and Ladon come barreling into the room. Ladon is carrying his wooden sword that the blacksmith made for him. Tia is in her favorite pink dress and dragging her favorite doll behind her. I open my arms, and Tia runs and jumps to me quickly. She nuzzles my neck and jaw, her little dragoness purring up a storm. My arms band tightly around her little body as my bear rumbles to her. Deep in my heart, I cannot wait to hold my own cub like this. "Papa Bear?" Tia says softly.

"Yes, little one?" I lean back and sit her on my thigh. Carefully, I sip at my bourbon and wait for her question.

"Can you teach me how to fish? Momma says you're the best fisherman in the family." Tia's pale-grey eyes shift to that of her dragoness as she studies me.

My eyes drift to Arnulf, then back to Tia. "I could, but let's have a bit of fun with it." My eyes drift between Ladon and Arnulf before looking back to Tia.

"Ladon and Arnulf are one team, and you and me on the other team, Tia." Tia starts bouncing up and down excitedly.

"We got this, Papa Arnulf." Ladon raises his fist to Arnulf, and they fist bump. "Tia's a princess. What can she do?" Ladon says smugly.

Just so happens, Aurora walks in on the tail end of what Ladon said. "What can a princess do?" Aurora asks as the rest of our bond mates enter the room.

Slowly, she stalks across the room, freezing the floor as she goes. Her arms shift to that of her gauntlets. "Technically, I am the only queen of the Ice Dragon court. I am still a princess in the Marelup court." Aurora smirks.

"Before I was queen, I took down a Wyrm Black Dragon, the great Nexus. He was undefeated before me." Aurora kneels to be at eye level with her son.

"Your sister, like me, is a direct descendant of the Blood Queen, the fiercest dragoness in history," Aurora says as she points between her and Tiamat.

"I know deep in my heart Tiamat will be a great warrior and queen one day. Her still having dragon scales in her human form tells me she will be even more powerful than I am one day." Aurora smiles, looking fondly at her daughter. Slowly, her eyes turn back to Ladon.

"Females are revered because the Goddess allows so few of us to be born. Treasure the females in your life always." She finishes speaking then kisses Ladon's forehead before leaving the room as suddenly as she came.

I'm gobsmacked listening to the way Aurora put Ladon in his place. He looks between his mother and his sister then back again. "Can we just go as a family? I don't want to compete anymore." Ladon kicks the ground staring at his feet.

"Wise decision, young prince," Arnulf says, attempting to keep a straight face looking between Tia and me.

Ladon smiles and nods as he leads us out the door. We follow him outside and to the stream not far from the outskirts of town. I was happy to find out that the other family members are already fishing in the stream. Tia screams happily, runs to the water, shifts her arms, and starts trying to catch the fish. Shaking my head, I duck into the shed we have out here, strip, and shift quickly. I amble out towards the others as my bear. Tia squeals and runs at me, trying to pull herself up onto my back. Aurora shifts her hands back and lifts Tia up, setting her behind my shoulders.

Carefully, I wade into the water and start fishing. With every fish I catch, Tia's musical giggles make my heart swell. Out the corner of my eye, I watch Aurora and imagine my cub growing in her womb. I huff a breath out of my bear's nostrils before I stick my head underwater and catch a nice-sized trout. Carefully, I approach Aurora and drop the fish beside her and tilt my head to the side. Tia is giggling her ass off as she watches everything I do. "Awe, Papa Bear is feeding momma." Tia exclaims as she slides off my back to go snuggle next to Aurora.

Once I'm sure everyone has gotten fresh fish and I've consumed mine, I head back to the shed and get changed. I really don't understand what Alaric's hang-up is about Tia seeing us shift is. Never in all of Aurora's years growing up did I ever hide anything from her. Personally, I feel Alaric is making a huge mistake hiding everything from Tiamat. My cubs won't be sheltered like that. I don't want their wedding night to be a night of terror because she sees her first penis. Thinking back, I don't believe we hid anything other than having sex from Aurora. We did the best we could for the situation that we were in for her.

Before leaving the shed, I grab a basket, throw some drinks into it, and carry it down to the stream. Using stones, I make a holder to put the basket in so that I can chill the drinks. Aurora starts to giggle, looking at what I'm doing. "Why didn't you ask me to chill the drinks for everyone?" she asks as she smiles at me and mouths *silly bear*.

"Honestly, love, I just don't want you overtaxing yourself, all things considered." Gently, I place my hand on her lower stomach and caress it.

Aurora stands up on her tippy toes and kisses my cheek. "Always so thoughtful of my needs. Thank you, love, for always putting me first." She kisses my lips gently, and in the background I hear Tia say *awe* and Ladon say *eww*.

Shaking my head, I move away slightly, then drop to my knees and kiss Aurora's lower stomach. "Why's Papa Bear kissing mommy's tummy?" Tia asks as she climbs into Alaric's lap.

Raising a brow, I look to Alaric, unsure if we were ready to broach this subject as a family. "Well, Tia, momma is carrying babies in her belly. Just like she carried you and Ladon," Alaric says as gently as possible.

Tia looks from Aurora to Alaric. "How did they get there?" Tia tilts her head slightly. "Did you put them there, Daddy?" Tia grips Alaric's beard staring into his eyes. She has him in such a grip it's almost impossible for him to move.

"Well, um… Aurora?" Alaric takes the easy way out, getting Aurora to navigate this one. Quickly, I get up and move out of the way and sit off to the side to watch this one.

"Tia? Father didn't gift me with babies this time," Aurora says, waiting to get her attention.

"Okay?" Tia responds as she releases Alaric and moves over to her mother, and places her little hands on the small bump of Aurora's stomach. "Who did it?" she asks innocently as she lifts Aurora's shirt to look. "I really don't see how they got in there," Tia says as she pokes Aurora's belly button.

Dominik almost chokes to death on his drink. Jayce hits his twin's back, trying to clear his lungs. Aurora rolls her eyes then looks back to Tia. Carefully, she sits down and pulls Tia into her lap. "Remember we had the talk about heat cycles?" Tia nods and still studies Aurora. "So if a mommy and her mate, or mates in my case, are left alone to do mate things, babies happen," Aurora says with a very serious face, though through the bond, we hear her laughing.

Tia nods and stands up. She looks at each of us in turn, and I feel like I'm standing before a firing squad. Tia moves to stand before me and lifts her arms. Hesitantly, I reach down and pick her up. "Did you give momma cubs?" she asks in a very serious voice. Her little fingers thread through my thick beard as she holds me hostage.

"Momma thinks so, little one." The smile that moves across Tia's lips brings me so much joy.

"Good!" she says with such finality. "They better be girls. If I end up with another smelly brother, I'm going to be mad." Tia says firmly, then gives my beard a tug. She leans in and kisses both of my cheeks, then wiggles to get down. To my surprise, that went much better than expected. That is until Tia tries to shove a piece of fish into Aurora's belly button, trying to feed the baby.

"Little one?" I say gently as I kneel beside Tia and take the fish away from her as Aurora laughs hysterically. "Mommy feeds the baby in her tummy. We just have to keep mommy fed." I smile as I watch Tia's expression change.

Without warning, Tia shoves the piece of fish in Aurora's mouth. Time seems to stop as we watch and wait for Aurora's reaction. Aurora's eyebrows shoot up, and she decides to start chewing the offered fish. "Thanks, sweetheart. The babies will love it," she says kindly with a smile.

Tia's head tilts. "Babies?" She looks at the small bell of Aurora's stomach then at each of us in turn. "Okay, who put another baby in there?" She jabs her finger in the direction of Aurora's stomach.

Alaric and Jayce almost choke on their drinks as we watch Tia walking around like a tiny general examining each of us in turn. I watch her move slowly, examining everyone, then she stops in front of Alaric. "Did you do it again, Daddy?" Tia stands there with her fists on her tiny hips, tapping her foot like Aurora does.

Alaric kneels before Tia, getting eye level with her. "I was with you, Grandpa, and Grandma when it would have happened, little one." Alaric raises his eyebrows, waiting for it to make sense to Tia.

Tia's little dragon comes to the surface, and scales ripple up and down her arms as she looks at all of her mother's mates. "Who did it?" she screams, and a small burst of frost shoots out in all directions from her.

Everyone's eyes widen at her display, and jumps back. "Little one, calm down. Some of your daddies can't survive your frost," Aurora says softly, trying to calm Tia down. She's scary powerful for such a little person.

"Sorry, Daddies. I just want to know what babies are coming." Tia pouts and sighs, then flops onto the ground with her arms crossed over her chest.

"Little one," Aurora says, then sits next to Tia. "I believe I'm carrying Dimitri's and Klaus's. So a bear and a Lycan baby," Aurora says with a sappy smile on her face. Her hand absently goes to her stomach and touches it lightly.

Tia pouts a little. "So we get a teddy bear and a puppy?" She raises an eyebrow looking at everyone to see if she's right.

Slowly, I move past the frost and kneel near Tia. "Baby bears are called cubs. If I'm not mistaken, Lycan babies are called pups," I say gently to Tia so she can learn the differences.

Her lips form the perfect little "O" as the information sinks. "So, does Daddy Jayce and Daddy Dom have puppies?" Tia asks innocently.

Dominik double blinks as he registers what Tia called him. He looks at Aurora, who's now white as a sheet. Then back over to me, hoping for me to fix the innocent slip up. Alaric is beside himself, Jayce and Arnulf are giggling with Klaus. I shake my head slowly and try to figure out how to fix this faux pas.

"Little one, how about we call Daddy Dominik by his full name. Momma and the rest of us call him Dom." I raise my eyebrows and look at Tia, trying to be gentle and serious at the same time.

Tia huffs and rolls her little eyes. "If I must." She smiles, then turns around, grabs hold of Ladon, and starts walking home.

We watch the twins walk off, apparently done with the family outing. It makes me wonder what the next set of babies will be like. I know those two are insanely close because they are both dragons. But a Lycan and a bear cub, I wonder how close they will be? I guess only time will tell. Everyone except Aurora grabs stuff to carry back. By the looks of it, she's going to need a nap sooner rather than later.

CHAPTER 52

Jayce

I'M SO EXCITED ABOUT THE NEW BABIES JOINING THE FAMILY, IT'S NOT even funny. With the help of Dominik, I set to converting one of the spare bedrooms downstairs into a nursery. We also planned to do a nursery for upstairs so we can stay with the pack while the babies rest.

There are so many plans that need to be made in the short period of time that we have left. I race around, gathering all the necessary items that will be used in both rooms. I try to do it when Aurora's either sleeping or out of the house to be a great surprise for her. Right now, she's out with Alaric and her two older children, so my brother and I sit here working on painting the walls and redoing the trim. We've already built two cribs upstairs and the two cribs downstairs.

We went with neutral colors in both rooms just in case of a little boy being born or if they're both little girls. I know that Dimitri and Klaus would be happy either way with whatever gender they end up with. I get that dreamy look in my eye apparently because

Dominik comes over and places his hand on my shoulder. "Are you okay, bro? You looked like you were off in your own world."

"Yeah, just daydreaming about one day having my own pups," I say and smile. Never in a million years did I think I would be a dad. Things thankfully improved with Tia and Ladon after the discussion Aurora had with them. So I kind of get to experience the dad thing now.

"Trust me, I'm right there with you, Jayce. I can't wait to see our babies." Dom comes over to me and hugs me tightly.

"We'll get there, little brother, don't worry." We break the hug and go back to work on the walls, making the two shades of forest green perfect. We wanted a warm woodsy feel to the bedroom.

Periodically I still get lost in my thoughts as I paint the walls. "We have much better odds next time, Dom," I say, shrugging my shoulders while I paint. To me, it honestly doesn't matter which of us fathered the next litter. Either way, the pups would be of my bloodline.

"Very true. I like these odds much better." Dominik smiles and winks at me. We work in relative silence for the next couple of hours, ensuring that the room is absolutely perfect. We return back upstairs to go over the other nursery making sure that the paint dried properly and didn't require a second coat.

Once all the paint is dry, we go out into the garage to grab the boxes for the babies' dressers as well as the changing tables. We acquired the help of other pack members to get all the boxes into the rooms they need to be in. Painstakingly slow, we assemble each of the items while assisting each other the best that we can.

It is late afternoon when our work gets interrupted by Aurora and the children. I was just putting up the last of the stencils on the wall, decorating it with different animals. One wall is done as a forest scene; another has the animals that each of us shift into. The third wall we are saving to put the babies' names on. The final wall we would leave for Aurora to do with whatever she wanted.

Tears shine in Aurora's pale-grey eyes as she looks on. Slowly, she enters the room and turns in a slow circle taking in all that my brother and I have accomplished while she was gone. Silently, she comes up and hugs and kisses both of us passionately, whispering her thanks.

Through the mate bond, she reaches out to everyone, summoning them into the room that she was currently in. As each of the guys enter, their eyes go wide as saucers as they take in what Dominik and I have accomplished. There is a series of high fives, back claps, and bro hugs to go around. Everyone was very impressed with what we did in the afternoon while they were gone.

My heart swells with love and affection from my bond mates. I didn't think this small gesture would mean so much to everyone. Dimitri gets bashful and crooks his finger, leading us out of the room that we were in.

He brings us down the hall to the last door on the left that now suspiciously has a lock on it. He unlocks the door, and oddly Arnulf enters first. We bring Aurora to the front and push her into the room before us and as if on cue, the lights flick on. In the corner of the room is a den with a nest inside. Aurora squeals with delight as she runs up and jumps into the pillowy softness that was made for her.

Her actions concern the rest of us. We are worried she will injure herself and or the babies she's carrying. We rush over and move the curtains aside to find her curled up in the middle of the nest, looking super comfortable.

Apparently, most of us had secrets today. In turn, we each turn and look at Dimitri, and he just smiles and shrugs his shoulders. The big guy doesn't do well with accepting congratulations or any kind of positive emotional feedback from the males in the family.

Arnulf surprisingly takes the lead and begins to explain everything that he and Dimitri had done. We stare in wonder as he points out all the little special things. He then explains what kind of products and materials were used in the making of the nest. You could tell that Aurora was exceptionally impressed by their craftsmanship by how she runs her hands over the bedding. Ever so carefully, she climbs out of the nest and then launches herself into Dimitri's waiting arms. She cries softly, thanking him profusely for all that he has done for her and the babies.

Being the honorable man that Dimitri is, he motions towards Arnulf and explains his part in the whole process. Aurora wiggles her way free from Dimitri's arms and goes and hugs Arnulf. She then comes over to me and tenderly kisses my cheek and then my lips, thanking me for what I did. She repeats the process with my twin, hugging him and kissing him, and thanking him as well. We go room to room upstairs and down, checking out the two new nurseries.

Klaus was exceptionally impressed by the color palette that we chose for both of the rooms. There are two shades of evergreen, one light, one dark, in both rooms. We alternated which walls had what colors. We alternated which wall was designated for what between the two rooms. Both rooms are the same, yet different in their own way. Alaric congratulates us and thanks us for the time and effort we put in to ensure that the babies had the perfect sleeping area. He's not even the male that fathered the children this time, and he's grateful for what we did. It just warms my heart to know that my brother and I's efforts are appreciated.

It's different being an Omega in this pack. I don't feel like I'm at the bottom of the ladder. I don't feel like I'm only useful for one thing. It's nice to be up at the top with those I love and all of us on equal footing. Klaus comes over and hugs me and then to my surprise, kisses me in front of everyone. It wasn't a soft, gentle kiss you would expect; this is full force, Klaus not holding back. He makes my toes curl, and butterflies rise up in my stomach. I can't help but wrap my arms around him and return his passionate kiss.

The kiss finally ends and I can't help but stare up into his eyes, lost. A slender hand rests on my shoulder, and I turn to look at Aurora, almost horrified at what we just did in front of her. Quickly, I look back to Klaus, and he is just as panic-stricken as I am.

"Don't worry, boys, I knew you two had a thing going and I'm fine with it." Aurora smiles at us and kisses us both, and then walks out.

Releasing the breath I didn't realize I was holding, my eyes dart back and forth between Klaus and Aurora. Shock doesn't even begin to describe how I'm feeling right now. Part of me feels as if my heart is soaring; the other half feels extremely blessed and grateful. Klaus hugs me tightly to him as we look to the others. The guys smile and high-five us and tell us that they knew. It's such a relief to get that off my chest. Aurora being okay with it makes it all that much better.

We spend a few moments alone before heading back up to the main part of the house. Tia and Ladon come running into the house. Tia is crying, and Ladon has three cuts across his arm. Aurora instantly flies into a rage as she drops to her knees in front of her children. "What happened?" Aurora looks Tia over then examines Ladon's arm before passing him off to Alaric.

I quickly go to Tia and cradle her against my chest before sitting across from Aurora. My wolf rumbles softly, trying to calm her. "Shadow man took Lia. We were playing under the peach tree, and he came up out of the ground and grabbed her." Deep in my heart, I have an idea about who she's speaking about. My fingers thread through Tia's hair as I try to soothe her.

Aurora's facial bone plates shift several times before she looks at me and Dominik. "Get Alex to go with you and search the area and report back. Oh, and find out when Alex wants to have his wedding too." Aurora's always multitasking if she can get away with it.

I quickly place Tia in Aurora's lap as Dominik and I head out of the house. Through the pack bond, we reach out to my brother and his mate to have them meet up with us. They arrive quickly, and we bring them up to speed as we walk towards the peach tree. The stench of sulfur and rot fills our sensitive noses. Dominik and I have smelled this before; the Strigoi have taken Lia. I reach out through the pack bond to Aurora and fill her and the rest of our pack mates in on our discovery.

We can clearly feel Aurora's rage through the bond, and she basically tells us to stay put. I raise a brow, looking at my brothers. We know that Aurora will go against medical orders and come herself. No sooner did I share that thought with my brothers and my future brother-in-law, Aurora arrives.

She charges over to the hole and starts searching around it. Her eyes raise up to the sky locating the sun. "More than likely, we will hear from them at sundown. They probably believe that they stole my daughter and will want me in exchange."

She raises a hand quickly and silences us all instantly. "We need to return and tell Anna what happened to her daughter. I also need to know if Lia has my scale with her or not before I attempt to locate her." Aurora turns quickly and starts heading back to camp without further adieu.

We lag behind the group, and when we arrive back at the pack house, Aurora already has Anna wrapped up in her arms. The child's mother is crying hysterically, and the father is speaking with Klaus and Dimitri. I pull my brothers off to the side as we wait to be needed. Alex and his mate pull out their phones, showing us their wedding plans.

We were so lost in the plans I didn't notice that Aurora was standing over us, looking over my shoulder at the plans as well. "The blue one would be best," she says and scares the hell out of all of us.

I clutch my chest as I turn to look at her, my eyes still wide from fright. "Excellent choice, babe. Um, does the little one have your scale?" Slowly, I tilt my head to the side, trying to get her back on track.

"In fact, she does!" Aurora smiles broadly. "The downside is all things considered." She motions to her stomach.

"I'll need Alaric and Nicodeamus to boost me; I don't believe I can do it alone." As soon as she utters their names, they move to her side, and we prepare for some freaky dragon location thing to happen.

CHAPTER 53

Aurora

Mother fucking bat-faced, deadhead bastards stole Lia. I swore to protect that sweet little baby girl, and I fucking failed her. Frustration boils within me like a cauldron, fueled by the bitter taste of failure. The knowledge that Lia, the innocent child I swore to protect, has been snatched away by those vile creatures stirs a storm of rage within my soul. With each step I take, the room feels like it's closing in on me, suffocating me with a sense of helplessness.

My senses are heightened, every nerve tingling with adrenaline and fury. The urge to unleash my pent-up aggression is overwhelming, a primal instinct clawing at the edges of my consciousness. But I know that giving in to that impulse will only lead to further chaos and despair.

As I pace the room, my hand instinctively drifts to my swollen stomach, a reminder of the new life growing within me. The weight of responsibility presses down on me like a heavy burden, a constant reminder of the stakes at hand.

Amidst the turmoil raging inside me, the scent of my approaching comrades wafts through the air, carrying with it the promise of sustenance and companionship. The tantalizing aroma of various meats and desserts fills the room, igniting a primal hunger within me. My guys return with a massive assortment of food to eat, and my stomach begins to growl in response.

Quickly, I start to dig in and eat a little bit of everything that's in front of me. I stab a raw steak and get ready to eat it, and the smell makes me nauseous. Furrowing my brows, confused, I try again, except this time my stomach turns to the point I can't stop. I roll to my feet and head straight to the garbage can and promptly lose my lunch. Up to this point, I have been able to eat everything I wanted to. Pouting, I look back to my lunch and sigh. I'm so hungry, and now I'm worried about eating.

Klaus and Dimitri rush to my side in a second, one rubbing my back while the other holds me steady. Jayce slowly approaches and offers me cold ginger water. I sip at it slowly and enjoy the cool, refreshing taste. Several minutes pass before my stomach settles; I sigh softly and feel relieved. How in the hell am I supposed to save this little girl when I can't eat?

Dimitri kisses my temple and pulls me to him. "Shh, love, all will be okay. We just need to figure out what this litter needs." He gently cradles me and keeps kissing my temple, trying to soothe me.

Klaus grabs ahold of my hands and holds them tightly. "We'll do whatever you need us to do. Just tell us." Klaus smiles and then kisses my lips gently. I'm so lucky to have so many good and loving mates.

Alaric brings the food tray over to me, minus the raw meat. So far, so good. I remain in Dimitri's lap and eat my lunch there. We move to the couch and watch a movie while waiting for my father's arrival. It's around four in the evening by the time he gets here. Alaric brings him up to speed while I use Dimitri as my personal pillow.

Father lays out an intricate plan in front of us. He is trying to pinpoint the exact location of the Strigoi without me having to tap into the scale. I know this plan isn't going to work. I know what I'm going to have to do to succeed. I wait and hear them out, just making sure that we haven't missed anything important up to this point. Lia's parents are in the room with us, listening. Both parents are still crying hysterically, just wanting their child back.

I look over at my own two children, and to be perfectly honest, I can't wait. I extend my hand out to Alaric and then to my father. Hesitantly, they both approach me and grab my hands. Within moments, I'm reaching through time and space, using the astral plane to locate a part of me. The signal is weak, but it's still there. I know that the little one is being held north of our position by about ten miles. There's a series of caves that run along the mountain base just on the other side of the lake. I give everybody the coordinates, and off goes both of my dragon guards on their mission. I sit back, a little more exhausted than I would have liked to be.

Jayce is at my side within seconds to give me a protein shake and ginger water. Dominik pulls me into his lap, taking me away from Dimitri. He's trying to cuddle me and make me feel better. I should be the one on the mission, not sending two of my guards. I slowly rub my stomach, calming my babies. These two little ones are taking a lot out of me, more so than the twins. I wonder if each litter is going to be different to this point. I can't eat my raw meat. I can barely stomach the smell of it, and it's my favorite. The mild amount of power that I exerted has exhausted me.

To my surprise, Arnulf is the one that comes and takes me away from Dominik. He carries me through the house to the upstairs bedroom and lays me down. He strips me bare, and here I think I'm going to get a little action. Instead, he decides to start massaging my muscles, trying to help me relax. All I know is my lids are getting heavy, and I can't fight the sleep that wants to take me.

I awaken several hours later with Arnulf and Jayce in bed curled up around me, tightly holding onto me. There's a flurry of activity downstairs that draws my attention. I wake both boys up and get dressed quickly, then head downstairs. Apparently, Dante and Edgar were successful; little Lia has returned home. Quickly, I wiggle free from the guys and get dressed in a comfortable blue gauze summer dress.

I go and sit in front of her, smiling. "You found me, Alpha, you found me," the little girl says, smiling before she wraps her arms around my neck. Tears of joy streak down my cheeks as I hold her tightly to me. Her tiny Lycan rumbles softly to me.

"I told you I always would. You keep this locket close to you at all times." Gently, I touch the locket. "Don't ever leave it at home," I say before I kiss her forehead and snuggle her tightly to me for a few moments.

Her parents promptly come and take her after I've checked her over; they can't stop thanking us enough for what we did. Motioning to Dante and Edgar, I stand and raise my fist to my chest. Bending deeply, I honor them and thank them for their service. Both males blush profusely and bow in turn to me. Slowly, I straighten up and wave goodbye to Lia and her parents.

I look at Dante and Edgar and then tilt my head to the side to go to the war room. Each one of my mates, I give them a slight nod and also the same head motion. I'm not using the bond, as I don't need others to know that we can all connect that way.

Once inside the war room, I click the lock and sit at my place at the table. "So, how many were there?" I ask as I look to Dante and Edgar. My eyes narrow as I prepare to brace for the worst possible answer.

"My Queen, there were only six. Though the cavern smelled far worse than that," Dante says as he moves over to the whiteboard and starts drawing the cavern's layout that they found Lia in.

Edgar moves up to the whiteboard next and draws the exterior of the area around the cavern. Apparently, the Strigoi had been busy changing the environment a little bit. Most of the area around the cave appears to be dead and/or rotting. Edgar crosses his arms over his chest and looks at me, shaking his head slowly. "We found the bones of many beings outside of the cavern. By the looks of it, there should be at least a dozen of those leeches in there." Edgar motions to the picture that Dante has drawn of the network of the caverns. "I believe the majority of them are deep within the cavern system. If we could take a Black Dragon or two and flood the tunnels with acid, that should help." Edgar moves and goes to take his seat at the table.

I walk over to the white board looking at everything they've drawn for me. As I do that, Alaric has the cavern map system out on the table. It's the map of what was done during Klaus's grandfather's time. I compare the two drawings and notice that additional tunnels have been drawn. "Gentlemen, it looks like the leeches have been in there for longer than we have suspected. We must reach out to the other dragon families and alert them."

I circle the differences on the whiteboard. "They need to check the caves near the strongholds to make sure they're empty. Apparently, the leeches aren't as dumb as we thought." I pace back and forth between the whiteboard and the map on the table, comparing and contrasting the two differences.

Since we moved here and I'd taken over as alpha and queen, I require all homes to dig bunkers just in case. My eyes raise and lock on Klaus's. "You need to alert all the families here; they need to go to ground tonight and lock up tight. I believe the leeches will bring the war to us."

I walk around the table again, then rest my hands on Dante's shoulders. "I need you to get Marco back here. Have him and his team lay a thick layer of acid around the perimeter." I flip the whiteboard over to the map that we have drawn of our small town. Then I take the green marker and draw where exactly I want the acid traps left.

"I know these bastards will dig underground and pop up out of nowhere. We will be ready for them." I say those words with all finality and seriousness. The guys nod at me and then take off to go start preparing.

I stand before Dimitri and look up into his hazel eyes, and smile. "I need you to gather all the unmated males, the ones without children and families. They will stand with us and fight tonight." I draw in a deep breath the lower my eyes. "Any who have children will not be in the fray." He nods his head at me and then bends down and kisses my lips

"As you wish, beautiful, but do not expect us to sit on the sidelines when there's a war to be waged," Dimitri says, crossing his arms over his broad chest, making himself look large and imposing.

My teddy bear cannot keep a serious face as I look up, smiling at him. "As you wish, handsome. But that means I get to play too," I say, and all the gentlemen start to protest. I raise a single hand and look at them all.

"What's good for the goose is good for the gander. If I'm supposed to be okay with you guys fighting, then I expect the same respect." I stand tall and proud at the head of the table. Both hands flat on the tabletop, and in my agitation my frost starts spreading upon it.

"I may not be able to shift and fight, but I have other weapons at my disposal. I'm two months along; it doesn't mean I'm dead yet." I move around the room and kiss each of my mates that are still present, and then leave promptly. I need to rest; I need to feed. Tonight, I believe hell itself is going to break loose.

CHAPTER 54
Nicodeamus

My daughter's tactical mindset has always impressed me. Even now, I can almost hear her thoughts as if they are my own as she assesses the situation that's been laid out before us. I watch her as she makes her plans and can see her studying every little minute new detail. Nothing has missed her gaze as she flips between the map from fifty years ago versus the one that was brought to her.

Tonight, I will send my mate to ground with my grandchildren. I would prefer to be sending my daughter to ground as well, but she makes a valid point. More than likely, the leeches are after her trying to get revenge by wiping out one of her strongholds. So if she stays topside, they will hunt her. It'll be easier for us to funnel and kill them if she's present. I have been in conference through the entire meeting with the other dragon councils, reaching out to those I am closest to. They, too, are prepared to assault the caverns near their homelands.

They also relay that their battle with the leeches was won far too easily, as if they were expecting it. We assumed that the leeches would be of a hive mind, where what one had learned, then they all know. And apparently, our assessment was correct. When in a swarm, dragons become of a hive mind, following blindly the most dominant and strongest dragon's orders. Tactically, it's a very bad idea. But if that dragon is a Wyrm Dragon with thousands of years of knowledge, then it's brilliant. It doesn't always work out that way, unfortunately.

The fae woman, Laurel, has appeared yet again and brings forth a scroll from the king of the fae, Oberon. Of course, it's my luck that it's magically enchanted only to be able to be open by the person it's intended to. I move through the house and go and find my daughter at the kitchen table eating again. She appears to be about four to five months pregnant by human standards. But because of who the fathers are, she's just barely two. Couple that with a multiple birth, she's much larger than she should be.

I present her with the scroll, and as soon as her fingers touch it, it opens up. I watch her eyes shift to that of her beast. My head, and I'm assuming her mates' heads, are filled with the knowledge sent to us. Oberon wants the last of the leeches dead. He is sending his best warriors to each of the dragon clans to assist with eradicating these leeches. This is the most excellent news. Aurora looks it over and reads the letter at least three times before pricking her finger and putting a drop of blood on it. I tilt my head to the side, curious as to why she did that.

"Daddy, he wanted to make sure that we are all serious about this assault on them. So to prove we are serious, he asked for a drop of blood to be put on the scroll." Aurora smiles, then shrugs.

"The drop of blood itself will alert him not only to the fact that I received the scroll but that I also agree with what he's getting ready to do for everybody. We don't have to wait for his messengers to return the scrolls to him for him to receive the answer." Aurora stands and touches my shoulder. "This was the quickest and most practical way."

I just nod slowly at Aurora and smile. "That is a brilliant plan that he laid out for us. I just hope this is the final battle for you, once and for all." I hug my daughter tightly and kiss her temple.

"I would like for you to know peace for once in your lifetime." A single tear rolls down my cheek, and of course, it's on the wrong damn side that I always have a hard time reaching with my right arm. Aurora quickly reaches for it and wipes it away for me.

"Daddy, you may not have been physically in my life my entire life, but you taught me so much when you were able to reach out to me." She smiles and hugs me again.

"You have done more for me than some fathers that are in their children's lives all the time." Aurora wraps her arms around my neck and hugs me tightly. I band my arm around her ribs and hold her flush to me. My poor baby girl is an emotional, hormonal wreck right now. What I find to be the second happiest moment, besides becoming a grandfather, she's over here crying during it.

All six of her mates come barreling into the kitchen, feeling her distress, and they find us hugging, both of us blubbering like idiots. Alaric is the first to break and start laughing at what they find.

"Here we go again, boys, someone get the kleenexes. Clean up, aisle two," Alaric says as he laughs. Jayce just shakes his head and pulls out a small pack of tissues from his back pocket.

"You guys still haven't learned what we need to have with us at all times for her. Please, I may not be the first mate, but I'm the best."

He smiles, beaming with pride as he walks over and hands Aurora a tissue and then one for me too.

I look over at Jayce and just start shaking my head. "Son, out of all of her mates, you're the most emotionally in tune with her. That is an absolute blessing and probably a curse." I toss my tissue away and then lay my hand on his shoulder. "I'd hate to feel the emotional roller coaster these next few months are going to give you."

"It's all good, Dad, and when it's my turn to be a father, I will bear the weight yet again, without problems." Jayce smiles and then moves to Aurora and kisses her belly.

"Don't worry, little ones. Daddy Jayce is on the job," he says and then moves to the refrigerator and grabs out Aurora's pomegranate juice.

Aurora raises an eyebrow at him, questioning what's in his hands. "Is that what I think it is?" She says, looking at him hopefully.

"Yes, it's your favorite juice; no, there's no vodka in it," Jayce says as he puts a straw into the bottle and hands it to her.

Aurora licks at her bottom lip and pouts, looking at him. We all know she's not serious; she would never drink while she's pregnant with the babies. Granted, she occasionally likes to lick a drop off of one of our fingers just for the taste but never more than that. She rubs her stomach gently and then looks at all of us. "We have about an hour before the sun's low enough for them to start moving. Make sure all the final preparations have been made, and we will meet up on the front porch in about forty minutes," Aurora says before she comes over and grabs my hand.

"Daddy, I need your help getting into my armor. Laurel brought me a new mithril that Oberon had sent for me, all things considered." I smile knowingly and follow her down the hallway to find Laurel in Aurora's upstairs closet.

Laurel bows her head graciously to me, then smiles. "Welcome, my King. My King has sent armor for yourself and for your daughter." She holds up two different sets of mithril, one that is in the shape of a beautiful gown, the other meant to protect my chest. I am quite impressed with its construction.

"Laurel, please pass on to your king my gratitude for this wonderful gift." She bows her head and then pulls over the dressing screen. I hear the *oohs* and *ahhs* of Laurel gushing over Aurora's belly. Never in a million years did I think I would get to see grand babies, and here I am again, awaiting the birth of more of my grandchildren.

Aurora steps out from behind the dressing screen, looking like a warrior queen. Her great-grandmother's ruby crown upon her head and her hair done in a braid around the top of her head. The new gown fits her perfectly, and I notice that there is extra chain mail around her midsection to protect the babies from all sides. I must remember to thank Oberon in person for this great boon he has given my family.

Once Aurora is settled, Laurel comes over and assists me with putting my armor on as well. Sometimes being a one-armed warrior is a bitch, but I've adapted and overcome my disability.

It's now that I look up and see Aurora has adapted her sash for her sword to be able to work around her pregnant belly. I can tell, though, she's not really thrilled with how it's sitting, but it's better than nothing. She gives me a terse nod, and we head downstairs to meet up with the others on the front porch.

Upon arrival, Jayce hands Aurora a chicken leg that she promptly eats while she's waiting. He continues to hand her food, and I'm guessing it's to keep her mind off of what's coming. My eyes dart around the porch, making sure that all of her mates are present. The only one I don't see is Arnulf. It's then I notice in the sky he and several of his brothers are flying around watching for the assault.

The cries of the Merlin falcons are heard long before you hear the cries of the Golden Eagles. Aurora lets loose a roar-howl of her own, pretty much assembling every species living in town. My mate Helle is at the door holding up my grand babies. Aurora pops the door open briefly, kisses both of her children quickly, and then orders Helle to go to ground. I didn't even get to say goodbye to my mate before she's swept away and down into the bunker. Tactically, I don't know if it was a good idea to send one of the War Dragons down there with her, but I understand why Aurora did it. The heir to the throne is in my mate's arms. Tiamat stands to inherit both the Ice Dragon throne as well as the Lycan throne. That is until Aurora gives birth to a female Lycan.

The roar of Marco's dragon fills the air as he and his team start to lay a thick blanket of acid as Aurora requested it to be. The screeches and cries of the leeches fill the air of those who try to breach the acid. Now that we start seeing the dirt move, knowing full well that they are tunneling to get to us. Aurora nods to Dante, and he shifts immediately, taking his dragon form to add extra protection. With the flourish of her hand, he starts setting the ground on fire around the Alpha House.

The fire prompts the leeches to come up out of their hiding spots, and the fight begins. Aurora remains on the porch, watching everything until she signals Marco, and he comes and picks her up. She sets herself behind his crown of horns to have the best and safest vantage point.

We all know she's able to siphon energy from the dragons if she needs it. With a raise of her hand, she starts sending ice spikes up through random leeches as they appear. She's working double time, impaling as many as possible, taking their heads from their bodies with the force of the ice. I watch her eyes take on an ethereal glow, and she spots her main target. Tomas is in the fray with the rest of his legion.

Aurora commands Marco to go forward, and as he does, she launches off of his head to go flying at Tomas. He was not expecting her to come flying through the air at him. He's tackled to the ground and quickly flips her off of him, and she lands with a hard thud.

I just about feel my heart stop in my chest, seeing her fly and fall onto her back. Several beats later, she's back up again, her face contorted in rage, her canines bared and dripping with venom as she charges forward. Her forearms are shifted into her gauntlets. Tomas, the poor bastard, doesn't turn in time to see her coming at him. Her hand punches through his chest. Her taloned hand sticking out of his sternum, his heart stuttering before the final beat ends. He turns to ash in front of her and falls away to nothing.

With his death, his legion starts to desiccate immediately. Like anything of a hive mind, you cut off its head, and it cannot function. But in the leeches case, you kill the leader, and the legion dies. Aurora stands still for a beat too long, and I become quite nervous about what's wrong with her. Klaus is on her in a second, and oddly enough, he cuts his forearm open and sticks it in her mouth. She drinks greedily at his open vein, feeding off his life essence.

Soon the color returns to her, and she licks his wound clean, sighing softly. He picks her up, carrying her bridal style as his beast back to the house. By the time she gets to me, she is completely asleep in his arms, and we dare not move her. I assist them in getting into the house and bring them into the living room. With some of the house staff's help, we drag one of the giant bean bags we had purchased for Aurora over. It takes four people to help Klaus sit in the bean bag as his Lycan holds Aurora to his chest. She's sound asleep, her beast rumbling to his.

One by one, the rest of her mates return as I sit there with the washcloth, cleaning off my daughter's exposed skin. Not a single mate questions as to why Klaus is still his beast with her sleeping on him. She felt better with her first litter with them sleeping as their beast; apparently, it's no different right now. We'll have to watch and wait to see what happens over the next few days, but the drinking of blood concerns me. I'll have to ask them later why that is and why that was his first instinct. For now, I'll just tend to my daughter, making sure that all her needs are taken care of while the boys go and clean up.

It's about midnight before Aurora awakens again, completely refreshed, bright-eyed and bushy-tailed, sitting there petting Klaus's beast as if he's a puppy. I guess to her, he is her puppy. Either way, he's enjoying the affection.

"Well, that went better than expected," Dominik says as he comes into the room. He heads straight to the refrigerator and starts grabbing out cold beers and a cold pomegranate juice for Aurora. He brings the juice over to Aurora and also hands her the beer for Klaus. She raises an eyebrow looking at Klaus, and then shakes her head slowly.

"Are you going to shift back, my love, or are you going to try to lick the beer bottle?" she asks as she taunts his beast with the beer. Carefully under her, Klaus shifts back to his human form and then smirks at her.

"I would rather have licked the beer off of you than to drink it out of the bottle, to be honest." Aurora just rolls her eyes at Klaus, and she leans back against him again, drinking her juice slowly.

Dimitri comes back in with some fried chicken and sweet potato french fries with coleslaw. Aurora's eyebrows shoot straight up as her nose twitches, smelling the food that's coming her way. Dimitri offers Aurora the plate and she takes it and kisses him gently. "Thank you, babe." she says, then starts scarfing down the food in front of her.

Sweet potato fries and some pieces of chicken get shoved into Klaus's mouth when he's least expecting it. We watch this comedy going on because he never knows when she's about to feed him. I would have to say it's an eighty-twenty split, eighty percent of the food going to Aurora, the other twenty percent randomly getting shoved in Klaus's mouth. Either way, they're both eating.

Arnulf comes in with several of his people, all raiding the kitchen looking for something to eat. Aurora starts to giggle as she notices that Arnulf had split the back of his pants somehow. With the occasional step, all you see is his ass crack. Then cheek then crack, then cheek then crack. She's in a massive giggle fit to the point Klaus has to take the plate away from her before she ends up wearing it all. We can't help but laugh, too, at her reaction to what she's seeing.

Arnulf realizes his pants are destroyed. His hands go to cover his ass as he runs out of the room. Aurora winks at us and follows him out of the room; I wonder what exactly my daughter is up to.

CHAPTER 55

Arnulf

As I HURRIEDLY TRAVERSE THROUGH THE HOUSE, A SURGE OF embarrassment floods over me, heightened by the realization that my companions had allowed me to walk around unaware of the state of my attire. The sensation of mortification prickles at my skin, mingling with the frustration of the situation.

Each step I take is accompanied by a sense of discomfort, the fabric of my torn pants chafing against my skin with every movement. The jagged edges of the tear catch on stray threads, adding to the disheveled appearance of my clothing.

Despite the reassurance that my bond mates have seen me in various states of undress before, the prospect of facing my mate in such a state sends a pang of insecurity coursing through me. I know that Aurora holds no judgment towards me, yet the thought of appearing unkempt in her presence gnaws at my confidence.

As I strip off the offending jeans, a wave of relief washes over me, the fabric feeling constricting and uncomfortable against my skin.

With a frustrated sigh, I toss them into the garbage can, eager to be rid of them once and for all.

Turning back to my closet, I rummage through the assortment of clothes, searching for something more suitable. Each garment holds a distinct texture and scent, triggering memories and associations with its wearer.

Jayce's sense of style is impeccable, his clothes exuding confidence and sophistication. Dom, on the other hand, favors a more rugged aesthetic, his attire reflecting his rebellious nature and edgy allure.

Dimitri's wardrobe is practical and utilitarian, his clothing designed for functionality above all else. Alaric, with his regal bearing, dresses with an air of elegance and refinement, his garments befitting of his royal status.

And then there's Klaus, whose flawless appearance seems effortless in any attire, his handsome features complemented by his impeccable fashion sense.

As I sift through the array of clothing, I can't help but envy the ease with which each of them carries themselves, their outfits serving as an extension of their personalities and individuality.

Here I am, the mate that's built the lightest out of everybody. I don't have the muscles that the bear and the dragon have or the wolves' definition. I just have a very fit build, light definition, light on the muscles. Light on everything as far as I'm concerned. I'm so lost in my own inner monologue that I don't notice until I turn around that my mate is standing there watching me.

"I'm sorry I came home with my clothes destroyed," I say softly as I lower my eyes, ashamed of the way I had looked earlier.

Aurora steps into my closet and wraps her arms around my waist, and lays her head on my shoulder. "My love, you can walk around this house buck naked, and you'd still be perfect to me." She slowly lifts her head and kisses my chest, my neck, and then my jaw. I can't help but make that whistling noise that my Eagle makes when he's excited. He's practically preening in the back of my head that our mate called us perfect.

As Aurora steps back, the air seems to crackle with anticipation, a charged atmosphere enveloping us both. My senses heighten, acutely aware of her presence and the subtle shifts in her demeanor.

I feel her gaze lingering on me, her eyes scanning my form with an intensity that sends shivers down my spine. The touch of her fingers against my skin sends a jolt of electricity coursing through me, igniting a primal urge deep within.

Her touch is gentle yet electrifying, trailing a path from my pecs down to my abdomen, leaving a tingling sensation in its wake. I can't help but tense as her fingers hover near my hips, a nervous energy coursing through me.

Then, without warning, she strikes, her hands darting out to seize me at my most vulnerable spot. The sensation is overwhelming, a rush of ticklishness flooding my senses and causing me to gasp for breath.

I collapse to the floor, my body convulsing with laughter as I struggle to protect myself from her relentless assault. Each touch sends waves of sensation rippling through me, overwhelming my senses and leaving me helpless in her grasp.

In that moment, all I can do is surrender to the onslaught, my laughter mingling with the sounds of the night as Aurora's mischievous laughter fills the air around us.

I'm more concerned about accidentally striking out and harming her and the babies than I am about my own body sustaining damage. I roll onto my back and try to shove her lightly just to keep her hands from those horrible tickle zones.

Aurora takes control and sits directly upon my crotch. She then places her hands flat on my pecs, using them for balance. She has that mild ethereal glow in her eyes as she stares down at me. My fight or flight instinct isn't as strong as it used to be, but it's still there for moments like this. She's looking me up and down as if I'm a snack or something delectable that she would like to devour.

Granted, I am a man, and I wouldn't mind my mate devouring me every once in a while. But being a much smaller predator than she is when she's shifted, I still get a little nervous. I trust her with my life and know that she would never do anything to harm me. But instinct can be a bitch at times and make you afraid over nothing.

Aurora's head tilts left and right and then back again several times, trying to assess the situation. "What's going on in that pretty head of yours, my love?" Aurora asks, then leans down the best she can, trying to reach my lips.

At this point, I realize that her stomach is just big enough that she can't easily fold over to get to me. In a feat of strength, I move us both so that I'm leaning against the wall. I'm using my shoulders as support just so she can curl closer towards me. Gently, I run my hands up and down her sides, massaging her back a little while I'm at it.

Her beast makes that rumbling purr that tells me she's pleased with what I'm doing. Leaning forward, I lightly nibble her jaw and then work my way down to her throat, sending goosebumps over her skin. She rolls her head back and away, giving me full access—a very submissive move. Honestly speaking, I'm not used to being the dominant one when it comes to us having an intimate moment. It's an interesting feeling being in control. Think I kind of like it. Pushing the boundaries just a little bit, I grip her hair in my hand, holding her head back. She growls lightly at me, and then a smile graces her perfectly delectable lips.

Definitely no rejection here whatsoever. I decide to be a little bolder, and I feel my canines descend. Leaning forward, I lightly bite her shoulder, and she starts squirming in my lap. I feel the moisture pooling between us. I bring my free hand down between us and start playing with that nub of sensitive nerves. She practically writhes in my lap, grinding hard against my swollen member.

At the rate she's going, neither one of us will last very long. I bite her shoulder harder and pinch that nub of nerves sending her over the edge. She's bucking and grinding down hard upon me. It takes all of my restraint to keep from blowing my load like a randy teenager.

I've had enough. I just have to have her. I reach down between us and push my jeans down and out of the way, freeing myself from its cotton confinement. Aurora sees what I'm doing and quickly rips her underwear free from her body, sending the tattered mass flying. Without any hesitation, she quickly impales herself upon my length and throws her head back, moaning loudly. Who says heaven isn't real? I found it right here in my closet. I change my angle slightly, to give her more of my length and grip her hips, helping her bounce up and down as quick as she wants.

We're both panting and moaning, grinding ourselves against each other as hard as we can. I can feel through the bond that we're both climbing to the peak at the same time, both of us within a breath of ecstasy. I lean forward, still masterfully moving her upon my length. My lips brush against her flesh with a feather-light touch to her throat, causing her muscles to clinch down tight around my shaft. I already feel my balls tightening, drawing up as far as they can. If we keep at it this way, I'll be done before she is. I refuse to come before she does.

I lean forward quickly and sink my canines into her neck, missing the artery but hitting a sensitive spot. She screams loudly, her voice carrying throughout the entire house as she digs her claws into my shoulder. Then it happens; she sinks her canines deeply into my flesh, setting off a cascade of orgasms between us. I can't tell where one starts, and the next one ends as we both bite harder on each other. Eventually, exhaustion overcomes the two of us, and we stop moving.

I pull a blanket from beside me and wrap it around the two of us, cradling my greatest treasure against me. We start to lick each other's wounds, and her beast's grumble soothes my bird. It's then we hear someone clearing their throat. Like two little kids who got their hands caught in the cookie jar, we lift our heads up quickly and look at the door. Alaric is standing there with his arms crossed over his chest with a knowing smirk on his lips. "So, maybe I should bust the ass out of my pants more often," he says jokingly as he looks between the two of us.

Aurora rolls her eyes and then hits him with a ball of frost. "Get the hell out of here," she says. Neither Alaric nor I can tell if she's joking or being serious. Softly, she yawns and buries her face against my throat, laying her head upon my shoulder. I guess I wore her out—score one for me. I'll take this minor victory when I can get it; it's not often that I don't tap out first. Alaric looks into my room then looks back at us. He disappears for several minutes and then returns with a bunch of pillows and blankets from my bed. He drops them on the floor next to us and motions for me to lay us both down.

"Make sure she rests well. Apparently, there's going to be a big celebration tomorrow for the defeat of Tomas," Alaric says and smiles

"You got it!" I say as I slowly maneuver us to lay side by side. Aurora moves and puts her head on my shoulder, snuggling in against me tightly. Half expecting to find one of the other mates popping in to share the snuggles with me, I look around. For once we're alone, and I'm kind of feeling very spoiled at the moment.

Softly, I began singing a song that was sung to me when I was younger, to soothe Aurora into a deeper sleep. I'm not sure how long it takes, but eventually, her beast stops making its happy grumbles, and she's silent. Her grip on my flesh has loosened, and the tenseness that was between her brows is gone.

Once I'm sure she's sleeping comfortably, I finally allow myself to close my eyes and take the much-needed nap with her. It's a new experience for me, just the two of us will be allowed this time alone. The last time I can remember us being alone was the night of the mating flight. Since then, there's always been somebody coming in after all the fun is over and sleeping with us. I know it's a pack thing, especially with the wolves, that they have to be close to their mate. However, I appreciate them giving us this time so we could just be. I drift off to sleep once I'm sure everything is perfect in my little world.

Arnulf

As I gradually awaken, the unmistakable aroma of sizzling bacon permeates the air, filling the room with its savory fragrance. It's a surprising scent to encounter in my bedroom, not typically associated with my morning routine.

Beside me, Aurora begins to stir, her movements slow and languid as she emerges from her slumber. I observe the subtle twitch of her nostrils, catching the faintest whiff of the bacon scent that hangs in the air.

Suddenly, her eyes flutter open, a spark of recognition igniting within them. A soft chuckle escapes her lips as she takes in our surroundings, her amusement evident in the laughter that follows. "I can't believe we ended up fooling around in the closet and then falling asleep here," she remarks, her voice laced with humor. "This is certainly a new experience, even for me."

As her laughter fills the room, I can't help but join in, the absurdity of our situation washing over me in waves of amusement. Despite the unconventional circumstances, there's a sense of intimacy and closeness that envelops us, turning this unexpected morning into a cherished memory to be shared between us.

She smiles and then kisses my nose, my cheek, and then my lips. "It smells like one of the boys brought me breakfast." She lifts her nose in the air and inhales. "Bacon." Deep sniff. "Eggs." Another deep sniff. "And smells like waffles too." She tilts her head several more times. "Yep, definitely waffles and maple syrup." She wiggles herself free from our little cocoon and then offers her hand to me. "Come on, let's go eat."

As we step out of our secluded sanctuary, I feel a mixture of contentment and exhilaration coursing through my veins. My disheveled appearance and stained clothes are a testament to the passionate night we shared, but I wear them with pride, devoid of any sense of shame.

In the room, the air is heavy with the lingering scent of our lovemaking, a heady mix of sweat and desire that hangs in the air like a tangible presence. Despite my state of bliss, a twinge of paranoia creeps in, and I find myself scanning the room for any signs of intrusion.

With each careful sweep of my gaze, I search for hidden threats, my senses on high alert. But as I find nothing amiss, a sense of relief washes over me, mingling with the lingering traces of passion and intimacy that still linger in the air.

Aurora's laughter fills the room, a melodious sound that pierces through the tension and soothes my frayed nerves. "What are you looking for, babe? There's no one else here but us." Her reassurance is like a balm to my restless mind, grounding me in the present moment and reminding me that in her arms, I am safe and loved.

As she sips at her ginger water, her eyes twinkling with mischief, I can't help but smile in response. In this moment, surrounded by the warmth of her presence, I am filled with a profound sense of gratitude and contentment.

"Okay, babe, not a problem." I settle down in the chair next to her and load up my plate. I even put a few slices of bacon with my food. Aurora looks at me curiously because normally I don't touch the stuff. I pick up the offensive bacon and wiggle it at her. Promptly she lunges forward and bites the bacon strip in half. I am mildly concerned for the health and well-being of my favorite member in the back of my mind. My free hand slides down and just makes sure that he's still intact. Once I'm sure everything's okay, I go back to feed her the other half.

Of course, she's laughing at me because she caught me checking. "Why on earth would I harm something that I love to use?" She tilts her head to the side and flashes me one of those dazzling smiles of hers.

I get butterflies in my stomach, and my heart flutters in my chest from being the center of her attention. "Well, babe, you see, the way you attacked that bacon was frightening. Thankfully, I was not holding up a breakfast sausage, that would have been way worse," I say with my eyebrows raised, trying to get her to relate the two things to my member.

She double blinks, looks at the bacon, and the breakfast sausage on her plate, then back to me, under the table, back to her plate. And in all seriousness, she looks at me, and she says, "Yours is bigger." I damn near choke on my orange juice. I'm coughing and sputtering, trying to clear my throat when the boys come waltzing in.

They all look from me to Aurora, and I'm still coughing. "What did you say to him?" Dominik asks.

Aurora holds up the eight-inch strip of bacon and wiggles it towards Dom. "I scared Arnulf when I bit the piece of bacon in half earlier. I then told him that he is bigger than the bacon." She motions to me while I'm still trying to clear my throat. "This is the result."

She smiles broadly as Dominik looks at the bacon, then down to his own crotch back to the bacon, then over to me. "Mother fucker! Why do I always have to be last in the goddamn lineup?" he says just before he storms out of the room.

I furrow my brows as the other guys all start laughing their asses off. "Obviously, I'm missing something here," I say as I look between the guys and Aurora. "Would somebody mind filling me in?" I ask curiously.

Dimitri steps forward and pours himself a glass of orange juice, and starts laughing. "Once upon a time in a castle far, far away, Aurora decided to put her mates in order according to the size of their dicks." He tilts his head to the side, waiting for it to sink in.

That aha moment hits when I look at the bacon, look down at my crotch, back up to Dimitri, and I just nod slowly. "Okay, so apparently I'm not last, and he is." I can't help but smirk at that news, I look over at Aurora, and she's still laughing hysterically. "I'm just curious, where am I on the lineup?" Raising a single eyebrow, I watch my mate for the answer.

Aurora takes a deep breath, and with all seriousness, she starts naming her mates. "Dimitri, Alaric, Jayce, you, Klaus and

Dominik." I look at Klaus, he shrugs his shoulders, I look at Jayce, he's smiling proud as a peacock Dimitri and Alaric both high five.

"Okay, I can live with that. Thanks babe," I say, smiling before I go back to my breakfast. Klaus kind of tilts his head looking at me, and then looks at my crotch and then back up again.

"So, if I understand this correctly, our resident eagle is bigger than two wolves." Klaus makes a statement instead of a question. He's looking at how much smaller my build is versus his build.

"Sorry to tell you, Klaus, but yes he is. It also helps that his body is much smaller than yours because I can fit around him better." She smiles and then lightly touches my cheek before stealing the last two bacon slices off my plate.

As I bask in the aftermath of my private victory, a sense of satisfaction washes over me, tingling along my skin like a warm embrace. The air in the room feels charged with an electric energy, crackling with the excitement of my achievement.

I revel in the solitude, savoring the rare moment of peace and quiet. The tranquility is palpable, wrapping around me like a comforting blanket, soothing my frayed nerves and easing the tension that had built up within me.

But it's not just the silence that fills me with contentment; it's the undeniable sense of accomplishment that courses through my veins. For once, I feel like I've come out on top, triumphant in a way that I've never experienced before.

And then, as if on cue, a sharp blow lands on the back of my head, snapping me out of my reverie. The sudden impact jolts me back to reality, dispelling the lingering euphoria with a swift and sobering reminder of the world outside my own thoughts.

As I turn to face Nicodeamus, a wry smile tugs at my lips, a silent acknowledgment of the playful reprimand. Despite the interruption, I can't help but feel a sense of pride swelling within me. After all, in this moment, I am indeed larger than life, if only in one aspect.

"I talked to Dom, kid, don't let it go to your head." As Aurora's dad addresses me, his words send a rush of heat to my cheeks, tinting them a brilliant shade of pink. The sensation of embarrassment washes over me, my heart pounding in my chest as I realize that Aurora's father may have caught on to our playful banter.

Amidst the laughter that echoes through the air, I can feel Aurora's amusement reverberating in the atmosphere. Her infectious laughter fills the space around us, nearly causing her to lose her balance and topple from her chair.

Quickly, Dimitri springs into action, swooping in to rescue Aurora from her precarious position. With a gentle yet protective gesture, he lifts her up and settles her onto his lap, ensuring her safety amidst the laughter and merriment.

"Silly woman, calm yourself before you hurt yourself and the cubs," As Aurora's emotions run high, a wave of tension fills the air, palpable even amidst the chaos of the moment. Dimitri's gentle nuzzle against her cheek carries a sense of reassurance, his words a soothing balm to her frazzled nerves.

But as the seconds tick by, a sudden shift in atmosphere takes hold. The unmistakable sensation of moisture against Dimitri's skin elicits a visceral reaction, prompting a mixture of surprise and disgust to ripple through the group.

With a grimace of distaste, Dimitri's expression contorts into an "eww" face, the evidence of our escapades now visible for all to see. The scent of the release lingers in the air, adding an unexpected element to the already charged atmosphere.

Amidst the chaos, laughter erupts from my lips, its sound echoing through the clearing. The tension of the moment is broken, replaced by the infectious energy of shared amusement.

"What am I missing here?" Alaric's voice breaks through the chatter, his brow furrowing in confusion. Suddenly, his nose twitches, catching a whiff of the heady, mixed scent of arousal lingering in the air.

With an exasperated sigh, he strides over to my bathroom, grabbing a towel and washcloth before returning to Aurora's side. "Go clean up," he insists, his tone firm but gentle. Yet, Aurora merely rolls her eyes in response, stubbornly refusing to comply as she shakes her head defiantly.

The tension in the room crackles with suppressed laughter as I watch the playful exchange unfold, a smile tugging at the corners of my lips. The interplay of scents and emotions fills the air, adding a layer of complexity to the already charged atmosphere.

"We need to get ourselves downstairs. There are still things that we need to take care of before the dignitaries arrive," Nicodeamus announces, his words cutting through the air with a sense of urgency.

Instantly, the atmosphere in the room shifts, and a wave of concern washes over us. I exchange glances with my companions, each of us mirroring the other's apprehension.

"What do you mean dignitaries?" I inquire, my voice laced with unease as I turn to face Nicodeamus.

"They were invited after the birth of the twins, or have you forgotten?" Nicodeamus's words hang heavy in the air, a stark reminder of our oversight.

A collective sense of panic grips us as we realize the implications of our forgetfulness. Aurora's sudden movement breaks the silence, her hurried exit signaling the urgency of the situation. Without hesitation, she bolts from the room, her footsteps echoing down the hallway as she rushes back to hers.

In the wake of her departure, a sense of urgency fills the room, propelling us into action as we scramble to prepare for the impending arrival of the dignitaries. The weight of our oversight hangs heavy upon us, driving us forward with a newfound sense of purpose.

"Thanks, guys," I say before heading into my bathroom to go shower and straighten up, making sure that I'm prepared for this visit that we all forgot about.

CHAPTER 57
Klaus

We all forgot about the dignitaries. Originally they were supposed to meet us at the Ice Dragon Court. I'm guessing since we didn't return with Nicodeamus to the castle, he rerouted everyone here. I hear through the pack link Aurora alerting all the wolves as to what's about to happen. My once tiny village has expanded to accommodate half of the Dire Wolf pack and a fraction of the rogue Lycans.

I am unsure of my mate's plans for all the wolves, but I know that she plans on calling all of the wolves home. We still haven't discussed where the new wolves will be going or how to assimilate them back into proper packs. Aurora has made arrangements for the last of the American Lycans to join us here. Perhaps some of the unmated wolves in my pack may find their mates with them. Plus, we have five pregnant females all in one house awaiting to give birth. Those pups will be given to families that can't have pups but want them. Two of my closest friends and my twin, Kaden, have found their mates because of this. Kaden is willing to raise the pup even though it isn't his, but his mate is still strongly against it. Aurora said we would take that pup as our own since it will be related to my brother's pups when they come.

Rooting through the closet, I finally find the dress uniform I had from all the political functions I attended with my father. It's a traditional three-piece suit with a tie and an appropriate cummerbund. I put on all of my metals and the sash. Those metals I had won through all the little skirmishes that we had fought years ago.

I double check myself in the mirror and then make my way downstairs to join the others. Once downstairs, I notice that Alaric had already pulled out all of his royal attire. Aurora is in a full-length gown, wearing her great-grandmother's crown. Dimitri is in the dress uniform of his people for the Royal Guard. Jayce and Dominik both are wearing their best suits, ties, and dress shoes. Arnulf is wearing a nice suit as well, but unlike Jayce and Dominik, he has a sash across his chest adorned with many assorted pins and ribbons.

Nicodeamus has pulled out of somewhere a crown and a rather regal-looking suit. We all assembled in the main hall of the Alpha House, awaiting the dignitaries' arrival.

Anna, who has become fast friends with Aurora, comes running in and whispers in her ear. We wait several moments. Aurora nods, and Anna goes running out of the house yet again, apparently on a mission.

Several minutes later, a powerful couple walks in with their young son closely at their side. Alaric rushes over and shakes hands with the man, and embraces him tightly. "Austin, I'm happy you made it. I hope that the winds were favorable for you." The gentleman, obviously the king of his clan, smiles at Alaric.

"Always, old friend. Being what we are, the winds are always in our favor." He smiles and then walks to stand before Aurora. Her head is held high, and her resting bitch face is on point. She slowly extends her hand out to the gentleman, who promptly takes it. He brings it to his lips and kisses her knuckles, and lowers his head and deferment to her. "It is an honor to meet a direct descendant of the Blood Queen herself. Thank you for allowing me and my family into your nest."

Aurora listens carefully to what the man is saying to her and then nods her head slightly. "You graced us with your presence, any friend of my husband's is a friend of mine." Her free hand comes up and lightly touches his cheek before she takes her hands away from him. Slowly, she turns and approaches the female.

The rest of us are on edge; Aurora doesn't usually get along with other females. For a split second, there is a battle of wills before the other female lowers her head and eyes. Aurora nods and then moves forward and gently kisses the female on both cheeks. "Welcome to my nest, Gisella. It's my pleasure to have you and your family here." Aurora looks down at the young boy whose jet black hair catches her attention. His eyes are as green as emeralds and wide open, looking up at her curiously.

"This must be your son, Draven." Aurora kneels down to get eye level with the young lad. She drops the resting bitch face and adapts a very friendly demeanor. "It's my pleasure to meet you, young prince." Aurora smiles softly. "Perhaps you would like to play with my son, Ladon? He could always use a friend his age."

The little boy's eyes light up, and he starts bouncing from foot to foot. Before we know it, he has his arms thrown tightly around Aurora's neck. She's smiling while he hugs her like she had given him the best present ever. "Thank you, thank you, thank you." he exclaims. He looks around quickly to see if the young boy she spoke of is anywhere in sight.

Aurora winks her eye at him and smiles. Her pale-grey eyes become stormy before an ethereal glow fills them. Soon, Ladon and Tiamat come running into the room. Tia runs and hides behind Alaric's legs, staring at the young prince. Her eyes are glowing like her mother's as she stares at him. Meanwhile, Ladon and Draven run out the door together to go play.

Aurora gives Alaric a knowing look then stands slowly. "Shall we adjourn to the banquet laid out in the great hall?" she asks cordially.

I watch Aurora escort the couple from the room and look to the others. "That was uncharacteristic of her," I say to no one in particular.

Nicodeamus comes over to me as Dimitri and Dominik greet the new arrivals. "She questioned me quickly about proper protocol. I educated her the best I could in such a short time frame," Nicodeamus says as if it was no big thing.

"How did she know who they were?" I tilt my head to the side, watching him.

"Alaric and I filled her in through the bond. She handled it quite well." Nicodeamus smiles and motions as several more dignitaries entered the Alpha House. "I believe we all have a role to play, son." Nicodeamus smiles at me then walks into the great room.

My eyes wander the main entrance for a minute before I turn and decide to follow everyone else into the great room. Aurora is speaking with three other women I can only assume are the wives of the other Great Dragon Houses that were invited. Along the wall is Dominik speaking with his brother, Alex, and his mate. I wander over slowly, not wanting to interrupt this family moment.

"Hey, Klaus! Great to see you not in the war room," Alex says to me, smiling as he kisses his mate's temple. "Oh, this is my mate James. James, this is Klaus, King Consort of the Lycan court." I double blink at the title, then look to Dominik, confused.

Dominik starts to laugh and shake his head. "Alex, he didn't know his title. Smooth move, brother." Alex's face goes pale as he looks from me over to Aurora then back again.

"I'm gonna be skinned alive," he says, still looking around nervously.

"Aurora won't skin you over a little slip. Besides, you're her mate's brother, you can't get much safer than that." I smile as I pat his shoulder before leaving to find Alaric.

Alaric is in deep discussion with the King of the Bronze Dragon court and two other powerful males. "Klaus, excellent timing! We have matters to discuss." He excuses himself from his current conversations and drags me through the house to the main floor's bedrooms. He reaches into the closest and pulls out a fancy suit, and lays it out for me. "You need to get changed, or Aurora will murder me." He winks before he adjusts his crown and tie.

I tilt my head and decide to get changed quickly without protest. It's very odd going from warrior alpha to being stuck in this three-piece monkey suit. Alaric moves in front of me and adjusts every-thing so that it's sitting properly. The suit itself is worth more than most of the things I currently own. Alaric throws a sheet over my suit and then proceeds to trim my beard, making sure it is well manicured. He looks me over one last time and then removes the sheet.

We start to leave the room when he stops and grabs two boxes I didn't notice on the table. He ushers us through the house and out into the gardens where Aurora is waiting at the altar with Nicodeamus behind the pedestal. Alaric walks with me down the aisle and moves me to stand before Aurora. Sometime during my wardrobe change, she went and changed as well. Her gown is as black as pitch and hugs her generous curves and the swell of her belly. Blood red roses are in her hands mixed with black calla lilies.

Nicodeamus raises his hand, and the guests quickly become silent. "We are gathered here today, after the victorious liberation of the Marelup castle. Today we witness the joining of two true and fated mates." Nicodeamus looks down and flips the page in front of him. "There has not been a Marelup descendant on the throne in over two hundred and thirty years, since the time of Queen Anca."

The crowd whispers, "May the Goddess bless and keep her."

Aurora's eyes get all misty, and I can't help but smile at her. Nicodeamus begins again. "Standing before you is my daughter and Anca's Heir, Aurora Marelup-Kraus, rightful Queen of the Lycan court. Rightful Queen as my heir to the Ice Dragon court."

Nicodeamus's voice is commanding and leaves no room for argument. "Before you stands Klaus Schmidt, Alpha of the German Lycan pack. Soon to be King Consort of the Lycan court."

My head whips back to look at the dead serious look Nicodeamus has in his eyes. Shit, this is really happening. "My daughter has chosen the ancient right of branding to anoint her new King." Alaric steps forward with the long wooden box and opens it.

Aurora slips on the leather gloves within and pulls out a small branding iron with the Marelup crest on it. "I, Aurora, last Marelup Heir, choose you, Klaus, to be my King Consort. To help me rule over our people from this day forth till our last breath," she says and extends a hand to me, palm up.

Carefully, I unbutton my jacket sleeve and roll it up, then repeat the process with my dress shirt. I lay my right forearm in her waiting hand and smile. "I, Klaus, Alpha of the German Lycan pack, accept the duties that come with helping you to guide our people from this day forth. I will support you and protect our people till my last breath." Once the words are spoken, she says to me through the bond that the branding will hurt. I subtly nod and smile.

With deft precision, she presses the brand in the exact same place as hers on my arm. I grit my teeth to keep from showing how much the brand hurts. A king cannot show weakness in front of others. The metal used is an ancient mixture that burns without fire and scars the skin black for life. As soon as Aurora pulls the branding iron away, she places her hand over it and sends a chill directly into my skin, stopping the burning immediately. She leans forward and kisses my lips passionately before pulling away and showing the crowd my new brand. Cheers erupt, and everyone stands, clapping for the two of us.

Aurora drags me forward to stand at the edge of the platform. Her pale-grey eyes look up to me adoringly. Through the bond, she speaks to me. *Klaus, it would be wise for you to address everyone gathered now that you have been crowned King Consort.* She remains smiling up at me and then kisses my jaw, the *oohs* and *ahhs* that erupt, giving me butterflies in my stomach.

I raise my hands up to silence the crowd. "Thank you to our friends and allies that have traveled near and far to be here for this momentous day." I motion towards Nicodeamus and call him forward with us. I then motion towards Alaric and call him forward with us.

"I have been thrice blessed in these recent days. Firstly, by receiving my angel who stands beside me from now until forever." I kiss Aurora's temple and smile, looking down at her.

"Secondly, I have been blessed with the gift of her father being present in our lives from this day forward. His wisdom and guidance will prove invaluable in the days to come." I motion next out and over the crowd.

"To all of you here that have not yet met everyone, my bond mates, my brothers in arms." I smile at them and bring my fist up and over my heart. "The five of them each have been a blessing in their own right. I don't know what I would do without them and their guidance." I can see that Jayce, Arnulf, and Alaric have unshed tears at the corner of their eyes. Next, I seek out where Dimitri and Dominik are standing. I raise my fist over my chest to them as well, no mate above the other.

"Let's have everyone adjourn back to the great hall. Let's eat, drink, and be merry. Tonight is a night for celebration," I say, smiling broadly, happy in the little surprise that was given to me tonight. Though, kind of like my mate, I don't really like being the center of attention. I am a warrior, not an aristocrat, just like she is. This will take some getting used to.

CHAPTER 58

Alaric

THE ATMOSPHERE IS CHARGED WITH A SENSE OF ACCOMPLISHMENT AS Klaus seamlessly navigates the social intricacies of the evening. Despite his upbringing as a warrior, he moves through the crowd with a grace and poise that belies his origins. Each interaction is executed with precision, a testament to his adaptability and determination.

Aurora's pride radiates from her as she observes Klaus's performance, her hand tenderly caressing her swollen belly. There's a softness in her expression, a mixture of admiration and affection, as she watches her mate effortlessly integrate himself into the gathering.

I approach her, drawn in by the warmth of her smile, and press a gentle kiss to her cheek. The sensation of her soft skin beneath my lips sends a wave of tenderness through me, and I can't help but feel a surge of affection for her.

"My love, how are you holding up?" I inquire softly, my voice filled with genuine concern. "Do you need anything for the babies?"

She smiles at me and then shakes her head no. "Just when I didn't think my heart could get any fuller, it does. What you and Dad did for Klaus was amazing," she says, smiling at me as she watches him make his rounds with the visiting dignitaries.

"Well, the fun has yet to begin, my love. Under the full moon tonight, you need to crown him as king. The ceremony can only do so much; the crown itself is what does the rest for your people." I motion to the second box—it's in my hand—then I motion out to Klaus. "In all the excitement, we forgot to place the crown on his head."

Aurora starts giggling, shakes her head, and shrugs her shoulders. "You can't honestly expect me to think straight carrying another litter of babies at this point in time, do you?" I start to laugh and shake my head no.

"Of course not, my love, though these are your people." I smile and tilt my head to the left, then back to the right again. "How is it that the Americans say? Not my circus, not my monkeys." I start to laugh and then poke her side gently.

"This is your circus, and these are your monkeys." The broad smile that graces my lips apparently infuriates my darling mate. She pokes my chest several times and utters a soft growl.

"Not funny, Alaric, definitely not funny," she says, inflecting as much anger as she can, trying not to laugh at the situation. Apparently, her poking my chest got Dimitri's attention.

"So what did the pretty boy do now?" Dimitri asks as he scoops her up in his arms and snuggles her to his chest.

"Well, to start, his royal highness here," Aurora jabs her finger in my direction, "allowed us to get away with ourselves, and I forgot to put the crown on Klaus's head." Aurora tilts her head, hoping for Dimitri to be on her side.

We all know he's going to be, but it's always interesting to see what that man comes up with. Dimitri strokes his beard and looks at me, then over to Klaus, then back down to Aurora. "Well, there's only three of us standing here that knew exactly how this was supposed to go. Only two of us were up on stage."

He looks between myself and Aurora and then back over to me. I think I'm in trouble. "There's only one of us that was on stage that isn't carrying multiple babies and isn't only constantly either thinking of dick or food. Gee, I wonder who that is?" Dimitri just crosses his arms around Aurora tighter and then tilts his head, staring at me.

"Well fuck, I guess I did bogart this one, huh? Okay, okay, I get it. I let things get out of hand." I raise my hands up in a placating manner. "It's all right. We'll fix it later, no big deal." I slowly move away from the snuggling pair and go seek out Klaus. He's standing with his brother Kaden, and Kaden has his brand new mate with him.

"Your Highness?" I say half-jokingly to Klaus and lightly bow to him with a big smile on my face, so he knows that I'm just messing with him.

"Why, hello, Your Highness." Klaus imitates me and then bows to me the same way that I did to him, both of us being asses about the title.

"Oh great! Not only is my brother Alpha, but now he's a King. There's going to be no living with him now!" Kaden says as he snuggles his mate. It's now that I notice she's one of the females we rescued.

"Leandra, how are you doing?" I ask cheerfully as I smile at her. Kaden is beaming with pride, and she looks absolutely miserable.

"Better as soon as that bastard's pup is out of me," she growls almost viciously, turning her head away quickly.

Her growls set off a chain reaction, heads turn, and that catches Aurora's attention. She grabs Dimitri's hand and waddles herself over to where we are as fast as possible. "What seems to be the matter?" Aurora asks gently. The way her eyes are narrowed, she already knows what's wrong.

"I want this thing out of me! I want the last of that bastard's taint out of me." Leandra starts crying and buries her face in Kaden's chest.

As she cries, her water just so happens to break. Aurora tilts her head, and then her eyes take on an ethereal glow. Elsa comes over quickly with some of her medical staff. They pick up Leandra and carry her back to the infirmary. Aurora sighs softly, then lightly rubs her stomach before looking at us. "She'll be okay. Unfortunately for her, she was too far along when we found her for anything to be done." I can tell the thought of a female wanting to kill her pup really affects Aurora. Tears are threatening to break free from her eyes.

Carefully, I pull her to me, and Dimitri snuggles in close from behind. One by one, all of my bond mates come to us, sensing Aurora's distress. We each lay a hand on her trying to soothe her beast. "I just don't understand. Life is a gift. Poor Emma and her mate can't have pups." Aurora sniffles as she rests her forehead against my chest.

"These poor pups didn't ask to be here. They don't deserve to die." She sighs softly and tightens her arms around my waistline.

"Love, Emma and her mate will be getting a pup as soon as it's born. As will the other two who want a baby." I smile down at her and kiss the crown of her head.

"I know, just Kayden's mate..." Aurora sighs. "I do and don't understand. I probably hate Vladimir more than everyone here." She slowly pulls away from me and looks at everyone. "I'll be okay. It's just, all life is precious." Aurora walks away, and Dimitri leaves with her.

Beneath the composed facade that Aurora presents to us lies a tumultuous sea of emotions, swirling with turmoil and uncertainty. The discovery of her twin's skeleton has dredged up a wellspring of grief and anguish, shaking her to the core with its stark reminder of a life cut tragically short.

As I observe her, I can sense the waves of sorrow and despair that wash over her, threatening to engulf her in their depths. The weight of such a profound loss hangs heavy in the air, casting a shadow over the room and dimming the once-bright atmosphere.

The thought of a life so young and innocent snuffed out before it could even begin resonates deeply within her, stirring up a tempest of emotions that rattles her cage to its very core. Each heartbeat echoes with the weight of all the death and destruction that has plagued us over the past two years, leaving an indelible mark upon her soul.

In the silence that follows, the air is heavy with unspoken grief, the weight of it pressing down upon us like a suffocating blanket. And amidst it all, Aurora stands as a beacon of strength, her mask of composure faltering only slightly as she grapples with the enormity of the pain that threatens to consume her.

As I navigate through the bustling party, a cacophony of sounds and sights assaults my senses. Laughter and chatter fill the air, mingling with the lively melodies of music drifting from a nearby band. The aroma of savory dishes wafts temptingly through the crowd, intermingling with the sweet scent of freshly baked pastries.

Amidst the jubilant atmosphere, I find solace in the knowledge that our hard-fought battles have yielded some semblance of victory. The once imprisoned are now free, their spirits unshackled from the chains of oppression. It's a bittersweet triumph, tempered by the losses we've endured along the way.

As I weave my way through the throng of revelers, I take a moment to express my gratitude to each person I encounter. Their unwavering dedication and sacrifice have been instrumental in bringing about this revolution, and I am humbled by their bravery.

I pause to exchange pleasantries with members of other dragon households, their presence serving as a reminder of the unity forged in the face of adversity. It's heartening to see Lycan packs finding refuge within their borders, offering hope for a brighter future amidst the chaos.

In the midst of celebration, I can't help but ponder the potential implications of this newfound alliance. Perhaps, with the integration of these packs, the longstanding issue of mate scarcity within the German pack may finally find resolution

I walk outside to find my son, Ladon, and Austin's son, Draven, playing by the koi pond. From my position, I watch the boys interact, having fun and roughhousing. In the shadows, my daughter. Tiamat, has taken a liking apparently to Draven. I move over and gently caress the back of her head to get her to look up at me. "Little one? Why aren't you playing with the others?"

"Daddy, the boys don't want me to play." Tia frowns and hugs my leg tightly. "They say it's not a princess's place to be able to play rough," she says again, rubbing her tear-stained cheek on my thigh.

My thoughts race as to how my mate would handle this situation. Aurora does not like when the boys feel that girls are not strong enough to do as they do. I reach down and cup my daughter's cheek and smile at her. "You are the direct descendant of the great Blood Queen. You bear her scales down your spine." I lightly trail my fingers over the scales that I just mentioned.

"In the years to come, you will surpass your mother and me by leaps and bounds. Pay no attention to the ramblings of silly boys." I smile as I bend down to pick my daughter up. I cradle her to my chest and kiss her cheek fondly.

"You are the heir to the Ice Dragon throne. As firstborn, you have the choice to rule or to abdicate the throne." I nuzzle her cheek gently. "When the time comes, and you choose your mate, I will respect your decision."

Tiamat makes that *eww* face as she looks at me. "Daddy, boys are disgusting. Yuck, why would I ever want one of them around me all the time?" She throws her hands dramatically up into the air and rolls her eyes exactly how her mother does.

"The only boys I don't mind around me are you and my other daddies. And sometimes Ladon." She smirks as she says that last piece.

As I observe the boys, a sense of pride wells within me. They play with their weapons, each movement a testament to their unique gifts. My son wields the power of ice with skill and precision, while Draven commands the crackling energy of lightning. Their camaraderie brings warmth to my heart, grateful that my son has found a friend who shares his extraordinary abilities.

The room is filled with the sound of their laughter and the occasional clang of metal against metal, creating a symphony of childhood innocence and boundless energy. I watch them with a mixture of admiration and nostalgia, savoring this moment of simple joy amidst the chaos of our world.

Beside me, Tia remains nestled in my arms, her presence a comforting weight against my chest. I glance down to find her sleeping peacefully, her soft breaths a gentle lullaby in the quiet room. It seems the events of the day have taken their toll on her, as they have on her mother and me.

With a tender smile, I carefully shift Tia in my arms, cradling her close as I rise from my seat. It's time to tuck my little princess into bed, to ensure she rests peacefully through the night.

As I carry Tia to her room, a sense of contentment washes over me. Despite the challenges we face, there is solace in the simple moments of familial love and unity. Tomorrow may bring its own trials, but for now, I cherish the tranquility of this moment, knowing that in the embrace of my family, life is indeed good.

CHAPTER 59
Dimitri

Swiftly, I catch up with Aurora and gently place my hand at her lower back, offering comfort. She slows her furious steps, and her shoulder's sag. "I don't understand, D." She sobs softly. "Life is so precious." She stresses the importance of life itself with that statement.

She turns to me, and her eyes are churning liquid mercury. The black dragon slits are barely visible with the amount of turmoil that I see within her gaze. Approaching slowly, I gently cup her cheek and thumb away the tears that have broken free from her eyes. She is my greatest treasure and my most precious gift. Never in all my years did I think I would ever be blessed with someone to love. Little did I know that I would get to witness her birth, raise her, believing that my only duty is to protect her. And as she grew, watch her become the strong independent woman that she is. I would love to believe that the values that Andre and I instilled with her made her the woman she is today.

On the flip side, genetics has a lot to do with the woman that she is. She is a direct descendant of one of the strongest dragoness's in history. Her father is one of the strongest kings in history. Her mother was the strongest and most respected Lycan ruler in the history of the Marelup throne. She was born for greatness. Originally, all I thought I was was a witness to it. Here I am standing with this little powerhouse in my hands.

Looking deeply now into her pale-grey eyes and I see my forever. My heart beats a little stronger, and I will live a little longer because of her and her love for me. I have been blessed multiple times over by this precious gift before me. My greatest gift to date, yet to be born. My future heir is growing in her womb. I cannot wait to see the babies that she will give us.

Softly, I kiss Aurora's full lips and elicit a slow growl from her. Her beast is happy with the affection that I'm showing her. We move and sit on a bench nearby, looking out over the gardens that Klaus and his grandmother had planted. Several of Aurora's favorite flowers that I had brought the seeds of now grow here where they do not belong. Aurora giggles slightly, seeing this now invasive species growing in a country they should not be in. "You guys would literally move heaven and Earth just to see me smile," she says softly as she leans against me.

"That is true. If we could, we would reign hellfire and brimstone upon the world to destroy whatever makes you cry." I kiss her cheek and hug her tightly to me. Out of the corner of my eye, I see a midwife approaching.

"Your Highness, the pup you were waiting for has been born." The midwife holds a little bundle up and out towards Aurora as she curtsies and lowers her head in submission. Aurora looks up to me and then over to the bundle, and she sits up slowly. Hesitantly, she reaches out and takes the bundle from the midwife. Carefully, she pulls the little bundle close to her chest and holds it tightly, looking down at it. The baby slowly cracks its eyes open and looks up at Aurora. Its eyes are sky blue, the same color as what was Sebastian's. Blue is a very unique color amongst the Lycan packs. It was highly uncommon, and only two bloodlines held it. Vladimirs and one other that Aurora did not tell me its name.

Aurora stares down at the baby and then sniffs its crown. Her beast rumbles very softly, and the baby responds almost immediately. I watch Aurora tilt her head several times, staring at the child. Carefully, she unwraps the blankets and inspects the child's gender. It's a little girl, yet another uncommon feat for the Lycans. Female births are so rare that they are revered amongst the pack. Kaden should be quite proud of his mate for bearing a female.

Hopefully, her next pup will be female so that Kaden will have a daughter of his own. It's kind of funny that most species strive to have males to pass on the family name. Amongst us, the shifters, since female births are rare, they are valued above all others. You would almost say that a female is a God compared to the rest of us. To be honest, males are a dime a dozen. With there being only one female born to every fifteen males, if not more, it makes it very difficult to find a mate.

I watch Aurora rock and hold the baby after she bundles her back up. It's funny to see this very lethal female go from being a phenom on the battlefield to this gentle creature before me. I guess it only makes sense with her dual nature to be dual in this as well. I kiss her cheek lightly and look down at the little one. "So what do you wish to name her?" I ask her gently.

Her eyes dart over the baby's face several times, and then she looks up to me. "She is of Vladimir's line. I do not believe that blood is a huge influence on someone. I believe that it's mostly how someone is raised that determines how they turn out," she says passionately as she nuzzles the baby's cheek ever so gently.

"She will know love, and she will learn to respect others. She will learn that life is precious and not to be taken lightly." She kisses the baby's forehead and then passes her back to the midwife.

"Please make sure that she's fed and held until she sleeps. Assign a nurse to her to remain at her side throughout the night." Aurora smiles as she looks at me and then looks back at the baby again.

"We shall call her Victoria, her name derived from the victory that released our enslaved people." The midwife receives the baby back and holds her tightly to her chest. "My Queen, what family name shall we give her?"

Aurora then looks at me then back to the midwife. "That will be determined. For now, just call her by her first name. I do not wish to assume that my mate will want her to have his last name." Aurora stands and gently kisses the baby's forehead one more time. "She cannot and will not receive my last name, for she is not a candidate for the throne."

The midwife nods gently and then hustles off with the baby back inside the infirmary. There's much to be done tonight, births that are happening. The party still wages on, and there's fun yet to be had.

I stand and offer Aurora my hand and escort her back inside. I give Jayce a nod of my head, and he puts on a nice slow waltz for Aurora and me to dance to. Gracefully, we slide and twirl around the dance floor. A smile never leaves her face as we move gracefully in time with each other. Halfway through the song, Dominik comes over and switches out with me mid-twirl. I watch them dance around the floor. It's a work of art.

She's giggling and smiling, and that's all that I could ask for. The next waltz comes on, and Arnulf takes her from Dominik, and the dance continues. Halfway through each song, a different mate switches out with the prior. Six songs in total are played before she ends up back in my arms again. Most of the dignitaries are starting to leave or head to the rooms that we are supplying for them. It has been a glorious day on many fronts. We have forged many new alliances and made great headway with doing exchange programs for the Lycans. Klaus is the most pleased that his people and others of his species will have the chance to meet and find love.

Aurora yawns softly and lays her head against my chest. Her body is slowly becoming heavy as she leans on me. It's been a very long day, and it must have been very tiring for her. According to Elsa's last reading, the babies can arrive within the next two to three weeks, putting her total time just shy of four months. Multiple births tend to shorten the gestation period. We invested in some of the high-tech ultrasound equipment to double check the babies' growth. I didn't tell Aurora yet, but she's carrying three babies this time. I'm curious to see how many are Bears and how many are Wolves.

The night comes to an end. Alaric and I slowly escort Aurora down to our bedroom. He takes her into the shower and helps her wash off while I prepare the room for bed. Our other four mates make their way down, bringing snacks and assorted drinks for us. Because knowing our mate before bed, she will get hungry, and we won't be ready. Klaus and Jayce fill the mini-fridge with juices and ginger water for Aurora. Dominik and Arnulf set up the snacks on the table near the bed. I'm in charge of turning down the sheets and fluffing the pillows, making sure the bed is ready for her. Klaus was absolutely brilliant when he bought the double king-sized bed for us. When we place Aurora in the middle, there is plenty of room for everybody to sleep on the bed simultaneously. Nobody has to be left out or shoved into a different room unless they want to be there.

We made provisions for Tiamat and Ladon to stay upstairs with their grandmother. Austin and Gisella, along with Draven, decided to spend the night. Draven is having a sleepover with Ladon tonight, and the poor nursemaids will be going out of their minds with two rambunctious boys.

Alaric walks out of the bathroom with our precious cargo in his arms, wrapped in her towels. He comes to stand before me, gently placing Aurora on her feet. Together we towel dry her body and her hair. Jayce comes over with a pair of her favorite boy shorts and a tank top just to try to keep her comfortable. Klaus comes forward with her cocoa butter and gently massages it over her stomach. If we listen carefully, we can hear him speaking to the babies in her belly. I don't know who's more excited about their birth, myself or Klaus. To be perfectly honest, I believe it's a tie.

Arnulf offers Aurora a snack and then sits next to her when she sits down and he feeds her. We sit back and watch them because their bond is still the newest. I've spoken with him at great length, and he is in no rush to father children yet. He feels the rest of us that have waited the longest deserve the chance to have ours first.

I love this man to death, his heart is huge, and he always thinks of everybody else first. We decided amongst ourselves that the twins will go next, and then Arnulf will have his time with Aurora alone. Alaric will have Dante fly them back to Arnulf's people so that they can spend a holiday there during her next heat.

For now, we make sure that she's pampered and fed, and it takes two of us to place her in the center of the large mattress. She wiggles for several minutes till she finds a spot that she's most comfortable in. We rock paper scissors to figure out who is sleeping where for the night. Arnulf laughs as he watches us try to figure out positioning. Aurora just shakes her head, watching us because this happens every single night.

"Okay, guys, let's just do this the easy way," she says, exasperated. "Dimitri, you and Klaus, since it's your babies that are making me uncomfortable, snuggle the closest." She tilts her head looking at us. "The rest of you just figure it out. I'm tired and uncomfortable; the babies are dancing all over the place." She throws her hands up several times during the explanation.

"I just want to sleep. Please let me sleep." Tears are threatening to roll down her cheeks, and we quickly scoot ourselves into position to not add to her stress. Aurora rolls close and puts her head on my chest, and Klaus scoots up behind her. In a matter of moments, she's out cold, snoring peacefully in my ear. At least one of us will have a solid night's sleep tonight.

CHAPTER 60

Aurora

I have to say, I probably had the best night of sleep that I've had in a long time. We made great headway yesterday, forging and solidifying more alliances than we had before. Slowly, I stretch my body and rub my stomach. Rolling over and finding only Dimitri still in bed with me, I look around the room, and nobody else is here. I wonder where they all got off to this early in the morning? I wake Dimitri up gently and kiss his cheek. "Hey, babe, everybody else is gone and it's not even seven a.m.."

Dimitri's large hands come up, and he rubs his face, clearing his eyes of sleep. My big, grumbly teddy bear smiles at me softly and kisses my temple. "They could be anywhere, love. I'm sure if we look for them, we'll find them." He's the first to get up out of bed between the two of us, and he goes about his morning routine.

I yawn for a second time and then slowly get myself out of bed. Dimitri's done in the bathroom, then I go take my turn and dress while I'm in there. I feel like I'm freaking huge; my stomach's enormous, my boobs are achy and sore. Miserable doesn't even begin to describe how I feel for the first few moments of being awake in the morning. Dimitri hands me my bottle of ginger water, and I sip it slowly like I do every morning.

A moan catches my attention, and my head whips around to the door leading into our spa chamber. I raise an eyebrow looking at Dimitri and start to waddle my happy ass over there. Curiosity is absolutely getting the best of me at this point. Thankfully, the door is dead silent when I go to slide it open. The sight before me makes my breath catch in my lungs.

My sweet Jayce is lying on his side on the massage table. Klaus stands in front of him with his rear end backed up to his crotch. Jayce pumps his hips, thrusting his cock into Klaus's ass with a punishing thrust. The momentum from Alaric, who stands behind Jayce, with his strong hand holding firmly to his hip bone, moving Jayce forward as Alaric takes from him his own bliss. At Jayce's head is Arnulf, getting the blow job of his life. Standing on a chair that defies all logic to me is Dominik having Klaus give him a blowjob. And not just any blowjob, he's going to town on him, deep throating him. Taking him as far as he can. I stare at this jigsaw puzzle of male horniness with sadistic glee.

Quickly, I raise a hand in silence to Dimitri as I allow him to peek over my shoulder at what I'm looking at. The panting, the moaning, the overall level of pheromones has me dripping wet. Dimitri eyes me, trying to clench my thighs tighter together to stop the throbbing in my molten core. Being the brilliant opportunistic male he is, he slightly bends me over, using the door frame for support and hikes my dress up. He drops to his knees and licks my soaking wet center.

It's obvious the moment that he shifts his tongue from human to bear. It's so much more broader and thicker and can reach much further inside of me. I bite my lip, trying to keep myself from outwardly moaning and disturbing the show going on in front of me. Several times the guys switch out and change positions. Each switch-up brings me closer to my peak as I claw at the door frame.

My first orgasm rips through me, and I feel as if my muscles will never stop spasming. Almost going weak in the knees, Dimitri grabs me and supports my full weight. He carefully cradles me to him as he sinks his length within me. Just the simple act of him breaching my entrance sets off another chain reaction of pulsing and throbbing, stealing my breath.

This time I can't help but cry out and throw my head back in ecstasy. As soon as the guys hear me, they all freeze mid-motion looking at me. Dimitri keeps his slow rhythmic thrusting to sustain the orgasm I'm having. I can feel my moisture running down the insides of both of my thighs and hear it dripping onto the floor. What can I say, my bear gets me? I watch the guys' noses twitch as they pick up on my pheromones.

It's at that moment that all hell breaks loose; Arnulf ends up taking flight for a few moments and backs away. While my other mates savagely start taking each other, fucking each other as hard as they can take. It's a thing of beauty when Arnulf gets back into the mix and offers his cock right to Jayce to suck.

Dimitri hasn't given me any indication that he was close to his peak. I swear the man's a machine. I watch the guys come in succession, one almost right after the other. Jayce looks how I feel at this moment, like a huge puddle of gelatin. He has the broadest smile upon his face as he flops onto his back, exhausted and sated. Klaus and Dominik come over towards Dimitri and me, both drop down to their knees, each reaching up to flick their tongues over my nipples. I cry out again as my orgasm rips through me, my muscles clenching and pulsating around Dimitri's thick cock. I could tell the moment the big guy's getting close. His grip on my hips has gotten tighter, and now Dominik and Klaus have to help support the weight of my upper body.

Dimitri reaches forward and sinks his canines in over his original mating mark on me. I raise up quickly, throwing my back against his chest, crying out for all I'm worth as probably the biggest orgasm of the day sweeps over me like a tidal wave. My heart is pounding in my chest, and my breath stalls within my lungs. Starbursts go off behind my eyes as I cling to Dominik and Klaus for dear life. One final thrust, and Dimitri seats himself deep within me. The throbbing pulses of his thick cock set off another orgasm within me. Jets of his seed coat my womb as my muscles try to milk him for everything that he's worth.

My body feels like molten Jell-o; soft, pliable, and deliciously relaxed. I know I'm going to be sore later, but it was absolutely worth it. Eventually, I feel Dimitri free himself from me. He reaches down and picks me up, carrying me past everyone to the showers. Klaus and Alaric race ahead of him to make sure that the water is to my liking. I hear somebody wake Jayce up and send him and Arnulf on a food and drink run.

There's a splat as what sounds like a body hitting the floor, and then Jayce laughs. His legs must have been more Jell-o than what he had originally anticipated, and that was him hitting the floor rolling off the table. When the shower's ready, Dimitri slides us in along with Alaric, and they start to bathe me. Klaus eventually climbs in. Thankfully, this is a huge shower. Dimitri supports my weight while Klaus and Alaric clean every square inch of my body. We step out of the shower, and Jayce is standing there with my favorite terry cloth robe.

He wraps my body up tightly and then begins to towel dry my hair as they walk me over to my chaise lounge. Klaus and Dimitri emerge with just towels around their hips, start plating food and drinks for me, and set them on the table. With a wicked smile on my lips, I look at the guys and raise a single eyebrow. "So? Looks like everybody had a very good morning."

Jayce, Klaus, and Arnulf blush furiously. All three of them look like the little kid that stole the cookies out of the cookie jar. "Um... Yeah, we did. I hope you don't mind," Jayce says as he wrings his hands in front of him nervously.

Tilting my head to the left, I look at him and smile. "Why would I mind? I honestly can't handle everybody right now." I rest my hand on my stomach. "These gigantic babies are taking up way too much room in my body." I smirk, looking over at Dimitri, who instantly looks guilty.

"How many times do I have to tell you guys that it's okay? Jayce, Klaus, you cannot change who you are." I smile at them before raising my glass and taking a sip. "I knew your tendencies long before we mated." I tilt my head again, looking over at Arnulf. "You're the wild card in the bunch," I say to him. "I think you're more curious about the lifestyle that Klaus and Jayce prefer to live. And trust me, this is the safest environment for you to explore it in."

My eyes drift over to Dominik, Alaric, and Dimitri. "You three are alphas in your own right. And Jayce being an Omega has a certain pull for you," I say with a smile as I look over towards Jayce, who's grinning like the Cheshire cat. My gaze returns to the other three I was just speaking to.

"Our little family has found a good and unique balance. I'm happy everybody is comfortable enough with who they are to be able to express themselves." I smile and start to dig into my breakfast, leaving the subject dropped because I feel I covered it well enough.

I finish breakfast and decide it's time to head out amongst the pack. Draven and Ladon are playing in the front yard with their toys. Tia is fawning over the new baby that the nursemaid has. Helle and my father are on the porch having their tea with their breakfast. So far, everything is right in my world, and I have no complaints. I go and sit on the porch swing to watch over everything for a while. According to yesterday's check-up, I have maybe a week, possibly two, left before these babies come into the world.

"Alpha?" There is a young woman and young man standing before me that I didn't notice before, both wringing their hands nervously.

"What seems to be the problem?" I ask as I sip my pomegranate juice down and lean forward the best that I can.

"There's no problem Alpha, we just wish to ask you a question." They look to each other, and the husband comes forward and drops to his knees before me.

"If it's at all possible, we would like to be put on the list for one of the pups being born. We've tried for years and have not been successful yet." Tears stream down the female's face, and I can see the male's struggle keeping his tears at bay.

All the available babies have been spoken for except for the one that I was choosing to keep for myself. The nursemaid anxiously looks at me and then down to the baby in her arms. A single nod is given, and she brings the baby over to the female. "I named her Victoria because she was born from the victory that we had just recently had. I would like to gift her to you to take care of and raise as she's your own," I say gently.

As soon as the last word was out of my mouth, the female turns to the nurse and takes the baby out of her arms. Joy doesn't even begin to describe the feeling of pure bliss and happiness that she's experiencing. I lose track of how many times the two of them said thank you to me at this point. I just smile and wave, watching them head home. Yet another good deed done. Time to people watch for a while.

CHAPTER 61

Dominik

EVERY TIME I THINK I HAVE MY MATE FIGURED OUT, SHE TURNS AROUND and does something else to surprise me. I was completely positive that she would be keeping the pup that was born last night for herself. Instead, she gave it to a childless young couple, and it warms my heart to see her be so compassionate.

Nicodeamus comes walking out of the house, fiddling with the bracelet we had found in the birthing cave over a year ago.

"You know, I haven't seen this bracelet in years. It used to be my mother's." He holds it out and offers it to Aurora, she in turn flips it around in her hand staring at it. I could almost swear one of the stones in the bracelet glows at her touch.

Nicodeamus smiles and walks closer to his daughter, examining her holding the bracelet. "Just as I suspected. It now belongs to you, Aurora." He smiles, takes the bracelet out of Aurora's hand, and places it on her left wrist.

"Once upon a time, this was your grandmother's and your great-grandmother's before her. The majority of the female dragons in our family have worn this bracelet." He rubs his thumb over the stones and then pulls his hand away.

"What do you mean, Daddy?" Aurora asks as her eyes remain locked on the bracelet, studying the one glowing gemstone.

"The stone itself will only glow with a certain bloodline. Once upon a time, there was a bloodline of dragons called Titanium." He gets a faraway look in his eyes as he stares off across the land. "The Titanium Dragons were the largest and the strongest." He draws in a deep breath and then looks out towards Tiamat, who's playing in the dirt with another little girl from the pack.

"She bears the markers of the Titanium Dragons. They retain scales on their body even in their human form." He tilts his head to the side as he waits for Aurora to understand what he's saying.

I scoot closer to Aurora and pull her onto my lap, careful not to harm her stomach. Gently, I rub my hands up and down her sides, waiting for the realization to hit. "So what you're trying to say, Dad, is this: my daughter is a throwback to the Blood Queen directly." Aurora's eyes move to watch Tiamat even more closely now.

Nicodeamus just nods his head and then motions to Alaric. "Most Ice Dragons, myself included along the way, have some Titanium Dragon in them. My bloodline more than most." He motions towards Ladon.

"Most times, the males will not show any of the characteristics of the Titanium Dragon. As an oddity, the majority of the Titanium Dragons were female." He chuckles to himself and shakes his head slowly.

"I will not be surprised when the day comes when she can collectively kick all of our asses. Part of me, I can't wait for that day to come." He smiles wistfully, looking at his granddaughter then over to his daughter. "Why do you think you're such a phenom in battle? You have the power of the Titanium Dragon, just not the form."

Aurora wiggles in my lap and then moves her shirt down to reveal a few of the scales that remain between her breasts. Her hands run up and touch the scales that remain behind her ears, just at her hairline. Realization hits that what her father is saying is true. She snuggles close to me, and I hold her tightly. "Father, what does this mean for my wolf, bear, and eagle offspring?" she asks curiously as she rubs her stomach.

"Sadly Aurora, it doesn't mean a thing. It won't affect them one way or the other; it may not even be a benefit." Nicodeamus says as he looks down at his hand and then back up into his daughter's eyes.

I kiss Aurora's temple and nuzzle her cheek gently. "All that matters, my love, is that the babies are born healthy. Their bloodline is what it is, and it's ours. That's all that matters." I nuzzle her cheek again and hug her. Aurora nods, slowly agreeing with me, and then slowly, a smile creeps across her lips.

"You know, Dom, think you've been hanging around your brother and Klaus way too much." She smiles and laughs softly as she pokes me in the chest. "Better watch out! You're going to catch feelings and stuff." She nips my chin.

"Next thing you know, my big bad enforcer is going to be singing kumbaya up in this mother." She sips her drink and starts laughing hysterically to herself.

I roll my eyes at my mate's antics and shake my head slowly. "Oh really now, beautiful? You don't think I'm the big bad enforcer anymore?" I raise an eyebrow, looking at her as my wolf's eyes blaze to the forefront, glowing golden. My canines descend as I stare at her, and I just smile. I run my tongue over the tip of one of my canines as I look her over slowly.

"I know someone who loves when I'm the big, bad wolf." On cue, my beast rumbles to her his deep, guttural growl and makes her squirm in my lap. She loves me taking her as the man, but also as the beast just as much. I can't help but keep my wicked grin upon my lips as I stare at her.

A soft blush crosses over her cheeks, and she looks down and away from me. Victory for me. "You know, Dom? You're the one who got me into those things." She tilts her head slightly, looking at me out of the corner of her eye. "I can't help it that my beast loves when your wolf pays attention to us." She turns and quickly nips my bottom lip before getting up and walking over to sit in a chair next to her mother-in-law. Poor Helle is five shades of beet red with her mouth hanging open in shock. I forgot mother did not know about those parts of our excursions.

"Dominik Angelis, what in the Goddess's name have you been doing to this poor girl?" My mother asks exasperated. Aurora sits there attempting to look as innocent as possible in my mother's presence.

"Nothing more than what she wants me to do, Mother, and nothing less. Besides, you want grand pups at some point, don't you?" I smirk, knowing that I hit the nail on the head. She wants the pups, and she wants them yesterday.

"That is beside the point, young man. I raised you better than this;

you chase your mate and take her as your wolf." Aurora goes into a giggle fit as my mother stares at her flabbergasted.

"To be honest, Mom, the chase really doesn't last long," Aurora says as her face turns beet red, and she starts laughing hysterically at my mom's shocked expression.

Poor Nicodeamus is sitting there with his hand covering his face trying not to laugh. I don't know what he's finding more comical: his mate's reaction, or his daughters. Both women have turned interesting shades of pink and red and a multitude of shades in between over the last ten minutes of conversation.

Aurora gets this look in her eye and then starts staring at Alaric, and his eyes widen. "There is no way on this Earth that you are ever attempting that! You will absolutely be impaled," Alaric says, almost frightened by what Aurora had shown him that she wanted to try to do.

I almost choke on my water that I'm attempting to drink. Aurora decides now is the perfect time to show everyone exactly what she was asking for from Alaric. I have no idea, nor do I ever want to know how large a dragon's dick is. That would be one thing that would scar me for life without question. My poor brother's head is on a swivel, whipping back and forth between Aurora and Alaric. I don't know if it's more curiosity or abject horror on his face; at this point, it's really hard to determine.

I noticed Aurora occasionally leaning forward and lightly gripping her stomach. I sit and stare at her, studying her movements closely. There's a tight clenching of the jaw, and slowly she rocks forward. She's either having Braxton Hicks contractions, or it's the real deal right now. I reach out to the other mates through the bond and inform them of what I'm watching. All eyes are on

Aurora, suddenly studying her every movement over the next ten to fifteen minutes.

"Angel? Is everything okay?" Klaus asks as he drops to his knees beside her. He lightly lays his hand on her stomach. We know the moment that he feels the contraction because his head whips around furiously, and he howls. He is summoning every possible medical person that is in the pack to get to the Alpha House as fast as humanly possible.

Aurora smacks him several times and shakes her head. "I'm fine. It's too early yet, send them all home." Aurora struggles to stand up; it takes Dimitri and Klaus to help her get to her feet. She takes about three steps off the porch heading across the road, and her water breaks.

"Son of a fucking bitch. What the actual fuck? Can't I do anything?"" Aurora curses up a storm because now the contractions intensify. "What the fuck are you guys standing there staring at me for? Do something." Okay, pregnancy number two, and she has gotten a lot more hostile.

It looks like a bad episode of The Three Stooges with the way everybody's running around in circles like chickens with their heads cut off. I rise up slowly, shaking my head, and go over and scoop up Aurora to carry her bridal style. Apparently, only myself and Nicodeamus have managed to keep a level head while this is going on. We look at the others and shake our heads slowly. Like seriously guys, this isn't the first time we've gone through this. He opens the door for me, and I bring her inside. We kick open the latch to reveal the hidden panel to open up the downstairs. I manage to get her down the stairs and into the large spa room we've built for us.

I strip her down quickly and go into the spa pool with her that we have here. The weightlessness does wonders for her, and she's able to relax. I move her into position so that her back is in front of one of the jets to massage her. My brother is the first to make it downstairs, bringing over towels, ice chips, and various other things he felt she might need.

We remain floating in the pool for several hours until, apparently, she is starting to get close to needing to push. "I need to get out of here. I need to hide." Her breaths come out in pants as she tries to convey what she needs from us. The light bulb goes on with Dimitri and he motions for me to give her to him.

Dimitri and Klaus share a look, and then the next thing I know we're sprinting down the hallway to the door that has a lock on it. Klaus unlocks the door, and lo and behold, there's a den that's been made for her. Klaus climbs in first, and Dimitri passes Aurora off to him. Aurora is still not comfortable, and she is still squirming. Thankfully, when the boys made the nest, they made it large enough for the two of them to be in there with her. Carefully, Dimitri climbs in and he leans Aurora back against him.

Elsa comes barreling in, and we stop her at the door. "I need to go examine her," she says, half panting from running from the other side of the village.

I take up my spot outside of the den and sit down. "I don't think that would be wise at this moment. This is going a lot different than the last time, and I'm not sure what she needs at the moment." I cross my arms over my chest and stay firm. Alaric arrives with clean blankets, a washbasin, and some water. Everyone that's not in the den is staying far enough away as to not upset her.

"Fine, then call me after they're born. I'll check them then," Elsa says before leaving the room and having a seat upstairs.

The combined grumbling of Dimitri's bear and Klaus's wolf has seemed to settle Aurora down. She's lying on her side with her head on Dimitri's chest as Klaus massages her thighs. We watch what we can from where we are. To be honest, other than myself, the others have a really poor view of what's going on.

My bond mates and I that are left on the outside, rotate in shifts to keep eyes on everyone. And we anxiously await the birth of the new babies into the family. It tugs at my heartstrings, thinking that myself and my twin are next to take the leap into fatherhood. Though, if you think of it as a big picture, we are already dads to the twins. We will be dads to the triplets that are coming now. From what I hear, it's a completely different feeling when it's your own blood. Part of me can't wait; the other part is that we can wait a little longer and help with the babies that came before ours.

CHAPTER 62
Klaus

The time is coming. We're curled up in the den with Aurora, giving her the support that she needs. I can feel the anxiety through the bond because our other bond mates aren't in here with us. I had suspected that she would want to isolate away from everyone and give birth alone. With most wolves, that is their preferred way of bringing new life into the pack.

Aurora positions herself so that her back is flush with Dimitri's chest, and I am sitting at her feet watching and waiting for the pups. To be perfectly honest, I'm not sure what the ratio of pup to cub is, but I guess we're about to find out.

Aurora's face starts to tense as she bears down with the next contraction. Dimitri is assisting her by holding her legs and letting her dig her nails into his forearms. He's wincing and gritting his teeth through every contraction right along with her. It also doesn't help that her nails sink deeper and deeper into his forearms muscles each time.

"Okay, everyone, I see the crown of the first head." I lower my body to see exactly how much further Aurora needs to go. "You're doing great, love, keep going."

She growls deeply, and her eyes turn liquid mercury as her dragon slits lock on me. "If you think you could do a better job, Klaus, let's switch positions. You try to push a watermelon out."

I wince at the description that she gives me of what childbirth feels like to her. I can really understand what she means at this point. Normally, her warm depths are snug and fit my member like a glove. Now, here comes a baby whose head is drastically larger than anything any of us are packing. It's an absolute miracle that females can do this. I will never admit to this, but I believe a thousand percent that females are the stronger gender.

Aurora screams pierce our ears and sends a chill down our spines. You would think somebody was ripping her apart. But then again, if you saw the size of the head she's trying to push out of her hoo-ha, you would believe it. The baby's head is finally free, and I put my hand under its head to support it. "Next big contraction, love, the biggest push that you can give me, and baby number one will be out."

Aurora takes several deep breaths and lightly rubs Dimitri's arms, and bears down again. I'm able to slip my fingers in between the baby's arms and rib cage to assist in sliding it out. Quickly, I use the little suction thingy my mother had given me and clear the mouth and both nostrils. The baby's cries fill the air, and Aurora smiles between pants.

I cut the cord, then pass Aurora the first baby, and as she is placed in her arms, she gives her a good sniff. "Odette, her name is Odette. She is of Dimitri's line." She takes several breaths and allows the baby to latch onto her breast and begin to feed. The big guy, meanwhile, has tears streaming down his cheeks. His large hand comes up and cups the back of the baby's head.

"I have a daughter," he says, his voice starting to crack, full of emotion as he tries to hold back the sobs that threaten to break free. They're tears of joy, and I can't blame him. I would be ecstatic too.

Aurora draws in a deep breath and grips her stomach as the next contraction starts again. "Okay, guys, enough smoochiness. The next one's coming." Aurora goes back to cycling between breathing and pants between pushes. This one seems to be coming faster than the first. She keeps pushing and pushing. Soon enough, the crown of the baby's head can be seen again.

"I see the next head," I say loudly, alerting the rest of the bond mates as to where we are in labor. I hear a cork pop, and Jayce giggle like a little schoolgirl. I guess he got shot by champagne. Aurora's eyes lock with mine, and she gives me a nod saying this is it. The next big contraction she bears down, and baby number two slides out screaming into the world. It's another daughter. I'm over here smiling like a damn fool seeing now that my mate has delivered two daughters back to back. It is a feat unheard of for my species. Like with the first baby, I sever the cord, suction the nose and mouth, and then pass her up to her mother.

Aurora sniffs the crown of the baby's head and then looks at me, smiling. "You have a daughter, Klaus. I would like to name her Kirra. Meaning, the first one from what I remember of the ancient dragonic tongue." Now I'm in the same place as Dimitri is. I'm over here blubbering like a damn fool. Tears rolling down my face and onto my chest. I scream loud enough for everybody to hear me. "I have a daughter!"

A second cork pops, and this time it's Alaric cursing. Apparently, he must have gotten hit. Arnulf is laughing, apologizing up and down for his poor aim. By the time the last baby is born, the rest of our bond mates will be drunk off their asses. It'll just be the three of us tending to the two babies. Aurora unlatches Odette from her breast and passes her off to Papa Bear. She next takes Kirra and latches her on to the opposite breast. Aurora sighs, contently lying back, resting against Dimitri.

There's a bit of a lull between births for the last one. It seems like forever before the contractions start again. Aurora is exhausted, and it is taking everything that she's got to get this last baby out into the world. Dimitri and I lock eyes, and then he brings his forearm forward. "Aurora, bite me and feed. You need the blood to sustain you right now. I'll be fine." She looks hesitantly at the offered forearm then back up to Dimitri.

With a decisive nod, she bites his arm, and I watch her drink from him. As she feeds from him, she regains color in her cheeks, and her breaths aren't as labored. It takes several moments before she's had her fill, and she licks the wounds that she created clean. The next contraction she has, she bears down and starts pushing. This little pup practically slides out since the other two were much larger than it is. I start to laugh because it seems like the baby was riding a slip and slide to get out. This little one is timid, it grips my finger tightly, seeming as if it is afraid to let go.

I cut the cord and suction out its nostrils and mouth. Yet again, a baby girl is born, a third miracle. But this one's not like the other two. She's not as heavily built, nor is she apt to scream once her airways were cleared. In the back of my mind, I wonder if this baby is sickly. I refuse to project that thought to anyone, not wanting to upset Aurora right now. I pass her up to Aurora, and she smiles, looking at the baby.

"Hey Jayce, would you mind poking your head in here?" The little girl has snow-white hair and pale-grey eyes like her mama. The other two both have dark hair.

Jayce pokes his head in and smiles, holding out a pomegranate juice. Aurora gently sits up, lays the new baby in her lap, and then passes me my daughter. I have a sinking suspicion I know what's going on.

"Jayce, get your ass in here," Aurora says firmly as she stares at our family's Omega.

Jayce climbs in, and in the meantime Dimitri makes his way out with his daughter to show her off. Aurora pats the spot next to her, and Jayce sits down, looking between the two of us curiously. "Jayce, I would like you to meet your daughter, Luna. I gave her the name Luna because of her birthmark." That being said, Aurora shows Jayce the single crescent moon on her wrist.

"Unlike my set of twins, your daughter will never hold a title, but like them, they have been touched by the Goddess herself." Aurora passes little Luna off to Jayce.

You would think that Jayce was hit by a Mack truck because of the shocked expression on his face. He keeps looking down between his daughter and Aurora and back again. "She's like me," he says sadly as he looks at his daughter.

"It's not often with the Dire Wolves that a female Omega is born. It's a blessing and a curse." Tears stream down his face as he slowly lifts his eyes to Aurora as he passes his daughter back to her.

"Thank you for this gift, my love. We will have to teach her how to protect herself." Aurora nods slowly as she watches Jayce leave the den.

"I would have thought he would have been happier. I didn't know that I would be able to birth an Omega," Aurora says sadly as she nurses the baby. "She will have the protection of her siblings, thankfully." She sighs softly.

"I will have to take extra care when it comes time for her to choose a mate. I do not want anybody that would take advantage of her Omega status to ever have control of her," Aurora says as she runs her fingers through the baby's snow-white hair. Slowly, I leave the den, leaving Aurora with her last daughter.

Elsa and Helle are in the room now. Jayce is explaining to his mother what's occurred. Dominik is excited for his brother. Jayce, unfortunately, is still sad. Helle is trying to comfort Jayce and explain to him how things are different now. Without his father's rule, there is no enslavement for the female Omegas. I move and get in front of Jayce and kiss his lips. "Love, our mate is saddened by your reaction to seeing your daughter. I don't understand what's going through your head, but Aurora feels like she failed you." Jayce's eyes go wide, and he looks back and forth between myself and the den that Aurora has refused to come out of.

"She never failed me. She gave me the greatest gift ever. You just don't understand what it's like to be an Omega." He sighs, and his shoulders droop down, his mother rubbing his shoulders. "I got lucky with the family I ended up with. Not all Omegas end up with such a glorious fate."

He starts to walk over to the den. "I will be damned if anybody ever mistreats my daughter," Jayce growls, and it's the first time there is any semblance of dominance coming off of him. He ducks inside to spend time with Aurora and his child.

Meanwhile, my grandmother already snatches my child out of my arms and somehow Dominik has Dimitri's child. For the next hour or two, we play pass the baby. Everyone gets to hold everyone else's child—all except for little Luna. Aurora seems fiercely protective of that little white-haired bundle of joy.

Eventually, Aurora emerges, cleaned up and in a different outfit that Jayce had brought into the den with him. Luna is still latched onto Aurora, feeding aggressively. Aurora's eyes are that of her beast as she scans the area for any possible threat. Helle hesitantly approaches Aurora to get a look at her granddaughter. As much as Aurora likes Helle instinctually, she lets out a low growl. "I'm sorry, I didn't mean that. This little one is going to need a lot of protection until she comes into her own or finds a suitable mate."

Helle nods sadly and lightly touches the crown of the baby's head. "I completely understand. I was the same way with Jayce when he was born. I had it easy, though; my mate rejected his Omega son," she says so sadly. "This little one has the full protection of the pack behind her and of the dragons. I would be concerned for those who attempt to get near her more than anything else."

Helle's deduction makes Aurora laugh. Gently, she lays Luna in her grandmother's arms. A light kiss is given to the baby's temple before Aurora backs up and sits in the rocking chair nearby. "I need to go shift in a little bit to make sure I heal up correctly," she says just before she yawns.

"I've ordered food to be brought down to you," Dimitri says. "Make sure you eat before you go out and shift and please take Alaric or one of the dragon guards with you." Aurora's eyes glow that ethereal white. It can mean only one of two things: either she would freeze something or would be summoning a dragon to her.

Several moments later, a knock sounds at the door, and she motions for it to be opened. On the other side of the door is

Marco, her Black Dragon. He holds a tray of food, brings it over, and sits it next to Aurora. His eyes flash to that of his dragon, and he looks around the room. I know that look; I've seen it before. It's the look of recognition for a dragon when it's found its mate. The question is, which one of these three little girls is it. Aurora looks back and forth and smiles, having seen it for herself. She motions to Helle, and she brings the baby back over to her.

Aurora stands slowly with Luna in her arms and looks up to Marco. She tilts her head gently to the side, exposing her throat for the briefest of seconds, showing that she means him no harm. She reaches out and puts Luna in Marco's arms. His eyes flash to that of his dragon again, and Aurora's eyes shift to that of her beast as she stares up at him. "She is yours to protect," she says sternly. "Do not let me ever find out that you defiled the sacred covenant in any way, shape, or form." Marco nods his head slowly, and a single tear rolls down his cheek.

"I understand, my Queen. Never in all my years did I think I would ever be blessed with a mate." He slowly lowers his head and kisses Luna's temple. "No offense, my Queen, but I will guard her from a distance. Please assign one of the War Dragons to her personally." He nuzzles Luna's cheek again and smiles.

"I want to do right by her, and to do so would be to give her time to grow into the woman that she's meant to be," he says reverently as he gently places Luna back into Aurora's arms. She smiles and then looks over to Jayce and then offers him his daughter. Without hesitation, Jayce comes running over and takes his daughter and goes and sits down and starts talking to her.

"I need to go shift, Marco, to make sure that I heal. I would wish for you to escort me outside and make sure that I'm fine." Her eyes take on the ethereal glow again, and before they are ready to leave, Dante arrives. Her eyes remain glowing as she stares at Dante, I'm guessing relaying to him everything that's just occurred. Dante's head whips back and forth between Marco and where Luna is, and he smiles. "Your secret is safe with me, my Queen," he says as he bows his head low and then takes a seat by the door.

Aurora and Marco leave quickly to go heal after she finishes eating everything that was on her plate. My grandmother finally gives me back my child, and I sit here snuggling my little Kirra. First one, what a perfect name for this perfect little girl. I couldn't be happier. Here we thought that it was only me and Dimitri that had fathered children. Jayce, his sneaky little self, somehow managed to slip in there and get himself a daughter. I guess next time around, it's just Dominik and Arnulf to start things off. Who knows, we each may get a couple of more children. All I know is I am thankful and grateful for the one that I've been given.

I look down at her little sleepy cherubic face and want to squish those little plump cheeks of hers. She has her mother's perfect cupid's bow as well as her full lips. She has my dark hair, and it looks like Aurora's light eyes. If you ask me, the perfect blend of the two. Dimitri comes and sits next to me, holding Odette. Her hair is a little lighter shade of brown than what Dimitri has, and again she has her mother's light eyes and perfectly shaped lips. I have a feeling that Dimitri and I will be beating the boys off with sticks in the near future.

"I know that look, Klaus," Dimitri says. "You're probably thinking the same thing I am." He smirks and then laughs a little. "No male will ever be good enough for our baby girls." He smiles, and I nod, completely agreeing with him

"You got that right, brother. They'll be nuns. We will lock them in a convent somewhere." I start to laugh, thinking about how bad I was as soon as I realized what my dick was for. I pale at that thought, yeah very much not good. "Hey, Grandma?" Elsa turns and looks at me. "At what age can I put a chastity belt on my daughter?"

Grandma throws a slice of pepperoni at my head; luckily, I catch it. "Never. Didn't work with you; it's not going to work with her." I tilt my head to the side, questioning what Grandma meant because I don't remember when we were wearing a chastity belt. Though, I do remember getting locked up when multiple females were in heat. I shrugged my shoulders, looking down at the little wonders between the two of us. Dimitri is nodding off with his daughter sleeping on his chest. It doesn't sound like such a bad idea right now. I scoot myself down and close my eyes. Thankful doesn't even begin to describe how I feel before I drift off to sleep.

CHAPTER 63

Jayce

Today I got to witness an absolute miracle. Aurora gave birth to my first child, a daughter. I didn't think my heart could get any fuller than it did today. The only thing that concerns me with her birth is that she's an Omega, like I am. It's the dawning of a new era with my mate as the Queen of the Lycans. I'm sure the way things were handled previously will never occur again.

I look down at the tiny miracle that is in my arms and can't help but smile. Luna's hair is as white as the freshly fallen snow, the exact same color as her mother's. Her lips are a delicate rose color much lighter than her mom's, but exactly the same shape. She slowly opens her eyes and gazes up at me. I am beyond in love with the little cherub in my arms. Her eyes are a beautiful grey-green which is the perfect blend of mine and her mother's eye colors. Her tiny hand reaches out and grips my pinky tightly. I can't help but smile as she looks up at me as if I am her entire world. Tears of joy slowly roll down my cheeks as I stare at my tiny blessing. She is the smallest of the three babies born, so she needs the most attention.

To say I was shocked that I had been gifted a daughter is an understatement. I didn't think what precious little time I had with Aurora would bring about life this time. I am beyond blessed and grateful that my little Luna is here. I noticed the look that the Black Dragon, Marco, had given her. The way his eyes had lit up upon seeing her. I know without a doubt that he is her mate. It gives me great comfort to know that she has one of the most powerful dragons I know as her mate. Despite all the rumors of how the Black Dragons are, he is a kind and gentle soul. He has served Aurora's family for generations. He is among the few to remember her grandmother, the Blood Queen.

Gently, I stroke the hair on the top of my daughter's head and can't help but smile when she coos at me. Aurora slowly comes over to where we are and extends her arms to me. I am not ready to relinquish my daughter to her mother, but I know this little girl needs all the nutrition that Aurora can give her. Reluctantly, I hand our daughter over and receive a kiss from my mate. She sits in the chair besides where I am, lowers the strap on her dress and begins to breastfeed our daughter. It always amazes me the strength and power that the females of our species have. They create life and carry it until it's ready to be born. They can nourish and sustain said life until it is able to fend for itself. I wouldn't exactly say fend for itself, but able to eat regular food.

Luna settles in and begins to feed. Aurora's beast starts to rumble softly to her daughter, soothing her while she eats. I can't help but smile, watching mother and daughter interact. Today was a day of miracles; not only were triplets born, but three daughters, which is absolutely unheard of for any of our species. Klaus's grandmother says only the strongest females can produce more than one daughter. I smile, looking at Aurora, knowing in my heart and soul that she is the absolute strongest female I have ever met in my existence. Shortly after Aurora's arrival, my mother comes down to sit with us while the baby feeds.

My mom is fawning over the baby as much as I am. We both have our concerns about her Omega status. But knowing that Marco is her mate, I am not as frightened as I was before. We sit there watching Luna as she slaps Aurora's breast several times. Aurora can't help but laugh at her tiny daughter's antics; after all, it is quite hysterical. To see the teeny tiniest baby, who's barely six pounds, slapping one of the most powerful beasts of our generation, it's comical. Aurora shakes her head and looks at me. "If I didn't know she was an Omega, I would swear to the Goddess above that she would end up being my competition one day."

Aurora's statement causes me to laugh, knowing full well that she is a Dire Wolf. Unless she has venom, she is no competition for Aurora's beast. "I wouldn't worry too much my love. If she takes after me, she'll be more than content just to sit on the sidelines and watch her siblings make asses out of themselves."

My mother starts to laugh and nod her head at my statement. "This is very true," she says as she laughs at me. "I remember all the times that after the fact, I learned that Jayce was the guilty one. Poor Dominik ended up getting punished for his brother's actions." As my mother said those words, I shrug my shoulders and attempt to look as innocent as possible.

Aurora starts to laugh immediately and raises an eyebrow looking at me. "You know it is true what they say. It's the quiet ones that you have to worry about." She gives me that knowing smile, remembering how I had woken her up a few months prior.

"You have no proof!" I say boldly as I stare at Aurora, who looks down at Luna and then motions with her free hand to the baby that is currently in her arms. "No proof you say, really?" I can't help but laugh and nod my head admitting defeat.

Aurora burps Luna carefully then gently hands her back to me. I sit there snuggling my daughter to my chest, singing to her softly. Aurora gets ready to leave and kisses me on my forehead before walking out the door. Shortly after she exits the room, little Tiamat comes in, dragging her dolly behind her.

Carefully, Tiamat climbs up onto the couch beside me, staring at little Luna in my arms, looking at her curiously. I tilt my arms just enough so that Tiamat can get a good look at her sister. "Daddy Jayce? Can I hold my sister?" she asks in her little squeaky voice that she uses when she really wants something.

I grab the boppy from beside the couch and lay it in Tiamat's lap. "You have to be careful, Tia. Luna is brand new and very fragile." Very slowly, I lower Luna to rest in the boppy. Carefully, I bring Tia's arms around to help support Luna's head and her legs. The boppy itself supports the majority of Luna's weight and keeps her safe from rolling off of Tia.

Ever so carefully, Tia lowers her face to Luna, and she kisses her forehead. "I will always protect you,' she says softly to her new baby sister. She nuzzles her cheeks, kissing her all over. It warms my heart watching this beautiful interaction between sisters. Deep down, I was slightly concerned about Tia being jealous of the new babies. Thankfully, she is proving me wrong, and knowing she is excited about them being here warms my heart.

Tia looks up at me and smiles. "Daddy Jayce, Luna looks a lot like Mama and me." She smiles, looking from me down to her sister and then back up again.

"She's not like me, is she?" Tia sniffs the crown of Luna's head before looking back up at me again. "She's like you. A wolf." Tia pouts slightly and then shrugs her shoulders. "It's okay. When she gets bigger, I can take her flying with me." She nods her head definitively, as if what she said will be taken as gospel.

I draw in a deep breath and slowly release it. "Little one, when you are a big dragon, you can take your sister flying as much as you want. Until then, we just need to make sure that she's kept happy and safe." Gently, I run my fingers through Tia's hair and then turn the rest of the way to face them both fully. I pull my phone out of my pocket and snap several pictures of Tia holding her little sister. Quickly, I send the images off to the rest of the family and wait for the responses.

It doesn't take long before messages start coming back. There are many *oohs* and *ahs*, and Dimitri sends me a picture of Ladon holding Odette. I show Tia the picture of her brother holding Odette, and she makes a scrunched-up face. "It's okay. I held her first." Tia has a slightly smug look on her face and then goes back to nuzzling her little sister. "Don't tell Mama, but Luna's my favorite."

I raise my eyebrows, shocked by Tia's admission. I wouldn't think that the Omega in the family would end up being her favorite. I thought either Odette or Kirra would have been more up Tia's alley, to be perfectly honest. But she's sitting here gently stroking Luna's cheek, lightly kissing her on the forehead occasionally. I think the favoritism has to do with the fact that out of the three babies born, Luna is the only one with the full head of hair. Don't get me wrong, the other two have hair, but it is rather short. Luna has several curls on the top of her head. If I wanted to, I could easily put a tiny bow in her hair.

Aurora comes walking back in, and the look on her face says it all. She is absolutely in love with the scene that is going on before her. She kneels before her daughters, kissing them both. "You make me so proud, Tia. Little Luna needs your love and protection as she grows up." Aurora gently cups Tia's cheek and kisses her forehead once more. Ever so gently, she scoops up Luna out of the boppy and brings her over to the rocking chair to feed her yet again.

I didn't realize it had been so long between her last feeding and now. Time seems to stand still as I spend time with my daughter. Unfortunately, they don't stay little forever, as evidenced by Tia, who is almost a year and a half now but the size of a six year old. It would be to Luna's advantage when she can spend time as her wolf to grow faster. Not that it's necessary, but it may make her life easier.

Tia hops off the couch and runs over to stare at Luna feeding from her mother. "Ah, gross, mom." Tia exclaims. "I thought milk came from cows, not from moms." Tia says, looking quite disgusted at the moment. She wrinkles her nose and hides her face in her doll. Aurora looks between the baby suckling at her breast, then over to Tia.

"I hate to tell you, sweetheart, but you and your twin fed from me for almost a month and a half," Aurora says with a smirk and a raised eyebrow. Tia sticks her tongue out, still grossed out. She takes her doll and swiftly runs out of the room.

Well, I'm quite curious to find out how Tia will handle it when she gets older. I look over at Aurora, and she's just shaking her head ever so slowly. "I don't know what I'm going to do with her," Aurora says jokingly. "In some ways, she's wise beyond her years. In others, she's more her shoe size than her age."

"To be fair love, chronologically, she's only a year and a half going on maybe two." I shrug my shoulders lightly, watching Aurora and the baby.

"You know, I keep forgetting that," Aurora says as she rocks the baby gently. "Her size throws me off every time," she says softly. I can see that wistful look in her eyes as she remembers Tia at the same age as Luna.

"I know, my love, but we did what we had to do to make sure that they were safe growing up," I say softly, my voice filled with some regret. "Looking back, I regret keeping them shifted for as long as we did. But it all worked out in the end."

"You're right, Jayce. Our people are free, Vladimir and Tomas are dead, and our family is safe." She smiles as she slowly stands and brings Luna back over to me. "The lunch wagon has two more stops yet." She smirks as she deposits Luna in my arms. Playfully she moos as she walks out of the room.

Slowly, I stand up and head over to the recliner and sit down. I lay Luna in my lap for a moment while I remove my shirt. Carefully, I unsnap the top she's wearing and lay her bare chest on mine for skin-to-skin contact. I grab the baby blanket I had on the table and lay it over her. Slowly, I lay the chair back and wedge myself and Luna in with pillows. It's time to nap with my number one girl. Tiny rumbles from her puppy make me giggle, and I kiss the crown of her head gently. My mom is still in the room with us as I decide to sleep for a little bit.

CHAPTER 64

Alaric

The last few days have been a giant swirl with all the hustle and bustle revolving around the three new babies in our lives. My two children have taken a great interest in the new offspring. It brings me great pride and comfort that both assist their mother in caring for the new little ones. Tia seems to be exceptionally attentive to Luna. It was a shock to us all that Luna was born an Omega. I would have assumed that given Aurora's dominant DNA, that daughter would have been an Alpha, just like her.

This afternoon, Ladon and I are starting his swordplay practice. Gus had given us a roe deer for lunch that we ate over an open fire with the rest of the bond mates. And then we went into town and got two wooden swords made by the blacksmith of all people. We walk back out to the training circle that we all usually spar in and take our stances.

Ladon attacks with force, strength, and precision for someone so young. I smile at his boldness as well as his tactical thought process. What he does not have in size, he makes up for in speed and agility. My father-in-law, Nicodeamus sits on the sideline with his mate, Helle, watching his grandson spar.

We take turns attacking and blocking for almost thirty minutes. Nicodeamus steps in and takes my place about halfway through the match. Ladon looks up to his grandfather, smiles and bows gently to him then stands en guard. Nicodeamus mimics Ladon's moves, and soon the strikes rain down furiously. I watch my son's footing and start to notice a pattern. His stance, his moves, and his reactions are exactly like his mother's. I tilt my head to the side, watching him even closer, now replaying in my mind all the times I've watched Aurora duel.

He mimics his mother, which means he will be a very formidable opponent at some point. Klaus casually strolls up next to me and takes a seat to observe the matches. "How's baby Kirra doing?" I ask him with a smile.

A bright, wide smile crosses Klaus's lips. The amount of pride that he has for his daughter is probably the same as I have for my children. "She's absolutely beautiful. She's more perfect than I ever thought possible." He smiles broadly and then pulls out his cell phone and starts showing me pictures that he's taken of his daughter. The baby isn't even a week old yet, and I'd have to say almost half of the pictures on Klaus's phone are of his child. Honestly, I can't blame him. I've ended up having to get more memory chips for mine.

Suddenly, in the middle of the match, Ladon stands stock still. An ethereal white glow surrounds his eyes as he stares off into nowhere. He whispers his sister's name, *Tia*, before dropping his sword and takes off running. I don't feel a disturbance in the bond, but that doesn't mean that there isn't one. Klaus and I look at each other and then over to Nicodeamus, and the three of us run off chasing after Ladon.

It doesn't take long before Aurora joins in the chase. Klaus looks at Aurora, puzzled. "I thought you had Kirra?" he questions.

"No, I left her with you," Aurora says with fear in her tone. We start to run faster, trying to catch up with where Ladon has gotten to. By the time we do, we're deep in the woods by one of the streams. Klaus's mother Agnes is frozen solid.

Tia is clutching baby Kirra who is soaking wet to her chest. She's shaking violently, holding her little sister, trying to keep her warm and to comfort her. Ladon moves in slowly and snuggles up next to his sister. Gently, he runs his fingers through her hair, trying to soothe her. "Tia, what happened"? Ladon asks softly

"I saw Grandma Agnes take Kirra off of Daddy Klaus while he was sleeping. Grandma Agnes never liked Mommy," Tia says, firmly gritting her little teeth as we watch tiny scales ripple along her skin.

"I didn't trust her," Tia says firmly. "So, without her knowing, I followed her. I did like Mommy does and I climbed the trees using my talons." To punctuate her statement, she shifts her free hand to her talons. "I stayed up high and watched everything that Grandma Agnes was doing." Tears start to roll down Tia's cheeks as she swallows deeply, looking up into both of her parents' eyes and then over to Klaus.

"I'm sorry I froze your mama," Tia says ever so softly, sniffling, trying to contain her tears. "But your mama tried to throw my baby sister into the water that's too deep and too fast. She called her an aboma-something."

Tia sniffles weakly again and snuggles her little sister, holding her as tightly as she can. "I did what I had to do, and I'm sorry," Tia says between sobs. "I froze your mama, Daddy Klaus, before she could kill my Kirra."

Aurora swoops in quickly and picks up Tia and baby Kirra all in one swoop. "You did good, baby girl, and I'm sorry you had to do such a big person thing."

Klaus moves over instantly and takes Tia from Aurora, leaving the baby with her mama. "There's nothing to be sorry about, little one. You did exactly what needed to be done. I wish with all of my heart that I could take this pain and memory from you," Klaus says softly as he rests his forehead against Tia's.

"I can help with that if you will allow me to do it." Arnulf, who apparently followed, says softly. "It's old magic, but not difficult to be done." He walks over to Klaus, gently touching the back of Tia's head. His eyes move over to Aurora, looking to receive her blessing. Reluctantly, Aurora nods her head, and Klaus hands Tia over to Arnulf.

I sigh softly, feeling like I'm on the outside looking in, that this is all just one giant, surreal nightmare. My baby girl, my innocent little daughter, just had to kill to protect her sibling. Part of me, I'm very proud of her for being able to do what had to be done. But as a father, I fear for her mental well-being over this. No child should have to carry the weight of having to kill. I walk over and gently rest my hand on Arnulf's shoulder and draw in a deep, slow, steady breath.

"If it's possible brother, please make her forget the kill, but let her remember that she saved her sister." Arnulf nods at his understanding and slowly starts to walk away with Tia, heading back towards the house.

Klaus is beside himself, looking at his mother, who is completely frozen in ice. Roughly he's running his hands through his hair, obviously not able to comprehend what she had attempted to do. I motion for Aurora and Nicodeamus to head back to the house. Nicodeamus gives me a firm nod and then wraps his arm around Aurora's shoulder and starts leading her back.

I approach Klaus and just pull him into a hug. There are no words to express how he must be feeling at this moment, torn between the love of a son or the love of a father. Whose life holds more value and whose doesn't? There's never a clear-cut answer when there's just family involved. It's either the person that gave you life or the one that you helped give life to. Myself, I've already proven this, will always side with that of my child.

Klaus looks up to me weakly; sad, broken, lost, and confused. "I don't understand," he says flatly. You can tell the amount of emotion waging war within him with the look of despair upon his face. "Why my daughter?" he asks as he drops his forehead to my shoulder.

"I have no answer, my friend. The only thing I know is that your mom was never fond of our mate." I hold him tightly to me, trying to give him comfort. It doesn't take long before Jayce comes bounding through the woods and steals Klaus from me. Our sweet little Omega is the perfect one to try to heal Klaus's wounds. I listen to them speak as we walk back to the house. Klaus is filling Jayce in as to what had occurred. Jayce's explaining to him that Tia had made the best decision at the time. Klaus knows and understands that to be true, but it's still rough knowing that your mother attempted to kill your child.

By the time we get back to the house, Klaus is relaxed; Jayce almost has him laughing. Jayce never ceases to amaze me. He seems like he's got the right answer for everything all the time, and I honestly don't know how he does it. As a family, we are truly blessed to be able to count him as one of ours. Jayce's mother comes out of the house and instantly wraps her arms around Klaus, holding him tightly to her, trying to soothe him. At this point, I'm not sure if it's everyone else needing the comfort because of almost losing the baby or the fact that everyone feels horrible for the decision that Tiamat had to make.

TIA IS as happy as a little girl should be. I don't know what Arnulf did, but he brought back my happy little girl. I shall forever be grateful to him for whatever mystic powers he used to make Tia feel better. One by one, Elsa pulls all the adults aside to discuss the events of tonight. But no one dares to discuss the events anywhere near Tia. Even after all was said and done, Tia is now sitting on the porch holding baby Kirra. She is sitting in between the two bassinets that are holding her other two baby sisters. She doesn't understand why, but she doesn't want to move away from her little siblings.

Aurora comes out of the house bringing tubs of ice cream, followed by Dimitri, who has the bowls and silverware. Without Tiamat knowing, we are celebrating her heroism. We are celebrating that she took it upon herself to follow her sibling and make sure she was safe. The amount of ice that little girl summoned in such a short period of time absolutely amazes me.

The ice is so thick, hard, and cold I believe she achieved permafrost.

I look up to Nicodeamus as he comes walking back from the spot in the woods. He and Dante are shoulder to shoulder deep in discussion. When he gets close enough, he opens his arm wide and kneels down. "Where is my favorite little angel?" He asks ever so gently. Tia's eyes light up as she slowly turns her head to look at her mama. Aurora gives Tia a knowing smile before she takes baby Kirra from her.

Once Tia is freed from her self-imposed responsibility, she runs to her grandfather and launches herself. She wraps her arms tightly around his neck and snuggles in close to him. "Yes, Papa?" she says ever so cheery.

Nicodeamus kisses her forehead and revels in the love and affection that his granddaughter is giving him. "One day, little one, you shall make a great and powerful queen. You bear the scales of your great-great-grandmother, the Blood Queen." He slides her over to the side so that he's able to hold her better on shifting her weight onto his hip.

"I just wanted to let you know that you make me so proud as the little girl you are becoming." Tia and Nicodeamus beam with pride as they look at each other. Slowly, frost creeps over the two of them, coating them both lightly. You can hear the soft rumblings of both of their dragons as they snuggle in the frost together. Nicodeamus's love for his family knows no bounds. He and I both agree that we would have taken Tia's spot without hesitation if given the chance. We would carry the burden of the death long before she ever should. But now we carry an even bigger burden: the knowledge of knowing we had one of her memories altered.

Slowly, I walk over to my mate and pull her into a hug, careful of little Kirra in her arms. "I have to say, my love, we raise some really good kids." Aurora smiles and kisses my cheek gently.

"It's like my father has always said: we must lead by example and try to use our hearts more than our fists." Aurora smirks. "I'm still working on that part, to be perfectly honest with you," she says, then she purses her lips attempting to look innocent. The rest of us all start laughing hysterically at her statement. Aurora's a "hit first ask questions later" kind of person.

"It's been a group effort, love," I say gently as I sweep my hand out, motioning towards all of her other mates as well as our extended family. "Sometimes it takes a village to raise a child. At the rate we're going, we're going to need an army, maybe two," I say laughing, trying not to be too serious.

Dominik rolls his eyes and just starts shaking his head. "Typical dragon, not everything has to be done by force," Dominik says, crossing his arms over his chest staring at me. "My father ruled by force and fear, it did not endear him to anyone." He goes over and gives his brother a side hug. "He damaged the family more than I can ever express." Jayce sits there and nods along with what Dominik is saying. Then I see their brother, Alex, and his mate come walking up, agreeing with what they overheard.

Elsa moves until she is standing in the middle of all of us, and she smiles. "I am grateful for the family I've been given. I received more grandsons than I ever thought I would have." She moves closer to the bassinets as well as Tia and Ladon. "I've been blessed enough to see great-grandchildren be born. My heart and my life are full." She slowly starts to move around, giving each of us a kiss on the cheek.

"Thank you, to all of you, for enriching our lives and freeing our people. I don't just speak for myself, but I speak for everyone whose lives you have touched." Elsa lightly bows to us, smiles, and then walks away slowly. It's not often that she stays to speak much on subjects, but we all listen when she does talk.

Dimitri takes his time handing out the ice cream to everyone making sure to serve Tia and Ladon first and then the rest of us who are gathered. The sun is slowly setting behind us, and the evening sky is bathed in a cornucopia of colors. It's the perfect ending to a day that could have turned out to be one of the saddest on record. Tonight, I shall count my blessings, not only for the birth of my daughter who saved her sibling, but for the gift of the family I've been given.

CHAPTER 65
Nicodeamus

THIS AFTERNOON'S EVENTS WERE SHOCKING, TO SAY THE LEAST. AGNES was the last person I would have thought would have attempted to attack my family. I know sometimes with wolves, especially females, the loss of their mate can drive them to the brink of insanity. I also picked up on the fact that she was not pleased that my daughter was not a purebred Lycan like her son.

Even with all those facts put aside, I never thought it would be a female who would have tried to kill a baby. Pups are so rarely born these days amongst the different packs of wolves that they are cherished. This one lone, borderline-insane female almost succeeded in killing off her son's first child.

If it hadn't been for Tia being attached as she is to her siblings, we might never have found Kirra. One would never look that closely, especially at a grandparent when it comes to someone going missing. If it was several months ago and the threat from all sides was still real, she never would have even been thought of. I watch my daughter with her mates all snuggled up around the five children. Poor Aurora is still crying, feeling like she's to blame for her child going missing.

Slowly and carefully, I approach my daughter and her mates and sit down nearby. "Little one," I say, gently trying to rouse her from her grief. Slowly her eyes rise, and she looks at me, but no words are spoken.

"I know that you blame yourself for what happened, but you cannot do this to yourself." I look down as Tia climbs into my lap. I wrap my arms around her to steady her on my leg. Softly, I place a kiss on her temple and just hug her to me.

"But Father, it is mine and Klaus's job to watch over our child. Just as it's mine and Dimitri's, mine and Jayce's and mine and Alaric's." She motions to each mate as she mentions their name. Each mate that has had a child, currently has a child sitting on their lap. Arnulf and Dominik are standing shoulder to shoulder, watching over everybody.

I lean down and whisper into Tia's ear and tell her to go to one of her other daddies so that they don't feel left out. Tia hops down quickly and runs over, and clings to Arnulf's leg. "Can we go flying?" she asks as she looks up to Arnulf. A broad smile crosses his lips as he looks down at her.

"If that is what you desire, princess, then yes, we absolutely can. Just double check with your mommy and daddy and make sure it's okay." He smiles and bends down and lightly pats Tia on her butt, sending her over to Aurora and Alaric.

"Brother, you're as much her father as I am," Alaric says, looking at Arnulf. "If you wish to take her flying, then do so. Just please bring one of the guards with you to make sure she remains safe." Alaric smiles and then looks down at Ladon.

"Son, would you like to go flying as well?" Ladon bounces up and down on his father's lap, nodding his head profusely. He leaps up quickly and runs over to Arnulf, tugging on his hand.

"Can I go too, please?" Ladon pleads, smiling and beaming up at Arnulf, who now has the broadest smile I've ever seen on his face.

"Of course, young prince," he says and does a light bow. Aurora is cracking up and shaking her head slowly.

"Oh please, not you too," she says, laughing as she's rocking Kirra. "Please don't give them both an ego. I already have one big lug with a giant ego." She pokes Alaric in the shoulder several times.

"Then there's this one," she pokes Dimitri in the shoulder, "who has an ego for a whole 'nother reason." She smirks, looking at Dimitri, and he just shrugs his shoulders.

"And then you have the underdog in the family." She points at Jayce. He blushes. She looks up into Arnulf's eyes and smiles at him.

"And then there's you, the wild card in the family." She smirks a little, scrunches her nose, and then looks over at Dominik. Her hand motions towards him. "Then we have the bad boy of the family."

I'm sitting here rolling my eyes at my daughter's description of her mates. She then sits there and pushes her foot against Klaus. "Then there's Mr. I'm-the-Alpha-when-it's-convenient." And she starts laughing at that, and so does he. We all know who's in charge of this family, and it's her.

Alaric gets up slowly and goes over to stand next to Arnulf. "If you don't mind, brother, maybe I'll come to stretch my wings with you. Hey, Dad, why don't you come with us?" I raise my eyebrows, slightly shocked because I'm not invited on these family excursions very often. I think it's mostly because they're not used to me having a second wing that my daughter so graciously was able to give to me.

Slowly, I rise and roll my shoulders and look over to my mate. She makes the shooing motion at me. I guess that's my cue to get out of her hair for a little bit. I nod at my two sons-in-law and follow them out to the large field behind the Alpha House. "Soon, gentlemen, we must address what needs to be done with Aurora's mother's castle. Either she needs to tear it down, or it needs to be fully rebuilt." Both boys look at me and nod slowly.

Alaric draws in a deep breath and nods his head again. I can tell he's in deep thought over this question. "After finding her twin within her mother's skeleton, Aurora is quite shaken. Part of her is not ready to return there for any reason." He shrugs his shoulders, assisting his son to undress to shift.

"The other part of her wants nothing more but to go back there and return her people to their ancestral home." He looks up at me and then shrugs his shoulders again. "I know the castle doesn't hold fond memories for many, but most that were harmed there are dead."

"I understand what you're saying, Alaric, but it's the birthright of the female Lycans in her family to inherit the title and that castle." I sigh softly and look back towards the house. "Klaus's daughter is next in line to inherit that throne. It's going to be up to Aurora and Klaus if they decide to continue on with that tradition." I make that statement reluctantly.

"In my heart, I know Anca would prefer for that title to be passed down from daughter to daughter. But with all things considered, we don't even know if Kirra being part dragon will have the same drive that her mother did." It was something about that subspecies of Lycan that the royal line took multiple mates. Klaus's bloodline is slightly different from Anca's. Instead of being your standard jet-black, long-furred Lycan, they have varying grey, white, brown, and black shades. Their fur is coarser with multiple layers, unlike Anca's bloodline.

"Might I make a suggestion?" Arnulf says reluctantly. "Maybe I could pose to Aurora summoning her mother from the great beyond again. And she can seek her mother's counsel as to what to do with the castle and the title." He dances from foot to foot, rather unsure of what our reaction to his suggestion would be.

"That is a brilliant idea, Arnulf! We'll leave it up to the current queen and the past queen to make that decision." I smile broadly because in one fell swoop, our newest family member solved our greatest problem.

Having lost track of what we were doing, we look down and find both children as german Shepard size dragons. I did not expect my grand babies to have grown so quickly in such a short period of time. My look of shock must have been evident because Tia comes over and starts rubbing her scaled muzzle against my thigh.

Alaric leads Tia away from the rest of us while we shift into our animals. Once the shift is complete, I roar, and Tia comes running over to me. I lie down slowly, and she climbs carefully up onto my back. The twins begin to preen my scales, removing any dead ones that they find. It feels so weird to have these little tiny talons cleaning my scales. When Alaric returns, he launches into the sky and roars for us to follow.

Arnulf's much smaller eagle takes off and starts gliding on the thermals. It takes me a few minutes and a slight running start to get off the ground. I am much more out of practice with flying than my son-in-law. Once up in the sky, the babies jump off my back and start flying on their own. I watch them circle and glide, enjoying the thermals between the mountains. We go up higher into the atmosphere. Eventually, I see Arnulf's eagle land on one of Alaric's horns as both babies take refuge on my back.

The evening temperature starts to drop, and the little ones snuggle in tightly between my wings. It's such a wonderful feeling to be able to experience this part of parenthood. In some ways, I wish Aurora had been born a dragon because she will never understand the intense bonding that takes place during flight. But in a way she does; she's taken the mating flight with Alaric, two of them in fact, and she knows how important it is. But one thing I've never gotten to do with her is taking her for a flight myself. I roar to Alaric that I'm returning, and I let him know what I'm planning on doing. He roars his response, and I go in and land behind the Alpha House.

Aurora and the guys come out just in time as Tiamat and Ladon go sliding off my back and run towards the house as their dragons. Aurora gets ready to head inside, and I blow a little frost at her feet. My beast rumbles at her, calling to her on a primal level. Her eyes shift and take on that ethereal glow. Before I know it, she's already running and climbing up my side to sit on my back. I turn my head around slowly and tilt it, wanting her to climb up and sit behind my horns. It takes her several seconds, and she gets what I mean and moves to sit upfront.

Carefully, I get a little bit of a running start and take off flying with my daughter. My heart is the fullest that it's been in my existence. I've been gifted with a strong daughter, a second chance mate, and grandchildren. I am the luckiest guy that has ever existed. I feel Aurora's talons cleaning my scales behind my horns.

It's such a unique bonding experience for dragons. It's a level of trust that is not easily given, nor is it ever taken for granted.

Through the bond, I feel Aurora's excitement and her joy. She tells me softly that she always wanted to fly with me. If I could cry in this form, I would be bawling like a baby right now. She wishes she had the gift of flight, but she is grateful for the life that she's been given. I express to her my gratitude for what she has done to heal me. She gave me back the skies and part of my life I didn't realize was missing. She gave me the gift of grand babies that I never thought I would ever see. From what Dimitri tells me, little Luna looks exactly how Aurora did when she was a baby. So in a sense, I have a second chance of watching Aurora grow up.

The sun has almost completely set, and the skies have changed from hues of red, orange, and yellows, to cool tones of various shades of blue and purple. The light wisp of clouds makes it seem like a beautiful painting made by the guy who always said, "let's paint a happy tree." We watch the remaining light from the sun fade from the sky. And the stars start coming out twinkling above us. Aurora and I stay in the air for much longer than I had originally intended, sharing the magic of twilight together. The moon is slowly breaking over the horizon, and in three to four days, it'll be a full moon.

One of the greatest gifts of the dragon bond is that we can see through each other's eyes. Especially the paternal bond between parent and child; it's the strongest. Aurora sees breaking over the horizon another dragon coming towards us. Her eyes narrow in on it, and she goes on alert.

I hear her clothes shred as her beast breaks loose of her human bonds. She does that roar-howl of hers, summoning the rest of the family and her guards to her. I feel her pulling on the bond of the dragons that follow her. It's a Wyvern that's coming after us. It just so happens to be the one she saw in Alaska. The same one that stole Sebastian away from her.

Daddy, paybacks a bitch. I just so happen to be that bitch, Aurora says to me through the bond. I feel her calculating the speed and the angle at which the Wyvern is traveling. It comes darting up towards us, trying to position itself over us. I go into evasive maneuvers, and when I flip upside down over top of it, Aurora let's go. She lands on the Wyvern's back and sinks her talons in deeply. The Wyvern is trying everything that it can to shake her off. Little does it know the more it struggles, the deeper her talons sink in. Alaric, Marco, Dante, and Edgar can be seen breaking through the clouds.

Soon as the boys are close enough, I roar to stop them. I don't need them interfering or possibly getting Aurora hurt while she most definitely has this under control. I watch her beast lean down and sink its canines into the back of the Wyvern's neck. Blood begins to spray and coat her white fur, painting it vermilion. She whips her head back and forth, violently shaking her head, tearing at the tendons and sinew that holds the neck muscles in place. I watch her reach down and quickly sink her talons into the throat of the Wyvern. She rips up and back, violently severing the main artery. At this altitude, the blood is freezing almost as soon as it hits the air.

The Wyvern starts to falter in its flight, and that is when Aurora runs and jumps off of its back. Part of me is ready to have a coronary thinking about my baby falling hundreds of feet. It doesn't take but four beats of Alaric's wings for him to catch up, flip upside down, and catch her in the air. Gently, his taloned hand embraces his mate as he holds her tightly to his chest. From this angle, it kind of looks funny if you think about it. The giant Ice

Dragon carrying a giant blood-covered Lycan hybrid like it's a doll. He slowly positions himself over Marco's back. Gently, he deposits Aurora onto Marco's back and decides to fly in formation with her guard. Let's face it, Marco is the biggest of all of us and with his acid breath, possibly one of the most deadly.

We watch the Wyvern crash into the side of the mountain, blood and guts splattering everywhere. The sickening thud reverberating through the mountainside. I watch my daughter walking along Marco's back, preening his scales as well. It's kind of funny watching her do it, mainly cuz his scales are almost the size of a shield.

The flight home was much faster than I had expected. I land first, then Alaric. Soon after comes Marco with Aurora on his back and then the two War Dragons—Dante and Edgar. Alaric is the first to shift back to his human form, and he rushes over to his mate's side. Aurora slides down and lands on her feet. Alaric checks her from toes to nose just before the rest of her mates run out of the house. That turns into a round of past the Aurora, so everybody has a chance to make sure she's okay. I look around quite puzzled because Jayce, oddly enough, is not outside.

We all walk inside, and in the main sitting room by the fireplace, Jayce is lying down as his wolf. He's curled up around the three new babies with two little dragons curled up around him. I guess after this most recent scare, nobody is willing to leave the new babies alone. You can't really blame them. You would think you'd be able to trust family. Quickly, Aurora runs off and showers and then returns much faster than anticipated. She slips herself into a recliner, and each male takes turns bringing her one of the new babies. Jayce almost whines because he doesn't want to shift back. So Dominik has the honor of carrying baby Luna to Aurora. Dominik is a huge mush when it comes to that baby girl. He's making funny faces and odd little baby noises just to hear her laugh. Promptly she grabs hold of his bottom lip and pulls. He starts to whine softly, and she giggles.

As soon as I set myself down, my mate, Helle, comes to sit with me. She curls up on the couch next to me and offers me a cold beverage. Dimitri hands me a pair of trunks—my dumbass forgot to get dressed. After each baby is fed, the guys promptly place them back with Jayce and the two older children. I opt to sleep in the living room tonight to watch over my little family. Dominik shifts as well and lies not far from the snuggle fest. Hopefully, tomorrow will be a better day with no danger. My poor baby girl needs to know what peace is.

CHAPTER 66

Arnulf

Watching over my family is one of my greatest joys. Each one of us has a specific skill set that makes us unique in our roles. I have taken the place of Andre, in the sense that I am the family's eyes and ears. I also take care of and protect the family on a mystic level. Alaric and Nicodeamus have come to me requesting to call forth Anca from beyond the grave.

I've done it once before, and I'll do it again for them since it'll help Aurora decide about her mother's castle. It's been almost a month since her last battle with the Wyvern. Her new babies are just about a month old and spend a little more time as their animals to have a sense of independence. Tonight is a full moon when the veil is the thinnest between the land of the living and the dead. We have gone out towards the lake in the clearing.

Water itself is a wonderful conduit for the spirits to pass through easily. Fire works as well, but it's harder to maintain their form in flames. Water itself can easily change to mist that they can hold and shape for themselves.

I watch Aurora with her five gathered children playing with each of them and having some fun by the water's edge. Her great dragon protectors Marco, Dante, and Edgar, stand guard in their dragon forms. This isn't the life Aurora had pictured for her children, but she's doing her best to ensure their safety. After the assault and the capture of the Marelup Castle, we were able to attain more physical items that belong to Anca. With these new items, I should be able to maintain her presence longer.

I watch Aurora look to the sky as we start to notice the haze around the edge of the moon, signaling that it's time. I gather everyone around in the designated area at the edge of the water. Slowly, I start to combine the herbs in the mortar and grind them fine with the pestle. Once they are properly combined, I signal for Aurora and Nicodeamus to add drops of their blood. I gather up the paste and put it in a small, thin, silk satchel. I take one of the lead fishing weights that Dimitri had given me and tie it to the strings that close the satchel.

Carefully, I pitch it into the water and start reciting the spell that I need to call forth the ancestor in question. It takes a good ten minutes of chanting before the water starts to bubble. I keep at it, pouring my intention into the words, trying to draw forth my mate's mother. Finally, a silken form starts to rise up out of the water. It slowly takes shape, and it's Anca. Even though she appears to be whole before us, the liquid form she has taken cannot leave the water's edge without dissipating back into nothingness.

The only thing that appears to be solid on Anca is her face. The rest of her body is see-through because of the water. We watch her smile and look to those gathered. Her eyes light up, noticing three new babies in the mix. She starts clapping her watery hands, sending sprays of water over all of us. Aurora can't help but giggle at her mother's actions. "Welcome back, Mom. As you can see, I've made a few additions to the family." Aurora brings each of the new babies over to her mother one by one for a closer inspection.

"What a glorious surprise. But I sense this is not why you called me here," Anca says as she tilts her head, looking at the last baby that Aurora has lifted to her. It just so happens that the last child is Kirra. Her little baby Lycan form has the same fur color and pattern as her father—grey and white. Anca smiles, looking over the baby. "She's just like you," she says gently. "When her time comes, she will seek her mate or mates. As of right now, she is the last heir to my throne."

Aurora smiles and then sighs deeply. "Mother, that is why I called you here," Aurora starts to say, so she hands Kirra back to Klaus. "The castle is in a horrid state of disrepair. Vladimir allowed those leeches to flood the lower half, thus weakening some of the foundation." She stops pacing long enough to gauge her mother's reaction before continuing.

"I've taken down the walls because they were destroyed not only by time but by us trying to get in." Aurora holds her head high, looking at her mother. "There's generations of beings that see the castle and the Lycan race itself as a blight because of what Vladimir had done." The look of horror that crosses Anca's face makes my heart clench in my chest.

"Do they not believe that you're different?" Anca asks, rushed. She clasps her hands in front of her, still the ever stoic queen. "Is there nothing that we can do to change their minds?" She looks to everybody else gathered, trying to discern their stance on the subject.

Dimitri steps forward and bows his head to his former queen. "My lady, many died at Vladimir's hands after your death. The forest and the villages stained with years of blood from his conquests." Dimitri looks back and motions to Klaus.

"His pack is one of the last few pureblood Lycan packs left in Europe. There are several other smaller packs but none of the old blood." Dimitri clasps his hands in front of him and bows, backing away after having given his report.

Anca looks to Aurora. "What do you wish to do about this, daughter?" Anca studies Aurora, she's standing tall, and shoulders erect, head held high. Whatever is going on in her head at this point, none of us are privy to.

"That is exactly why I called for you to be here, Mother. Several revelations were made after we finally gained control of the castle." Aurora drew in a deep breath, trying to steady herself. "The first is the damage to the castle is far worse than we had expected, but not beyond repair."

She turns and looks back at us, and I move up slowly to take her hand just to offer my support. "The second revelation is that I was supposed to have a twin." She drops her eyes immediately after saying that, tears start to roll down her cheeks in earnest.

I look up, watching for Anca's reaction to what Aurora had just said. Tears stream down her face almost as quickly as they do her daughters. "I did not know. You have to believe me, baby girl, I did not know." Anca says those words between sobs, drawing out tears from all of us. There's not a single dry eye on the beach except for the children who don't understand.

Aurora draws another deep breath and nods slowly. "I would not expect you to know, Mother. Back then you did not have the technology that we do now. We will never know what happened inside your womb other than whatever it was that caused me to shift and rip my way out."

She sighs softly, unable to keep her mother's gaze at this point. "I'm sorry I killed you; I didn't mean to," she says as her voice breaks with the weight of the emotion that she's carrying. Quickly, all of her mates run up and lay a single hand on Aurora, trying to soothe her. And this is exactly why I am so adamant about maintaining the entire family's health and well-being. She carries the burden of regret and guilt that she may have been the one responsible for her mother's death.

"Shush, little one, it was not your fault. I started feeling odd halfway through the evening." She lightly runs her hand over her head and then looks back down to Aurora again.

"To be perfectly honest, I think I was poisoned. It's probably what prompted you to be born early." She looks over to Nicodeamus, staring at him almost intently. "Do you remember anything odd that night? Do you remember me through the bond feeling off at all?" She decides to try to probe Nicodeamus's memories, prompting him to hopefully remember parts of that night.

He raises his hand and strokes his beard, and begins to pace. "Come to think of it, you did feel a little more lethargic than usual. You started out the night feeling okay, but towards the end you started feeling like all you wanted to do was sleep." He furrows his brows, still in deep thought, trying to remember all of the details.

It's now that it dawns on me what might have occurred. "If I might interject, it sounds like either deadly nightshade or hemlock was used. Both have an odd effect on those of wolven blood." I hold tightly to Aurora as I look at her mother.

"Symptoms would be lightheadedness, dizziness, sudden weakness, and fatigue. All of these things and the change of Aurora's internal environment would have prompted her to shift and try to survive," I say as I kiss Aurora's temple, trying to reassure her that none of this was ever her fault.

She looks up between her mother and me, then back over to her father. "Do you think it's possible, Father? Why would Vladimir try to kill the child that was supposed to be his heir?" Aurora poses a great question with that one line.

Nicodeamus starts to pace again and then stops in front of Anca. "Vladimir had many enemies; I'm almost certain that your father's the guilty party."

The look of shock crosses Anca's face as she stares at Nicodeamus. "Let's look at it this way: your father was not thrilled with how Vladimir took you as his mate. In my heart, I believe he was only trying to rid himself of Vladimir's seed."

Nicodeamus mouths the word *sorry* to Aurora. "Unfortunately for his plans, he did not expect the child within you to be mine. Fortunately for Aurora, she was strong enough to remove herself from the poison. Unfortunately, killing you in the process, Anca." Several tears roll down Nicodeamus's cheek as the full weight of the revelation hits him. Anca's own father was responsible for helping to end her life as well as Aurora's twin.

I could feel the rage bubbling underneath Aurora's skin as it all sinks in. Her eyes whip frantically between myself and her other mates and then over to her mother. "So it seems I'm not fully responsible then. Grandfather has a lot to answer for," Aurora says in a very hostile tone.

"Don't worry, little one, I will handle him when I leave here tonight. The killing of babies is frowned upon by the Elder God's. Somehow he managed to make it into Elysium." Anca's rage is almost as palatable as her daughters. The water begins to churn almost violently. It looks as if it's the waves upon the ocean crashing upon the shore of the lake.

It's now that I step forward and start to silence the lake. Unfortunately, when a spirit gains too much power, especially using water as a conduit, it could be quite dangerous for those who are living. "Anca, it's time for you to return. Before someone you love becomes mortally wounded."

She looks around quickly and sees what is happening to the lake around her. Immediately, she assists with silencing it. "I am truly sorry; my temper got away from me. Do what you will with the castle and the title, daughter." She looks down and back at the water and then back over towards Aurora again. "If that part of the monarchy must die with you or me, then so be it. Speak with those who still remain living around the castle and see what they think."

She opens her arms wide and sends a cool breeze towards us. "I will always love you, little one. Now I must go search for your sister in Elysium." Now that liquid form of Anca falls back into the lake. The lake itself is calm and flat as a sheet of glass. The moon's reflection dances on the light ripples of the water as we stare at it, waiting to see if anything else was to occur.

"Well, my love, I'm sorry she didn't exactly give you an answer, but at least you know that no matter what you decide she will support you in it," I say softly just before I kiss her cheek and release her. The typical game of pass Aurora occurs as each one of the mates takes their turn. Each male is hugging and kissing her and reassuring her that she has their full support.

I turn around and smile, laughing that the three new babies are surrounded by Tia and Ladon. They have their own two little personal dragon sentinels. It's a beautiful sight to behold. We know that no matter who's born in what order, they will always have someone older than them watching over them. Nicodeamus starts to usher us all back to the house, saying it's time for us all to sit and have a long, serious conversation.

I love and hate these meetings. Mostly because they all set my bird on edge when tempers start to flare. I honestly know nobody will hurt me, but it's just pure instinct. Dominik and I both grab one of the new babies. I take Luna, Dominik takes Kirra, and Nicodeamus takes Odette. We take them all downstairs to the nest that had been prepared as their birth site. Dimitri has replaced all the soiled pillows and linens with brand new extra fluffy ones. We get Tia and Ladon dressed for bed and have them curl up in the nest with the other three babies. At least with those two there, if something goes on, they can reach out to their mother, father, and grandfather to alert us to what they need.

We stay on the lower level and move to the sitting room, leaving the nest room door wide open for us to hear. Aurora stands at the head of the table with Alaric and Nicodeamus at the two closest seats to her. The rest of us file in, taking random seats. "I haven't come to a decision lightly. I want to rebuild my mother's castle and the town that used to surround it." She pulls the map out in front of her, looking over the land. "I want to reestablish a Lycan stronghold near the castle. Klaus's brother, Kaden, will move into the castle for now.

"Love, have you spoken to Kaden about this?" I tilt my head slightly as I study my mate. Aurora smiles and looks down at the map.

"I gave Kaden and his new mate a permanent home in the castle. I told them to choose which suite they want on the third floor to be theirs." Aurora smiles as she looks between Klaus and me. "I couldn't think of a better pair to watch over the castle for me." Aurora shrugs slightly, then looks back to the maps.

Klaus wraps Aurora up in a big hug and kisses her silly. "We can move the American Lycans to the village by the castle. I do have some fantastic news." Klaus smiles broadly. "Between the once rogue Lycans and the American Lycans, more mated pairs were made." Klaus moves to go stand near his twin as he enters.

"Thank you, Aurora and family! You have made the European packs whole again." Kaden bows before taking a knee before Aurora and gently holding her hand. He presses his forehead to the back of her hand. "You have my undying loyalty and gratitude for what you and your family have accomplished for all of us. You saved us from an eternal war that has ravaged these lands for over two hundred years." Aurora gently runs her fingers through Kaden's hair.

"You are most welcome. Without your pack and your brother at my side, I may not have made it this far," Aurora says softly as she watches Kaden look up at her slowly.

Aurora assists Kaden to stand. "Let's usher in a new life of peace. Please take your mate and the others to the castle and start the reconstruction." Aurora smiles sweetly. "I'll send Edgar with the plans in a few days' time. Dimitri's people will join you shortly to assist."

"Thank you, my Queen." Kaden bows and leaves as swiftly as he had arrived. Aurora disperses the meeting for tonight. Tomorrow is a new day with a ton of changes on the horizon.

CHAPTER 67

Aurora

Morning, my least favorite time of day, ranks right up there with pack politics. I wake up in a tangle of limbs between my mates and my five children. I can barely move. Today is the day we return to my mother's castle and see how far Kaden and the Bears have gotten.

I wiggle myself free and tiptoe across the floor to the bathroom and take care of my morning necessities. A quick shower later and I feel like a new woman. The only thing missing is my coffee. I come out of the main part of the Alpha House and into the kitchen, catching my mother-in-law and my father sitting at the table having a quiet breakfast together.

"Good morning, everyone," I say with my semi-serious grump. They murmur their good mornings, barely forming words. I guess they are having a morning like I am. Jennifer brings me my coffee as well as my favorite—French toast with bacon. I'm halfway through my first cup of coffee when Dimitri makes it upstairs from our little love nest.

"Good morning, love," he says softly as he kisses my temple and hugs me to his body gently. He sits next to me at the island table, and Jennifer brings him his coffee and his honey-covered toast. I can't help but start to giggle, seeing what he's having for breakfast. "What seems to be so funny, my love?" Dimitri asks, raising an eyebrow.

"Well, you see, I just find it funny what you're having for breakfast. Little stereotypical, don't you think?" As I scrunch my nose, looking at him, then down to the honey-covered toast, then back up again, I tilt my head to the side and smile trying not to laugh.

Dimitri looks at his toast before taking a bite, and then it hits him. He smirks while chewing his bite and then starts shaking his head slowly. "Yeah, you got me. I can't help it. I love sweet, sticky things." I almost inhale my coffee, my poor father wasn't so lucky as he does inhale his coffee, and my stepmom laughs hysterically at him. Poor Jennifer comes back to the counter three shades of red as she wipes up after my father's mess.

I'm just shaking my head, trying not to spit or inhale my coffee. I settle down enough to finally swallow the gulp that I have in my mouth, and then I look over at poor Jennifer. "Yeah, you guys really need to learn not to drink when I'm involved in a conversation." My father, of all people, should know this by now since he's almost drowned at least six times. I start laughing softly before taking another sip of my coffee.

"The things that come out of your mouth… your mother would have been blushing," Nicodeamus says semi-sternly but with a smile on his face, so I'm quite confused.

"Really, Dad?" I tilt my head, looking around Dimitri at my dad. "You helped to create me, and you're telling me she would have been blushing about what I said." I lightly touch my chin with my index finger as I stare at him. "I've overheard some of the things you've said to Helle; you're definitely not innocent."

I raise an eyebrow staring at him as he starts to stutter. "Well, yeah. I guess you have a point there," Nicodeamus says, trying to hide his blush as he goes back to sipping his coffee.

I lean forward a little further to try to catch Helle's eyes. "I know what Daddy said to you the other day that had you blushing furiously," I say with a sadistic smirk and smile like Harley Quinn.

Helle starts to sputter and cough and then turns a bright shade of crimson. "Um, I don't know what to say to that, daughter." She looks frantically between my father and me. Dimitri has his hand up, not wanting to look in their direction, trying to shield his eyes.

"It's all good, Mom. Besides, you gave me the twins. Life can get no better than this." I smile broadly and throw my arms out dramatically in a tada motion. I'm still smiling broadly as I stare at her, and again her face goes through several shades of pink and red before she looks down at her food.

"You're welcome?" She sighs softly then starts laughing. "I've heard what my boys have said to you," she says and smirks. I shrug because quite honestly, there's no shame in my game. I've got six mates, and I somehow manage to juggle them all.

"And?" I smile, tilting my head, looking at her.

"Did they give you any brilliant ideas of what to do with Daddy dearest?" I ask as I purse my lips looking at her. Dad again starts to choke on his coffee. Dimitri starts smacking him on his back, trying to help him clear the coffee from his lungs. Helle and I look at each other and then bust out hysterically laughing.

Several coughs later, my father looks angry. "I'm glad my misery is bringing you guys such great, jovial moments." he says sarcastically as he looks between the two of us.

"Aw, poor Daddy. You want to take my new mommy to your room and have her kiss it and make it all better?" I say as sweetly and as sarcastically as I can possibly manage. I purse my lips at the end, almost like I'm getting ready to kiss somebody, and then rest both my fists under my chin, trying to look as innocent as possible.

Dimitri just shakes his head and lowers it. I know at this moment he does not know what to do with me. "You know, baby girl, most kids would be grossed out by their parents having sex." He just tilts his head, looking at me, and smiles.

"Yeah, I know. But thankfully for them, I am not the normal child, and I honestly don't give a fuck. I don't care if we walked in on them boning in the middle of the living room. I'd just be happy Dad is alive and able to get laid." I throw my hands up in the "so what" position. My poor father is five shades of red, staring at me jaw dropped, eyes bugged, completely shocked by the words that came out of my mouth.

Alaric apparently came in on the tail end of my tirade. His face is beat red, and he's just looking between myself and my father, trying to figure out what exactly just happened. "Good morning?" he says hesitantly, as he cautiously walks his happy ass into the room and has a seat next to me.

"Morning, babe," I say as I bounce in my seat and lean over and kiss his cheek. "D thinks I'm going to be grossed out by Dad and my new mom going at it like a pair of rabid bunnies in the middle of a heat cycle." I shrug my shoulders as I stare at my husband. He's wearing the exact same expression my father has, jaw dropped, eyes bugged out. I really think I'm missing something here.

My father clears his throat and then turns to face me. "Little one, I know that you were raised in a different time than myself, Alaric, and Dimitri. The level of openness and comfortableness that you have with sex is quite shocking to me." He tries to speak as softly as possible, trying to get me to understand where he's coming from.

"Okay?" I say, still quite puzzled and really just not getting what he's trying to tell me. "So do you want me to like, tone it down a little bit, or just not talk about sex in front of you and my new mom?" I ask as I look at them, my head tilted to the side, my brows furrowed. I am absolutely confused as to where this morning has decided to take a turn to.

Dimitri gently grips both of my shoulders as he turns me fully to face him. "It's not that, my love," he says softly. "Just because you're comfortable talking about them having sex and knowing that they're having sex, doesn't mean that they are comfortable discussing the subject around you." Dimitri is staring at me, hoping I connect the dots and that it makes sense to me.

I ponder what he says for several minutes as I finish eating my French toast. The kitchen is so silent you could hear a pin drop. The rest of my mates slowly emerge from our bedroom, dragging the children along with them. I'm still lost in my own thoughts to the point that I don't even notice everybody filling the room. Jayce and Klaus have the babies sitting around their table off to the island's side along with Tia and Ladon. I briefly look over at my children and notice that Luna is sitting between Tiamat and

Ladon. I don't know if it was the way that Tiamat wanted them to sit or if it was Luna's choice to sit between them.

Eventually, I came to the conclusion that Luna wanted to sit there. And upon further pondering, I realized how uncomfortable I made my father and Helle this morning by being okay and open with them having sex. Slowly, I lower my head and sigh. "I'm sorry, Mom and Dad, if I made you uncomfortable. I didn't mean to do it. I really gotta start realizing that not everybody is as comfortable with everything as I am." I get up from my seat and go over and hug it out with my dad and Helle. They tell me that they understand and that they're thankful to know that I do. I move back over to the table where my babies are sitting and check on everybody.

"How's my babies?" I ask as I watch Jayce and Klaus feeding all the little ones. Tiamat has taken it upon herself to sit there and feed Luna. I can't help but laugh, and my heart swells at the amount of love at this table. Ladon occasionally reaches over and helps feed Odette.

After all of the pain and suffering that I've dealt with in my entire life, this singular moment has become one of my favorites. My older children help the younger ones, and two of my mates are taking the time to feed the babies. The others are hanging out with my dad and new stepmom.

Several moments later, Dante and Edgar enter the kitchen dining area and place their orders with Jennifer. Curiously, I look around to see if Marco happened to follow them. My two War Dragons start discussing the planned flight back for today to go see the renovations on my mother's castle with the guys . Halfway through the discussion, Marco makes his appearance.

His eyes lock on Luna immediately. I can see the love and adoration in his eyes that he has for my daughter. He must be in his own personal hell having to watch and wait for his mate to grow and mature. I don't know how he's doing it, and I give him credit for the amount of strength that he must have to be able to wait this long. Jayce notices Marco enter the room and carefully removes Luna from her seat. Presently, Luna's about the size of a two-year-old. We had her stay as her wolf long enough to make it easier for all of us to care for them.

Luna squeals and throws her chubby arms out as she goes running the best she can towards Marco. He opens his arms wide as Luna crashes into him. She squeals and plants fat baby kisses all over his cheek, wrapping her little chubby arms around his neck. I hear his dragon croon to her, showing her the love and affection only a mate can. It makes me emotional watching this moment. Tears slowly trickle down my face as I watch the two of them interact. Selfishly I want to keep her as her wolf and help her grow quickly and mature faster so that they can be together. But it's not fair to Luna to miss out on all the fun things that children get to do. I'll help speed the process up slightly, letting her leapfrog a few years here and there. Instead of an eighteen-year wait, he might only have six.

Marco must have noticed me watching him with Luna because suddenly his stance stiffens. I smile and raise a hand to him, letting him know that everything's okay. He sighs softly, thankful that I'm not angry. My heart aches for the two of them. At least I know one thing: my Omega daughter will be taken care of by one of the best men I know. Marco smiles at me before he kisses the crown of Luna's head and carries her back over to Jayce.

Jayce and Marco hug it out before he leaves Luna's side. Almost instantly, Luna begins to cry because Marco had to go. I sigh softly and call Marco over to me.

"Yes, my Queen?" Marco says to me curiously as his eyes never leave my daughter.

"I would like to make sure that Luna's first flight is a comfortable one." I draw in a deep breath, looking at him before looking back over to Jayce and signaling for him to join us. "I would like to make a request of you, Marco."

"If it's within my power, my Queen, I will do anything that you ask of me." He raises his fist to his heart and bows his head slightly to me.

I slightly bow my head to him and then look over to Jayce. "Marco, will you do me the honor of carrying both of my precious Omegas? I would like for Luna and for Jayce to ride with you on this trip." I smile softly and raise my hand to stop him from speaking. "It'll be Luna's first flight, and it's not natural for a Dire Wolf to be in the air." I lightly rest my hand on his forearm before continuing. "Although your bond with her is fragile, it's still enough that it may keep her wolf settled."

Marco smiles, trying to hide how happy it makes him that he'll be able to carry his young mate. I see the sly smile from her father, Jayce, seeing what I'm doing. Marco drops down to one knee before me and lowers his head. "You honor me and trust me greatly, my Queen. Thank you for this great boon you have given me," he says solemnly. "If there is ever anything that you wish of me, big or small, do not hesitate to ask; it is yours."

Gently, I rest my hand on top of Marco's head and according to his people's custom. I slide my hand down his face to caress his jaw and lightly pull up to allow him to stand again. "You honor me. I am blessed that a man as good as yourself is to be the mate of my most gentle daughter."

Marco blushes then joins Dante and Edgar. I shake my head, slowly watching the guys interact. I send Klaus over to hang out with the others as Jayce and I finish feeding the children and then clean them up. For our benefit, the guys begin to speak louder, projecting their voices. From what I hear from the conversation, we leave in less than an hour. My father plans on meeting us there, he has things to finish after our last visit. Honestly, I don't blame him, I kind of don't want to go either, but I have to because it will be Kirra's castle one day.

The guys start prepping to leave, dividing up who is flying with who. I'm over here with Jayce and the babies trying not to laugh. Marco is taking Jayce, Luna, Dimitri, and Odette. Alaric is taking me and his two children as well as Dominik. More than likely, Arnulf will shift and fly for a bit then land on my gauntlet. Dante is trying to get Klaus and Kirra to fly with Marco so that he and Edgar can be on security. Klaus finally gives in and heads to start packing bags for himself and his daughter. I can't help but shake my head as Jayce and I leave to go pack. The next few hours are going to be the longest hours of my life.

CHAPTER 68

Dimitri

Two hours, thirty-eight minutes, and nineteen seconds is what it took for us to finally get everyone packed and loaded onto the backs of the dragons. It doesn't help that almost half of us that are going are children. According to Aurora, I must have achieved sainthood at this point in my life at least a dozen times. Between her and her antics and now her and her children's antics, I'm almost at my wits' end. If they weren't so stinking adorable and one of them was mine, I think I would have lost my mind days ago.

I join Jayce and Klaus on Marco's back for the ride out to Aurora's mother's castle. Little Luna squeals with delight as she sits behind Marco's crown of horns on her father's lap. They have such a unique situation. She wasn't even an hour old and he knew that she was his. I noticed Marco isn't flying how he normally flies with the dips and the waves and the sudden turns. No, he is flying extra careful and a little slower than usual.

Alaric occasionally roars at him, trying to get him to pick up speed. Marco roars right back at him, challenging him to force him to move faster. I think only Aurora knows the reason as to why he's flying much more carefully than usual. On the other hand, my daughter is looking around curiously but has the same self-preservation that I do. Bears should not be flying.

I glance over to my right and observe Tiamat and Ladon flying right alongside their father. Aurora is hooping and hollering, ecstatic that her babies are currently flying. Arnulf is flying right along with the children, keeping pace with them. Now it's Alaric's turn to slow down to a snail's pace just so his children can get flight time. Part of me, I want to laugh and make fun of him because of the way he was yelling at Marco. The other part of me is just grateful that Aurora thought of something without alerting Alaric to the real reason as to why Marco is going slower.

A little over an hour later, we can see the castle on the horizon. My people and Klaus's people have done a wonderful job starting to repair the spires that were almost to the point of disrepair. Dante and Edgar roar their greeting to those that are on the ground. The dragons that had stayed behind roar back, letting us know that it's safe to land. Alaric lands and lies down quickly, allowing Aurora and Klaus to slide off his back. Soon after they are clear, Alaric shifts back to his human form and watches his children land.

Marco waits until both babies have landed and have cleared the area before he starts his descent. Little Luna is laughing hysterically as he swoops in gently and lands. I have never remembered the big guy making such a gentle landing in the entire time I've known him. He waits patiently until Aurora comes over to receive the baby from Jayce.

Once Aurora is at his side, ever so carefully, he lowers his head and allows Jayce and Luna to slide off safely. Slowly, he extends his wing for myself and Odette to get off of his back. His eye follows Aurora and Luna until they are at a safe distance away, and I'm safely off of his back. When he is sure that I'm clear, he shifts back to his human form and accepts the clothing from Alaric quickly.

I watch Marco hesitate for a mere moment, staring over at Aurora and Luna. Luna locks eyes with him and starts making the come here motion with her hands. There are only a few moments of hesitation on his part before he turns and obeys the little princess. Luna squeals with delight as Marco comes up alongside her. He lightly kisses the crown of her head before bowing gently to Aurora and walking off to continue where he was needed to be.

He looks at little Luna the same way the rest of us gaze at Aurora. My mind is telling me that it's physically not possible at her young age for him to acknowledge a mate bond with her. Shit, Aurora notices the way I was staring at the interaction.

Aurora suddenly changes course and comes right to Odette and me. Either I'm in deep trouble, or I noticed something I shouldn't have. She snuggles up alongside me and kisses me on my pulse point. "So, what do you think you just saw?" she asks, tilting her head to the side, staring at me.

The smart answer for me to say would be that I'm glad we have such attentive guardians. But being a father now, my concern far outweighs what may be in my best interest. "Was I seeing what I think I saw between Marco and Luna?" I tilt my head slightly to the side and raise an eyebrow. My little Odette thankfully is fast asleep in my arms and is unaware of what's going on around her.

"Perhaps, perhaps not," Aurora says in her typical riddle. What I've learned over the last two-hundred and thirty years with her, usually the first half of the answer is the correct answer. So with that being said, I am right. She is his mate, and how the fuck does that work? Cautiously, I nod slowly, pretending I didn't solve her riddle.

"If you say so, sweetheart, eventually what's actually going on will come to light." I shrug my shoulders and just smile at her. I've got her now. Concern flickers over her angelic visage. And like a little girl, she asks me not to tell. "Alaric can't know yet. It's only you, me, Jayce, and of course the other dragons that know what's going on. I'm almost afraid of how he might react," she says as she lightly strokes my forearm. Her concern is understandable and warranted. When it comes to the children, Alaric's temper is very short, and his urge to protect them is quite strong.

"You know we have to tell him at some point, right?" I say softly to her because I notice him looking in our direction. I pretend to point to something on Odette's forehead that actually is not there just to act like I was showing Aurora something. She catches on quickly and pretends to look at what is supposed to, in theory, be there.

"I know, just give me some time to figure out how without him wanting to battle Marco. Luna isn't even his, but I know because she's mine, he will go to extreme lengths to make sure that she's safe." She rocks little Luna in her arms, staring down at her smiling. "I've been so afraid for her. She's not a warrior like me, and I'm afraid she may not be able to protect herself in the future. I'm so thankful that someone I trust is going to be her mate and the one to protect her from now on." Aurora smiles softly and sighs. "I'm kind of shocked, to be honest. I didn't think the bond could snap into place or be recognized with someone so young."

"I agree. This is something that you must question your father about in private and find out exactly how that works." I gently rub her shoulders, trying to give her some semblance of comfort. I look back towards the group, and Jayce and Alaric are coming right at us. Immediately, Aurora offers Jayce his daughter; he smiles and starts making the cutest little baby noises at her. Luna, in turn grabs him by his beard and puts squishy little toddler kisses all over his face.

Jayce walks off with Luna towards the castle, and I watch Aurora's eyes take on their ethereal glow. Marco's eyes immediately begin to glow, and he goes to follow Jayce and Luna. Aurora winks at me as she nabs Alaric before he has a chance to question anything he saw. I watch them walk off before I head towards the bears from my village. Renee, apparently, is in charge of her mate's part of the reconstruction of the north spire. I wave at Renee, and she comes running over quickly.

"Morning, Dimitri. Oh my! Is that the new cub? She's so precious." Renee gushes and looks at me for permission to touch Odette. I nod slightly and gently touch the crown of Odette's head. Hesitantly, Renee lowers her face to sniff at the crown of Odette's head. A smile spreads across her lips as she backs away slowly. "Such a precious little angel. You have mine and my mates' protection for her. She needs something, you just let me know."

"Thank you so much. You and your mates honor us." I bow the best I can with my daughter in my arms. Carefully, I turn and head back to the main entrance. I see all the improvements that have been made already. The stonework is exemplary; you can barely tell where the new stone meets the old stone. Brock, one of the German Lycans, uses a power washer to clean the stone so that they blend nicely.

Walking through the front doors brings back memories of the night Aurora was born. The archways have been repaired as well as most of the original interior design. The original paintings of Anca's family have been fully restored by one of the local artisans. I study each image carefully, remembering the fallen. Not a single person up on these hallowed walls is left alive. Be it from the ravages of time, or they were killed the night of the invasion.

Nicodeamus has headed up a team specifically just to gather the remains of those who were left behind. With him being the oldest of us, he would have a sense in a memory of where he saw his comrades die. It's a little dark and morbid, if you ask me. Instead of remembering the good times, to only see the bad.

I'm thankful Aurora has no memory of that night. It was not something I would want her to bear. I wander my way into the throne room and find our young queen sitting there, nursing Luna. Aurora smiles softly at me and makes the shush motion at me. Apparently, little miss Luna is asleep.

Carefully, I approach and look down at the precious little angel in her arms. She is almost the spitting image of her mother at that age. Jayce comes up slowly and offers to take Luna from Aurora. Carefully, the exchange is made, and Jayce goes to take Luna to put her to bed.

Aurora smiles at me and makes the gimme motion with her hands as she stares at our daughter. Gently, I place Odette in her waiting arms. Aurora moves her top and latches Odette in place. My daughter feeds ravenously from her mother's chest. Size-wise, she may be that of a two-year-old, but chronologically she's barely five months. Aurora wants to give them at least one more month of breastfeeding before she stops. Klaus's daughter has other plans; Kirra refuses to breastfeed any longer.

I leave Aurora and Odette and head down the hall to the Grand Ballroom. Within the ballroom, I find Nicodeamus, Dominik, and Arnulf directing the woodworkers and the other artisans on how to renovate the room. Nicodeamus is telling the story of the original renovation of the Grand Ballroom. He tells them in-depth about what the stained glass used to look like and how the floors use to be. He describes the various vases and other ornamental decorations that line the mantle of the great fireplace in great detail.

It's now I notice that Nicodeamus has Aurora's sketchbook in front of him. Apparently, through blood memories, she saw the castle how it used to be and drew it for him. She made adjustments as to how things can be modernized and made more her style. I start flipping through the book as I get up alongside him and note the subtle changes that she's made instead of putting the ornaments back on the ledge that runs the room's perimeter. She has decided to spread out part of her and Alaric's skull collection in the Grand Ballroom.

Shockingly, Klaus is making arrangements for a new chandelier to be made for the center of the ballroom. The one that he's having commissioned has skulls in the center with beautiful lighting around the perimeter. In a rather creepy move, he wants to put lights inside of the eye sockets. I know my mate would absolutely love that setup. Part of me is slightly concerned about everybody else's perception of the chandelier itself.

After what seems to be a couple of hours of discussion and meeting with other artisans, Aurora finally arrives in the ballroom. Lightly, she trails her fingers over Klaus's shoulders, looking down at the sketch he has in front of him. She squeals with delight seeing what he is preparing for her. She hugs him tightly and kisses both of his cheeks before moving over to stand next to her father.

Nicodeamus points out the different designs that he already has the artisans working on. A slow smile creeps across Aurora's lips as she comes up and kisses her father's cheek before moving to me. "What do you think about it, D?" She moves away from all of us and opens her arms wide, and spins slowly. "I want to bring it back to the grandeur that it was when my mom lived. I can see it now, people dancing and drinking and celebrating again." The ethereal white glow surrounds her eyes, and she shares a vision with all of us.

An orchestra sits in the corner playing her favorite song, "Clair de Lune." She's dancing gracefully, being passed between each of us. Our children dart in and out between the party-goers, giggling happily. Her father and new stepmother are dancing closely, whispering sweet nothings in each other's ears. The biggest thing that I take away from this vision is the amount of love she feels for everybody.

Slowly, we're pulled from the vision and back into reality. One by one, we turn to look at each other and smile. I feel through the bond that the other mates who are not in the room with us shared the vision as well. We've decided that we shall make her vision come true—the amount of joy that vision gave her as well as us must happen. Aurora moves over to Dominik and whispers in his ear, then departs with him. I raise a single eyebrow looking over at Nicodeamus, who by the way, is also confused by the quick departure. I guess we're going to have to wait and find out what she's up to.

CHAPTER 69

Aurora

I'VE DECIDED TO TAKE OVER THE THRONE ROOM THIS AFTERNOON. ALL five of my children play in front of me with their various toys and imaginary games. I've managed to drag my guitar into the throne room and set it up. This is one of the few rooms that the guys have managed to set up with electricity. On the roof of the castle itself, we now have solar panels to power everything since it'll be virtually impossible to run power lines up here. Carefully, I sit back and tune my guitar, figuring out exactly which song I want to play today.

I'm not playing because I'm upset, nor am I angry. It's not really based on an emotion this time. It's one of those times I just feel like I need to play. Tiamat comes and sits next to me, picking up the smaller child-sized bass guitar that I had gotten her. I smile softly at her and then reach down to set her up with her own amp. I finish tuning my guitar, then reach over and assist Tia in tuning hers. Now it's time to try to figure out exactly what I want to play this afternoon.

I have to figure out a song with ample lead guitar and a good bass line to it. "Mommy?" Tia says, looking up at me as she sits with her bass guitar and her lap. "What song are we doing?" She tilts her head slightly to the side as she looks up at me with my own grey eyes.

"Good question, baby girl; Mommy is still trying to sort that out at the moment." I start tapping my finger against my chin, pondering as to which song I really want to do. Regardless of whichever song I decide to choose, I still have to teach Tia how to play it. I start tapping my foot on the ground, trying to figure out what to play.

Several moments pass as I ponder the playlist for this afternoon. I finally decide to settle on Audioslave's "I am the Highway." Gently, I rest my fingertips on Tia's temples, and we lock eyes immediately. I teach her the song the best way I know how, infusing her mind with the knowledge of how to play the instrument in her hand. Through the mental bond that we have currently forged, she shows me exactly what she must do. I smile at her and give her a nod.

We start off playing the song, and the intro reverberates through the hall setting the mood. I cheat a little bit, use my Alpha power, and project what Tia and I are doing. I reach out to all those bonded to me either by the pack or by mating. Whether they are dragon or wolf, everyone will hear what we're playing.

Just before I start the opening lyrics, all of my mates arrive in the throne room. I'm sitting on one throne, and Tia is on the other. The guys and my father do a double take, looking between the two of us. Purposely today, I dressed Tia similar to how I'm currently dressed. We're both wearing our black leggings and a red sweatshirt, both of us barefoot, sitting the exact same way on the thrones.

The lyrics are haunting as well as meaningful. It's about a journey, one that I now know all too well. I've experienced love and loss. I've experienced great joy and the opposite, great pain. I'm hoping that we finally know peace and my children can grow without fear in the upcoming years. The throne room slowly starts to fill with our friends and allies. Work is officially stopped now, and everybody's listening to the impromptu concert. We finish the first song, and pretty much everyone is clapping and cheering for us. I smile in motion to Tia, letting her take her first official bow.

"Mommy? Can we play another song everybody really likes, like that one?" Tia smiles as she looks at me, and I could see that making the others happy through music has made Tia happy.

"Of course, baby girl, what would you like to play?" I ask as I smile, looking at Tia. She sets down her bass guitar and starts pacing in front of the throne. She has that serious look that I end up having when I'm deep in thought, and it doesn't escape the guys. I smile wickedly at my daughter and motion for her to approach me. Again I place my fingers on her temple, and my eyes take on their ethereal glow, and I pass the knowledge of the next song on to her. Tia starts to laugh because it's one of her favorites. She runs back up over to her throne and waits for me to count it off.

I start counting it off by tapping my foot on the floor, and then I start singing. The second song chosen is Evanescence's "The Chain." Tia joins me this time with the lyrics, following up right behind me, helping me sustain the notes and making them even more haunting. She fills in on the chorus with me, and to my surprise, Ladon joins in.

Slowly, I start to freeze the throne room to the point that snowflakes start to fall from the ceiling. My youngest children run around trying to catch the snowflakes on their tongues while Tia and I play the song. It's a wonderful feeling having my entire family here playing the song, bringing everyone together. Until a little while ago, I did not know my father and his mate had arrived, but apparently, they had snuck off and somehow beat us here. I watch my father hold his mate tightly as we sing our hearts out.

Tia and I, both at the end of the song, decide to breathe fire in the middle of the throne room, going out with a bang. We high-five and start to laugh to ourselves. Jayce is ever thoughtful and comes over with glasses of water for the two of us.

I rest my guitar on my throne, and Tia does the same. We go down amongst our people and accept thanks. We hug it out with several friends and family members before everybody disperses and goes back to work. It was absolutely lovely to be able to liven the day up and bring a little bit of joy to everyone's day. The guys all depart, going back to their chores and jobs that they have given themselves. My father and his mate decide to take the children out into the courtyard to play for the afternoon.

I have the urge to explore the castle further, so I begin to walk towards the east wing. Arnulf decides to come with me. I reach down and grab his hand and hold it as we walk through the halls. Room by room, we take the time to explore everything. Several rooms have hidden corridors that I was unaware of. Some of the corridors only go a few feet and hide treasures we didn't know existed. Others brought us out into other rooms that you were unaware had a secret passageway.

Finally, up on the second floor, we are going past yet another one of the studies. Apparently, my mother's family loved collecting books on all different subjects. I find a room on the second floor that appears to be an art studio. Carefully, I start taking the sheets off of the various pieces of art. Under one of the sheets, I find a painting of my father and mother. It brings a tear to my eye to see exactly how happy they were together. Tears threaten to break and roll down my cheek when Arnulf comes to my side and hugs me just in time.

"She was beautiful. You look almost exactly like her except you have your father's eyes and his lips. Well, and obviously his hair color as well," Arnulf says as he gently touches the different features that he's pointing out. It's nice seeing a picture from when she was alive versus just a spectral form. They were so happy. If I didn't end Vladimir's life myself, I would still be seeking vengeance for her. I move through several other paintings, deciding that my father and mother would be moved to the main hallway. Some of the other older paintings would be removed.

I'm not on edge for once in my life, and I'm not constantly scanning or searching for impending danger, figuring now everything is safe. This room is much larger than I initially thought because apparently, part of it runs behind the room next to it. Just as I'm reaching up to take a sheet off a statue, I feel the press of cold steel against my throat and an arm band around my rib cage.

I reach out through the bond to my mates, alerting them as to what's going on. The male lowers his mouth close to my ear and whispers. His foul breath washes over me, turning my stomach almost instantly. "If you scream, I will kill you where you stand." His voice is familiar, and I search my memory to try to figure out who it is. And then it dawns on me, he's one of the young males that I spared.

I hear my mates come running towards the room I'm in. Once they break into the room, the man presses the blade to my throat, drawing a blood rivulet from my flesh. "If you move one more step, I will end her where she stands."

Klaus is the first to be able to formulate words. "Why are you doing this?" He says forcefully, "You're free now. You don't have to fight anymore." He's practically yelling. Anger tinges his voice bringing forth the growl of his beast. Alaric rests a hand on his shoulder, trying to calm him before he does something irrational.

"Oh, so it's okay for you to kill off my people and my family in the name of this hybrid bitch. But, it's not okay for me to seek revenge for the deaths of my family members?" He presses the blade a little further, and I feel my blood seeping out more.

I wink at the guys and slowly concentrate on having my scales rise up through my skin to protect my fragile throat. Thankfully, Gallus's present strengthened my scales, making them almost bulletproof. Once I'm sure my throat is protected, and he is unaware of the scales, I smile at my mates. "Please do what he says," I say, acting like I'm frightened.

I feel the male standing behind me relax slightly when he believes that I will not fight him. And that's his biggest mistake. I don't think this male is aware of the spines that my beast had acquired. I get that Hannibal Lecter and Harley Quinn had a baby kind of smile going, and instantly my father and Alaric know what I'm about to do. Without warning, I shift, the spines that run down my back shoot out—they're four to five inches in length—and impale the male. He has multiple holes from my spines running from his groin up to his eye socket. His body twitches, hanging off of my spines, bleeding his viscous fluid down my back in warm rivulets.

Dimitri and Alaric come to my side and remove the man's corpse from my beast's back. He lands with a wet thud on the ground in the puddle of his own blood. My poor white fur is stained vermilion, and I didn't even get to fight. How disappointing. I shift back to my human form and look from my mates to my father. "Send the War Dragons and Marco to detain all those that I spared, throw them into the dungeon until I'm able to check them. Make sure that none of them are going to betray us again." My voice is but a growl, echoing my beast as I speak to everyone. The stupid male underestimated me, betrayed my trust, and attempted to kill me in my own home. I will not take that chance with my children running around.

We race through the halls back to where Helle is with the five children. We find two burned corpses and three others with blackened veins from Helle's toxic bite. Tia and Ladon are in their dragon forms, standing protectively over the other three babies who have shifted to their animal forms.

All I am feeling is a burning rage; it's another five males that I spared. They've pretty much just issued a death warrant for the rest of them. There may be no saving any of them. Klaus, Jayce, Alaric, and Dimitri go tearing out of the room to serve out the sentences for the last nine that are alive. I go over and start checking my babies over quickly, making sure that none of them are injured. The only one that has any kind of a mark on them is Tia. Apparently, she deflected a blade with her scales. It's a slight cut, nothing too deep that won't heal over time. But she may end up with a wicked scar to remind her of her heroism today. Ladon refuses to shift back as he stays curled up around little Luna.

I look over at my mother-in-law, or stepmom—however, you want to call her—and smile. She shifts back to her human form and tries to find something to wear. My father is quick to offer her his button-down. "You know, daughter, you ought to get dressed as well. It's unbecoming for the queen to run around naked." I roll my eyes as Dominik takes off his hoodie and hands it to me. Slowly, I shake my head at the two of them and then slide it on.

"Am I being too brash ordering the deaths of the last nine I spared?" I pose the question in the open air for anybody to answer me. Dominik is the first to come and stand before me and look me square in the eyes.

"My love, they went after you as well as your children. I would be more than happy if you burned them all to ash. Anyone who goes after children does not deserve to live. To take the life of an innocent is uncalled for." Dominik smiles and gently kisses my cheek. Quickly, I wrap my arms around his neck and hug him tightly. His strong arms band around me and crush me to his chest as his wolf starts to rumble to me. I close my eyes, just reveling in the feeling of having my mate's arms around me. Eventually, I feel the heat from Arnulf as he presses against my back, hugging up against me.

"Whatever you decide is best for our family and the kingdom, my people and I will support any and all of your decisions," Arnulf says softly as he nuzzles my cheek. The whistles and keening call that his bird makes always brings a smile to my lips. I know that they're happy noises for his shift, so it makes me happy as well. Eventually, we break apart and I just sigh softly looking at the carnage my children and stepmom caused.

I break away from the guys and run over to Helle and give her the biggest hug that I could possibly give her. I thank her over and over again for her defense of my children. She's in tears over the fact that Tia got hit with a blade and that she wasn't fast enough. She tells me about how brave and strong both my dragon children were. On the other hand, my father is sitting there with his chest all puffed up doing the "that's my grand babies" thing that he always does. Helle and I stay wrapped up in each other's arms for several moments, both of us blubbering like giant babies. My mates return covered in blood but no worse for wear.

"Is it done?" I question. Helle and I both turn to face them simultaneously, waiting for an answer from someone.

Alaric comes from behind Dimitri, drops to one knee, and holds up a head. "He's a direct descendant of Grigore's line. I'm unsure of his relation to Vladimir, but I could almost assure you he is more than likely one of his children. He was cursing your bloodline for tainting Lycan kind." Alaric's eyes shift to that of his dragon the minute that sentence falls from his lips. "I couldn't have him speak about my beloved mate that way. My dragon and I would not allow those venomous words to fill the air any longer."

I move forward and gently cup both of Alaric's cheeks and lean down and kiss him lightly on his lips. "Thank you, my love, for protecting my honor." My eyes drift to my other mates and I smile.

"Thank you for keeping our family and our people safe. I am so blessed to have all of you in my family." I move to each mate, kissing them and letting them know how thankful I am for what they've done. My eyes find my father staring at us.

I start to walk over towards him and smile. "I need your guidance, Father, as to what I should do. I believe we have eliminated the threat for this moment. But you have seen more wars and battles than any of us here." Gently, I grab my father's hand, looking up into his eyes. He tilts his head several times, then he nods slowly.

"My advice to you, daughter and my sons, seek out all those who have not been with us from the beginning and isolate them. Trust is earned and not freely given." He looks around the room and then back up to me again. "We should summon more of our dragon guards to be here. If we can get a Spectral Dragon here, that would be most helpful as they can sense lies."

"That won't be necessary, old friend." The melodic tune of Oberon's voice fills the hall. My head whips around to stare at him. He materialized literally out of nowhere. "It's a pleasure to see you, young queen, and congratulations on regaining your mother's castle," he says as he spreads his arms wide, looking around the room and then back over to us. He has that dramatic flair with everything he does, and it's definitely a whole new level of showmanship.

"It's a pleasure as always to see you, King Oberon." I bow my head slightly to him, never taking my eyes off of him. "Are you able to assist us in our current predicament, trying to sort out those who may be betrayers?" I tilt my head slightly as I look at him.

"It would be my honor to assist you," he says with a flourished bow. "Let's make haste, Nicodeamus. I will need your assistance in navigating the castle," he says as he sweeps into one last bow before following my father out of the room.

I raise a single eyebrow and look between my mates and narrow my eyes slightly. We're all on the same page right now. Something's going on behind the scenes that we are unaware of, and that's why he's here. For now, we will remain vigilant and see what happens.

CHAPTER 70
Klaus

We become aware of Oberon's arrival and go listen to what he has to say. Especially after what happened with the Lycans that we had spared, we're concerned there may be others plotting silently in the shadows.

Jayce's mom is kind enough to take all of the children back to their playroom while the adults handle these pressing matters. There's a study on the first floor that we tend to use for our meetings, so I head there immediately. Nicodeamus is already there and has checked and made sure that there are no additional passageways into the room.

Oberon has put himself at the head of the table, sitting with his legs crossed, sipping on what I guess is a glass of white wine. He regards everybody as they enter and then motions for everybody to sit. I can see the tick in the corner of Aurora's eye, which generally tells me she is not pleased with how everything is starting. Oberon, unbeknownst to him, is sitting in her chair. I can watch the various emotions flicker over her face as she tries to maintain the aura of calm that she needs for this meeting. I decide now, feeling that I may as well test my metal. I stand before everyone at the end of the table, directly facing Oberon. "I assume you have heard about what transpired here." I tilt my head slightly to the side, looking at him. "From what I understand, you would be able to tell who is friend and foe?" I raise the question gently, not wanting to aggravate the ancient before me.

He smiles, sets his glass down, and then plays with a strand of his long, white hair. "But of course, young one," he says with the flourish of his hand. "That is exactly why I've come." He smiles and lightly lowers his head to me before looking back up.

"I am here to assist the young queen as well as protect and preserve her valuable bloodline." He makes a circle with his hand over the top of the table, and under it, shimmering into view is a scroll. Aurora, who is sitting off to his right, leans over to look at the scroll and then quirks an eyebrow up. Her eyes dart between her father and Oberon, then back down to me, then back over to the scroll. By the way, she's looking at it I can only determine she cannot read what is on it.

Nicodeamus, who is sitting on Oberon's left, leans over and looks at the scroll as well. He furrows his brows, staring at it quite curiously. "Dear friend, is there a way for you to translate this for all of us to be able to read?" he asks cautiously, not wanting to upset or aggravate the ancient before him.

Oberon laughs a little. "Silly me, I keep forgetting that not everyone can read ancient Elvish." He throws his hands up in "the oops, my bad" position and then runs his hands over the scroll again. Within a few moments, the scroll is in English and able to be read by everyone.

Oberon slowly sides the scroll over to sit in front of Aurora. I watch her eyes dart left to right as she reads through the scroll. Through the bond, I can hear her clear as day as she reads the contents out loud for us. The details within tells the story of the creation of the Blood Queen. Aurora's great-grandmother didn't just happen; she was thoughtfully engineered by the fae.

This new news is shocking to us, and Aurora looks between her father and Alaric. The repercussions that this could have on the twins are incredible. Aurora's eyes read down to the line describing the mark of the Blood Queen. Those that can tap into her power usually bear the mark of the crescent moon on their body somewhere.

Aurora quickly looks to her wrist, and sure enough, she has a very faint crescent moon. Her eyes glow and take on that ethereal quality that we know all so well. Shortly after, both Ladon and Tia show up. Aurora carefully grips their wrists, examining them. Both twins bear a double crescent moon on their right wrists. Aurora motions for both of her children to show Oberon their wrist. He examines both of the children's wrists and then Aurora's. He reaches out and then grabs Nicodeamus's as well. His is the faintest of the four of them. Tia has the darkest marking out of the four of them. It's still faint in comparison to a tattoo but yet dark enough to be seen easily.

I move closer to the group, looking over exactly what Oberon is examining. "What does this mean for my family?" I ask as I put my hands protectively on Aurora's shoulders, standing behind her. I'm willing to do anything necessary to keep her and all of our children safe.

Oberon smiles and then reaches out and touches my hand. "Young king, you are doing exactly what needs to be done. You are supportive of your mate and protective of any of the children born into this union. These two," he motions to Tiamat and Ladon, "will need a lot of guidance and training as they grow in age. Nicodeamus, yourself, and your son-in-law, Alaric, will need to teach these two how to use their frost and their flames wisely. Aurora, you will need to work with your daughter on some of the gifts that she has, for her brother does not have them," he says gently as he scoops Tia up and sits her in his lap. He pulls the back of her collar on her shirt to the side, looking down her spine, taking note of the scales present even in her human form.

"She is almost an exact replica of the Blood Queen. She bears the scales of her great-great-grandmother," he says as he shows us the line of scales across Tiamat's shoulders and the set about three to four scales wide running down her spine. "She will have access to powers and gifts that the rest of the Dragons in this room do not. You must protect her fiercely; she is the deadliest of all of you." Oberon smiles and gently rests his fingertips on Tia's temples.

"I have already foreseen who her mate is. He is born of a great house and is a blend of two dragon species. He is approximately three calendar years older than she is." Oberon gently hugs Tia holding her to him. "Princess, you will need to learn all that your parents and grandfather can teach you. There will come a time that you will need to do everything within your power to protect yourself." He kisses her cheek gently as she turns to face him.

"What do you mean, Obie?" Tiamat asks. She gently places both of her hands flat on his cheeks smiling up at him. Chronologically, right now Tia appears to be about the size of a six-year-old child. Unlike her appearance mentally, she is far advanced for her age.

Oberon smiles at the nickname that Tia had given him. "Young princess, I cannot tell you everything that I've seen in the future. But I can tell you this: your future mate is a good man. He comes from great parents as well as a peaceful and powerful kingdom." He smiles as he places his hands over Tia's hands on his face. "Do as your father asks to be able to protect you. Please, do not be angry at him over the extreme measures he may take in the future." Oberon's eyes move to lock with Alaric's. "Everything that is going to be done from this day forth has your safety in mind, princess." Oberon gently kisses Tia on her forehead. And then he gently passes her back over to Aurora.

Oberon's eyes take on a blue glow as he turns his palms upward. We can feel the power stretching and radiating off of his form. Nicodeamus smiles and then alerts us through the bond that he is reaching out, sensing who still has malice in their heart.

Just shy of fifteen minutes later, Oberon's eyes stop glowing, and he smiles, looking at us. "All of those that you have in the dungeon should be sentenced to death immediately. They are the last of the uprising that was about to be staged here in this very castle. Two of them were plotting to murder the children; the rest figured that they can take out Aurora in her sleep," Oberon says with the finality that sends a chill down my spine. My nerves are on edge now, thinking about all the times that we could have possibly come into harm's way.

"If I understand correctly, ancient one, if we eliminate those in the dungeon, we should be safe?" I say because I'm pretty sure I already know his answer.

"Simply put, yes." He smiles and claps his hands and then rises from his chair. "Eliminate these threats, and your home will be safe. The Winter Palace is your next visit; there may still be some that might cause issues there as well." He starts to head towards the door and then stops. "I will meet you there next month on the full moon. Together we shall seek out the last of those who wish your bloodline harm, young Queen," he states just before he drops into a flourished bow. As he moves to stand up straight, his form shimmers and then vanishes from sight.

"I don't think I'll ever get used to seeing that with him," Arnulf states flatly, being the mystic of the group, magic usually upsets him slightly. "I hope that he's wrong; I really don't want the children growing up in fear," Arnulf says softly, sighing at the end of his statement. He runs his hands through his hair and then looks at the rest of us for our reactions.

I move from where I'm standing to go and give Arnulf a hug. "Don't worry, with the eight of us here we will do everything within our power to keep all of the children safe." I embrace him a little tighter for a few more moments before releasing him.

Dimitri moves forward and places his hands flat on the tabletop. "I will send the War Dragons to finalize the executions. After that, I believe it would be wise for us to head to the Winter Palace and clean house there too." His eyes drift over to Alaric, who nods slowly in agreement.

"I believe you're correct, old friend. We will handle the Winter Palace and then the Summer Chalet." Alaric begins to pace the room before coming back to stand next to Aurora. "All kidding aside, my love, I believe our safest bet is to move everybody to either the Summer Chalet or the Winter Palace. That is until either you're done having children, or the children are old enough to protect themselves."

You can almost see the gears turning in Aurora's mind as she weighs the options out before her. "Sadly, I believe your deduction is the most accurate and safest course for our family." Aurora stands slowly and begins to pace around the table. "In the interest of safety for all the children born and yet to be born, we should move swiftly." Aurora moves to come and stand before me. "Appoint your grandmother as pack master for the German Lycan pack."

I lower my head to my mate and raise my fist to my heart. "Your wish is my command, my angel. As you have spoken it, it shall be done." I furiously began to type on my phone, sending the message to my grandmother, alerting her about Aurora's wishes. Through the pack bond, I hear Aurora reach out to both the American and German Lycan packs. She tells them that my grandmother, Elsa, shall be pack master in her absence. That Elsa's word is law and carries as much weight as her own. Any who rise up against her shall meet her talons. The respective pack members answer one by one, agreeing to the terms set forth by Aurora. Her eyes meet mine, and she nods.

She moves to stand before Dominik and Jayce taking both of their hands. "Your brother, Alex, will remain in power as my proxy for the Dire Wolf pack." Her eyes take on the ethereal glow as she uses Dominik as an anchor to reach out to the Dire Wolves. She sends word to the pack, advising them that Alex is still in charge of them. Dominik backs Aurora up immediately, telling them that his brother is still his proxy in his absence. His word is their law and to go against him is to stand against the crown. The Dire Wolves all are in agreement and understand what needs to be done.

Aurora looks to Alaric next; their eyes start to glow with that ethereal halo around the whites of their eyes. They're reaching out to all of the dragons and dragon-kin, alerting them about what is about to happen. Aurora smiles as she sits there, I'm assuming making plans for transport for all of us.

"Is everything set?" I ask them as their eyes lose that ethereal glow. I look carefully now, between myself and the other mates, and then back over to the two of them. They nod their head slowly, then Aurora starts to head for the doors.

"I'll have the babies ready within the next thirty minutes. After that, we leave for the Winter Palace," she says, so sure of herself that she will be able to get the babies ready and out the door in less than thirty minutes. The other mates and I start to place bets as to whether or not she'll be able to accomplish this feat.

CHAPTER 71

Aurora

I leave the study swiftly, and in my mind's eye, I reach out to all five of my children. Each one always has a bag ready to go if we need to leave in a hurry. I task Ladon and Tia to gather the three youngest ones and bring them downstairs to the main courtyard. I give Marco the task of assisting children and the babies with their bags and bringing them downstairs with them. I next reach out to my mother-in-law, advising her to join us with my father in the Winter Palace journey.

In less than twenty minutes, I have my entire group, minus my mates ready to go. My father has shifted, and his mate is riding behind his crown of horns. In his taloned hand are their bags ready for the trip. My children sit with their bags in front of them, waiting for their fathers to arrive.

With five minutes left to spare, my mates make it downstairs, each of them bickering, saying they can't locate the children. My five little cherubs are here sitting with their bags in front of them, waiting patiently. Being the wise-ass that she is, Tia decides to stand up and drag her bag behind her in front of her father. "Daddy, what took you so long? You're a boy." she says in a huff with her little hands on her hips. She's emulating me perfectly; it's kind of hysterical. Alaric is shocked, looking from his daughter to the other children and then up to me. I smile at him and tilt my head to the side, motioning to all the children with their bags.

"We've been waiting for you guys for almost ten minutes now. What took you so long?" I pose the same question to all of my mates, looking at each one in turn. Jayce, Arnulf, and Klaus look ashamed of themselves for having taken so long. Dimitri and Dominik just shrug their shoulders, both of them with two bags apiece. I could almost bet the second bag has weapons in it. I shrug my shoulders slightly. And Alaric just stands there, bag in hand, coffee mug in the other, and I just tilt my head looking at them. "Did you remember to bring everyone coffee?"

He sheepishly looks down at his coffee and then holds the mug out to me. "No, my love, but here, take mine. I'm sure you need it more than I do," he says with a smile on his face, trying to hide that he did not think to bring everybody coffee. I take the mug from him, take a sip and then hand it back.

"No love, it is you that needs it more than I do; I'm not the one flying," I say with a smile as I look at him. He chuckles slightly and then hands me his bag. He finishes off his coffee quickly and then looks at the War Dragons, motioning for them to shift.

Slowly, I walk over to Marco, who is holding Luna, and I take her gently from him. "All right, big guy, time to get this little bundle of joy to the Winter Palace." I smile as I talk to him. He nods slowly and then walks away from us. Shyly he looks over his shoulder at us, and I put my hands over Luna's eyes. He nods his head at me and smiles before he shifts.

Once Marco is fully shifted, I motion for Jayce to approach. I hand him Luna and start to guide him back over towards Marco. "My love, yourself and our little princess will ride with Marco. Dimitri and his daughter, as well as Klaus and his daughter, will also be joining you on Marco." As I name my other mates, they come walking over with their daughters in their arms. "Time to load up everyone. We need to get going." I smack each of my mates on their asses, sending them scurrying up Marco's wing.

Jayce remains standing next to me as I tilt my head, looking up at Marco. I wiggle my finger at him and get him to lower his great head. I take Luna from Jayce before he starts to climb onto Marco's neck. With great skill and excellent balance, he walks his way up to the crown of horns and sits himself down. I nuzzle my daughter several times and kiss both of her cheeks. Her little chubby hands grip my face as she plants big wet, baby kisses on my face. Marco senses what I need to do next, and his tail comes around to my side. Carefully, I step on the flat portion of his tail, and he raises us up level with Jayce. Ever so carefully, I hand my daughter over to her father and make sure that they are safely snuggled in place.

Slowly, Marco lowers me back to the ground, and I walk to stand in front of him. Gently, I place my hands on his great maw to stroke his heavily armored scales. "It's time to head off to the Winter Palace. I want you to wait to land last." Ever so slightly, I feel his head nod before I release him and set off on my next task.

I look over at Dante and Edgar and nod my head to them, signaling for them to take to the skies. They start circling the castle courtyard, waiting for the other dragons to launch. I signal the four Gold Dragons that will be escorting us to take off as well. Alaric already had the contingent of four additional War Dragons for this flight waiting for the rest of us to launch. The last two to launch would be Alaric and Marco.

I move swiftly over to Alaric's side and scurry my way up onto his back and then walk up to his crown of horns. I motion to Marco for him to launch next. As soon as he's airborne, Alaric and I follow. The War Dragons fly in formation around my father, Alaric, and Marco. We fly slowly over various mountain ranges and hidden lakes and streams and en route to Siberia's Winter Palace.

We skirt China's edge, knowing full well that the Chinese Dragons don't always appreciate other dragons in their airspace. A decisive move made by Alaric and my father, we head up into mother Russia, where the Ice and Gold Dragons thrive. We remain high enough in the air that it allows us to be able to circle over the Kremlin. It's such a beautiful palace, ornate and decorative, yet has such a foreboding history. We head further into Russia's airspace, heading towards Siberia.

We go past Chernobyl and the abandoned towns around it. At the height that we're flying, we are in no danger of any radiation harming us. It's just amazing to see what's left of that part of history. We take the time to explain to Tia and Ladon what had happened in this once-thriving mecca. Both children listen intently as we relay the history of the area to them. Ladon has millions of questions that we keep trying to answer for him before he fires off his next question.

After answering my son's fifty million questions, he finally lays down to take a nap. I'm not sure which one of us is more thankful to stop talking, myself or my mate. But we are quite overjoyed at the silence we are now experiencing. On the other hand, Tia is standing up, holding on to her father's horns, looking at the winter wonderland around us. Spring has not yet touched this part of Siberia, and it's a huge blanket of snow.

We spot in the distance a herd of oxen and yak moving through the tundra in single line formation. I know the dragons that are currently carrying everyone must be hungry from the long flight. I reach out through the bond and advise those that are carrying the family to land. We land far enough away from the herd, and I spread out a blanket to sit all the children on. Thankfully, it's a very thick wool blanket with a fur backing, so I snuggle all the little ones into the middle.

Once I'm sure the little ones are snuggled, I throw an extra blanket over the top of my five children. I have Jayce and Dominik shift and curl their wolven forms around the blankets. Myself, Klaus, and Dimitri shift and take on the form of our beasts. Arnulf, who's not built for this weather, climbs into the blankets with the babies to keep them safe. It's time to hunt.

The dragons take to the sky and one by one start to pick off oxen and yaks for themselves to eat. In the process of them culling the herd, they drive the rest of them towards us. In the interest of protecting the children, I have Dimitri and his Great Bear stand guard by them. Klaus and I split up and start stalking one large oxen in particular.

You can tell this mammoth beast has escaped being hunted numerous times. Claw marks from what I assume to be Polar Bears mark this ancient warrior's back and shoulder. Today is not his lucky day. Klaus and I are quick and light on our feet as we separate him from the rest of his herd. He makes the mistake of focusing on Klaus since he's the one able to be seen easily. I launch myself from out of nowhere and land on the beast's back. I sink my talons in deeply and start to bite at the back of his neck.

The oxen starts to buck and spin, throwing his weight around, still trying to keep Klaus in his line of sight. Blood sprays everywhere, painting the snow and my fur vermilion. My adrenaline's pumping, and my heart thunders in my chest as I hold on for the wildest ride of my life. Surprisingly he throws himself on his side, trying to dislodge me. Little does he know that gives me the advantage. He's semi stuck on his side and slightly weakened from the blood loss.

I take advantage of his miscalculation and lunge, sinking my talons through his thick fur and into his flesh. I have never met an animal with such a thick hide on it before. It takes some effort to slice through till I hear the gasp from its trachea. I keep telling myself a little further, a little harder, a little deeper as I push my talons in. Eventually, I throw myself from his body, and he stands up and wobbles. Blood is pumping out with every beat of his heart, staining the snow at his feet.

One last great huff of breath escapes the hole in his throat before he falls to the ground. He huffs several more times before he expires and lays down dead in the snow. Klaus and I make short work of breaking up his body to drag it back to the children. We quarter it and sink our talons into the hunks of meat. We return to the babies and call them out so that they can eat. Dimitri wanders off and starts to bite into the carcass to drag it back to us. Thankfully, before he's even halfway back, Alaric lands and takes the oxen in his mouth and carries it back over to us, making Dimitri's job that much easier.

The babies eat their fill, while Arnulf eats snacks out of his bag. It would not be wise for him to shift in this weather because he may just freeze to death. When we are sure that everyone has eaten sufficiently, we pack everyone back up onto their dragons and take off again. It's not much further to the Winter Palace. It takes us only maybe another thirty minutes in the air to get there.

Upon arrival, one of the duke's that are good friends with Alaric is waiting in the courtyard for us. As everyone shifts, he passes out robes for us to wear. "Greetings and salutations to my King and Queen," he says, then bows deeply. He stands back up and offers us warm beverages that one of his assistants was holding for us. I take the offered beverage and sniff at it several times before deeming it safe to drink. He looks at me oddly, not used to the fact that I just don't trust.

"Please follow me. I will have the staff set up baths in the master suite for you to get cleaned up and rest a little bit before dinner. We will be serving caribou later tonight with several different desserts," he states formally as he reads off the scroll that was handed to him. "If there's anything that you wish of us, please let someone know." He bows again graciously before heading back into the castle. I raise an eyebrow looking at Alaric because I'm just not used to this level of formality.

He raises his shoulders and shrugs slightly, looking at me. For him, everything's back to status quo because this was the castle that he was raised in. We enter the castle and the entryway is exactly how I remember it: beautifully polished floors, a winding staircase going up to the second floor, the study directly off to our right where the guys will have their meetings. I trail upstairs to the master suite with all five children in tow. My little hellions are still coated in blood from their meal from earlier. We definitely did get some odd looks when the children disembarked.

I guess you can say we're not your typical royal family. I'm not stuffy, nor am I all about the pomp and circumstance. Most of my mates did not grow up royal, and neither did I. We're back in the same master suite that we were in previously, and it's still just as gorgeous as it was the last time. The bathtub is big enough to be a small swimming pool, and we set it up so that I can bathe the children first because it's almost their bedtime. After their bath, we will be all set up for bed, and then the adults will be off for dinner.

CHAPTER 72

Alaric

It's such a strange homecoming, returning to the castle of my birth. My friend, the Duke, addresses me as King even though he knows that my title is King Consort. I don't mind the difference in titles; after all, it is just a title. I am not of royal lineage nor of noble birth. My father had stolen the mantle of king, sending Aurora's mother to an untimely death because of his betrayal.

I watch my mate conduct herself around the others. It's definitely a huge change for her to be acknowledged as a ruler in an actual palace that doesn't hold bad memories. Well, not as bad of memories as the ones in her mother's palace. She moves our children swiftly into the palace and up to our suite. The fun memories of things that have occurred here, I can only hope we get to relive some of them again.

Apparently, during my inner monologue, I lost track of where my mate currently is. I go searching around our room, trying to see exactly where she had gotten herself off to. I start to hear the splishing and splashing of the bathtub and the giggles from our children. Bath time has always been one of our family's favorite times. Not only do the children get bathed in their human form, but they also get bathed as their animals.

To start off, Aurora has Tiamat and Ladon in the tub with her. She's scrubbing the children's bodies one by one, making sure that they are completely clean. Tia and Ladon's hair is a few shades lighter than mine but still darker than their mothers. If I had to give Ladon's hair color a name, I would say it's a medium ash blonde, whereas Tia's is a light ash blonde. Where Tia has curls, Ladon's hair is straight while her eyes are grey-blue. His are a grey-green like mine.

Once their human forms are completely cleansed, Aurora has them shift to their animals. Ladon's dragon, now about the size of a german shepard lays on the steps waiting his turn. While Tia's dragon lazily floats around the pool, slowly wiggling her way away from her mother. Aurora giggles while chasing after Tia with the scrub brush loaded with soap. She finally gets a hold of our wayward daughter and begins to preen her scales with her talons. Aurora has a small pile of dead scales on the edge of the tub that Jayce promptly takes away.

Furiously, Tia is scrubbed and then allowed to dunk under to remove the soap from her scales. Shortly after, she trades spaces with Ladon. He just lays there and lets his mother do whatever she wants to him. I know I personally enjoy it when my scales get preened. His scales were not as bad as Tia's since he recently had gone through a growth spurt and had all the dead ones removed. Aurora scrubs them and then dunks him under and sends him off to exit the tub with his sister.

The process is repeated a little faster with Odette and Kirra. Both little girls love bath time. Odette has honey brown hair that has a wave to it like her father's and warm hazel eyes, also like her father's. Whereas Kirra has the same ringlets that Tia has, and her hair is a light brown with a few streaks of white similar to her mother's hair color. Both little girls enjoy their tub time and get bathed as humans and as their animals. Once they're done being washed, their animals climb their ways out of the tub and go to sit by the hearth to dry off.

The last one is always the most skittish, poor little Luna. For this, Jayce strips and gets into the tub with Aurora and Luna. While one parent holds the child, the other one washes. The poor little girl is so frightened. It must be tough being an Omega, always afraid of something happening, always concerned that things aren't just so. Aurora must be noticing my thought process, and she growls lowly at me. Through the bond, she tells me that the way I'm staring must make Luna uncomfortable. I walk away slowly and return to the main part of the castle finding Nicodeamus and his mate sitting at the table already beginning their dinner.

I take a seat not far for them, and the young man comes out and takes my order. "So, Father?" I say softly to Nicodeamus. "Anything you notice that may be slightly off here?" I ask in a low enough tone not to alert anyone else to where my thought process is going. He looks around and then back at me.

"No, not yet. Then again, we also just arrived," he says low.

Helle waves her hand slightly to get my attention, and I give her a little bit of a nod, letting her know that I'm listening. "It looks to me like the staff has diminished greatly." I start to ponder what she said as I look around, and I'll be damned. For someone that's never been here, she hit the nail on the head. We are definitely short some staff members.

"I see what you mean," I say to her. "We're going to have to investigate that a little further don't you think, Dad?" I say to Nicodeamus.

He nods slowly and then looks around the room. "Definitely a little bit of an oddity but not uncommon. Quite often, when there's a power shift, there'll be a change of staff. Some very loyal to the original people that held power in the house will leave others hopeful or thankful for the change will remain. I wouldn't bother seeking out those who left, to be honest," he says as he swirls the amber liquid in his glass.

"You want only those who are going to be loyal to you and to your mate left in this house. Not those that could possibly be a potential problem," he states flatly, leaving no room for questioning or argument. Although at this point, I would tend to agree with him. We don't need anybody to start problems, especially with all the children that we have now.

"I thank you, Father, for your wisdom and guidance. It's proven yet again to be most invaluable." My statement makes Nicodeamus smile broadly. Proud that he was able to help and that I'm taking his word seriously. "I will, however, have to go tell my mate about this," I state softly. It always concerns me having to bring up matters of state with her. Sometimes she becomes like the red Queen from that children's story and starts yelling "off with their head."

It doesn't take long before Aurora and the rest of my bond mates arrive for dinner. Through the bond, I fill everyone in as to what Nicodeamus and I and his mate had discussed. You can watch the random emotions flicker over Aurora's features as she takes it all in. Thankfully, I do not see any form of anger; it's more curiosity and questioning than anything else. This is great progress for her.

Usually, I'm concerned about her wanting to destroy everything and pick up the pieces later.

She taps her finger on her chin before looking between myself and her father. "Oberon is due to arrive here in a few days. Upon his arrival, we will throw a banquet so that anyone and everyone who is part of the Dragon Court will be present in one place." Aurora lightly taps her fingernails on the tabletop as she sorts through what she wants to say next.

"Once gathered, Oberon should be able to tell us who is and who is not loyal to our cause," she says definitively with the firmness not normal in her tone. She looks back over at her father, locking eyes with him; he nods slowly, agreeing with her statement. Her eyes drift slowly to each of us, just seeing where we all stand with her proposed idea. One by one, we each nod in agreement with her. Her thought processes are sound, and with the aid of Oberon we should know who the betrayers are in a matter of moments.

"Personally, I hate relying on him for everything," Aurora says with a slight huff. "But on the other hand," she says and flourishes her hand shifting it immediately to her gauntlet staring at her talons.

"I'm quite thankful that he is doing this, and we're able to resolve the issue peacefully." She shifts her hand back to normal and then looks up at us. "Contrary to popular belief, I do not enjoy killing, nor do I like taking lives that could have been spared," she says and smirks.

"Then again, some of them were fun." She coughs and says, "Sebastian." Then continues to cough, trying to cover up that she said his name.

Most of us laugh at her antics; only her father appears to be a little concerned. "Daughter? Why was he the most entertaining?" he asks, puzzled by her actions.

"That's quite easy, Daddy," Aurora says sweetly, then stands and walks over and leans on Dimitri's shoulders. "So, you see, It was me, D, and the twins going into the throne room. There's Bash and all of his false swagger trying to look like he's Mr. GQ and all that."

She smirks and starts laughing. "How I was ever attracted to him, I have no goddamn clue," she says and shrugs and runs her fingers over Dimitri's shoulders.

"Anyway, the first words out of his mouth was him asking if the baby's his. Then, of course, my big teddy bear here," she says and hugs Dimitri's shoulders. "Takes full credit for the paternity of Alaric's babies." Aurora starts to laugh.

"The look on his face was absolutely priceless,' she says as she stands up to her full height and does what I can call jazz hands in a dramatic flare. "So, you know, of course, me being me, I just had to kiss D in front of him." Aurora smiles broadly. I can only imagine the over the top kiss that she did with Dimitri to set Sebastian off.

"So now he's all messed up in the head. Dimitri's happier than anything, and I'm just sitting back here wanting to kill him," she says and shrugs her shoulders lightly.

"So you guys know me," she states. "I suck at being patient,' she says flatly with a roll of her eyes.

"I had to wait for that idiot to think that he had a shot at me again. But to be perfectly honest, it really didn't take that long." She shrugs her shoulders and then picks up a glass of wine and takes a sip. Now she's starting to pace around the table as she tells her story, and it's getting more interesting by the minute.

"So by this point, I already sensed that he had some more men behind one of the hidden passageways. So I reached out to you," Aurora says, then runs her hand over Nicodeamus's shoulders.

"So daddy dearest if you remember you go on your mission to take out the assholes that are looking to take me out. Definitely an excellent and solid plan." They high-five and share a good laugh.

"Dominik and I had watched the movie "300." When I killed Sebastian, I was thinking about that epic scene where the bad guys were at the pit. So I ripped out his heart, cut off his head, and then kicked his chest, knocking him backward. I kind of wanted to yell that same battle cry from the movie, but we're definitely not in Sparta." Aurora continues to laugh as she walks over to me and then climbs into my lap.

She stares up into my eyes and kisses my cheeks several times. "I think you would have been laughing hysterically," she says softly as she nuzzles my cheek and neck. I wrap my arms tightly around her and hug her flush to my chest.

"I absolutely would have, my love. It must have been an epic sight the way you dispatched him." I run my fingers gently through her hair as I now look up to her father. "We need to get together later and make a list of the local nobles that we should invite here for the banquet. By my guesstimate, Oberon should be here in two to three days. So in about five to six days, we should have the banquet."

"Son, I agree," Nicodeamus says as he strokes his beard. "I believe we should probably set my mate with your children and the two War Dragons in the playroom for the banquet," Nicodeamus states as he looks between all of us gathered. Aurora starts to shake her head no.

"We need your mate present, Dad. I will send Marco, Edgar, and Dante to watch my children. Not that your mate is incapable of protecting them, but she is your mate and should be seen at the gathering." Aurora crosses her arms over her ample chest, looking at her father, expecting him to argue with her. I run my hand over her lower back, trying to soothe the tension I feel building.

Nicodeamus rises from his seat and walks over to where we are sitting. He drops down to one knee in front of his daughter and places his forehead on her knees. "I agree with you fully, daughter, and I am sorry to have started making arrangements without your input." Aurora smiles softly at her father and runs her fingers through his hair. Lightly, she reaches under his right arm and pulls so he will stand.

"Daddy, there's nothing to forgive; you are so used to being in control of everything that your council is most valuable." She smiles at her father and then stands and embraces him tightly. She bounces up and kisses his cheek and then pulls back to look at him. "Besides, who else would I want by my side if we have to torch the entire banquet hall?" she asks with a wicked smile and a slight giggle to her speech. It's moments like this I can't tell if she's joking or being serious. By the look on Dimitri's face, I'm pretty sure she's serious.

The rest of the meal goes off without a hitch, and no more discussions of plans occur. We share a few good laughs at each other's expense and prepare to retire for the evening. Tomorrow should be a rather interesting day, to say the least.

CHAPTER 73

Aurora

THIS MORNING IS NO DIFFERENT THAN ANY OTHER MORNING. I'M awakened by a minimum of two to three of my children jumping on me, trying to wake me up. Thankfully, Klaus is smart enough to come in trailing behind the babies with a big cup of coffee. I noticed now that none of my other mates are still in bed with me. Dirty rats bailed before the babies were able to get them too. It is what it is, I suppose. I snuggle up with the three littlest ones as they all try to hog my pillows and blankets.

Jayce brings me breakfast in bed, and now I know the guys are up to something. He sits down beside me and starts to set the tray across my lap. I notice that Arnulf is coming in, bringing extra coffee with him. I narrow my eyes looking at my three mates that are present.

"Okay, guys, I know you're up to something," I say as I look between my three gentlest mates. My eyes pin each one in place, waiting for one of them to crack. It's kind of interesting to see that it's Arnulf who cracks first.

"Sweetheart, I know what this must look like to you, but we come in peace," Arnulf says as he raises his hands in a placating manner. He then crawls up from the foot of the bed and sits in front of me. I narrow my eyes, slightly observing him, studying him for any signs of weakness.

"Are you sure that's what's going on right now?" I ask, dropping my voice at the end, attempting to sound docile.

Jayce reaches out and takes hold of my hand, and envelopes it in both of his. "We know that today is the day of the banquet. Oberon arrived early this morning, and we've already set him up with one of the master suites." Jayce offers me my coffee, and I sip at it, slowly digesting everything that he said.

"Okay?" I tilt my head to the side, looking between the three of them. "I assume that's not the only thing that's going on right now." I keep my eyes narrowed, looking at them this time; it's Klaus that caves in. "Oberon brought a dress and a new crown for you. He requests that you wear it for the banquet tonight."

I attempt to keep my face in a neutral position as I look over back at Jayce. "I assume you've seen this gown and the crown that goes with it?" I ask as I sip again at my coffee.

"I did indeed, my love," he says with a great big smile on his face. "You are absolutely going to fall in love with it. It's a gown fit for a warrior queen like yourself." He slowly brings my hand up to his lips and kisses it. "When you're ready, we'll bring the gown in and help you get ready for tonight. But for now, we're here to help you relax."

Shortly after he says the word relax, my new stepmom—his mother—comes walking in. "The babies are going to stay with me today until it's time for the banquet, and then they will go with your dragon guards," Helle says with a smile. Odette, Kirra, and Luna jump off the bed and go running to Helle. I smile, watching my children willingly go running to their grandmother.

"Okay, boys, I guess I'm all yours. What are we doing?" I ask as I lean back, finishing off my coffee and handing the empty mug to Klaus. Jayce removes the tray from my lap. And then Arnulf slowly starts pulling the blankets down the bed, removing them from me.

Klaus extends a hand to me and bows slightly. "Well, we thought of starting the day off with a nice hot shower, full body massage, and well, who knows what else," he says with a sly smile.

I slide off the bed and into Klaus's waiting arms. I snuggle up against him tightly and wrap my arms around his waist. "Lead on, gentlemen. I'm all yours," I say with a smile. Jayce swoops in and bows down, and sweeps me up into a bridal carry, stealing me away from Klaus. I can't help but start to laugh that my most gentle mate has just stolen me from his boyfriend.

Arnulf runs ahead of us and into the bathroom, starting up the hot water in the mammoth shower that we have. He strips down immediately and beckons me towards him. Reluctantly, Jayce sets my feet on the ground and allows me to go to Arnulf. I remove my nightgown and throw it to the floor off to the side. I take both of Arnulf's hands as he pulls me into the shower with him. He sits me on the shower bench and takes his time wetting my hair, and then starts to massage the shampoo into it. I close my eyes, enjoying the feeling of his fingers digging into my scalp.

I feel him gently rinse the soap for my hair, and then the click of the top of the conditioner bottle sounds in the shower. I feel him starting to massage the conditioner into my hair. Suddenly two sets of lips latch onto both of my breasts. I open my eyes slowly and look down to find both Jayce and Klaus suckling at my breasts. This is definitely a new development. These three have never attempted anything with me together.

I'm moaning softly as I feel Jayce's hand slide down my lower stomach to find my moist center. Slowly, he inserts two fingers into me and starts pumping them gently while his thumb massages my clit. My breathing becomes erratic as I start feeling the coiling tension of my impending orgasm. Arnulf brings his mouth down and covers mine, kissing me deeper than he normally does. I feel his rigid member against my side, gently pulsing against my ribs.

Jayce picks up the pace, and I can feel the early onset flutters of my canal trying to grip at his finger. Klaus releases my breast and uses his fingers instead to torment my nipple. He's quite sneaky when he turns around and sinks his teeth in over his mating mark, sending me over the edge with one of the most powerful orgasms I've had in a while.

I cry out in ecstasy as my hands grip at the bodies that surround me. I have one hand buried in Jayce's hair while the other hand holds Arnulf's ass tightly. I cry out in the throes of my orgasm into Arnulf's mouth. He swallows down my cries and seems to be spurred on by it further. He starts to grind his hot cock into my ribs—I can feel it starting to weep and become slick.

Jayce finally stops his assault on my poor pussy, allowing me to slowly come down from the euphoria I am feeling. The guys take both my arms and assist me in standing. They finish washing me off and then pull me towards the massage table, wrapping me in the softest towel I've ever felt. If this is how they're going to be before every banquet, we may just have to have more banquets.

I look at the massage table before me. The bottom end looks like it splits and can spread open. The top part looks like your typical massage table with a hole for my face to go down into. The guys assist me in sitting up on the table and then steal my towel from me. "So? What do you three have in mind now?" I ask, smiling, looking at the three of them. Anticipation is now getting the better of me. No matter what they decide to do to me, it really doesn't matter because I know it will be done out of love.

Klaus moves forward and pushes me so that I lie down flat on my back on the table. He removes his belt and brings both of my wrists together, and uses his belt to restrain my hands. I raise an eyebrow to look at them curiously because I'm not a fan of being restrained. Thankfully, I trust them, so I will allow them to do whatever they wish to me.

While watching Klaus with rapt attention, Jayce and Arnulf apparently get the bright idea to take the belts from their pants and restrain my ankles to the table. This is getting to be quite interesting. I wonder what exactly inspired this type of play from the three of them. Once fully restrained, I lie back, attempting to relax, watching them.

It's Arnulf that remains at my feet then pushes the two parts of the table apart from each other. He moves himself between my legs to my fully exposed core. The keening call of his bird fills the bathroom, and I can tell that he's very excited. Klaus takes his shirt off and uses it as a blindfold on me. Now, all I have is my sense of touch, my sense of smell, and hearing.

I can feel Arnulf lower his lips to kiss my bare mound as his tongue darts out to lick at my sticky sweet essence. I draw in a sharp breath as he moves to slowly slide the head of his cock between my folds. The anticipation is killing me. Two sets of lips descend on my breasts, again sucking and nibbling at my nipples. I'm trying to writhe and grind to get some sort of penetration out of Arnulf, but yet he still just teases me.

I breathe in deeply and let out a soft moan as he slowly presses his length within me. Jayce and Klaus's hands roam my entire body as Arnulf sets the world's slowest, most teasing pace known to woman. I feel every inch of him sliding deep within my hot depths. I attempt to tighten my internal muscles to hold him in there to spur him to move faster. But with as restrained as I am, there's not much I can do except for feel. Klaus and Jayce begin to move and kiss and nip at my flesh.

I hear the bathroom door open, and by scent I know it's Dominik. I feel him approach and stand by my head. His big strong hands slide down my shoulders and over my breasts that his brother and Klaus had abandoned. Suddenly, his lips descend upon mine, and his mouth assaults mine furiously; our tongues battle for dominance, caressing and sliding over each other.

I guess with the addition of Dominik now, Arnulf has been inspired to pick up the pace. He starts to set a punishing rhythm, making the table squeak as it moves across the floor, propelled by his thrusts. Dominik pulls away from me for a moment, and then I feel the head of someone's cock against my lips. Tentatively, I lick the tip and taste its salty essence. By scent, I know it's Dom, and he slowly attempts to push his length into my mouth.

Arnulf and Dominik work in unison, assaulting me from both ends—when one thrusts in the other one withdraws. I feel that familiar tingle start to spread through my lower abdomen down into my thighs. My breaths become erratic, and I start panting. I open and close my hands rhythmically, wishing I could grip on to somebody. Arnulf cries his release just as my orgasm overtakes me. My muscles clench and milk his length for all that it's worth. Euphoria spreads through me like a warm blanket caressing me and holding me tight. I cry out around Dominik's throbbing shaft. Mercifully, he withdraws and allows me to catch my breath. I feel someone slide down my body, nipping and licking all the way to my engorged mound. Arnulf's now flaccid cock falls free from my depths. I feel empty, but I know it won't last long. He kisses my thigh and moves out of the way.

Someone moves between my legs and thrusts into me in one smooth motion, burying himself to the hilt. I feel my juices run down between my thighs and onto the bench below me. His fingertips dig in, gripping my hips tightly, almost to the point of bruising. My Dominik knows exactly how I like it from him: rough, aggressive, and possessive. I feel a set of mouths return to my nipples, licking and sucking at them. Jayce's and Klaus's hands roam all over my upper body as Dominik sets up a punishing pace.

I can feel him reach down and bite at my lower rib cage, sending sparks of desire through my body. I honestly don't know how these guys do it to me every single time. Just when I think I'm done, they ramp me up again, prime for another massive orgasm.

Jayce and Klaus must sense that I'm stuck from reaching my peak, and they both start to move towards my shoulders. I feel their lips descend on my neck, and my body starts to respond immediately with rhythmic pulses fluttering around Dominik's thrusting cock. My back starts to bow off the table as I start climbing towards my peak yet again. That all too familiar heat that flushes my body washes over me in a gentle wave. My muscles start to coil tighter and tighter, milking Dominik's cock for every drop that it contains. His thrusts start to become erratic, and I know that he's just as close as I am. At that exact moment, Jayce and Klaus both bite me over their mating marks sending me plummeting over the edge, crying out as my orgasm overtakes me. Lights burst behind my eyes as I feel every muscle in my sex clench tightly and pulse. Not too long after I reach my peak Dominik roars out as I start to feel the pulsing jets of his seed spurting within me.

I feel him press gentle kisses against my abdomen up to my rib cage. His hands reach down and undo the restraints at my ankles as Jayce and Klaus undo the ones at my wrist. I am thoroughly sated and ready to take another nap. But I'm pretty sure my guys have another plan for me. Klaus scoops me up in his arms and carries me back over to the shower where it all began.

Klaus and Jayce help me shower, and while in there, those two sneaky bastards decide it's their time to play. I hear Jayce giggle as he stands in front of me, and I look over my shoulder to find Klaus with a bottle of lube in his hand. I'm seriously starting to question where these boys have all these bottles of lube hidden throughout the house. It's as if a lube fairy comes along and miraculously drops it off to them in their time of need.

Jayce slowly lifts my left leg and holds it to his thigh as he thrusts up into me. Several strokes later, I feel Klaus starting to massage my rosette, preparing the muscle for entry. When he feels he's got me nice and loose, he lifts my other leg that Jayce isn't holding and aligns himself up with my back entrance. In one fluid motion, he slowly breaches that tight muscle, inching his way within me. I gasp at feeling so full and throw my head back to rest it on Klaus's shoulder

Jayce brings his free hand up and starts to massage my left breast while lowering his head to take the other nipple into his mouth. As soon as the guys feel that I'm relaxed enough, they decide to start setting their pace. It's not the same punishing pace that Dominik likes to set, it's slow and gentle. Each thrust is drawn out ridiculously before slowly pushing back in yet again. I don't honestly think we've ever made love in the shower standing up, so this is a first for us.

They take excellent care of me, making sure to draw out my pleasure as long as you could possibly believe. Without the two of them supporting my weight, I think I would have been a mass of Jell-o on the floor. I rest both my hands on Jayce's shoulders and stare into his eyes as they pick up their pace. All of us are getting close to the end, barely able to keep from having any erratic movements. My guys tighten their grip on me. I'm the first to cry out, screaming their names at the top of my lungs as a mind-blowing orgasm rips through me. Every muscle in my body seems to contract rhythmically and in time with my heartbeat. My vision's almost blurred; my breaths are just barely panting. Shortly after my orgasm crashes over me, Jayce and Klaus come almost in unison. They embrace me tightly between them, hugging not only me but each other as well.

Out of the corner of my eye, I can see them kissing over my shoulder. It makes me smile to see that there's so much love between them as well as with me. They slowly allow my feet back on the floor as their now flaccid cocks fall free from my body. We take several more minutes to clean each other up, removing most of the evidence of our fun time. I kiss both of them passionately and then leave them to their own devices in the shower as I go to get prepared for the evening.

Honestly, I hate getting dressed up but hopefully, I won't have to do it too often. I return to the main bed chamber and head into the walk-in closet. The stunning blood-red dress that Oberon has sent for me is absolutely breathtaking. It also looks like I'm going to need a Lego master to get it on me. Thankfully, I have the two royal seamstresses as well as Helle present to assist me with this debacle. I can't wait for the boys to see me in this.

CHAPTER 74

Jayce

AFTER HANDLING AND SEEING TO AURORA'S NEEDS, KLAUS AND I REMAIN in the shower taking care of each other for at least the next thirty minutes. Apparently, for tonight, Oberon had set up a second room for us guys to go into to get ready. Within the room, there are different tuxedos for us to wear. Each one varies in shades of grays. The only one who doesn't have a fully grey tux is Alaric, who has blood-red lapels.

The rest of my bond mates are in different states of getting dressed; most of us have the pants and the dress shirt on. One of the male tailors are present in the room with us, helping us get our fancy buttons, tie clips, and cufflinks on properly. For some ridiculous reason, Oberon thought that today would be a great day to wear a cummerbund. The cummerbunds are a mix of slate grey and crimson.

I could tell by the colors chosen for us that Aurora's gown more than likely would be some shade of blood-red. "Well, it's obvious, guys, she's going to be wearing a gown, more than likely according to the accent colors, some shade of red," I say almost sarcastically as if they should know by what they're wearing. Each one looks suspiciously down at his outfit and then back over to me as I motion to the color of the cummerbund and the color of the bow tie that we're wearing.

"That would be the most logical answer," Klaus says as he looks at his cummerbund.

"I was wondering why my suit had this ridiculous colored lapel," Alaric says, looking from his lapel to the cummerbund then to the tie in his hand. I roll my eyes and shake my head at him.

"Obviously, Alaric, since you are King of the Ice Dragons, yours would have more color to it than ours." I roll my eyes slightly after uttering the sentence in a rather uncharacteristic ballsy move for me. He looks at his outfit more closely then studies everyone else's. It suddenly must make sense to him as to why his outfit is different.

We're finally all dressed when Oberon comes walking in—his robes for tonight are the same colors as our tuxes. His flowing robes are almost iridescent in color, one direction looking grey while the next movement takes on a beautiful crimson color. "Greetings and salutations to Your Highnesses," Oberon says in that melodic voice of his as he sweeps into a bow gracefully. Slowly, he stands back up and looks at us. "I'm so pleased to see that what I arranged for you fits so well," he says with a smile and a flourish of his hands.

"Our young queen is ready and waiting for her king to come and get her," Oberon says as he pointedly looks at Alaric. "After all, this is the Winter Palace once known as the Ice Dragon Castle. It would break protocol and tradition for anyone other than the King Consort to escort the Queen," Oberon says in a stately manner as he motions towards the door for Alaric to get his ass moving. It takes several seconds before Alaric fully connects the dots and takes off out the door in a hurry.

"Your Highnesses," Oberon says in a much gentler tone. "Upon the table, there are new crowns for you to match your queen. She would like for all of you to match," he says. And as he waves his hand, the lids from the boxes all pop off and disappear into a shower of glitter.

I'm the first to creep over and take a good look at the crowns he had brought for us. They are similar in design to the crown that the Blood Queen once wore. I look at Oberon questioningly, and he just smiles at me. "Aurora is going to wear her great-grandmother's crown tonight. I just so happened to polish it up a little bit and adjust its sizing to fit her better." He smiles and bows before promptly leaving the room. Within each box is a card with a name and a crown specifically for each of us.

I reach for my crown, and just as he said, it's exactly like the one that was once the Blood Queen's. I walk in front of the mirror with it and set it upon my head. Miraculously the crown moves and resizes to fit my head perfectly. Now I'm really pondering if the crowns can do this. Why is there one specifically for each of us? I can't help but ponder that as I watch everyone else slowly put theirs upon their heads. I will have to ask Oberon about this later.

We take the side corridors heading towards the throne room. The handmaidens usher us in to line up on either side of Aurora's and Alaric's thrones. She and Alaric have not yet made their appearance into the throne room. Nicodeamus is already sitting at Aurora's right-hand side. We get moved and shuffled around to fill in the five remaining seats. Each seat is its own throne, but not as big as Alaric and Aurora have.

The music changes, a beautiful fan fair starts to play, and then the music changes yet again to the song "I am the fire" by *Halestorm."* I smile at the song choice as the doors open wide. Alaric and Aurora walk in hand in hand, smiling. It's now that I notice their hands are shifted to that of their gauntlets. And at this point of the song, the singer says *she is the fire.* Aurora and Alaric raise their empty hand, talons facing up, and blue flames rise at least a foot above their open palms. The *oohs* and *ahhs* that fill the throne room are almost deafening.

Aurora is extruding an aura of confidence and dominance as she walks down the aisle towards the throne. Her head is held high as she maintains the flames as she walks. Her gown is full length with a train. The bodice of the gown appears to resemble dragon scales. The rest of the gown appears to be made of thousands of tiny rubies sewn into the material. She ripples and shines every step she takes; the material seems to flow like blood behind her. Upon reaching the throne, she and Alaric release each other's hands and hold their taloned gauntlets in front of them, allowing the fire to rise. Aurora looks over to her father, and Nicodeamus shifts his hands to that of his gauntlet, and then the flames rise from his hand as well.

Be it a show about or just a sign of unification, it was definitely an impressive feat that gained everyone's attention in the hall. Aurora and Alaric quickly shift their hands back, extinguishing the flames, as does Nicodeamus. They slowly take their seats, and as they sit, we all sit in time with them. Aurora does a very slow nod of her head, and the entire room sits at her command.

I can feel the power radiating off of my mate. She uses every ounce of her dominance to make sure that everyone realizes there shall be no one that stands against her. Nicodeamus rises and addresses the court, thanking everybody for their arrival and taking part in the celebration that is taking place tonight. He announces the complete victory over Vladimir as well as the Strigoi. He names several of the war heroes present in the Dragon Court that assisted in our endeavors. As each of the males comes up, Aurora stands with Alaric, receiving the various pins and medals to place on our allies.

I, myself, and the others were not aware of the awards ceremony that was taking place. It's a nice way to show that people are appreciated and see who is or is not on our side. Oberon periodically comes over and exchanges trays with Alaric, providing him with more medals and ribbons for Aurora to hand out. I can almost bet these little trinkets she's handing out are enchanted. I would dare place a wager that these will be another way for Oberon to weed out anyone who may commit treason against us. A gift to be given in good faith also serves as a little spy to make sure nothing negative happens to our family.

Oberon announces for everybody to retire to the Grand Ballroom for dinner and drinks and engage in dancing and frivolity. Aurora nods slowly and then rises up, taking hold of Alaric's hands. Dimitri and I flank them as they head down the hall and into the ballroom.

The floors are freshly redone in the cedar planks that Aurora had wanted. It's a beautiful blend of red cedar as well as white cedar. The intricate designs flow across the space. As we move towards the front of the ballroom, it's now that the design becomes evident. The pattern mimics dragon scales and is only visible from where Alaric and Aurora are sitting.

Speaking of the happy couple, they drink and eat at the head table, watching the festivities. Nicodeamus and his mate Helle are sitting to their right, also enjoying themselves. Queen Gisella and King Consort Austin are sitting to Aurora's left. It seems the two families are quite close, from what I can tell. I know that our little girl, Tia, was quite taken by their son, Draven. Oh, Goddess above, please let him be her mate. He comes from such a good family. I look up and see the questioning look in Aurora's eyes as she follows my gaze towards Gisella and her mate.

I make the come here motion with my finger and Aurora giggles as she excuses herself from the conversation. Quickly, I meet her halfway, and she wraps her arms tightly around my neck. Her delicate scent is slightly enhanced with honeysuckle. Slowly, we dance gracefully around the ballroom. I am blessed to have this time with my mate; not only are we enjoying ourselves, we are scoping out the attendees. Aurora's beast softly purrs in my embrace, making me feel like I'm the king of the world. Her lips gently kiss me on the underside of my jaw before she runs her nose along my jawline. Whispers move through the crowd seeing our exchange. The queen is being submissive to her Omega. I wink at Aurora, and she smiles against my throat; Alaric's plan is working.

Shortly after the whispers start, Alaric raises his hands and the music changes. He slowly steps down from the royal table and extends his hand in Aurora's direction. She smiles and tilts her head looking at him. Gently, she kisses my cheek then moves to Alaric. Her movements fluid and graceful as she dips into a low bow. Her eyes are downcast, and a smile graces her lips. Playing submissive has become a game between Aurora and Alaric, getting ready for this very moment.

Old school protocols suck. With most dragon houses here being well over the five-hundred-year-old markers, they are stuck in the old ways. Aurora remains bowed low before Alaric till he gently touches under her chin to get her to rise up. Aurora stands up, back straight, and her chin held high. Alaric lowers his head to her and then bears his throat in a move that shocks the entire gathering. Aurora's eyes shift to that of her beast and she stares down at her mate.

"The days of subservience are over." Aurora's voice booms as the temperature in the room drops swiftly. "My great-grandmother, the Blood Queen, bowed to no male!" she says as she helps Alaric to stand at her side as her equal. "I will not stand idly by allowing these archaic traditions to weigh down my daughters," she says boldly as her hands shift to that of her gauntlets.

The double doors to the side of the ballroom open, and Dimitri and Dominik enter with all of Aurora's children. Her daughters each are wearing crimson dresses, a nod to their mother's gown. Little ruby crowns rest upon their heads as they walk hand in hand towards their mother. Marco walks beside all of the princesses, allowing Luna to hold his hand as they walk. Ladon is in an exact replica of his father's suit; he also has a ruby crown upon his head. Aurora motions for her children to line up around her as she looks at the audience. A quick wink to Tia and she shifts her arms to match her mother's gauntlets. Tia's eyes move to her brother, who removes his suit jacket, handing it off to Dominik and rolling up his sleeves. He looks up to Alaric and receives a smile and a wink; Ladon shifts his arms to that of his gauntlets, as well.

Aurora steps forward and motions back to her children. "Some call me a mutt, an abomination," she says with a sexy smirk.

"Well, I am here to tell you this abomination took down Nexus, Vladimir, and united the Great Dragon Houses." Her eyes scan the crowd as the aristocrats start talking to their guards who were at the various battles to verify Aurora's statement.

"We are entering a time of peace and growth; I would love for this to continue for generations to come." She smiles as she steps back to her children. "Any who wish to challenge me for the throne," she pauses dramatically and arches an eyebrow, then makes a sweeping motion with her hands, "meet me in the ring tomorrow morning. I will gladly show you what this abomination can do." Aurora smiles sweetly, then shepherds her children to the main table and gets them settled.

Her ever watchful eyes scan the room slowly. Through the bond, she reaches out to myself and Dominik and asks us to shift and sit on either side of her children. We do so without question and rush over to the table once we return to the ballroom. I choose to sit on the same side that my daughter is on, and Dominik ends up taking the opposite side.

We stay as our wolves for the rest of the evening, ensuring no one that isn't safe gets anywhere near the children. I look up and watch my daughter as she attempts to feed herself at the table. She keeps looking down at me and dropping scraps of food to me. The kid already has the idea to feed what you don't like to the pet in the house. I shake my massive head and then rest my muzzle on my daughter's thigh.

Gently, her tiny fingers run through my thick fur, and I hear her ever so softly going, "daddy daddy daddy." It's amazing how one so little knows who I am even in this form. The majority of the night goes off without a hitch, and we all head off to bed. Dominik and I decide to stay with the children as our wolves tonight to make sure that nothing happens. I know for a fact that my mate has just pissed off a few of the dragon households. I won't be shocked if somebody doesn't make an attempt either on her life or one of the children's. I guess we'll just have to wait and see.

CHAPTER 75

Aurora

Morning's here, and I couldn't be more excited. Maybe it's the sick side of me that loves the idea of going to battle. Or it's just the fact I want to see exactly how many houses stand against us. My mates bring me my breakfast and I eat it in my room with them all present, along with our children. I don't bother to choose an impressive outfit for this morning because in all reality, it's going to get shredded the minute I shift.

As we start to head down to the arena, my father, Marco, Dante, and Edgar flank us as we move through the halls. I start humming to myself Danzig's "Killer Wolf." It's a classic and quite honestly, I quite love the song and the tone of his voice—whoa, baby, is his voice sexy. We make it down to the arena and I step into the ring. My eyes scan the bleachers looking to see how many of the houses are present. I hold my head up high and raise my arms, instantly dropping the temperature in the room. I can do the most evil thing possible and start pulling on their beasts to make them realize exactly how powerful I am. I contemplate this idea for several moments before deciding that this is not the ruler I wish to be.

Two men come stepping through the double doors on the opposite side. Ah yes, the house of Equus. They are a bunch of power-hungry fools. "What is one lone hybrid going to do against the likes of us?" Tegan asks without a hint of remorse. His twin, Liam, steps forth and lightly bows his head. "You know we have to test you." he says in a tone that tells me he's really not sure this is such a good idea. At least one of the twins might have brains.

I smile and lightly dip my head to them. I see the panic on Gisella's and Austin's faces. The house of Equus comes from the same island of the Bronze Dragon Kingdom. They are shocked and appalled, rightfully so, that one of their noble houses dare to stand against me.

I lightly bow my head to Gisella and Austin and mentally send a message to Alaric to repeat to them. I watch the moment the words leave his lips, and they both nod and bow their heads lightly to me. I just pretty much informed them that the house of Equus will be short two heirs by the end of this morning.

Now I'm pretty sure that these two are a mix of Green and Bronze Dragons. To me, it says their dragons will have a decent size and no real punch to their hits, and they are not immune to ice. I'm seriously contemplating not even bothering to shift for this battle; I can end it quickly with just a thought. But now, I will give my people the battle that they are looking for.

Tegan and Liam end up shifting at the same time. As I suspected, both of them took more after the Green Dragon side than the Bronze, according to their coloration. I shift to my beast, and I watch as Liam raises his head sharply in shock as to what he's seeing before him. By my coloration alone, you can pretty much assume I have an ice weapon. You can also tell my lineage of my great-grandmother, the Blood Queen. She was the most vicious dragon in the history of our people.

I practically snarl as I look at them with a feral grin. Standing still, I click my talons together, waiting to see which of these two males will make the mistake of charging. Tegan is the first to attack, and I'm quite thankful for it. I may be able to spare Liam if he knows what's good for him. I dodge out of the way of Tegan's breath weapon, then roll and jump to launch up onto one of the pillars in the colosseum. I remain on the pillar for a moment till he whips his head around and starts blowing his breath weapon at me.

As soon as his maw is wide open and the moment I see fire coming at me, I jump. At this point, I am soaring through the air in his blind spot. He won't realize that I'm almost on him till shortly after he closes his mouth. I land with a thud just above his nose. Quickly I sink my talons into his skin as I make my way up his maw. He starts thrashing his head around wildly, trying to shake me loose, but I refuse to let go. I see Liam suddenly start to back up into a corner. He shifts back to his human form and just stays pressed against the wall.

Tegan keeps thrashing his head around, still trying to throw me off. He takes several stumbling steps forward and attempts to ram his head into the wall. Just before he does, I flip myself around behind the two pitiful horns on his head. He crashes his own forehead into the sharp corner of the pillar, cracking his skull and allowing blood to ooze down his face. He starts to wobble, disoriented from the impact, and I go to work.

My big decision for this is: do I freeze him and then break the ice or do I rip his throat out and bathe the arena in blood? I'm going for option B. I slide down his neck as he still thrashes. He tries to bring his clawed hand up to grab me, but instead all he does is catch his own scales. I get underneath his jaw hanging upside down and lash out with my talons quickly. I catch part of the artery on the left side of his throat, watching the blood shoot out in spurts.

I maintain my grip and then reach out with my other taloned hand and slice the artery on the right side. As his heart beats, spurts of blood escape through the incision in his throat. Every beat, another spurt. I just hang there upside down, watching him bleed out slowly. I leap off his body when I feel him starting to get woozy. I land on all fours and start growling at him with my tail thrashing wildly behind me.

Several minutes later, his body crashes to the floor. The arena goes dead silent; you can hear the lub-dub of his heartbeat as it starts to stutter and falter. I'm not merciless, so I stare at him for several more seconds before shifting back to my human form. Quickly, I raise my arms up, sending a giant ice spike up from the floor through his chest, impaling him to end his suffering.

Alaric jumps down into the arena with me and throws a robe around my shoulders. I look back at Liam, and he comes crawling over to me on his hands and knees. He starts begging for forgiveness, telling me that his brother bullied him into standing against me and that he really didn't want to do it. I sense that Liam is an Omega, and just with that knowledge, I know that he had no choice but to follow his brother's instructions. Gently, I place my hand on his head and bid him to rise.

When he's standing almost at eye level with me, he can't maintain eye contact. He tries twice but can't look for more than several seconds, which further backs the proof that he is an Omega. I gently kiss both of his cheeks and tell him that he's forgiven. I tell him to go back to his family and tell them about the boon I have given him. He drops to his knees and kisses my hands before getting up and running out of the arena quickly. I look back to Alaric before he starts to yell.

"Anyone else wish to stand against our queen?" The anger coming off him in waves is almost unbearable. He's getting so tired of me having to fight constantly just to keep our people and us safe.

We watch the arena for any signs of someone coming to challenge me next. When nothing happens, he turns slowly in a circle before announcing. "The battles are over. We will all have lunch together, and at the next sign of any kind of betrayal I will wipe out an entire bloodline," he says sternly as he snuggles me against his side. Alaric is finally acting like the king that he should have been born to be.

Alaric leads me back to our suite and into the master bathroom. Jayce and Dominik already have the shower running and set to the perfect temperature. I drop the robe to the floor and head straight for the shower, where my boys pamper the hell out of me.

"I'm sorry, my love, if I could do these battles for you, I would," Alaric says solemnly as he lowers his head, semi-defeated.

I quirk an eyebrow looking at him, and then tilt my head to the side. "We both knew coming into this that I would be faced with challengers almost constantly. That is until they have faith that I am not like Vladimir and that as a hybrid, I can follow the old dragonic traditions," I say, trying to soothe his nerves as Jayce works the shampoo through my tangled bloody hair.

Alaric comes to stand outside the stall leaning his forearm against the wall and then presses his forehead to his forearm. He sighs softly, then looks over at me. "I know, but it's still not fair.

Females are not supposed to be the ones that battle. But, for some reason, most of the males have no respect and raise a talon to my mate." He says on a huff, half-sounding sad. Out of the corner of my eye, I see Klaus come over and start to rub his shoulders.

"I know with my people, females are revered, honored, and spoiled rotten. The fact that the dragons have no problem battling her concerns me greatly for Tia's sake," Klaus says as he rests his forehead against the back of Alaric's shoulder. I watch his arms slowly snake around Alaric's ribs and hold him tightly.

"I know, and that's the one thing that scares me about my daughter being in the world. Who's to say someone isn't going to challenge her, figuring that they may be able to conquer her." Alaric lifts his head and looks at me. And I see the fear in his eyes.

"I'm not as worried as you are, my love," I say softly, leaning my head back as Jayce massages my scalp and starts putting the conditioner in my hair. "I've already foreseen who her mate is. He comes from a great house with wonderful parents. We just have to wait until the proper time for them to meet," I say with a gentle smile upon my lips as I wait to see Alaric's reaction.

He whips his head up and looks at me, eyes open wide, jaw slack. It takes several moments for him before he's able to formulate words. "You know who it is already?"

I nod slowly. "If my vision is correct, I believe, eventually, Tia will end up a bride of one of Gisella's sons," I say with a smile. My words bring Alaric comfort, and he nods slowly.

"I wouldn't mind her marrying into that house. They're good loyal friends and have offered us a ton of aid when we needed it." He smiles as he straightens up and pats Klaus's hands on his chest. "I would be honored if one of their sons became our daughter's mate."

"As would I, but keep in mind that not all visions come true." I raise both eyebrows at him. "Dominik and Jayce will tell you that once upon a time I saw myself giving birth to a boy and a girl, one with white hair, one with black. The babies I saw were twins, and that has not come to pass." I tilt my head to the side for him to gain some understanding.

"Sometimes these premonitions are more wishful thinking than actual for telling the truth about the future." I smile as Jayce finishes rinsing my hair. I step out of the shower and into the waiting robe that Dominik has for me.

"Well, for our daughter's sake, I'm going to wish that your dream comes true," Alaric says as he gently kisses my temple and then walks off with Klaus hand in hand. I have a sneaking suspicion my mate is going for a little stress relief, and Klaus has offered himself.

Dimitri comes walking in with food and beverages with all the little ones in tow. All of my children are shifted to that of their animals and running amuck through my massive bathroom. I can't help but laugh watching each one of them as they play and roll around with each other. Arnulf moves over to the extremely large tub in the room and starts filling it. "I promised the children they can play in the water for a while as you eat your breakfast. I hope you don't mind," he says with a smile and playfully motions his head towards the tub. I nod gently, and he continues to fill the tub with just enough water that even the littlest one can stand without their head going under.

One by one, Arnulf brings each of the children into the tub and then sits on the stairs splashing water at them playfully. He is such a great father to the children. He plays with each of them equally and has no favorites. But I have a sneaking suspicion that will change when he has one of his own. They continue to play and splash while I eat my meal. Eventually, my father comes wandering in with his mate.

"I hope you don't mind my intrusion, daughter, but I wished to see how you were," Nicodeamus says as he sits on the bench close by, dragging his mate into his lap.

"You're never intruding, Father, that is unless it's the bedroom and I have the door locked." I smile and laugh, and he just shakes his head at me. "The battle went much easier than I suspected this morning, and I was quite shocked to find that only one house stood against me," I say before I bite into the strip of bacon.

"I was kind of shocked myself to see that the house of Equus decided to try to stage a coup. They are not the smartest nor the strongest of the dragon families. But I do have to say you handled it beautifully." My father reaches over and grabs a biscuit off the tray, and starts snacking on it. "You showed mercy that even your great-grandmother wouldn't have. You are making a statement that you bear her power but not her blood thirst. You may just win all the houses over on that stance alone."

"I don't wish to be a tyrant," I state flatly as I stare into my coffee mug. "I don't wish to have to rule the kingdoms with my talons. I wish for peace and prosperity for our people more than anything else in the world." I take a small sip of my coffee and then hold the mug between both my hands. "These species have known nothing about war and loss for the last two generations. I wish to change their perception of the Lycans, as well as the Dragons." My eyes move to Arnulf as he plays with the babies and then back to my father. "Change begins with me, and I will be damned if my children will have to do as I have done the last two hundred and thirty years."

"You have no idea how proud it makes me to hear you say those words," my father says with a smile as his mate leans into his side, holding on to him tightly. "We shall make the change happen slowly but surely so that everybody is happy and comfortable. I do suggest, though, reparations to be paid to the families that lost members in Vladimir's coup." His eyes drop down to the mug that he had picked up. "Money doesn't fix things, but it can help elevate the living conditions that those who were left behind are living in."

I ponder my father's statement and think it over thoroughly. "I believe what you said has a lot of merit, Dad. Quietly take a poll and see which species besides the Great Bears have been afflicted the most by Vladimir's actions. The Great Bears need to have their village rebuilt as well as brought up to more modern conveniences." I sigh softly.

"They took the greatest hit because of Vladimir slaughtering their people pointlessly." I stare down at my mug before taking another sip. My eyes drift up, and I look at Dimitri who is now smiling proudly at me.

"I am most grateful to you, baby girl, for looking out for my people. They may be resistant to change, but I will help you all that I can." He smiles and bows slightly to me.

"I know that you wish to try to heal old wounds quickly, but to be honest, actions speak louder than words, and it's going to take time for my people to trust anybody outside of their community," he says as he pulls his daughter, Odette, out of the tub and starts drying her off.

Nodding slowly, I remain watching him. "Would you be so kind as to go speak with your people and advise them as to what I wish to do for them?" I ask, sounding slightly unsure of myself. "For a fact, I know the bears will be quite resistant to any help given to them by someone who even has a drop of Lycan blood in their bloodline."

"We will smooth things over with them. Me going alone will not make the statement that you wish for change. It'll appear as though you are scared to go stand before them," Dimitri says as he stares down at his daughter, drying her off. "Whenever you're ready, we can go, or you can invite them here or to the Marelup Castle, whichever you're more comfortable with." Dimitri raises an eyebrow at me and I nod slowly.

"We will go meet with your clan tomorrow afternoon." I reach out to Arnulf through the bond, requesting he sends a message to Dimitri's clan. "Today, we spend time as a family and figure out how to help everyone."

CHAPTER 76
Dominik

I spent the better half of the day yesterday planning for the trip down to see Dimitri's clan. We enlisted the help of several other dragons just to be able to spread the family out and ensure our safety. The flight over was easy and quick, and the children enjoyed it immensely.

Aurora was on Alaric, directing him to where there was a clearing big enough for the dragons to land. Once everyone disembarks their rides, the extra dragons take off, leaving us with just our family—Edgar, Dante, Marco, and of course Nicodeamus and my mom. Dimitri shifts almost immediately once we come to the stream that Aurora had told us about. He rises up on his hind paws and roars several times, announcing our arrival

Several minutes pass before a chorus of roars answer him. At this point, his daughter, Odette, has weaseled her way out of her clothing and shifted to that of her bear cub. The cute little darling toddles alongside her father. Poor Dimitri has to walk painfully slow for her to keep up. It was probably the most adorable thing watching that little cub trying to keep up and attacking her father's hind leg.

I look over to see Aurora smirking and shaking her head, trying to stifle a laugh. "So, sweetness, what's got you borderline cracking up over there?" I ask as I give her a dazzling smile and a wink. I know something's going on that I don't know about, and I'm quite curious to find out what it is.

"Well, you see," she says as she walks up alongside me. "Little Odette is purposely attacking her father because she wants a ride. Dimitri told her if she shifted, she was going to walk the whole way as her bear to be properly introduced to the clan."

Aurora starts laughing. "Odette has my wonderful temperament and because her daddy's not listening, she has decided she's going to keep biting him until he lets her get a piggyback ride." As soon as Aurora finishes the sentence, she starts cracking up laughing.

Dimitri's head whips around and glares at her and issues a soft rumbling growl. Which has the absolute opposite effect that he was hoping for: she starts cracking up even harder. She's full-on belly laughing with tears streaming from her eyes, almost ready to double over holding her stomach. I just raise my brows and look between Dimitri and Aurora, then over to Alaric, and he just shakes his head, looking at me.

"Aurora can't take him seriously," he says to me and starts laughing himself. "She knows all too well all she has to do is nip him, and he'll pretty much roll over and give her his belly," Alaric says, still laughing. Dimitri turns and growls at Alaric this time.

He growls right back at him and then starts laughing harder. "Yeah, bring it, furball. I'll roast your ass," Alaric says with a chuckle.

Even though Alaric is joking, both of Dimitri's eyebrows shoot up in mock shock. Then I hear the familiar crack of Aurora's hand slapping Alaric on the shoulder. "You will do no such thing. Do you want me to put you on a ban? Because I will!" Aurora says, raising her eyebrow and crossing her arms over her ample chest.

I just look between the two of them, and I have got to ask the question. "Love, what the hell do you mean by putting him on a ban?" I ask with the utmost level of confusion evident in my voice.

"Well," she says as she uncrosses her arms and does the "oh well" with her hands palms up facing the sky. "Being put on a ban means this: no playing hide the sausage, no riding the pony, basically zero sexual contact with me." She smiles and then blows a kiss at Alaric and tilts her head while looking ever so sweetly.

"Just think of it this way, Dom," she says, then snuggles up against my side. "He fucks up; it's your gain." She smiles and then nips at my jaw before bouncing off.

The look of shock on Alaric's face is quite comical. I don't think the king has ever been put on a ban or ever grounded in his entire existence. The fact that Aurora just stated that as if she had planned it definitely threw him off his game.

I look over at Jayce, and he starts laughing. "Don't look at me, cause if she puts him on a ban, I know she's going to make me put him on a ban." Jayce turns around, looks at Alaric, and mouths *I'm sorry.*

Alaric quickly turns and looks at Klaus. Klaus looks shocked; his eyes dart between Jayce and Aurora and then back over to Alaric.

"Oh no, my friend, I'm Switzerland in this shit. She put you on a ban; he put you on a ban. I'm going to just go on strike altogether because, yeah. You both scare me." Klaus throws his hands up in defeat, trying to show that he is not contesting or fighting anything. He is unwilling to be involved in this conversation.

Alaric huffs and walks off, dragging his son Ladon behind him. I look over to my brother and he's slowly passing a sleeping Luna over to Aurora. She smiles as she nuzzles her littlest toddler and then looks up at me. "You're next, Dom, you're next." Her eyes flare when she says the word next. I know in my heart that she absolutely means it when she says it. I see Arnulf sneak up alongside her and give her a peck on her cheek. "Yeah, you too, big guy." She lightly punches him in the shoulder as she situates Luna in her arms.

I watch little Luna play with her mother's hair as we walk towards the village that is now in sight. By the time we reach the first row of houses, Luna has part of Aurora's hair braided. A big burly man comes out to greet Dimitri and Odette. Not knowing the new man, Odette's little cub scoots underneath her father and peeks out from beneath his chest. Aurora walks up and lays a hand on Dimitri's shoulder. "It's good to see you again, Alpha Karl," she says with a slight dip of her head.

"Congratulations on your decisive victory. I must say it was quite impressive." He slightly bows his head, never taking his eyes off of Aurora. It's now that I figure out as to why she's holding Luna. Her instinct to protect Luna and shield her from things is what is going to keep her massive temper in check. Especially since my niece is an Omega and scares very easily.

Aurora looks over to Klaus and motions for him to take Dimitri and give him his clothes. Both the guys wander off into the woods briefly before returning with a fully dressed Dimitri. On the other hand, Odette has decided to remain as her cub, now hiding between her mother's ankles. "Karl, old friend," Dimitri says in a booming voice as he extends one hand and then wraps his arm in a modified bro hug around the Alpha. They greet each other and start speaking in their native tongue.

Aurora rolls her eyes and looks at the two of them. "You two jackasses do realize that I can understand you perfectly? And to speak in your native tongue is pointless and rude?" The Alpha looks up, shocked, as his eyes dart between Dimitri and Aurora.

"This is an old dialect; there is no way someone as young as you could possibly know what we're saying," he says harshly. Aurora turns to me, kisses my cheek, and puts Luna in my arms. *Uh oh, shit just got real.*

She goes to stand before the Alpha and stares at him. Her eyes shifting to that of her beast as I watch the scales ripple down the back of her neck, disappearing into her shirt. I can see the twitchiness that she's getting in her hands as she opens and closes her fist several times, trying not to shift to her gauntlets. Aurora answers the Alpha in the ancient dialect, stunning him immediately. Shortly after, an almost oppressive wave of Alpha power booms out from her, causing him to waver. Little Luna tenses in my arms as I turn my back to shield her from the brunt of it. "Just because I am young does not mean that I am not knowledgeable."

Aurora goes on to list Karl's entire bloodline back almost a thousand years. She then decides to start spewing the knowledge of the clan going back to its beginnings. The Alpha is stunned completely and left rendered speechless. Even Nicodeamus is shocked at the history she is verbalizing. I can only assume that this knowledge came from Gallus. She looks over to Dimitri, then bows her head to him ever so slightly, and then presses her nose under his jaw. Soon as she makes contact with Dimitri, the wave of power ceases. She moves quietly back over to Alaric. Along the way, she grabs Luna from me.

"Please, forgive me for my insolence. I meant no disrespect for someone as knowledgeable and powerful as you." He sighs with his eyes still downcast, completely defeated. He somehow managed to remain standing during Aurora's wave of power that I must question later. "The meeting hall is ready for us to sit and chat. But realize, there are others older than I, that are more set in their ways and their beliefs about the Lycans." His tone is completely defeated; his shoulders are not held as proudly as they were before. He moves slowly, carefully pacing his steps over to the meeting hall.

Dimitri scoops up Odette and carries her, following directly behind the Alpha. Soon after, his daughter and granddaughter come out to meet him. He quickly does introductions and lets them meet Odette as well as the rest of the family. I'm watching the entire clan, and I still feel as if something is bound to happen. Maybe it's my years of being an enforcer, or it could be the years of constantly having battles within my father's pack.

Once inside the meeting hall, Dimitri stands before all of the elders and starts laying out the plans that we had all gone over yesterday. We figured as a family it would be better for Dimitri to relay the plans to his people than for any of us to do it. Aurora has both Luna and Odette in her lap; both girls are watching their Papa Bear intently.

I can tell the moment that Aurora starts putting thoughts and ideas into Dimitri's mind. His eyes take on that slight gold glow of his bear as they speak. The course of the conversation almost immediately changes which throws the Alpha off. "What is the meaning of this?" the Alpha says as he stands, looking between Aurora and Dimitri. "Are you this wolf's puppet?" he asks, slamming his fists down on the tabletop.

Dimitri stands abruptly, sending the chair he was sitting in flying backward. Fur ripples up and down his forearms as he stares at the Alpha. "I am no one's puppet," he says with the distinctive growl of his bear evident in his voice. His eyes are glowing brightly as he stares at Karl. Dimitri does not notice that a slight tinge of frost is starting to coat the table surrounding his hands. I raise an eyebrow looking at Aurora and motioning with my eyes to Dimitri's hands. She smiles and nods and gets that sadistic look in her eyes. She's obviously up to something.

"I shall tell you what. I shall leave the meeting since Karl is obviously threatened by an Alpha female." She looks at Dimitri and raises a brow. "Just remember, love, WWAD," she says and ends it with the most sick, twisted smile I have ever seen grace her ruby red lips.

Dimitri gives her a curt nod, and she leaves with Alaric, my brother, and Arnulf in tow. "Why are these two still here?" he practically snarls as he looks at Klaus and me. Well, he doesn't realize that Aurora pretty much just gave the kill order for the Alpha if he gets out of line. "And what is this WWAD mean?" he asks, still snarling, looking between myself and Dimitri. I just start to laugh.

"The short version," I say, sounding way too jovial. "What would Aurora do?" I smile as I feel my canines descend, and I give him a wolfish smile. "You have a thing against wolves, yet, it was my people. My Dire Wolves were the ones who stood guard around your people during the assault on the castle. And now you attempt to shun me, my mate, my brother, as well as my bond mate Klaus." I narrow my eyes as I look at him. He's starting to realize how deep of a hole he has just dug himself into.

CHAPTER 77
Dominik

DIMITRI LOOKS DOWN AND NOTES THE FROST AROUND HIS HANDS AND smiles. It's that kind of smile that even Hannibal Lecter would probably be afraid of. "Elders, Alpha," Dimitri says in the most commanding voice I have ever heard come from him. "I wish to invoke the right of challenge." The room explodes in shouts and hushed whispers as everyone looks around, chatting with each other. I can feel through the bond that Aurora is ecstatic with Dimitri's request. At this point, Klaus leaves the room taking his daughter with him quickly.

Alpha Karl stands there, fur rippling up and down his arms and the bridge of his nose. The rage coming off him is quite palatable in the air. "How dare you!" he says, enunciating each word tinging the syllables in venom. "You leave to work for the wolves! You abandon the female carrying your child, and you dare come in here requesting to battle me?" he says, his bear's growl evident in his voice as he stares at Dimitri, attempting to intimidate him.

The oldest elder stands now; his arthritis-ridden hand sticks out from the long sleeves of his robe as he raises it to silence the room. "The Kovac line is the oldest of us all. If he had been present before your father, he would have been Alpha, and his bloodline would be in charge right now." The elder says as his eyes begin to faintly glow. "I have seen three Alphas come and go over my life-span. None as disrespectful as you are Karl," he says with a slight tremble to his voice due to age.

A second elder, just slightly younger stands next. He lowers his head as he looks at Dimitri. "We, the elders, approve your request to battle. It's about time someone shows this male what it means to be a real Alpha." Dimitri stands tall, then raises his fist over his heart and lowers his head in deference to the elder. All six of the elders repeat the exact same motion that Dimitri had done. The current Alpha, Karl, is sputtering, unable to form words. He's practically foaming at the mouth with how angry he is.

"We'll see you in the ring, I suppose," I say with a smile as I walk over to Dimitri and pat him on his shoulder. Dimitri just smiles at me and nods his head before we leave the room peacefully and quietly. We start walking towards where I suppose the challenge ring is. There's Aurora with the rest of the family in the stands, each with clusters of oak leaves to act as pom poms.

Aurora comes over and jumps up into Dimitri's arms quickly and kisses him. "I'm so proud of you," she says as she smiles brightly up at him.

"I'm only doing what's right, baby girl. Nothing more, nothing less," Dimitri says as he presses a kiss to Aurora's forehead. She smiles and then suddenly bites her wrist and shoves it in Dimitri's mouth. His eyes widen in shock as we see some of her blood dripping out of the corners of his mouth. Through the bond, I hear her explain to him what she's doing. Even though he does not need the edge. Her accelerated healing factor would be quite beneficial for him to have for when the fight is over. She goes on to say that it's easiest now to give him her blood than when there's a crowd.

I watch him take several large gulps before he removes her wrist from his mouth and licks the wound to seal it. She bounces up on her tippy toes and licks her own blood off of his face. It's probably the most erotic thing that I've watched in the last thirty-six hours. She smiles and then smacks him on the ass. "Now be a good teddy bear and beat that asshole's ass and become Alpha," she says much more jovially than she would normally say.

"If you feel he's a threat, eliminate him," she states plainly. She nuzzles him underneath his jaw, showing him affection, and with the gathering bears shows she's submissive to him. They know what a powerhouse she is, and for her to bow to him only adds to the fear she's trying to spread.

Dimitri removes his shirt and hands it to her, and she clutches it to her chest tightly. He then walks into the center of the ring after kicking off his shoes. Aurora comes over and hops into my lap, wrapping her arms around my neck. "Don't worry, Dom, he's got this," she says, smiling as she rubs her face along my cheek. She's extra affectionate, so I can only imagine that there's another heat cycle on the horizon. It's been almost six months since the babies were born. And almost a month since the last one stopped nursing. It's about that time.

The old Alpha enters the ring and shifts, wrecking the clothes that he was wearing. Aurora tilts her head, studying him, quite puzzled. Her laugh carries across the challenge ring. "He's so tiny. It's cute!" she squeals when she says the word cute, which gets her a deep growl from the now-shifted Alpha.

Aurora seriously doesn't care. "My baby girl's going to be bigger than that." She starts to laugh harder then throws her arms up in the air.

"What the hell. You call that a Great Bear." She points right at the alpha. "He's mediocre at best." She screams at the top of her lungs as she bounces in my lap, unfortunately, causing a very painful erection. "Oh hell. Even I'm bigger than that when I shift." she says as she now suddenly stands up and has her ass in my face.

Alaric and the rest of the guys are watching Aurora taunt the Alpha. All of them laughing hysterically because what she's saying is true. Being the red-blooded male that I am and that peach of an ass in front of me, I grip her hips and then bite her firmly. I draw blood and get a squeal from her as she sits back down suddenly. "Naughty naughty, little mate," I say to her, whispering in her ear.

Slowly, I take the tip of my tongue and trace the outer shell of her ear down to her neck. I then half bite my mating mark, causing her to shiver almost uncontrollably in my lap. "Now be a good girl, and sit here for Daddy, and maybe later I'll give you a treat," I say, hoping that the offering of naughty sex would appease her for now.

Aurora's eyes turn back to me suddenly. She raises an eyebrow, and I just nod at her; she can see I'm not joking. She nods emphatically, agreeing and suddenly being the most quiet, perfectly behaved female I have ever seen in my entire life. Just as I regain my focus on the ring, Dimitri's bear bursts into existence. The earth shakes as his front paws hit the ground. He's almost twice the size of the other bear in the ring. Aurora claps her hands and then looks back at me quickly, making sure that she's not overstepping the bounds that I'd set for her. I want her to be proud of her mate. I want her to show her support, so I smile and give her a nod.

Dimitri charges the Alpha before we know it and bowls him over, almost launching him into the air. We hear the crack of several bones as Karl hits one of the pillars outlining the arena. Dimitri raises up on his hind paws and roars again, swiping his paws in the air, taunting the downed Alpha. The Alpha gets up quickly and charges, trying to ram his head into Dimitri's stomach. Dimitri takes the hit and then lands full force on the Alpha's back. He splats him to the ground and moves quickly to protect his stomach. He brings his massive jaws down on the back of the neck of the current Alpha. He starts applying pressure, growling, trying to force his submission. Aurora is bouncing in my lap, clapping her hands furiously as she watches the scene unfold.

After what seems like forever, the Alpha shifts back to his human form, which for them is the sign of submission. Dimitri backs away and lets him up. Aurora starts stepping down off the bleachers when another bear tackles her to the ground with his mouth around her throat. He's made one vital mistake, though. Aurora is on her back, therefore able to attack him directly. She remains compliant for several minutes, which shocks the rest of us.

I start to move forward, and she raises her hand to stop me; she's got a plan. The bear that's holding her throat can't see her face or her eyes. She winks at me, and just as the old Alpha starts taunting Dimitri, Aurora's hands fly up and shift immediately. She sends her talons through the bear's throat and through his chest. Blood spurts out in all directions, coating her and the ring in blood. The bear that had her did manage to puncture her neck in three places, but nothing life-threatening.

She throws the bear off of her with the help of Alaric and me. We flank her immediately as she walks towards the old Alpha, still bleeding.

"Oh, how the mighty have fallen," she says. Her eyes move to the elders, who bow their heads, pretty much giving her permission to seek her revenge. "You dare attack a royal," she says softly as a pleasant smile slowly creeps across her crimson lips.

She reaches up and touches one of the holes in her neck. It's slowly starting to close; she looks at her own blood on her fingertip and then licks it off slowly. "Your guy managed to draw blood; I'm impressed. But not impressed enough to spare your life," she says ever so calmly. Slowly she shakes her head from side to side as she stares at him.

"Hey, D?" Aurora says while Dimitri remains behind the old Alpha. "Remember how I explained that new trick of mine." Dimitri nods, Aurora smiles. "Do it," she says with such finality and smile.

Dimitri's eyes start to glow like that of his bear, you can hear the rumble from him. We feel a pull through the bond from him as he starts to gather strength, for what, I'm not sure. Suddenly, he hits the Alpha in his back flat palmed. Shockingly enough, I'm sprayed with blood as I now see a large spike of ice sticking out of the Alpha's chest with what's left of his heart around the tip. All of our eyes go wide, even Nicodeamus is shocked. Aurora starts to clap her hands, looking at Dimitri as the Alpha falls to the ground.

Dimitri stands there shocked. Looking at the palm of his hand, wondering exactly how he did that. Aurora smiles and goes up and hugs him tightly. "Apparently, I can do my ice attack remotely," she says and smiles. "I tested it when we were in the meeting hall. When I had you freeze the table."

She smiles ever so sweetly. "Just now, yeah, that was all me using you to impale him." Dimitri smiles and then leans down and gathers Aurora up in a passionate kiss. We just start laughing because the freak factor just went up by twenty. When I didn't think our family could get any stranger, here we are kicking it up a notch, taking it to the next level.

The elders approach and advise the clan that Dimitri is now their Alpha. Dimitri blinks his eyes twice and releases Aurora, smiling with a slight blush to his cheeks. He embraces his countrymen one at a time. Each of them swearing fealty to him and to our family. He walks off with the elders to relay our plans to help rebuild the clan. Aurora smiles and looks at me and then waggles her eyebrows.

"So?" She bites her bottom lip seductively. "When do we get to play there, Daddy?" she asks.

Ever since one of the little girls in our family called me Daddy Dom, it's now become Aurora's new favorite nickname for me. Part of it freaks me out, the other part makes me hard as a rock.

"Later, sweetness, later," is all I say to her before smacking her on her ass.

One of the elders breaks off from the pack and decides to give us a clan tour. We go from house to house, meeting each of the families. Most are thankful that Dimitri and Aurora removed the tyrant from his rank. There's only one house that's still upset that there's a Lycan in control. But as the elder put it, they lost most of their family members because of Vladimir. It was going to take a little bit before they decided to trust again.

Aurora hands off her daughters to Arnulf, and the four of us wolves go out to hunt. Alaric and Arnulf remain behind, helping to prep for the big banquet that we were going to have in celebration of Dimitri taking over. The four of us roam over the countryside for what seems like hours. We successfully manage to kill four wild boar and a stag. Aurora's beast shoulders the stag as Klaus takes two of the boar. Jayce and I pick up the last two to carry. We make it back to camp and the local butcher smiles, clapping loudly. He's ecstatic that we have plenty of fresh meat for the celebration.

We party into the night as Dimitri gets to hang out with his clan. Aurora stays with all five of her children, almost isolated away from the rest of the group. My brother and Arnulf sit by her side, helping with the children. Alaric and I stand shoulder to shoulder, watching her and the others at the party. "Is she alright?" I ask softly, hoping for Alaric to shed some light on what's going on.

Alaric draws in a deep breath, and his eyes glow faintly. Within moments Nicodeamus approaches and looks between his daughter and us. "Ah, I see what concerns the two of you." He sighs and sips at his whiskey. "She's allowing Dimitri to have his moment in the sun. And she knows most of the bears aren't comfortable with the wolves' presence." Nicodeamus sighs and looks between Dimitri and Aurora.

Dimitri notices the looks that Alaric and Nicodeamus keep giving me. He slowly approaches and then looks over at Aurora. "Why is she sitting with the children over by themselves?" He furrows his brows, just as confused as the rest of us.

"I don't think she wants to steal your thunder," I say softly and keep an eye on Aurora and the children. Jayce has pulled Aurora and Luna into his lap, kissing both of their temples.

"Bullshit!" Dimitri says firmly before walking over to Aurora and the children. Odette immediately latches onto her father. Aurora and Jayce start to laugh at the little one's antics. We can see the range of emotions that cross Aurora's face as she smiles up at Dimitri. He kisses Aurora's full lips before coming back over to us. "No problems, Luna is anxious, and Aurora is making sure she feels calm and safe." He smiles as he snuggles Odette tightly before heading back over to his other daughter and grand-daughter.

Aurora's eyes glow faintly, and soon Marco is by her side. He kneels before her and lowers his head to her. Luna practically launches out of her mother's arms and into Marco's. I'm shocked witnessing the exchange. My eyes quickly dart over to Nicodeamus. He smirks and shakes his head. "She's his mate. Until she matures, she will seek him out for comfort but not understand why."

Nicodeamus smiles just before he kills off his drink. "When she gets close to maturing, Marco will be sent to either the Winter Palace or the Summer Chalet." Nicodeamus smiles and sets his glass down.

"He's lucky to have lived so long without a mate. Luna is blessed to have such a good, strong male," Nicodeamus says before moving off to join Dimitri.

The rest of the night goes off without a hitch. Aurora has finally accomplished what she had set out to do. All of her mates are in positions of power within their own species. Now is the time for change and growth for all involved.

CHAPTER 78

Aurora

WE ARRIVE HOME AROUND LUNCHTIME, AND WE SETTLE BACK INTO THE Alpha House with the German Lycan pack. To be perfectly honest, I feel the most at peace here and the safest. Deep in my heart, I know this is where I was always meant to be. The guys are off getting things settled, and I'm in the kitchen cooking for everyone. I already called the butcher, and he dropped off some fresh stag meat for me to prepare.

Elsa and Helle soon join me and act as my sous chefs, chopping and marinating what I need done. I've decided to prepare a stag carbonnade with all the fixings. Tia is helping Odette and Luna with peeling the potatoes and putting them in the cutter. Elsa pulled out a child-safe cutter. All they have to do is drop the potato in and press the handle to make slices. Tia is such a good big sister, and I know she will be a wonderful mother one day.

Ladon finally joins us with Kirra in tow. I hand them the cloves of garlic and put them in charge of peeling them and putting them in the press. I watch them work together, and they divide the job up between them. All of my children are helping with the dinner, and it makes my heart swell. I kiss my stepmom and Elsa on the cheek and step outside to where the stag is hanging.

I size up the stag then head back inside to grab large pots and trays. The picnic table becomes my prep station. I shift my hands to my gauntlets and start butchering the stag into the prime cuts of meat. Boris, the butcher, returns to see if I need help, and he stops dead in his tracks watching me. "My Queen?" he says hesitantly as I cut the back strap free.

"Oh! Hi Boris. This is an excellent stag you brought me. Please tell me you and your mate will be joining us for dinner tonight?" I ask ecstatically, hoping he says yes.

"Um, but of course, my Queen. Are you sure you want commoners to dine with you?" He furrows his brow, looking at me puzzled.

"The entire village is invited. You're just the first I've seen to ask. I'm sorry if that threw you off," I say, trying to calm down my excitement.

"I still don't understand, my Queen. I am no one." Boris lowers his head and closes his eyes. Quickly, I shift my hands back to human and gently cup his cheek.

"Your family has been loyal to my family since day one. You are not a no one. You made sure I was properly fed with both of my pregnancies when my mates couldn't hunt." I smile and kiss his cheek. "I am honored to know you and your family, Boris," I say softly to him as I notice Klaus coming around the side of the house.

"Boris and his father made sure my mom was fed when she was

pregnant with Kaden and me. You are a treasure, ole friend," Klaus says and embraces a blushing Boris.

I return to the stag and go back to butchering. It takes me the better half of an hour to remove all of the usable meat. Back into the kitchen, I take trays of meat in to set on the prep island. The kitchen staff looks at me strangely as I and the other women in the family work on making dinner for the pack.

In the middle of cutting onions, a pair of hands slide over my eyes. To be honest, I can't smell jack shit except for the onions. I know it's not a pack member or one of my mates that's covered my eyes. Carefully, I lean back against a firm chest that's almost the same height as mine. "Hi, Ellis." I say with a squeal. Quickly, I spin in his arms and hug him tightly around his neck.

Ellis starts laughing and holds me tightly to him. "How are you, sweetness?" he asks sweetly and kisses my cheek.

"I'm good, E, what's shaking?" I ask as I smile, looking up at him.

"Not much, just come for a visit and to hang out," he says as he smiles broadly at me.

"Good. Stay for dinner, the girls and I are almost done. So get out of the kitchen and go join the guys." I shoo him out of the kitchen and into the backyard, where everyone has started gathering. We finish the final preparations for the meal and all the sides before we have the kitchen staff help us bring it out.

I even managed to sneak in chicken schnitzel, one of Klaus's favorites, into the mix. Dom and Jayce love how I make my mashed potatoes. Dimitri loves the chocolate cake I make for dessert. Alaric loves the cheddar and broccoli soup I make, and Arnulf loves the string beans with cranberries and almonds. I made sure each of my mates had one of their favorites made for them for this dinner.

The kitchen staff finishes with setting the buffet-style meal up, and they give me a smile and a bow. "Go eat with everyone else. This is as much for them as it is for you too," I say softly, and they all look at me shocked. Gently, I herd them towards the door, so they can go enjoy themselves too. Once the house is empty, I run to our room, pull on my favorite leggings and my favorite Grateful Dead shirt that reads hug me, love me, and take me on tour.

I run through the house barefoot and grab my full wine glass on the way out the back door. I'm greeted by thunderous applause and people yelling my name. Taken back, I lean against the house and look at all the smiling faces.

"Daughter?" my father says softly as he places his hand on my elbow and starts to lead me forward. "You have managed to unite the clans once more." He releases my elbow and motions to the mix of species that are in my yard. "You and your mates managed to bring peace to the lands and free those enslaved." Dad kisses my temple and moves off into the crowd.

"Thank you, one and all for everything that you've done for my family and I." Using my Alpha powers, I amplify my voice so everyone can hear me.

"I wish to usher in a time of peace and prosperity for all the clans." I open my arms wide, motioning to everyone.

"My mates and I have plans to update existing villages as well as restore the one at the base of my mother's castle." My eyes glide over the crowd, and I smile seeing the excitement and happiness on all of their faces.

"It's time to call our people home. Bring the clans and bloodlines of the old back to their ancestral home." Cheers erupt as everyone celebrates the idea.

"If anyone has family outside our borders, call them home. They will have a home and work to support themselves." My eyes land on my mates, several of them with tears in their eyes from joy.

"Call home the Dire Wolves, the Lycans, the Bears, as well as the Eagles. All are welcome here," I say with a few tears escaping down my own cheeks.

"Over the next five years, I hope to have all of our loved ones back where they belong. Father, Alaric call home the dragons and dragon-kin, we will welcome them with open arms." Alaric wipes the tears from his eyes. I know several of his cousins were banished because of his father.

"Tonight, we rejoice and spend time with our loved ones. Eat, drink, and be merry." I say just before descending the stairs and into the crowd. I have to laugh; if you put the me from three years ago in a crowd like this, I would have freaked out. Now, I love being with my people. *My people...* there are so many species here all at once, and I consider them all mine. I'm passing out hugs and handshakes to any and all who wish to get close to me. My mates are looking at me like I'm a pod person.

I find Dimitri and Nicodeamus standing shoulder to shoulder, watching the gathering. "Looks like everything worked out in the end," I say softly and lean against Dimitri to watch the crowd. Alaric is hanging out with Ellis. Dom, and Jayce are with their brother and his husband. Klaus is with Elsa and his twin, talking over the dessert table. Arnulf is with his clansmen off to the side, skittish guys the whole lot of them. Slowly, I raise my wine to my lips and take a sip.

Dimitri's thick arms band around me, holding me tightly to him. "Da, it did, love. This is how it used to be before Vladimir. All the species interacting and enjoying time together." He bends down and kisses my temple. "We can't fix what was done, but we can make sure it never happens again," he says before he rests his head on top of mine.

"This is how it was always meant to be, little one," my father says, smiling. "I'm glad I've lived long enough to witness it again. We do need to weed out the wicked on the dragon council, but that can wait." Dad raises an eyebrow looking at me. If I'm reading the look right, he wants to personally clean the house with me at his side.

"Let's give everyone some time to enjoy the peace before we go stirring the pot, so to speak," I say with a smile upon my lips. It'll be fun going against the council, especially since none of them can stand against me because of Gallus.

All I get is a nod from my father before he walks off to go find his mate. I didn't think second chance mates existed. Apparently, they do, and dad was lucky enough to get one. It almost makes me wonder if my father was meant to have a harem of his own. It's not uncommon for dragon males to take multiple females for the continuation of their species. My eyes glance around the surroundings, taking in the interactions of those gathered. All of the species of old have arrived and are enjoying themselves.

Eventually, Klaus comes over and steals me away from Dimitri, and brings me over to the dessert table. He takes a tray and loads it up with delicious treats to head over to the table my other mates are already sitting at. Dimitri joins us, as well as all five of my children. I can't help but smile, looking at everyone interacting, finally able to relax. I know historically, these times of peace don't really last. But we will enjoy it for now and make sure that we set everything up so that my children are prepared for whatever may come.

Sometime in the early morning light, the party starts to disperse. I know here in Germany some of the discotek's run till seven a.m. So it does not shock me that Klaus's pack is used to partying well into the next morning. I stifle a yawn and use my hand to cover my mouth. The guys give me a knowing look, and Alaric sweeps me up into his arms and starts to carry me inside.

I'm brought downstairs and into the main sleeping quarters, where we all tend to rest with the babies. My children are already asleep, curled up into a tight ball, snuggling against each other. It doesn't take much for the rest of us to climb in and surround the children, each of us with our hands on one of them. As soon as I'm surrounded by warmth, I quickly fall asleep.

We sleep until early afternoon when we are finally awakened because the littlest ones are hungry. We head upstairs and rejoin the land of the living. My home is filled with some of the local females bringing different trays of assorted foods and leaving them on our center island. Uncharacteristically for me, I go and quickly embrace each of them. At some point in my life, I have to put myself out there and trust those outside my bond.

OVER THE NEXT SEVERAL MONTHS, we complete my mother's castle's reconstruction and have a grand opening celebration. We were lucky to find out that some of the American Lycans had true mates within Klaus's pack. And the ones that did not match up with those in Klaus's pack matched up with some of the rogues we had rescued. Between the now blended packs, they divided themselves up between the original village and the new one that we had built at the base of the mountain of my mother's castle.

We founded several other small villages en route to my mother's castle for the Dire Wolves from the Americas. We discovered more Dire Wolves in mother Russia and the Netherlands. In light of the discovery of the new packs, I called a pack run. We had a great gathering on the eve of the Wolf Moon and ran as one pack. It was a great hit, and many of those that did not have their true mates found them that night. It was a fantastic event that led to many happy endings.

I STAND NOW on the balcony of what would have been my mother's bedroom. The room has been reconstructed and renovated up to the most current technologies. I look into the Grand Courtyard, watching everyone interact, seeing the joy and elation on everyone's faces. I shall pray to the Goddess above that this time of peace lasts. I don't foresee anything bad on the horizon for once in my life. But in my heart, I know that Goddess forbid something does arise, I have a legion at my side willing to do what is necessary to protect all of those who need protection. We are blessed beyond measure, and I will not let the sacrifice of those who died be forgotten. The north wall that surrounds the castle has been reconstructed. Pallets of blocks were delivered to each of the clans before the wall was built. Instructions were left to carve the name of the loved ones lost on a stone. The finished wall serves as a memorial to all of those who were lost along the way.

Quickly, I head down and into the courtyard to the memorial wall. Nicodeamus is giving a grand speech about the thought behind the construction of the wall. Jayce and Dominik stand at the ready and upon my dad's signal, they pull the ropes. The tarps fall, and all of the names are visible for all to see. Someone apparently took the time to paint the names of the fallen to make them stand out more. The biggest stone bears my mother's name. Hesitantly, I reach out to touch it then notice my sister's and Andre's stones are under my mother's. Tears roll freely down my cheeks as I stand there, touching their names.

"Angel?" Klaus says softly just as he wraps his arms around me. "We put your mom's and sister's ashes behind their name stones. Dimitri had Andre's ashes, so his are there as well." Klaus kisses my cheek before he passes me off to Dimitri. Each of my mates holds and kisses me before passing me off to the next one. We stand in silence, looking at the memorial till my father speaks.

"You have done a wonderful thing with this memorial. It means a lot to your people that the fallen will not be forgotten." Dad smiles at me, and I move to embrace him tightly.

"So many died because of that mad man, and I didn't want them to be lost to history," I say as I lay my head on my father's chest.

"It may take a generation or two before the Lycans are fully trusted again. But I know Klaus and I will do everything within our power to prove that not all Lycans are evil." I peek over at Klaus, and he nods, agreeing with me.

Slowly, I release my father and move to stand with the wall at my back. "We will remember the fallen. Today will be marked as a day to celebrate them from now until the end of time," I say loud enough for those gathered to hear me. Cheers erupt, and instantly, a moment of mourning turns into a celebration.

Change is possible as long as everyone is willing. It doesn't matter if you're a bear, a wolf, dragon, or eagle. All of us are created equal in the Goddesses' eyes. It doesn't matter who you love as long as you love with all your heart.

CHAPTER 79
Epilogue Welcome Home

ONE YEAR LATER - TIAMAT

THE LAST FEW NIGHTS, I've felt like my blood was on fire. My dragoness calls out in my dreams to a male I do not know. The only thing I do know is that he's mine or meant to be mine. His back is thick with muscles, still lacking definition from his apparent youth. He never faces me, no matter how much I scream for him. I need to get to him, find him. The desperation I feel is from my dragoness. She wants her mate, and for some reason, she has an idea where he is.

This morning is worse than the others; my bones feel like an electrical current is running through them. My muscles burn and feel as though they are being ripped apart. Restlessly, I flop around in bed till I feel myself hit the floor. I can't open my eyes and wake up from this painful nightmare. The most blood-curdling scream escapes my lips, and it doesn't even sound like it's me. My nightgown is tight and feels as though it's constricting around me like a snake. A loud ripping noise is the next thing I hear, and the restrictive fabric is gone. *What's happening to me?* I'm terrified. I shift my arms to my gauntlets and attempt to summon my dragoness's scales to protect me.

My muscles tense, and my back arches off the ground with the surge of power that's going through me. Voices are soft at first, then sound as if they are underwater. Hands lay upon my flesh, and I know it's my mother. "She's frightened; get me her blanket. Dad? What can we do?" My mother's voice is clear because of direct contact, but everything else is garbled. I feel something get laid on me, and I can only assume it's my blanket. The next set of hands I feel on me is my brother Ladon's. I can feel his fear through our bond. *What's wrong? Why is he scared? Someone answer me, please.* I can feel the pull of my brother, and soon I'm in the astral plane with him.

My eyes finally focus, and my brother is a full-grown man standing before me. "Ladon? What's happening? Why can't I wake up?" I rush to my brother and into his waiting arms. He holds me tightly, letting me cry it out.

"Grandpa says you're going through your first ascension. He said that you seem to take after our great-great-grandmother the Blood Queen, which means you have one more ascension to go through," he says calmly as he kisses the crown of my head. It's now that I realize I'm much taller than I was earlier.

Backing away quickly, I start to study myself closely. I have breasts larger than my mother's and very long legs. It seems I've hit adulthood literally overnight. I stare at my brother in disbelief and then examine myself again—so many changes from yesterday to today.

"Why can't I wake up, Ladon?" Sighing softly, I look to my brother, and he frowns.

"I'm not sure, Tia. Grandpa and Mom don't understand. From what Papa Bear says, Mom never went through anything like this." He shrugs lightly, then looks around the Astral plane. "Where's your dragoness?"

At my brother's question, I look around, trying to locate her. His dragon stands tall and proud behind him. He's huge compared to how he used to be. I stare at my brother's dragon in wonder.

That is, till I feel my dragoness approach. She's heavily armored and larger than my brother's dragon, almost by a whole head and shoulder. Her coloration is different as well. She has more silver to her scales, and they seem to have a much more aggressive appearance to them. She also has what looks like a frill that runs from the top of her head to the tip of her tail. Her frill has a faint tinge of purple along the edges. On top of her head are two huge horns that start out a silver purple then turn black at the tips. Her wings are more rounded than my brother's dragon, and she has two talons on each versus his one. Her scent has even changed; she smells like it does just before a rainstorm. That scent of rain has now become my new favorite smell, that is, besides the smell of my mate. His scent has been haunting me since that first dream; he smells like sandalwood.

My eyes drift back to my brother to see the look of shock on his face. "Tia, your dragoness is huge! Fuck! Look at her!" Ladon flails his arms around wildly as he looks between our dragons. My dragoness moves over and curls around Ladon's dragon slowly; she extends a wing over him and almost covers him entirely. Females are supposed to be smaller. *Why is mine larger?* I feel a pull back to the real world from my mom, and I go willingly.

Slowly, I awaken and look around the room with blurry eyes. My skin still feels as though it's on fire, and I start rubbing my arms. To my surprise, my skin has a light layer of dragon scales. Everyone is staring at me in disbelief as I look over my adult body. My mother shoves my father Dimitri's shirt over my head, and it hangs on me like a dress.

My dragoness is roaring in my head, begging me to let her out to go find our mate. My mom senses the struggle within and tries to use her Alpha power on me. I lock eyes with her and do not bow or break under pressure. A deep rumble builds in my chest as I feel my flames wanting to escape. The room temperature starts to drop suddenly, and I know what my mom is trying to do. I narrow my eyes then take off, running for the balcony door. Running as fast as I can, I launch off the balcony rail, and my dragoness explodes into existence. We are a freaking mammoth, several pumps of our large wings, and we are up in the clouds.

I roar louder than I've ever roared in my life. The power this adult body holds is no joke. My dragoness tells me we must turn south, and I listen. We don't know why we must head that way, but instinct drives us in that direction. It doesn't take long for Marco, my father, and my grandfather to try to block my path. The three of them are blowing their breath weapons at me, and the only one that concerns me is Marco. Sadly, through my distraction, I didn't notice my brother till he was almost on top of me. He comes at me quickly with his talons extended, intending on stopping me in any way possible.

We're locked in an aerial battle, talon to talon, and I have him upside down. I won't hurt my twin. I love him too much, but I also won't allow myself to lose to him either. During my distraction, I feel something land on my back. Suddenly, there's a piercing pain, and I release my brother quickly. I do several barrel rolls and finally, dislodge whatever was on my back. I turn to pursue my attacker and realize it's my mother free falling. Her great white hybrid beast falling quickly. Without hesitation, I fold my wings tight to my body and dive after her knowing I'd gain on her quickly. My taloned hand reaches out and plucks her out of the sky, and I pull her close to my chest. Quickly, I open my wings and slow us down, then rise back up into the sky. Mom's talons sink into my hand again, and I angle my head to look at her.

Through the bond, I hear her say, *I'm sorry, it's for your own good.* There's remorse in her beast's eyes as I feel myself getting sleepy.

My dragoness is roaring in my head about an ice sleep that we must fight. I'm so tired, though. We're starting to lose the fight. I see my father, grandfather, and brother on the ground blowing their breath weapon at the ground, trying to build a large cushion of snow and frost. I open my hand, and my mother's beast climbs up my scales onto my back. Through the bond, I can feel her panic; she's unsure if we're going to land alright. It's getting harder to keep my eyes open, and it feels like my head weighs a million pounds.

Several circling attempts happen before I'm finally low enough that I'm not going to get hurt if I fall. I feel my mother's talons sink into my dragon hide just before the darkness takes me. Sleep pulls me under quickly as my body crashes into the pile of snow my family had made for me. Just before everything goes completely black, I see my mate one last time. The man seems to be struggling just like I was, but I can't get to him... I can't wake up.

I watch as Oberon appears in a shimmering mist not far from where Tiamat crash-landed. "You need time to grow, young one. The mind must catch up with your body," he says musically as his glowing hand touches the temple of Tiamat's dragon. His eyes turn to me, and he bows his head. "Young Queen, I must confess, I did not foresee the resurrection of the Blood Queen's line in your daughter." His eyes drop as his lithe hand glides over Tia's scales.

"What do you mean resurrection? What have you done, my King?" Alaric asks, trying to reign in his temper.

Oberon keeps his glowing hand upon Tia's temple; slowly, his lavender eyes lock with Alaric's. "The world needs a protector, a guardian, besides your mate. Which, I must admit, we engineered her birth as well." Oberon narrows his eyes in thought for a moment before continuing.

Alaric's and Nicodeamus's tempers radiate from them like the waves of the ocean. "So my mate died, so you could create a hybrid so you could bring back the Blood Queen?" Nico asks through gritted teeth.

"Essentially, yes," Oberon says with a scary finality. "Though this knowledge will not be yours after I leave. The only one to remember will be Aurora. She must protect Tiamat at all costs." Oberon's lavender gaze moves to me, and he tilts his head, studying me.

"You cannot tell anyone of the future your daughter holds. Just like her knowledge of her mate's location will be hidden from her until the time is right." Oberon slowly removes his hand from Tia's dragon's temple. "She must sleep through each of her heat cycles till her twenty-fourth birthday; after that, I will make it possible for her to locate her mate."

He turns his head until he looks at Alaric, Nicodeamus, and Ladon. "Sleep and forget all that you learned here today. You must keep the princess pure and strong until she meets her mate. Protect her at all costs," Oberon says and waves his hand. As his hand passes each male, they crumpled to the ground, fast asleep.

"I do not envy the burden you now carry, young Queen, guard your secrets well," Oberon says before disappearing in a shimmer of glitter.

I stand there up to my knees in snow, gobsmacked by the information relayed to me. My daughter will be stronger than all of them combined. I walk over and lightly run my hands over Tiamat's scales. Not long after Oberon's departure, the guys slowly start to awaken and hold their heads. Protective details are created. Each day a different family member will stay with Tia until it is safe to awaken her.

IN A LAND across the sea and far away, Oberon appears in a young man's bedroom. He looks down at the male that one day will be Tia's mate. Lightly, he touches his temple, taking away his dragon's ability to navigate to its mate that it met in his youth. "Forgive me, young Prince; what I do is the best for the two of you. Ladon Kraus is your best friend and eventually the key to finding your mate." He runs his glowing fingertips over the young man's forehead.

"Yourself and your mate shall be the most powerful the world has seen in generations. Be patient, learn and grow into the warrior she will need you to be, the warrior she deserves." Oberon rests his palm flat over the prince's heart. "Bide your time; family is everything and your mate the most precious treasure you could ever hope for."

Oberon removes his hand from the prince's chest then looks back to Queen Gisella. "He will rest peacefully now and no longer attempt to fly off to find her. They will meet when the time is right. I swear." Gisella nods slowly, and then Oberon vanishes in a wisp of glitter.

PART TWO
Bonus Scenes

It's been a very long time since these scenes have been seen. These were the four bonus scenes requested by readers. So now for the first time in print here they are.

Enjoy.

CHAPTER 1
Dimitri's POV

Ice Dragon Chalet

Night of the Wolf

November 30, 2019

I sit on the bench near the window watching as Aurora gets her wig pinned in place. She is almost a mirror image of her mother. Nicodeamus voices exactly what I'm thinking as I watch Aurora prepare for tonight's farce. "Da, except Aurora is a wee bit taller and has more muscle tone." My tone is reverent as I compare Aurora to her mother. I can't help but feel that something is missing as I watch her mentally prepare herself for tonight.

I made sure I talked to her about how sexist Bane is and how little value he places on females of any species. Nicodeamus kisses Aurora's cheek and moves away just in time for the twins to bring in a tray of food from the Prince. Alaric has thought of just about everything, even invoking the old tradition of wearing the cloaks for the procession. It will be to our advantage to be able to hide Nicodeamus for as long as possible.

Aurora is already pissed off about having to hide everyone and now add to that her having to destroy a dress she actually likes. I never thought I'd live to see the day she would like to wear a dress. Aurora moves around the room adjusting our cloaks making sure everyone looked perfect. I have to give Aurora credit she hates being handled but she allows the handmaidens to adjust her dress and train. I'm shocked when she sets her wedding procession the same way her mother did, I briefly look to Nicodeamus and we start to laugh. Our laughter causes Aurora to growl at us, then Nicodeamus tells her what she's done. I guess history can repeat itself.

Aurora smiles and bares her canines at us, her beast made her eyes bleed liquid mercury within those fathomless orbs black dragon slits adorn the centers. Aurora is pleased with her upgrade and moves to apply her blood red lipstick. I swear to the Gods that girl loves to tease me, she knows that she looks damn sexy with that color. I'm already on high alert after the five minute warning knock had come a few moments earlier. My bear is on edge and wants us to shift to protect her.

Aurora tells us it's time to reign in blood then turns around and starts humming "Heathens". Shit I thought we were going to start singing a little Slayer "Reign in blood" yet another perfect song for our girl. Aurora looks so detached from what's going on around her, she calls it a resting bitch face, I call it someone is going to die face. We arrive at the double doors standing there in silence as we wait to be brought in.

Go time, we move as a singular force and immediately whispers erupted throughout the hall. Aurora is a carbon copy of her mother, right down to her I don't give a fuck attitude. I watch Bane's reaction from under the hood, apparently the photos we faked didn't do Aurora justice. I can understand where he's coming from, I feel like I've gone back in time looked at Aurora with that wig on. I watch Aurora play the part of the submissive female. It makes my stomach turn watching that strong female act like a weak dejected woman.

Bane starts to man handle Aurora like a worthless piece of meat and my blood boils, my bear and I want to rip him to pieces. I watch the twins flinch and tense as they fight their animals trying to restrain them from attacking Bane. The idiot finally acknowledges Aurora is Anca's daughter then verbally degrades her next. How Aurora is keeping her cool right now is beyond me, I'm ready to rip Bane's spine from his body and beat him with it. Bane finally makes his smartest move to date and hands Aurora over to Alaric.

WE LISTEN to the Friar proceed with the ceremony as planned, blah blah blah.. I swear I can't even hear his words anymore. Its like listening to Charlie Brown's teacher talking. He finally says the line we were all waiting for. "Speak now or forever hold your peace."

AURORA RIPS off her wig and the rest of us throw the cloaks as if they were on fire. My bear is ready to destroy anyone that even attempts to come at Aurora. I watch Aurora and Alaric shift their arms to their armored gauntlets, their long black talons glisten in the light. Nicodeamus and I move forward together, he announces who he is and the confusion is evident in the crowd. Nicodeamus is the true Dragon King.

CHAPTER 2
Arrival in America

KLAUS

North American Lycan Camp

I was summoned into my father's quarters in the middle of the night. Apparently, an old ally he long thought was dead lives and needs our assistance. My twin and I take as seat at my father's desk waiting for him to speak. "Gather four of our finest fighters quickly, the lost Princess and its our ancestral promise to protect her bloodline." My father says sternly his inflection suggests great concern.

"What do you mean the lost Princess? The Marelup heir died with her mother the night of the attack." I say questioning my father's intel. It's common knowledge around here that none of that blood line lives to this day.

"My boy what I'm about to tell you two remains in this room do you understand me?" My brother and I nod at our father and lean forward. He's definitely piqued our interest. "The Princess ripped her way free of her mother's womb at the time of the attack. Apparently, the stressful situation caused the baby to shift and rip its self-free. Nicodeamus sent me a video that he was sent of his daughter. I am not at liberty to show it to you. But be warned the stories of a great white lycan beast are true. The Princess is a hybrid of lycan and dragon. I'm sending you two and another four to America to help protect her. Apparently, there's traitors in their pack and Nicodeamus is concerned for his daughter's safety." My father crossed his arms over his barrel chest looking between my brother and I. We both nod at our father and get up to leave.

"We will bring you honor father and serve the Princess well." I extend my hand to my father sealing my promise to him. My brother and I make haste leaving my fathers home. I send my brother to gather the most loyal solders we have and load everyone up into the van.

It didn't take long to make it to the local airport, apparently a man named Jayce had secured six first class tickets for myself and my pack. We went though the normal airport bullshit and boarded our flight. My father had texted me the contact numbers for Dominik and Jayce, apparently, they are two of the princess's mates in charge of our transport.

I watch out the window as the plane flies over Mother Russia, the entire country is covered in ice and snow. Rumors of dragons living within the boarders has been around for generations. I watch the miles fly by and soon we are crossing the Pacific Ocean. It's not natural for a wolf to fly and to be honest I'm really not comfortable with it.

This flight feels like it's taking **F O R E V E R ...** At some point I must have dozed off cause my brother decided to punch my shoulder to wake me up. I jolt awake and look around searching for the problem. My brother is sitting there laughing his ass off at me and I punch him back. Fucking stupid brother, I swear if mom didn't make me promise that I wouldn't beat his ass he would be crying right now. We disembark the airport looking like a strong man competition is in town. Right at the gate is a man with dark hair and hazel eyes holding a sign with my name on it. From the description I was given I recognize him as Dominik. I roll up my right sleeve and show him the crest of my father's pack. He then rolls up his sleeve to show his pack mark as well. Dominik then turns his head to the side and pulls his collar to the side to show me Aurora's bite mark. Identity's confirmed we depart for the pack lands in which we will be staying.

We pull through the gates to the pack lands and I look around. The American Lycans are puny and appear to be half starved. Poor scrawny things, they are a shadow of the beasts they should be. Dominik parks the vehicle and we start walking towards what appears to be the main pack house. My twin is close on my heel as we approach the mountain of a man I come to know as Dimitri. Stories I was told as a pup had him as the Queens personal guard. How does he still live and look this young? Dimitri gives us the rest of the report of what's going on around here. It's much worse than my father had originally anticipated. Dimitri brings me forward and introduces me to Nicodeamus, the fabled Dragon King. This ancient warrior holds his remaining arm out to me and shows me his brand. I in turn hold my arm our showing him the brand of my father's pack. Once our identities are confirmed we embrace briefly then turn to leave the building we were in front of.

Nicodeamus stops us in front of the small cabin's door, the sweetest scent I've ever smelled fills the air around the building. Suddenly the door flies open, and a heavenly angel stands before me. I feel as though the world had stopped. This was it the moment I had been waiting for my entire life. She's it. I watch her ruby red lips pop open and her mouth falls open. My angel blinks her eyes several times before opening the door wide to let us in. Her father and I enter the cabin and I watch the Princess closely. Her eyes are pure silver orbs, reflective and secretive.

A few moments later she speaks to me in my native tongue, her German is perfect as if she had been speaking it her whole life. Aurora motions to the couch and I'm quick to oblige, her scent is intoxicating. I know it's because she's mine, but for some reason she's not reacting the way I am. Aurora walks into the kitchen and returns with three beers. I watch Aurora first set the bottles down then shift her hand into this armored taloned gauntlet. Shocked isn't the word I'd use to describe how I feel watching her coat the bottle in frost before handing it to me. I watch her move to a recliner and sit down, she looked to her shifted arm and returned it to human then showed me the Marelup brand.

I moved quickly and dropped to my knees before her, cautiously I rest my forehead on her knees in subjugation. I look up to Aurora my wolf came to the forefront, I had to test her make sure she is whom she's supposed to be. I lower my eyes quickly and apologize profusely for my attempt. Aurora shocks me by running her fingers though my hair, I look up at her in awe. This powerful female caresses my head as if I'm precious to her. We stay in this moment for to me what feels like forever. Something suddenly changes and she pulls her hand back as if she was burned. I'm told to retrieve my men, so I do so promptly. I return to find the Princess standing in the kitchen in nothing but a robe.

I explain to my men that she's the true heir and then I hear it start, her shift is being painfully slow for our benefit. Her beast is huge, mammoth, an impossible thing to behold. Her lycan dwarfs all of ours, its head is wider and her muzzle longer. Her body is the perfect mix of dragon and lycan, those battle ready gauntlets look even more impressive together with her long black talons on display. We swear our loyalty to the Princess on the spot. There's a bigger mystery besides who is the traitor, like why does my mate not see me as hers?

CHAPTER 3

Alaric – Birth of his children

I feel the slight tug from Aurora when she reaches out through the bond to gauge my location. It makes me smile that she seeks me out upon waking. Not long after she reached out to me, I feel her pain and discomfort. The dual whines of Dominik and Jayce confirm my suspicions, Aurora is in labor and she's been hiding her discomfort from us. I feel through the bond how intense her contractions and I warn the twins I'm about to pick up speed. I'm closing in fast on the castle and I feel the fear from Dimitri about what may come. I summon other dragons to aide in transporting my family and providing security. Dante and Edgar and the first to shift in the courtyard leaving ample room for me to land.

I land as carefully as I can and apologize to the twins, I see Aurora being escorted out and watch her double over from a contraction. Fuck I wish I could hold her, comfort her in some way. I lower my head to her, and she cries she can't climb, fuck. Slowly I open my hand and extend it to her curling my pinky to make a seat for her to sit on. Once safely in my hand I close my fingers around her, her complaint about the temperature is handled immediately. I turn and launch into the sky clutching the hand that holds my mate tightly to my chest. I am flying faster than I usually do with the twins on my back to its urgent that I get Aurora to the cavern. I land inside the cavern and thankfully Dante beat me there with Nicodeamus. I open my hand the minute Nicodeamus is ready to receive his daughter from me. Dominik and Jayce slide off my back and go to help with Aurora. Her pained cry wanting, no needing me to shift prompts my shift to be faster than its ever been before. The minute I am able to lay my hands on her the pain lessens and its tolerable for her. Dominik shifts to his wolf and lays down to carry Aurora into the cavern.

The rest of my bond mates arrive soon after we make it to the waters edge, Klaus and I escort Aurora into the water trying to soothe her. Nicodeamus explains how special this place is to his family and what its able to do for a female. Instinctually Aurora wanted the water long before knowing what I could do. Watching my beloved mate go though all this pain to bring our child into this world is the hardest thing I have ever done. I constantly push all my love and gratitude to her as the guys switch out taking turns touching Aurora. Eventually her beast urges her to climb onto the island and we follow her. In my heart of hearts I am scared for my love after what had happened to her mother. Without warning her forearms shift to her armored gauntlets and she digs her talons into the earth under her. The contractions are getting stronger and the odd shapes her stomach is taking it frightful.

I'm in constant contact with Aurora when Klaus calls me to him. Slowly I turn my head to look at him and the fear that flashes in his eyes for a mere second scares a few years off of my life. I pass the juice I was holding off to Dimitri and head back to where Klaus is. Gently I rest a hand on Aurora's hip and take a peek.

To say I'm in shock seeing the white scales of my daughter's dragon peeking out with every contraction. Slowly more and more of her head is exposed, she's the cutest little thing I've ever seen. Then reality hits me, what damage is her scales and claws doing to Aurora's insides? "Everything is ok love, we see the baby's head, that's all." I move forward and kiss Aurora's temple. I smile at her trying to reassure everything is ok.

I can feel when Aurora starts to get tired and then the faint pull of her trying to syphon energy off of any available dragon. "Man down!" I yell watching one of the black dragons that accompanied us drop in the tunnel. I turn my head just in time to watch my little Tia slip free of her mothers' body. Klaus wipes her off quickly before Aurora picks her up. Little Tia has mostly dragon feature with some wolf fur and wolf hind paws. She's absolutely perfect in every way possible. Nicodeamus lowers his dragons head to look at the baby and my little girl blows a small plume of fire at him. *That's daddy's girl!* I say to myself as I move off the island and shift to my dragon. I lower my head and open my mouth and like a good little hatchling she climbs in without fear. I carefully lower her to the ground allowing her to get to know mine and Nicodeamus' dragons.

Aurora's scream catches my attention, my head whips around to see her in labor again! There's a second baby coming holy shit! I shift quickly and scoop up my daughter and carry her back to the island. I put Tia down and take the Dominik's spot and start pouring water over Aurora's back to keep her comfortable. The moment baby number two slides free I'm almost hit with a plume of blue flames. This baby is all its mother, it came into the world ready to fight.

Carefully I pick up baby number two and flip it around several times. I look at the shape of the baby's cloaca and know that it's a boy. The little man blows another plume of flames in my face, I shift my eyes to that of my dragon and assert my dominance, my little man settles down quickly after that. "He's going to be a tough one." I tilt my head looking at her and she's really not catching on.

"Aurora love I know you're tired, but you have a son to help me name." I pass our son to her watching her nuzzle him and then I can see the excitement on her face when she finally gets it that he's a boy.

Aurora names our son and he goes off to play with his sister, it's now that we notice she's bleeding more than she should be. I feel like my heart damn near stopped. Aurora moves off the island and into the main cavern where her father is in his dragon form. I look my mate over, and her beast has changed again, its bigger and its scales are heavier and more aggressive looking.

I know that look on her face she's searching for something in her father's memories, he bathes her in flames healing her wounds and accelerating the healing of any internal damage. I watch her tilt her head several times and then I hear it. The familiar click of a dragon's ignitor, I'm expecting Nicodeamus to bathe her in flames again. Shockingly, it's Aurora who lowers her head and blows frost flames across the cavern floor before her. We all jumped back a bit watching her freeze everything before her. The babies are the first to approach her and they all sniff and lick at each other. We watch Aurora shift and make the baby's shift to human right along with her. Will wonders ever cease?

CHAPTER 4

Thana

HAPPENS BEFORE KLAUS CHRISTMAS AND BEFORE DISCOVERED

My morning starts like any other morning: coffee, a shower, and then head out the door. I plan to walk to the bakery for a muffin and a snack before I head to the park to read. As I stroll towards the center of town, it gives me time to reflect on the past week's events.

I still don't know who is stealing my shit at work. Raphael is ridiculously handsome, and it's distracting when he's in my wing. Having drinks with Christian and his squad was a riot, especially because of the karaoke. He told me there are bars like that all over China and Japan. Apparently, it's a common after work activity to go bust out a song.

My phone buzzes, and I pull it out of my pocket to see who it is. Mark's sent me yet another meme about coffee and books. He likes to make fun of the reverse harem books I read, but he doesn't know why I enjoy them. Most Nephilim end up in a polyamorous relationship, so I figured I needed to do some research.

When I get to the bakery, I see Jayce rushing around and Klaus trying desperately to calm him. The bell rings and the scent of baked bread assaults my senses as I watch the two love birds fuss at one another. Jayce is talking to someone on the phone, his tone frantic. Klaus looks like he's going to pull his hair out strand by strand.

I have to help.

Striding over to Klaus, I take his hands and hold them, so he stops yanking at his hair. "What happened?"

His gaze is full of fear. "Aurora is in labor, and we're three hours away."

I flick my eyes over to Jayce, hating the tears that run down his cheeks. "Theres more than that happening. Tell me, maybe I can help?"

At my offer, he stops pacing. His eyes open wide when he remembers I'm a nurse, and he abruptly hangs up on the person he was speaking to. Facing me, he gives me a pleading look. "The baby is stuck."

His admission makes my chest constrict. Lycans frequently have difficulty with carrying babies to term and, even worse, issues giving birth. Aurora may not be a pureblood Lycan, but even a drop of their blood increases her chance of birthing issues. I weigh my options as I pace across the bakery floor. If I shadow walk to her, it means I have to embrace my darker nature. I've suppressed it for so long, but this is an emergency. "Where are they?"

"They are in Dominik's pack. It's an hour past my pack lands." Klaus sounds defeated, and his acceptance that either Aurora or the baby could die decides for me.

"Lock up. I will get us there as fast as possible. Take me to the darkest part of the store." My nerves get the better of me as I watch them get their business shut down. I feel jittery, but my best friend and her baby need me to be strong right now.

"Are you sure, Thana? We don't want you to get in trouble." Jayce bites his bottom lip, clearly worried about what Azrael will do to me.

Taking a deep breath, I nod. "Let's go before I chicken out." Klaus takes me to the storage room and turns out the lights. The shadows whisper, and I feel them seep into me. "What you see today cannot ever be shared with anyone else."

My friends nod their heads as I unfurl my wings. Flexing them several times, I extend my hands to draw them to me. I wrap my wings around us all to help lessen the effect of the shadows. Luckily, I went to Dominik's house for the Easter hunt this year, so I know where I'm going.

"Close your eyes and hold on tight. It will feel like the initial drop of a roller coaster." After warning the guys, I focus on my intended location. Sifting through the shadows is the quickest way to get anywhere without being seen.

In a matter of seconds, we manifest in a closet in Dominik's home. I open my wings to see Klaus stabilizing an unsteady Jayce. "We're here."

As the words leave my lips, they rip the door open and a furious Dimitri stands in front of us with his bear damn close to breaking free. "Thana..." Dimitri growls. His bear settles when he sees Klaus and Jayce with me. "What have you done?"

Pushing my shoulders back, I stare up at the mountain of a man. "Aurora needs me, and I'm here. Consequences be damned." I allow my eyes to blacken as I stare up at him, unwillingly to budge on the topic.

Sighing, Dimitri grabs my hand and drags me through the hallways to the bedroom where Aurora is struggling. I watch her, my heart in my throat, and allow myself one moment of fear before I turn coldly clinical. "I need hot water, clean towels, and a coffee." My last demand makes Alaric do a double take, but he and Arnulf take off to gather the supplies, regardless.

"How's my bitch doing?" I joke as I look at my best friend.

Aurora grunts and forces a grin. "Peachy keen, fluffy. How the fuck did you get here so fast?" A contraction hits her, and she lets out a long, low growl. Dominik is holding her hand as she crushes it, wincing from his place by her bed.

"You needed me; fuck the consequences. I shifted us through the shadows." I point to Jayce and Klaus with a grin.

Aurora relaxes a little once she sees her two wayward mates, giving me a nod. She screams again as another contraction hits her. Arnulf returns and offers me my coffee and Alaric has everything I asked for and sets it up on the side table. Chugging my coffee, I finish it quickly, then head into the bathroom and wash my hands before heading over to Aurora.

I pull back the sheets and look the situation over, assessing what I need to do next. "Let's move her to the edge of the bed so I can get this baby out." This is going to be much tougher than I originally expected because I can see the baby's heels.

The guys jump into action and maneuver Aurora into place, chuckling as I joke with her about getting all up in her business. Turning to one of her mates, I point to the several areas of stretched skin. "Alaric, I need to you chill this area right here."

Alaric touches where I asked, numbing the skin so I can continue to get Aurora ready. I smile when Arnulf offers me sterile gloves, sliding them on with a snap. Once I'm prepared, I inch my fingers in along the legs of the baby.

My eyes shift to the chrome color of my powers, and I can see the life force of the baby. It gives me a faint outline of how it's positioned inside, so I know how to adjust. With gentle turns and twists, I get the baby lined up, and it progresses more easily. Reaching into the birth canal, I position the baby's arms, making minor adjustments with every contraction.

After a few agonizing moments, the baby slides free. Lifting it up, I clear the airway and we hear her first cries. Smiling with relief, I cut the cord before offering her to Aurora. I pass my hand over the child, using my healing light to make sure that she's completely healthy. "You have a beautiful daughter."

Dominik stares at his little girl in wonder, then looks up at me with a grateful smile. "I don't know what we would have done without you. Klaus's grandmother is at the castle of wolves. She won't be here for at least another hour, even if she flies."

When he describes what happened before I arrived, I realize without my intervention, the baby would not have made it. It makes the risky decision to come here seem worth it. I couldn't have lived with myself if my friend had lost her child because I wasn't brave enough to defy the edicts.

After Aurora passes the placenta, I heal the damage from childbirth, smiling as I watch her feed her new daughter. I wash my hands in the basin after I remove my gloves, whispering to my friend. "What are you going to name her?"

"I'm not sure. Do you have a suggestion?" Aurora kisses her daughter's cheek as she replies, not taking her eyes off the nursing infant.

I look at the babe in her arms, considering as I see how enamored Dominik is with her. "How about Isabella? You can call her Isi or Bella or Bells for short?"

"That's perfect. Isabella, you shall be, little one." Aurora burps her, grinning broadly before offering her to me.

Cradling the baby in my arms, I unfurl my wings and rock her. Kissing her temple, I whisper her name to imbue it with power. Either at birth or later, I bless each every child I help bring into this world. "You're going to do great things, little one."

I flex my wings once more before putting them away. Aurora's house is one of the few places I can expose my wings without breaking angelic law. With these males already mated, I am not breaking protocol at all. I will miss that freedom when I leave. "I should get going."

Greeting Aurora's other children as they come running in, I walk around the room to give my friends their hug good-bye. I watch the large family with a pang of jealousy—I don't know when or if I'll ever have something like this myself. Once I've said farewell to everyone, I head back towards the hall closet I manifested in when we arrived.

"Thana, wait!" Dominik shouts over the pounding of his boots behind me.

I stop with my hand on the doorknob, spinning to face him. His tone has me prepared to rush back into the room where my friend is. "Did something happen to the baby? Am I still needed?"

He laughs as he holds his hands up in supplication. "They're fine. I didn't mean to scare you."

It takes a moment to catch my breath—fear had almost closed my windpipe. Tilting my head to the side, I study him, wondering why he came rushing out.

"I want to give you a gift. I appreciate all you do for our family." His fist is closed around something small, and he's looking at me with an earnest expression.

"You don't have to give me anything; you guys are like family to me." I step towards the closet, but something tells me he won't let this go.

"I get that, but I wouldn't feel right. Take this as my token of my gratitude." Dominik places something small and warm in my hand. When I open it, tears well up in my eyes. The key to the black SRT Hellcat sits in my hand.

"Dom, you can't be serious! This is your baby! It's your favorite possession." I offer him the key back, unable to fathom such a generous present.

Aurora wobbles over, wrapping her hands around mine. "She's yours. I've been wanting to give her to you for a long time, Thana."

I lunge forward and hug them both, unable to find the words to express how I feel. This is the kindest thing anyone has ever done for me. I've delivered a majority of their children, but I didn't expect anything in return, much less something so valuable.

"Come on. Let's go introduce you to your new ride," Dominik says as he takes my hand. He leads me down the hall, not commenting on my stunned silence.

Just outside the front door is Aurora's lifted black diesel—nick-named Black Beauty aka the Beast. The sleek jet black SRT Challenger—aka the Harlot—is right next to it. They named the Challenger after the song "The Beast and the Harlot" from A7X, which is one of Aurora's favorite bands. Approaching it reverently, I run my fingers over the curves of the car.

Dominik watches me with a big grin. "I can tell you're gonna love her like I do." He steps over and opens the driver's door to show me a perfect interior I couldn't see because of the blacked-out windows.

Sliding into the driver's seat, I press the brake and clutch pedals and the roar of the engine makes my heart race. The rumbling purr rattles my very soul and I can't help the manic smile that crosses my lips. Wiggling the shifter left to right, I look up at Dominik. "Anytime you're in the area, please come visit your car. I know she'll miss you."

He nods, laughing as he shows me the spare fob in his hand. "I intend to. Thank you again for all of your help, Thana. I don't know what we would do without you."

Turning to face him, I beam. "I love you guys. If you need me, I'll always be there." My word is my bond, and Dominik knows I'm serious.

"Enjoy the rest of your day off. I'm sure Aurora will video call you later."

Saying goodbye is never easy, but I know I have friends for life in Aurora and her mates.

I flip through the channels until I find the Black Veil Bride's 'Fallen Angels'. It's the anthem of my life, and I sigh in happiness.

Dominik closes the driver's door as I drop into first gear. Mashing down on the pedal, I launch onto the road.

The roar of the engine rivals my loud singing. The song I love so much is about not being accepted for who you are, and it feels like they wrote it for me. All four of the band members are Dark Nephilim, so they know how I feel.

According to GPS, I have an almost four-hour drive back to reality. Grinning, I look at the screen, accepting the challenge—*I'll beat that time in minutes to spare.*

About the Author

Serenity Rayne spends most of her time either howling at the moon or creating cheeky crafts in her lair. Since she published the first book in the bestselling Aurora Marelup series, she's released sixteen more books while surviving being a nurse during the COVID-19 pandemic.

Serenity writes strong women who find their way in the world through blood and fire, learning to love and trust the men who adore them. Her books also feature positive LGBTQ representation, loss, and all the emotions that transcend species. Though her catalog has been focused on paranormal why choose and horror, she is now branching out to write contemporary why choose as well. She lives on a farm with dogs, chickens, peacocks, a one-eyed horse, and her son, who is way more like her than he wants to admit.

Signed Books and Merch

www.SerenityRayneRomance.com

This is the only place to get official Serenity Rayne Merchandise as well as book swag and signed books.

If you would like this **LIMITED** edition 5 year anniversary edition in print. My website is the only place it will be offered.

Follow Serenity Everywhere:

Facebook: Serenity Rayne

Readers Group

Twitter: Author Serenity Rayne

Instagram: Author Serenity Rayne

Goodreads: Serenity Rayne

BookBub: Serenity Rayne

Amazon: Serenity Rayne

Website: https://www.serenityrayne.com

WebStore - https://serenityrayneromance.com/

Also By Serenity Rayne

Pre-orders:

Children of the Moon - Full Moon

Coveted By The Alpha Pack

The Aurora Marelup Holiday Edition

Hybrid Royals - World at War

Shifters:

Claimed by the Alpha Pack

Embraced By the Alpha Pack

Children of the Moon: New Moon Rising

Children of the Moon - Waxing Crescent

Her Elemental Mates

The Aurora Marelup Saga

Ascend

Hunt

Fight

Attack

Welcome Home

Klaus Christmas

Princess Lost

Destiny Found

Tiamat

The Dark Angel Chronicles:

Discovered

Innate

Balance

Destroyer

Daughters of the Destroyer - Nikita

Stand alones:

Heart Shaped Box

Blood Moon Pack

Once Upon the a Raven